THE WHITE TOWER

THE ALDORAN CHRONICLES
- BOOK ONE -

written by

MICHAEL
WISEHART

Copyright

THE WHITE TOWER is a work of fiction. Names, characters, places, and incidents are products of the author's imagination or are used fictitiously. Any resemblance to actual locales or persons, living or dead, business establishments, or events, is entirely coincidental.

ISBN-13: 978-0-9981505-1-2
Copyright © 2016 by Michael Wisehart
All Rights Reserved
2nd Edition

Cover Art by Michael Wisehart
Cover Illustration by Jack Adams
World Map by Michael Wisehart
Map of Easthaven by Elwira Pawlikowska
Map of Aramoor by RenflowerGrapx

Printed in the United States of America

THE WHITE TOWER

THE ALDORAN CHRONICLES
- BOOK ONE -

Books by
Michael Wisehart

Map of Aldor – West

The Five Kingdoms of ALDOR

Map of Aldor - East

E OF THE
NORTH

ANGORAN MOUNTAINS

MEERWOOD

BAY OF MIST

ISLE OF
TALLOS

WELLHOLLOW

CRYSTAL
LAKE

S I D A R A

GRASSLANDS OF
TEKOA

SIDARAN
FOREST

BELVIN

EASTHAVEN

FLORAN

SAEIDA

REED MARSH

WOODVALE

HIGHCREST

SIDARAN
FOREST

KARISS

EAST
RIVER

RIVERTON

MTS

IRASETH

WHITE
TOWER

BRAEDON

WINDMEER

THORNWOOD

RAZOR SPINE MTS

HARAN

I A

CARRAN

RHYNDIR

KOALL

DORMANE

GOREN

O Z R I N   S E A

B R I S T O N

RAINE

VINTEN

RIVERLANDS

DELYUM

LAKE
YARBIN

BALMIR

DUPORT

AZMAR

FAYBURN

RHUNARIN OCEAN

THE BLUE ISLES

Map of Aramoor

1. LUMBER YARDS
2. THE ROCKSLIDE COMPOUND
3. LANCER CORPS
4. THE GUILD
5. WILDFIRE COMPOUND
6. LANCER BARRACKS
7. SANDSTORM COMPOUND
8. BAYSIDE
9. THE TEMPLE
10. KING'S SQUARE
11. AVALANCHE COMPOUND
12. SHIPPING YARDS
13. THE PIT
14. THE ROYAL PALACE
15. THE GRANARY
16. OLD MERCHANT DISTRICT
17. THE WARDENS

BAY OF TORRIN

ARAMOOR

Map of Easthaven

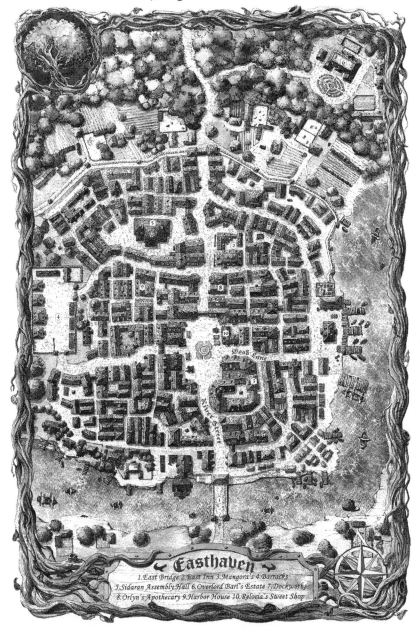

Easthaven

1.East Bridge 2.East Inn 3.Mangora's 4.Barracks
5.Sidaran Assembly Hall 6.Overlord Barl's Estate 7.Dockworks
8.Orlyn's Apothecary 9.Harbor House 10.Reloria's Sweet Shop

Foreword

THIS SERIES IS not your typical *follow-the-hero-on-their-journey* story. It has a larger scope with multiple storylines that weave together as the series progresses. For those of you who prefer to keep up with each character as they read along,

I have added a *Character Glossary* at the back.

"What has been created in the laws of nature holds true in the laws of magic as well. Where there is light, there is darkness, and where there is life, there is also death."
— *Aerodyne: First of the Wizard Order*

Chapter 1 | Nyalis

NYALIS HEARD THE cry of the corax behind him, and the sound of their approach sent a shiver racing down his spine. They were still some distance back, but it wouldn't take the winged trackers long to catch up. The thought of what would happen if they found him was as chilling as the patches of ankle-deep snow threatening to slow his pace.

Few had ever seen the corax's dark wings. Those who had seen them, lived only long enough to regret it. Nyalis knew all too well what these creatures were capable of, having been hunted by them before. They were the eyes of the White Tower, a twisted amalgamation of night-raven and reptile. Their dark, guttural caws echoed off the mountain peaks behind him, clear as the baying of bloodhounds.

Nyalis shoved his fear aside and willed his legs to keep moving, each step agony as the frigid mountain air cut his face and burned his lungs. Moonlight lit the path ahead. He glanced over his shoulder, but the towering stand of ancient redwoods kept the creatures blocked from sight. Before he could turn around, his foot got snagged on a root, and he fell.

Quickly, he clutched the tightly wrapped bundle to his chest before landing on his side in a pile of snow against one of the massive trees. Pain shot through his shoulder as he pushed himself up into a sitting position and leaned against the rough bark.

Two little hands shot out of the wrapping and grabbed hold of his white beard, forcing him to grit his teeth against the pain of pulled whiskers.

"That's quite the grip you have there, little one," Nyalis whispered, untangling the babe's tiny fingers. He tried to stand, but his legs gave way and he plopped back into the snow, deciding a short rest was in order. His entire body ached from the strain, a sharp reminder of his old age.

Lifting his head, he studied the star-filled sky through the coverlet of branches. *Night already?* Where had the time gone? Nyalis had been on the run for three days, and his pursuers were showing no signs of letting up. He knew they were close. He could feel them in the short hairs on the back of his neck. With the last of the sun's rays having slipped over the horizon hours before, his best chance to catch a glimpse of the Tower's winged hunters would be to spot their silhouettes against the dimly lit heavens.

If the stars began to wink, it was time to move.

Nyalis took a deep breath and looked back down at the squirming bundle in his lap. It had been more years than he would like to admit since he had cared for a child. He had forgotten how demanding they could be. "I'm sure you miss your mother," he said, as if the drooling, wide-eyed face staring up at him could understand.

He wrapped the swaddling back around the child's shivering body. Nyalis paused when he caught sight of the strange mark developing on the boy's right shoulder. He traced the darkened area with his finger. "It would appear I was right about you after all, my little faeling."

Nyalis patted down the babe's unnatural shock of white hair and tucked his arms back within the warmth of the wrapping. He tried rubbing the soreness from his aching calves. When that didn't work, he stood, shook the snow from his robes, and pushed on.

He had found the boy's mother just in time to help her deliver, but even with hands as skilled as his, there was no stopping the outcome. Magic, like nature, demanded balance. The price for bringing something as powerful as this faeling child into the world had been her life.

Nyalis fought his way through the dense brush at the edge of the tree line. He was about to lose his temporary shelter from the corax's hungry eyes.

With a sharp tug, he pulled his robe free of the prickle vines that had latched on and turned to stare out at the chasm before him. It was a breathtaking sight, there at the edge of one of the peaks within the Northern Heights, the tallest of Aldor's mountain chains. The mountains were awash in moonlight and backlit with a million stars.

Careful not to slip on any of the loose rocks and plunge headfirst over the side, Nyalis skirted the large boulders lining the front of the pathway and started down the narrow snow-covered trail that meandered along the face of the cliff.

Even during the summer months, the crests of the Northern Heights were covered in snow, but here, at the beginning of the month of Èldwin, the chances of an unexpected storm blowing in from the north were all but certain. A simple change in pressure could cause an avalanche. Nyalis prayed that the weather held out long enough for him to get off the mountain.

The wind tugged at his robes like a ship's sail, threatening to pull him over with every rising gust. Raising his free arm, he gathered the air in front of him and wove it into a barrier, deflecting the dangerous drafts sweeping across the side of the mountain. The continuous push of the wind against his shield kept him balanced as he descended. It was a basic magical weave, taught to first-year apprentices, but sometimes the simplest things worked best.

With one arm out for balance, he hugged the child close and edged his way forward. There was little leeway for maneuvering with a solid wall on one side and a sheer drop on the other. The trail wasn't much wider than his feet.

Preoccupied with trying to work his way around a pile of fallen rocks, Nyalis stumbled and lost his balance. His heart leaped into his throat as he desperately grabbed a small niche in the rock and yanked himself back against the mountain's face. His hands were trembling as he glanced over the side. The drop was so deep, he couldn't see the bottom. He took a couple of moments to catch his breath, then pressed on.

Up ahead, the path widened and split. The soreness in his arms had lessened, but only because they had gone numb from the child's weight and the cold. Nyalis wiggled his fingers, attempting to circulate the blood. When that didn't work, he lifted his free hand to his mouth and blew, hoping to find some warmth.

He cocked his head and listened. He could still hear the corax's cries faintly over the heavy wind. They were circling somewhere to the west, but their steady sweep of the mountainside was heading directly for him.

Using the fork as an opportunity to divert his pursuers, he sent a touch of magic into the right branch. Just enough to whet the appetite. "That should keep them busy for a while," he mumbled as he tightened his grip on the child and headed into the opposite branch. He knew it would eventually wind its way out into the foothills below. Flicking his wrist, he conjured a ball of golden light to illuminate the way ahead.

The rock loomed above him, cutting off all sight of the night sky and hiding him from the watchful gaze of the corax. In a way, it reminded him of the wizard's stronghold of Aero'set. Nyalis longed to be back within the protection of the fortress's great walls. He yearned to walk its many halls, to spend his days combing through the libraries, seeking out new information to aid him in his struggles. It had been far too long since his last visit.

Aero'set was a place of magic. It was a place where dreams were born, where young men and women had come to train in order to earn the right to be named wizards. It was a place of wonder and excitement, but most of all, for

Nyalis, it was home.

Unfortunately, those days had long since vanished into memory. Now all was silent. Nyalis had been there all those centuries ago when the keep had been locked away out of time and reach, awaiting the day it would once again be needed.

That day was not far off.

The child whimpered, pulling him from his reverie. He readjusted the cloth, blocking the babe's view, which seemed to appease him, if briefly. "Hungry again, I see," he said, pulling a small plant from one of the inner pockets of his robe. "Wish I had something a bit tastier than costa root to offer you." He bit off the stem and allowed its bitter juices to run into the babe's mouth. The child's face puckered, but his hunger clearly outweighed the unpleasant taste, and he sucked on the end, making gurgling noises as he did.

The two continued on as Nyalis studied the stone ahead for anything he recognized. He was beginning to wonder if he had taken a wrong turn when the walls finally began to widen.

An early morning sunrise lit the way ahead, its colors washing across the open rock, revealing an end to the passage. He let his ball of light disappear as he crept his way to the opening.

Nyalis waited within the shadows, wary of what might lie ahead. He closed his eyes and reached out with his mind, scanning the open area in front of him.

He couldn't feel the presence of an aura, dark or otherwise.

Ahead lay a gradual slope of scree and small shrubs stretching clear to the forest below. There was a considerable amount of open ground to cross before reaching the large copse of elder pine at the bottom, and the thought of leaving the cover of the mountain didn't sit well with Nyalis's already frayed nerves. But if he could make it to the river and the waiting boat, they would have a chance.

Holding the child close, he left the confines of the rock and made his way down, still scanning the naked expanse around him for any sign of pursuit.

Halfway down the slope, the child grew restless and thrashed inside the swaddling. Nyalis didn't dare stop to calm him. Instead, he hugged him tighter and pushed on.

The child squealed.

Nyalis nearly tripped trying to cover the child's mouth with the cloth. "You've got to keep quiet."

The child wailed, his eyes filling with tears.

"What's wrong with you? You're going to get us—"

The air behind them began to tingle.

Nyalis spun and wove a shield as a wave of energy raced down the slope toward them. He sensed it more than saw it as the surge flew across the ground, kicking up piles of dirt and dust in its wake. The air in front of Nyalis hardened, absorbing the brunt of the impact, but it still sent him tumbling backward.

He shielded the child with his body as they rolled across the sharp rock. The pain was enough to steal his breath. Quickly, he scrambled to his feet, testing his arms and legs for injury. Nothing felt broken. Blood ran down the side of his face, and he wiped it away, discovering a nasty gash on his forehead.

At the top of the slope, three black-robed bulradoer stepped out of the shadows of the open fissure, their hoods raised. The corax had led them right to him.

In the ancient tongue, bulradoer meant *the departed*. They were a sect of dark-magic wielders employed by the White Tower. It was ingenious, really. While the White Tower feigned abhorrence of magic and its wielders, it secretly recruited and trained those same wielders for its own use.

The child continued to cry in his arms, but there was nothing Nyalis could do about it now.

How did they find me so fast? he wondered. Then he saw them. Two sniffers, shuffling just behind the bulradoer, seemingly reluctant to leave the darker shadows of the mountainside. They must have somehow managed to catch the scent of his magic from the left fork.

Sniffers were hideous beings, twisted by magic to serve a single purpose: to hunt down the ven'ae, those who had the ability to wield magic. Both sniffers stood at least eight feet, their flat noseless faces held high as they caught the scent of his magic.

Nyalis was a match for any of the bulradoer, but facing all three, with a pair of sniffers and a full praad of corax—well, that was a different matter altogether.

The Tower's trackers shrieked as they circled his position, letting him know they were still there. As if he needed reminding.

Nyalis raised his free hand and sent a wave of fire flying up the hillside toward the bulradoer. The flames ignited the brush in front of them, burying the dark wielders in smoke.

Using the distraction, he tightened his grip on the child and made a dash for the tree line below. He needed to reach the river and his boat before they caught up with him. Glancing over his shoulder, he could see he hadn't stopped them long, as they broke through the dying blaze in pursuit.

The corax shrieked and dove.

Nyalis ran as fast as he could, the tree line only steps away. He raced through the underbrush, leafless branches slashing at his face and forearms. Behind, he could hear the corax following him into the trees.

With his free hand, he conjured fists of air and sent them careening into his pursuers, hoping to slow them down. His efforts only drove them into a further state of frenzy as they voiced their thirst for blood.

He clearly wasn't going to outrun them, so he turned to face them. Quickly, he wove a net of magic that stripped the bark off a dozen trees and sent it tearing into the oncoming gale.

The reptilian birds shrieked as the projectiles tore through their ranks, striking half of the praad. Those worst hit tumbled to the forest's floor, many missing wings, heads, and feet. Mutilated bodies convulsed as the trees and ground were painted red with their blood, the stench of death strong enough to choke on.

The remaining corax fled.

Nyalis took a deep breath to steady himself. The constant use of magic was beginning to take its toll. In the distance, the sniffers and the bulradoer were just breaking through the first of the trees.

Hugging the child close, he turned and ran.

Chapter 2 | Nyalis

DAWN BROKE THROUGH the forest canopy, filling Nyalis with hope. He could sense the waters ahead urging his weary feet to keep moving. The blood running down his face had painted his beard, and the pain from a hundred tiny injuries tore at his thoughts, threatening to overwhelm him.

Were all his efforts to keep the child out of the White Tower's hands for nothing? Perhaps today would mark the end of the Aerodyne wizard line. If he were to be defeated, would he have the courage to do what was needed? Could he kill an innocent child to save humanity?

Nyalis could hear the river ahead, but he could also hear the sniffers closing in behind him. The hair prickled on the back of his neck, and he ducked. A wave of heat billowed overhead, singeing his white hair. The fireball splashed into one of the trees on his right, immediately igniting the thick bark. Nyalis raised his hand with a whispered word of warding as he ran past.

His spirits lifted when he broke through the brush and spotted the swift-flowing water. But there was no sign of his boat. He paled when he realized he had exited too far north. He could see the small skiff downriver, but it was too far to reach before the bulradoer were on him.

He had nowhere to run.

Frantic, he spun, his eyes darting from trees to brush to embankment as he searched for a place to hide the child. He settled for tucking the babe up under the roots of a fallen tree.

Determination guided his steps as he marched back into the forest. He let his magic seep into the ground as he went, its tendrils spreading through the root systems of the giant trees. He waited just inside a small clearing within sight of the river, continuing to extract as much life from the sleeping forest as he could. He would need it for what he knew was coming. The essence of the giant trees' strength flowed into him, renewing him, bringing his weary thoughts into sharp focus. His skin tingled as he drew in as much as he could hold.

The sniffers slowed when they saw him, spreading to either side to flank him.

He let them come. Nyalis had trained himself to survive. He had studied the teachings of the five great war wizards of old: Pax'Sool, Rascalian, Telvarran, Ballidor, even the mighty Aerodyne himself. He had studied their tactics. Though he could not bring to bear half the magic they had been able to wield, he was dangerous nonetheless.

The three bulradoer stopped at the edge of the small opening when they saw him waiting. The tall one in the middle took a step forward, his voice the sound of one used to being obeyed. "Give us the marked one, wizard, and we will let you live."

"How very generous of you," Nyalis said. "I have a counterproposal. Walk away, and I will let *you* live."

The taller bulradoer waited a moment, then responded with a simple nod to the sniffers. They charged.

So much for diplomacy. Nyalis readied himself. He was only going to get one shot at this; a mistake would doom more than just himself and the child. He forced a final pulse of magic down into the trees as the first sniffer slashed at him with its elongated claws.

Nyalis ducked underneath the first creature but caught a blow across his left shoulder from the second. He cried out as the force of the hit spun him around, nearly causing him to lose his footing. He couldn't expend his magic for healing or even to lessen the pain. He didn't have enough to spare. Instead, he used it to fuel his rage.

He hit the first sniffer with a wall of air, slamming it into one of the trees. It didn't kill the creature, but it did knock it off balance enough for him to dive out of the way of the second as it swung for the side of his head. Its claws passed close enough for him to feel the air on his face.

He couldn't wait any longer.

Nyalis stumbled backward and lifted his hands, releasing the magic within the trees. The ground around the creatures' feet began to move. All three bulradoer backed to the edge of the clearing, immediately weaving shields as roots burst from the ground and wrapped around the two sniffers.

The creatures thrashed, trying to rip themselves free from the entangling roots, but the more they fought, the tighter the roots took hold. The sniffers howled in rage, but their howls soon turned to shrills of pain as, one by one, their limbs were ripped from their bodies. Pretty soon, they made no sounds at all.

Silence returned to the small glen as the roots withdrew into the rich soil and disappeared from view. What remained of the two sniffers was scattered across the open ground between Nyalis and the bulradoer.

Nyalis wrinkled his nose at the foul smell, keeping his guard up as the bulradoer cautiously made their way back into the clearing.

"Impressive," the shorter one on the left said as she pulled back her hood to reveal a head of curly red hair. "But I'd wager that took about everything you had left."

Nyalis was stunned by how young the woman was. She couldn't have been much more than twenty. Her unique raspberry eyes shone bright with gold flecks as she stared him down.

"I have plenty enough to dispatch you three," he lied.

The other two followed her lead and removed their hoods as well.

The man in the middle, who had been the first to speak, took another step forward. His smooth, pasty complexion gave him the appearance of someone recovering from a severe illness. He had a sharp face and an even sharper nose.

The man on the right was shorter, stockier, and wore a thick beard that covered the majority of his face. The little that was visible was pockmarked. His skin, unlike the others', was coarse brown and as rough as untreated leather.

Nyalis wove another shield—smaller, more maneuverable—and attached it to his left hand.

Instead of attacking, each of the three wielders pulled something from beneath their robes.

Nyalis took a step back. *How did they acquire ter'aks?*

The short, bearded man on the right held a plain silver rod about the length of his forearm. It was etched in runes. The woman carried two more, one for each hand. They were shorter but bore similar runes. The tall man in the middle gripped the hilt of a bladeless sword.

Somehow, the White Tower had uncovered weapons from the time of the Fae. Nyalis had thought he was the only wielder alive to still carry one. He had been counting on this should his efforts to escape the bulradoer fail.

The bulradoer conjured their ter'aks by calling their names in the ancient tongue.

"*Ravinar,*" the pale man said, and a double-edged blade of orange flame protruded from the hilt.

"*Cryora,*" the woman whispered, and two whips of flame nearly as red as her hair snaked across the ground, igniting the fallen leaves they touched.

"*Zurok*," the short, bearded man said, conjuring a battle-axe of green flame from the end of the thick silver rod.

It had been almost a thousand years since faerie weapons were last used. Nyalis reached into his robes and drew his own ter'ak, calling its name. "*Taraneel.*" A double-edged longsword of golden flame stretched from the hilt. He raised the sword in front of him. Unlike weapons crafted of wood and iron, ter'aks could be wielded with a single hand. The only weight each possessed was that of the hilt, making them very maneuverable and very dangerous.

Nyalis could already feel the heat from the weapons on top of the patches of flames rising from where the woman's whips touched the ground.

"Last chance, wizard," the pale man in the middle said. "Give us the child or die here."

Nyalis raised his sword. "We'll see who lives and who gets left behind."

The young woman drew back her whips and hissed as she lashed at him from the side.

Nyalis used his shield to deflect the strike, sending the tip of the fiery brand into a nearby tree, igniting the leaves. The pale man came at Nyalis head-on, swinging his sword with both hands. He clearly intended to end the fight by severing Nyalis's head, but Nyalis caught the man's sword with his own. Sparks of flame shot out upon contact, and Nyalis winced at the intense heat as he angled his sword to deflect the other. It slid to the side, and Nyalis took the opportunity to shuffle to the right. The bearded man and his green axe hung back, clearly waiting for the opportune moment to strike.

Nyalis couldn't afford to stay in one place for long. He wouldn't last three flicks of a horse's tail if he was forced to fight all three at once. The energy he had taken from the trees had helped overcome his weariness, but he had no idea how long that would last.

This time, it was Nyalis who charged as he unleashed a barrage of strikes and thrusts at the tall man, forcing the bulradoer to go on the defensive. Each time their blades met, they hissed. Nyalis could feel the air crackle with excess magic.

Nyalis sidestepped, keeping the tall man between himself and the woman's whips. She had the most leverage, and he wanted to stay as far from her reach as he could.

Angling his shield, Nyalis struck the pale man's next thrust away, driving the man's sword into the ground. The leaves immediately caught fire, and Nyalis used the distraction to dart away, spinning just in time to face the bearded bulradoer and his battle-axe.

The short man had thought to move behind Nyalis and catch him off guard. Nyalis had been ready. He turned and swung at him, forcing the surprised bulradoer to block instead of strike.

Nyalis circled the short wielder, positioning the bearded man between himself and the other two. The lower branches of the trees were on fire, the morning air growing uncomfortably hot. Sweat poured from his brow, making it hard to see.

The bearded man charged. He was powerful, his axe swinging with relentless fury. Nyalis raised his shield, struggling to stop the fiery weapon from splitting him like a piece of wood. Even with Nyalis's shield, the bulradoer was all but driving him into the ground. Nyalis was barely able to stand; his legs were shaking, about to give way.

Nyalis moved as if to attack from the right but feinted and swung left. The short bulradoer lowered his axe in time and deflected the blow, sending green and gold sparks in all directions, lighting more of the forest on fire.

The man was unrelenting. He had tremendous strength. His strikes weren't fancy or swift, but they were powerful. Nyalis did his best to dodge the blows as opposed to blocking them. However, he nearly missed an underhanded swing the bulradoer snaked at him, and by the time he had lowered his shield, the force of the hit threw him from his feet.

Nyalis smashed into one of the great pines behind him with a grunt and landed in the dirt. The pain took his breath. The ter'aks might not have had much weight, but the force being used to wield them was very real.

Gasping for breath, Nyalis tried to shake off the wave of nausea threatening to overcome him. He tried moving, relieved to find he still could, though the arm holding his shield felt like it had been fractured.

The other two bulradoer waited for the bearded man to finish him, apparently giving their comrade the chance for the kill.

Nyalis struggled as if to stand, then fell back to his knees. Seeing his opportunity, the bearded bulradoer charged.

Nyalis rose to one knee, but instead of blocking, he threw his air shield like a disk. It sped across the ground, leaves whirling in its wake.

Clearly not expecting such a bizarre maneuver, the bulradoer didn't lower his axe far enough, and Nyalis's shield hit him just below the knees. The man shouted as his legs were ripped out from under him. The force of his forward motion flung him through the air, and he landed face-first in front of Nyalis. His axe slipped from his fingers, and the ter'ak's blade vanished.

Nyalis leaped to his feet and plunged his sword through the bulradoer's back, pinning him to the ground so quickly, his body didn't even jerk. The skin around the blade hissed, but there was very little blood. The heat had cauterized the flesh and set the robes aflame.

A high-pitched shriek was the only warning Nyalis had, and he quickly conjured another shield and turned. He raised it just in time. The lash from the woman's whip ricocheted off his guard like a crack of lightning and struck her across the side of her face. She screamed, and her whips blinked out. She didn't even bother wiping the blood. All reason fled from her raspberry eyes as she called her whips back to life and attacked.

Nyalis swung his shield left and then right, almost tripping over his own feet as he tried to keep her from splitting him in two. The woman's eyes burned hotter than her weapons as she whipped her lashes around, searching for a way to break through his defenses. He fought to keep his feet under him, his legs already shaking.

He backed against one of the trees, using it for support as he concentrated on keeping the fiery brands away from his body. Limbs fell where her whips struck, and the smoke from their burning had grown almost too thick to breathe.

It took everything he had just to counter her advances; his fractured arm was in agony, each stroke of the whip sending a lance of pain down his left side. Sweat poured from his face, coating his body. Even as light as the ter'ak and shield were, keeping them up and moving would soon be more than he was capable of.

"I've got the child!" the tall bulradoer shouted behind them. Both Nyalis and the woman froze.

Keeping his shield up, Nyalis stepped back and glanced over his shoulder. The tall bulradoer lifted the cloth-wrapped bundle into the air, and Nyalis gasped.

Before Nyalis could move to intercept, the woman shouted in triumph and launched another barrage of attacks, this time trying to cut Nyalis's legs out from under him. He dropped to his knees and blocked, nearly growing faint from the impact on his arm. He rolled backward, and the lashes scorched the ground beside him. He was halfway to his feet when the pale bulradoer behind him started screaming. The two fighters stopped once again.

Nyalis made it to his feet and moved out of striking distance of the woman's whips before turning. The babe was now lying in the grass without its swaddling, and the taller man was standing beside him, staring at his own hands.

The smoke was so thick, it was hard to see through, but it looked like the flesh on the bulradoer's hands was falling off in clumps around the bone. The bulradoer screamed and ran for the river.

"What did you do to him, wizard?" the young woman behind him shouted, raising one of her whips as if to strike.

Nyalis turned and raised his shield. "I did nothing," he said, glancing over his shoulder momentarily to look at the bulradoer, now neck-deep in water. "It was the child."

The woman pointed at him with her whip but kept her distance. "What are you babbling about?"

"The child . . . is a faeling," Nyalis said, sucking in air. "He's . . . magic-born."

"We know what he is, you old fool!" she spat. "What did he do to Bellar?"

"I suspect Bellar was the one who did it."

"Quit talking in riddles, whitebeard, or I'm going to cut you in half and feed you to the corax!"

"The child's magic is pure," Nyalis said, dragging the explanation out as long as possible to catch his breath. "It hasn't been corrupted like those of you who serve the Tower. My guess is that when he touched the child, his own polluted magic could not coexist with magic in its purest form, so it tried to correct itself by peeling off the taint." Nyalis shrugged. "It would seem the Creator is smiling on me today."

The woman's face twisted, and she snapped her whips into motion. Not bothering to fight back, Nyalis concentrated all his effort on holding her off. He danced, ducked, spun, and rolled, giving every last ounce of strength his body possessed to keep from being cut in two.

His magic was nearly depleted, and the pain from the cuts, gashes, and fractured arm numbed his senses.

Seeing an opening in her increasingly reckless attacks, he lowered his shield and raised his ter'ak just in time for one of her whips to wrap completely around the blade and meld. Before she could respond, he snatched his arm back with all his might and jerked the whip from her hand. The fire immediately vanished as the silver rod hit the ground behind him. She screamed in fury and nearly took off his head with her other whip.

Nyalis dove to the ground with a shriek of pain and rolled as the whip flew over and sliced clean through a thick mountain fir. The enormous tree toppled, forcing the two to dive in opposite directions as it crashed to the forest floor.

It was just the distraction he needed.

Nyalis struggled to his feet, half delirious, and ran for the child. Placing his ter'ak back within his robe, he scooped the babe and his discarded clothing up in his arms and sprinted along the river with as much speed as his aged legs would carry him. He barely spared Bellar a glance as he raced by, though he could hear the man sobbing as he held his hands under the water.

"That's what you get when you mess with a wizard," Nyalis shouted, then promptly tripped on a rock and flew face-first into the soft mud of the riverbank. "You old fool!" he hissed at himself as he climbed back to his feet, checking to make sure the babe wasn't injured.

He could see his boat ahead, water lapping against the stern. Behind him, the woman's curses broke from the trees as she gave chase. If he could just reach his boat, he might escape with his life, something he had not expected. Unfortunately, she was gaining on him, aided by her younger, more stable legs.

He half hobbled, half ran down the embankment. His heart sank. He was going to make it, but not in time to push off. In a miserable sort of way, he briefly wondered if it wouldn't be easier to just let her end it. A quick snap of her wrist and his problems would be over. No more sleepless nights, no more trekking over mountains, no more relentless pursuit to protect a world which cared nothing for its own protection. Why was he killing himself? Nobody would thank him for his efforts.

Then he felt a slight tug on his bloodstained beard and smiled.

Reaching the boat, Nyalis quickly placed the naked faeling on top of a folded tarp and turned to face the young woman. What was he going to do? She was far too close for him to shove off without her whip cutting the boat in two. His magic was too depleted to weave a shield and much too drained to conjure his ter'ak. The noise of the river's flow pulled at him, and he paused. *It wouldn't take much*, he thought, *just enough to slow her down.*

Not wasting time to think it through, Nyalis stretched what little magic he had left out to the river and gathered its strength, pulling in the water's life much the way he had with the trees. He didn't have time to grab much. He could feel the water's force, the power it yielded as it moved its body along the winding path. Using the river's energy, he raised both hands, and the water near the edge began to shift direction.

Nyalis waited until the bulradoer was almost on top of him. She raised her whip over her head, and he sent a wave of water slamming into her side, throwing her into the mud and dousing both whips in the process. Every last strand of her curly locks was plastered to her face.

Nyalis turned and pushed the small skiff off the bank and into the swift current. He struggled over the side and collapsed into the bow. He didn't have the energy to even lift his head to see if the bulradoer had made it to her feet or was giving chase, or if they were still close enough to the bank for her to reach them with her whip. At that moment, none of it mattered.

Pulling the child down into the bottom of the boat with him, Nyalis closed his eyes and listened to the sound of the river as he lapsed into unconsciousness.

Sometime later, Nyalis struggled to raise his head. He pushed himself into a sitting position against the seat. The sky was clear and the air warm as the current guided them along. His nap had restored a little of his magic. He could feel it moving within him. He needed nourishment if he was going to recover any further.

He pulled out one of the last remaining costa roots from his robe, bit off the end, and squeezed what milk he could into the babe's hungry mouth. The naked child squinted against the light of the setting sun, bubbles seeping from a toothless grin.

He stared at the child's head of white hair and smiled. "That simply won't do, now, will it?" The last thing he needed was to have gone to all this trouble to rescue the child and then have something as mundane as the color of his hair give him away. "Hmm, I think I might have enough magic for this." He placed two fingers on the soft crown of the child's head. Focusing, he mumbled a simple incantation, and the boy's hair shifted to a modest ash blonde. "Yes, I believe that will do nicely," he said, inspecting his work.

After spending a considerable amount of time squeezing the last drops of the root's milk into the child's mouth, then wrapping the now-ratty swaddling around him to ward off the evening air, Nyalis sat back against the seat with a weary sigh and pondered his next move.

The boy had to be protected, which would require that he be kept hidden as long as possible. And there was only one place he could think to do that.

Easthaven.

Chapter 3 | Ty

$\mathcal{T}$HE WOODS SURROUNDING the small clearing were silent, as if nature was holding its breath.

At least, that's how it felt to Ty as he watched his brother raise his large ash bow and sight down the slender shaft. A single bead of sweat slid toward the corner of his brother's eye, but Breen ignored the sting, keeping his concentration locked on the target as he waited for the right moment to draw.

Ty had to admit, his brother was a born hunter, but Breen's skill would never let him feel the forest the way Ty could.

Ty had always known he was different. Apart from the soft features and sandy-blonde hair, he could see, hear, and feel things no one else could. Living in a world where magic was outlawed, Ty had learned very quickly to keep his abilities hidden, even from those he cared about most—especially from them. It was the only way he could protect them.

Perched like a big clumsy bird a pace or two up the bough, Ty closed his eyes and reached out with his senses. Everything slowed as he worked to isolate the voices—the whistle of the wind, the song of the birds, even the monolithic redwood—that called his name.

One by one, the chorus of life faded, leaving only the rhythmic beating of his own heart. His pulse raced as his mind stretched across the wooded glen, searching for that lone voice. The voices he heard weren't expressed in words but feelings. After years of practice, he was learning to understand them—and respond in kind. Once he found the voice he was looking for, Ty opened his eyes.

Caution. Thirsty. Unknown smell. Caution! The stag's head jolted upward as it sniffed the gentle breeze.

Ty watched from the corner of his eye as Breen held the nocked arrow. His breathing was steady, rhythmic, and his broad shoulders pivoted as he followed the stag through the brush. Breen drew the bow's string to his cheek and waited for a clear shot. Ty continued to gently nudge the buck with his mind, enveloping him with a sense of security.

Everything is quiet. You're safe. Water nearby.

A searing pain shot through Ty's right arm. He yelped and grabbed his shoulder, almost flipping himself backward out of the tree.

Breen, startled by the outburst, released his arrow early and missed.

As swiftly as it had appeared, the pain ceased. Ty looked up, but the deer was gone.

Breen turned around, fire in his eyes. "What in the flaming pits, Ty?! That was our meal for the next couple of weeks!"

Ty flinched. His brother's brown-and-green sleeveless tunic revealed arms layered in muscle. Ty had always wondered why he couldn't have been born to look more like Breen. No matter how much he ate or lugged around the feed barrels from the barn, he wasn't anywhere close to matching his brother's size.

"I'm sorry, Breen. My arm . . ." Ty rubbed the back of his shoulder. "It started burning again." It wasn't long after his sixteenth birthyear that the strange sensations had begun.

Breen ran a hand through his shoulder-length brown hair and huffed. He finally hooked his bow on a branch and scooted up the bough beside him. "Here, let me take a look," he said, yanking down on Ty's collar. "Hmm," Breen grunted as he poked Ty's back with his thumb.

"What's wrong?"

His brother scratched at the three-day growth on his face. "Well, if I didn't know any better, I'd say this birthmark of yours has gotten . . . bigger."

Ty twisted his head around like a grey owl to get a better look. "What do you mean, *bigger*?"

"I mean it looks like it's grown since the last time I saw it." His brother released Ty's shirt. "Maybe it's not a birthmark at all?" Breen said casually. "Maybe it's a gruesome skin disease and pieces of you will start falling off, or perhaps it's the mark of the Defiler." Breen wiggled his fingers at Ty, making an eerie noise.

Ty punched him in the shoulder. "Stop it, Breen! That's not funny."

Breen smiled and slid back down the limb, grabbing his bow. He slung it across his back and looked off to the east. "We need to move if we plan on making it home by supper. Don't forget that tonight's Performance Night."

Ty grunted. "How could I forget?"

"You'll do great," Breen said as he swung out of the old white oak. "They say the first time is always the hardest."

"I'm not so sure I want to do this," Ty admitted, running his fingers across the wooden pipes of his homemade flute in his jacket pocket. "You know I don't like playing in front of people." Ty dropped from the limb—not quite as gracefully as Breen, but at least he didn't twist his ankle this time—and ran to catch up.

"Sorry about the deer."

His brother put his big arm around him. "We'll get 'em next time."

Without a fresh kill to drag home, Ty and Breen made good time getting back to the main road. No sooner had they stepped onto the single dirt lane than they could feel vibrations in the hard clay. Ty could sense the horses even before the sound of their hooves had reached them. There were at least nine or ten.

They stepped off the road and waited for the riders to pass. The hairs on Ty's arms shot to attention when he saw them. The riders were all wearing the distinct white mantles of the Black Watch.

"Don't say anything," Breen warned as he took off his bow. "If they stop, you let me do the talking."

Ty nodded.

Living this far out from the White Tower, few had ever seen the white riders, but everyone knew of them. He wondered what the point was in calling themselves the *Black* Watch if all they ever wore was white, but he wasn't about to bring it to their attention.

"I mean it, Ty! Don't you say a word."

"Fine," Ty hissed, feeling on edge. Unlike Breen, the only weapon he carried was his belt knife, but that wouldn't be much use against a group of armed men. "What do you think they're doing out here?"

"Same thing they do everywhere, I reckon. Looking for wielders."

Ty felt his stomach lurch as the riders came to a stop. He counted ten of them before the cloud of dust blocked his view. When it settled, he noticed a small figure at the center of the group, a woman. Her hands were bound and her mouth gagged.

"Saleena?" Breen mumbled half under his breath. He looked shocked.

"Saleena? Who's Saleena?"

"Hush, before you get us both killed . . . or worse."

Ty wondered what could be worse than being killed. He also wondered why his brother appeared to recognize the Black Watch's prisoner.

"How far to the nearest town?" a rough-looking man at the head of the group asked.

Ty noted the guard's posture—stiff as a tunic fresh off the drying line, with back erect and nose in the air. He looked like a bull deer in rut, and probably just as dangerous.

"The nearest town is Easthaven," Breen said, pointing east. "Take this road to its end, then head north. Can't miss it."

Ty snuck another look at their prisoner. The man noticed.

"Get a good look, boy," he said with a sneer, one hand resting on the hilt of his blade. "It'll be the last time you'll see this one. Chased her halfway across Sidara, we did, finally caught up with her just east of Reed Marsh." He glanced over his shoulder. "Have to gag them like that to keep them from using their dark powers on you."

"What'd she do?" Ty asked, forgetting his promise to his brother. He could feel Breen tense next to him.

"This one's been practicing magic on children." The soldier leaned forward, the rough leather of his saddle creaking under his weight. "Townsfolk said they'd seen her offering unnatural healings and unholy charms." He spat onto the road.

The lady fidgeted in her saddle, tears rolling down her cheeks and soaking into her gag. She shook her head, and one of the other guards backhanded her across the face.

Ty started forward, but Breen grabbed his arm. Before he could jerk away, something warm stirred inside him. It was similar to what would happen when his magic was released, but much stronger. He bit down on his tongue, fighting to hold it in check.

"Don't get any wise ideas, boy!" The rider fixed him with a hard stare. "This one would sooner kill you than look at you." Leaning back in his saddle, he wiped his forehead with the back of his glove, streaking the previously caked road dirt clear to the side of his face. "Either of you heard of any magic being practiced round these parts?"

"There's no one at Easthaven with magic," Ty blurted out a little too desperately. Breen tightened his grip on Ty's arm, nearly ripping the sleeve of his faded blue tunic.

"Is that so?" The large man studied Ty's face. "And I'm sure that two upstanding citizens like yourselves would do their duty and report them if there were, correct?" He turned and winked at his comrades.

Their snickers did little to help calm Ty's anger. He took a slow breath. Something still didn't feel right. The heat building inside him felt stronger than anything before. He took another slow breath, in through the nose, out the mouth.

"Yes, sir," Breen interjected, clearly not wanting to give Ty the chance to open his mouth again. "We are good citizens of Aldor. We don't hold to those who practice the dark arts. Dangerous folk. We're mighty thankful to have the protection of the Black Watch." Ty's brother offered a quick bow.

Ty clenched his fists but finally bowed as well.

The man held Breen's gaze for a moment longer before turning back to Ty. "What's wrong with you, boy? You look sick."

Ty could feel Breen shaking his arm, but the strange heat building inside of him was making it hard to focus. He closed his eyes and took another gulp of air. *What's wrong with me?*

"Don't mind him, sir. He gets nervous around strangers."

The white rider stared at Ty a moment longer before grabbing his reins. "Well, you wouldn't want us to get the impression you was keeping secrets, would ya? You know what happens to those who harbor wielders." The man sliced his thumb across his neck. "I'm sure we'll be seeing the two of you again." He snapped his reins, and his horse leaped forward, his men trailing right behind.

Ty couldn't help but shudder at the thought of what they had in store for the poor lady. He took another deep breath, and the heat finally abated. He didn't know if it had risen because of the riders or his anger, or if it had been a random coincidence. He didn't like not knowing, or worse, not being able to control it.

Breen waited until the Watch had disappeared around the next bend before turning on Ty. "I told you to stay quiet!" he snapped, veins bulging in his forehead.

Ty swallowed. "Sorry, I don't know what came over me."

"Obviously." Breen pointed in the general direction of where the riders had just been. "They could have taken us right then and there, locked us away in the White Tower, and there's nothing anyone could have ever done about it. You of all people need to be more careful."

Ty lifted his head. "What do you mean 'you of all people'?"

Breen paled. "I . . . I just mean that . . . that you tend to get overly excited and let your gums go to flapping before your good sense catches up."

Ty studied Breen's face. He knew his brother was right. He had to learn to control his temper, especially when he happened to be one of those very wielders the Black Watch was looking for. He was not some great wizard, but even his small ability to communicate with living things would get him locked away.

With the way people seemed to fear those with magic, he felt his decision to keep his gifts hidden, even from his family, was the right one. And with the Black Watch now threatening to round up any wielders living in Easthaven, his days of going off into the woods to experiment with his magic had come to an end. If he couldn't learn to control whatever was happening to him, he was going to be in real trouble.

Breen picked up the pace. "We need to get back to the house. Father needs to hear about what just happened."

Ty scrunched his nose. "Why? What's he going to do? And how did you know that lady back there? Who was she?"

Breen didn't respond.

"What's going on, Breen?" Ty demanded. "Why aren't you saying anything?"

Breen never slowed. "We need to get home."

Chapter 4 | Ty

AS THEY ROUNDED THE last bend, Ty could see the family cottage just ahead, tucked away on the edge of the Sidaran Forest.

Their home was quite spacious for average wood folk, with three bedrooms, an indoor washroom, kitchen, and a sizable living area. The walls were crosshatched cedar planks and river stone, capped with a densely thatched roof, but little could be seen through the greenery crawling its way across the top. The cottage looked as though it had grown with the rest of the forest.

"Breen, slow down! It's not like the Black Watch is coming over for dinner," Ty grumbled as his brother's longer legs outpaced him.

"Hurry up. Father's going to want to know about this."

"Why? What's he going to do? He'll just lock us in our rooms until they're gone." The thought of being cooped up in the house was excuse enough *not* to tell their father.

Ty followed Breen up the stone path and through the front door.

Adarra, Ty's sister, only a couple of years his senior at eighteen, lifted her head from her spot on the sofa. She was reading another one of the large tomes she always seemed to have on hand. She tucked the loose strands of chestnut hair back behind one ear, revealing a light dusting of freckles. One look at the two of them and she went back to reading.

"I was beginning to worry," their mother, Nilla, said as she stepped in from the kitchen, ladle in hand. She was a short woman with a kind face framed by the same straight chestnut hair as Adarra, though hers bore a few hints of grey. She claimed that Ty had been the one to give them to her.

"Supper will be ready shortly."

Ty closed the door as Breen unstrung his bow and laid it in the corner. "We ran into a little trouble on the road."

"Trouble?" Ty's father, Kellen, looked up from his seat by the fire, where he was busy whittling a small piece of wood. As always, he chewed on the stem of his long pipe to better concentrate. "Not more poachers, I hope?" Ty's father was the overlord's gamekeeper, as was his father before him.

"They were poachers, all right," Breen said as he plopped down on the bench in front of the window. Ty sat in the rocking chair next to him. "Poachers of the Black Watch variety."

His father's hand faltered with the knife. Ty heard a deep intake of breath come from the direction of the kitchen. Even Adarra lowered her book.

His father leaned forward in his seat. "The Black Watch, here?"

"Creator help us," Ty's mother said, moving farther into the main room.

"Yes," Breen said. "And it gets worse."

"Worse?" His father spared a troubled glance at Ty. "How could it get much worse?" That was the same thing Ty had wondered.

"They have Saleena."

"Bog toads!" Ty's father jumped to his feet, startling Ty. His father was a big man and towered over him, much like Breen did. "I told that foolish girl to stay put, that I would be back for her. But when I did, she was gone. It's not my fault she went and got herself captured again."

Ty looked from one person to the next. What were they talking about?

"Did they have a sniffer?" his father asked, pulling his pipe from his mouth and pointing it at Breen.

A sniffer? Ty shoved a strand of blonde hair from his eyes. *What's a sniffer?*

"No, just the guards. They said they found her east of Reed Marsh."

His father leaned against the hearth. "She must've gotten nervous and tried making a run for it."

"Foolish woman." Ty's mother shook her head, swinging her ladle around the way she used to when threatening one of them with a good spanking. "If she would have just listened, we could have found her a safe place to relocate."

"They asked for directions to Easthaven," Breen continued. "Said they were looking for other wielders."

A glimmer of hope registered in his father's eyes as his fingers traced the edges of his groomed beard. "Good. My guess is, they will search the city and surrounding community before moving on. That could give us a few days to do something about Saleena."

Ty couldn't take it any longer. "What is going on? Who's Saleena? And what in Aldor is a sniffer?" His eyes darted around the room as he waited for someone to answer.

His parents shared a hesitant look. Ty's mother shrugged. "He's sixteen. I'd say he's old enough."

"Old enough for what?" Ty asked. "Will somebody please tell me what is going on around here?"

His father sighed. "Nilla, would you get my bag ready?"

"Of course, dear," she said on her way back to the kitchen. "Adarra, come give me a hand?"

Adarra reluctantly laid her book aside and followed her into the kitchen.

"Breen, I need you to saddle my horse."

"You want me to come with you?"

"No. Go to Performance Night. No need to draw any suspicion by not showing up. I'm going to work my way around town and see if I can't find out what our guests are up to before I see the council. Hopefully, we can come up with a plan that won't risk our entire community."

Breen nodded and left, letting the door shut behind him. Ty rocked anxiously from one foot to the other. His father finally sat back down and motioned for Ty to join him. Anticipation swept over him as he sat on the bench his brother had previously occupied.

There was a spark of fear behind his father's sharp emerald eyes. Those eyes, like his brother's, were another reminder of how different Ty was from the rest of his family. Ty's eyes, while just as bright, were sapphire blue. He knew he wasn't their real son. They had told him so when he was old enough to understand.

Ty used to daydream that he was the long-lost heir of a wealthy nobleman, that he had been kidnapped by a band of marauding gypsies and sold on the slave market for food, which was loads more exciting than the truth—that Ty had been dropped off by a kindly old gentleman who had found him in the woods.

Having resigned himself to the fact that he would likely never discover who had given him life, Ty didn't push the matter further. He came to realize he didn't care who his birth parents were. This was his real family, and they were all that mattered.

"Ty," his father began. Ty could tell he was weighing his words with care. "What I'm about to tell you is very dangerous. It's a secret known only to a few. There are a great many lives that depend on it remaining so." His father waited, expression serious. "Do you understand?"

Ty nodded. "Yes, sir."

"Like your brother and sister before you, we were going to wait until we felt you were old enough before revealing what I'm about to share with you. In fact, your sister was nearly seventeen before we told her. But from what you've told us, the White Tower's reach is clearly spreading, and waiting any longer could prove even more dangerous."

"Why would our family be in danger?" Ty asked nervously. "We don't have anything to do with the White Tower." Did his parents already know of his ability to communicate with animals? Would the White Tower come after him if they knew? He couldn't understand why they would; it wasn't like he was anything special. How dangerous could it be to talk with tree-rats and forest-conies?

His father took a deep breath. "Our family is part of a secret group that helps hide wielders from the White Tower."

Ty didn't move. He was too stunned. His family hid wielders?

"Easthaven, like a lot of other larger cities across Aldor, has places of refuge for magic wielders. We call them Harbor Houses. What you need to understand is that most of these wielders haven't done anything wrong. They're no more dangerous than you or me. But because they were born with a special gift or, like Saleena, have been spotted using a new kind of herb to heal what other physickers cannot, they get branded as ven'ae and are rounded up by the Black Watch."

Ty leaned forward in his seat. "What happens to them?"

His father scratched the back of his neck with the stem of his pipe. "We don't really know. At one time, they were held and tested, just to see if their gifts were safe or not. Those they believed to have nonviolent abilities were released on their word that they would never use them, while others who were said to be too dangerous to release were either locked away or executed."

Ty shuddered at the thought.

"Aldor used to be a land rich with magic after the arrival of the Fae. But what we didn't know was that the magic they brought with them could turn even the most righteous of men into tyrants." Ty's father studied his face for a moment before continuing. "Magic can lead to corruption, son, and the more magic we allow around us, the more dangerous it is for our world—"

"Yes, I know," Ty interjected. "And now we are living in the splendor of the Third Age," he said, quoting his teachers, not bothering to hide his sarcasm. "An age of peace without the dangers of magic." Ty sighed. "We already learned about the evils of magic in school."

"Yes, but"—his father leaned forward and jabbed his pipe at Ty to make sure he was paying attention—"is what you learned the truth?"

Ty was afraid to respond. What answer was his father looking for?

"The truth is, Ty, that magic is just that . . . It's magic. It's neither good nor evil. It's a tool, like your mother's rolling pin, or Adarra's books, or even Breen's bow. Evil does not come from the tool but from the one who wields it. Magic, like anything else in this world, can be used for both purposes. Does that make sense?"

Ty considered for a moment. "Yes, sir. I guess I never really thought about it. I just thought magic would eventually corrupt anyone who used too much of it." Ty had always been careful not to use his magic too readily, afraid of getting the taint he'd been warned about in school. "Then why are they telling people that magic is so dangerous?"

"Fear."

"Fear?"

"If those who covet power can make you afraid of the very thing that can keep them from obtaining that power, then half their battle is already won. You'll be surprised what people are willing to do, or give up, in order to feel safe." His father laid his pipe on the stand beside his chair and stood as Ty's mother entered the room with a satchel in hand. "It's the oldest trick in the book, son." He took the bag and tucked it under one arm before turning to kiss Ty's mother.

"There's fresh bread," she said, "a couple of slices of the white cheese, and a cut of salted pork for your supper, and some mulled cider to wash it down. Just promise me you'll be careful. Do you hear me, Kellen?"

"Nilla, you are a blessing from the Creator."

"I know." She leaned in and kissed him once again, this time not releasing.

"Okay, you can stop now," Ty protested, eyeing the tips of his boots, trying to keep from watching the garish display of affection.

His parents chuckled as they parted, and his father ruffled the front of Ty's hair.

Adarra came back in and picked up her book about the same time the front door opened and Breen stepped through.

"The horse is ready."

"Thank you, Breen." His father laid a hand on Breen's shoulder. "By the way, how was the hunt? Any game?"

Breen looked at Ty and cocked an eyebrow. "Not exactly."

Ty sighed. "It was my fault," he said, slumping in embarrassment. "Breen had his eye on a large buck, but . . . my shoulder started hurting again." He rubbed the offending area ruefully. He stopped when he saw the look shared between his parents. It was a look that said they knew something.

"Guess we can't get them all," his father said. "We'll go out again next week." He stuck his pipe in one of the inner pockets of his overcoat. "Have fun in town tonight. I'm sorry I won't be there to see you perform, Ty, but I know you'll do well."

"Should we be going into town tonight, with the Black Watch there?" Ty's mother asked.

"I think right now the safest thing for us to do is to keep up appearances," his father said. "There will be folks at the performance expecting to see you. We don't want people asking questions. I'm sure you'll be fine for tonight."

Ty sighed. He had almost hoped his father would have told them they didn't have to go. The last thing he wanted to do right now was perform.

"You're right," his mother conceded, still not looking like she was quite convinced. "Your father needs to be on his way, and you need to get some supper in you before we head into town."

"I'll try to be back before morning. It all depends on how long it takes the council to discuss our options." His father started to leave, then turned. "Breen, do keep your brother out of trouble."

His father's smile might have been light, but his tone definitely wasn't.

Chapter 5 | Ty

TY AND HIS FAMILY traveled a good three miles before the forest opened and they took the main road leading into Easthaven. Their pace was slow. Ty's mother didn't want to wrinkle her good dress any more than necessary.

"Come on, Waddle," Ty said with no small amount of frustration. He gave the overweight horse a firm nudge with his boot. "You're falling behind. Again."

Straight ahead was the East Hill Orchard. Ty wasn't sure why they called it an *orchard* since it held nothing more than a sprinkling of apricots, interspersed with a couple of mulberries. In the center of the sad cluster, at the highest place of honor, was a rather large cherry tree. The honor was clearly undeserved, considering the last time it had produced anything worth eating was nearly a decade ago.

The road skirted the edge of the orchard before cresting a small rise that gave them a clear view of Easthaven in the valley below. The Sidaran capital was nestled comfortably into the elbow of the East River, like a jewel wrapped in blue velvet.

The only access for miles on this side of the river was the East Bridge. It was a good fifty feet in length and wide enough to fit a pair of tinker wagons. Ty idly watched a couple of flat barges pass underneath the bridge as he made his way across.

The city proper held a variety of shops, craftsmen, and residential living areas ranging from the wealthy estates off River Street to the back-alley shanties behind the larger storefronts. There was a full garrison where the Sidaran lancers trained, a patroller office, which doubled as the local courthouse, and one good inn, which of course could only have been named the *East* Inn.

Ty found an empty hitching post outside the three-story inn. He had just tied Waddle to it when something hard bounced off his head.

"Ow!" He clapped a hand to his head and spun around. "Who threw that?"

Breen shot Ty a serious look and jerked his head to the left. Ty turned and saw three white-clad figures trotting down the road in their direction.

"Blazes!" he squawked, then followed his brother's example and ducked under his horse. The three men rode past. If they had recognized the brothers, they didn't acknowledge it. They simply turned down the next street and vanished from sight.

"That was close," Ty said, peeking out from under Waddle's chin. The horse was busy nibbling on his hair. Ty swatted him away. Waddle just stood there with a smug look on his face, so Ty stuck his tongue out at the blasted animal. He attempted to straighten the part that Waddle had mussed.

"Here, let me see it." His mother dipped her hand in the rain barrel and successfully flattened the rebellious strands. "There, that's better," she said with a satisfied smile.

There was a small line already forming at the inn's entrance. Ty's mother stopped to chat with Bue Aboloff, the innkeeper, as he stood greeting people at the door.

"Ah, I see you've brought your pipes with you, Master Ty," the innkeeper said, a jovial smile on his round face. "Will we have the pleasure of hearing you play tonight? I've heard good things."

Ty smiled and stroked the long wooden tubes sticking out of his jacket pocket. "I'm considering it, Master Aboloff."

"Good, good. I look forward to it."

Adarra slid by and headed inside the open foyer, another thick book out and open in her hands. It was a wonder she managed to keep to her feet, the way she kept her nose stuck in her book.

Once inside, Ty scanned the room for an empty table, which proved to be more difficult than he had expected. The soft light from the candles and table lamps showed the place was filling quickly. He glanced up at the second-floor balcony, but there appeared to be even less available seating up there.

Breen grunted. "I knew we should've left sooner."

"It'll be fine," his mother said, waving to a friend off to the right. "You three find a table and I'll catch up with you in a bit." She disappeared into the crowd.

Ty pointed to an empty spot near the front. "There's one up there."

Breen turned around to see where he was pointing. "Grab it before it's taken. I'm going to wait for Fraya."

At Fraya's name, Adarra looked up from her book and grinned.

Ty grabbed his sister's arm and pushed his way toward the open seats, reaching the table just ahead of a group of elderly women who were having a difficult time squeezing through the crowd. Feeling a little guilty, he gave them the table and settled for one near the side entrance on the right.

By now, the room was so packed, it was hard to hold a conversation unless you were willing to lean across the table. Normally, this wouldn't have been much more than an annoyance, but tonight, many of the women were wearing their most inviting attire, presenting quite the eyeful if they happened to lean too far. Then again, Ty was sure it had something to do with the unusually high turnout of men.

Ty was still scanning the room to see who all was there when Breen approached with a raven-haired girl on his arm. Fraya was looking quite pretty this evening, with her straight black hair parted to the side with a bright yellow bow.

With Breen's build, he had never lacked for girls fawning over him. But he had never been interested in the overly affectionate types. Fraya was different. Since her mother's passing, she had shouldered the load of keeping up the household for her father and three younger siblings.

"Good evening, everyone," Fraya said. Ty waved as Breen held her seat. Ty noticed her hand brush across the top of Breen's fingers. "Why, thank you, Breen. You're quite the gentleman," she said as she sat.

Breen's cheeks reddened, and Ty shook his head.

"Hi, Fraya," Adarra said with a warm smile, lowering her book partway.

"My, don't you look pretty tonight," Ty's mother said as she joined them. She winked at Breen, who flushed an even deeper shade of red.

"Can I get you something?" a young serving girl asked, her lanky features and auburn hair declaring her one of the Aboloff children.

Fraya ordered a mint tea, while Adarra and their mother ordered the apricot.

The girl looked across the table at Breen and Ty, waiting for their orders, a cordial smile plastered to her face. Breen looked tense as he fumbled around the front of his coat.

"Get what you want, Breen," their mother said as she dug in her carry bag. "I can cover it."

"No, I've got it." Breen's face was really glowing now. He pulled a couple of coins from one of his pockets. "Cider, if you have it." The girl nodded and smiled.

Ty joined his brother in ordering the cider. It wasn't his favorite, but it was better than the tea. Bue Aboloff tended to use too many cloves in the brewing, leaving it with a strong aftertaste.

The girl performed a sidestep that was meant as a curtsy but looked more like she had tripped on her left foot. "I'll be right back with them." She turned and disappeared back into the crowd.

"She's such a sweet girl," Ty's mother said, looking in his direction. He pretended he didn't notice.

"We found out the reason for the large crowd," Breen said. "Fraya heard that Overlord Barl is planning on attending tonight. He's coming to support his daughter's performance."

Ty's stomach lurched. "Lyessa's going to be here?" *She would pick tonight to show up,* he thought. *Just to spite me.*

"What's wrong?" Fraya asked.

"Ty was going to play tonight," Adarra answered, nose back in her book.

"That's wonderful," Fraya said. "Breen has told me how well you play. I'm looking forward to hearing you."

"Well, you'll have to keep looking," Ty said. "It won't be tonight. Not if *she* shows up."

His mother sighed.

Ty was saved from any further discussion by the arrival of the serving girl with their drinks.

Breen pulled out three coppers to cover his and Fraya's drinks, while Ty's mother counted out four more to cover hers, Ty's, and Adarra's. Ty blushed. In all the excitement, he had forgotten to grab his coin pouch before leaving the house.

"Thanks," he mumbled. "I'll pay for yours next time. I promise."

His mother raised an all-too-knowing eyebrow.

As soon as he lifted the cider to his lips, the crowds parted, and Overlord Barl walked in, heading slowly for his reserved table at the front. Just behind him was Lyessa, hanging off the arm of some guy Ty didn't recognize. She glided through the crowd, forcing Ty to twist in his seat to get a better view. Who was she with?

Lyessa was almost the image of perfection, with her sparkling emerald eyes and long flowing curls—only instead of being sun-kissed, they were an angry red. Ty figured the Creator must have had a sense of humor, since he had gifted her curls to match her temperament.

It was hard *not* to stare at her. The eighteen-year-old moved with such grace that she drew every eye in the room. Her dress, though quite modest with its long silky sleeves and conservative neckline, demanded attention. Its burnished-gold color accented her hair all the more, flowing behind her as she walked. As much as Ty hated to admit it, she looked stunning.

"Speak of the Defiler . . ." Ty said, putting a hand in front of his face as they drew closer, hoping she would pass by unnoticed.

"Hello, Ty," Lyessa said, making a beeline for their table. "I haven't seen you here in a while."

Lowering his hand, Ty smirked. "Lyessa." He glanced to either side of her. "No poor peasants to flog tonight, I see."

Adarra kicked him under the table. "Ow!" He glared at his sister. "What was that for?"

"Be nice," she hissed softly.

"Oh, where are my manners?" Lyessa cut in. "Have you met Aiden?" She snuggled closer on her escort's arm. "His father owns half the millworks in Sidara." She gestured to their table. "This is Breen, Adarra, and their mother, Mistress Nilla." Lyessa offered a polite bow in Ty's mother's direction. "And, of course, we can't forget Ty."

"No, we wouldn't want to do that," Ty mocked under his breath, and he was about to say more when he noticed his sister had closed her book. She was staring at Lyessa's escort with an expression Ty rarely saw from her, except when discovering a new book she had to have.

Breen stood and bowed. "It's nice to meet you, Master Aiden." Aiden returned Breen's bow, though his was much slighter.

Why is Breen bowing to this foolish nincompoop?

Breen gestured across the table. "This is Fraya."

"I was sorry to hear about your brother, Fraya," Lyessa said, surprising Ty. "He will be truly missed." She actually sounded sincere.

Breen took his seat again, and Aiden offered a polite nod to the table.

"It's very nice to meet you, Master Aiden," Ty's mother said. "I hope you plan to stay awhile."

Aiden tightened his grip on Lyessa's arm. "Yes, there are many things about Easthaven that I find quite appealing."

Ty tried not to gag.

Adarra presented her most charming smile as she continued to stare. Ty didn't know which was sadder: his sister's bizarre infatuation with this overdressed oaf or Aiden's lack of response to her attempts to catch his eye.

"I see you brought your flute, Ty," Lyessa said. "Will you be gracing us with a song?"

"Hardly," he said, trying to cover the offending instrument. "I just forgot to take it out of my pocket before we left."

Lyessa shrugged. "Well, it's probably for the best. I wouldn't want you to be self-conscious about having to perform the same night as me." She smirked. Ty felt his blood boil at the unspoken challenge. "Father just purchased me a new half-harp and requested I play it tonight."

Ty couldn't take it any longer. "I wouldn't care if your father could afford to get you a *full* harp with a ten-piece band and a pair of dancing tenors! It will take a whole lot more than that to challenge me."

His mother gasped. "Ty!"

Aiden glanced nervously at the surrounding tables while Breen and Adarra merely shook their heads in embarrassment.

Lyessa released Aiden's arm. "Is that so? You think you can show me up with your little wooden pipes?"

"I know I can." Ty started to rise from his seat, but his mother pulled him down.

"Then get up there tonight and prove it."

"I will!" Ty exclaimed.

"Fine!" Lyessa said, allowing Aiden to lead her away.

"Fine!" Ty shouted, coming the rest of the way out of his seat.

Their table was quiet, and so were half the surrounding tables. All eyes were on him as he sank back into his chair.

Fraya cleared her throat. "I guess I'll get to hear you play after all."

"What?" Ty paled as he realized what had just happened. *Blazes! She did it to me again!*

Adarra sighed and lifted her book.

Ty glared at the back of Lyessa's red curls, watching as they bounced all the way to her seat. He slowly traced a finger over the pipes of his flute. He would show her. This was going to be a performance she would never forget.

Chapter 6 | Kellen

KELLEN ADJUSTED HIS HOOD as he crossed the empty street. He turned into a dimly lit alley behind some shops on the west side of town and stopped at a darkened doorway. He knocked in three short bursts, waited a moment, then knocked once more.

"Who ith it?" came a raspy voice from the other side.

"It's Kellen." He could hear the brace being removed from the inside before the door slid open. Light from inside spilled across Kellen's face as Eliab, an elderly man with a thinning head of grey hair and a full beard, peered out. He carried a large double crossbow tucked under one arm. He opened the door the rest of the way and ushered him inside.

Kellen cast a quick glance back up the alley to see if he'd been followed before stepping inside.

Eliab propped his crossbow against the wall and bolted the door. "Thollow me, Mathter Kellen," the man said with a wide, toothless smile. "They're already here."

"Thank you." He trailed his guide into a back room and through a door leading to the cellar below. He followed the man down. The temperature dropped with each step. The stairs ended in an open area that looked much like any other shopkeeper's cellar, with boxes and barrels sprawled across the floor, each one meticulously labeled. But this wasn't just any shopkeeper's cellar. This was the Easthaven Harbor House.

Both sides of the cellar were lined with rooms. The council used them as temporary housing for wielders before they were moved to a safe location somewhere within the Sidaran borders. Each room was equipped with a single cot, a small table, and a chair.

At the back of the cellar was another door. This one leaked a trickle of light around its edges. Eliab knocked. Without waiting for a response, he turned the handle. "Mathter Veldon," the old watchman said to a stout man sitting at the head of a long table. "Mathter Kellen hath arrived."

"Thank you, Eliab," Veldon said in his deep, booming voice. "That will be all."

Eliab bowed and shuffled out of the room, shutting the door behind him.

Veldon, the local portmaster and official head of the Easthaven Wielder Council, rubbed a faded handkerchief across the top of his balding head. He had a thin jawline beard that did little to hide the girth of his cheeks. Around his neck hung two silver chains. One had a small flint rod; the other a wedge of steel.

The room never seemed to change much. Three six-tiered candelabras lined the center of the table, their warm glow giving the room a relaxed feel. Six of the ten chairs were filled, one by a woman Kellen didn't recognize. By the faint creases around her eyes, she didn't appear to be much younger than he was. Her short-cropped hair was as white as a midwinter's snow, a highly unusual trait for someone without great age. In fact, he'd only ever heard of one other person who had it.

The color and length of her hair, however, were not what kept his attention. It was her amber-colored eyes, eyes that seemed to absorb all action within the room. The restless eyes of a predator. Kellen looked away, not wanting to stare.

"This saves us the trouble of sending for you," Veldon said, motioning for Kellen to join them. "How'd you hear about the white riders?"

Kellen took a seat near the opposite end of the table. "My boys were returning from a hunt this afternoon when they came across them on the road. Breen said they had Saleena." The others stiffened in their seats. "The guards were bragging about having caught her just east of Reed Marsh. Said they were planning on rooting out any other wielders in the area."

Veldon leaned forward, the edge of the table jabbing at his midsection. "It appears you know more than we do." He glanced at the others. "Has anyone heard from our recent batch of refugees?"

"Not yet," Reloria said across the table from Kellen. She had a frustrated look on her face as she tried unsuccessfully to adjust her brightly colored hat. Kellen couldn't remember the last time he had seen the sweet-shop owner without one, but they never seemed to match her outfit. Either she was completely colorblind or she enjoyed making a rather pronounced statement. Knowing Reloria, it was probably a little of both.

"We've had no report of seeing the Black Watch from any of the other wielders," Orlyn added from his seat between Reloria and the mysterious white-haired woman. The older man's staff rested against the back of his seat. It was nearly as tall as he was, with faint carvings that ran the length of the wood.

"Good." Veldon released the flint and rapped his knuckles on the table. "I would hate to think we had a leak."

"Well, that's all well and good," Feoldor grumbled on Kellen's right, the usual scowl on his face, "but what I want to know is . . ." He stopped scratching at his bushy side whiskers and pointed at the white-haired woman on the opposite side of the table. "Who is this? This is council business, Veldon, and

I demand to know who this woman is and why she's here." Feoldor looked around at the others. "Blood and fire, people! The woman knows who we are! Am I the only one who sees a problem with this?"

Orlyn shifted uncomfortably in his seat, no doubt because his chair was just to the left of the newcomer. "Feoldor has a point. Our secrecy is what keeps us alive and effective. This is highly irregular, Veldon." He tugged at his baggy earthen-green robe. "It should have been discussed beforehand."

"I agree," Reloria added. "We should have been informed prior to this meeting."

The only two members silent through the whole affair were Kellen and Gilly. The dwarfish man seated next to Veldon on Kellen's side of the table simply smiled. Gilly had a thick head of dark hair and even thicker eyebrows. His childlike mannerisms often gave him the appearance of being younger than he was. As usual, Gilly seemed content to play the spectator. Kellen knew the socially awkward man had little love for being around other people and preferred the solitude of his river, but with this being an important meeting, his presence had apparently been requested.

Veldon raised his hands to gather everyone's full attention. "I apologize for the break in protocol, but with the Black Watch having now made it as far as Easthaven, I thought it prudent to skip some of our regular formalities."

The portmaster lifted his gaze to the other end of the table. "Kellen, you've been rather quiet. Did you have anything to add?"

Kellen scanned the faces, considered the outcome of picking sides, then decided on a more direct approach. "You could start by introducing her."

"Well, if you all would give me the chance." Veldon wiped the top of his head one more time. "Her name is Sheeva, and she's from Briston. Duport, to be precise. She came to me about a week ago—"

"And how, pray tell, did she know who you were?" Feoldor asked. "Do you have a sign over the docks that reads *shipping* on the left, *wielding* on the right?"

Veldon groaned. "Lugar, the head of the Duport Harbor House, who happens to be a trusted friend, heard of her predicament and sent her our way." Veldon leaned back in his seat. "If Lugar trusts her, that's good enough for me."

"What predicament?" Feoldor asked.

"I'll tell you as soon as you stop flapping your jaws."

Feoldor crossed his arms but obeyed.

"Like I was saying, Sheeva arrived last week with a little girl she had saved from an assassin's knife. The child had been discovered to be a wielder and was set for execution. The overlord of Briston, as we know, has little tolerance for magic."

"Didn't he recently lose his wife?" Reloria asked.

"He did," Orlyn interjected. "And to a charlatan posing as a healer. The man had promised to possess a rare herb that could cure the plague, of all things." Orlyn, who also happened to be the local apothecary, shook his head. "What kind of opportunist would make claims that outrageous?"

"A stupid one," Feoldor added.

Reloria sighed and popped a sweet in her mouth.

"Anyway," Veldon continued, "I received word a couple of days ago that there was indeed a bounty being offered for the capture of this little girl, as well as the white-haired woman harboring her." He glanced in Sheeva's direction. "And since it bore the royal seal of Briston, I would say her story appears to be true, at least on that account."

Something about the story still bothered Kellen. "If I may interrupt," Kellen said. "I'm going to need to know a bit more than that if I'm going to place my life and the life of my family into the hands of this council."

"Aha!" Feoldor beamed with satisfaction. "You see, someone around here finally shows some common sense."

Reloria rolled her eyes. "Oh, shut it, Feoldor, and let the man talk."

Kellen turned back to Sheeva. "What bothers me is how Overlord Meyrose knows not only that someone is protecting this girl, but exactly who it is and what they look like. How does he know so much about you?"

Sheeva returned Kellen's gaze. "Because I was the assassin he hired to kill her."

Reloria nearly choked on her candy while Orlyn made a quick slide to the opposite end of his seat.

"Until recently, I've been in Overlord Meyrose's employ," Sheeva said, no emotion on her face. "I'm very good at what I do, and this usually allows me a certain measure of leeway to choose what jobs I want. However, when I learned that my target was an eleven-year-old girl and a wielder, I refused. Needless to say, Meyrose didn't appreciate my reluctance and put a bounty on my head in turn."

"That's all we need," Feoldor grumbled. "A wanted assassin with a price on her head, and by the flaming overlord of Briston, no less."

"I'd rather her be on our side than not," Orlyn said.

Feoldor shrugged, which was as close to an agreement as Orlyn was going to get.

"Speaking of young wielders," Reloria said, "what of Ty?"

"Aye," Orlyn chimed in. "We've never had a full patrol from the White Tower in Easthaven before."

"I don't believe he's in much danger at the moment," Kellen said.

"Have you gone completely daft?" Feoldor spouted. "It's those goat-licking vermin from the White Tower we're talking about! Here! In Easthaven! Of course he's in danger!"

"Watch your language, Feoldor," Reloria said, glaring at him from across the table.

"It was Saleena they were after," Kellen said. "And if she had listened to me, they wouldn't be here at all. As it is, there's not much we can do but keep an eye on them while they're here. Besides, if I were to restrict Ty to the homestead every time there was a whiff of danger, he'd be asking questions I don't believe he's ready for."

"It's been sixteen years, Kellen," Orlyn said. "We can't keep him in the dark much longer. The boy needs to know who he is and where he came from."

Kellen sighed. "I know. The wizard said that he was going to come for him one day. I'm afraid that time might be close."

"Perhaps it was a mistake to have kept this from him," Reloria said, but it was more a question than anything.

Kellen didn't agree. "Why lay that heavy a burden on such young shoulders? Is it so wrong to want him to feel normal, to have friends, fall in love, to live his own life?"

Veldon rested his forearms on the table. "No, it's not, Kellen. But therein lies the problem. He's not normal. I understand wanting to shelter him from the truth, but there comes a time when doing so will only prove more harmful. As Orlyn said, Ty needs to know who he is."

Kellen lowered his head. His friends spoke the truth, whether he was willing to accept it or not. If he was honest, he was afraid that the truth would cost him his son. Like any father, he wanted his children's lives to outshine his own, but with Ty, that reality was as dangerous as it was probable.

The White Tower was hunting him. That alone was enough for Kellen to want to shield Ty from the truth as long as possible, to protect him from the burden he would one day bear. Kellen knew he couldn't shelter his son forever; he just wasn't ready for *someday* to mean *now*.

Chapter 7 | Kellen

"**N**OW THAT WE'VE** gotten that out of the way," Veldon said, "introductions are in order."

Feoldor groaned and leaned back in his chair.

Veldon turned to Sheeva. "With an association as dangerous as ours, we feel the best way to reassure those we are working with is to require each member of this council to be wielders themselves. Greater risk, greater loyalty. Normally, we require a grace period for new members wanting to join, but I trust Lugar with my life. And if he says you're okay, then I agree."

He cleared his throat. "I guess I will go first. My name is Veldon, and as you know, I own the Easthaven Dockworks. I am also an incindi."

Kellen had always enjoyed watching Veldon's gift. Everyone except the white-haired assassin relaxed in their seat, waiting for what they already knew was coming. Sheeva, on the other hand, remained poised as if to strike or run.

Veldon raised his right hand. Around his second finger was a uniquely designed pewter ring with a small crystalline center. It pulsed a deep red as he aimed it at the flickering lights of the large tallow candles lining the middle of the table. The flames blinked momentarily, then detached themselves from their wicks and rose into the air. The portmaster spread his fingers, and the flames grew brighter.

Kellen watched the flickering lights float above their heads. He looked across the table at Sheeva. Her face was still expressionless, but her eyes were wider than usual.

A gust of wind whipped across the room and extinguished the flames, blanketing the room in darkness.

Feoldor chuckled.

"Feoldor." Sparks illuminated Veldon's face as he struck the flint and steel hanging from his neck. Kellen watched as they developed into a ball of flame. Veldon sent the small flame bouncing across the candelabras, relighting each as it went.

Feoldor lowered his hand back to the table rather nonchalantly. Just visible beneath his sleeve was a brass bracelet bearing a single clear stone. He cleared his throat. "My name is Feoldor, and I run the best glassworks in town. As you can tell, I'm a vanti."

"Which, in Feoldor's case," Reloria said, "means he's full of hot air."

Kellen smiled. Reloria always found every excuse to needle the outspoken man, which was hardly difficult to do. The two had been playing this game for years, ever since she had lost her husband, and him, his wife. Most of the council had bets on how much longer before the two would finally overcome their petty bickering and tie the knot.

Feoldor huffed and went back to fiddling with his bracelet. Reloria, on the other hand, leaned forward in her seat to get a better look at their guest, offering Sheeva a warm smile. "My name is Reloria, dear, and I own the sweet shop in town. I'm a telasero, which I admit is not as glamorous as some of the others. In fact, most wielders have no idea what a telasero is." She waited to see if Sheeva would say anything, but she didn't. "Well, it means I have the ability to control taste."

Kellen could tell by the puzzled look on Sheeva's face that Reloria was going to have to demonstrate. Reloria reached inside her rather large carry bag, which looked to have been sewn from a number of discordant fabrics, and pulled out a wrapped pickle. She cut a slice and offered it to Sheeva.

The white-haired assassin lifted the pickle, sniffed, and promptly wrinkled her nose.

"Go ahead, try it," Reloria said.

Sheeva stuck the pickle in her mouth, her face contorting at the taste. It was the single largest emotion Kellen had witnessed from her so far.

Reloria rubbed her fingers across a small crystal amulet hanging loosely around her neck and closed her eyes. The stone sparked to life, emitting a faint golden pulse.

Sheeva's expression softened. "Tastes like . . . toffee."

Reloria smiled victoriously.

"I guess I will go next," Orlyn said in his raspy voice. "My name is Orlyn, and I am the town apothecary. My simple ability lies with vegetation. I'm a floratide."

"More than simple, I would say," Veldon said as Orlyn slipped his hand into one of the many pockets of his baggy robes and pulled out a small clay pot. It had always astounded Kellen, the number of bizarre and utterly random objects Orlyn managed to keep hidden away within his saggy attire. He seemed to have something for every occasion.

The pot was filled halfway with dark, rich soil. Orlyn placed the small container on the table and held out his hand to reveal a seed pinched between his thumb and first finger. He gently tucked it into the soft dirt, pressed down with his thumb, and retrieved his staff from behind his seat. The staff was wrapped with rows of carved vines. Interwoven within the vines were runes. Kellen had asked the apothecary about them years ago, but the old man had only shrugged and said the staff had been handed down in his family for generations, and he didn't know where it had originated.

The crystal crafted into the top cast a light-green flicker across the side of Orlyn's face as he tilted the head of the staff downward and tightened his lips in concentration. Everyone leaned forward to watch as the soil around the seed shuddered and a small sprout poked its head through the dirt. The stem raced up, sprouting leaves until a flower with gold-and-lavender petals exploded from the end.

"I never get tired of that," Reloria said, beaming.

Orlyn slid the planter in front of Sheeva. "For you, my dear. A beautiful flower for a beautiful lady."

Sheeva bowed her head slightly. "Thank you." She left the gift sitting untouched in front of her, looking as though she wasn't exactly sure what she was supposed to do with it.

Kellen glanced around the room. That only left two more.

Veldon poured some water into Gilly's cup. "Go ahead, Gilly," Veldon urged. "Show the nice lady what you can do." Gilly wasn't exactly simple, but having been raised into his adult years by parents who thought that hiding him away from everyone was the best way to deal with his gift, he wasn't exactly normal, either.

Veldon glanced at Sheeva in an apologetic manner. "Gilly is rather shy. Since the death of his parents, he's lived by himself upriver and doesn't usually come to town, except on special occasions."

Gilly, whose head barely reached Kellen's waist, was one of the most timid men Kellen had ever had the privilege of knowing. But what the little man lacked in social skills, he made up for in kindness. Even now, as he stared at his cup of water, his face held an infectious smile. It reminded Kellen of Adarra every time she discovered some new tidbit of information from one of the countless books she was always reading.

"Anytime you're ready," Veldon said.

With his short, pudgy fingers, Gilly retrieved an uncut crystal from the inner pocket of his cloak, which he pointed at the cup. The stone glowed a pale blue, and water in the cup began to whirl and stretch, forming a miniature funnel as it rose over the lip. Gilly's eyes were bright with laughter, like a child playing with a new toy. Abruptly, the swirling motion slowed and then stopped as the water turned from blue to translucent to white, hardening into ice.

Sheeva studied Gilly with the same appraising look she had given everyone else in the room.

Still beaming from ear to ear, Gilly stowed his crystal back in his pocket without saying a word.

"Gilly's a voda," Veldon added, since the little man was clearly not going to speak. "One of the strongest I've seen, I might add." The portmaster turned to Kellen and raised his arm. "That just leaves our gamekeeper."

Kellen reached into his pocket and pulled out a small copper coin. He'd performed this trick a number of times. He held it up for everyone to see. "Who wants to do the honors?"

No one volunteered.

From the other side of the table, Sheeva's hand went up. Kellen tossed her the coin, which she plucked easily from the air. She looked it over and then cocked her head as she glanced back in his direction.

Kellen smiled reassuringly. "Just toss it up whenever you're ready."

Her eyes narrowed as if measuring the risk involved, but eventually she flicked the coin upward. It almost reached the rafters before gravity took over and brought the coin plummeting back toward the table. Before it landed, Kellen drew a small dagger from his cloak and flung it across the table, catching the coin mid-rotation. Coin and dagger flew across the chamber, spearing one of the wooden beams that framed the room.

Sheeva left her seat and retrieved the dagger from the wood. She slid the impaled coin free and inspected it. "Impressive," she said, flipping the dagger from handle to blade with the movement of one who was obviously familiar with its feel. After taking her seat, she leaned across the table and held the knife out to him, handle first.

"Thank you." Kellen slid the blade back inside the folds of his jerkin. "You can keep the coin."

"Master Kellen isn't like the rest of us," Veldon said. "He doesn't require a transferal crystal to use magic. His magic is innate, a rare trait nowadays. And as you've just witnessed, he has perfect aim. He can pin a fly to the wall with anything you place in his hands. He draws quite the crowd during Easthaven's archery competitions." The portmaster winked at Kellen before turning his attention back to their guest. "That just leaves you, my dear, if you would be so kind?"

All eyes were on their newest member, waiting to see what sort of magic she possessed. Kellen was especially interested in a gift used by an assassin.

Sheeva gave a slight nod, and the space around her body shimmered. It was like looking through a piece of broken or warped glass, then she disappeared. Chairs scraped across the floor as the council members jumped to their feet. Feoldor cast around nervously, ready to bolt, while Gilly ducked under the table. Kellen reached for his knives when the space Sheeva had been occupying distorted, and she came back into view, never having left her seat. Veldon seemed to have been the only person not affected by her rather unique gift. He must have seen it when she had come to him to hide the young girl.

Once the room quieted, Veldon spoke. "I guess you can now understand her previous employment." He glanced at Sheeva. "Not that I'm condoning it, of course. But if you're going to be an assassin, what could be more helpful than not being seen?"

More than a few eyebrows rose at his offhand comment, but he continued. "Someone with your ability could make a useful addition to our group."

"If we can trust her," Feoldor was quick to add.

Veldon didn't reply. Instead, he leaned forward and placed his elbows on the table. "Let's get down to business, shall we? The question is, how are we going to help Saleena without drawing attention to the wielders here in

Easthaven?"

Kellen packed his pipe from the pouch in his side pocket and lit it using one of the nearby candles. "I might have an idea."

Chapter 8 | Ty

BY THE TIME THE performances were ready to begin, Ty had broken out into a full sweat, and it had nothing to do with the number of people in the room.

Noreen Aboloff ascended the stage and gave her ritual greeting. She made sure to include a special welcome to Overlord Barl and his lovely daughter Lyessa and thank them for their faithful patronage. The audience cheered, and Overlord Barl raised a hand in thanks, not bothering to stand.

Ty barely noticed the weaver's three daughters as they sang "Breaking of the Dawn." He did note that the arrangement's difficulty seemed to surpass the girls' skill, but the crowd cheered graciously anyway.

Next was a rather impressive flutist who mesmerized the audience as he rolled up and down the melody of a tune Ty didn't recognize. He dropped a few notes along the way, picking others up in their place, but it was for the most part rather well played, and Ty halfheartedly clapped with the others as the man left the platform.

After the flutist, Justice Tirfing's wife recited a section from Islow's *Love of the Fallen*, a depressing sonnet about the loss of true love. There were a couple of sniffs, some eye-wipes, and more than a few yawns from the men as she finished and returned to her seat.

Ty stiffened. He suddenly realized he had no idea what he was going to play. Panic set in. His mind raced through an assortment of possibilities, each one perfectly acceptable any other night, but none good enough to squelch Lyessa. *Why did I ever open my mouth?*

Three or four more selections were announced, and the performers came and went, but Ty didn't notice. He was focused on more important matters, like how he could sneak out the back door and still save face.

The innkeeper's wife announced a short intermission, and the serving girls made their rounds. What if he told them he was feeling sick? It wasn't too far from the truth. If he backed out now, he'd never hear the end of it from Lyessa. His mouth was dry. Ty lifted his mug and looked inside. He'd finished the cider some time back and was too embarrassed to ask his mother to buy another round.

The performances continued for at least another painful hour before Noreen made her way to the stage to announce the evening's three final performances. First was Master Ethen, a local carpenter. He shuffled through the tables on his way to the platform. After taking a seat, he opened a finely crafted case and produced a beautiful hand-carved five-string vielle and bow. With careful precision, he ran his fingers across the strings, twisting the tuning pegs at the top as he did.

A voice rang out from the back of the room. "Play us a fun one, Ethen. None of that snobbish stuff!"

"Yeah," another agreed. "Give us something we can sing to."

More than a few hardy ayes came from the anxious crowd as Ethen accommodated his audience with a town favorite: "Bart the Fool." No one had ever managed to record all the verses to the song, since every family had a verse or two of their own passed down from generation to generation.

Lifting his bow, Ethen drew the crowd in by playing a couple of rounds with just the vielle. Once he was comfortable with the level of participation in the room, he unleashed his strong baritone.

> *There once was a fool named Bartimus, a wife he went to find.*
> *He left his home, his work, his friends, his fam'ly all behind.*
> *And on the way he met a Fae, who told him of a place,*
> *Where there were girls with golden curls . . . but growing from their face.*

By the second round, the people were clapping and singing along. The way Ethen's bow flew across the strings hauled Ty out of the gloom he had been wallowing in and set his feet to bouncing under the table. Soon he was clapping along with everyone else. The driving rhythm made him want to get up and dance.

> *He heard a maiden had been taken by a dragon 'cross the sea,*
> *And so he tracked the creature down, in hopes to set her free.*
> *But after he had slain the beast, things went from bad to worse.*
> *For the dragon was no dragon . . . but the girl under a curse.*

By the third round, the townsfolk were out of their seats and standing in the aisles. There was a growing crowd of men up front who had locked arms in a line, kicking up their heels in a dance. Even the occupants at Ty's table belted out a verse or two.

> *Bart the Fool, he never quit, his searching carries on.*
> *From town to town he travels round, his stay is never long.*
> *So if he comes a knockin' on your door . . . don't let him in.*
> *But lock your daughters in their rooms and promptly warn your kin.*

The crowd called for more, but Ethen waved kindly and placed his instrument back in its case so the next performer could take their turn. Ty envied his choice of song. No performer had ever left the stage to silence after a few verses from "Bart the Fool." Now if the Creator would only bless him with such a stroke of insight.

Next to last were the Aboloff children as they laid aside their aprons and donned a set of rather unique costumes to reenact the *Tales of Prysipitus*, a short but emotional fight scene between the hero and the evil sorcerer. Small pieces of confetti flew across the stage, landing on those seated closest as the magical scene was revealed. Their performance was warmly applauded as the children bowed and exited the stage.

Noreen climbed the steps one final time to make a full introduction for their special guest musician. She gestured to a table near the front center. "And now we welcome Lady Lyessa, who has graciously offered to tickle your ears and warm your hearts this evening with her harp. Please give her a round of applause."

The audience clapped with excitement, Ty especially, as it appeared Lyessa hadn't told Mistress Aboloff to put him on the schedule after all. He breathed a deep sigh of relief as he watched Aiden help Lyessa to the stage, her instrument tucked safely under his arm. Ty found himself wishing Aiden would trip and land on the stupid thing.

Lyessa took her seat, and Aiden lowered the harp to her lap, then returned to his table, where Overlord Barl sat waiting with a proud grin.

From the moment her fingers touched the strings, the audience was hers. Each note demanded praise. The music radiated through the East Inn like dawn's light greeting a new day—warm and filled with promise. Ty couldn't help but stare at the intricate way her fingers seemed to float up and down the strings, producing sounds and rhythms so enchanting, they gripped his very soul.

Time itself seemed to slip into darkness as his burdens and fears dissolved like new-fallen snow across the embers of a dying fire. As the final notes faded, the people bounded from their seats with an ovation worthy of the High King himself. It was honestly earned, in Ty's humble opinion, but his heart sank.

Still under the trance of her music, he found himself wishing—no, pleading—for more. Ty was suddenly jerked from the entrancement by the sound of his name being called. He looked up at the stage. Lyessa was pointing in his direction. He would have shrieked if he could have caught his breath long enough to do so.

". . . and he has promised to make this night one we will never forget. Please give him a warm welcome."

The smug look on Lyessa's face as she left the stage had Ty's teeth grinding.

The crowd erupted with applause. He glanced around the table at the half-hearted smiles dripping from his family's faces. His mother even gave him a sympathetic pat on the arm. What could he do? He didn't dare back down now.

Ty stood from his seat and made his way slowly to the stairs and up to the platform. He still had no idea what he was going to play. He tried rubbing his sweaty palms down the legs of his trousers, but it didn't help. Finally, he lifted the set of wooden pipes his father had made for him from his pocket and turned to face the crowd. He nearly dropped the flute at the sight of so many people.

A cough from somewhere in the crowd signaled the audience's growing impatience. Ty tried to smile, but his lips didn't want to part. They were frozen in place, much like the rest of his body—as stiff as the back side of Crystal Lake at the height of winter solstice, three feet deep and covered in snow.

Ty's glorious victory was falling to pieces all around him. He was going to be the laughingstock of the entire town. For the rest of his life! Every time he'd pass someone on the street, they'd say, "Look, there goes the kid who froze." Worse yet, Lyessa would hold this over him. Forever!

At that thought, a jolt of desperation drove the joints in his arms to lift the eight-stemmed flute to his dry lips. He had no idea what to do. No idea where to begin. And certainly no idea why he had ever volunteered to do this in the first place.

He took one final glance around the room. Not able to risk postponing any longer, Ty closed his eyes, took a deep breath, and blew across the open ends. His family all said he had a natural gift. No one had ever needed to teach him. The music had always been there. On the other hand, he'd never had to perform in front of anyone but his family.

The notes were soft at first, dark and somber with a hint of nervous hesitation. But from somewhere deep within, he could feel a stirring, like a wild animal desperate to be free of a poacher's cage. It started as a warm tingling sensation, and much like throwing kindling on a pile of glowing embers, a flame ignited.

Struggling to hold at bay whatever was fighting to break free, Ty's music shifted to that of the forest. It was only natural, for it had always been the forest that brought him a sense of calm, of peace. Whenever he felt the pressures of life becoming too heavy, he could find his solace in the trees.

The music quickly took on a life of its own. The rising fire within him found a release through the notes, the heat of his magic escaping through his lips. Without warning, the pain was back, searing deep into his right shoulder. But unlike earlier that day, he wasn't about to let it quench his momentum.

He pushed through the burning.

The melody was unfamiliar, but with each note, he could see the swaying of the trees, the leaves dancing to the beat of the wind; the animals as they scurried about, searching for food; birds snuggled in their nests, singing in another day.

Realizing he hadn't heard a single peep from his audience, he opened his eyes wide enough to see if the faces held any sign of enjoyment. What he saw caused his lips to nearly slide off the wooden tips.

The East Inn was gone.

Or at least, the building was. The people were all still seated in their chairs, standing in the corners, or leaning against where the walls used to be. But instead of a hazy, crowd-pressed room, they were surrounded by a quiet autumn glen. One Ty recognized. It was the hideaway spot he frequented in the woods behind his house. The place he escaped to when he wanted to talk to the animals.

Fear alone kept him playing.

Strangely enough, no one seemed to be screaming in terror. There were no women fainting in the aisles, no children clinging to their mama's skirts, no men reaching for their swords or yelling for the torches to be lit. Could they not see what was happening? Why was everyone just sitting there? It was as though the entire assembly was in a trance.

Some of the kids pointed at the animals, but other than that, no one seemed to be all that upset by the fact they were no longer where they were supposed to be. Maybe *he* was the one imagining it all?

Afraid of breaking the moment, Ty played on. He couldn't help but wonder, though, whether what he was seeing was real or just an elaborate illusion. Beads of sweat broke out across his forehead. His throat was parched and his lips chapped, but he kept playing. It felt like he'd been playing for hours. He poured all his concentration into the music as his mouth flew up and down the ends of the pipes. The notes came forth like colors on a canvas, each one blending with the next to form a mosaic in time. Maybe *he* was the one in a trance.

The music continued to flow out of some unseen place inside him. It was a once-in-a-lifetime work of art, a masterpiece that was sure to cost him his life. For as soon as he stopped playing, the townsfolk would no doubt recognize what had happened and, without even waiting for the Black Watch, would most certainly hang him from the nearest tree, then kill his whole family for good measure. The thought of Overlord Barl demanding his family's execution forced him to keep playing.

Unexpectedly, the world around them changed. The sky grew dark. The leaves that were once lush and green withered and fell from the trees. The birds no longer sang their happy tune, and a deadly hush fell over the small glen.

Dread took over. He could feel himself tiring. Reaching deep inside, he plundered what little energy he had left to keep going. How could he make everything go back to the way it was? How could he bring everyone back to the inn?

As if in answer to his plea, one by one the trees vanished, and the small glen folded in on itself. In the blink of an eye, the dark-stained walls of the East Inn snapped back into place. Ty didn't know if he needed to be impressed, relieved, or terrified—perhaps a little of each. Glancing around the room, everything appeared to be as it was before.

He wanted to exhale a huge sigh of relief, but he suddenly realized he was nearly out of breath.

Ty poured everything he had left into the final notes of his song and then released the pipes from his mouth, half expecting the crowd to wake from its trance and rush the stage. His arms dropped like stone weights to his sides. "Please, don't let them remember," he prayed, reciting it over and over again as if his desperation would be enough to persuade the Creator to be lenient.

Giving up all hope, Ty closed his eyes, bowed his head, and waited for the inevitable.

He waited, but nothing happened.

He waited longer—still nothing. No stampeding for the doors, no demands for his head. There was simply silence, which was even more disturbing.

Before he had a chance to open his eyes, a roar of applause thundered across the room. It grew so loud, it shook the platform he was standing on. Opening his eyes, he saw there wasn't an occupied seat in the house. Everyone was on their feet clapping, shouting, banging their mugs on the tops of the tables, waving handkerchiefs and ribbons in the air, whistling, and stomping their boots on the hard wooden floors. He didn't know what to do, so he bowed from the waist. A bit clumsily, but not enough to cause embarrassment.

The crowd cheered all the harder, so he waved. He couldn't believe it; they loved him. Had the Creator answered his request? Was the audience completely oblivious to what had just happened? Even Lyessa was applauding with surprising vigor. And to think he had almost talked himself out of playing tonight. He continued waving to the crowd as he descended from the platform.

It was like a dream. Maybe it was a dream. Apart from the terror of having used magic in the middle of Performance Night—and having done so with the overlord of Sidara sitting not two tables away—Ty felt quite exhilarated.

Stepping down from the stage, Ty wanted nothing more than to rush home and try out this newfound ability. But he knew he couldn't. Not with the Tower's guards let loose on Easthaven. Then it hit him. Had any of them seen? Had they been in the audience?

He panicked. What if he couldn't control what was happening to him? What if next time, he wasn't so lucky? Ty didn't know how much longer he could hide who he was from his family. It might, he thought, be time to tell someone.

Chapter 9 | Valtor

"I DO NOT EXAGGERATE, Your Eminence. If you do not deal with him now, you're going to have another uprising on your hands."

Valtor took a deep breath. "Thank you, Marta," he said, laying a gaunt hand on her shoulder. "Your insights have been most valuable." Marta had been with him from the beginning. She had been one of Valtor's greatest allies in his fight to take over as the new Archchancellor of the White Tower. She was one of the few he had allowed inside his personal chambers.

The rooms above the central gathering hall had belonged to the archchancellors for centuries, each one lending their own unique touch. Valtor cared nothing for amenities or comforts. He only cared about his work. Because of this, he had removed the former archchancellors' draperies and sofas, pillows and cushions, replacing them with tables and shelves and desks full of books, parchments, and artifacts—ancient relics of a time long forgotten.

"You know how close Medarin and Archchancellor Bezaleel were," Marta said, interrupting Valtor's deliberations. Her smile faded, replaced by the same worried expression Valtor was used to seeing. "He's now claiming to have proof of your involvement." Marta shook her head, her long grey hair falling across her dark robe. "If it were me, I would have put an end to him a long time back."

"Even Medarin has his uses," Valtor said, turning to look at his staff. The silver wolf head at the top stared back at him as if wanting to be fed, though it already held a large bloodstone between its teeth.

When he didn't say more, she nodded. "I just thought you should know."

Valtor smiled. "I count myself lucky to have such an attentive friend."

Marta's smile returned as she bowed. Without another word, she left the room and headed down the stairs to where the others were waiting.

Valtor sighed as he adjusted the folds in his robe. She was right. Medarin had outlived his usefulness. Valtor had kept a close eye on Medarin, making note of the places he went, the people he associated with, and then kept an eye on them as well. One by one, Medarin's co-conspirators had been brought to light and disposed of. But time was running out. Valtor needed to ensure the Tower's unity.

He left his chambers and made his way down the stairs to the large vaulted room at the bottom, where the three branches of the Tower conducted their meetings. Four windows on the left side emptied pale light across the floor as he glided toward the long marble table in front of the hearth. He passed a few empty seats on the way—seats once occupied by those who had thought to be rid of him.

Quietly, he made his way to the head of the table and took his seat, enjoying the warmth of the fire beside him.

Ten of the thirteen seats were filled by the heads of the Bulradoer, the Legate, and the Inquisition. Despite the power their positions granted, they shifted uneasily as they waited for him to speak.

Valtor studied the faces of the men and women gathered around the table. Some faces he trusted, while others . . . He spared a passing glance at Medarin, lingering only long enough to make the bulradoer squirm.

Since Archchancellor Bezaleel's *untimely* demise and Valtor's rise in station, the White Tower had nearly doubled in size. Bezaleel had been soft. He had pandered to the throne in Aramoor in hopes of gaining favor at court instead of focusing on his rightful duty to build the Tower's ranks. He had still held to the old ways—that the White Tower should be controlled by the jun'ri, and that magic should be purged from Aldor at all costs.

Valtor, however, had dedicated his life to the liberation of the ven'ae. The jun'ri had persecuted those with magic for centuries, forcing them to go into hiding. He was finally giving them a chance to reclaim their rightful place in the world. Being a wielder himself, he could understand their plight. He had lost his family as a young boy, or more correctly, his family had lost him. As soon as they had realized what he was, they had tried to drown him to be rid of the taint of being associated with the evils of magic. He had learned quickly whose side he wanted to be on.

Thinking about his younger self brought Valtor back to the main reason for gathering this assembly in the first place.

"Sixteen years," Valtor said, scanning his audience, meeting each eye in turn. "Sixteen years, and what do we have to show for it? How hard is it to find one single child?"

"Why should we care?" Medarin grumbled under his breath at the other end of the table.

"What was that, Medarin?" Valtor asked, leaning forward in his seat as he glared at the man. The miter on top of Valtor's head tilted forward ever so slightly. The cursed thing never would stay in place.

The short bulradoer glanced at the other faces around the table, looking for support. "I said, why does it matter? When Bezaleel was archchancellor, you wouldn't have found us wasting our time looking for some stupid child. We would have been out there kicking down doors and rounding up wielders."

The others looked from Medarin to Valtor and back again.

"And if your goal is to make an enemy out of every citizen in Aldor, then that is exactly what you should do. Precisely the kind of backward thinking I'd expect from a supporter of Bezaleel."

Medarin's eyes grew hot, his fists clenched tight on the table. "Bezaleel was ten times the chancellor you'll ever be!"

Valtor twisted the knife. "Bezaleel was a fool!"

Medarin's eyes widened. Valtor could almost hear his teeth grinding. "At least *he* didn't have to resort to murdering his predecessor to gain *his* title!"

And there it is.

Valtor lifted his staff, and the bloodstone between the wolf's fangs pulsed a deep red.

Medarin had gone too far to stop now. Leaping to his feet, he conjured a ball of green flames and threw it at the head of the table.

Valtor met the attack with a shield of air that sent the blaze ricocheting into the side of the hearth beside him. Pieces of stone and wood flew on impact.

Those sitting around the table jumped from their seats to move out of the way. Valtor drew magic from his staff and reached out with his other hand, binding the magic to the bulradoer's neck before Medarin had a chance to attack a second time. Valtor clenched his fist as if gripping an invisible object, and Medarin choked. With a swift jerk, Medarin was lifted into the air, his seat toppling over as the man tried to free himself from the invisible noose around his neck.

The others stood in silence. No one attempted to come to the bulradoer's aid.

A good sign, Valtor thought.

Valtor suspended Medarin over the table, letting the little man perform the hangman's dance in front of the others. Like a marionette on his master's strings, Medarin flexed and kicked as he struggled to breathe, his body convulsing. His face whitened, and his lips turned blue as he tried unsuccessfully to scream. A soft gurgling sound followed by a bubbly white paste were all that was left of the bulradoer's attempt at life. Medarin's body went limp, his eyes open, terror stamped on his face.

Valtor released him, and the bulradoer landed on top of the marble slab.

No one said a word. Instead, they quietly retook their seats.

At the end of the table, the Legate Superior smiled. She wasn't the only one who seemed pleased by his actions. Valtor examined each face in turn but didn't find a resentful countenance amongst them. It would appear he had quelled the last of the dissenters.

Valtor sighed as he leaned back in his chair, the miter shifting again. "We need that faeling child found," he said, continuing his prior conversation as if the dead body was nothing more than a decoration. "Aerodyne has special plans for him."

All eyes quickly shifted from Medarin to Valtor.

Marta was the first to speak. "Is it true that the confinement spells have begun to fail?"

Valtor waited a moment to reply, giving the room a chance to build anticipation. "It is."

Conversation buzzed at the possibility of Aerodyne's return. Some whispered of the end of the jun'ri, others the power they would hold. Some talked of rewards they would be granted for having remained faithful to the cause. Valtor let them have their excitement.

"What of Aramoor and the High King, Your Eminence?" a member of the Legate asked, directing Valtor's attention back to the present. "Rhydan has never trusted the White Tower. We could work a lot faster if we weren't having to constantly worry about drawing the attention of the throne."

Valtor rested his elbows on the table's cold surface. "There is more than one way to defeat an enemy. Why fight an unnecessary battle when you can use others to do it for you?"

"Is this the reason for your recent interest in the High Prince, Your Eminence?" one of the inquisitors asked.

Valtor smiled. "I certainly don't keep Dakaran's acquaintance because I enjoy his company. He is a means to an end." Valtor shifted his attention to Marta. "How is our recruitment faring?" As head of the Legate, she was in charge of the Tower's records.

"Enlistment within the Black Watch is up, Your Eminence. Many are crossing the border from Cylmar in order to join. Apparently, work in their kingdom is scarce. We are also seeing growth within the bulradoer ranks. It seems when given the choice to join our fight against the jun'ri or be sent for purging, wielders tend to choose the former."

A couple of the inquisitors chuckled amongst themselves.

Valtor nodded. He hated losing wielders to purging. But at least with the guidance of Aerodyne's grimoires, they had learned to separate the defiant ones from their magic and store it for future use. They had managed to gather quite the collection of magics over the last couple of years. The wielder, of course, rarely survived the process.

"However," Marta continued, "there are still some who would rather undergo purging than to help us fight against our oppressors."

"And how is the Inquisition handling these resisters?" Valtor asked, his gaze falling on the white-robed delegation sitting at the far end. "Have you been able to convince them of the value of our cause?" Valtor was amazed by the reports of ven'ae who actually fought to protect the very people who wanted to destroy them. They were little more than a nuisance right now, trying to hide potential wielders from the Tower's grasp. But if left alone, they could grow into something more dangerous.

An inquisitor on the right cleared his throat. "A few hours on the rack has persuaded many to recant, Your Eminence. We have one wielder, though, who you might find of interest. He's a metallurgist and, from what I've heard, a gifted weaponsmith."

"A metallurgist? Interesting. Who is in charge of his interrogation?"

The man glanced at his fellow inquisitors before replying. "Sylas, Your

Eminence."

It wasn't the first time he'd heard that name. "I hear he is quite talented in the art of persuasion," Valtor said, drumming his fingers on the arm of his chair.

The inquisitor smiled. "If anyone can get a man to talk, it will be him. I've never seen an inquisitor more dedicated to—or in love with—his job."

Chapter 10 | Ferrin

𝔗HE SCREAMING HAD RETURNED.

They say the threat of pain is even more persuasive than the pain itself. Whoever *they* were, they had clearly never spent any time on an inquisitor's rack.

Ferrin's head slammed back against the metal rungs, strands of red hair hitting him in the face. He squeezed his eyes shut, tears welling at the corners. He hated the sound of his own voice. Worse, he hated the satisfaction it gave his torturers.

He snapped his mouth shut, teeth grinding against the pain as the fat inquisitor ran a stone blade across the tender muscle of Ferrin's chest. The knife bit deep, sending warm blood down his stomach, saturating the tattered remains of his trousers.

Ferrin had to say this for the Inquisition—they had turned the collection of information into an art form.

He remembered the first time he had been brought into the Hall of

Inquisition. Marched in along with the others and divided into two groups—those willing to join the White Tower and commit to its cause, and those brave enough to say no. Ferrin was surprised how many were prepared to simply give up their freedoms and join. But there were plenty like himself who didn't—those still willing to fight.

Those who didn't bow to the Tower were made to watch as the inquisitors gathered information from other wielders who had made the same choice. First, the only sound from these witnesses was a soft whimper, but that soon gave way to uncontrolled sobs as the Tower guards fastened one prisoner after another to the large wire racks and began their interrogations.

Legs and arms were spread and bound by heavy iron manacles, allowing access to the soft inner muscles. These were pricked, punched, sliced, stabbed, or, in some cases, ripped from those being questioned. The screams and the overpowering smell of urine, vomit, and blood were enough to dissolve the courage of even the strongest. Once all hope had been ripped away, all that remained was to give in to the White Tower's demands.

Yet there were a few who continued to hold out.

Ferrin spat a mosaic of red across the front of the inquisitor's white robe, earning him a heavy backhand to the face. *It's the little victories that keep us going,* he thought, curling his lips into a defiant smile.

"Why do you test me, swordsmith?" The inquisitor rubbed at the stain, but that only further smeared the blood into the once-pristine garment. He gave up with a sigh. "Just tell me what I want to know, and all these . . . pleasantries . . . will cease." The inquisitor's tone was compassionate, like a father chastising a child, but the smirk on his face was anything but. He was clearly enjoying himself.

At first, Ferrin had questioned the reasoning behind the Inquisition's use of *white* robes. Surely it must take an enormous amount of work to keep them clean. But after the first inquisitor stepped through the door to question him, still wearing the blood from his previous interrogation, it became all too clear.

The inquisitor Ferrin had dubbed Cheeks—since those on his face rivaled the padding of the ones on his backside—stared at him through dark, swollen eyes. His pasty complexion gave Ferrin the impression that the man hadn't seen the sun in three or four decades. Tattoos covered much of his face and bald head. All inquisitors had them, but Cheeks had more than most. Ferrin had no idea what the tattoos meant; position within the Inquisition, perhaps. Regardless, at the moment, he didn't really care.

There were thirteen torture chambers within the Hall of Inquisition. If you'd seen one, you'd seen them all. Ferrin would know. The rooms were small and circular. A man could stand in the center and walk no more than five paces before hitting a wall in any direction. The rack was positioned at the center of the room with a stool for the inquisitor, as well as a small table on which to display the tools of their trade.

Cheeks paced in front of the rack, waving his blade around like a conductor would a baton, urging his musicians to give him more. "How many other wielders are there in your city? What are their names? What can they do? Where do they live?" The questions were endless, always seeming to work their way back around to one in particular: "What can you do for the White Tower?"

Like so many others before him, Ferrin fought to safeguard the identities of the wielders he knew. He would not be the one responsible for their imprisonment and torture. Above all else, he had to protect the one good thing left in his life: his twin sister, Myriah. She was the only member of his family left. He was fighting for her.

He just didn't know how much longer he could hold out.

In the two weeks since his arrival, Ferrin had been questioned by every interrogator the Inquisition had to offer. He wasn't sure why they had singled him out for such a privilege. Each inquisitor had left him that much closer to breaking. All it took was one session with Cheeks to know they had saved their best for last.

Ferrin was amazed that he had yet to be permanently maimed. He supposed the inquisitor was saving that particular pleasure for later. Maybe he wanted to start small and work his way up? Whatever the reason, Ferrin was thankful that nothing had been severed yet.

Most prisoners only lasted a day or two before breaking. Others confessed their own mothers were the spawn of the Defiler before the manacles even had a chance to click shut. Ferrin figured the threshold for his endurance might have been a little too high. Thankfully, the pain from Cheeks's latest work had begun to dull, as it did after each of his cuttings, bringing with it the barest of respite and allowing Ferrin's mind to work its way back before being subjugated to another round.

Cheeks held out the small stone dagger. A drop of fresh blood fell from its tip and landed on the inquisitor's forefinger. He turned it around, examining it. "So, what else shall we cut today? Hmm?"

"How about my beard?"

Cheeks roared with laughter, clapping his hands together. He struggled to catch his breath, a difficult task for a man of his girth. "I see your sense of humor is in full force today, smith. Good, good. I have rather enjoyed our time together." He wiped tears from his bright blue eyes.

Ferrin watched as the inquisitor scanned his body, studying the many afflictions Ferrin had already endured. Patches of hardened white skin crossed his chest, stomach, arms, and legs, indicating previously explored territories.

Cheeks stepped back from the rack and settled himself onto the stool. It groaned in protest. Ferrin wondered how much more pain and suffering the poor seat could endure before its legs finally buckled.

"You have no idea how insufferable it can be to cut someone who doesn't have the . . . how do I put it?" He chewed on his lower lip. "The proper constitution."

"I completely understand," Ferrin said through gritted teeth, fighting to hold back the wave of nausea threatening to overwhelm him. "You have my deepest sympathy."

"Yes." The inquisitor grinned. "I believe you do understand."

Swiveling in his seat, Cheeks unrolled a leather satchel across the table on his left, displaying an alarming number of tools. His fingers slid affectionately over each one, like a new husband admiring the curves of his wife's body during their bonding ceremony.

Ferrin glanced from one instrument to the next: a small poker, a short single-edged blade, two pairs of iron tongs, a hammer, a heavy clipper, whipping straps, a sturdy saw, and an assortment of wooden wedges ranging in both length and girth. *Quite the impressive selection,* he thought, quashing the rising fear.

Only a short time before, he would have been going about his own daily routine—igniting the coals in his forge, arranging hammers and tongs, choosing what strips of iron to smelt, and preparing lengths of steel for shaping. He loved the blistering heat of his little smithy in the heart of Rhowynn. Now here he was, nothing more than fodder for another type of forge, one in which they heated, hammered, and shaped human beings.

Cheeks looked up from his doting, his seat giving an uncertain squeal. "I have a surprise for you today, my proud smith." He reached inside one of the inner pockets of his white robe and pulled forth, with flair worthy of a troubadour, a new instrument. "I call it . . . the wiggler." He held it up for Ferrin to inspect.

Ferrin had to admit that it was a well-crafted piece. It had a robust iron handle with finger grooves for comfort and a soft leather grip. But instead of a blade, this particular tool had a thin steel rod that coiled in a circular fashion until it reached its point at the end.

"I call it the wiggler because once I punch it through the gut," he said with a sharp, thrusting motion, "I can wiggle it to the left, and wiggle it to the right, and play with all kinds of fun things in there." He giggled with delight.

"Your happiness brings tears to my eyes, Inquisitor."

Cheeks beamed. "I want to introduce you to someone, smith." The stool sighed with relief when Cheeks hefted himself from it and shuffled across the room to the chamber's one door. Giving a tug on the latch, he swung the door open, revealing a young girl. At least, Ferrin thought she was a young girl. Her clothes hung loosely on her thin, half-starved frame. She kept her head bowed almost reverently, but Ferrin could see the edge of a large bruise near one eye.

"Come in, come in." Cheeks held out his arm, beckoning her forward.

She slid into the room with hesitant steps, never once raising her gaze above the floor. "This is Rae." The inquisitor put a sweaty hand on her shoulder and shoved her the rest of the way to the rack. "She's here for you."

Ferrin raised his head, the only thing he could move. "I would give you my hand in proper welcome," he said with a forced smile, "but, uh . . ." He wiggled his bound arms inside their shackles. "As you can see, I'm kind of tied up at the moment."

Cheeks jabbed Rae in the shoulder. "See, I told you he had a sharp wit."

The girl lifted her head slowly, warm torchlight washing across her face. She wasn't quite as young as Ferrin had thought, maybe early twenties, but she was thin enough to seem at first no more than twelve or thirteen. Ferrin didn't think she was much longer for this world.

She looked to be from one of the southern islands. Her skin was the color of warm caramel, and her dark hair looked like it had been cut with a dull knife by someone who had indulged in a night of hard ale. It hung at varying lengths, the longest nearly reaching her shoulder. Oddly enough, her eyes weren't brown but pale green. A unique trait for an islander. There was no emotion on her face, but her eyes screamed of loathing. But of what? Ferrin? The Inquisition?

Ferrin frowned when the inquisitor's words sank in. "What do you mean, she's here for me?"

"Don't get your hopes up," Cheeks said with a wink. "She's here to help me with my work."

Ferrin glared at the inquisitor. "You're going to make her watch, you sick spawn of a faerie?"

"Now, now," Cheeks said with a wry smile, waving a plump forefinger. "No need for name-calling. Even if she was a sorry excuse for a human being, she was still my mother." The smile faded. "Where were we? Oh, right. We were deciding where to use my new instrument."

Cheeks walked over and cranked the large wheel attached to the right side of the rack, and Ferrin was lifted into an upright position. "That's better," the inquisitor said, securing it with its chain. He turned back to the table holding his array of instruments. "My young friend here has quite a remarkable gift," he said, pointing the wiggler at Rae. "Don't you, my dear?"

Rae said nothing. She stood on the far side of the rack as Cheeks shifted his attention back to Ferrin. "But unlike you, we have allowed her the use of a transferal. I would hate to think of the havoc you could wreak in here if you still had yours." Cheeks slid his fingers along the thin, winding shaft of the wiggler, paying special attention to the coil, finally coming to a rest at its pointed tip.

Cheeks walked over to Rae and carefully slid the instrument down the front of her shirt, tugging lasciviously at her top button. He smiled as he withdrew a small crystal hanging from a sweat-tarnished chain.

Ferrin recognized the crystal for what it was.

After his parents had died, his uncle, not wanting magic under his roof or the wrath of the White Tower brought down on his head, had sold Ferrin to a traveling peddler. It was Pinon who had given Ferrin his first transferal and explained that what Ferrin possessed was not a curse, but a gift. Pinon had warned him to keep it hidden.

Obviously, that hadn't worked too well for Ferrin.

"Yes, she has quite a useful gift," the inquisitor continued. "I would tell you all about it, but . . ." Cheeks leaned in, his warm breath reeking of garlic and rotten meat. Ferrin had to swallow against the bile in the back of his throat. "It would be so much more fun to show you." With that, he raised the wiggler and rammed it into Ferrin's stomach.

Ferrin screamed, his head snapping backward to once again bounce off the rack's metal bars. Spittle flew from his mouth as he gasped for breath, concentrating on nothing, everything, anything but what the inquisitor wanted. Names. He must protect his sister. He must protect Myriah.

He could feel the inquisitor twisting his instrument around inside of him. It was excruciating. He'd never felt anything so terrible in his life. Somewhere in the distance, he could hear Cheeks's voice: "Who are the wielders in your city? Do you have any family? Are you ready to join the White Tower?"

Nausea swept over him like a tidal wave, and he emptied what little remained in his stomach across his chest.

Cheeks chortled with perverse pleasure.

Everything faded, sounds muffled. The pain was beyond what he could bear. Ferrin's body began to convulse, then everything went black. There was silence. At last, it was over.

Ferrin's eyes burst open as he inhaled a torrent of life-sustaining air. A thick haze coated everything. Sights, sounds, even his sense of smell was muted. He felt nothing. *I must be dead.*

Cheeks's pale face popped into view. "Ah, there you are. Almost lost you," he said with a chuckled.

Ferrin felt his heart sink. "Wha . . . what happened?" Without warning, all the pain and agony he had suffered from his previous cuttings came flooding back, searing his senses once again. It was overwhelming.

"Quite the rush, isn't it?" the inquisitor said, eyes gleaming.

Through the pain, Ferrin felt something soft and cool slide across his chest. He tilted his head. Rae had the palm of her hand pressed against the open wound from Cheeks's blade. Her eyes were closed, brow furrowed in concentration. Ferrin found himself caught in a confusing mix of emotions. He knew he should be screaming out in pain, but her touch was all his tormented mind wanted to focus on.

The inquisitor studied Ferrin, no doubt trying to determine where next to ply his trade. This should have terrified Ferrin, but right now all that mattered was the gentle caress of Rae's hand on his skin.

Icy cold washed across Ferrin's torso, and he gasped in shock. It was as if hot and cold, night and day, had collided on his skin.

A soft lavender glow had enveloped Rae's hands. The light spread into the muscles and tissue of his chest. He watched as the sinew knit back together. It was incredible.

The pain that had threatened to drown him moments before had eased to little more than a dull ache. He felt euphoric, as if someone had administered a dose of laudanum or cannabis. He was almost willing to go back under the inquisitor's knife just to feel her magic once again. Almost.

She removed her hands from his chest, and Ferrin saw that even the skin had resealed, leaving only the smallest trace of a scar. The hole in his stomach from where the wiggler had entered was also gone.

He looked up and into the little healer's pale-green eyes. He was about to thank her when her legs buckled, and she collapsed to the floor.

"Not again." Cheeks huffed as he finished wiping the remaining blood from the twisted poker. He took great care to make sure each tool was properly cleaned and stowed back within his instrument roll. He obviously cared more for his tools than he did for his help.

Waiting until he had finished cleaning and replacing the utensils, Cheeks waddled across the room, opened the door, and called to one of the white-cloaked members of the Black Watch outside. "Take Rae back to her chambers and see that she gets something to eat. Can't have her dying on us, now, can we?"

Ferrin watched as the guard threw her limp body over his shoulder and carried her off.

"Just think of all the fun I would miss if our detainees expired every time they received a little prodding," Cheeks said as he shuffled back to his table, rolled his leather satchel, and secured the straps. "We are through for today, my dear smith. How did you find my new device? Be honest, now. Did it live up to its name?"

"Why don't you release me, and I'll show you?"

Cheeks doubled over with laughter, his hands gripping the rolls around his waist. "I do so enjoy our time together, smith. More than any other, I daresay. You'll make sure to get plenty of rest, won't you? I want you good and ready for our next session."

And with that, he was gone.

Straining his neck, Ferrin wiped the blood from his mouth on his shoulder while waiting for the Tower guards to take him back to his cell. He took a deep breath and exhaled slowly. He wondered how much more he could take, how much longer he could hold out.

I'm wearing them down, he thought.

He chuckled, amusement teetering dangerously close to insanity, as he listened to the growing sound of heeled boots.

Chapter 11 | Ayrion

AYRION STOOD QUIETLY at the center of the practice ring as hushed whispers skittered across the inner courtyard of Aramoor's royal palace. He hated being put on display. He had better things to do with his time than fight for the amusement of others. But the king had ordered a ring set up next to the palace to allow the nobles, as well as traveling dignitaries, a chance to see his fighters at work. As much as Ayrion could see the benefits, he still loathed being the one doing the performing.

Today, the courtyard was filled with Elondrian lancers—decked in their formal crimson-and-gold uniforms—there to cheer on their fellow comrades as they faced the king's Guardian Protector. On Ayrion's right, a cluster of High Guard gathered to watch their leader defend his title. Ayrion nodded at his overcaptain, Barthol, a bear of a man who smiled and nodded in return. Ayrion was the youngest man ever to command the king's elite fighting force. The sole duty of the High Guard was the protection of the king. Many a lancer had longed to wear those coveted black uniforms with the silver falcon.

Ayrion shifted slightly to get a better look at the wide terrace on his left that overlooked the courtyard from the second floor of the palace. The crowd it held differed greatly from the excited but disciplined lancers beneath. Lords and ladies pranced around in fine suits and puffed lace as they waited for the exhibition to begin.

Ayrion had a clear view of the balcony. As always, the central gallery was reserved for members of the royal family and their guests. Rhydan, High King of Aldor, sat at the center, his gaze proudly taking in the scene below. Queen Ellise sat to the king's left, her silver-streaked hair not detracting from the remarkable strength seen in her sharp eyes.

Their son and only living heir, Dakaran, sat stiffly on his father's right, his face fixed with a scowl. Ayrion couldn't remember the last time he had actually seen Dakaran smile, except when attempting his latest short-lived romantic conquest. Behind the prince stood his new advisor, Valtor, the archchancellor of the White Tower. He wore the crimson robes and miter of his office, both emblazoned with the Tower's insignia: a blade piercing a rising sun. His black hair cupped the sides of his gaunt face, making his coal-rimmed eyes look even more sunken. He appeared to be even less excited about being there than Ayrion was, if that was possible.

Ayrion caught sight of the ambassadors on the far side of the balcony, and his fingers tightened on his sword. The ambassadors rested comfortably on plush benches canopied by silk sheets, while children scurried around the railing in front of them, hoping to gain a better view. Ayrion was reasonably sure it was due to the ambassadors' arrival that he was standing on display in the courtyard rather than attending his duties.

Ayrion shifted again, continuing to scan each face as his eyes moved down the long line of nobility, finally coming to rest on a small group of young ladies off to the side. The queen's ladies-in-waiting. *Where is she?*

He smiled when he saw her.

Amarysia's rich honey-golden hair waved in the cool afternoon breeze as she stood alongside the other young women, awaiting the upcoming event. She smiled back when she noticed him looking. Somehow, the thought of those deep blue eyes staring down at him had Ayrion more anxious than the armed men he was about to face.

Behind him, Ayrion could hear the crowd part. He turned to see five men move through the spectators and step into the ring. Each wore the Elondrian crimson-and-gold tabard over their leather and chainmail armor, their swords drawn and ready.

Ayrion could feel the metal grip of his blade through his glove. He didn't see the need to draw its twin, so it remained in its sheath on his back—for now. His sword rested at his side, his long black leather coat bouncing against it in the cool breeze.

The five soldiers spread out in front of him, causing the surrounding crowd to quiet in anticipation. Ayrion took a deep breath and waited for them to make the first move. He could hear soft murmurs from the balcony by those laying wagers on how long he would last. As a way to increase the excitement, Ayrion had given his challengers permission to use whatever force necessary to win. He had learned from his years living on the streets that nothing drew a crowd more than the chance to witness death, disturbing as it was.

The lancer on the end charged, but Ayrion stayed where he was. They were testing him by sending just one. He fought the urge to defend himself. He hated this part.

Without flinching, Ayrion watched as the soldier raised his blade and lunged. Before he could get his sword into place, the lancer's steel hit him mid-chest, driving straight through and out the back. Screams erupted from the balcony as Ayrion coughed blood, nearly blacking out from the pain. Death had become a close friend.

Suddenly, everything around him shifted. The sword in his chest vanished, the pain was gone, and the lancer was back beside the others, getting ready to charge.

Ayrion's whole body was shaking. He took a deep breath to steady his nerves. His visions had been the same since he was a child, giving him a few seconds' warning against danger. Magic had saved his life more times than he could count and had helped him earn the title Guardian Protector. However, if anyone were to find out about it, he'd lose more than his position.

The lancer attacked again—or, more correctly, for the first time.

He waited till the last possible moment, then pivoted on his left foot, letting the soldier's blade slide by as he spun to the lancer's side.

Go for the head.

The soldier's blade was still extended when Ayrion finished his spin and punched the unprepared guard in the right side of his face. The man's head whipped to the left, and he slumped to the ground, unconscious.

Turn around! he shouted at himself mentally.

Ayrion spun, raising his blade just in time to deflect the next attacker, who had thought to catch him with his back turned. The second lancer struck three times, each driven with lethal intent. Ayrion used his sword to beat each strike away from his body. His opponent pushed all the harder, trying to overwhelm him with brute force as he swung for Ayrion's neck, not seeming hesitant in the least.

Underneath. Go underneath.

Ayrion ducked under the man's next swing, feeling the blade passing just overhead. Using the lower position to his advantage, he kicked the lancer's feet out from under him, and the man hit the dirt hard. Ayrion grabbed the lancer's sword and threw it out of the ring. With nothing left to defend himself, the soldier quickly backed away, moving for the safety of his friends. Ayrion let him go.

Applause drifted down from the balcony. Some of the ladies leaned over the balcony railing to make the best use of their low-cut necklines.

Ayrion ignored them all, glancing instead at the king.

Rhydan and Ellise seemed more interested in the ambassadors' reactions to the fight than the fight itself.

Ayrion stepped over the first lancer and walked out to face the remaining three. The three men spread out to flank him as they moved forward together, no longer willing to fight one-on-one.

Finally, Ayrion thought, *some challengers whose sense outweighs their pride.*

Ayrion drew his second sword from its sheath. He could get away with one sword against two opponents, possibly even three, but he wanted this to be over quickly. He waited to see what the men would do. He didn't have to wait long. They came at him all at once. It took a great deal of concentration to keep his swords up and moving, blocking, parrying, deflecting. Before one vision had ended, three more had taken its place. He blocked left and ducked right, spun, blocked again. They were coming at him from every side. He couldn't focus—too many visions to handle.

Unable to concentrate, he forced them down, relying instead on his second gift.

His mother had called him a repeater. Most fighters had to practice hours every day to learn how to fight both with weapons and without. But for Ayrion, his body only needed to perform an action once, and then he could repeat it without fault.

Ayrion let his body take over. His arms and legs seemed to move on their own as he fought his way in and around his opponents. He didn't want to permanently injure the lancers—which made it even more challenging—so he used the flat of his blade to strike instead of the edge. It was fast enough that no one could tell the difference.

The three lancers were holding their own. They fought using direct tactics. One to draw the attention at the front, while the other two came from the sides. Ayrion smiled. He recognized Commander Tolin's training. The lancers gritted their teeth, grunting in frustration at not being able to bring him down. They'd swing left. He'd dodge right. They'd thrust. He'd sidestep. They'd kick. He'd twist and spin out of the way. His former mentor had taught them well.

But not well enough.

One by one they dropped. First, the man on the left. His guard opened during an attempted head strike, and Ayrion kicked him in the gut, dropping him to his knees as he gasped for breath. The second attempted to do the same to Ayrion, but Ayrion caught his leg and ripped it out from under him. The lancer landed on his head, and Ayrion kicked his sword to the other side of the ring.

With only a single lancer left, Ayrion released his visions. The third man came at him with everything he had. He swung left, right, overhead, thrust, kick. Ayrion didn't even raise his swords. He used his visions to keep just out of reach, never letting the blade touch him.

The crowd shouted, jeered, and eventually laughed as the lancer fought like a madman without landing a single blow. The soldier was so winded and unnerved at hitting nothing but air that he finally dropped his sword and raised his hands in defeat. He walked away, shaking his head.

Cheers erupted from the audience as Ayrion turned and bowed toward the center terrace and the High King, who looked rather pleased as he glanced in the ambassadors' direction.

Ayrion spared a quick glance at Amarysia. She smiled, but it looked more out of relief than excitement. It had only been a couple of weeks since their first official meeting. The queen had asked him to escort Amarysia to one of the shops in the merchant district as a personal favor to her. Ushering young women around Aramoor was about the furthest thing from one of Ayrion's duties as he could get. The reason was painfully obvious, not to mention embarrassing. Although, in the end, the queen's not-so-subtle way of setting the match had turned out in Ayrion's favor.

He smiled as he watched Amarysia join the other ladies as they moved in behind the queen. Now that the spectacle was over, the nobility shuffled back indoors, and the lancers returned to their duties.

Overcaptain Barthol stepped into the ring. "Those are certainly some fine blades."

"I won't argue with that," Ayrion said as he inspected the steel. Not even a scratch. Ayrion's swords were of unique design—steel as black as midnight flared out from the handle like dark flames from a dragon's maw. The grip, crossguard, and pommel had been fashioned in the shape of a dragon in flight, its wings overshadowing his hands. Ayrion had never known workmanship so fine. He slid them back inside their sheaths.

"Any idea what this was all about?" Barthol asked as he helped an unsteady lancer to his feet and pounded the man's back, trying to dust off the dirt. The lancer winced as Barthol's mallet-sized palms landed. "I don't mind the break, but it seems an awful waste of time to organize for some quick entertainment."

Ayrion returned the lancer's sword. "My guess is, the king wanted us to put on a show for the ambassadors." He nodded toward the empty terrace. "No doubt to instill a little caution before they report back to their overlords. Force them to think twice before planning any incursions into Elondrian territory."

Barthol grunted. "If it were up to me, I'd march the lancers over there and show them why messing with us is a bad idea."

Ayrion smiled. His hulking friend was one to act first and ask questions later.

"How are you feeling?" Barthol asked as they waited for the rest of the procession to go inside.

"A little stiff," Ayrion admitted, rolling his shoulders.

"Yeah, you looked a bit floppy out there. And there *were* only five of them."

"Only five, huh? I thought I did pretty well keeping the crowd entertained—"

"Well, they were just lancers. It wasn't like you had to stand toe to toe with any real fighters." Barthol tugged at his belt, trying to look sincere. He fought as hard as he could to hold the serious expression, but it soon gave way, and the two began to laugh.

"I best finish my rounds," Barthol finally said. "Unless you need me here, *sir.*"

"Don't let me stop you."

"Very good, *sir*," Barthol said, standing at attention. "May I be dismissed?"

"Get out of here," Ayrion said, kicking at his friend. "I'll see you at lunch."

Barthol hopped out of the way of Ayrion's foot, then offered Ayrion a deep, groveling bow before leaving.

Ayrion chuckled as he watched the big man head toward one of the west towers. He took a moment to glance around the now-empty courtyard. He was surprised by how fast it had cleared. Instead of heading for the palace, Ayrion turned and walked in the direction of the lower gardens, a routine he had incorporated after each fight. He found it helped him relax. The gardens were quiet, a couple of visitors here and there, but for the most part, he found himself alone with his thoughts.

Yellow sprays of wintersweet floated on the breeze, their heady scent more welcoming than the overpowering perfume of the ladies at court. His feet crunched on the white gravel that filled the maze around the lush flowerbeds, cultivated shrubbery, and groomed trees. Ayrion stopped to admire one of the larger pools and the bright yellow-and-teal fish within. It wouldn't be long before the water was iced over, the chill in the air warning that fall was nearing its end.

He was halfway back to the palace when a member of his guard rounded the corner of the arched trellis and approached.

"Sir, the king requests your presence in his study." The young man saluted, his right fist across his chest. Ayrion returned the gesture before dismissing him.

Knowing the king, he probably wished to congratulate Ayrion on his performance and, in a roundabout way, check to make sure he was unharmed. Ever since the king had taken Ayrion under his wing as a boy and given him a position in the palace, he had kept a close eye on him.

Ayrion crossed the courtyard with its statue-lined pavilion and entered the foyer. His boots echoed off the checkered marble tile as he headed for the staircase on the far side. He took it to the fourth floor and made his way down a labyrinth of warmly lit hallways, each as lavishly decorated as the next.

He rounded the last corner to find Prince Dakaran skulking a few doors down from his father's study, a large goblet in one hand. He looked to be well on his way to full intoxication.

"Well, if it isn't the almighty Ayrion," Dakaran said, his words already beginning to slur. "The king's *Guardian Protector*. I see you managed to outshine your opponents once again." He raised his glass in salute, his unsteady hand sloshing some of its contents onto the lush gold-and-crimson carpet.

"I did what was asked of me, nothing more."

"Yes, the pride of Elondria. The Dark Warrior. The man who can't be beaten. How does it feel to be my father's champion?" Dakaran snickered. "His favorite lapdog. Tell me, does he pet you on the head when you're good?"

"You're drunk, Dakaran."

"So glad you noticed."

"I'm not talking to you when you're like this." Ayrion moved to pass him, but Dakaran cut him off.

"Where are you going?"

"I have a meeting with your father."

"How lucky for you," Dakaran said, his voice raised loud enough to be heard from one end of the hall to the other. "It appears I wasn't invited!"

Two of the High Guard, who were presently standing outside the king's study, turned to look just as Dakaran pressed Ayrion up against the wall. Ayrion held out his hand for them to stay where they were. This wasn't the first time he'd had to deal with Dakaran's temper. The prince's breath was as strong as a vintner's.

"What makes you so special?" Dakaran asked. "Even as children, you always got away with everything. The perfect little boy that Father thought could do no wrong."

"I don't know what you're talking about."

"Our adventures. You remember our little adventures, don't you?" Dakaran said, releasing Ayrion long enough to pat him on the cheek. "Sneaking outside the palace with Kira and Reevie and Po. You remember. Except . . ." Dakaran looked both ways down the hall as if he were about to divulge some great political intrigue. "Whenever we were found out, you were conveniently never around, leaving me to take all the blame." He smiled and took another sip of his wine.

"Dakaran, we were kids, and the only reason I was rarely caught was because I wasn't foolish enough to brag about it. Now if you don't . . . mind." Ayrion tried to push Dakaran to the side. He knew the only way to keep this from escalating was to leave.

The door to the king's study opened, and Rhydan stepped out along with a couple of the ambassadors.

"Oh, I do mind!" Dakaran said, not having noticed the audience behind him. "You might have everyone else around here fooled, but not me!" He spilled more of his drink, some of it falling on the lace sash around his waist.

Ayrion shook his head. He almost felt sorry for Dakaran. "And you wonder why your father doesn't want you in the meeting? Look at you. Five minutes with the ambassadors and you'd likely start a war."

Dakaran stepped back and threw his cup at Ayrion, but Ayrion ducked and the goblet bounced off the mural behind him, adding a much-needed dash of crimson to the battle scene.

"What's going on out here?" Rhydan demanded, a glower on his face as he marched toward them.

"Nothing!" Dakaran spat, stumbling backward slightly. "We were just having our own little meeting. And you weren't invited."

"Grow up, Dakaran," Rhydan said, "before I send you to your room."

Ayrion didn't think that humbling the prince in front of the others was the best remedy to the situation, but at this point, he wasn't sure what was.

Dakaran ground his teeth, both fists clenched. Ayrion was afraid Dakaran was going to do something stupid. But seeing half the ambassadors standing in the hall behind them, he finally turned and stormed off.

"What was that about?" Rhydan asked, staring after his son. The king's eyes looked tired. Ayrion hadn't noticed how weary Rhydan had become. Even with his grey hair, the king had always held a strong bearing, thick in the chest and arms, with a stout chin. But now, he looked like a man who had too much on his mind.

"He didn't appreciate being excluded, Your Majesty."

Rhydan sighed. "If he'd pull himself away from his drink long enough to handle a simple conversation, I wouldn't have to." He shook his head. "I don't know what I'm going to do with him."

"I find the odd spanking here and there works well," one of the ambassadors said, drawing a few chuckles.

"Maybe when they were five," another replied. "But when they're old enough to spank you back, it's generally too late."

"I say we stick them in the ring and let them fight it out," the stocky ambassador on the end said in a strong Cylmaran accent. He seemed to be glaring at Ayrion. Ayrion wasn't sure if it was just the man's normal look or if he was upset with him for some reason.

The king didn't respond. He simply smiled and ushered the men back into the study. Ayrion followed just behind.

Rhydan's study was a large room with a vaulted ceiling layered in crosshatched beams of rich mahogany. To his right was an inlaid wall of shelves crafted of the same dark wood, which housed an impressive selection of books. The right wall boasted an enormous map of Aldor, depicting its five kingdoms, natural landmarks, cities, towns, and villages. Ayrion had spent many an hour studying the illustration. At the heart of the map, marked with gold letters, was his home—Aramoor.

The king walked to the head of the room and stood beside a hearth large enough for several grown men to fit inside. He lifted a glass of wine that had been sitting there and motioned for Ayrion to join them.

"Guardian, I would like to introduce you to our esteemed guests." All four of the ambassadors remained seated in their cushioned high-backed chairs around the fire.

"It would be an honor, Your Majesty." Ayrion walked around to the front of the small gathering and bowed, low enough to be considered respectful of their position but not so much as to be groveling for attention.

The king started with the man on the left. "We have Ambassador Gyin of Briston, Ambassador Belkor of Cylmar, Ambassador Lanmiere of Sidara, and Ambassador Nierdon of Keldor." The king motioned in Ayrion's direction. "Gentlemen, I give you Ayrion, Guardian Protector to the Crown." Rhydan glanced at Ayrion. "The ambassadors were most impressed with your display earlier."

Ayrion bowed once more. "I thank you, though I'm certain these gentlemen have no doubt witnessed demonstrations more remarkable than that."

Ambassador Nierdon, whose hair hung like curtains down the sides of his long face, crossed his legs, absently dragging a finger around the stem of his goblet. "Ah, the self-deprecating warrior . . . You're a dangerous man, sir."

"Only to those who wish harm to my king."

"And loyal, I see," Ambassador Lanmiere said. He was older than the other three, with a demeanor that seemed more approachable. "It is indeed reassuring to see the wisdom in the king's choice of champion."

Ayrion bowed his head to the Sidaran ambassador. "I thank you for your kind words."

Ambassador Gyin, a rotund individual with a flushed face, lowered his goblet. "Wherever did you find him, Your Majesty? *Hup*," he half burped, half hiccupped. "His eyes are quite . . . unique."

"Quite unique indeed," Nierdon echoed with a raised brow. "A trait I know all too well, as his people live in our former capital. Am I correct in saying you are Upaka?"

"I am, sir," Ayrion acknowledged. "Although it has been many years since I've seen the Lost City."

Ambassador Belkor lowered his glass. "The Upakans are nothing more than mercenaries. A pack of rabid mongrel dogs if you ask me." Even for Cylmarans, the ambassador's forwardness was surprising.

No one spoke, waiting to see how Ayrion would respond.

Belkor didn't back down. He fixed Ayrion with a harsh glare.

Ayrion smiled. "I've found, Ambassador, that it is the mongrel which tends to be the most dangerous. They have not been bred into servitude and stupidity, which makes them . . . unpredictable. Yes, I believe if I were a betting man, I'd take the mongrel over the pedigree every time."

"Ha!" Lanmiere roared. "He's got you there, Belkor." He gestured with his glass. "If I were you, I'd think twice before insulting one of the Upakans when there's nothing more between you than a beaker of fine wine."

Ayrion caught the ghost of a smile on the king's face. "Well, I believe adequate introductions have been observed," Rhydan said, nodding to Ayrion. "Thank you for your presence, Guardian."

Ayrion bowed. "By your leave?"

The king nodded, and Ayrion offered another bow to the ambassadors, if not quite so formally.

As Ayrion retraced his steps, he wondered what maneuvering the king had hoped to achieve with this second spectacle. Feeling more drained now than he had after the fight, he hastened his departure.

Chapter 12 | Valtor

VALTOR STOOD AT his table, reveling in the new manuscripts they had uncovered while excavating the tunnels below the White Tower. From what he had translated so far, he believed they held key information about the power established during the time of the Wizard Order—arcane magic that had long been forgotten and was believed destroyed during the Great Purge.

At Dakaran's request, Valtor had been allotted rooms within the palace. Since getting himself assigned to the prince's staff as chief advisor, Valtor had enjoyed a freedom within the royal court that he hadn't previously held. His political maneuvering was finally beginning to bear fruit.

He congratulated himself on setting the pieces in motion. Pieces that had led to him saving Dakaran's life outside a local brothel the prince was known to frequent. He'd swooped in at what had seemed to be the last moment, heroically rescuing the prince from a mugging Valtor himself had arranged.

The ruse was easily accomplished. The prince was a drunkard with a wonderous air of selfishness that took Valtor no effort at all to manipulate.

Valtor dipped his quill in ink. He paused, carefully studying the runes found in the ancient manuscript before translating them into one of his larger journals. Each new spell he managed to conjure found its way into his journals for future reference. One of his latest discoveries was called a Shak'tor; the drawings alone—depicting half-human monsters—were enough to encourage Valtor to take the risk and attempt the new piece of magic when he next found the time. As soon as he had set pen to page, his chamber door flew open and Prince Dakaran stomped in.

"The arrogance! Who does he think he is?" Dakaran didn't bother shutting the door.

Valtor's fingers tightened around the quill, nearly snapping it in half. There were times he wondered if putting up with Dakaran's pettiness was really worth the hassle. It was beyond him how a king like Rhydan or a queen like Ellise could have sired such an oaf. Then again, it was this pettiness that was helping Valtor get what he needed.

"Who are we discussing, Your Highness?" Valtor asked, walking over to close the door. One of Valtor's initial goals had been to turn the prince against his father, but he found Dakaran had nearly done that himself. It wouldn't take much to push him just a little further.

"Ayrion!" Dakaran snapped, pacing the floor. Valtor could see the prince had been at the wine again. His speech, although coherent, was dragging. "And my father . . . Blind fool! He showers him with praise! Always has. You'd think *he* was the crown prince!"

Valtor massaged his temples as he walked back to his table. "I can see the appeal."

"What was that?" Dakaran spun on his heels.

"I said, I know how you *feel*."

Dakaran studied the Archchancellor a moment, then shook his head. "I want him gone."

"Of course, Your Highness," Valtor said almost sympathetically. "Might I ask how Your Highness would suggest this happen?" Overthrowing Rhydan would prove a whole lot easier if the Guardian Protector wasn't around to stand in the way. There was something about the man that didn't feel right. Something other than his heritage.

Dakaran swung the blue velvet cape from his shoulders and tossed it across the nearest chair. "I don't care if you have to stick him while he's sitting in the privy doing his morning business. I want him gone."

Valtor offered a slight bow of his head as Dakaran made his way over to Valtor's mixing table and began rummaging through some of the glass decanters. The jars came in an assortment of shapes and sizes, holding anything from pickled human remains to deadly insects and poisonous plants.

"Don't you have something you can use in all of this . . . stuff?" Dakaran asked as he continued his inspection. "What are these relics, anyway?"

"I am a collector of rare items," Valtor said, glancing at the jars to make sure there was nothing there to lead Dakaran to believe otherwise. "Some I use in herbalism. Others are just for my amusement."

Dakaran picked up a jar holding an adult tranochis: a green ten-legged spider about the size of a child's hand. It had a red double triangle on the outer abdomen. Valtor had purchased it from a collector who frequented the Caldera, a place most stayed well clear of. And considering the man he'd purchased it from had lost one of his ears, three fingers on his left hand, and half of his right foot, it was easy to see why.

Dakaran shuddered and carefully placed the jar back on the table.

"I'm sure I have something in here I could use." Valtor closed the large volume he'd been studying. "But I wouldn't advise it, at least not at present."

"And why, oh illustrious advisor, would you not?"

"The last thing we need is for the Guardian Protector to be assassinated. That would put the entire kingdom on high alert, making life even more difficult for us. Besides, the last thing you want is for him to look like a martyr."

Dakaran grunted.

"Patience is not a virtue to use sparingly, my prince." Valtor took a stack of notes from the table over to a nearby shelf and slid them between two leather-bound volumes. "Your time will come. Acting hastily will only land us in the dungeon, or perhaps on the chopping block."

"What in the name of Aldor is this?"

Valtor sighed and turned to see what the prince was referring to.

"What dark nightmares were these conjured from?" Dakaran asked, flipping through Valtor's journal.

Valtor's breath caught in his throat. Quickly, he scuttled back to the table and confiscated the book. He glanced at the page the prince had seen. It was his latest entry, including the drawings of the Shak'tor. The borders of the page were lined with ancient runes.

"Ah, these are merely . . . bedtime stories used to frighten naughty children, Your Highness, nothing more."

"What language was that?"

"Just an old dialect from the Westlands." Valtor closed the book and placed it on the shelf. "I told you, I collect ancient relics." He turned back around. "Where are we with the Cylmaran ambassador?" he asked, changing the subject. "Belkor, isn't it?"

Dakaran retrieved a ceremonial dagger from off the shelf, examining and then replacing it. "Yes, he has agreed to meet with us on Seventhday after the evening meal."

"That's good news. We are going to need Cylmar's help if we are to get you your throne. If that is still what you desire?"

Dakaran seemed hesitant as he stared at the shelf, not really looking at anything in particular.

"Of course, you can always wait and see if your father will willingly turn it over to you when the time comes. Then again, from what you've been telling me . . ."

Dakaran clenched his fists. "He might give it to someone else."

"Someone like . . ."

"Ayrion."

Valtor smiled. "The law gives your father that right, as long as the Provincial Authority agrees." The Provincial Authority was the ruling body of Aldor, made up of the four ruling overlords and the High King.

"You don't need to remind me."

"If I were you, I'd take every opportunity to rebuild your relationship with your father. At least for now."

The prince grabbed his cloak and threw it across his shoulders. "I don't see that happening anytime soon."

"It won't if you don't try, Your Highness. Eventually, you'll learn that politics is nothing more than politely agreeing with fools, showering praise on mediocrity, and shaking hands with people you'd like to stick a knife into. It's a dangerous game of pretend. And if you can't pretend to get along, you *will* lose."

Chapter 13 | Ferrin

ERRIN SPAT BLOOD. He was on the rack. Again.

Apart from a few noticeable differences—the torch holder was fastened to the right side of the door instead of the left and the rack set to the opposite side of the entrance—the interrogation rooms were exactly the same. Ferrin could have sworn that even the large bloodstain on the floor was of similar size and placement.

I'm still alive, he kept telling himself, a chant of hope to ward off the desperation threatening to consume him. Cheeks had graciously spared him the wiggler this session. It probably had something to do with Ferrin almost dying during their previous encounter.

Instead, the inquisitor had decided to test Ferrin's reaction to heat. His experiment consisted of testing the length of time he could maintain Ferrin's hand over a torch's flames before Ferrin either passed out or ignited.

Ferrin's luck being what it was, he didn't pass out.

After the demonstration was over and Ferrin hadn't given in, Cheeks left

Rae to fix the damage while he packed his tools and moved on to the next victim.

Ferrin grimaced as two of the guards hefted his aching body from the rack. They grabbed his worn tunic from the floor and jerked it over his head. His sweat-soaked hair was plastered to his face.

Each guard took an arm and hauled him from the room. "Looks like they still couldn't get him to talk," said the guard on his left. "I told them not to bet against the smith, but would they listen? No."

"Give it time," the other guard replied. "They all talk eventually."

Too weak and battered to move his legs, Ferrin let his feet drag across the stone floor of the dimly lit passageways as the Tower guards carried him back to his cell. They were joined by a third guard.

"This way," the guard said, leading them in a different direction. "I've got orders to move him."

Why the change? he wondered. Ferrin shivered as they took him outside and across one of the open battlements, toward a tower on the adjacent crosswalk— one he wasn't familiar with. The wind bit into his flesh as it whipped across the parapet in howling gusts. He took a moment to admire the view as they crossed the enormous walkway. They were hundreds of feet in the air, looking out over the mountain fortress.

He remembered his first impression of the White Tower, having seen it through the bars of his prison wagon as they wound their way out of the Pass of Arnon. It was a solitary pillar of stone protruding straight out of the ground and nearly touching the sky. It was a monument to another age—an age of wonders, an age of true power.

Surrounding the central spire was a vast network of crenellated walls, stone parapets, and lesser towers, each connected by long, open walkways like the one they were crossing now. Most had been built into the side of the mountain. He turned his head. They seemed to be heading away from the main tower.

There was strength to the ancient design that reminded him, in a way, of dragons. He wasn't sure why, considering the mythical creatures were just that: mythical. Perhaps it was the stone heads that decorated the upper spires. The monstrous elongated faces reminded him of some of the drawings he'd once seen in a book that was supposed to depict what the ancient creatures had looked like.

The Tower had no outer defenses; not that they were needed. The entire fortress was completely encased by sheer cliffs. The only way to reach it was through a solitary pass that was connected to the fortress via a monolithic bridge. Ferrin could see the garrison stationed on the outskirts of the Tower below them.

They reached the other side of the battlement and stepped inside the next building. Ferrin's teeth were still chattering even after they had shut the door, blocking the harsh mountain wind.

"So . . ." Ferrin said, his breath coming in shallow rasps due to the rather long march from the lower chambers. "What will I . . . be dining on . . . this evening?" Rae's gift of healing did wonders for the outward afflictions to the body but very little to affect the inward aches of fatigue and hunger. "A few hours on the rack . . . can really . . . work up a man's appetite."

The guard in front turned his head, the cut of his uniform and stripes on his arm declaring him to be a captain. "How long are you going to hold on to that sense of humor, smith?"

"As long as I can."

From the silhouette cast by the torchlight, Ferrin had to admire the captain's rather bulbous nose. It was a snout of indescribable proportions. It was an incredible work of art. The masters would have charged double to paint such a portrayal. Nostrils sounded like a good name for the captain, he thought. He played around with the idea a moment longer before coming to an agreement. *Yep, Nostrils it is.*

They were climbing again. The higher they ascended, the more his teeth chattered. "Maybe this time I'll get a room with a view."

"I'm sure there'll be a nice view of the gardens," Nostrils said.

Ferrin was starting to feel a little apprehensive. Why would they suddenly be changing where they kept him? What was he going to find when he got there?

Nostrils stopped outside a row of closed doors, very similar to the hall of cells he had formerly inhabited. The captain pulled out a key and unlocked the door, pushing it open far enough that it squealed on its hinges. Ferrin didn't even get a chance to look inside before the guards tossed him in, where he landed hard on the stone floor.

"Your meal will be along shortly. Hope you have a strong appetite. I heard the cooks are whipping up a special treat for tonight."

"That does sound delightful," Ferrin said with a grunt as he rolled over. "Could you do me the favor of informing the cooks that they forgot to remove the whiskers on the last one they served?"

One of the guards snickered. "Get some rest. You'll need it for tomorrow."

The three men left, taking the light with them as they swung the heavy door shut. Once again, Ferrin found himself alone in the dark with nothing but his memories to keep him company. Still lying on his back, he glanced up the single arrow slit above him and the faint trail of moonlight that seeped through. *So much for the view.*

As his eyes began to adjust to the dim light, he lifted the bulk of his torso on one thick forearm and scanned the room. It was similar to the others—four paces across for the width and maybe six for the length. The walls seemed to bleed moisture, keeping their occupants somewhere between sick and dying. A pallet of straw had been strewn across the floor, no doubt to allow the residents to find a small escape from the damp and thereby stave off their eventual passing long enough to complete their interrogations.

The pungent odor produced from the combination of human waste collecting in the corner and the stink of unwashed bodies had been unbearable when he first arrived at the Tower. Now it was but a mere irritation, dulled by time.

He grunted at the stabbing pain in his lower chest. *Broken ribs, no doubt.* He lifted his torn tunic and carefully prodded the rest of his upper body. "Oh! Yep, they're broken." The little healer had expended her magic earlier that day. By the time she'd made it round to Ferrin, she only had enough left to tend to the more serious damage on his hands.

"What's your name?"

Ferrin started. He sat up, eyes darting around the room for the origin of the raspy voice, finally locating what looked like a figure huddled in the shadows on the far side of the room.

"Ferrin," he replied hesitantly.

"Ah, Ferrin." The old man repeated his name, rolling it around in his mouth as if sampling some new exotic delicacy. "It's a strong name," he said, "a name that bears with it a true calling and purpose."

Ferrin snorted.

"I see a solitary stone," the man said, "which, if removed, will collapse a kingdom. I see a future that rests in balance on the edge of a blade, a blade tempered by magic. The future tips one way and then another, never quite revealing its outcome. Hmm, most curious indeed."

Ferrin strained to get a better glimpse of his cellmate. "Try seeing us a way out of here while you're at it." *Just my luck,* Ferrin mused. *They stuck me in a cell with a lunatic.*

"My name is Azriel," the voice said as the man forced himself into a seated position. Chains clanged heavily on the stones around him, while the glint of the moon divided his upper half with its soft, pale light.

Ferrin grimaced at the sight of the man's face. Withered with age, it held a gauntness that clearly showed the malnourishment he'd suffered. But it was not the skin-wrapped skull, or the scars of prolonged cuttings, or even the patches of hair that had fallen away from rot that drew Ferrin's attention; it was the old man's eyes. He'd never seen eyes so green, like the first rich sprouts of emerald lace at the height of spring. Intense. For reasons unknown to Ferrin, it made him want to turn away, as if they were gazing right into his soul.

"I'm a seer, and I have been waiting for you far longer than I care to admit."

"Then you're an idiot or a pretty terrible seer. You could have just as well saved us both the hassle and paid me a visit at home instead of waiting till I ended up here." *The poor fool really has lost his mind.*

"We all have a destiny to fulfill, my young friend, if we would follow the Creator's path. Mine is to guide others like yourself on their way."

"There'll be no further talk of the Creator here, old man. He has abandoned us." Ferrin was sick and tired of hearing about how the Creator loved them, how the Creator had a plan, how there was some overall grand purpose as to why the Creator had given him his gifts. He'd heard enough of that from Myriah. The Creator could take a flying leap.

The Creator's will was nothing more than a weak man's attempt at justifying why he was being strapped to a metal bed and his body used as a whetstone for the inquisitor's blades. He wasn't in the White Tower because of some divine intent: He was there because a would-be friend had set his heart on Ferrin's sister. That and those stupid swords.

"Nonsense," the old man said. "The Creator is everywhere."

"Then He has turned His back on us. What kind of benevolent being would subject us to this? Answer me that!" Ferrin felt a sharp pain in his chest, and he bent over. The *Creator* was now affecting his broken ribs. He took a deep breath and let the feeling subside.

"It is not for us to know His ways, only to believe they are for the best. It wouldn't be called faith, otherwise."

"*Blind* faith, you mean," Ferrin sneered.

"I do not pretend to know why He has put you here," Azriel said, "but my journey has already been laid out."

"To sit here and suffer? Is that the purpose your Creator has for you? I would say you got the short end of the stick there, my friend."

The old man chuckled. "I guess it could appear that way to those without faith."

"What are you trying to say? That you think there is some divine purpose behind my being here?" Ferrin would have belted out a hard laugh if his chest didn't feel as though it had been trampled by a herd of desert sherakin.

"Is it truly that hard to believe?"

"I'm nothing more than a poor swordsmith who finds himself locked in the White Tower, waiting to be purged . . . and for what? For nothing more than being born with something others weren't." Ferrin cursed himself again for having used magic to create those two blades.

"You listen to me," Azriel said with a stronger tone. "The Creator does not endow such blessings without purpose. The outcome of an entire battle could fall on the edge of a single sword, no matter its size or strength. Have patience, my young friend. Your time is coming."

"Time?" Ferrin twisted, then coughed as the pain from his ribs flared once again. "Time for what?"

"Your destiny."

"My destiny? Is that something you have seen?" Ferrin asked mockingly.

"Possibly."

"Possibly? How could it be *possibly*? Either you saw it or you didn't."

"I'm a seer," Azriel said with a smile and a slight shrug. "What I see can be interpreted many different ways."

Ferrin shook his head. *Great! I wonder if it's too late to request another room.*

Chapter 14 | Saleena

"I WON'T ASK AGAIN," the man in white said. "Who's been helping you? Are they in Easthaven?"

The questions never seemed to stop. Why couldn't they just kill her and get it over with? Saleena struggled against the ropes; her wrists and ankles burned from where the skin had been rubbed through.

When she wasn't being interrogated, the Black Watch kept her in one of the cramped storage rooms in the Easthaven barracks, tied to a chair and left to sit until they were ready to go again. That had been three days earlier. At least, she thought it had been three days. She wasn't sure. Delirium had begun to set in. She tried sleeping during the times she was left alone, but the constant cramping in her muscles made it fitful at best. She didn't know how much more she could take.

"I don't . . . know . . . anything," she managed with a hoarse whisper. She tried swallowing, but her mouth was as dry as the birch bark powder she used in some of her poultices.

Pain flared on one cheek.

The guard raised a gloved hand and struck her again. Her head whipped to the side, eyes watering, ears ringing. Slowly her vision cleared and the stinging dulled, joining the litany of pains from the other beatings she had endured over the last few days. At least it had only been beatings—so far. She didn't want to think what else they might do to her if she didn't start providing them with answers.

Strangely enough, Saleena found herself wondering what she looked like. She knew what she felt like, but she was strangely curious as to how her pain would translate in a mirror. Was there permanent damage? It was one thing to look at a wound, or injury, or illness and diagnose the symptoms from what she saw, but when you couldn't see anything, it was certainly more difficult.

She could taste the dryness and feel the lightheadedness that came from dehydration. The pain in her jaw was dull , which meant it probably wasn't broken, but the bruising would be significant. Both her eyes were swollen; no guessing needed there. Her ribs were another story. The ache was intense. If she had to guess, one or two might be broken, but she wasn't sure. As long as she didn't move too far to the right, she could manage it.

She wanted to laugh, but she didn't have the energy. Here she was, tied to a chair, being beaten by the Black Watch, knowing that the only future that awaited her was a slow and painful death inside the White Tower. Yet instead of trying to figure out how she was going to get out of this mess, she was busy trying to diagnose her condition, like she didn't already know—pretty flaming hopeless! *At least it's better than focusing on the pain,* she thought.

"Are you listening?" the guard asked, pulling her from the momentary drifting of her thoughts. Another blow sent her head reeling and scrambled them altogether. She could taste blood. In some small way, she was thankful for it. The blood made up for her lack of saliva. She rolled it around on her tongue, then tried to swallow.

"I'm not a wielder. Why won't you believe me?" Tears moistened her cheeks. She wished she could reach them with her tongue, even though she knew the salt would increase her thirst.

"That's not what we heard. We were told you had been healing children with spelled potions, tonics laced with dark magic."

"I'm a healer. Nothing more."

Saleena had lost both her parents to winter fever when she was ten and was taken in by an aunt and uncle who lived in Kariss. Her uncle had been the town physicker, and her natural curiosity encouraged him to teach Saleena his trade. She had been a quick study, soaking in all the information she could. It was exciting to see how a single root, or piece of bark, or leaf, if used properly, could cure illness, calm emotions, and increase life.

Unfortunately, it was her unending curiosity that had attracted the White Tower. When her uncle's age began to hinder him from keeping up with the work, Saleena took over the business. Her use of tonics and tinctures had earned her quite the reputation as a healer. Her name became synonymous with *miracle worker*. Infuriated that some slip of a girl had done what they could not, some of the local healers began claiming she was using the dark arts.

"Were there sympathizers here in Easthaven hiding you?"

Her vision cleared enough to see Hatch, the captain of this Black Watch unit, leaning against the door. His arms were folded as he watched his men question her.

"No one helped me."

"Then how did you escape?" Hatch asked. "You overpowered five of my men and disappeared into the woods in the middle of the night without help?"

She tried moistening her tongue with her blood once again. "Yes. I did it . . . on my own."

"Is that so? Then why do my men talk of seeing a large hooded man leading you off?"

Saleena didn't respond. Whatever happened, she wasn't going to betray the one person who had tried to help her.

Chapter 15 | Kellen

KELLEN KNEW THEY were running out of time.

The Black Watch seemed to have finished most of their inquiries within the city and were now questioning residents just outside of Easthaven. Once they were finished—depending on what they found—the Tower's guards would move on, taking Saleena with them. If the council was to pull off a rescue, it needed to be soon.

Easthaven might have been the capital city of Sidara, but its size was nothing compared to that of Aramoor or Rhowynn. It wouldn't take the Black Watch long to complete their work. For his family's sake, Kellen wanted nothing more than for the white riders to be done and gone, but for Saleena's sake, he needed them to remain where they were long enough for the council to play out their heist.

There were still a few pieces to the puzzle that needed to be put into place before the council was ready to attempt a rescue. Liberating a prisoner right out from under the Black Watch's noses was going to be challenging enough, but doing it *and* making them believe that Saleena had managed to escape on her own would be trickier still.

Kellen swung himself off Your Highness, a chestnut stallion whose proud bearing had earned him the name. He tied the horse to an empty hitching ring, then headed up the steps of the East Inn.

One of the benefits of living in a city like Easthaven was that Kellen could always find ready gossip if he looked, and there was no better place for uncovering loose lips than this inn. He stepped inside and scanned the room, letting his eyes adjust to the dim lighting.

Sadly, today, the place was rather empty. There were a few scattered regulars around the bar, and a single table near the front with a few people who looked to be merchants enjoying a late breakfast or possibly an early lunch, but not much other than that.

Kellen sighed. He didn't see anyone he recognized. He was about to leave when he spotted someone at a table near the back, just right of the stage. She was strategically placed against the wall so she could keep an eye on everyone while she ate. Recognizing the cropped hair, he started across the room.

Sheeva watched him like a hawk, her posture stiffening as he approached. The light from the candle on the table reflected in her amber eyes, giving him fair warning.

"Mind if I join you?" He gestured to an empty chair.

She nodded with enough enthusiasm to cause any sensible person to walk away. Undaunted, Kellen pulled out the chair and sat. She kept a watchful eye on his hands, so he folded them on the table.

"I thought you were going to do something about that," he said, staring at her white hair.

Without saying a word, Sheeva leaned over and grabbed a wool knit cap off the chair beside her and stuck it on her head.

Kellen chuckled.

"Can I get you anything?" one of the Aboloff children asked, having seen him come in.

"I'll take a warmed cider if you have it."

"We do." The little boy scurried off toward the kitchens, and Kellen turned his attention back to the assassin.

"I hope you're finding Easthaven to your liking?"

"It's . . . quiet," she said, her tone giving no indication whether she thought that a good thing. Her eyes were full of energy, the only part of her that held any hint of emotion.

"You're a Night Walker. Correct?"

Before he had a chance to say anything more, her figure warped and vanished.

Kellen quickly turned to see if anyone had seen, but no one was looking in their direction. "Hold on. I want to show you something," he said softly. He withdrew a silver chain from around his neck and laid the pendant on the table, jewel facing upward. He kept his hand on the chain as he rested his elbows on the uneven table surface and waited for her to respond.

"Where did you get that?" she demanded softly, somewhere to his left.

Kellen didn't move. He continued to stare straight ahead. "If you would be so kind as to retake your seat, I'd be happy to tell you." He kept his voice calm and reassuring, much like when trying to coax a wild animal out of its hole.

He covered the pendant with his hand as the young waiter reappeared with his drink. He slid the coins he had placed on the table into the palm of the waiter, who bowed. "Thank you most kindly, sir," he said, glancing at the empty chair across from him. "Did your lady friend leave?"

"She'll be right back," Kellen said with a smile. The boy nodded and departed.

Kellen sat silently and continued to wait, staring patiently at the wall in front of him. All at once, his view of the wood paneling was replaced by Sheeva's carefully blank face.

"I have never seen a moonstone in the hands of a foreigner," she said, taking it from him and rubbing her fingers across the smooth pearl surface. "It signifies a great debt."

"I'm hardly a foreigner," Kellen said, urging the conversation on. "I was born and raised—"

"Foreign to the Night Walkers."

"Ah." Kellen nodded. "There has been a story passed down in my family for generations, of the birth of the Night Walkers. Few have heard the tale or know of their existence. In my own defense, the story has possibly degraded with the telling, but the amulet is proof enough of its validity."

The stone seemed to brighten. If one didn't know better, they'd think it was merely a trick of the light. Sheeva's amber eyes shone faintly as well; whether they simply mirrored the stone or they actually glowed, Kellen wasn't sure.

"The story takes place over a hundred years ago, deep in the heart of the Sidaran Forest. My great-great-grandfather saved a Night Walker from a band of poachers."

Sheeva's face twitched. Kellen couldn't tell if it had been a smile or a frown, or if she just had an itch.

"Now, everyone knows that Walkers are part wraith. They pass through walls, make themselves invisible, and fly through the night, feasting on the blood of their victims. The only time you see one is the moment before you die." Kellen was pleased to see a hint of wry amusement on her face.

"However," he said, "I don't put much stock in folklore, faerie tales, or children's fables. Still, I have come to realize that even the most bizarre of legends has a kernel of truth buried somewhere deep within."

He cleared his throat. "As I was saying, the evening was cool and the moon bright. My grandfather had been tracking a ruthless band of poachers for three days near the foot of the Angoran Mountains. He knew he was getting close.

"He was skirting a copse of pine when he caught a glimpse of their campsite, or what was left of it. There were bodies everywhere, most of them scattered around the dying embers of their campfire. It didn't take him long to see there was no life left in them. He was about to leave the protection of his hiding spot and get a closer look when he caught a glimpse of someone half sitting in the shadows. Whoever it was appeared to be wounded. My grandfather figured there must have been some kind of falling out, and this one had been the only survivor. The man didn't look like he was going to make it through the night.

"My grandfather was about to leave when he heard a voice call out. 'I can see you. You might as well come on out,' he said. So, as quietly as he could, my grandfather made his way across the camp to where the figure waited, with his back propped against an old stump.

"By the time my grandfather reached the man, he had gone silent, and his head was slumped to the side. Naturally, he thought the man was dead. He started to feel for a pulse when the man's eyes opened. And there they were," Kellen said, pointing at Sheeva's eyes, "two glowing yellow orbs staring back at him, like those of a large mountain cat. He, too, had a full head of white hair."

Kellen paused to take a sip of his cider. "My grandfather had grown up hearing the scary tales of the Night Walkers, but he just couldn't bring himself to leave the man there to bleed out. So, he managed to build a stretcher with a couple of thick limbs and his cloak, and dragged the man back to a small cabin he used on his longer treks. The man had several knife wounds, some cracked ribs, a broken arm, and what looked to be deep gouges in his leg from a bear trap. It was three days before the Night Walker's fever broke and his breathing steadied."

Kellen took another slow pull on his tankard, not wanting to rush the story. "My great-great-grandfather had lost his first wife in a raid, and with no children, he had plenty of time to help nurse the man back to health. Living on his own like he did, he probably enjoyed the company.

"It took a week before the Walker would say more than two words, and longer still to get a complete sentence out of him. But, with time and trust, he eventually opened up. His name was Arnoni. My grandfather constructed a simple crutch, and the two of them spent hours walking through the forest. My grandfather told of the tragedy he had endured, while Arnoni told of how he had come to be snared by one of the poacher's traps. He said the winter had been a harsh one and food was scarce, so he had decided to try finding game farther south, even though it was forbidden."

Sheeva's mouth tightened.

"It was during one of those walks that Arnoni told my grandfather of the origin of the Night Walkers."

Her face tightened even further.

"Arnoni said that the Night Walkers had been *created*. That their blood had been mixed with that of dragons, or some such creature that had come through the tear between realms. He said the wizards were trying to create the perfect soldiers to fight against the faeries, but after centuries of being used as warriors, his people had turned on their masters and fled to the mountains, vowing never to use their abilities for killing again."

Kellen finished the rest of his cider. It was good cider. "Arnoni gave my grandfather the amulet. He said it was a life-bond between them, and it signified the bearer as a friend and brother of the Night Walkers."

"It's a lovely story," Sheeva said rather coldly. "But for all I know, your grandfather was the poacher, and after killing Arnoni, took the amulet for himself."

"We both know this amulet can only be given, never taken, or it loses its light." Kellen placed the amulet back around his neck, tucking it safely under his tunic. Sheeva watched with a hint of longing as the jewel slid out of sight.

"You know your lore, Master Kellen; I'll give you that. When do you plan on sharing this information with the others of your council?"

Kellen leaned back in his chair and smiled. "I won't . . . if you tell me a story in return."

Sheeva glared. "What do you want to hear?"

"I want to know why a Night Walker has forsaken her people's path and is now selling her services to the highest bidder."

Sheeva glanced at the now-stowed amulet, then lowered her eyes to the table. She paused a moment before answering. "I had a twin brother."

She said nothing further for an uncomfortable amount of time. Kellen was wondering if she would say anything more when, finally, she continued. "Some hunters found him playing near the lower foothills of the Northern Heights, west of Rhowynn. Recognizing him for what he was, they thought they'd have some fun. So, they gave him a head start and then hunted him down like an animal." Her voice was flat.

"I found him two days later. They had hanged him from a tree and gutted him like a deer."

Kellen's stomach churned. His was wishing now that he'd never asked.

"I tracked them for three weeks through the Slags to a village called Norshag. I spent days watching them, studying them—their movements, their habits, where they liked to eat, where they spent their evenings drinking and their nights carousing. I knew them better than they knew themselves. And I used it against them.

"The first one, I slipped a toxin called hemper vine in his evening meal. It's a slow and excruciating way to die. I sat with him in his room for hours, feigning to be a physicker of rare herbs, wiping the sweat from his brow as the poison devoured his insides.

"The second man was the first's younger brother. He wasn't exactly all there in the head. I had mercy on him and slid my blade through the back of his neck while he slept.

"The third man, though, I saved for last. He was a cruel sort of creature. Every night he would visit the same whorehouse to claim the attention he could never receive from any respectable woman. By the time his activities were finished, the poor girls had been beaten bloody.

"One of those nights, I switched places with one of them. She thanked me profusely and fled.

"I waited until he had stripped himself and was demanding my full attention. I tied his arms and legs to the bedposts. He thought it all quite exciting." Sheeva's smile was disturbing. "It wasn't until I had him securely bound that I revealed who I was and who my brother had been." She cocked her head to the side. "I don't think he realized what was about to happen until I raised my blade and made the first incision."

Kellen was surprised by Sheeva's sudden openness, especially given the grisly details. Was she really all that worried that he might reveal her past to the others if she didn't? Kellen didn't believe she was trying to intimidate him, although he didn't rule it out.

"I took my time with him. I don't believe I've ever heard such colorful examples of language as what poured from his mouth. He passed out a few times, and I revived him with a bottle of hartshorn. Shortly after, his language became incoherent garbles and screams as I worked my way from one side of his body to the other." She leaned forward and let her elbows rest on the table. "I am quite skilled with a knife." Her face had resumed the emotionless mask Kellen was used to seeing. He didn't know if he should be impressed or horrified.

"As you can imagine, because of my actions, I am no longer allowed to return home. So, I do what I've found I'm good at—killing." She looked back down at the table. "How's that for irony? I tracked down and killed the three men who murdered my brother, and then I took their place."

They sat in silence. Kellen wasn't quite sure what to say.

She regarded him with an unreadable stare. "I've never taken a mark that didn't deserve it, though. I know that's not a justification, but it's my way of holding on to what little honor I still have. When I realized my latest target was nothing more than a young girl, who a powerful man felt threatened by simply because of the way she had been born, I took her and ran."

"Where is she now?"

"In Master Veldon's care. The kind of life I live doesn't lend itself to children."

"Maybe it's time to consider a change."

Sheeva didn't respond. She stared at him a moment and then glanced back down at the table.

Kellen finally pushed his seat back and stood. "I probably should be going. It was nice talking with you, Sheeva. I hope you plan on sticking around." She looked up but didn't say anything, so he turned and headed for the front doors.

Once outside, Kellen shook his head. "That was . . . intense."

"Ah, just the man I was looking for."

Kellen turned. He stiffened at the sight of three men crossing the street in his direction. Their white mantles rustled in the early afternoon breeze. The man in front was taller than the other two, with a thick black goatee and hair that fell to his shoulders.

Kellen crossed his arms as he waited, letting his hand slide beneath the front flap of his cloak. His fingers stroked the handle of his largest blade.

"I've been told you're the man I need to see when it comes to traveling the forest around these parts."

Kellen released his grip on the knife. "I'm the overlord's gamekeeper." The three men stopped a few feet away. "The name's Kellen."

The man in front regarded Kellen with a scrutinizing gaze. "Aye, you have the look of a hunter. I'm Captain Hatch. My men and I are in need of someone who knows their way around these woods. We've been charged with searching the city and surrounding countryside for wielders or those harboring them. Do you have a horse?"

Kellen glanced to his left, where Your Highness stood watching them with an air of indifference. "I do."

"Good. Make yourself available this afternoon. Be at the barracks in one hour."

Kellen held back his anger at being ordered around like one of the captain's soldiers. "Yes, sir." He offered a respectful bow. "I would be more than happy to assist our Black Watch protectors with anything they need."

The captain studied Kellen's face a moment, then turned and walked away, his subordinates in tow.

Kellen left Your Highness in front of the inn and quickly made his way down River Street. This might be the break the council had been looking for.

Chapter 16 | Kellen

AN HOUR LATER, Kellen rode through the front gates of the Easthaven Barracks. After securing Your Highness, he scanned the buildings for any sign of the Black Watch. There were a few lancers in their green-and-yellow livery scattered around the outer buildings, but no sign of the white riders anywhere.

Kellen stepped into the barracks office.

An elderly guard lifted his head from the stack of papers on his desk. "How may I help you, sir?"

"My name is Kellen. I have a meeting with Captain Hatch."

"I see." The clerk set down his quill. He had a sour look on his face at the mention of the captain's name. "I'll see if he's available." He gestured to an empty bench along the adjacent wall. "It shouldn't take long." The man's tone said otherwise.

Kellen thanked him and took a seat.

The clerk marched down the back hallway and knocked on the last door on the left. Not waiting for a reply, he stuck his head inside. Kellen couldn't quite make out what the man was saying, but he did hear his name mentioned. The clerk closed the door and returned to the lobby with a surprised look on his face. "The captain will see you now, sir." He plopped back on his stool and lifted his quill.

Kellen walked down the hall and knocked on the door he'd seen the clerk use.

"Come."

He opened and stepped inside. The room was rather plain for an office, not much more than a desk, three chairs, a small shelf, and a window that diffused the sun through a buildup of grime.

"Right on time," Hatch said as he leaned back in his chair. "I like that. I believe you can tell a lot about a man by his time of arrival. A man who arrives late is lazy, self-indulgent, and has a total lack of respect for the other party. However, a man who arrives too early is either eager to get their business over with or attempting to curry favor." Hatch leaned forward. "But a man who shows up precisely when he is expected can follow instruction."

Kellen nodded. Hatch had obviously given the subject some considerable thought.

The captain studied Kellen a moment longer, then fetched a roll of parchment from the shelf. He spread it out on his desk, using a bottle of ink and a blade he pulled from inside his cloak to hold the corners in place. It was a detailed map of the southeastern section of Sidara, including Easthaven.

"This is where we've searched so far." Hatch circled places on the map with his finger—Reed Marsh to the west and the Sidara-Briston border to the southeast. "How familiar are you with this area here?" He pointed to the forests between Reed Marsh and the southernmost edge of Crystal Lake.

"Very familiar," Kellen said.

"Good. We'll leave after lunch."

"Leave?"

"Yes. You'll be guiding us through that region."

Kellen glanced back down at the map. "If I knew a little more about what we'll be doing, it might help."

"Oh? And why is that?"

Kellen wondered if he'd made a mistake in asking. "Well, if you were planning on taking a full squad with us as opposed to a small company, it could affect the choice in route. A small party can pass through terrain that a larger one would find difficult. If we plan on being out for a certain number of days, I would need to consider the best places to find water and shelter. Also, if you had something specific you were looking for," Kellen hinted, not wanting to come right out and say it, "it would help me in planning our route."

Hatch didn't say anything, but the way he was staring had Kellen poised to grab one of his knives.

"I see the overlord made a wise choice in his gamekeeper."

Kellen relaxed.

The captain grabbed his knife from off the table and stuck it back in his cloak. He rolled the map but left it on the desk, and passed Kellen on his way to the door. "Come. We will speak over lunch."

During their short meal, Kellen and Hatch spent the majority of their time discussing the best course of action. Kellen then gathered what supplies he thought they would need from the barracks warehouse, and five of the white riders mounted their horses. Hatch rode alongside Kellen as they headed out the northern gate.

They left Easthaven and traveled north toward Crystal Lake, then cut west as they searched the outlying districts. Being a member of the Easthaven Council had its perks. One being that Kellen was aware of the wielders in the community and where they lived, having relocated many of them himself. Because of this, he was able to steer the Watch away from those particular locations.

"Weren't there ten of you?" Kellen asked offhandedly.

"The rest are guarding our prisoner."

"All those men to watch one bound woman?"

Hatch stiffened in his saddle. "How did you know it was a woman?"

Kellen laughed. "Captain, even a city our size would be hard-pressed to miss a contingent of the Tower's guards riding through, especially when they have taken a young woman prisoner. We might be the capital of Sidara, but gossip still travels faster than a racehorse around here."

The captain relaxed in his saddle.

"I still don't see how someone that small could be so dangerous," Kellen said. He needed to coax the captain into revealing something the council could use to rescue Saleena.

"I see you have never run into a wielder before," Hatch said, glancing sideways at Kellen. "Thank your Creator for that. I've seen a single wielder take down an entire company of battle-hardened armsmen without breaking a sweat."

"How is that possible?"

"They use the powers of the Defiler; how else? But once we've taken them to the White Tower, they can be purged of their evil."

"Purged? I hate to sound like a backwoods simpleton, Captain, but what exactly is this purging you speak of?"

Hatch gave Kellen a sharp look. "Easthaven might not be the largest city in the five kingdoms, but it can't be so small as to not know of the White Tower's mission?"

"I beg your pardon, Captain. I did not intend to imply I knew nothing of the Tower or its benefit to our land. But I am unfamiliar with this term *purging*."

"I see. Purging is a name for the process the Tower puts wielders through to give them a chance to live a normal life. It eradicates their dark spirits."

"Interesting," Kellen said, somehow managing to sound excited while at the same time wanting to strangle the man for his role in it. "How does it work?" Kellen was genuinely interested in finding out. He had never talked to someone associated with the White Tower before.

Hatch scratched the side of his face. "Well, I'm not exactly sure. That's the Legates' job. I just round them up."

"Have you ever seen a wielder return home after this purging process has been completed?"

Hatch opened his mouth but didn't say anything. He twisted his reins in his gloved hands. "No. But that's no surprise. We spend most of our days out in the field. I don't keep up with the wielders after I've turned them over to the Tower. That responsibility belongs to someone else."

In a way, Kellen could understand the man's reasoning. When Kellen apprehended poachers on the overlord's property, he turned them over to the city patrol for confinement. After that, Kellen's job was done. He had little say in the justice that was levied on the poachers afterward.

Hatch then shared with Kellen how his brother had been killed by a rogue wielder in his own hometown, and how he had joined the Black Watch shortly after.

"As long as there are wielders out there, our lands will never be safe," Hatch said. "So I will get up every morning, as I did the last, and do whatever I must to ensure our people's protection."

Most of the Tower's guards had joined either due to a strong but misguided belief in the corruption of magic, or because of a direct encounter with a wielder that had ended poorly, as was the captain's case.

After an entire day of direct and indirect questioning, the only thing Kellen really had learned was how ignorant the Black Watch were of the inner workings of the White Tower, and those who ultimately made the decisions. As long as the guards got their pay, they didn't seem to care what else took place. The Tower obviously kept them in the dark to prevent them from asking too many questions.

Chapter 17 | Kellen

I 'M STARTING TO BELIEVE this part of the world is so secluded that even the ven'ae wouldn't come here," Hatch remarked as they rode back through the barracks gates empty-handed. Again. He had called an early end to their search, allowing them to make it back well before the sun dropped.

The last couple of days had proven no more fruitful than the previous. Kellen had escorted the Watch through the surrounding countryside while they scoured for wielders. The majority of their time had been spent navigating the forest without so much as a flicker of magic in sight. The few smaller communities Kellen had led them to were barely large enough to be considered villages—scattered homes around a freshwater stream. The homes were in poor condition, the people even more so.

"Your services will no longer be required, Master Huntsman," Hatch said, swinging off his horse. "We will be heading south tomorrow into Briston."

Kellen offered Hatch a polite bow, nervously glancing around the barracks.

"I'm glad to have been of assistance, Captain. If there's anything else you might—"

A bell rang out from somewhere within the thick stone walls of the barracks, and a single Black Watch guard burst from one of the buildings farther down, their hood raised to hide their face. The uncharacteristically small guard glanced in their direction, then sprinted for the north gate.

Kellen wrung his hands. They had returned too soon.

"Who was that?" Hatch yelled, running toward the building the figure had just exited. "Check on the prisoner! Hurry!" Two of his guards drew their swords and charged into the building. Kellen dismounted and ran to catch up. He glanced over his shoulder as the runner exited the north gate. *Run, Saleena, run.*

"Everything okay, Captain?" Kellen asked as he watched two of Hatch's men emerge from the building.

"That *was* the prisoner, sir! Soren, Jaylen, and Heglith are unconscious, and her ropes look like they just fell off. It must have been her magic."

"Leave them!" Hatch bellowed. "All of you, follow me! Huntsman, grab your bow."

Kellen ran back to his horse and retrieved his bow and quiver before rushing to catch up. "Of course, he had to choose today of all days to come back early," Kellen said to himself. He reached the south gate in time to see Saleena dart down an alley three or four streets up, heading east toward River Street.

"This way!" Hatch shouted, charging down an adjacent lane that ran between homes. "We'll head her off!"

Kellen ran after them, offering a silent prayer for Saleena as he did. They scrambled down the narrow alley, dodging boxes and crates and stacks of garbage that had been laid out by the residence for disposal. The lane ended at an intersecting alley. Hatch took the left route, then cut right at the first adjoining street, angling them back toward the shopping district.

Kellen, with his long legs, caught up with the captain as they broke from the alley onto the main promenade, not far down from Mezard's Chandlery. He glanced to the left and caught a glimpse of Saleena sprinting across River Street and into a dark alley next to Orlyn's Apothecary.

"Hurry!" Hatch called out over his shoulder as he ran for the side street Saleena had just taken. Kellen was on the captain's heels, dodging horses, small carriages, and carts as they ran toward the alley's entrance. Shoppers scattered to make room for the men in white.

"Father!" Kellen stopped at the sound of his name and turned. Ty was coming out of Reloria's Sweet Shop a few doors down with a small bag in hand. His son started in his direction.

"No! Go home, Ty!" With his bow still firmly gripped in one hand, Kellen turned back around and ran. He spared one more glance over his shoulder. Ty was still moving after him. "Go home!"

He had fallen behind because of Ty, and he needed to catch up. What would happen if they caught her before she reached the docks? Would he be forced to let them have her? He tried not to think about it. He wanted to curse Hatch for putting him in this predicament—not that the captain knew it.

The cobbles flew by as their steps echoed off the surrounding buildings. The alley was cast in shadow, the sun blocked by the three- and four-story dwellings rising to either side.

Kellen managed to pull alongside the captain just as he spotted Saleena ahead, and put on a burst of speed. The captain and his men were panting hard, but it didn't slow them down. Their prey was just in sight.

Ahead, Saleena was struggling to maintain her pace. Her arms and legs flailed around in the large white trousers and tunic. She looked ready to trip at any moment. She stumbled out of the alley and on to Lynden Street, pausing to catch her breath as she turned and looked back down the lane. *Run, you silly woman, run!* She had barely turned to leave when a lantern hanging from one of the walls in the alley behind her exploded. The flames ignited a stack of crates that had been inconveniently placed across the alleyway.

Hatch roared as he came to an abrupt halt, his men stumbling into him as he pulled back from the blaze.

"It's the Dark One's own fire!" one of the men bellowed. "She's going to roast us alive!"

"Pull yourselves together, you spineless targs!" Hatch bellowed. "Or I'll give you something to really fear!"

Kellen could barely see Saleena through the smoke as she crossed Lynden and headed east on Bullmar.

"She's making for the river!" Hatch turned. "Down there!" They retraced their steps; this time the captain took them left down another narrow street, where they dodged half-empty boxes and barrels of litter as they cut across to a parallel road. Kellen was growing winded by the time they made it back around to Lynden. The crates one street over were still burning as they passed.

Bullmar ended at the edge of Veldon's dockworks. Saleena was tearing down the wagon trail toward the three wooden piers below. Kellen's knuckles were white from gripping his bow. What if Hatch ordered him to shoot her instead of capturing her?

"We can't let her reach the water!" Hatch yelled, motioning for his men to follow.

Kellen slowed so as not to overtake Hatch. The captain was clearly not used to running, as his breath was coming in wheezes. Hatch stopped as they approached the loading bay in front of the piers.

"Careful," he cautioned, raising an arm to warn the men behind him. "An animal is most fierce when cornered." Hatch cast a wary look at Kellen. "Have your bow ready, Huntsman, in case we need it."

Kellen grimaced but nocked a shaft anyway.

Saleena was standing on the far end of the pier, watching as they approached the front end of the docks. She kept looking to the water, as if judging whether or not to leap in. She looked at Kellen, recognition setting in.

Her eyes were begging him to save her.

The men cautiously stepped onto the wood-slatted platform. They didn't say a word. The dock groaned under their feet as they slowly edged their way forward, water lapping against the posts. The tension was as thick as the perspiration pouring from their faces.

"Stop!" Hatch brought them to a quick halt with a wave of his hand. The men cast about, heads darting in all directions. "What's that?" Hatch looked out beyond the piers. The others followed his gaze across the wide expanse of the East River, where it appeared waves were surging *toward* the docks.

Before the men could question what they were seeing, a heavy gust of wind hit them and they nearly lost their balance. Some scrambled for the sides of the pier to find something to hold on to, while those farther back made it onto land. Kellen bent to brace himself against the gale.

"How is she doing this, Captain?" one man yelled. "She's never shown any signs of having abilities like these."

Kellen held his hands in front of his eyes to shield them against the torrential wind. It howled as it flew across the water. Saleena stood at the end of the pier with her arms stretched out in front of her. Her mouth was moving, but Kellen couldn't hear anything over the howl of the wind.

A hand grabbed hold of his shoulder, pulling him backward as they moved to get off the dock. "She's conjuring a whirlwind!" Hatch shouted. "Shoot her before she destroys us all!" Hatch had a crazed look in his eye. Kellen recognized the desperation. The other guards scrambled to get off the pier as well.

"No one said anything about shooting an unarmed woman!"

"Are you blind? She's a wielder, and she's going to kill us all! Now shoot her! That's an order!"

"Father! Don't!" Behind them, Ty came running out of the storm like a specter, causing more than a few of the guards to jump in fear. One of them swung his sword at Ty but was too off-balance to land the strike.

Kellen hit the man in the side with his elbow and sent him rolling before he could swing again. "That's my son!"

Kellen panicked. Ty's insatiable need to know what was going on was about to get them both killed.

Ty moved between Kellen and the pier. "You can't kill her!" His blonde hair whipped across his face, but his eyes held strong.

Hatch didn't hesitate. He reached over and grabbed Ty by the scruff of his tunic and shoved a knife to his throat. "Shoot her, Huntsman, or I kill the boy!"

Kellen froze. What was he going to do? Hatch was leaving him no option.

The captain looked like he'd lost all reason. He stumbled sideways from the force of the wind but quickly regained his footing, not letting go of Ty.

Kellen turned back toward the pier, his arrow nocked, and looked at Saleena. Her arms were still waving. He drew, then hesitated.

"Father, no!"

"Shut your mouth, boy!" Hatch took a couple of steps to the left, giving Kellen a clear view of his son's face with the dagger pressed against his neck. There were tears on Ty's cheeks as he shook his head, urging Kellen not to do it.

By then, water covered the majority of the pier. "I said shoot her!"

Kellen looked back down the dock at his target. "Creator, forgive me," he said, and released the string.

Ty screamed, and everything went deathly still.

The wind and the waves evaporated. Kellen and the others watched as Saleena, with a look of both shock and horror on her face, glanced down at the large shaft protruding from her chest. Her body went limp and her eyes closed as she fell backward into the chilly waters.

Kellen was the first to reach the end of the pier. He watched as her body was pulled beneath the rolling waves. A few bubbles made their way to the surface, and then there was nothing.

One of the guards stepped forward to take a look. "At least she can't do any more damage."

Hatch watched the water lap against the pier's footings. "True." He turned to Kellen and cleared his throat. "I, uh . . . I hope you understand why I had to do that," he said, releasing Ty and placing his knife back in his coat. He didn't wait for Kellen to answer. "An excellent shot, Huntsman. My compliments." Kellen and Ty watched as the captain and his men made their way back down the pier, their boots scuffing on the loose boards as they went.

"You . . . you killed her."

Kellen leaned against one of the pier's posts to steady himself. His heart was pounding. "I'm sorry, Ty. I didn't have a choice. They would have killed you if I hadn't." He watched as Ty stood, staring at the empty space on the dock where Saleena had been moments earlier. He tried putting his arm around his son, but Ty shrugged it off.

Kellen took a deep breath. "Come. It's time I introduced you to some people."

Chapter 18 | Ty

THE SUN HAD FINISHED its journey for the day as the beautiful wash of orange, purple, and gold waned from the sky.

Ty took a deep breath to steady his nerves. He tried focusing on the cobbles in front of him, studying each stone as he passed. Anything to keep from picturing the look of horror on Saleena's face when she had slipped into the icy waters of the East River. Would he ever forget that look?

"Who was she?"

His father hadn't said a word the entire walk back from the docks to the East Inn.

"Who was the woman you . . ." Ty didn't finish.

His father stopped, taking a moment to study the uncommon sight of nearly vacant streets. Ty assumed it had something to do with the company of Black Watch running through the center of town, shouting with swords drawn.

"She was someone I rescued from the Black Watch a few weeks back," his father finally said. "I hid her and led the guards on a wild chase to keep her safe. When I went back for her, she was gone."

"Why were they hunting her? What could she do?"

"That's just it. She couldn't do anything. She wasn't a wielder."

"Then why were they after her?"

"Because someone claimed she was. They saw her use some new kind of treatment to heal a child, something other physickers had never used before. And nowadays all it takes is for someone to be *suspected* of being one of the ven'ae to make it so." His father snorted in disgust. "The White Tower has everyone so scared of the idea of magic that people can hardly sneeze around here without worrying they're going to be turned in for associating with wielders. They've turned us all against each other."

They continued down the west side of River Street. A few of the shopkeepers were closing their doors as customers made their way home. Ty could see Waddle still tied in front of Reloria's Sweet Shop. He was the last one there. Ty thought he looked rather lonely. They were only a couple of storefronts away when his father turned abruptly and headed across the street.

"What about—"

"Leave Waddle. We'll come back for him later."

Ty hoped he was still there when they did. He waited for a carriage to pass, then followed his father across. From there, they headed south and slipped down a side street next to the tannery.

"Where are we going?"

"I'm taking you to meet the council."

Ty's breath caught in his throat. *Finally,* he thought. Ever since first hearing about their existence, he had wanted nothing more. Maybe they could explain what was happening to him! But then he remembered. He still hadn't told his family about his magic yet, and he wanted them to be the first to know.

Why was his father even on the wielder council? His father didn't have any magical abilities. It must have been because he was the overlord's gamekeeper and his knowledge of the land was useful in locating the ven'ae.

"You deserve some answers," his father said over his shoulder. "Not everything is as it appears."

What did that mean? Ty picked up the pace to match his father's longer strides. They traversed half a dozen back lanes and side streets before finally making their way down a small alley behind an artillator shop, with its stacks of bows and arrows dimly visible through opaque window panes.

The air in this section of the city was rancid. The smell of human waste emanated from the narrow trenches on either side of the street, where residents had emptied their chamber pots. He clamped a hand over his nose and kept walking.

The alley was dark. A few lanterns hung in front of entryways, revealing doors lining the backs of obscure shops and personal residences. His father stopped in front of the second-to-last door on the right, knocked three times, waited a moment, then knocked once more.

"Who ith it?" called a rough voice from the other side.

"Kellen."

Ty could hear scraping noises coming from the other side of the door just before it opened. Not wanting to linger in the dingy alley any longer than he had to, he followed his father inside.

"Ith good to thee you, Mathter Kellen," the older man said, sticking his head out the door to see if anyone was about.

"It's good to be seen. Especially after the evening we've had."

"Aye, I geth it ith."

Ty found himself curious of the cause of the man's slurred speech. After dropping a wooden beam back across the door, the elderly man turned and smiled. His toothless grin ended Ty's guessing.

"Eliab, I'd like to introduce you to Ty, my youngest." He felt his father grip his shoulder. "Ty, this is Eliab. He's the gatekeeper for the council. In his younger years, he was the overcaptain of the Sidaran forces."

That must have been a long, long time ago, Ty thought as he watched the old man smack his toothless gums. It reminded him of a weasel he had once seen preparing to relieve some poor creature of its eggs. "It's nice to meet you, Master Eliab." Ty started to hold out his hand but hesitated when he saw the large double-bolt crossbow tucked under the man's arm.

Eliab took his hand and shook it. "Ith good to meet you, Mathter Ty. Mighty fine young man you have here, Mathter Kellen."

"He is, indeed."

"After hearing about thith evening'th predicament, I can thee why you brought him by." Eliab laid the crossbow back on the table and headed into the next room. "The counthil ith already here and waiting."

"Good." His father motioned Ty forward with a nod. "This is one of the Harbor Houses we have in Easthaven. It's also the primary location we use for our meetings." They followed Eliab into a back room and down a flight of stone steps into the cellar below.

"We use this location to hide wielders who have been discovered and need a safe place to stay until they can be relocated."

Ty followed the two older men through a maze of boxes and barrels. They stopped outside a closed door on the other side of the room, and Eliab knocked.

"Come in," came a low voice from the other side. Eliab opened the door and stepped back to let Ty and his father pass.

"That will be all, Eliab, thank you," said a short, stocky man standing at the far end of a long table.

The old toothless gatekeeper laid an encouraging hand on Ty's shoulder as he passed. He shut the door on his way out. Ty stepped out from behind his father to get a better look at who all was in the room. His head shot up. "Mother? Why are you—" Then he saw Breen and Adarra. His whole family was there. Even Fraya, Breen's girlfriend.

He scanned the room. He recognized a few of the people as local shop owners. His eyes widened at the sight of Miss Reloria. Her head was topped with the same bold yellow-and-lavender lace bonnet she had been wearing earlier when he had visited her shop.

There were others he didn't recognize, including a strange woman with short white hair and yellowish eyes. He pulled away from her harsh stare and continued counting the faces until reaching the end of the table. His jaw went slack, and he took a step back. He couldn't believe it. Sitting in a chair on the far side of the room was Saleena—and she was very much alive!

"What? How?" was all Ty could get out.

"Master Kellen." Saleena tried standing, but her legs gave out, and she collapsed back in her seat. "I don't know if I should hit you or hug you." She actually had a smile on her face as his father walked over and laid a hand on her shoulder. He didn't seem all that surprised by her being there.

"I am glad to see you alive, Saleena."

Ty took a step forward. "I don't understand."

"It's a long story," his father said, "but one I'm sure you're going to enjoy." He stood and gestured to some empty chairs at the table. "Take a seat. We have a lot to discuss."

Around the room, the others exchanged eager glances as they took their seats. For some reason, Ty felt this had more to do with him than Saleena.

After everyone had found a place around the long table, Ty's father turned to him. "First of all, Ty, you need to know that none of what happened tonight was your fault. Everyone here had a hand in it. In fact, why don't we all *briefly*"—he gave Feoldor a sharp look—"tell our part in this elaborate ruse." He glanced at Ty and smiled. "I believe you will rather enjoy this."

His father didn't say it, but Ty could tell he was proud of whatever it was they had done. "Why don't you start?" his father said to a tall grey-haired man sitting on the other side of the table. Ty noticed the large beautifully carved staff leaning against the back of his seat.

The older man nodded politely and folded his hands on the table. "My name is Orlyn, and I own the apothecary on River Street. I'm a floratide." He saw the confused look on Ty's face. "It means I have a gift with plants."

Ty perked. He had a gift with plants as well. Maybe he was a floratide?

"Your father gave me the task of rendering our jailors catatonic."

The man sitting next to Orlyn, with the disheveled hair and side whiskers, grunted. "What in the name of Aldor is cata . . . ton . . . whatever? Speak plainly, man, or the boy ain't gonna have any idea what you're talking about."

Orlyn raised a bushy eyebrow. "Well, for the less educated in the room," he said, casting a sidelong look at his neighbor, "it means unconscious."

The man folded his arms and mumbled something under his breath. Ty wanted to chuckle but resisted.

"As I was saying, my job was to find a way to eliminate Saleena's captors. The best way to accomplish this was to place yularis in their evening ale. And because I happen to be on good terms with the barracks cook, I was able to slip my embellishment in their drinks." Orlyn finished with a slight bow of his head.

"Which leads us to the next stage of our story," Ty's father said, pointing to Miss Reloria.

With a smile, the sweet-shop owner expounded further. "The only unfortunate downside to Master Orlyn's concoction was that a mere whiff of yularis would have sent them into convulsions from its unbearably foul taste. So, being the only telasero around these parts, I was tasked with taking a pitcher of rancid ale and reconstituting it into something fit to drink. I also added a touch of cloves and honey. It was undoubtedly the finest drink they will ever have the pleasure of forgetting."

"What's a telasero?" Ty asked, feeling a little embarrassed for not knowing more.

Reloria smiled. "It means I can control how things taste."

Ty nodded. Now he knew why her shop was so popular.

"Once we had managed to dose the guards' drinks," his father said, "we needed to get someone into the room to free Saleena. That is where Sheeva came in." He gestured with his head down the table at the strange white-haired woman. Ty shivered when she looked his way. He felt like she was looking right through him. He wondered why she didn't talk. The others seemed excited to relay their parts.

His father spoke for her. "As the cook walked into the cells with the Black Watch's evening meal, Sheeva followed him in."

"How did she do that?" Breen asked, leaning forward in his seat on the other side of Ty. Apparently, Ty wasn't the only one who had been kept in the dark concerning tonight's events.

"I'm glad you asked." His father gestured to Sheeva. "Would you mind?"

Ty, along with everyone else in the room, turned to look at Sheeva. He had just locked eyes with the woman when the air around her seat started to distort, like looking at his reflection in the water and then dropping a pebble through it. In the blink of an eye, she vanished. Ty gaped.

"What the—" Breen slid his chair back from the table. Ty's mother and sister gasped as they stared at the empty chair in disbelief.

"It's one thing to hear about it," his mother said, "but it's quite another to actually see it."

Moments later, the place around Sheeva's seat distorted, and she reappeared.

"That was amazing, Miss Sheeva," Ty's sister said, pulling out one of her journals and scribbling something inside. "Could you tell me how it works? What does it feel like? Have you always been able to—"

"That's enough, Adarra," Ty's father interrupted. "You can question the poor woman later."

One look at Sheeva and Ty didn't figure his sister would ever get the chance.

"As I was saying, once Sheeva made it inside the barracks, she waited until the guards had emptied the entire pitcher. It didn't take long before they were lying facedown in their own dribble. She then helped Saleena into one of their robes and had her run for the docks."

"Wait," Breen said. "That doesn't make sense. Why dress her up and parade her through town? Why not just sneak her out another way?"

Ty's father smiled.

Ty had been wondering the same thing.

"What do you suppose Captain Hatch might have thought if he'd come back and found his men tied and unconscious on the floor?"

"He would have been suspicious," Ty quickly interjected, beating his brother this time.

"Right. If she had simply vanished, they would have thought she'd been rescued by someone in town, which means the Black Watch would have continued their searching. We needed them to believe it was all Saleena."

"And that is where I took over!" the impatient man beside Orlyn chimed in, looking rather distraught at not getting his turn.

"Not quite," said the stocky man at the front. He wiped his hand over the bald area on the top of his head and fiddled with a small piece of metal hanging around his neck.

"Veldon is correct," Ty's father cut in. "As determined as our beloved Captain Hatch was, he and his men managed to gain considerable ground in their chase—"

"And would have intercepted our fugitive," Veldon said as he waved his hand over the flame of a nearby candle, causing it to stretch to nearly three times its normal height, "if not for a timely explosion that forced them to retrace their steps."

Ty's eyes were bulging as he watched the flame dance around on its wick. Beside him, he could hear Adarra scratching away in her journal.

Veldon smiled. "I'm an incindi, which means I have the ability to manipulate fire."

"Can you create it as well?" Adarra asked, her hand flying across her paper.

"No, I need its spark—"

"Adarra, we're never going to get through this if you keep interrupting."

Ty's father gave her a stern look, then motioned for Veldon to continue.

"The fire in the alley gave us enough time for Saleena to reach my docks."

"Which leads us to Feoldor," his father said, glancing at the man on Master Orlyn's left.

Feoldor, with a grin that spread clean across his face and quite possibly around the back of his head, clapped his hands together. "Right! Now for the good part." Some of the others rolled their eyes. "My job was not only to keep the Black Watch away from Saleena but to do it in a way that would leave them believing she was going to destroy them all if they didn't act. And let me tell you, son," he said, looking directly at Ty, "that was no small feat. I had to keep them from getting close enough to notice that she was not the real threat. And I did it with this." He raised his hand, and a sharp gust of wind whipped around the room. "I'm a vanti."

"Feoldor!"

Feoldor quickly lowered his hand when he saw the look on Reloria's face as she tried holding her hat in place.

"Sorry," he said with a cheeky grin.

"I guess it's my turn," his father said as he rested his elbows comfortably on the table. "My job was to kill Saleena." Ty was stunned by his father's matter-of-fact confession. "Or, at least, to appear that I had." His father's smile vanished when he looked at Ty. "What I did not expect was to see my son come bursting out of the storm to save the fair damsel like Felix the Great."

Breen clapped Ty on the back and winked. "Ty the hero."

Ty, feeling rather flushed, merely smiled and shrugged it off. He was glad no one except his father had actually witnessed the incident. If they had, they would have seen how completely terrified he had been.

"I must admit," his father said, "when Hatch grabbed him and demanded I shoot Saleena or watch Ty die, it nearly stopped my heart."

Everyone gasped.

"So, I did the only thing I could. I drew the string, took aim, and released—"

"And that," Feoldor butted in, "is when I cut off the wind so as to appear as though it had indeed been conjured by our young Saleena here."

"It was most convincing," Ty's father agreed.

Ty watched as Saleena's hand rubbed across the place on her chest where the arrow had been. "I guess it's my turn," she said, "since I was the one standing there with a shaft sticking out of me. Although I must admit, I don't remember much of anything after that." Her eyes seemed to glaze over as she relived what had happened. Tears streaked her cheeks. "I remember pain," she said, "and falling. It seemed like I was falling forever, and then, darkness."

Fraya reached out and squeezed Saleena's hand.

Reloria pulled a swatch of material from her handbag, unfolded it, and removed a small piece of what looked like green taffy. Saleena graciously accepted the sweet and smiled when she tasted it.

Ty could only see one flaw in their story. "If you shot her, then why isn't she dead?"

"Because, like your brother, that is my gift. We have perfect aim."

Ty glanced at Breen then back to his father. Now it all made sense. All those years of Breen constantly beating him at targets, all those years of wondering why he couldn't seem to do the same. As woodsmen, Ty had to admit that seemed an exceptional gift to have.

"My shot had to be precise. I had to make sure that I not only kept from piercing anything vital, but that I gave her time to finish the last two steps of our plan."

"Last two steps?" Ty was confused. "But we all saw her sink into the river and disappear downstream. Even if the arrow didn't kill her, she would have drowned."

"That is where I pass the story off to our little friend over there." His father pointed toward the small man seated on the other side of Orlyn near the head of the table. "Gilly, if you would."

"When the beautiful lady fell into the waters, I caught her," Gilly said with a smile so warm, Ty couldn't help but be drawn in. "I made a bubble for her to breathe on the soft bottom. And I carried her away from all those mean men."

"And he walked her right out of the river like a water faerie," Fraya added, offering a bright smile down the table for Gilly, who playfully waved in her direction. "He brought her to where I was waiting in a wooded area outside of town. After I pulled the arrow from her chest, I set about healing her wound."

Healing her wound? Ty looked at Breen and then back at Fraya. "Are you saying you're a . . ."

"A wielder?" Fraya smiled. "Yes."

Ty couldn't believe it. Was everybody a secret wielder? Why was he the only one who didn't know about any of this?

"Thankfully, Master Kellen is an excellent shot, or my job would have been impossible," Fraya admitted. "There are some wounds so severe, they can kill the healer as well as the victim."

Had Breen known about her involvement? Ty turned to look at his older brother, but Breen was too busy smiling like a lovesick oaf to notice.

"You know the rest," his father said, relaxing in his seat. No one spoke for quite some time, content to revel in a job well done.

Ty was bursting with questions. But first, he had his own to share. This was his chance. He just couldn't figure out where to start. *Here goes nothing.* He opened his mouth but was cut off when his father spoke first.

"Ty, there is another reason why I brought you here tonight. There's something we've been meaning to tell you for some time now, but . . ." His father shared a look with Ty's mother, and she nodded for him to continue. "Ty," his father said, "you're a—"

"A wielder!" Ty exclaimed.

Chapter 19 | Ty

THE ROOM WAS QUIET.

No one said a word—no doubt too stunned by Ty's sudden outburst.

"I'm sorry," Ty said, feeling more than a little embarrassed. "That wasn't exactly how I had meant to say that. I actually had this nice little speech prepared, but . . ." He shrugged.

His mother reached over and patted him on the arm. "It's fine, sweetheart. We already knew."

Ty scanned the faces around the table. Why were they all smiling? Did *everyone* know? How had they found out? He had been so careful in keeping it hidden.

"There's something you need to know about how you first came to live with us," his father said, his smile gone.

Anytime someone started a conversation with *there's something you need to know*, it was sure to be something he didn't want to.

"Your mother and I weren't exactly honest about how you arrival in

Easthaven."

Ty looked at the two of them. "What do you mean?"

"The elderly gentleman who gave you to us wasn't a traveling merchant like we said."

"I knew it! I'm some kind of royalty, aren't I?"

Adarra giggled.

"What?"

"No, Ty," his father said, shaking his head. "You're not royalty. At least, none that we know of—"

"Then what's all this about? If the man wasn't a merchant, who was he?"

His father sighed. "He was a wizard."

Ty didn't bat a lash. *A wizard?* His father was a wizard? Or was it his grandfather, perhaps?

"His name was Nyalis," Ty's father continued, settling back in his chair. "When he first arrived in Easthaven, you couldn't have been more than a few weeks old. He looked like he'd just walked out of the Pits of Aran'gal after spitting in the Defiler's eye."

"Why? What happened to him?"

"He didn't talk about it, other than to say that he had rescued you from wielders who worked for the White Tower."

"The White Tower?" Ty felt his chest constricting. "Why would there be wielders working for the White Tower? I thought you said the White Tower purges wielders." A thought struck him. "Did they know I was a wielder? Were they trying to purge me?" If Ty hadn't been afraid before, he certainly was now. "Why do they want me? I'm nobody. All I can do is talk to animals."

"You can talk to animals?" Breen asked, suddenly scooting forward in his seat to peek around their father.

Some of the others scooted forward as well.

Ty glanced around the table at the attentive faces. "Well, yes, sort of. It's not like they talk the same way we do, but I can understand their thoughts and communicate with them."

"That's very impressive," Orlyn said with a curious smile.

"Not really." Ty rolled his shoulders. "It's not like I can summon fire or conjure a windstorm. Although I did have something happen to me during Performance Night that I'd never had happen before."

"Really? And what was that?" Adarra asked, still scribbling away in her journal.

"What happened, Ty?" his mother asked. Her voice sounded concerned, not so full of curiosity like his sister's.

"I'm fine." He caught himself rubbing his arm. The mark had now covered the entire shoulder and was working its way down. "I don't know what happened. I was in the middle of playing my pipes when . . ." He bit his lip.

"When? When what?" Breen asked.

Ty wasn't sure how to explain it. He didn't understand it himself.

"Well, speak up, boy! Don't just leave us swinging in the wind!" Feoldor's face looked ready to pop.

"When I sort of made the East Inn . . . disappear."

The room went deathly quiet. He could have heard Adarra's quill drop. In fact, he thought he did. The looks of astonishment on everyone's face made Ty slink back a little farther in his seat.

"You did what?" The sleeves of Orlyn's robe flopped across the table as he leaned forward.

"I don't know. One moment, everyone was sitting there listening to me play, and the next, we were all sitting in the middle of the Sidaran Forest."

Breen grunted. "Ty, I think I would have known if—"

"Hush, boy," Orlyn said, raising a hand to Breen. The apothecary's eyebrows hung low over his eyes as he turned back to Ty. "What happened next?"

"What do you think happened? I closed my eyes and started praying that everything would go back to normal and that no one would remember what happened."

"I don't remember any of that," Breen said.

"Do you know something about this, Orlyn?" Ty's father asked.

The older man leaned back in his chair and nodded. "I believe I do. I think Ty is a mentalist."

His mother looked concerned. "A what?"

"I believe Ty can plant thoughts in people's minds as well as extract them. A mentalist can make people see things that aren't real."

"That's amazing, Ty!" his sister said, her eyes back on her parchments once again.

"Yes," Orlyn said, "and extremely dangerous."

Veldon wiped the top of his forehead with his hankie. "I've never known anyone to possess such a gift."

"Aye," Orlyn agreed. "That was a skill the Defiler was rumored to have used against his enemies—those whose minds were weak enough to be controlled."

Ty's mouth went bone dry. They had just compared him to Aerodyne, the vilest person to have walked Aldor.

"Be very careful how you wield that, young man," Orlyn said with a stern look."

Ty gulped. "Do you think that's why the White Tower wants me?"

"We aren't sure," Ty's father said. "The wizard was a little less forthcoming than we would have liked—"

"He was downright dodgy, if you ask me," Feoldor said.

"What he did tell us was that you were special and that we were to keep you safe."

Ty's mother poked her husband in the side with her elbow. "Tell him the rest."

"I will if you give me a chance," he said, turning to look at Ty. "Nyalis also said that when the time was right, he'd . . . he'd be back to get you."

"Get me?" Ty didn't like the sound of that. "You mean I'll have to leave here?"

His father shook his head and shrugged.

"What if I don't want to go?"

"Don't you worry about it, Ty," his mother butted in protectively. "You won't be going anywhere if I can help it."

Ty's head was reeling. Everything was spinning out of control. Who was this wizard, anyway? If Ty was so important, then why hadn't this Nyalis person raised him himself? Why had he left Ty to grow up in Easthaven?

Orlyn stood from his seat and grabbed his staff. "It's getting rather late, and I must be up early to open my shop. Besides, by the look of it, I think our young Ty here has had quite enough news for one night."

"I believe you're right, Master Orlyn," Ty's father said, following the older man up. "I think we could all do with a good night's sleep."

Feoldor stifled a yawn and scratched his whiskers. "How about I see you home safely, Reloria?"

The sweet-shop owner twisted her hat back and forth to make sure it wouldn't fly off. "Well, since you asked so politely."

The rest of the council said their goodbyes and left.

Ty was in a daze for the entire ride home, his mind struggling to accept everything he'd been told. The one thing he knew for sure was, no matter what happened, he wasn't about to leave his family.

Chapter 20 | Valtor

THE NORTHEAST QUARTER of the palace was quiet by this time of the evening. The royal family had retired for the night, so most of the staff were either turning down their own sheets or conducting last-minute preparations to ensure the next morning's duties went off without a hitch.

Valtor's staff tapped steadily along as he trudged down the lonely corridors, occasionally passing a random kitchen scullion or palace maid. No one dared cast an eye in his direction. Most went out of their way to keep to the opposite side of the passage as they scurried past.

He rounded the corner and stopped in front of a brightly colored tapestry, one of many that lined the palace walkways, spreading bits of unwanted cheer with its ghastly profusion of color. This one in particular draped from the ceiling clear to the floor. A draft caused the bottom of the material to move ever so slightly. Its golden tassels tickled the corridor's white marble floors like the fingers of a celebrated musician would the polished ivory of a pianoforte. Something only Valtor would have realized, since the instrument had long since been lost to the ignorance of the Third Age.

He waited and listened for any sound of approach. Satisfied that he was alone, he reached behind the fabric and flipped a hidden release. The wall gave way with a soft click. A draft from the hidden passageway threatened to topple his miter as he moved the drapery aside with his staff. Stepping through, he slid the hidden panel shut behind him.

Valtor lifted his hand and a soft orb of green light rose from his palm. He carefully picked his way through the narrow passages. Dust covered the hem of his scarlet robe as it dragged down the steps behind him. Silence enfolded him like a coffin, giving him time to organize his thoughts as he anticipated the night's activities.

He kicked at a large rodent that darted past his feet. "I hate rats." He sent a ball of flame at the helpless creature, searing it to the side of the wall.

Finding these hidden passages as a boy had been a stroke of luck. He had discovered the tunnels while he was still living on the streets. As a teenager, he had stolen a skiff in an effort to dodge the city patrollers, and while trying to find a place to hide, he had found a set of caverns in the lower mountainside, just under the massive bridge that connected the city of Aramoor to the royal palace.

The tunnels had obviously been added centuries earlier, after Aramoor was attacked by the Khul hordes from the far north. Valtor had spent years mapping out the labyrinth of passageways leading up through the palace. The expanse was a great maze of corridors forgotten by time. It was amazing that something so intricately constructed, a web of veins running throughout the palace's body, could go so completely unnoticed. All it took was for a single generation not to pass on the knowledge for it to be lost.

The secret passageways had been instrumental in Valtor's rise to power. He'd listened in on private meetings of state, caught officials in compromising positions—even the occasional assassination hadn't been completely out of the question.

The familiar smell of rot and mildew pulled him away from his musings. Salty moisture saturated the air the deeper he went. The rear tunnels flooded periodically throughout the day with the tide, leaving them in a constant state of dampness. He crossed another landing and entered the stairwell on the opposite side before continuing downward. Torches lined the stone walls of these lower passages. Faint human cries echoed up, growing louder the farther he descended. Valtor released the sphere, and the green light faded into nothingness.

Ahead, the winding stairs came to an end. His feet and legs cried with relief as he reached the bottom.

Sparing a glance at the staircase behind him, he gripped his wolf-head staff all the tighter. He would eventually have to climb his way back to the top, unless he decided to take one of the boats docked in the channels farther down. But that would require being rowed all the way back out and around to the entrance of the bay, and from there renting a carriage back up to the palace. He didn't care for the wasted time, or coin, or the questions it might cause. With an irritated huff, he limped his way forward, the silver tip of his black staff clicking as he walked across the chamber.

Only one other passage led in or out of the room. Three tables lined the right wall, surrounded by members of the Legate in their official black robes.

They bowed upon his approach.

"How is our collection coming?" he asked.

"Splendid, Your Eminence. A new shipment was boated in last night."

"Glad to hear it." There was always a fresh supply of unwanteds to be had, those who no one would miss. He had felt somewhat like a traitor at first, using the very street folk he'd grown up with as a child, but there were times when harsh sacrifices had to be made. And with a city the size of Aramoor, who would ever notice?

The legate motioned him toward the doorway leading into the lower dungeons. Valtor had converted these vaults to something more suitable for his own personal use years before. They hardly compared to those of the White Tower, but at least the screams of his subjects couldn't be heard this far down.

Another flight of stairs carried them down to the holding areas. The wails of fear, demands for release, and incessant cries for mercy coming from below were beginning to weigh heavily on Valtor's already stretched nerves. He placed a bony finger against his right temple and pressed, trying to relieve the growing ache.

The cells he passed were nothing more than iron cages, each large enough to accommodate up to eight comfortably. But, with *comfort* not being the overall intent, the prisoners had been packed in like lobsters in a trap.

Valtor took a left at the end of the wide hallway, stopping just outside an iron door. It, too, had been tainted from the moisture that lingered down there, its edges showing discoloration as flakes of metal gathered on the floor below.

It was this room that caused not only the prisoners but the guards as well to tremble with fear. The guards called it Tir'Ross Moktor—the room of a thousand nightmares. What went in didn't always come back out, and if it did, it wasn't the same.

The legate pushed open the door and stepped out of the way so Valtor could pass. "Ah, home at last," he said as he took it all in. At the back of the chamber was a closed door. Behind it, he could hear the mixture of clanging metal, scraping wood, and feral noises all harmonizing like a pharyngeal choir.

He walked over to the two waist-high restraining tables that stood in the center of the chamber and propped his staff against one. Valtor turned to the legate who stood waiting just outside the door.

"Fetch me one of the younger ones."

"Yes, sir."

"And send for Rowen. Tell him his training continues."

"Right away, Your Eminence." The legate turned and disappeared from view, leaving Valtor alone with his thoughts as he tried his best to drown out the incessant whining, begging, and fits of crying wafting from the nearby cells outside. Unable to do so, he finally shut the iron door, dimming them to little more than a buzz in the background.

"Much better," he said with a smile as he turned back around to face Tir'Ross Moktor. "Time to get started."

The light from the bracketed torches sent eerie shadows around the large stone room. The many desks, tables, and random cabinets placed intermittently about the chamber held an array of candelabras. The left wall was lined with shelves holding a wide variety of artifacts, books, relics, and potions necessary in the use of his craft.

There were no tapestries, no murals, no paintings of any kind to add a dash of decorative color to the chamber. The only contrast to the drab greys and browns of the stone and wood was the red that stained the floor around the two restraining tables.

He wound through several rows of bookshelves, finally reaching the barred door on the far side. He unlocked it with a large key he kept on him at all times and pushed the door open with his foot, allowing light to spill into the darkness beyond. It had been several weeks since he had been in the lower tunnels beneath the palace, and he wanted to make sure everything was in order.

Stepping inside, Valtor frowned at the smell. He needed to remember to have Rowen muck the place out. What was the point in having a pupil if you couldn't put him to good use? Valtor waved his hand through the air. "*Voyestra.*" The darkness dissipated as a couple of torches flared to life.

The storage room was lined with cages and crates of all sizes and shapes, each holding a unique specimen. The creatures grew restless as the light filled the room, adding wails to the buzzing from outside.

"Did you miss me?"

Near the front were the more common everyday animals: dogs, cats, birds, snakes, frogs, lizards, and a slew of other smaller creatures only found in the wild, untamed areas of Aldor. Farther back, the cages grew in size, as did the animals within.

At the very back, hidden within the shadows, were Valtor's most prized possessions. They were of his own design, creatures unlike any seen by human eyes in over a thousand years.

They were a twisted blend of many varieties, much like throwing random ingredients into a bowl and hoping the outcome would be edible. It rarely was. The corax—the Tower's winged trackers—had been one of his first successes but not his last.

Finishing his rounds, Valtor left the room and closed the door. He twisted the key, listening for the click of the lock before returning it securely to the confines of his inner cloak.

He made his way to the podium at the head of the restraining tables and opened the large leather-bound volume resting on top. The tome was one of a set he had found, along with numerous other items of ancient magic within the Chamber of Purging. He flipped through the pages, looking for something specific.

The ancient manuscripts were written in a very old dialect of Fae. It had taken him years to interpret, and even then, he only had a partial translation. As far as Valtor could tell, this particular grimoire detailed the manipulation of magic in ways long since forgotten. Its author, the former First Wizard, had been forced to work in secret after a few of his side projects had come to light. Valtor could relate. It seemed he was destined to follow in his mentor's steps.

The creak of rusted hinges had Valtor lifting his head. A skinny young man, barely twenty, entered. His clean-shaven face gave him the appearance of a mere youth, though the grotesque deformity on the left side ruined that impression. It was like a thick blister that had been left to continue growing, each year getting a little bigger. It was quite a work of art, reminding Valtor of one of Raguel's later paintings, once the artist had taken to the bottle after the death of his wife.

"Ah, Rowen, do come in." The Archchancellor waved his young acolyte over. "I have a list of items I need you to collect from the shelves while I prepare for our first subject."

His protégé smiled broadly, fetched the list, and started gathering the necessary items from the shelves on the left wall. Valtor looked on approvingly. The young man was astute, earnest, and above all, completely loyal. It was amazing what a small amount of kindness and appreciation could do for someone who had never known any.

Valtor returned his attention to the grimoire, searching the pages, finally coming to a stop on the runes he was looking for.

"Ah, here we go." He skimmed a gaunt finger across ancient text that skirted the edge of a horrific hand-drawn illustration. "Yes, this will do nicely."

"What is it?" Rowen asked, his arms laden with supplies. "What are we going to make this time? A six-legged lizard-goat, a winged constrictor? I know—what about a two-headed chirping donkey? That might be rather interesting, don't you think?"

"Interesting, perhaps. But hardly useful." Valtor continued to work his way down the page. "We will be attempting something no one has accomplished in at least fifteen hundred years." He paused for emphasis, glancing up from his place in the book. "We are going to create a Shak'tor."

Rowen peered out from behind the cabinet. "A what?"

"A Shak'tor." Valtor realized he was going to have to explain. "The Shak'tor were created during the Second Age, at the height of the Wizard Order. Of course, like most unfamiliar magics," he said with a huff, "it was forbidden since it involved the blending and manipulation of animals and humans."

Rowen stepped out from behind the row, his attention obviously piqued. "Is that even possible?"

"Yes. But it's not without risk. This is by far one of the most dangerous incantations developed."

"Why?"

"Because we are dealing with a living soul. Definitely not something to be taken lightly, but"—he glanced back down at the open page—"with the right elements, the spell has proven extremely effective in the past." Valtor continued to scan the document. "Hmm, this might be cause for concern. It says here that during earlier trials, the wizards found they were incapable of controlling them, and they were destroyed."

"The wizards or the creatures?"

Valtor grimaced as he studied the text. "Doesn't say."

He scanned farther down before flipping the page. "Ah, hold on, here we go. Evidently, they determined that to control the beasts, they had to use their own blood in the mix. Whoever's blood was used, that individual would be granted the ability to bend the Shak'tor's will to their own."

Valtor tapped his finger across the top edge of the podium. "Interesting."

Rowen quickly shuffled over to where Valtor was reading. "What is it?"

"It says here the more willing the participant, the more successful the transformation."

"Willing?" Rowen laughed. "Who in their right mind is going to willingly volunteer for this?"

"It's all about the presentation, my young apprentice. You'll be surprised what people are willing to do under the right circumstances."

A knock sounded from the other side of the metal door.

Valtor lifted his head. "Come in."

The door opened with a noticeable whine, and the legate stepped inside with two members of the Black Watch following close on his heels. In between the guards stood a little boy, shivering from cold or fright, or both. In a way, the boy almost reminded Valtor of himself at that age: short, skinny, with dark hair and dirty cheeks from a lack of bathing.

"No, please, I don't want to go in there!" the boy cried, trying to pull himself back, bare feet sliding across the stone floor. He couldn't have been much older than ten or eleven. His clothing, what little there was, was dirt-stained and worn, and his skin had discolored splotches from living on the streets.

Valtor sighed and gestured toward the wooden table on his right. "Let's get him situated, shall we?"

"No, please!" the boy cried. "Please, don't hurt me! I promise never to steal from the bread cart again!" Tears streaked his filthy face as his sobs became more frantic. "I don't want to die!"

"There, there, now," Valtor said in a soothing voice as the guards lifted the boy onto the table. "No need for those tears. I have no intention of killing you." He laid a comforting hand on the boy's shoulder. "I'm going to give you a gift."

The boy stopped thrashing and looked up. "Really?" He wiped a torn sleeve across his wet nose and sniffed. His red eyes met Valtor's. "What kind of gift?"

"The kind that won't let anyone hurt you." Valtor knew all too well what it was like living without a home or family, being taken advantage of by everyone, including those you lived with. It was a harsh life on the streets, where the weak were cast aside.

The child paused a moment to think, staring at his bare feet as they hung down from the table. Valtor could see the wheels in the child's head turning. "You mean like Master Sil'foren?"

"Master Sil'foren? Does he hurt you?"

"Yes, he's a very bad man. He hurts all the kids. If he catches us, he makes us work in his mill. And he beats us if we don't load the sacks fast enough." The boy raised his shirt to show the ugly scars.

"That's terrible," Valtor sympathized. "He's an evil man indeed to hurt little boys like you."

The child sniffed another run of snot. "He is."

"Well, where are my manners? My name is Valtor," he said with a sweeping bow. "What's your name?"

"I'm Rat."

Valtor grimaced. "Rat? What a horrible name."

"They call me that 'cause I can squeeze into places most others can't."

"Well, I'm not calling you Rat. Don't you have another name, like Narris, or Jin, or Dezryk?"

"My mother used to call me Tate."

"Tate. Yes, now that's a good, solid name," Valtor said, placing his gaunt hand on the boy's shoulder. "I like you much better as a Tate."

The boy smiled, but after looking at the men surrounding him, it faded quickly. "So . . . where's my gift?"

"Ah, I have it right here," Valtor said as he walked back to where the thick volume lay open. He raised it into the air for the boy to see.

"A book? How is a book going to keep Master Sil'foren from hurting me?"

"It's not just any book," Valtor said. "It's a book of magic."

Tate's eyes widened. "You can teach me magic?"

"Well, not quite. But I can use magic to make you big and strong so that Master Sil'foren won't be able to hurt you. In fact, when I'm done, *he* will be afraid of *you*."

"He will?" Tate obviously liked the sound of that, but there was still a hint of hesitation in his eyes as he glanced nervously at the book.

"Of course, if you are too afraid to help your friends, that's understandable," Valtor said. "Not everyone can be brave."

"No. I want to help," the boy said with a little more enthusiasm. "I want to be big and scary. Then I can protect the other kids."

Valtor smiled. "That's exactly what I wanted to hear." Turning away from the boy, he caught his pupil's eye and winked.

Chapter 21 | Valtor

"**H**AVE THE LEGATE bring me one of the older ones," Valtor said as he returned to his book.

"Of course." Rowen left off gathering Valtor's ingredients to have a word with the legate while the guards laid the boy on the wooden table and secured the leather straps.

"Why are they tying me?" Tate asked.

"It's only for your protection," Valtor said, looking up from behind the podium. "We wouldn't want you falling off and getting hurt, now, would we?"

"I guess not." Tate's hands were shaking.

"Nothing to be worried about, my boy. Pretty soon, you'll be bigger than any of the other kids out there. When Master Sil'foren sees you, he'll wish he'd never laid a hand on you or your friends."

The boy's shoulders relaxed a little, and his fingers, which had scrunched into a ball, uncurled.

"Is it going to hurt?"

Valtor sighed. "Like my father always told me when I was about your age, 'nothing great is ever accomplished without a little pain.' And we are about to do something great." Valtor stepped away from his book. "You're not having second thoughts, are you?"

"No, sir."

"Good, good." Valtor walked over and patted the top of the boy's head, regretting his decision when his hand came away with grease and dirt.

The hinges of the metal door squeaked, announcing the black-robed legate with an older man in tow. The man looked to be a vagabond—so many of those they brought in were. The vagrant half limped, half stumbled across the room, propelled forward by the guard's grip on his arm.

They fastened him to the drainage table, which was constructed of rough metal and molded to fit the shape of a man. A furrow ran along the center of the table, ending in a funnel that connected to a trough underneath.

Rowen helped the legate and the guards snap the last clasp into place around the old man's legs, securing him firmly to the table. Valtor inspected their work. Although he was quite a bit shorter than the mold, the table had been designed to allow the manacles to be adjusted for height, so it wasn't of much importance.

"Excellent."

"Thank you, Your Eminence," the legate said, and then stepped away.

Valtor tried to collect his thoughts, but it was rather difficult to do, given the extent of the magic he was about to attempt. He was about to shape a living body and soul to his own will. He wondered how those wizards during the Second Age had ever come to discover such levels of magic. It had to have been revealed to them by the faerie.

". . . big and strong." Tate's voice interrupted Valtor's contemplation. He realized the child was trying to explain to the old man what was happening. "That way I can protect my friends."

"Son, nothin' good comes of magic. I'm tellin' you. You can't trust anythin' these people be a-sayin'."

"No! You're wrong!" Tate shot back. "He's a nice man, and he wants to make me strong so I can help my friends!"

"No, boy, he doesn't. He wants to experiment on you and turn you into somethin'—"

"The boy has heard quite enough of your lies!" Valtor broke in. "You're just trying to keep our Master Tate here from doing what he knows is right." He stepped between the tables, careful to keep his back to the boy so he couldn't be overheard as he addressed the old man. "If you say one more word to scare him, I'll have my assistant slit the boy's throat and go get another. You understand?"

The old man glanced over at Rowen, who had produced a hidden dagger from the sleeve of his robe and was running his thumb along its outer edge.

"Do we understand each other?"

The vagrant nodded.

Valtor smiled. "Good." He turned and stepped over to Tate. "He won't bother you anymore. I think he might be one of Master Sil'foren's friends."

Tate peered around Valtor to get a better look. "I don't remember seeing—"

"He was obviously trying to scare you so you wouldn't let me help. He doesn't want you to stop Master Sil'foren. He wants to keep your friends working in the warehouse."

Tate's eyes darkened.

Valtor smiled and made his way back to the podium.

"Let's begin."

The legate took a seat at a desk in the far corner and organized his quill and ink.

Two guards positioned themselves at the door, their hands resting loosely on the hilts of their swords as they watched the proceedings. Their postures portrayed battle-hardened warriors, but their faces gave the impression of defectors ready to cut and run at the first sign of trouble.

Valtor pointed to the back of the metal table where the old man lay quivering. "Is the collector clean? If we contaminate the ingredients, we'll be forced to start over."

Rowen knelt and inspected the trough directly underneath the funnel. He put a fresh jar down just in case.

"When I tell you, I want you to place the ingredients from the list I gave you into the stone basin." Valtor raised a finger of warning. "This is important. You must add the elements in the order I gave you and in the exact amounts I gave you. Nothing more. Nothing less. You understand?"

Rowen spared him a glance as he arranged the items in order on the table beside the stone basin. He nodded once he was finished.

"I mean it," Valtor said. "The exact amounts I've written."

"I understand."

The waist-high stone basin looked more like a hollowed-out altar than anything. It seemed to have grown right out of the floor itself, as if the stones had risen and taken shape.

"Wait to add each item until I tell you. I have to match each element with a specific rune, in precise succession, or this isn't going to work. If not performed correctly, it could kill everyone in here."

The room grew very quiet; all heads shifted in his direction.

Rowen peered over the top of the empty basin and looked in. "This seems a bit silly. I feel like we're making a witch's brew."

"Silly or not, if this is what the grimoire says, then this is exactly what we're going to do."

The room remained eerily silent as they began. Valtor grabbed a piece of chalk and joined Rowen at the basin. At his nod, Rowen poured in the first ingredient while Valtor bent to write the required rune on the altar's side. He took great care that his inscription was accurate, reproducing every line and curve and space as precisely as it was diagrammed in the book.

When he finished, he stood and called out the rune's name in the Old Tongue. The chalk glowed, and the first element inside the basin ignited and bubbled. As swiftly as it had flared, the rune faded and vanished. Even the chalk inscription disappeared, making room for the next.

Rowen continued adding elements while Valtor copied the appropriate arcane symbol to the altar's side. Each new rune blazed as its name was called, then vanished into the ether, leaving room for the next.

The ingredients merged within the basin. Sparks burst from the top, floating toward the ceiling. There was a distinct hum now emanating from the stone cauldron.

Rowen took a few steps back and glanced at Valtor.

Valtor paused as well when mist poured over the lip of the stone and rolled across the floor around them. *Interesting,* he thought.

The legate lifted his feet off the ground to keep them out of the vapors while continuing to scribble his notes.

Within the mist, Valtor could feel a dark, almost vengeful presence. It was too late to turn back now. He was determined to find a way to keep magic from being exterminated.

Rowen added the last of the elements to the bubbling amalgam.

After watching the last rune spark to life and fade away, Valtor stepped back to the book and reread the section. Satisfied that all was in order, he raised his head from the age-worn pages and nodded at his assistant.

"We're almost done."

"Now what?"

"The final ingredient," he said, moving to the drainage table.

"Please, you don't have to do this," the old man said. "I'll do whatever you want; just don't hurt the boy. He doesn't deserve this. Have mercy."

Rowen sneered.

"I assure you, I have no intention of hurting the boy," Valtor said, laying a gentle hand on the man's trembling shoulder. "Like our young Master Tate said, I only want to make him strong so he can defend those in need."

"What's going on?" Tate asked, his voice trembling. "I thought you were going to make me big."

"Don't you worry," Valtor said. "That is exactly what we are going to do. Now I want you to look over there for a moment." Valtor pointed at the wall on the opposite side of the room.

"Why?"

"It's important that you trust me, Tate. Now look over there." Valtor conjured a noise barrier between them so the boy wouldn't hear what was about to happen.

Tate turned his head away from the other table just as Rowen drew his blade, covered the old man's mouth with his hand, and slit his throat.

The vagrant convulsed on the table, gasping for air and coughing blood before finally going still. The blood flowed into the thin trough underneath the body, collecting in the clay pitcher beneath the table.

"What's going on? Why did everything get so quiet?" Tate asked.

"Nothing to concern yourself with. You just keep looking at that wall." Valtor turned to the guards by the door. "Take him away."

The guards untied the old man and dragged his body back out the door.

"Can I look yet?" Tate asked.

Valtor glanced at his apprentice.

"It's done," Rowen said, lifting the clay pitcher out from under the table and placing it on the rim of the hollow altar. His fingers tapped impatiently on the side of the urn.

"Yes, you can look now."

Tate turned around. "Where's—"

"He didn't want to help," Valtor cut in, "so we sent him on his way."

Valtor grabbed the book off the podium and walked over to the basin to get a better look. He motioned for Rowen to add the blood. Rowen emptied the pitcher, and they both stepped back. When nothing happened, he walked back to the basin and looked inside. The concoction had now taken on a decidedly red hue.

Valtor held out his hand. "Give me your blade."

Rowen produced the sharp instrument with a flick of his wrist. The speed of it made Valtor a little uneasy. He raised his hand out over the brewing amalgam and made a small cut on the inside of his palm. He handed the knife back to his assistant, then balled his fist and squeezed out a few drops of his own blood to finalize the mix.

Valtor glanced over his shoulder. Tate's eyes, like all the others in the room, were fixed on the cauldron.

"Dip a cup," Valtor said as he walked over to where the little street urchin lay bound on his table.

Rowen followed with a cup of steaming potion in hand.

"Cut off his shirt," Valtor said. "And mind you, don't cut him."

Rowen slid the blade from the top of the boy's tattered tunic to the bottom, exposing his dirty chest and stomach.

"What are you doing?" Tate asked, sniffling. "Why are you taking off my shirt?"

Valtor laid a hand on the boy's shoulder. "I'm going to keep my word and make you big and strong. But you need to be brave for me. Do you think you can do that?"

Tate nodded.

"Excellent. I knew you had it in you." Valtor dipped a brush into the cup and sketched a single rune across the boy's chest.

"It tickles."

"Yes, well . . ." *Not for long.* "All right. There is only one more thing you need to do, my boy."

"What's that?"

"Drink this."

Tate's eyes bulged. He pinched his mouth closed and shook his head with an emphatic *No!*

"Come now, Tate. Don't let something as simple as taking a drink stand between you and stopping Master Sil'foren from hurting your friends. The power is there for you to have. You just have to take it."

The boy's head finally tilted. The nod was small, but it was there nonetheless. He opened his mouth slightly, and Rowen quickly poured the steaming mixture inside. Tate spat and coughed, but Rowen pinched his nose, forcing him to swallow. As soon as the cup was drained, Rowen released him.

Tate gagged.

By this time, the guards at the back, along with the legate, had moved forward to catch a better view of the proceedings. To Valtor's surprise, nothing happened.

Then the boy's entire body went taut. His back arched off the table, his chest pushing against the restraints.

"What's happening?" Rowen asked, eyes sparking with anticipation.

Valtor remained silent as he watched.

The leather around the boy's chest buckled under the strain until it snapped, causing everyone in the room to back away, Valtor included.

Tate's skin darkened, and hair sprouted from his body in matted clumps.

"What's happening to me?" came a guttural growl of a voice, barely understandable, barely human.

Valtor shuddered. Still, a part of him was fascinated. He couldn't pull his eyes away.

The boy's arms and legs lengthened and thickened. The straps holding his legs in place ripped apart as he rolled off the table and onto the floor, where his limbs continued to twist. All the joints in his body snapped.

"Make it stop! Please, make it stop!" His voice grumbled like rocks being rubbed together. The skin around his body appeared to be ripping in places as if it was too tight to hold what was growing inside.

The cries and growls and screams finally faded. Tate, or whatever it was, appeared to be dead. It lay prostrate on the stone floor.

No one moved.

The creature finally stirred. It no longer bore any semblance of humanity, except maybe in the eyes as its head rose and it scanned the room, marking those who stood near. It was bigger, much bigger than what Valtor had expected. Gradually, it pushed its way up to all fours, then continued to rise on its two back paws. It was easily two times the height of any man, with claws the size of a human finger.

Raising its matted head, it sniffed the air and then spread its lips, baring its massive canines.

Pulling himself together, Valtor took a step forward. The movement brought the creature's attention around with a swift snap of its head. Seeing Valtor, it sprang into the air, over tables and chests and cabinets, landing directly in front of him.

Valtor tripped over his own feet as he stumbled backward into a bookshelf, his miter flying in the opposite direction.

Rowen tried to rush the creature, but the Shak'tor backhanded him and sent him flying through the air to land on a table at least ten feet away. Rowen moaned and went still. The creature roared and started for the misshapen young man.

"No!" Valtor shouted, trying to keep his knees from knocking. The creature turned and headed back in his direction. It spread its jaws and roared. Saliva hit Valtor in the face. He could see the hatred it had for him, but before it lunged, Valtor raised his cut hand and showed it to the Shak'tor.

He wasn't sure what was required to control it. He didn't even know if he had gotten the incantation right. For all he knew, whoever had scribed the book had added that part just to play a sick game on the one stupid enough to try it. Either way, he didn't have much choice, and so, with arm outstretched, he waited while the creature leaned its muzzle over and sniffed his open palm.

He figured either it would work or he'd soon be missing a hand.

The Shak'tor hovered for just a moment, its enormous teeth only a few inches from his fingers. Then it reared and howled before slowly bowing its head.

Out of the corner of his eye, Valtor could see Rowen begin to stir. Realizing he had been holding his breath, Valtor exhaled, and struggled to regain his footing. He looked deep into the creature's eyes and smiled.

"My dear Tate. I told you I would make you big and strong."

Chapter 22 | Ty

TY WOKE TO THE sound of Breen dressing. Not feeling quite so energetic, he waited until his brother had left the room and shut the door before stretching and throwing back his covers. The light was just creeping in over the sill as he fought to open his eyes.

He lay on his back and watched the early morning rays press through the split shutters of his bedroom window. The dust sparkled as it floated from one beam to the next.

He smiled. He had the whole day to himself. After his experience with the Black Watch the previous evening, he needed to go somewhere to relax. Somewhere quiet enough to hear himself—

"Ty! Are you in there?" Adarra bellowed from the other side of the door. "We have a lot to talk about today! Get up!"

"Ugh." Ty rolled over and pulled his covers back over his head.

After a leisurely breakfast of hot porridge and honey, with some cold milk to wash it down, Ty headed for the woods. Unfortunately, he was accompanied by an older sister who was acting like she had just been bequeathed the royal library in Aramoor. Her lust for the knowledge she thought he possessed flickered in her eyes as she strolled alongside him, crossing the small wooden bridge behind their cottage.

Giving up on blowing a few loose strands of hair from her face, Adarra finally tucked them behind her ears so she could see to scribble on the loose sheets of parchment she carried with her.

She took a seat on an old log and laid her small stack of paper on top of a thick hardbound book. "So, when was the first time you knew you had magic?"

Ty huffed. "Do you really need to keep a written record of my life? What happens if someone reads it and discovers what I can do?"

"Who would ever want to read my journals?"

She has a point, Ty thought. His sister had no friends, for that very reason. She spent all her time doodling, documenting, and contemplating deep thoughts.

"Besides, once I finish writing it down, I'm going to burn it anyway."

"What? Why would you go to the trouble of writing it down if you're just going to burn it?"

"It's the only way I can remember it."

Ty cocked his head to the side. "That doesn't make any sense."

"It does if you're a memoriae."

"A what?"

"A memoriae. Someone with the gift of memory."

Ty perked. "You have magic?"

"Of course, featherhead. Why do you think I'm constantly writing everything down?"

"Because you're weird?"

Adarra looked like she wanted to throw her quill at him. "No, it's because my gift allows me to remember everything I see. So, if you were to simply *tell* me how your magic works, then I'd likely forget it later. But if I write it down where I can see the words on the page, then I'll remember it forever." She narrowed her eyes, trying to read his face. "Understand?"

"I guess. Seems like a strange use of magic, though, just to be able to remember things."

"Hardly," she huffed. "Knowledge is power. Think about how long it takes a physicker to learn their craft. Imagine how much better it would be for someone who didn't need to spend precious hours poring over old medical journals while their patient lay dying in the next room. If they had my gift, they would have the answer in moments."

Ty conceded with a bob of his head. "I guess you're right. So, you can really remember everything you've ever written down in your journals?"

"I can remember anything I've ever read or seen."

Ty pinched his chin. "What book is that?" he asked, pointing down at her lap.

"*Scagoria's Guide to Herbalism and the Art of Natural Healing.*"

"How many pages does it have?"

"Three hundred and nineteen." Her eyelids narrowed. "Why?"

Ty leaned over and grabbed the book before she could stop him.

"Hey, what are you doing?" she asked as she tried to catch the loose parchments that had been on top.

"I want to see for myself."

She offered a mischievous grin. "Don't believe me?"

He opened the book to somewhere in the middle and scanned the left side. "What does it say on page one hundred and forty-eight?"

Adarra's lips pursed as she glanced down at the mulch of early winter leaves lining the small path ahead. "Which paragraph?"

Ty looked up from the book. "Are you serious?"

"Which paragraph?" she asked again. "There are five. Should I recite them all?"

Ty glanced back down at the heavy book. She was right. There were five paragraphs. Could have been a lucky guess, though. He scanned the opposite page to count the number of paragraphs there. Most pages probably had only five or six. That wouldn't be too hard to figure out. "All right, what does the second sentence of the third paragraph say?"

Again, her lips stiffened. "It says, *The elderberry has traditionally been used to treat pain, swelling, infections, and skin conditions—*"

"All right, all right, I believe you," he said as he snapped the book shut and handed it back to her. "That's pretty incredible."

Adarra merely smiled as she placed the heavy book back under her papers.

"To answer your question," he said, "I'm not really sure when I first knew I had magic." He tried to recall the earliest moments he had recognized his gift for what it was. "When I was younger, I didn't understand that what I was doing was magic." He paced back and forth, dry leaves crunching under his feet.

Like the flickering dance of a red flit hummingbird, Adarra's fingers flew across the paper with rampant speed.

"Honestly," he continued, "I can't remember a time when I haven't been able to communicate with the life around me." He stopped to watch a couple of tree-rats scurry through the branches over their heads, playing a hazardous game of tag. "It didn't take long to figure out that I was the only one who *could* hear them."

He kicked a couple of rocks down the path, watching them skip and bounce and finally come to a stop. "I figured it was probably best to keep it to myself. I didn't want everyone to think I was . . . weird or something."

Adarra shook her head. "Well, we already knew you were an odd one." She snickered as she playfully kicked a small pile of leaves in his direction. "So, when you talk about listening to nature . . . what's that like? Can you actually understand the animals when they make noises? You said they don't talk like we do, so how do you know what they're saying?"

"They don't exactly communicate with a spoken language. It's like they talk with their emotions or instincts. I can hear when they are hungry, or tired, or scared. I know if one of them has a mate or a family." He shrugged dismissively. "I can't explain it other than that."

"Interesting." Adarra waved her hand for him to continue.

"Now, with the trees and plants, it's even more instinctive—"

"Whoa, wait!" His sister's head shot up, interrupting her scribing. "You can talk to the trees? You can actually hear plants? Ty, that's incredible."

He grinned.

"When they communicate, it's mainly about their basic needs at the time. Like sunshine, water, air, good soil—that sort of thing." He watched his sister's expressions go from anxious to excited to exhilarated with each new tidbit of information. "They tell me when they are thirsty or content, when they are enjoying the nutrients of the sun or feel the rise of a storm."

"With so many voices all talking at the same time, doesn't it get . . . I don't know, rather confusing, or loud?"

"At first it was overwhelming, but I've managed to find a way to drown most of them out when I want to. Just don't ask me how I do it." He stopped for a moment to try coming up with a logical metaphor. "It's like when you hold something in your hand for a long period of time without moving it, and pretty soon you can't tell it's there anymore. It's the same way with the noise. I sort of grow numb to it."

Adarra finished scribbling a couple more lines before dropping her arm and fixing Ty with a look of absolute determination. "Push me."

"What?"

"You know, with your magic. Push me."

Ty smiled. He had been wondering how long it would take before she got around to asking about that.

After taking a moment to clear his mind, Ty tried focusing on a single image—the same small glen where he had taken the people during Performance Night. Nothing happened. He tried again. This time, he searched for that strange warming feeling he had experienced when he had pushed everyone the first time. Again, nothing happened. Ty opened his eyes and shook his head. "It doesn't seem to be working."

"Why don't you try playing your pipes? That's what brought it on the first time."

Ty had forgotten about his flute. "Good idea." He grabbed it from its place inside his pocket, then closed his eyes and let the music flow out of him. Immediately, the warming sensation returned. It was like a small burning in the pit of his stomach that spread upward and out, sending a wave of heat throughout his extremities.

He conjured the image in his mind. The sound of Adarra's gasp forced him to open his eyes. He had done it again. They were back inside his hideaway spot.

He stood at the bottom of a small, open hollow surrounded by white birch trees that had grown between a set of protective hills. It was like a giant hand had reached down and scooped out the dirt and left the little vale there for Ty to enjoy. The floor was carpeted in lush grass and winter jasmine.

"Ty, this is unbelievable." Adarra laid her parchment, quill, and ink aside and stood. "It looks like we are really there, or here, or I'm not sure how you would describe it." As soon as she stepped away from the log, it disappeared, along with her writing utensils. She quickly felt around for them, and when her hands touched them, they reappeared. "Hmm? That's clever."

Adarra let her parchments disappear once again. She turned back around to where Ty was still playing. "See if you can stop playing and keep the image here."

He wasn't sure if that was possible, but he gave it a try. Instead of stopping altogether, he slowed the music and then softened it until it was barely audible. The mirage was still in place. Finally, he released his lips and held his concentration on the image. It remained.

"You did it."

"I did." He was beaming. "It worked."

"Let's try something else," she said. Ty could see the wheels in her head turning. "Instead of a location, try picturing an inanimate object."

Ty focused on stopping the magic, and the glen folded in on itself. It was easier that time. "You mean like a spoon or something?"

Adarra crossed her arms. "I'm sure you can get more creative than a spoon."

Ty thought about it for a moment, and after making his choice, he held out his hands and concentrated. The space above his palms shifted, much the same way it had when Sheeva had vanished. A moment later, a large hardbound book appeared.

Adarra's eyes widened as she grabbed it out of his hands. Glancing at the front cover, she quickly turned around to see if her volume of *Scagoria's Guide to Herbalism* was still resting in its place on the old log. It was. And yet she held a complete replica in her hands.

"Ty, how did you . . ." She opened it up; the pages were filled with text. "You realize what this means, don't you?" Ty shrugged. "You've only seen one page of this book, and yet you somehow replicated it down to Scagoria's very own hand strokes. That means you must be using my memories to create this."

"Is that good or bad?"

"I don't know. But it's fascinating. I'll have to put some thought to it. Try something else."

Ty didn't even have time to think about another object when a bowl appeared in his hands, steam wafting over the rim with a wooden spoon stuck from the top. He glanced inside. "I guess I was hungry." The magic didn't seem to take as much concentration on his part once it was there. It seemed finding it and calling it up was the hardest part.

Adarra cocked her brow. "You're going to have to be careful what you think about. Who knows what you might conjure."

Ty hadn't thought about that until now. "That's a good point. This could get really—"

Adarra let out a yelp and raised her hand to her mouth. Ty turned around and yelped as well when he saw Lyessa standing there beside him. She was dressed in a full evening gown, but unlike the conservative cut of her usual style, her deep blue dress was rather provocatively revealing. Ty's face turned red. "What the . . ." Quickly, he swiped his hand at the image, and it vanished.

Adarra lowered her head, pretending to look at her parchment.

"I can explain." Ty's face was completely flushed. He could feel his temperature rising. The burning sensation inside had grown considerably.

"Ty! What is that?"

"What is what?" He spun around. "I don't see anything."

"No! Your hands! Look at your hands!"

Ty raised his hands and shrieked. They were on fire. But unlike any fire he'd ever seen, these flames were a vibrant blue. As fast as he could, he waved them in the air, trying to extinguish the image like he'd done with Lyessa, but this time, the push didn't leave.

"Help! It won't quit!"

"Ty, let me see that!" Adarra hopped up from her seat. "I don't think that's a push."

"What are you talking about?"

"Ty, I can feel the heat."

"I don't feel anything." He glanced at his flame-covered hands. There was no warmth. They tingled just a bit, but that was all. "When I made you see the book, did you feel it?"

"You're right. I did feel it."

"Then how do we know if it's real or not?" He pulled his hands away to keep from burning her.

Her brow wrinkled in thought. "Try using it to affect something," she said, glancing around the small dirt path, "something real." She looked over her shoulder. "Like those leaves over there."

There was a small pile of leaves in front of a large palmetto. He started to raise his arm when a lance of flame unexpectedly released from his right hand and hit his sister.

She screamed as her dress went up in blue fire.

The flame on his hands disappeared immediately.

Adarra dove to the ground and began to roll as fast as she could. "Help! Put it out! Put it out!" The flames continued to burn.

Ty dove on top of her, trying to douse them with his hands. He could feel the heat this time. His hands burned as he worked to extinguish her clothing.

By the time they managed to snuff the fire out, his sister didn't have much more than her undergarments left. Thankfully, the damage to her skin hadn't been too severe.

"Are you trying to kill me?" She scooted quickly to a safe distance.

"I'm sorry," he said, making sure to keep his hands lowered. "I don't know what happened." He took a step toward her. "Are you all right?"

"No! Stay back!" she said, holding up her hands to stop him. "Don't come any closer."

She actually looked frightened of him.

Ty backed away. He'd nearly killed his own sister. For the first time, he was scared of *himself.*

Chapter 23 | Rhydan

HIGH KING RHYDAN rolled over on their canopy bed, wrapped his arm around his wife, and pulled her close. "I wonder if anyone would notice if we stayed in today."

"Highly doubtful," she said, playing with his beard. "Though I must admit the thought is tempting."

Rhydan didn't say anything. He simply stared at his wife. Ellise was beautiful. Her silvery hair fell below her shoulders. Rhydan loved running his hands through it. He breathed her in, the smell of lavender from yesterday's bath still clinging to her nightgown. He had been most fortunate in his choice of wife. He depended on her.

Ellise burrowed farther down under the thick coverings on their bed. Rhydan had left the curtains on his side open that evening to let in the warmth from the fire in the hearth. Unfortunately, all that was left were the embers.

"Do you have anything special planned for the ambassadors' last week?" she asked.

"I thought about taking them on a hunt. The grouse are good this time of year, and our spaniels could use a little exercise."

"They aren't the only ones," Ellise said with a small poke to his waistline.

"Watch it, woman."

"How can I not?"

Rhydan chuckled. "A diversion would be a welcome change from these constant meetings where nothing worthwhile ever seems to be accomplished."

"Just make sure they don't shoot each other," Ellise said with a teasing smile. "Although, I don't believe many would complain if a stray arrow were to strike the Cylmaran ambassador."

Rhydan laughed. "Treacherous talk. I'm thankful you're not my enemy, dearest."

Ellise stroked the tip of Rhydan's nose with her finger. "And don't you forget it."

He grunted. "You wouldn't let me." He kissed her forehead, and they lay there a few more moments, enjoying the warmth of the comforters.

An hour later, Rhydan found himself dressed, fed, and sitting in his study.

"I would like us to make our way north to Lord Tulvik's estate this afternoon," Rhydan said to the two men sitting across from him. "Commander Tolin, I would like you to arrange for a full lancer escort." Rhydan raised a hand. "I know it's not customary to use a full guard for a simple hunt, but I would like to give our guests one more show of strength."

"Yes, Your Majesty. Might I suggest Overcaptain Asa with Second Company?"

"I'll leave the details in your capable hands, Commander, although I would like you to join us." Commander Tolin was a bear of a man, almost half a head taller than Rhydan. He had a short, well-groomed beard that softened a strong jaw, and his thick hair—showing more than a touch of grey around the temples—was pulled back and tied off neatly. His face bore the scars of battles fought in Elondrian service, the most notable of which narrowly missed his left eye.

Tolin stood and bowed. "It would be my pleasure, Your Majesty. I will see to the arrangements."

"Thank you, Commander." Rhydan watched Tolin leave. Tolin was one of the finest men Rhydan had ever had the privilege to work with. Not only was he fearless, but he had a good head on his shoulders, and his men loved him.

Once the doors had closed behind Tolin, Rhydan turned to Ayrion. "Considering your last encounter with our esteemed ambassador from Cylmar, I want your presence felt at every available opportunity. I want to keep Ambassador Belkor off balance. The raids against our border communities have grown of late."

Ayrion nodded. "They've been sending slaves through the Black Hills since I was a child." He had a vague look in his eyes.

"What are you thinking about?"

Ayrion seemed to return from wherever his mind had wandered. "I was just remembering my time spent on the *Wind Binder* as a young boy, sailing the Shemoa River with Captain Treygan and his crew. We faced Cylmarans even then."

Ayrion hadn't spoken much of his past, and Rhydan had never pressed him for it. He figured when he was ready, he would share it.

"The only thing men like Overlord Saryn respect is someone more dangerous than they are," Rhydan said. "We need to remind Ambassador Belkor who they are dealing with before more drastic measures are required."

"As your Guardian, it is my solemn duty to stand by your side, Your Majesty."

Rhydan smiled. "I would like to believe it is for more than mere duty that you do so, Ayrion."

The young man opened his mouth, closed it, then steeled himself and spoke. "There is no one I respect more, Your Majesty. You saw something in me that . . . well, you gave me a purpose. For that, I could never begin to repay you except through my service."

Rhydan leaned back in his seat with a heavy sigh. "There are times I wish . . ." He lowered his head. "No matter. No sense dwelling on what is not." He smiled at the young warrior in black. "Your service honors me, Ayrion. It always has. If only my own flesh and blood could do the same."

"I am sure the prince cares in his own way, Your Majesty."

Rhydan lowered his head. "I fear I've been far too lenient with him. My own father cared more for his position than his family, and I vowed I wouldn't do the same. Perhaps that was a mistake."

"If Your Majesty hasn't already, I would suggest inviting Dakaran to join us on the hunt. It might give you the opportunity to mend some fences."

Rhydan nodded. "It's been a long time since my son joined me on a hunt. I remember how much he used to love them." His smile slowly faded. "He's grown so distant of late. No matter how much I try to include him in the royal affairs, he's either too busy, too tired, or too full of wine." Rhydan couldn't remember the last time he'd seen his son without a glass in his hand. He wished a little of Ayrion's dedication had rubbed off on Dakaran. It was one of the main reasons he'd chosen Ayrion as a playmate for his son when they were children.

"I had hoped that Dakaran's recent act of selecting a personal advisor had signified he was going to turn his life around and finally start preparing for when it becomes his time to rule. Instead, he seems to be getting worse." Ellise had counseled him that Dakaran needed a firm hand. "I'm worried it might be too late."

"When it comes to family, Your Majesty, I don't want to believe that it's ever too late."

Rhydan smiled. He knew how hard that must have been for Ayrion to say, given his past. He took a deep breath and decided to change the subject. "The queen tells me you have been seen on more than one occasion in the gardens with a certain young lady."

Ayrion's cheeks flushed slightly. "Oh. Uh . . . Yes, Your Majesty. I find her company quite . . ." He looked like a bag snatcher caught still holding the bag. "Rewarding," he finally said.

"Rewarding?" Rhydan laughed. "Not quite the word I might have used for a beautiful young woman, but maybe things have changed since I was young."

Ayrion didn't reply, choosing instead to study the fabric on the arm of his chair.

Rhydan shook his head. The man would rather take on an army of Scorvinians out of the Westlands than discuss matters of the heart.

"Well, I'm sure you have plenty to do before the hunt," Rhydan said, still smiling. "I will release you to it before I embarrass you further."

Ayrion, not quite leaping, stood to his feet. "By your leave, Your Majesty."

Rhydan nodded, trying not to laugh as Ayrion made a strategic retreat for the door.

With the last of his appointments for the morning taken care of, Rhydan decided that instead of a written invitation, he would invite his son personally.

He knocked on Dakaran's door, waited a moment, then entered.

His son's room was lavishly decorated, everything trimmed in gold and accented with purple. Plush rugs lined the floor, and thick draperies hung from the windows and bed. Rhydan could hardly make out the shape of his son amidst the pillows.

Dakaran slid off his enormous four-poster bed, stood, and bowed, looking quite surprised by the visit. "Your Majesty."

Rhydan could see his son was already in a mood. "Dakaran, in private, I'm your father, not your king."

"Rather hard to distinguish the two."

"Perhaps that fault lies with me," Rhydan said with a sigh of regret as he stepped farther into the room.

Dakaran looked stunned by the admittance.

"My father, your grandfather, was an ambitious man. From the day I was born, he groomed me, pushed me, forced me to measure up to his expectations. He believed that discipline and control were the ways to shape a boy into a man." Rhydan glanced at Dakaran. "I didn't want to make the same mistake."

Dakaran stood there in silence.

Rhydan couldn't tell if he was wanting to say something or still trying to rouse himself from another night of hard drinking. He finally waved it off. "The past is the past. I was hoping you would join me and the ambassadors on a hunt. I would enjoy your company. It's been quite a few seasons since we've shot together."

Dakaran plopped on the edge of his bed. "Is this a request or a command?"

Rhydan felt his composure begin to slip. "It's a request from a father to his son. I'll leave it to you," he said as he turned and headed back to the door. "We leave this afternoon. Lord Tulvik has opened his estates to us for this evening, so we can get an early start of it tomorrow." Rhydan didn't wait around for his son to provide another sarcastic remark. He hoped Dakaran would accept his offer, but he didn't harbor much hope.

Chapter 24 | Ayrion

THE MORNING SEEMED to have flown by, much faster than Ayrion would have liked.

Shade was saddled and waiting when he arrived at the High Guard stables. The stallion was eager to go, pulling at the reins that Loren, one of the royal hostlers, held. Loren was taller than Ayrion and lanky, with flyaway brown hair and a smooth face. He offered the reins to Ayrion as he approached.

Ayrion took them, patting Shade's strong neck as he moved around to the front. Shade nuzzled Ayrion's palm.

"Hello, old friend. I've missed you too."

Shade was a magnificent animal, everything a warhorse should be: strong, enduring, intelligent. His coat was the color of midnight, save for a single strip of white that ran from his forelock to the tip of his nose.

Ayrion glanced over his shoulder at Loren. "How is he?"

"Ready to go, sir. I took the liberty of warming him for you."

Ayrion clapped Loren on the shoulder. "Good man." Loren hadn't been with them long, but he had a good feel for the animals. Ayrion appreciated that.

"Thank you, Guardian."

Ayrion mounted and rode toward the front gates, Shade's shoes echoing off the courtyard stone. Commander Tolin was saddled and chatting with Overcaptain Asa as Ayrion made his way to the front of the two lancer companies waiting at the gatehouse walls.

Asa was a commoner, but he had quickly risen through the lancer ranks to a position normally held by lesser nobles. He was short but well built. His two distinct features were the full ducktail beard hanging from his chin and the jagged scar that ran from the top of his right eye, down, and across the side of his right cheek.

The overcaptain had opted to not wear his eye patch, something he enjoyed doing to unnerve those around him with his empty socket. From the way Asa continued to glance over his shoulder and smile at the ambassadors, this was clearly one of those times.

Ayrion reined in beside Tolin. "Everything in order?"

"Everything but those royal pains in my backside," Asa said, spitting in disgust. There was no need to guess who he was referring to.

Tolin smiled. "I can't say that I disagree with the sentiment. But we have a duty to perform, and we will perform it to the best of our ability no matter how distasteful we might feel it is."

Asa grimaced. "I would never shirk my duty, Commander. I just don't got to enjoy it, that's all."

Tolin chuckled.

"I believe the king is ready," Ayrion said, noticing as Rhydan looked back in their direction. Ayrion left Tolin and Asa and rode ahead to join the king at the head of the procession.

"Looks to be a beautiful day, Your Majesty."

The king shaded his eyes with his hand. "Hopefully it will hold out for our sport tomorrow as well." He turned in the saddle and looked back down the line. "Is the commander ready?"

"He is, Your Majesty."

"Good. Let's be on our way."

Ayrion motioned for his guards to move out.

They had just reached the bridge gate when a solitary rider rounded the inner wall behind them, heading in their direction. Ayrion shifted in his saddle to see Dakaran trotting up to take his place behind his father. He couldn't help but notice the king's smile.

To the rear of the ambassadors rode the High Guard, their black capes billowing out behind them, a not-so-subtle reminder of the elite forces Elondria had at her disposal. Following behind them came the gamekeeper, who was so bent with age that the man could barely see over his mount's head. After him, the crossbowmen, the spaniels and their handlers, and finally the lancers.

All together, they made quite the impressive parade as they crossed the bridge connecting the palace to the main part of the city. At Ayrion's command, the High Guard split, half taking up position in front of the king as they entered the city proper. The citizens of Aramoor lined the streets and cheered as the king passed. Rhydan returned their greeting with a smile and wave. He truly seemed to care about the people, and they respected him all the more for it.

Ayrion had spent countless hours attending the king's weekly open sessions in which anyone, regardless of station, was free to enter a petition. The king and queen couldn't personally attend to everyone, but it let the people know they had the right to come should they feel their situation required his attention.

Ayrion could remember a time when the king had given the order that his own coffers be opened to help build a home for unwanted children. Having been one of those boys years before, Ayrion knew firsthand what a difference a chance like that could make.

It took a couple of hours for the procession to travel King's Way from the palace to the city's eastern gate. The massive wall that surrounded the Elondrian capital was a testament to the wonders magic had been capable of in times past. The wall was thick enough for three men to walk abreast at the top. Ayrion could only guess at the labor its construction had required. Those living within were all but guaranteed a peaceful existence, for since its construction after the Wizard Wars, the wall had never been breached.

Turning north, the hunting party followed the road leading through the open plains above the city. The grasslands were lush and green all the way to the Tansian River. After crossing, they headed into the lower woodlands below the foothills of the Sandrethin Mountains. The day was still warm by the time they arrived at Lord Tulvik's estate, or as warm as it could be this late in the season. The leaves had already turned, and many had begun to fall.

Lord Tulvik was a gracious host. He spared no expense for the king and his guests, even giving up his own quarters so the king could enjoy the mountain view from his chambers. After dinner, Commander Tolin posted a watch. The rest turned in for the evening. It would be an early rise if they planned on reaching the best cubbies before the day warmed.

After eating with his men, Ayrion took a stroll outside and found the commander leaning against a tree just outside the main gate.

"I hope the weather holds for their sport tomorrow," Ayrion said as the two gazed up at the star-filled sky.

"It's not the weather we should be concerned with," Asa said, coming up behind to join them. "It's the incessant yammering from those flaming ambassadors. That one from Briston just doesn't know when to shut up. The only time his gob wasn't flapping was when he was filling it with more wine."

Ayrion chuckled, then glanced at Tolin and noticed the man wasn't smiling. "What's wrong? The ambassadors getting under your skin as well?"

"It's awful quiet out there."

"You've been cooped up in that city for too long," Asa said. "It's supposed to be quiet out here."

"It's too quiet."

Ayrion joined the other two in looking at the surrounding forest.

"When was the last time you heard anything?" Tolin asked. "I don't even hear the insects."

Asa shivered. "You're right. It's as quiet as the training grounds during mealtime."

"I'm glad it's not just me," Tolin said.

The hair on the back of Ayrion's neck stiffened. "Something's out there."

All three men stood as still as possible as they scanned the trees. Ayrion had the greater advantage with his Upakan eyes, but even he couldn't catch a glimpse of what was making his skin crawl.

Soon enough, the typical forest chatter started up once again.

"Whatever it was," Tolin said, "it must have moved on."

"They say the black bear numbers are up this year," Asa commented, still staring out at the trees with his one eye. "Probably smelled Tulvik's cooking and came to get a better look." He clapped Tolin on the shoulder. "Well, I'm off to bed. Gotta get my rest while I can."

Tolin yawned. "I believe I'll join you. You coming, Ayrion?"

Ayrion took one last look at the surrounding trees, then turned and followed the others back through the gate.

Ayrion didn't sleep much that night and was up before the sun the next morning. After a quick but hearty meal, the hunting party was mounted and back on the trail.

It appeared to be the perfect day for a hunt. The sun was shining, and the cool breeze blowing in off the snowcaps kept away most of the insects. The ash, silver maple, and slippery elm gave way to sugar pine, fir, spruce, and mountain hemlock the farther they journeyed.

The old gamekeeper rode on ahead to scout the game. Ayrion turned to check on the king and found him busy trying to keep a conversation flowing with his son. Ayrion thought it best not to interrupt. Dakaran was at least attempting to be civil. The ambassadors seemed content to talk amongst themselves, pointing out the landscape or the occasional animal that passed within sight. Only one of the ambassadors watched Ayrion. Ayrion could feel the Cylmaran's hateful gaze stabbing at his back like a hot iron poker. What was driving the man to loathe him so?

About an hour into their journey, Ayrion spotted the gamekeeper standing by his mount on the side of the road.

"I believe he's found our quarry, Your Majesty. We should go on foot from here."

Ambassador Gyin, who had barely managed to stay on his horse with his rotund belly bouncing around at every dip and turn, protested. "On foot? I can't see why we shouldn't be able to shoot these birds from a horse just as easily as from the ground."

"That would be the case were we in a field, Ambassador," Ayrion said. "But in the woods, the noise of all the horses would undoubtedly frighten off any creature long before we were within shooting distance."

"Well, just how long of a walk are we talking about here?"

Ayrion sighed. "As long as it needs to be, sir, but I would hope not far."

The king gracefully swung down from his horse. "Come now, Gyin, I'll be more than happy to entertain at dinner this evening with the heroic tale of our hunt. Not leaving out, of course, the fearless ambassador who stayed behind to watch the horses."

Gyin grumbled under his breath as he awkwardly slid off his mount.

Ayrion motioned for the dog-handlers to follow the gamekeeper up the faint path.

The bowmen locked back the strings on their crossbows, then loaded them with blunt-head quarrels. Anything wider would strip the meat off the bird, especially in the hands of inexperienced hunters.

Once the bows were ready, the party made their way up a gentle slope that wound farther into the lower foothills. Ten lancers selected by Overcaptain Asa were left in charge of the horses, while those remaining followed the party as they headed deeper into the trees, keeping their distance so as not to startle the hunters' game.

The trail opened into a large meadow. There were a few trees that dotted the otherwise barren landscape. Thick grass covered the terrain, with some dense brush along the outside edge. Ayrion could see why the gamekeeper had chosen it. It was prime for cubbies. The dogs strained against their leashes, eager to be after their quarry.

After a brief discussion with the handlers, Ayrion walked back to the ambassadors. "Our gamekeeper believes there is a covey nesting in those shrubs on the far side. If we keep our noise to a minimum, he believes we should be able to approach to within thirty paces before releasing the dogs. Once released, you'll get one shot, maybe two, before the birds hit the tree line."

Nierdon, the ambassador from Keldor, took a step forward. "What happens if we miss?"

"Then you will hand your bow back to the bowman and he'll give you a fresh one. The grouse will fly only far enough to perch in the nearby trees. If all else fails, this is only the first stop."

"First stop?" Gyin's head lifted. "I hope you don't expect us to go traipsing all over the mountainside like a pack of wild goats!"

"For pity's sake, Gyin," Lanmiere said. "The fresh air might do you some good, not to mention the exercise."

The other ambassadors stifled chuckles while Gyin huffed and tugged on his trousers.

"Ambassadors, please take your crossbows," Ayrion said. "We will be walking in silence the rest of the way. I'll raise my hand when we get within shooting distance." He demonstrated the hand motion. "When I lower it, they will release the dogs. The rest will be up to you."

The king took the offered crossbow. "Thank you, Guardian. I believe they get the picture."

Ayrion hoped so. He was tired of acting like a mother hen trying to round up her brood of wayward chicks.

The rest of the party retrieved their weapons and walked all abreast, making sure no overenthusiastic hunter released his quarrel into another's unsuspecting back—whether by accident or not.

With each new step, the tension grew. Ayrion wanted to laugh. One would have believed they were marching into battle against a horde of rock trolls, not a nest of defenseless grouse.

Tolin, Asa, and the lancer company remained at the wood line, not wanting to disturb the nobility's sport. The High Guard followed a few steps behind the nobles, giving them plenty of space to enjoy their hunt.

The pace was slow as they crossed the open meadow. Ayrion walked a few steps in front of the gentry. Up ahead, the veteran gamekeeper knelt to study some tracks in the soft dirt. He turned and looked at Ayrion. Something was wrong. The look on the man's face forced Ayrion to stop.

The forest went still.

Ayrion's hand slid toward his blade. It was the same feeling he'd had outside Lord Tulvik's estate. Something was watching them. He raised his fist, signaling the hunters to stop.

"What's wrong?" Ambassador Gyin asked under his breath. "Where are the birds?"

"Hush, you fat fool," Belkor spat.

Ayrion scanned the forest ahead as he cautiously retreated toward the king. He drew his swords.

The dogs started growling, and their lips curled as they stared ahead at the tree line.

The king's finger gently stroked the tip of his crossbow's release clamp. "What is it, Guardian?"

"Something's wrong."

"I don't hear anything," Ambassador Lanmiere whispered.

"Exactly. Ambassadors, please get behind my men."

Chapter 25 | Ayrion

T HE HIGH GUARD had barely gotten in front of the ambassadors when an enormous misshapen creature burst from the thick brush. The beast towered over the elderly gamekeeper. With effortless precision, the monster rammed its massive claws through the old man's chest and lifted him off the ground.

Ambassador Gyin shrieked in terror.

The creature flung the old man's body and turned to look at them. It reared on its haunches, releasing a bloodcurdling roar that sounded like something between the challenge of a feral beast and the pain of a creature so badly formed that every movement was agony.

Ayrion froze. He didn't believe what his eyes were seeing. Something like this beast shouldn't exist. It looked completely amiss, a patchwork of a dozen different animals mashed into a vaguely human, vaguely canine shape. Layers of muscle wrapped a skeletal structure that bulged oddly, as though there were extra bones trying to push through the skin.

The dogs tucked tail and ran. Ayrion wondered if they weren't the smart ones. He could hear Tolin from the other side of the meadow, shouting for Asa to bring the horses. Light armor clanked as Tolin and his lancers charged. It was up to Ayrion and the guard to hold the creature off until they arrived.

Taking a deep breath, he pushed everything from his mind.

The creature was a least twenty paces from the men. It scanned the cluster, coming to a stop on the High King. There was some kind of intelligence at work behind its dark eyes. It had not been a mere quirk of fate that had brought this beast across their path. It had been hunting them. Ayrion dropped into a crouch, swords at the ready, and reached out with his senses, waiting.

Beside him, he heard the ring of the king's sword as it cleared its scabbard. Even Dakaran had drawn and was ready.

The creature roared once more, then attacked.

Crossbow bolts whizzed by Ayrion's head, narrowly missing him. The ambassadors, who had never seen real combat, had fired without so much as taking aim. It was sheer luck they had managed not to shoot each other—or him. Behind them, the dog-handlers decided their dogs had shown the most sense, and fled.

Ambassador Gyin threw down his bow and ran after the handlers.

"Gyin! You coward! Get back here!" Ambassador Belkor shouted, his voice shaking with anger and fear.

The creature was more agile than Ayrion would have thought possible, considering its size. It closed the distance between them with a few lunging strides. It was going to plow straight through them. Ayrion threw himself into the king, barely knocking him and Dakaran to the side before the beast barreled over the guards. Two of Ayrion's men went down, crushed under the beast's feet. The other four hacked at the creature, trying to stay clear of its deadly claws.

The bowmen fired a volley from the ambassadors' reserve bows, then rushed to reload. The creature retreated slightly when the bolts hit, but they seemed to have little effect. If a direct volley didn't bring it down, they were in trouble.

The beast turned and swung at Ayrion. His magic saved his life as he ducked underneath. Its claws caught one of his men in the chest and threw him. He landed in a heap and didn't get back up. Ayrion dove underneath the next swing and cut a deep gash along its lower arm. The creature's skin was thick, much tougher than should have been possible. It howled and reached for him again, but Ayrion leaped backward, and it grabbed another of his men instead. The creature bit through the guard's neck and threw his body over its shoulder.

It spun and locked eyes with Ayrion, baring its bloody fangs in defiance. Whatever intelligence drove this creature, it was now changing tactics and coming for him.

This suited Ayrion just fine. If he could keep the beast's attention, it would give Tolin and his lancers time to reach the king. He angled left, studying the creature: the way it moved, the reach of its claws, the way it coiled to attack. As hideous as it was, there was something about its eyes. They seemed . . . almost sad. If he didn't know any better, he would have thought the creature had no more desire to be in this battle than they did.

Ayrion felt the tug of his magic. Seeing the vision, he readied himself for the attack. Sure enough, the creature dove. Ayrion spun to the left, sidestepping the creature's arms and cutting into the thick muscle of its left leg. Again, his blade didn't cut as deep as he would have liked. The creature reeled and caught Ayrion in the arm, its claws ripping through the leather of Ayrion's coat and raking his shoulder. It was faster than anything Ayrion had ever faced. He stumbled backward but fought through the pain. He could feel warm blood running down his arm. What was it going to take to kill this thing?

The creature struck again, not giving Ayrion a chance to catch his breath. Ayrion raised his blades, having seen it coming, and deflected the oncoming arm. He spun, hoping to catch the beast from behind, but tripped over the body of one of his men and went down. Instincts saved his life, and he rolled as soon as he hit, narrowly escaping the creature's claws as they buried themselves in the back of the fallen man.

Ayrion flipped back to his feet, swords raised as the half-animal, half-human monster shook the dead guard from its fingers and twisted toward him. He saw over his shoulder that Tolin had managed to get his lancers around the royal family and their guests. Tolin was calling for a squad of polemen to join him.

The creature, seeing the lancers, pulled back toward the woods. Ayrion wondered if it was attempting to flee.

Tolin and his men formed a line to either side of Ayrion. The commander grunted. "I tell you, these grouse get bigger every year."

The creature continued to back slowly toward the brush.

"Why isn't it—"

A roar from behind them answered Tolin's question before he had a chance to ask it. Two more creatures flew out of the trees on the other side of the meadow and hit the rear of the lancers protecting the king.

It had been an ambush all along.

Ayrion barely had time to turn when the first creature attacked. It lunged at Tolin's men. Three lancers were ripped apart before Tolin managed to thrust his halberd into the creature's shoulder and force it back. The beast screamed and split Tolin's weapon in half with its hand. It kicked out with its hind leg, and Tolin hit the ground.

Ayrion dove between Tolin and the beast. He stood over his mentor, striking away the creature's attempts to reach him, giving Tolin enough time to get back to his feet. Ayrion's swords countered, deflected, and hacked at the beast's arms. "Get in here and help me!" he yelled at the remaining lancers. "I must reach the king!"

Tolin's men fought their way in, jabbing at the creature from all sides and giving Ayrion the time he needed to make a break for the battle taking place on the other side of the meadow. The remnants of the High Guard and lancers were managing to keep the two beasts at bay, but at a high cost.

Horses thundered into the meadow on Ayrion's right as Asa and his men arrived.

"Sergeant, take some men and help the commander!" the overcaptain barked as if it were no great thing to be fighting ten-foot-tall half-human monsters. "The rest with me!"

Ahead, Ayrion could see Rhydan and Dakaran swinging their blades in wide arcs, fighting to keep out of the way of the creature's claws. Lanmiere and Belkor stood over a wounded Nierdon, brandishing polearms reclaimed from fallen lancers.

Rhydan was as close to a father as Ayrion had known since coming to Aramoor. That above everything else drove his legs to go faster. One of the creatures had pushed its way through the guard and was shoving the ambassadors aside to get to the king. Ayrion sheathed his swords and grabbed a fallen halberd. He darted between the king and the monster and drove it into the creature's abdomen. The pointed tip bit into the creature's flesh but not deeply enough to have killed it. What sort of magic was driving these things?

The beast recoiled, and Ayrion lost his grip. The shaft hit him in the chest and sent him spinning. He had seen it coming, but he couldn't move or it would have hit the king. Ayrion felt like he'd cracked his ribs, the pain causing his eyes to water. He had barely caught his breath when the creature lunged again.

Ayrion yanked the king out of the way and rolled underneath as the beast severed the head of the lancer next to him, spraying Ayrion and the king with blood. Ayrion's shoulder was throbbing. He could feel his own blood dripping from his hand as his vision clouded at the edges. *No!* he shouted at himself. He couldn't afford to lose consciousness now. He slapped his face to focus. He had to find a weak spot or they were all going to die.

He hopped back to his feet. The creature stared down at him. It appeared to be smiling, or as close to it as it could manage. Ayrion held its gaze. There was something about those eyes. *The eyes!*

The beast reared to strike but was stopped by Asa as his mounted troops joined the fight. The one-eyed overcaptain swung his heavy battle-axe, spewing language so foul it would have made a Tallosian blush.

The two beasts regrouped to face the additional troops.

Ayrion circled back to where the creatures were battling the mounted regiment. He couldn't wait for them to come to him. He freed his blades and waited for the closest beast to turn. But instead of continuing its fight with the cavalry, one of the creatures split off from its partner and made an unexpected dash back toward the king. Only this time, Ayrion was on the opposite side of the battle.

Ayrion tore through the fighting, dodging the mounts to avoid being trampled as they cantered to get at the beast. Pain shot through the entire length of his arm. He could barely breathe from the strike to his ribs. How could he have been so stupid? He had thought he could fight the creatures while they were safely away from the king.

He pushed through the last of Asa's men and charged. Ayrion's men were going down left and right. Ambassador Lanmiere was thrown through the air, landing a few feet in front of Ayrion. Ayrion didn't bother stopping. He leaped over the injured man and kept going.

The creature swung at the king, but Dakaran shoved his father to the side, getting knocked down in the process. Ayrion didn't have time to be shocked. He slid between the creature's legs while its back was turned and cut as deeply as he could just behind the knees. The creature shrieked and lunged. His magic kept him from being ripped in half.

He dodged and cut, spun and thrust, not giving the creature anything to hit. He plunged one of his blades into its lower abdomen, causing the beast to double over far enough for Ayrion to drive his second straight into its eye.

The creature howled as the steel buried itself to the hilt. It stiffened, then hit the ground.

Behind them, the second creature bellowed with rage, throwing itself at the mounted lancers with abandon. Whatever intelligence had been driving it vanished, and instinct took over.

Asa's men tried circling the creature, but it tore through them, not caring if it felled man or horse.

Ayrion retrieved his blades and turned to see Shade racing across the meadow, freed from the lancer who'd been holding him. Ayrion ran to meet him. Grabbing the saddle horn, he swung his legs up. On the left side of the field, Commander Tolin was limping heavily on one leg while he and his men did everything they could to hold the first creature back.

Ayrion directed Shade straight at the second beast.

Asa took a hit and was thrown from his mount, spouting curses the whole way down. There was now nothing left between the creature and the king. Ayrion dug in his heels, and Shade rammed the beast in the side just as it was about to take a swing at Dakaran. The force of Shade's body and a precise thrust of Ayrion's blade knocked the creature sideways, giving the lancers a chance to skewer its legs with their halberds. With a shriek, it fell backward.

"The eyes! Go for the eyes!" the king shouted as he rushed forward and thrust his blade into one of the beast's sockets. Dakaran, Belkor, and what remained of the lancers joined the king. Within moments, they had hacked the creature apart.

The remaining beast on the other side of the meadow roared and punched through what was left of Tolin's lancers, scattering them like leaves in the wind. It picked up speed, ignoring the bolts and spearheads bristling from its skin as it charged straight at the king.

Ayrion kicked Shade into motion. The warhorse bounded forward, his nostrils flaring, dirt flying in all directions as he fought to give Ayrion every last bit of speed he had.

Fifteen paces. Ten paces. Five. Ayrion stood from the back of his saddle and leaped into the air, both blades drawn.

The creature raised its claws to rip him in half, but Ayrion struck first, driving both swords straight through the creature's neck. He landed, rolled, and vaulted back to his feet with swords still in hand.

The creature's last breath came out as an eerie sort of whimper.

"Close ranks! Close ranks!" Commander Tolin shouted as he and what was left of his men limped their way across the meadow to join the king.

Those still standing quickly formed a small circle, shoulder to shoulder. No matter their title, whether king, ambassador, or lancer, they stood side by side with sword or halberd in hand, waiting to face down whatever might be coming next. Ayrion and the one remaining member of the High Guard stood in front of the king.

After a long stretch of silence, one by one, the birds began to sing.

Chapter 26 | Ayrion

THE MEADOW smelled of freshly turned earth and death. The metallic stench of blood was only slightly lessened by the cool breeze coming off the mountains behind them.

Ayrion's shoulder ached. He had cleaned the lacerations as best he could and had tied some material he had cut from one of the dead men's shirts around it to stop the bleeding. His coat, however, was going to need a miracle from a master leatherworker if it was to survive.

Commander Tolin sent some men to scout the surrounding wood to make sure there were no other creatures lying in wait, while the rest gathered the wounded and began setting up a temporary camp near the center of the meadow. The commander wanted to stay as far from the tree line as possible.

After seeing to the fallen, Ayrion sat down to clean his blades. While he did, he kept a close eye on the king. He wasn't about to let him out of his sight.

"Those have got to be the best investments I have ever made," Rhydan said as he walked over to join him. Ayrion started to rise, but the king motioned for him to remain seated. Rhydan lifted one of swords and inspected the black steel. "If I had only known the kind of craftsmanship the smith was capable of, I would have ordered one for myself. I still might."

Ayrion could tell the king was trying to sound upbeat. "They are indeed beautiful weapons, Your Majesty." Ayrion raised a hand to block the setting sun from his eyes. "Where did you have them made?"

"I was told they came from a small shop in Rhowynn, nothing too special about the place or the smith, other than people claimed he could forge steel in a way that made it almost indestructible. Of course, I was skeptical at first, but . . ." He shrugged. "I figured it couldn't hurt to try. If the smith had turned out to be less than worthy, I could have always given the swords to one of the overlords as a gift."

Ambassador Belkor grunted as he walked by, apparently not amused.

Ayrion balanced the other blade in his hand. "I would say he lived up to his word."

"Aye, indeed he did. With talent like that, I'm going to have to track the man down and offer him the position of royal weaponsmith before someone else steals him away."

Commander Tolin limped over with a little help from a large halberd.

"Do we know how many casualties yet, Commander?" Rhydan asked.

Ayrion sheathed his swords and offered the commander his seat. "We lost all but two of the High Guard, Your Majesty."

Tolin sighed. "We also lost the better part of two companies of lancers and three of our five bowmen. The last time we saw the dogs or their handlers, they were heading for the road. Probably halfway to Lord Tulvik's by now, along with our Keldoran ambassador. He passed us, running like the Defiler had called his name."

"We need to send some men to make sure he's found," the king said. "It's easy to get lost in these woods."

"I've already seen to it, Your Majesty." Tolin bowed and limped over to where Overcaptain Asa watched as the healers continued to work on his men.

Rhydan waited until Tolin was out of earshot before turning back around to Ayrion. "To be honest, I can't blame the ambassador. One look at those creatures and I was nearly ready to join him." He took a deep breath. "I can't tell you the last time I was so frightened. Not just for me, but for my kingdom—for all our kingdoms. Something is changing," he said. "I can feel it."

Ayrion could only nod.

Rhydan beckoned Ayrion to follow him to where Dakaran knelt, studying one of the beasts.

"I don't know what to believe anymore," Rhydan said. "I heard stories growing up about the creatures that were here before the Great Purge, but to be honest, I never gave them much credence. I thought they were just old tales the common folk used to gain a few drinks at the tavern or scare their children into obeying. But here we are, standing next to not just one but three." They rolled the creature over to get a better look. "These things aren't natural."

Ayrion knelt across from Dakaran. "I agree. They look to have been created by something extremely dark."

The prince stiffened.

Ayrion lifted his head. "Did you notice the way they seemed to be focused on you, Your Majesty?"

"I did. And I certainly don't like the implication."

Ayrion stood back to his feet. "Neither do I."

Rhydan turned to his son. "What do you think, Dakaran?"

The prince didn't raise his head. He traced a finger down one of the creature's bloody claws. "I think we need to start allocating more resources to the White Tower. We need to be rid of magic once and for all."

Rhydan didn't respond.

When his father didn't say anything further, Dakaran added, "I think we are lucky to be alive."

Rhydan laid a hand on his son's shoulder. "Truer words were never spoken."

Ayrion shadowed the king as he left Dakaran to check on the ambassadors, whose wounds were being tended.

"Your Majesty." Tolin bowed upon the king's approach. "I sent lancers back to Lord Tulvik's to procure wagons to carry our dead and wounded."

"Good. I want to make for Aramoor as soon as possible. I won't feel safe until we are back behind our walls."

"Yes, Your Majesty."

"Assemble the men. I'd like to say a few words."

"Right away, Your Majesty."

It took about a quarter hour for everyone to assemble. Rhydan raised his hands to quiet them down. "Soldiers of Elondria," he started, then sighed. "Men . . . I want you to know that a grateful king stands before you today. A prouder king you could not find in all of the five kingdoms for the sacrifice and courage you have shown here. I consider it my privilege and my honor to be counted amongst you.

"Our loss today is great." Rhydan paused to scan the battleground, where many of their dead still lay. "Many of you will bury friends, comrades, fellow soldiers." He took a deep breath. "But they were more than that. They were our brothers. The bonds forged in battle cannot be broken, and at no time is that union more felt than when they are taken from us."

Rhydan's face hardened, his words sharp. "I do not know from where these creatures came, nor what we have yet to face, but this one thing I promise you: as long as we stand side by side, those who seek the destruction of Elondria and her people shall rue this day!"

The men raised their fists to their chests in salute. Many were barely standing, some only with the help of fellow armsmen. Ayrion could see the pain in the king's eyes as he looked at his men. Ayrion knew that pain. He felt it. It was the pain of losing men under his command, men who trusted him, followed him. Men who had given their lives for him.

Rhydan bowed his head. "May the Creator gather our heroic fallen into His bosom. May He grant them rest from their labor and peace from their troubles, and may we strive to live our lives in a manner that will not bring them shame."

A soft rumble of agreement passed through the ranks before the king dismissed them.

"A moving speech, Your Majesty," Ambassador Lanmiere said, adjusting the sling wrapped around his arm.

"No less than they deserve."

One of the lancers made his way over. "The search party has returned, Your Majesty," he said, indicating a group exiting the forest behind them. Asa directed the men to the king to give their report. The party sergeant dismounted and approached, bowing to the king.

"Your Majesty, we found the Keldoran ambassador. Unfortunately, it appears the creatures found him first. He must have run right into them as they were preparing their attack from behind. We collected what little we found to return to his family for burial."

The king lowered his head. "I feared as much."

The sergeant bowed again, and the king dismissed him.

"This isn't going to sit well with Overlord Meyrose. I will need to send a dispatch to him as soon as we get back."

The prince spoke up. "It might be prudent to leave out the ambassador's overabundance of self-preservation."

"Self-preservation?" Belkor spat. "The man was a spineless coward and a glutton to boot. He got what he deserved, if you ask me."

The king's eyes flashed. "Then I guess it's good we're *not* asking you, Belkor. As much as I disagree with the manner in which Ambassador Gyin conducted himself, my son is correct. For the sake of peace, I will merely declare him as one of the many fallen during the battle."

"Your Majesty," Tolin said with a slight bow. "The wagons have arrived from Lord Tulvik. It's time we escort you back to Aramoor. I'd prefer not to get caught in these woods after dark."

Rhydan nodded. "I couldn't agree more, Commander. Make sure to bring the creatures as well. We should let our people study them."

Tolin bowed and limped his way toward the wagons.

It was well after dark by the time Ayrion and what was left of the hunting party rode back through the palace gates.

They were met by the queen and her staff. The only sign the queen gave that her composure was a lie was the speed at which she strode across the courtyard. She held her head high and kept her voice calm, her eyes scanning the king's body. "Are you injured, my lord?"

"Nothing worthy of song," Rhydan said.

"And how is my precious son?" Ellise asked, now studying Dakaran.

He was halfway off his horse before the animal had even come to a complete stop. "He's alive, if barely," Dakaran said, sounding irritated. He handed off his horse and stomped toward the palace.

Ellise smiled and placed a hand on Rhydan's leg.

"If I had known you'd be so passionate over my returning," Rhydan said, "I'd try being gone more often." He dismounted and engulfed his queen in a warm embrace.

"I save it for times when I am in deep distress over your safety, my lord. Don't expect such treatment every time you leave my sight." She pulled out of his arms to inspect him once again. "You are well, then—truly?"

"I am, and thankful to be home."

"As am I, dearest."

"There were many who were not so fortunate, I'm afraid."

"We will honor them, then," she said. "I will ensure their families are cared for." She linked arms with her husband and led him toward the palace entrance. "Come inside. I'll have some hot water drawn."

Ayrion dismounted. He was about to help Tolin unload their fallen when he felt he was being watched. He turned to find Amarysia standing at the outer edge of the courtyard. Her posture was stiff, and she curled a strand of blonde hair around her fingers, a nervous habit that made Ayrion smile.

When she saw him looking, she rushed over and threw her arms around him. "I was so worried. As soon as the lancer sergeant delivered his message to the queen about your attack, I feared the worst."

She smelled incredible. Of course, anything other than the blood, sweat, and mud caked to his clothing would. "Can I kiss you?" he asked hesitantly.

She pulled back slightly and looked up at him. "Do you have to ask?"

"Well, we haven't been seeing each other that long, and I—"

He was cut short when her lips pressed to his. Everything melted away. His fears, doubts, worries, everything was gone for a brief wonderful instant. He never wanted it to end.

Ayrion held her for a moment before finally pulling away.

"What's wrong?"

"I stink."

Amarysia wrinkled her nose. "That's for sure." She took a step back and looked him over, noticing his arm. "You're hurt." She reached out to touch it, but he stopped her.

"I'm fine. There's no need to worry about me."

"How can I help it when I know you as I do? If there is fighting, you're going to be in the middle of it."

He smiled. "You'd better catch up with the others before the queen sees you're missing. I'll see you tomorrow."

Amarysia sighed. "Ever the soldier." She kissed him on the cheek and then walked across the courtyard.

Ayrion watched her fall into the back of the small processional behind the king and queen as it made its way toward the southwest pavilion. Once she had moved beyond sight, he walked to where Commander Tolin was directing the unloading of their men.

Tolin cast a wary eye in Ayrion's direction. "Do you ever get the feeling that the stars are out of alignment?"

"Not until recently," Ayrion said, joining his former mentor. Together they watched as the lancers lifted the bodies of the fallen from the wagon beds, laying them in neat rows across the lower bailey. Others wrapped them in sheets, making ready for their families to claim. They looked like caterpillars in white cocoons, waiting to open and fly away—but they never would.

Chapter 27 | Valtor

VALTOR WATCHED FROM his chamber window as the soldiers below stretched the row of dead across the courtyard. He cursed inwardly as the king made his way back inside the palace. "All for nothing," he said to himself. "What a waste."

He turned away from the depressing sight with a heavy sigh. He had to figure out what to do about Dakaran. The fool had taken off to join his father on the hunt without telling Valtor. When was the last time he had done that? This had been his one opportunity to be rid of Rhydan without anything pointing in his direction. Now he had the prince to deal with. Not only had Dakaran been unexpectedly put in harm's way, but he had already caught a glimpse of the creatures from Valtor's books.

How was he going to explain that away?

Valtor walked back over to his mixing table and studied the bubbling liquid he had been dipping his vial into. It looked nearly ready.

The door to his chambers flew open behind him and slammed against the back wall with an echoing thud. Valtor flinched, and some of the contents splashed across the table, very near where he had placed his miter. The liquid hissed as it ate through the wood, filling the room with a pungent odor.

Valtor didn't need a seer to know what was coming. He placed the half-filled vial in a stand and turned to face the prince. Dakaran had his sword out, rage etched across his face.

"Your Highness," Valtor said with a deep bow. "I'm glad you are well. I feared the worst."

"Are you, Valtor?" the prince seethed, backing Valtor into the wall. "Or are you disappointed I managed to survive?" Dakaran raised his blade to Valtor's throat, forcing Valtor's head against the cold stone.

Valtor gulped and feigned a look of distress. Dakaran was typically easy to persuade due to his inebriated state. But at the moment he appeared to be quite clearheaded. "I'm afraid I don't understand—"

"Don't give me that, you maggot! I was almost mauled to death by three creatures that looked to have come straight out of the Pits of Aran'gal."

"I . . . I don't understand. What does that have to do with me, Your Highness?"

"It has everything to do with you!" Dakaran spat as he pressed the blade closer.

Valtor's tactic wasn't working. Dakaran's eyes were clear. Valtor felt a trickle of blood running down his neck from where the blade had pierced his skin. He fought to keep his anger in check. It would be so easy to kill the prince, but unfortunately, he still needed him.

Dakaran held Valtor's gaze. "At first, I thought I was dreaming. Monsters as tall as a single-story home living in the woods just outside of Aramoor? How was that possible? Then I remembered that book of drawings I found on your shelf the other day. Those creatures looked pretty flaming similar!" Dakaran leaned forward, their noses practically touching. Valtor searched for any hint of wine on his breath. "You'd better explain quickly. After what I've been through today, my sword arm feels unsteady. I would hate for it to slip."

Valtor swallowed. For the first time in a long time, Dakaran was as sober as a Wengoby priest. He had hoped Dakaran would see the light on his own, but in his current frame of mind, the man was more likely to slit Valtor's throat than anything.

Valtor didn't have time to worry about manipulation; if he didn't get the prince under control, all of his work could be for nothing. Carefully, he opened himself up to his magic and let it gently caress the prince's thoughts. This was another secret he had discovered in Aerodyne's grimoires. It wasn't as though he could see what a person was thinking and control it. It was more like he could direct a person's emotions, guide them toward a desired response. It was tricky to use, and Valtor was far from mastering it, so he settled for simply nudging the prince in the right direction. It was most effective if the target's will was weak. And lucky for him, Dakaran wasn't known for his strength, but his sudden rage made influencing him a challenge.

"You are correct, Your Highness," Valtor said in a calm voice. "I conjured those creatures. When I heard the king was taking the ambassadors on a hunting trip and the Guardian Protector was going with them, I couldn't pass up the opportunity. You made it quite clear during our last meeting that you wanted the Guardian and your father gone, so I—"

Dakaran pushed his elbow against Valtor's chest. "Ayrion, yes. But I said nothing about my father. And why did your pets come after me?"

"How was I supposed to know you would be going on the hunt? Honestly, when was the last time you and your father did anything together? By the time I found out you were going, it was already too late."

Dakaran loosened his grip but only slightly. Valtor continued to soothe the prince's frayed nerves.

The prince pulled his sword away from Valtor's neck but didn't lower it.

Valtor pushed his magic just a little more, dulling the anger driving Dakaran. The pieces were on the board and falling into place. In order to make the next move, Valtor needed Dakaran to wear the crown.

"Do you want to be king or not?" Valtor asked.

Dakaran raised his head. Valtor could see the longing in his eyes. He knew how badly Dakaran willed it to be so. But there was something else there as well: hesitancy.

Valtor continued to stroke the back of Dakaran's mind, letting his magic worm into his emotions. "Elondria needs strength, Your Highness. Cylmar mocks us by pillaging our borders. Every day Overlord Saryn grows bolder, and your father does nothing. It makes him look weak. It won't take much longer for the other kingdoms to rise against us. Aldor needs a leader."

Dakaran took a step back, running a hand through his hair and tucking one side behind an ear. "I don't know. This is all happening too fast."

"If you want to implement change, you need to move those standing in its way. We have a plan, a way to bring the kingdoms of Aldor back under one rule, starting with Cylmar. You know that. That's why this meeting with Ambassador Belkor is so important." Valtor felt Dakaran's control slipping, so he pushed deeper. "The people of Cylmar are looking for a benevolent leader to direct them down a different course." Valtor smiled. "Who better than you?"

Dakaran stared at the floor in silence. Finally, he took a step back and sheathed his sword, allowing Valtor to finally breathe a little deeper. Without saying anything, Dakaran turned and headed for the door.

"How did our good friend Belkor fare today? I trust he wasn't too grievously wounded, was he? I would hate for that to affect our meeting tomorrow."

"Belkor's fine. He's one of the few who managed to walk away without so much as a scratch."

The prince left, not bothering to close the doors behind him. Valtor rested his hand on the table and smiled.

Chapter 28 | Ellise

ELLISE'S COMPOSED CALM lasted until they reached the royal wing. Once there, she dispatched an army of servants to haul hot water so Rhydan, who was covered in sweat, soil, and blood, could bathe. If she had left it up to her husband, he would have plopped right down in their bed, bloody clothes and all, and fallen asleep. She wasn't going to let that happen.

Besides, she still had to find out what had taken place on their hunt. Rhydan wouldn't want to tell her, wouldn't want her to worry, but she needed to know, and she wanted to ease some of his burden by letting him talk about it.

She followed her husband into their washing chamber and helped him remove his clothes as the servants filled the large pool in the center of the room. It had been cast into the floor during the palace's reconstruction after the Wizard Wars and was one of her favorite amenities.

Centuries earlier, when magic was still permitted, the pool had been filled with water by pipes that ran inside the walls and up to the top of the tower, where they had built enormous water basins for catching the runoff during each storm. Now, filling it was a strenuous, time-consuming effort of carrying heated buckets from one side of the palace to the other.

Rhydan started down the marble steps into the foaming water and promptly began to dance around. "What are you trying to do, woman, cook me alive?"

"Hush your whining, you old goat. There isn't enough hot water in all of Aramoor to soften you up. You're about as tender as boot leather."

She moved one of the candles she had instructed the servants to place around tub. The soft light reflected off the marble tiles, adding a warm ambiance to the room. She hoped the hot bath and calm light, and the essence of lavender and chamomile she had ordered placed in his water, would lessen some of the day's burdens. He enjoyed the pampering, even though he'd never openly admit it.

Rhydan whimpered as he eased into the tub, foam pouring over the sides and onto the floor. With a satisfied moan, he rested his arms on the sides and leaned his head back against a folded towel.

Ellise allowed herself a small smile of triumph. She took a seat on the cushioned stool in the corner and let the silence stretch on for several long minutes before finally speaking.

"Start from the beginning, dear."

He closed his eyes and told her of the hunt, of the appearance of the creatures, and of the ensuing battle for their lives. He shared his men's courage, the Guardian Protector's feats, even the sad outcome of the Bristonian ambassador.

Ellise listened carefully, not interrupting. She soaked it all in, every horrifying detail. Her heart was panting by the end as she realized how close she had come to losing her entire family. She took a moment to calm her nerves before speaking.

"You certainly know how to put wrinkles on my face, dearest. When the messenger first arrived with news of the battle, I didn't know what to think. I even went so far as to ask the Creator for help."

Rhydan lifted his head. "When was the last time you did that?"

"It's been a while," she said nervously as she gnawed on her lower lip.

He blew away the bubbles gathering under his chin. "You're biting that lip again, Ellise. What's on your mind?"

"I fear we are at a crossroads. A beginning—or maybe, more accurately, an ending."

He stopped playing with the bubbles. "An ending to what?"

She rose from her seat and walked over to one of the large windows that looked out onto the Bay of Torrin. The bay had been named after the first High King of Aldor. *Fitting,* she thought. Torrin had cut the city away from the rugged terrain much like the tides of the Rhunarin Ocean had carved the inlet deep into the coast.

Ellise stared out across the moonlit breakers. How could she explain all the thoughts swimming around in her head? She looked at the ships moving through the harbor, carrying supplies along the southern coast. She rested a shoulder against the gilded edge of the window's frame and watched the water below crash against pillars of rock.

"I believe we are reaching the end of another age, my love." She turned to face him. "We may find ourselves facing things we never knew existed—like today." Rhydan's face darkened. "I came across several volumes in the library that spoke of how it was at the end of the Second Age just before the great Wizard Wars. How they—"

"Not again, Ellise. It seems every conversation we have of late comes back around to faeries, magic, and years gone by. If I didn't know any better, I'd wonder if you would rather have been born back during a time when magic ruled the world."

She waited. The years had taught her it was best to let him get it out, leaving him free to listen and consider her words. She loved him deeply, but sometimes he could be the most stubborn of oafs.

"Are you quite finished?" she asked, crossing her arms. His grunt was the only answer she knew she was going to receive. Her husband had always been a man of action. He lived in the moment. If he saw something that needed fixing, he fixed it; a problem that needed solving, he solved it, or at least tried. It made him a strong king. But those same characteristics also made him narrow-minded. His focus was on the present. The past was best left in the past, and the future could worry about itself.

"Considering what you told me happened today, we would be wise to heed the information our historians have given us. Besides, I saw those creatures down there. We're not living in the same world as we did when we were children."

Rhydan looked up from the thick horse-hair brush he was scrubbing across his bloodstained arms. "Did you find something in there about these creatures?" For once, he actually seemed interested.

"There have been references. But what I find most disturbing is the similarities I see between now and what it was like near the end of the Second Age. It was around that time when monsters like those were first seen. I don't think it's a coincidence." She grabbed her seat and dragged it to the side of the pool. The metal tips scraped across the tile with a grating noise. "Hear me out, my love."

"It appears I don't have much choice. You've—"

She narrowed her eyes, and he shut his mouth.

"I know you don't wish to speak of your forefathers' mistakes, but how else can we learn?"

Rhydan sighed. "It's not that I don't care. It's just that . . . well, I don't understand it." He stopped his scrubbing once again. "Look at me. What I know is what I can hold in my hands." Brandishing the scrub brush like a weapon, he continued. "I understand the feel of a sword, the weight of its balance, the edge of its blade." She could see regret in his eyes, the kind that came with memories.

"I know nothing of magic," he admitted, lowering the brush back into the water. "How can I begin to combat something I don't understand? I'm too old to go learning something new."

"Hogwash!" She splashed a handful of water in his face. "If you're too old, then that would make me too old. And I'm not too old, I assure you." She went to splash him again, but before she could get her hand in the water, he grabbed her arm and jerked her headfirst into the soapy bath, silk nightgown and all.

"Rhydan!" she roared as soon as her head broke the surface. She swung her hand with all her might, trying to slap him, but her hair was plastered to her face and her blow met nothing but air. Shoving her sodden curls aside, she tried again, only to find herself wrapped in his arms.

"You brute!"

"A brute, am I? Maybe I should act more like it." He shoved her head to the side and ferociously started nibbling at her neck. She broke into a fit of laughter, kicking her legs back and forth underneath the water.

"Stop it!" she demanded, pulling away from a sloppy kiss. "I'm trying to have a serious discussion with you. If I didn't know any better, I would think you'd been into the brandy again."

He pecked the tip of her nose, then finally released her.

Deciding there was no reason to leave the warm water now that she was in it, she shrugged off her drenched nightgown and tossed it on the already-soaked tiles. Scooping up the bar of soap, she began rubbing it across her stiff shoulders.

She decided that confining him to his bath gave her the best time to share her research. An opportunity like this might not present itself again, and it seemed he was willing to listen, at least.

"As I was saying, the histories tell us that the Second Age was an extremely prosperous time. They thought magic was the answer to everything. Not rich enough? Well, a simple spell here, an incantation there, and your financial worries are over. Someone is sick? Call one of the gifted arcane healers. You have someone you're infatuated with and you want them to feel the same? No problem. Just whip together a special potion and they're yours."

"If only it *were* that easy," Rhydan mumbled.

"What was that?" she asked, poking him with her big toe.

"Nothing, nothing."

She gave him a harsh glare, let it linger a moment longer, then continued. "Like I was saying . . ." She glanced down at the bubbles around her shoulders. "What was I saying?"

Rhydan laughed. "You were saying how our problems were finally over."

"Right. Magic had come, and they couldn't have been happier. There were wondrous accomplishments during that time—monumental buildings constructed, impossible depths explored. Did you know they even built flying ships?"

"You're having me on."

"No, really," she said, moving her hands over the top of the bathwater. "They had huge schooners that could float on the air like ours do on the water. They built great cities with vast networks of tunnels deep below the surface of our land! There was wealth beyond anything we could imagine—and food in such supply that all of our vast warehouses could not contain it!"

"Slow down, woman," her husband said, waving his hands at her. "This all sounds a little overreaching. I think I would have known about flying ships if they had existed."

She splashed him hard. "And just how would you have known? I've been trying to tell you about this for years, and all I ever get from you is some regurgitated nonsense about how magic only corrupts."

"If it doesn't corrupt, then how do you explain what happened to us today?"

She paused a moment to think. "Magic is just a tool. And like any tool, what is used to create can also be used to destroy."

He surprised her with a thoughtful nod.

She wanted to jump up and dance around in the tub. It was the first time her husband had actually shown any sign of agreeing with her on this subject.

"It now seems that magic is beginning to reveal itself once more. And after seeing those creatures, I believe we have come full circle."

Rhydan exhaled slowly as he stared at the elongated reflections emitting from the candles around the tub. "I can't argue with that. And as much as I'm loath to admit it, perhaps it might be prudent to hear a bit more. The surest way to defeat an enemy is to know it. And the surest way to *be* defeated is not to."

Ellise smiled. She could see the weariness in Rhydan's eyes. She slid up against her husband, letting her head rest against his shoulder. "Thank you for listening."

He wrapped an arm around her and hugged her tight. "I wouldn't be half the king I am without you."

Chapter 29 | Valtor

VALTOR LOCKED THE door to his chambers, then crossed to the far corner of his workshop. Unlike the rest of the room, which was crowded with shelves and tables, this corner only held a tall, flat object draped in a heavy canvas. He pulled the canvas back and let it fall to the floor, kicking up a spray of dust that made him sneeze.

He stared at his reflection in the uncovered glass. The mirror was old, very old, as shown by the tarnished coating of the gold filigree frame. Ancient glyphs decorated the outer edge, written in a language few scholars would even recognize. This was one of the lost Mirrors of Maon, better known as the Traveling Mirrors.

Valtor found it hard to believe the object had been created nearly two thousand years before, when wizards had moved freely through the kingdoms. It was how they had managed to keep the peace for so long. Never knowing when a wizard might make an appearance was a great deterrent against revolts. But at the end of the age, after the devastation left by the Wizard Wars, the jun'ri had ordered the mirrors they could find destroyed. A few still remained, like the two he had found in the lower vaults of the White Tower.

Valtor had spent years searching for more. A few of the ancient manuscripts spoke of a stronghold built by the Wizard Council and some of their faerie allies. It was said to have been the birthplace for many such magical items, but he could find no reference to its location, only its name: Aero'set. Valtor concluded that it was either shielded by some form of magic, or perhaps destroyed during the final battles of the Wizard Wars.

Thankfully, two mirrors were the minimum number needed for traveling. Each mirror had its own name etched in runes at the top. All he needed do was to call the names of the mirrors in the correct order, and he could pass through unharmed.

The runes around the frame were Fae glyphs. The way they rolled off the tongue, Valtor thought it likely the names were those of faeries from around the time they had been created. Valtor had spent hundreds of hours calling out various possible names, hoping to somehow awaken a third mirror. He considered himself a fair linguist and well versed in the histories of the Second Age, but he doubted the wizards would have named the mirrors something he might stumble across by chance. They were too valuable.

Valtor grabbed his wolf-head staff and called out the names of the two mirrors, starting with the one in front of him. *"Galaerion Sugethru. Nothleen Filaurel."*

The glass sparked to life.

His reflection vanished, replaced by an empty room. A lone torch mounted next to a closed door cast shadows across the stone walls and floor. Once the mirror's surface stilled, Valtor took a quick glance around his chambers, then stepped through. He shivered, a chill running through his body. It felt like walking through water without getting wet.

Once on the other side, Valtor watched the image of his chambers fade, leaving his own dark reflection in the glass. He wasn't all that fond of traveling by mirror. He always feared the possibility of one of them failing while he was in between. He had never read what would happen if something like that were to take place. He wished there had been more written about them, but for now, he was grateful for the convenience. Traveling from Aramoor to the White Tower on horseback would have taken weeks.

Shaking off the discomfort, he headed for the door.

Before leaving the room, Valtor held his hand out and summoned an orb of sea-green light. He found the color soothing. Quietly, he wound his way through the dark upper corridors of the White Tower. It was the ultimate contrast to his life in the royal palace. There were no lavishly decorated chambers trimmed in gold and draped in velvet, nothing but discolored walls of cracked stone, coated in layers of web and dust. He took a deep breath and smiled. He was home.

Upon reaching the central levels, he extinguished the orb. Many of the lower rooms and hallways were already awash with bracketed torchlight. The lower levels had a richer architecture. Instead of stone, the floors and walls were constructed with marble.

Rounding the final corner, he stepped out into the Tower's throat. The large, open circle at the center of the construct looked as though it had been left by the passing of an orm, an enormous sand worm found in the outer reaches of the Wengoby Desert. It cored the Tower, beginning at the ground level and extending to the uppermost chambers. The view from the higher levels was dizzying. Even from the lower levels, a fall would prove fatal.

Valtor crossed the open second-floor walkway, where he could see the Black Watch below as they rotated positions in front of the grand entrance. He headed beneath the arches on the other side. A yawn escaped his lips as he strolled down the corridor toward his chambers. He wanted nothing more than to crawl into bed, but he had a meeting with the Legate Superior that he had delayed long enough. At the end of the corridor was a set of double doors. The guards on duty bowed and opened them.

"Tell the Legate Superior I will see her now," Valtor said, entering the room.

"Right away, Your Eminence."

The doors shut behind him, the sound reverberating off the walls.

The room was spacious, a vaulted ceiling that reached up into darkness. Brass chandeliers tarnished with age hung from long chains, filling the room with their light. Worn drapes decorated the sides of tall stained-glass windows, their colors faded with time.

Valtor had never allowed any of the ancient adornments to be repaired or replaced. There was something about surrounding himself with originality, knowing that he was looking at the same decorations as wizards of years past. It gave him a sense of purpose, a link to those he so admired.

As he moved across the cold stone, Valtor's red robes billowed out behind him like they were caught on an evening breeze. He raised his hand toward the large open hearth on the left side of the room. "*Voyestra.*" Flames erupted from the previously stacked kindling and logs. In front of the fireplace was the long white marble table they used for Tower meetings. Surrounding it were thirteen chairs made from the same smooth stone, reminding him that he had a vacant seat that needed filling.

He reached the other side of the room and entered an open staircase leading up to his personal chambers, comprised of his private study, washroom, and modestly decorated sleeping chamber. Much like his workroom in Aramoor, his study held a large assortment of shelving for all manner of oddities he had accumulated in his search for lost pieces of magic.

Long wooden tables lined the back corner, each covered with thick tallow candles that bled colored wax down brass sconces, gluing them to the surface underneath. Open books lay scattered across the tops of each table. There were copper pots, pewter urns, and cruses of every size and shape, most only half filled. Their contents would have made a rather disgusting stew. There were large insects of all varieties, both living and not. Pieces from human bodies, some still fresh. A few urns held decomposed mire or sludge that smelled as though it had been harvested from the foulest of bogs, while others were filled with rich topsoil or clean sand.

Valtor opened a glass cabinet on the far wall, its shelves lined with a variety of tinctures, tonics, distillations, and extracts for every possible use. The best-stocked apothecaries would weep with envy at the rare potions he had at his disposal.

Pulling out a crystal decanter, he poured a dark amber liquid into a nearby goblet and took a quick sip of the strongly spiced wine. With a soft moan, he slid into his favorite chair in front of the hearth. He frowned at the cold stone. *Why can no one manage to keep a simple fire stoked around here?*

Irritated, he raised his hand. "*Voyestra,*" he said, and the flames burst to life. He released a long, slow exhale as the warmth invaded his skin.

Valtor heard the doors of the main chamber below open. He gathered his thoughts as he drained the rest of his goblet, wishing he could stretch this rare moment of rest a little longer. With a grunt, he lifted himself from the comfort of his cushioned spot in front of the fire and set his glass down.

He took a moment to straighten his robes, then gathered his miter. This being an official meeting with the Legate Superior, he needed to keep up appearances. Even there amongst his inner circle, he found it helped to reinforce his authority. Appearance was everything—something his father had instilled in him at an early age. His father's words were there as a constant reminder: "If you ever want to get anywhere in this life, Milo, you must look the part." Milo was the name given him by his parents. It was a weak name, one he had no intention of being associated with, especially considering what his parents had done to him. Once on the streets, he had changed it to something more suitable—Valtor.

His father had been a tailor to the wealthy. He used to say even the poorest back-alley waif, if placed in a new suit of clothes, would be respected and admired. Men and women would look him in the eyes when he passed. They would offer to open his door, pull his seat, shine his shoes. "It's all about perception, Milo," he would say. "You can control the way people perceive you by the clothing you wear."

Valtor let his fingertips slide down the thick velvet folds of his robe, enjoying the texture as he descended the steps one at a time. He held his head high as he emerged into the main assembly chamber. For everything his father had been wrong about, he had gotten one thing right: perception was indeed the first step to power.

The Legate Superior, who wore her official black robes with gold trim around the sleeves and neckline, bowed at the waist as Valtor strode across the room toward the head of the table. Marta waited for him to sit before lowering herself into her own chair.

"Has there been any backlash to my dealing with Medarin during our last meeting? You have the ears of most. What are your thoughts?"

"I believe you've managed to weed out the dissenters, Your Eminence. If there are others, they are either too few or too scared to stand against you."

Valtor studied the woman's face. "Good. I don't need their respect, but I do need their obedience."

Marta nodded. "And you will have it."

"What else do you have to report?" he asked.

The elderly woman folded her hands in her lap. "The flow of information has been quite steady, Your Eminence. The inquisitors have been rather successful in recruiting new wielders to our cause and obtaining useful confessions. It seems there are indeed a growing number of ven'ae not only in Elondria, but throughout Keldor, Sidara, Cylmar, and Briston as well."

"That is good news indeed." Valtor leaned forward.

"Confessions, however," she pointed out, "can be tricky to sort through. It's quite amazing how loose the lips become when faced with an inquisitor's touch. Often, the confession will be misleading if not outright false. There are those who'll confess to anything, whether it be the truth or not, just to escape more time on the rack. If we were to act on all such information, we would be rounding up half the population." She chuckled lightly.

Valtor sighed as he twisted his staff on his lap. "We need more wielders if we are ever to have a chance of protecting ourselves against the jun'ri."

Marta rubbed her chin. "My only fear is what you mentioned in our last meeting. We don't want to catch the eye of the king and have him decide to re-implement the Inspection Squads."

"Leave that to me. I want you to focus on gathering stronger wielders. Which reminds me," he said, arching one brow, "has there been any progress in bringing the swordsmith over to our cause? It's been a long time since we've had a true metallurgist at the Tower."

"The smith is proving to be . . . well, quite resilient, Your Eminence."

Valtor's smile broadened. "I'm glad to hear it. The stronger they are, the more useful they become." He took a moment longer to enjoy the fire before finally coming to his feet. "Keep me apprised of his progress. I want you to focus all your energy on this man. He's important to me." Valtor corrected himself. "To all of us. We are going to need his abilities in the very near future." He turned and headed back toward the stairs leading to his upper chambers. "Don't fail me, Marta," he warned as his staff echoed off the tile.

"I won't, Your Eminence."

Chapter 30 | Ferrin

S NAP!

Ferrin's head slammed against the back of the rack, every nerve in his right hand on fire as he fought to break free of his shackles. The pain was excruciating to the point of delirium.

"Okay, okay, okay, I'll talk, I'll talk!" Ferrin tried to swallow, but his throat was too swollen from screaming. "What do you want to talk about? You want to discuss the weather? Fine! Looks to be a wet one today. I saw a front coming in on my way across the battlements earlier. Bit of a nip in the air." Sweat poured from Ferrin's brow. "Maybe you'd rather discuss the lack of proper sanitation in this place? You're right, it's appalling. My room hasn't been swept in ages. And when was the last time you emptied our chamber bucket? Anything else you want to talk about? Let's talk!"

Ferrin gritted his teeth and glanced at his ruined finger. It was bent awkwardly to the side, rather grotesque. His knees buckled. His heart was racing faster than a prize stallion flying down the home stretch at the Rhowynn

Festival of Lights.

His mind wandered back to his home. He had always loved the city festivals, especially those in the fall: the changing of the colors during the month of Kùma, the abundance of exotic foods, the garish decorations. It made him feel like anything was possible.

Ferrin closed his eyes and tried to will himself there. He tried to remember the sights, the smells, the sounds of excitement and laughter. People enthralled in the joy of putting aside their work and reveling in a bit of honest distraction. He remembered his booth, selling his latest work, with his sister there beside him.

He had been especially fond of Overlord Agnar's annual tournaments. The games fascinated Ferrin, especially those involving the sword. He had always told himself he'd enter the competition one day, but he never did.

Ferrin strained to hold on to the memories, to keep his focus on anything but the present, but the intense pain kept pulling him back.

"Why aren't you talking?" Ferrin muttered, his eyes swelling with tears. His mouth was as dry as a sun-bleached bone. "I thought you wanted to talk! I'm ready. Come on, you flatulent pot-licker, let's talk!"

"My dear smith, I assure you, we will talk. But I fear you aren't quite ready yet."

Cheeks slid his finger down Ferrin's forearm, across the steel manacle holding his wrist in place, and lightly stroked the top of his hand. The touch was tender, as soft as a lover's caress.

Snap!

Ferrin screamed. "Stop! Wait . . . just wait!" Tears blurred his vision of the bald man, his tattooed face just in front of him. "Please, just wait!"

He tried to catch his breath, hoping the pain would subside. He couldn't believe how similar the sound was to that of a thick twig being split between two hands. A simple bending of the wood until the tension reached its breaking point, and then—

Snap!

He screamed again, his back pressing so tight against the rungs, it actually drew blood. He could feel it running down his back. He closed his eyes. He didn't dare look at his fingers. Seeing them would make the pain even worse.

"Now, let's start again, shall we? Who are the other wielders living in Rhowynn? I'm sure you can give us names. A city that size is bound to have at least one wielder council, if not two or three."

Breathe, Ferrin, curse you. Just breathe. Ferrin fought to control his sanity. He was on the verge of losing consciousness. He prayed for it, begged and pleaded for it. But unfortunately, the Creator, if there was such a being, remained silent. *Maybe I could just give him one name. That wouldn't be so terrible, would it? Someone I don't even like . . . perhaps Garreth. Yeah, I could give him Garreth's name.* Ferrin took another deep breath, fighting back the temptation to give in.

"I told you. I don't know any names," he said, sweat dripping from the end of his nose. "I kept to myself. It's not like we all get together on Sixthday for a game of batmyth or something!" Actually, that's *exactly* what they did. He did have those he knew within the hidden wielder communities. A few he would have considered friends, like Ellson, even if the man tended to cheat while they played.

No. Ferrin couldn't betray them. Most importantly, he couldn't let the Tower find Myriah. His twin sister looked up to him, relied on him. He had to live. He had to get back to her.

Cheeks paced in front of the rack, his hands folded behind his back. "Everyone breaks. I have dedicated my life to the study of this phenomenon. How much torture can one body accept before its mind betrays its heart?"

An image of Myriah flooded Ferrin's thoughts—same fair skin as Ferrin, same thick red curls. Identical, except for the eyes. Hers were much kinder.

She was the one good thing left in his life.

Ferrin had to find a way to escape. The White Tower obviously wanted his skills. How long would they be willing to wait before killing him and moving on?

The inquisitor stepped to the other side of the rack and stroked the fingers on Ferrin's other hand. "How about a change of subject, then; maybe that will stimulate some answers?" Cheeks slid his hand around Ferrin's small finger and waited. He seemed to be taunting him.

"What are you waiting for? You got a question, or do you just enjoy holding my hand?"

Snap!

Ferrin screamed and Cheeks paused to inspect his work.

"Now for the important question," Cheeks said with a wry smile, as if waiting to bring it up until Ferrin was near the point of breaking. "Have you given any more thought to joining our cause? The White Tower could use a man of your talents." He paused a moment to look Ferrin in the eyes. "Why put yourself through this, smith? Join us. If not for yourself, then do it for all those other ven'ae out there who are unable to stand against their jun'ri oppressors."

Ferrin laughed through gritted teeth. "Do you even hear yourself, you pompous offspring of an overfed dung beetle? You open your mouth and what comes out is pure prattle. You want me to join the White Tower to help the ven'ae, and yet it's the *White Tower* that is hunting us down, you stupid sack of orm larva."

Snap!

"I'm going to kill you!"

Snap! Snap!

Ferrin's head bounced off the wire rack, his screams echoing off the stone walls around him. Cheeks squeezed the fingers on Ferrin's left hand, and he nearly bit through his tongue.

The inquisitor sat there for an uncomfortably long time, studying Ferrin's face. He must not have been able to find what he was looking for, because he finally turned and stepped off the rack.

"Rae! Clean up this mess."

The door opened, and the little healer stepped inside. She looked at Ferrin. Her eyes seemed blank, no expression. He would have expected revulsion, at least, or perhaps pity. Instead, he found only indifference. It was probably the only way she could keep from going mad.

Cheeks donned his richest smile. "I want to do this again." He collected his tools from the table and tucked the case under his arm. "I do hope you come to see the value in what we are offering you. The Archchancellor is a patient man."

Ferrin thought he could hear a hint of fear at the mention of the Archchancellor.

"Everyone has a weakness, smith. Finding it is the fun part."

Chapter 31 | Ty

A DELIGHTFUL AROMA from across the street pulled Ty from his deliberations. Once again, he'd found himself reliving the incident in the woods with his sister. He couldn't seem to get the image of her standing there covered in blue flames out of his mind. It haunted him.

He turned and glanced across the street at Reloria's Sweet Shop, thankful for the momentary distraction. The colorfully painted images of sugar sticks and chocolate drops made his mouth water on cue. It took every ounce of willpower he had not to cross the road. He still had work to do.

He looked down at the list of items his mother had asked him to purchase and realized he was nearly through. Eagerly, he folded the slip of paper and stuffed it back inside his brown overcoat, giving Reloria's shop one more longing glance before pressing on. The sooner he finished, the sooner he could stop for a treat.

The day was a little warmer than it had been, the sun bright and cheerful in the sky. The streets themselves were bustling with activity as the beautiful weather seemingly drew the people of Easthaven out of their homes.

Ty reached the last shop on the west side of River Street and wrinkled his nose as he caught a whiff of the sickly sweet smell of fermentation drifting from the vintner on his left. Not wanting to linger, he made his way across the street. Master Orlyn's shop was the next one down. The sign out front depicted a wooden mixing bowl surrounded by sprouts of valerian. The gold letters at the top spelled out *APOTHECARY*.

He stopped partway across the street to allow a carriage to pass, then turned at the sound of horses' hooves. Four men rode out from behind the Justice Hall, heading in his direction. Their white mantles were enough to send Ty scurrying. He had no intention of running into them again.

He ducked around the carriage and hopped onto the sidewalk, almost colliding with a well-dressed lady who was balancing a large number of bags and packages in her arms. Ty mumbled an apology as he rushed inside the shop and shut the door.

The riders didn't stop.

Realizing how crazy he must have appeared, running in the way he had, he turned to see if anyone had been watching. His luck was holding. It looked as though he was the only customer.

He took a moment to look around. It was the first time he had ever been in Master Orlyn's shop. It smelled like the forest. The walls and shelves were lined with ivy. Colorful blooms of gold and purple sprouted from each vine—something Ty had never seen before, and considering his home was covered in ivy, he felt he would have. There were even a few shoots rising between the floorboards at his feet. It was captivating.

Ty knew at once. Other than Reloria's, this was by far his favorite shop in town.

He took a moment to browse the jars of aromatic plant life on the first aisle.

"Well, hello, young Ty. How are you today?" Ty looked up to see the old apothecary heading toward him, his baggy robes sweeping the floor.

"I'm doing well, Master Orlyn," Ty said, digging into his coat for his list. "I was told to get some sage, some mugwort, chickweed, and also some cor . . ." Ty gave up trying to pronounce what his mother had written and handed Orlyn the folded parchment.

"Ah." The apothecary pointed at the sheet with a flicker of amusement on his face. "Coriander." Master Orlyn inspected it further. "Hmm, I should have all of this. If you'll give me just a moment, I'll pull them for you."

Before Ty had time to even nod his thanks, the man was off.

Ty decided to keep perusing. He had made it as far as the right wall when the bell on the shop's door rang and two ladies entered. Ty could hear them gossiping away as he quietly examined the contents on some of the lower shelves.

After a couple of minutes, one of the ladies shrilled, "There is magic being used in this shop!" Ty tripped over one of the jars he had been looking at and fell face-first into the adjacent shelf, nearly tipping it on his head. From his hands and knees, he peeked through a dusty niche to see what was happening. He caught a glimpse of Master Orlyn hurrying down one of the aisles toward the two women.

"What seems to be the problem, madams?"

"There is magic being used in this establishment," the lady on the left huffed again, trying to find a position that would allow her to look down at the apothecary. A rather difficult task, since Orlyn was nearly twice her height. "I have a mind to report this to the magistrate."

Ty craned his neck to see what they were referring to. All he could see were more shelves.

"Madam, I'm sure there's a reasonable explanation."

"Rubbish!" she said, wielding her handbag like a weapon at the tall apothecary. "I know magic when I see it. And I am a woman who knows her duty."

Ty moved some of the containers to get a better view, but he still couldn't see anything that would have hinted at magic.

Orlyn produced a kerchief from his robe and wiped his brow. "If you would be so good as to explain what you saw, I will be only too happy to help you in any way that I can. But I'm sure the city patrol would be quite put out to find you had wasted their time without evidence."

"Hmph!" She crossed her arms. "Are you accusing me of lying, apothecary?"

"No, ma'am." Orlyn nervously tugged on his long beard. "I just want to keep you from looking a fool by bringing something to the officials without having investigated it properly."

The lady and her friend seemed to consider his words a moment, but not wanting to concede the point, they merely nodded.

He bowed slightly. "Thank you. Now please explain what it is you think you saw."

"I didn't *think* I saw anything! I saw what I saw!"

"My apologies." Orlyn dabbed his forehead once again. "Please forgive an old man his fumbling use of words."

The ladies appeared to be satisfied, as the short, thin one doing all the talking stepped forward and pointed at one of the potted plants on the third shelf up. "Right there. That's where I saw it."

Ty peeked out from the aisle to get a better look.

"Saw what?" Orlyn asked.

"Those plants right there. They moved." She turned and looked at the other woman. "You saw it, didn't you, Felina?"

"Indeed I did, Helene," the lady said emphatically. "They twisted around and pointed right at us." She shivered as she looked up at the two large red-and-black plants.

"Ah, now I'm beginning to see." Orlyn stepped around to the yellow-stained clay pot and pulled it from the shelf.

Both women quickly backed away.

"No need to be frightened. This is a rare form of flora known as Dragon's Breath. And even though it bears the name of a mythical creature, it harbors no magical properties. It was so named because of its aversion to heat. It only blooms in cool climates. My guess is you got a little too close and your breath caused it to retract, hence its name," he admitted with a look of humorous guilt, "Dragon's Breath."

For the first time since walking in his shop, the two women were speechless—if only for a moment.

"Why, I never!" Helene grabbed hold of her companion's arm, and they scurried out the door. Ty couldn't help but laugh at Master Orlyn's joke. The old man winked at him, then went about replacing the plant.

"Having the Tower's riders in town has got everyone on edge, it seems," Orlyn said as he continued to fill Ty's order.

Ty marveled at how the old man seemed to know precisely where all his merchandise was located. He didn't even get the chance to look at everything on the first shelf before Orlyn had returned to his desk at the front of the shop and signaled Ty to join him.

The apothecary wrapped each of the herbs individually in oiled parchment before rolling the entire bundle in a wax sheet and tying it off with a piece of string. "That will be four coppers."

Ty counted out the few remaining coins in the pouch his mother had given him. *I hope I have enough left for a sugar stick.* He laid the coins down on the counter and grabbed the bundle.

"Thanks for the help, Master Orlyn."

"You're most welcome, young Ty. Visit anytime."

"Thank you, I will." Ty closed the door behind him and stepped back out onto the crowded sidewalk. He started back toward Wood Lane, dodging the other townsfolk as they went about their business. How could people stand living in such a crowded place?

He made it back to the main intersection at the center of town and turned left. The spice merchant was the last shop on his list. He crossed the street, trying to avoid an oncoming wagon loaded with pumpkins—no doubt heading for Mezard's Chandlery—and stepped inside the spice shop. He didn't waste time getting the last couple of items on his list. He was in and out before the particularly strong odors had him sneezing.

With nothing left for him to purchase, Ty opened his small coin pouch and counted out the coppers. He had just enough to make a quick stop at Reloria's.

He was tucking the pouch back into his tunic when a familiar voice ahead caught his attention. Lyessa and a couple of her friends were just crossing River Street. They were laughing loudly and heading straight for him.

In no mood for another jousting of wits, Ty spun around and wove his way back through the oncoming crowd and turned down the first alley he came to. The sign over the closest door was so faded with age that he couldn't tell what kind of shop it was. At the moment, he didn't care. Opening the door, he rushed inside. Before he could get the door shut, Lyessa stopped and looked right at him.

He quickly closed the door. Had she seen him? He couldn't see how she would have missed him. Lyessa wiped a fold of red hair from her face as she studied the fronts of the small shops. Eventually, she shrugged and kept going.

Ty exhaled his relief before backing away from the door. He turned to get a better look at his surroundings.

The room was dark. The windows had been draped over, and the only light came from a few candles placed haphazardly around the shelving. He was reaching for the handle to leave when, from the back, an aged voice broke the silence.

"The shop's open, boy, if you care to look."

Ty turned around. There was someone slouched in a rocking chair near the back, the floorboards creaking as it moved. Half her body was masked in the shadows, and a black shawl was draped across her lap.

"Thank you, ma'am," he said, feeling uneasy.

Not wanting to cause offense, Ty decided to have a quick look around and then be on his way. As his eyes adjusted to the dim light, he started making his rounds. The room held an impressive assortment of oddities: some gaudy jewelry, dusty chalices, crystal orbs, daggers with strange emblems, and an unusual collection of exotic herbs and insects.

After seeing a cluster of what looked to be shrunken heads hanging from some string in the corner, Ty quickly turned to make his exit, but a small shelf of old books caught his eye. Before long, he found himself excitedly flipping through the titles written on the fading spines. The titles were barely legible. He quietly read each one to himself as he thumbed through them. *The Foresight of Divination, Poison: The Lost Art, Reshaping the World, Elixirs of Life, The Marked Ones . . .*

"Who or what are the Marked Ones?" It was a rather strange assortment of titles to have in a public shop, Ty thought. Then his eyes caught the second-to-last volume, and the hair on his arms stood up. *The Hidden Magic of Fae.*

"Magic . . ." How was a shop like this allowed to operate right here in the middle of town?

Ty pulled the volume from the shelf and opened it, dust flying into the air and around his head. He sneezed and wiped his nose.

"What'd you find there, boy?"

Ty jumped when he realized the old lady was now standing beside him. *How long has she been there?*

She hobbled a little closer, her cane tapping on the wooden floorboards as she reached out with what had to be the oldest, most shriveled hand Ty had ever seen and flipped the book to its cover.

"Ah, I see you have an interest in that which is most dangerous."

"Uh . . . no, I was just looking."

"More like you were drawn," she said, studying his face.

Ty swallowed. "What do you mean . . . *drawn?*"

She cackled. "Not just anyone can find this place. Only those with the gift."

"It's not that hard to miss," Ty pointed out. "You're right in the middle of town."

"Ah. That's the fun part. What you see as a shop, others see as nothing more than part of the building next door."

Ty cocked his head. Was she saying the entire building had been infused with magic?

"Don't believe me? Then ask yourself why your little redheaded friend didn't see you."

"How did you know about . . ."

The old woman smiled. "Those without the gift can't see the shop. They are compelled not to. A little bit of magic I learned years back." The old woman stepped closer to Ty. "Let's talk about you, shall we? There's something different about you, isn't there?"

Something about the old woman made Ty anxious. He wasn't sure whether it had to do with the way she had crossed the room without him knowing, or the repulsive way her wrinkled flesh seemed to hang from her bones, or the fact that she kept inching closer to him when she thought he wasn't looking. But before he could excuse himself, the old woman's head shot upward, and she sniffed the air.

His eyes widened. *Yep, definitely time to go!* Ty thought. He slapped the book shut, tossed it on the shelf, and bolted for the door. He didn't make it two steps before the old woman had grabbed ahold of his arm.

He tried to pull himself free, but she was much stronger than she looked. Her withered hand was clamped around his wrist like an iron fetter.

A strange sizzling sound caught his attention. It sounded like a wedge of pork grease on a hot pan. The old woman's eyes widened, and she jerked her hand away, releasing a horrific shrill that turned Ty's blood to ice. She lifted her hand and gawked as clumps of skin around her fingers and palm started sloughing to the ground. "It's you!" she screamed, pointing what remained of her ruined hand in his face.

If Ty's eyelids had opened any farther, his eyeballs would have fallen out. He dashed for the front of the shop, threw open the door, and ran like he'd just seen an old lady melting in front of him. He didn't even take the time to spare a glance behind to see if she was in pursuit.

Ty charged out of the alley and plunged headfirst into Lyessa, knocking her clean off her feet and into the arms of one of her three companions.

"Ty! What the blazes?" she cried out, trying to gain her composure. She dusted off her rumpled dress. "I thought that was you I saw earlier. Where'd you go?"

Ty didn't answer. He kept glancing over his shoulder, half expecting to see the frightening old woman come flying out of the dark alley behind him.

Lyessa peered around him. "What are you looking at?" Her expression was just as befuddled as his. "You look like you just tried absconding with the butcher's daughter."

Without saying a word, Ty turned and half walked, half ran in the opposite direction.

Lyessa left her friends standing on the corner and chased after him. "Where are you going?" she demanded, trying to catch up. "The least you could do is have the decency to talk to me after you assaulted me back there!"

"Sorry, I've got to go." Ty abandoned the entire notion of stopping at Reloria's. All he could think about was getting home.

"Sorry? Is that all you have to say?"

As soon as he reached Waddle, he untied the reins and mounted. "What more do you want?" he asked, turning back around to take one last look at the alley beside the spice shop. Nothing looked amiss. Lyessa's friends were standing there chatting while townsfolk walked past, no one the wiser.

"A simple conversation would be nice."

He was surprised by her offer to talk, perhaps even eager to take her up on it—but not enough to overcome the fear of what he'd just seen.

"Sorry," he said as he turned Waddle's head around, "but I have to go."

"What? Right this very moment?"

Digging in his heels, Ty spurred his horse into action. "Some other time!" he shouted back to her, sparing a quick glance over his shoulder. Lyessa was still standing there, looking more disappointed than angry.

To his surprise, he found he wanted to turn his horse around and go talk to her, but he didn't. He couldn't. He had more important things to worry about: Who was that old woman? Why did she seem to know him? And why, in the name of the Dark One, did her hand start dissolving? Was it something he'd done? Had he somehow invoked his blue fire without noticing?

His sister's screams echoed in his mind. He almost felt guilty for having hurt the old lady, but then he remembered the hungry look in her eyes when she had grabbed him. His remorse passed quickly.

He needed to get home and tell his parents.

Chapter 32 | Valtor

VALTOR FELT THE tug of the incantus crystal. *What does she want now?* he wondered. He didn't need to guess who it was. There was only one other person who had one.

He walked over to one of the shelves and opened a silver box. Inside rested a tubular piece of quartz, black as coal. He laid it on the table, and it started to vibrate.

Grabbing his staff, he aimed the wolf's head at the long piece of quartz. "*Ocnubian . . . Mangora.*"

The crystal began to rotate, faster and faster, until it was spinning so quickly he could hardly tell it was moving. It looked like a solid piece of dark glass without the reflection. Pretty soon, it rose into the air, and an image appeared in the glass. It was like looking through a window. He saw a cloaked figure in a dark room lit by a single candle. But unlike the Mirrors of Maon, Valtor couldn't reach through.

"This better be urgent, Mangora. I was in the middle of—"

"I found him," she said, out of breath.

"Found who?"

She leaned forward and pointed a hooked finger at him. "The faeling."

Valtor's fingers clenched around his staff. "Are you sure? How do you know?"

Mangora raised her hand.

It was even uglier than usual. The flesh seemed to have melted together around the palm and fingers.

"Thankfully, I still had some hedimari loam left from my travels in the Blasted Lands," she said, prodding at the concoction she had plastered over her ruined flesh. "It's going to leave a nasty scar, though."

Given how ugly her hands were, Valtor doubted anyone would notice.

"Where is he?"

"Easthaven."

"Easthaven? Why would he be in . . ." Then it dawned on him. "Of course. Nyalis wants to keep him close to the forest."

"What would you have me do?"

"Keep your eyes on him." Valtor leaned forward and cocked a single brow. "*All* your eyes."

Mangora smiled. "They are already watching. When should I expect you?"

Valtor shook his head. "I cannot leave. My task is progressing here. By winter's end, Aramoor will be broken and a new High King established. It will be up to you to bring the boy to me. Do you think you can handle that?"

"Are you questioning my abilities?"

"No, but we have had others try and fail. We cannot afford to act too hastily. It could drive the boy back into hiding or, worse, give cause to alert Nyalis. I don't want that timeworn fool of a wizard getting in my way."

"I can handle him."

"Don't underestimate him, Mangora."

"I have no intention of doing so."

Valtor began gathering some of the scattered documents on the table. "Do you have those you can trust to help you with this?"

"I have all I need to get the job done."

"Then let me know when it's finished." He fixed Mangora with a harsh glare. "And for all our sakes, you had better not fail." He swiped his hand in front of the image. "*Sikreeyo Padorum.*" Mangora and the room disappeared as the crystal slowed. He held out his hand, and it dropped into his palm. It was still cool to the touch.

Stepping away from his table, he placed the crystal back in its container and made his way down the open stairwell of his chambers. The clacking of his staff against the stone tiles filled the empty assembly room below. He waved his hand, and the large double doors at the front opened.

The two guards in their pristine white uniforms jumped to attention and stepped aside as he swept by. His course was set—no delays, no deviations, no distractions. His grip on the staff tightened. It bit into his palms as he tried to keep his hands from shaking.

On through the torch-lit passageways he strode. On through the winding stairwells he climbed. Countless doors passed in the darkness as his steps directed him deeper into the Tower's fortress. The farther he went, the more lifeless it became. The room he sought was deep within the mountainside. Dust lay thick on the floors, disturbed only by his passing. It had been a long time since he had walked these halls. The silence was almost oppressive.

The footprints in the dust stopped outside a large set of double doors. They were simple wooden doors by all accounts but protected against intrusion with a powerful, ancient magic. Had anyone tried to enter without releasing the spell first, they would have been killed immediately.

Even though he had found the incantation for lifting the spell in one of Aerodyne's journals, it still gave him pause whenever he used it. Carefully, he raised his hand and spoke the incantation to lower the wards. A dark layer of green mist materialized like a wall in front of the room. Valtor's entire body tingled from standing so close. It hummed for a moment, then vanished into the floor, leaving him free to pass.

There had been many wards placed throughout the ancient keep, preventing access to all but those who could defuse such magic. A few of the wards were of Valtor's making, but many had been conjured centuries earlier. Some of them were well beyond his capabilities to master, and thus the contents of those rooms remained a mystery, untouched by time. They had been created by wizards of the Second Age: wizards whose power and control over the elements matched those of even the Fae themselves.

Valtor had discovered this particular room and its warding in one of the many journals of magic he had found inside the Chamber of Purging during their renovations.

Taking a deep breath, he opened the door and stepped inside. *"Voyestra."*

Torches in rusted brackets burst to life, revealing the extended chamber beyond. It was a circular room, the outer perimeter comprised of the same dust-covered floors as the corridors. However, the floor at the center was made of white marble. The sharp contrast of color, and the fact that no dust touched its surface, was not the only thing that made this part of the room stand out.

Surrounding the circle of white were thirteen enormous pillars with veins of red marble running throughout. Atop the pillars were thirteen stone-faced gargoyles, each one as haunting as the next. They were referred to in Aerodyne's journals as the Watchers. They, too, had been warded in case of a breach. If someone were to step within the circle, someone with an aura not in line with Aerodyne's will, the stone creatures would come to life and destroy them.

Entering the white tile had always been an exercise in overcoming fear for Valtor. He found himself staring at the immobile statues above, wondering if they were looking down at him. A couple of times, he could have sworn he saw their eyes move. Pushing his fear aside, he crossed the white stone to a raised dais at its center, four feet off the ground.

Hovering at the center was an onyx basin wrapped in intricate gold runes.

The reflective black bowl was filled with a silver liquid. The Waters of A'sterith, the journals had named it. He remembered the first time he laid eyes on the basin and its contents, how excited he had been. Stretching out his hands, he whispered, "*Iryseth a' Daomon.*"

Stepping back, he watched as the silvery water within stirred. Above the basin, the liquid began to take shape, coalescing into the form of a figure wearing a hooded cloak. There was no face, no hands, no feet. Only nothingness rested beneath its folds.

Valtor kept his head lowered. "Lord Aerodyne, I await your command."

"What failings have you come to report?" The Dark Wizard's voice filled the chamber, resonating his power in such a way that Valtor had to focus just to keep his knees from trembling.

Valtor retreated a couple of steps before answering. "My lord, I wish to report that the faeling child has been found." He hazarded a quick glance toward the basin, where the stationary image of the former First Wizard stood waiting, buried beneath a silvery shroud.

The image slid forward slightly in the bowl. "At last. I was beginning to wonder if my trust had been misplaced."

Valtor shivered.

"Where is the boy?"

"He is in Easthaven of Sidara, my lord."

The room boomed with laughter. The sound was neither joyous nor pleasant. "Nyalis has wisely kept him close," Aerodyne said. "He is, of course, using the ven'ae to keep the faeling hidden."

Valtor nodded. He didn't know how Aerodyne might have known that, but he wasn't about to dispute it. He tried straightening his back where it ached from the stooped, subservient stance.

"Nyalis is the last of his kind, a dying breed," the apparition continued. "In his effort to tend to my prison, he has forgone the opportunity to train another."

"Yes, my lord."

Aerodyne lifted a robed arm and pointed at Valtor. "I want the faeling alive and unspoiled." The silvery figure shrank back into the basin once again. "He is vital to my release."

"Yes, Lord Aerodyne."

"Failure will be dealt with most severely." The wizard raised his arm.

Valtor fell to his knees as an onslaught of pain exploded through his mind. It was as though someone had reached inside his head and squeezed. Dropping his staff to the floor, he raised both hands and pressed them against his skull. His breathing had gone from sporadic, to chaotic, to nonexistent as he leaned forward and screamed in agony.

And just as quick as it had appeared, the pressure was gone.

"I have waited sixteen years for you to deliver the faeling to me. Don't fail me again." The figure melted back into the basin and out of sight.

Valtor's breathing was ragged. Drool dripped freely from his mouth, and his face was drenched in sweat. He rubbed his hand across his wet chin and found it was covered in blood. There was a sharp metallic taste in his mouth. Upon inspection, he found there was blood seeping from his nose and ears. What did this mean? Aerodyne had never been able to touch the land of the living before. His prison must truly be deteriorating.

For the first time, Valtor felt doubt. He wondered if his path was leading him in a direction he would soon regret.

He struggled back to his feet. Like it or not, he had gone too far to turn back now.

Chapter 33 | Nilla

NILLA CROSSED OVER Aldcliff and took a street that ran behind a couple of the less-frequented shops on the northwest side of Easthaven, heading for the residential district. She had left her horse tied in front of Mezard's Chandlery and opted to tote her basket of baked goods for Saleena instead of trying to direct her mare through the tight passageways between buildings on the seedier side of town.

After hearing that the peculiar shop owner had somehow recognized her son for what he was, Nilla, along with her husband, had insisted a council meeting be called. She had decided to leave a little earlier than usual to check on Saleena. The young healer had been holed up in the cellar of the Harbor House and was to stay until the Black Watch finally decided to leave Easthaven. The last Nilla had heard, the council had no idea when that would be—only that they couldn't take the chance of transporting her while the Tower's guards were around.

Nilla had packed a basket of food for the young woman. The council did its best to look after those under its protection, but most of the council were men and tended not to think beyond keeping its charges sheltered from the Tower's reach.

Her thoughts strayed back to her son. If half of what Ty had told them about his run-in with the old woman was true, there was a good possibility Ty would not be able to roam free in town himself anymore. The last thing they needed was for someone to recognize him for who he was: a wielder. At least while the Black Watch was in Easthaven, the strange shop owner, whoever she was, might be hesitant to get involved, lest they take her as well.

From the description Ty gave of her shop, with its bizarre artifacts, books, weapons, and desiccated heads, it was pretty clear the woman leaned toward the darker side of magic and likely had no intention of giving the Black Watch cause to take notice.

Nilla feared it would soon be time to get the wizard involved. She wasn't sure how much longer Easthaven would be able to harbor her son safely.

A stray alley cat knocked some trash from the top of a barrel, causing Nilla to jump. "Pull yourself together," she chided herself. She had always been a worrier. Being married to someone like Kellen, who could calmly face down an angry bear without thinking twice, had been both a blessing and a curse. Her husband had mellowed her anxiety somewhat over the years, but when it came to her family, her nerves stayed on edge no matter how calm he was.

When her parents had told her they had found her a husband, it had taken her everything not to run away from home. The last thing she wanted was to be tied down to some big lout who wanted nothing more than for someone to cook and clean for him. At least, at the ripe old age of fifteen, that was what she had believed marriage was supposed to be about for a woman. That's what it had been for her parents.

She remembered the first time she had seen Kellen. He was the biggest man she had ever laid eyes on, though in reality, Kellen was only a year or two older than her. His mother had passed away when he was just a child, and his father had left when he was barely in his teens, which forced him to grow up sooner than the other boys his age.

Even as a young man, Kellen had been the best tracker this side of Reed Marsh. It ran in his blood. His father, and his father's father before him, had been gamekeepers and woodsmen for the Sidaran overlords. When Kellen inherited the position, the overlord also granted him a large cottage and the land around it for his use. As long as Kellen remained gamekeeper, the property and the job would be his to pass on to future generations.

After one look at Kellen's station, Nilla's father had been first in line to offer his daughter as a wife to the gamekeeper. Kellen had always been shy around girls. He never took to the traditional view of courtship and was normally too busy to bother. Trying to get two words out of him was like trying to coax a raccoon out from under the house. In fact, the first time the two of them had spoken was the day before their wedding.

Kellen had come out to the house to see about any final preparations. He had pulled her to the side, with her father's permission, to speak with her alone. Nilla was shorter than the other young women, which made his height even more intimidating. The size of his hands frightened her. The thought of what he could do to her if he ever became violent was terrifying. She craned her neck just to look into his eyes when he spoke. His words, however, for the first time made her dare to hope that life with Kellen may not be as bad as what she was expecting.

"You don't have to marry me if you don't want to," Kellen had said. "I won't force you."

Looking into his eyes, she saw something she had never seen in her father's: compassion. Not that Nilla would have said no, even if he looked like he was ready to throw her over his knee and paddle her right there. The fear of what her father would do to her if she did was more than enough for her to go through with it.

As it turned out, it was the best thing that had ever happened to her.

Nilla smiled and quickened her pace through the maze of lonely back alleys. The icy wind threatened to strip her of her basket on more than one occasion. That same wind seemed to be keeping the good citizens of Easthaven indoors, leaving her a clear path to the Harbor House.

Once inside, she followed Eliab down the stone staircase to the cellar below.

"Mith Thaleena ith right thith way, Mith Nilla," the old gatekeeper said. He had his double crossbow tucked under his arm like a third appendage. Nilla couldn't remember ever seeing him without it.

Eliab stopped outside a door on the left side of the room and knocked.

"Just a moment," a voice called out from the other side.

Nilla turned at the sound of a door opening behind her. She passed a quick glance over her shoulder in time to spot the elusive Sheeva entering a guest room on the other side.

Saleena's door opened, and Nilla turned back around. Saleena was a pretty girl, at least a head taller than Nilla. Her long, dark hair was down, probably trying to cover the extensive bruising still visible from her time with the Black Watch. Fraya had healed the worst of the damage, but she was letting Saleena's body take care of the smaller injuries on its own. Nilla wondered if Saleena had anyone waiting for her back home, or if she'd ever be able to return.

"Please, come in," Saleena said with a gesture for her to enter.

Eliab bowed and headed back to the stairs.

Nilla stepped inside. The room wasn't much to look at—cramped with a cot in the corner and a short table with one chair. Then again, it was only meant as a temporary shelter until a more permanent situation could be found.

She walked across the room and laid her basket on the bed. "I brought some roast venison, fresh rye, and a wedge of cheese. It's not much, but . . ." Nilla took a seat on the edge of the bed and gestured for Saleena to join her.

"Thank you, Your Ladyship."

"Ladyship?" Nilla laughed. "I'm no lady, dear. My husband and I are simple folk. Just call me Nilla." She pulled out the loaf of dark rye and offered it to Saleena.

The young healer tore off a piece and wolfed it down, smiling sheepishly as she did. "Master Orlyn might be one of the sweetest men this side of the Angorans, but he can't cook worth a hoot. He won't let me out long enough to do it myself, either." A look of horror crossed her face and she threw up her hands. "I'm not complaining, mind you. I'm very grateful for everything the council is doing for me."

Nilla chuckled. "Don't you worry about it; I completely understand." She almost laughed at the absurdity of *her* telling someone else not to worry.

"How long do you think I'll need to stay down here?" Saleena asked, stuffing another piece of bread and cheese in her mouth.

"As long as it takes, I guess. Now that the Black Watch believes you are dead, they will be moving on soon enough, at least we hope. Once they do, we'll find you a new place to live. You'll have to change your name, and most importantly, you'll have to give up medicine."

Saleena stopped chewing. "Give up medicine? I can't do that. It's my whole life."

"It won't be much of a life if the Black Watch nabs you again and carts you off to the White Tower. I have a feeling you won't be doing much healing from your cell."

Saleena grunted, twisting what remained of the loaf of bread in her hands.

Nilla padded Saleena's leg. "My dear, you have your whole life ahead of you. It doesn't have to be about an occupation. Having dreams is a wonderful thing. But what good are they if you don't have anyone to share them with? Who knows, maybe those skills of yours will be needed again. Or perhaps you'll find a different set of dreams."

Once Saleena had finished eating, the two women joined the other members of the council in the meeting room. Most of the council was there, save Gilly, who needed the solitude of his river after the last council session, and Reloria, who was too busy at her shop to get away.

Nilla took a seat next to her husband, and Saleena took the one beside her.

Ty had been left at home with Breen and Adarra. It was best that he remain out of sight as much as possible for now.

Feoldor scratched the whiskers on the side of his face irritably. "I'm telling you, it's time to contact the wizard."

Orlyn leaned forward in his seat on the other side of the table and glanced toward its head. "As much as I hate to agree with Feoldor, it is no longer safe for Ty here in Easthaven."

"There, you see," Feoldor said, sweeping a hand in the apothecary's direction, "even greybeard knows when to see reason."

Orlyn reached for his staff. "Call me greybeard once more, you sorry excuse for a vanti. At least I don't look like a chipmunk."

Beside her, Saleena chuckled lightly at the two's banter.

"That's enough," Veldon said from the front, clearly not in the mood. He nervously fiddled with the piece of flint around his neck.

Nilla was growing anxious. The bickering wasn't helping, whether playful or not. She took a deep breath. She didn't know why she kept letting herself get so worked up. What had she expected? That her family would spend the rest of their lives in protected bliss? That the White Tower would eventually give up their search? That Overlord Barl would somehow keep the Black Watch from ever entering their city?

She looked up as Kellen's fingers interlocked with hers. Her hand seemed so small in his. She smiled.

"Kellen," Veldon said.

Kellen squeezed her hand, then turned.

"What are your thoughts? This is Ty, after all. Do you believe his account of the old woman and her shop?"

Kellen glanced at Nilla to get her response. She nodded. They didn't need a long conversation to get their thoughts across to one another. After so many years together, a simple look was enough most of the time. "I believe him," Kellen said. "He hasn't given us cause to doubt his word before."

Veldon nodded, and then rubbed the top of his head. "Then I'd say we haven't much choice. We should use the horn."

"The horn?" Saleena asked.

"The wizard gave us a way to call him," Nilla said, turning in her seat to look at Saleena. "In case of emergencies."

Saleena glanced around the table. "I know I'm going to sound silly asking, but how is he going to hear it?"

Orlyn cleared his throat. "We're not quite sure."

"Oh." Saleena didn't say anything more.

"We also need to send someone to check this woman's shop," Nilla said. "If she knows Ty, then it's likely she would recognize myself or Kellen." Nilla looked across the table at Orlyn. "Perhaps . . ."

"No need to say anything more," Orlyn said. "Feoldor and I will check it out."

Feoldor huffed. "Thanks for volunteering me."

Nilla caught Feoldor's eye, and he squirmed in his seat. "I'd be only too happy to help," he said, fiddling with the bracelet on his wrist that held his transferal crystal.

"Orlyn, if you please," Veldon said with a nod.

Orlyn reached under the table and withdrew a rectangular box about the length of a man's forearm. He placed it on the table in front of him. There didn't appear to be a lock, hinge, or seal of any kind. In fact, Nilla thought it looked like nothing more than a simple block of sanded wood. Apart from a couple of strange symbols carved into what she thought was the top, there was nothing extraordinary about it.

Orlyn grabbed his staff. The crystal at the top radiated a vibrant green as he placed his free hand on top of the box. Nilla had been there the day Nyalis had first presented them with the magically sealed case. Orlyn spoke the incantation the wizard had given them.

"*Vera Sintorum.*"

The gold runes flickered to life along the edge of the box, revealing the outline of a lid. A latch inside the container clicked, and Orlyn released his staff, letting the crystal's light fade. He removed the lid and laid it on the table.

Inside the box was a curved horn made of ivory. The ends were gold-plated. Orlyn lifted the horn and offered it to Kellen.

"Ty is your son. It should be your choice."

Kellen took the beautifully sculpted artifact and studied it for a moment, turning it over in his hands. He then turned and handed it to Nilla.

It felt cool in her hands, delicate. She was suddenly inundated with doubt. Did she really want to do this? Was it truly necessary? She knew the wizard had said he would be back one day to take Ty. Did that have to be now? Once she blew the horn, everything was going to change.

She glanced at her husband and saw the answer in his eyes. There was nothing more important than her son's safety. No matter what happened, she had to keep him safe. She lifted the end of the horn to her lips, took a deep breath, and blew.

The horn didn't make so much as a peep.

The members cast quizzical glances around the table.

"I didn't hear anything," Saleena said.

"What happened?" Feoldor asked. "Did you blow?"

"Yes. I blew as hard as I could."

Kellen took the horn and examined both ends. "I don't see any blockages."

Feoldor grabbed the horn from Kellen. "Oh, here, let me show you how it's done." He sucked in a large gulp of air and expelled it as hard as he could.

His face turned red by the end of his blow. Again, nothing happened. Feoldor shrugged, obviously embarrassed at having done no better. He handed it back to Kellen. "Wouldn't it be just like that old codger to give us a defective horn?"

"What now?" Veldon asked.

Orlyn took the instrument and placed it back inside the box. "Now we wait and see."

Chapter 34 | Ferrin

FERRIN FELT SOMETHING prick his arm, pulling him from another fit of restless sleep.

He lay there on the cold stone for a moment, trying to decide if what he had felt was real or just another dream. The cold wind howled eerily through the room's single arrow slit, making it impossible to truly fall asleep.

He felt it again. This time, the pain was sharp, much more than a prick. He smacked at the source like he would at a blood gnat trying to fill its belly. However, instead of a squishing sound, there was a squeal as his hand wrapped around a large rat. It had apparently decided that Ferrin was more appealing than the bucket of dung sitting in the far corner.

He grabbed the rat by the head and snapped its neck, then threw it against the wall. The pail in the corner clanged, letting him know he had hit the mark.

"I see you finally caught our little friend," Azriel said from his side of the room. His chains clanged against the floor as he struggled to lift himself into a sitting position.

Ferrin wiped the hair from his face. "He mistook my arm for a serving tray."

"Ah, I guess he finally realized the little meat covering *my* bones is too tough and moved on to greener pastures." Azriel's laugh turned into a fit of coughing.

Ferrin crossed the room to see if there was anything he could do to help the old seer, but Azriel waved him off. "Don't you worry yourself over me. I'm too ornery to die."

Ferrin grunted. "Now, *that* I can believe." He turned and walked back to his bed, which wasn't much more than a clump of straw, barely enough to ward off the stone's cold chill.

"You never did tell me why they keep you chained like that," Ferrin said, the arrow slit above his head allowing just enough light to see by.

Azriel rubbed at the thick manacle around his neck. "Because they fear me. I'm a powerful sorcerer, after all."

Ferrin snorted. "Yes, you looked very powerful over there mounted to the wall."

"I'm chained because not long after they brought me here, I managed to escape."

Ferrin stopped fluffing the straw and raised his head.

"What's wrong?" the old man asked. "You look like you just sucked a bad egg."

"You escaped? How? How did you get around the guards? For that matter, how did you get your hands on a transferal?"

Azriel raised his hand. "One question at a time. This old mind doesn't run as fast as it used to." He paused. "As a seer, I see things—"

"You don't say."

Azriel ignored him. "I see past things. I see present things. I see future things. Actually, I guess the future things are more like possibilities than actualities, but we'll save that topic for another time." Azriel looked at Ferrin.

"Understand?"

Ferrin shook his head.

"Good. I'd be afraid if you did. You're not a seer, after all." He studied Ferrin's face for a moment curiously, then shook his head. "As I was saying, I see things, things no one else can, like when they were going to send only one guard to escort me to the Chamber of Inquisition, and when that same guard would be startled by something and turn his back to me. I could also see which corridors and stairwells would be left unguarded. Granted, I don't normally get such vivid foreshadowing. They usually come in small clumps. But this time, it was enough for me to find my way out."

Ferrin smirked. "Then why are you still here?"

"Well, no one's perfect. Although I like to think that some of us are a bit closer than others." He offered Ferrin a quirky smile. "Anyway, once I reached the outside, the extent of my visions was over, and I was forced to go the rest on my own. I hadn't made it halfway to the stables when a guard spotted me on his way to the privy. Imagine that," the old man balked. "All that work, and I was caught by a man with a loose bowel." Azriel threw his shackled hands in the air. "You can't tell me that wasn't some kind of higher power. The Creator had a good laugh that day at my expense."

Ferrin stared in astonishment.

"Well, my boy, are you going to say something? A moment ago, I couldn't get you to shut up."

"How did you get your hands on a crystal?"

"Ah, now that's a good question," Azriel acknowledged with a raised finger. "And I guess the easiest answer is . . . I didn't."

Now Ferrin was confused. "What do you mean you didn't?"

"I mean I didn't have to. My gift is innate. I don't need a faerie rock."

"Faerie rock?"

"Yes, faerie rock. Those little shards of crystal that give you access to your ability." Azriel smiled sadly and shook his head. "You mean to tell me you've never heard the term *faerie crystal* before?"

Ferrin shook his head. He was beginning to understand how in the dark he truly was. He had never been one for all that drivel. He had never cared all that much how the world worked, or what the purpose to life was, or if there was some higher plan or destiny for him. As long as he could keep food on the table and a roof over his head, he was more than satisfied.

"Where did you think your magic came from?" Azriel asked. "It came from the Fae, when they broke through to our realm thousands of years ago."

"Everyone knows that," Ferrin said.

"One thing you might not have known is that everything about their realm is based on magic, and the transferals, as we call them, are pieces of their realm brought over to help aid us in our use of magic."

"So my metallurgy isn't me? It's just a piece of rock?"

"Well, no, it's mostly you," Azriel said, rubbing his hand down his long, disheveled beard. "The crystals form a bridge to your magic. When magic was first introduced to our realm, it started to seep into things, living things. And we were no exception. Pretty soon, there were humans being born with magic, which in turn is what led to the war and the founding of the Wizard Order.

"Like everything in life, you have good and evil. Some of the faeries were content to coexist with humans, but most believed that because of the faeries' abilities, they should be able to rule over us. And they did—at least until the Wizard Order and its faerie allies drove them out and sealed the breach."

"How do people know if they have magic?" Ferrin asked.

"In a way, you can sense it. You, for example, were born with the ability to manipulate metal ore. But even before you had ever come in contact with a transferal, I bet you could sniff out metal like a basset hound could a fox. Most people have no idea they have magic at first, since what they feel is something they've had since birth and don't know any better.

"Those born with a certain gift are able to sense that gift but not manipulate it. Right now, you can probably tell me where every piece of metal in this room is, the type, consistency, and probably age, but," he said, raising a finger, "you can't manipulate it. You could stick a voda in the middle of a desert and they could point out precisely where the water is under the sand, but they couldn't bring it up.

"Then there are a few, like myself, who were born with what we call innate abilities. We don't need a transferal for our gifts to work. Our magic is solely self-contained."

"Must be nice."

"Understand, I'm not saying that my magic is more powerful; it just isn't dependent on the crystals. And before you ask, I have no idea how or why that works. There are also different forms of magic. For example, there are runes and incantations. These are all forms of magic that can be learned."

"So, can anyone perform magic?"

"No. Only those born with it. You were born with a propensity for metallurgy. So, given the right amount of time and study, you could eventually learn other forms and variations of magic as well. The difference though is that those with an aptitude for a certain gift will have a stronger control over *that* gift than those who merely learn to manipulate it through runes and incantations. For example, you could learn to control fire, but you would never be able to employ it the way a true incindi could.

"Either way, this learning of other magical forms is how wizards were made in the old days. There were great schools of wizardry where the ven'ae could go to learn, but the Great Purge put an end to them centuries ago."

Ferrin remained quiet, trying to absorb everything the old man was saying. There was so much he didn't know. He wondered if his blissful ignorance could be better described as complete stupidity. After all, he was here because of these strange gifts.

"What you ogling at, son? I know I'm not the prettiest thing to look at, but I'm a far sight better than you."

"Oh, sorry," Ferrin muttered. He hadn't realized he had been staring. "I was just thinking," he said finally.

"Independent thought, hmm." Azriel's eyes brightened with sarcasm. "A rather dangerous pastime, to be sure. It can lead a man into all kinds of trouble. Take me, for example. I thought I should use my gift to help others. Now look at me." He raised his iron-bound arms into the air. "I'm chained to a dungeon wall with nothing more than a dead rat and you to keep me company. And don't ask me which is worse." He coughed out another laugh.

Ferrin couldn't help but smile at the old man's tenacity. Ferrin only hoped he could bear his time in the Tower with as much dignity as this withered old seer had. "If only I could get my hands on one of those crystals," he said finally.

Azriel's head leaned back against the stone wall, watching him with a gaze intense enough to be staring straight into his soul. "Oh? And what would you do with the crystal if you had it? Unlock my chains? Rip open the door? Storm the castle?" He cackled.

"What's so funny?"

"Do you even know where you are?"

"Where I am? What kind of ridiculous question is that? Of course I know where I am. I'm locked in the White Tower with nothing but a dead rat and you to keep me company. And I *can* tell you which is worse."

Azriel laughed. "But do you know *where* in the Tower you are? I'm sure that once you managed to get beyond that door, you have an escape route planned. Of course, you know where the guards are, what their rotation is, how many on and off duty, where to find supplies, clothing, and transportation to get you beyond the Pass of Arnon. For that matter, do you even know where the front door is?"

Ferrin felt like the tail end of a donkey at this point. He actually hadn't given it much thought beyond breaking free of his cell. "Okay, I get your point." He scratched at his thickening beard.

"As I was saying, thinking can lead to trouble. However, if those thoughts are nurtured, cultivated, and well planned, they could lead to great accomplishments. Every amazing achievement man has wrought began as a single idea. It's what separates us from the animals.

"Unfortunately, our thoughts can be self-centered as well. They can betray us, manipulate us. Just remember, every form of evil we find in our world started as a single thought." The old man shook his head. "Listen to me, preaching again. I'm probably the last person who has that right."

Ferrin lifted his head. "No, you're right. There is wisdom in what you say. I've always been one to act with little thought to the outcome. Unlike you, I decided to use my gift, not for others, but for myself. With my gift, I could create weapons that were lighter, stronger, and more durable than my competition's. My reputation grew, and so did my head. The gold was too tempting, and so was the recognition for my work. My sister warned me, but I didn't listen. In fact," he admitted with a slight grunt, "it was my crowning achievement to be contracted by the High King himself for a pair of swords."

"You don't say."

"It's also, no doubt, what landed me on the Tower's watch list in the first place." He shrugged. "And the rest is history. I lost my home, my gold, my business, and will probably lose my life. All because, as you say, I didn't stop to think."

"We wouldn't be human if we didn't make mistakes, my boy. Thankfully, the Creator can take our lapses in judgment and use them for something good."

Ferrin took a deep breath. "I'll be honest—"

"That's always a wise choice."

Ferrin sighed. "Right now, I'm having a hard time seeing what that could be."

Azriel's head lowered. A moment later, it lifted, a hint of amusement flashing across his eyes. "Well, just think. If you hadn't been so selfish and went and got yourself caught by the Black Watch, you would never have had the great privilege of meeting me." The old man's smile was so pitifully sincere that Ferrin immediately laughed, which caused the seer to laugh, ending in a fit of coughing, gagging, and eventually hiccups, which in turn brought on even more laughter.

Once the amusement had ended, Ferrin rolled over on his back. He wondered if it was luck or something else that had landed him in the same cell as this crazy old seer. Either way, he was determined not to waste what time he had. He had nearly broken during his last round of interrogations. He didn't know how much longer he could hold out.

Chapter 35 | Ayrion

AYRION TOOK A DEEP breath and closed the door to the king's study.

It had been a long meeting. After the troubling events of the past week, he had half expected the discussions to last clear through the night. As it was, the king wasn't feeling well and suggested they resume in the morning.

He decided to take the northern route back to his chambers. Apart from the guards stationed on patrol and a few of the overnight staff preparing for the following morning, the palace appeared to be asleep.

Ayrion came to the end of another quiet hall. Here, the sconces had not been maintained as meticulously as those in the more traveled areas. More than a few had burned out, leaving the lonely corridor cut with shadows. He turned right and spotted a figure slipping out of one of the storage rooms ahead, a large sack slung over their shoulder. Whoever it was wore a dark cloak with the hood up.

Ayrion quickly moved against the wall and watched as the figure entered the stairwell on the far end of the passageway. He followed, keeping to the shadows as he moved down the corridor. What was someone doing back here at this time of night? Whoever it was clearly didn't want to be seen and knew the palace well enough to avoid the staff.

Ayrion trailed the hooded figure down the stairwell. Instead of getting off at the next floor, they descended all the way to the bottom, which led to an outer passage behind the kitchens. The person stopped just outside the cook's entrance and pressed their ear against the door.

For a brief moment, Ayrion felt like he was a child again, chasing his friends around the darker recesses of the palace, looking for a good place to hide. He was half tempted to jump out and yell "Gotcha!" But as fun as it might have been to scare the blazes out of whoever this was, he decided to hold back and watch. If this turned out to be something more than one of the cleaning staff helping themselves to a couple of extra blankets, he wanted to let it play out and see if there were any others involved.

The thief shifted the half-filled sack to the other shoulder and stepped through the door. As a child, some of Ayrion's favorite places to hide had been the palace kitchens. The smell of the exotic foods being prepared was beyond anything he could have ever imagined while living on the streets. Ayrion had been sure that when he died, the afterlife couldn't have fared much better.

Slipping into the room, he worked his way along the back wall behind large crates of fresh sea crab and watched as the thief went about filling their sack with whatever food they could get their hands on. The cloak shifted, and he realized the thief was a woman.

He crept a little closer, hoping to find a better vantage point to see who was behind the hood. Slowly, he peeked out from behind a pair of stacked barrels, but there was no one there. His eyes darted around the room, but the piles of boxes, barrels, baskets, and crates had hidden her from view. Careful to keep to the shadows, he worked his way through the maze of food stores, poking his head up every now and then to see if he could spot the food bandit, but he had somehow managed to lose her.

To his left, he heard the creak of the loading door, which led out to the lower courtyards. Ayrion smiled. He had taken this route on several occasions to get to the stables. Quickly, he worked his way around to the back entrance and slid the door open just enough to peer through. He could see the woman crossing the yard toward the back of the stables. She must have had a horse already waiting for her.

He was enjoying this cat-and-mouse game a little too much. It had been years since he had had reason to think and move the way a street rat would.

Opening the door the rest of the way, he stepped out and stood with his back against the stone wall, keeping out of the light from the torch poles lining the inner courtyard. Within moments, the cloaked thief rode out from behind the stables. She looked to be heading for the main gate.

The direction she was taking would lead her right past where he stood. He flattened himself against the wall. He could feel his swords pressing against his back. He hoped his dark clothing was enough to keep him hidden.

As the woman passed, she turned her head just enough for him to catch a glimpse of the face beneath. His mouth dropped. He couldn't have been more surprised had it been the queen herself. There was no mistaking those bright green eyes and tuft of golden hair. It was Amarysia. Why was she sneaking around in the middle of the night, pilfering wares like a common bag snatcher?

This was far too interesting to leave unresolved. Ayrion raced across the courtyard and grabbed the first mount with a saddle. Being the Guardian Protector had its perks. Loren, who happened to be on duty, waved.

"You want me to saddle Shade?"

"No time," Ayrion said, and spurred the horse into action.

Ayrion took the central route past the upper gardens and across the front courtyard. He wanted to make sure he didn't lose Amarysia before she crossed the palace bridge. If she made it into the city before he did, there would be no use following.

Thankfully, he reached the outer bailey in time to see her horse passing under the main gates. Urging his own mount on, he followed her across the enormous structure connecting the island of rock to the mainland, then into the city.

He followed her for the next hour, staying far enough back to not be seen or heard on the empty streets. She didn't seem to be in a great hurry. After passing through the upper north quarters into Bayside, whose wealthy mansions overlooked the harbor, she skirted the west side of the merchant district and headed south into Cheapside.

Cheapside, for those living in the lower regions of Aramoor, was known as the Maze. It was a city within a city. The compact housing of the lower class was fraught with interconnecting ways, streets, side passages, and narrow alleys hardly wide enough for a grown man to fit through. A person could easily get lost for days, never finding their destination.

Ayrion knew the Maze like the back of his hand. He could remember his time with the street tribes: the battles fought, the friends made, the lessons learned, many of which had helped him rise to where he was today.

So many memories. It seemed a lifetime ago, or maybe someone else's life altogether. It had been too long since his last visit with Reevie and Sapphire. Ayrion regretted that his duties as Protector had forced him to neglect his childhood friends.

He urged his horse to go a little faster, concern growing the farther they traveled into the Maze. This was a rough section of Aramoor. A person could be mugged, stabbed, and tossed into the bay without anyone knowing. They were approaching one of the vacant shipping districts when Amarysia finally pulled back on her reins. She stopped in front of one of the smaller stone buildings and climbed down. Part of its walls had begun to collapse from neglect. Ayrion thought he remembered it being a warehouse at one time. Why, of all places, would she be going there?

Ayrion led his horse off to the side of a building a few streets down.

Quietly, he worked his way around to the building opposite where she stood. He kept his eyes open, scanning every window, every door, every dark corner and hole for signs of movement. A person who let their guard down this close to the Warrens was a person not long for this world. With practiced feet, he moved along the fronts of the derelict structures, his Upakan eyes keeping him from stumbling over loose boards and scattered debris.

To his surprise, he felt as though he were coming home.

His first full year in Aramoor had been spent in a small room under an abandoned granary not three blocks away. The time he had spent there as a boy had been some of the best and worst of his life.

The front door of the building Amarysia was facing opened, and three cloaked figures stepped out. One was a little taller than her, the other two shorter. Ayrion crouched and waited. They didn't appear to have ill intent. Their hands were empty at their sides, and their posture, though alert, was carefully nonthreatening.

The taller individual offered a quick greeting. Ayrion was too far away to hear what they were saying, but after a short chat, Amarysia unhooked the large sack from her saddle and fell into step behind them as they entered the three-story building.

He scanned the building, looking for a way in, and noticed that the door on the second-floor balcony was ajar. After taking a moment to make sure he was alone, Ayrion raced across the alley. He hopped up on a pile of crates, jumped, and grabbed hold of one of the crossbeams sticking out from under the balcony floor. Using it as leverage, he swung himself up to the railing, and from there it was a quick leap over.

He smiled. It had been a long time since he had made use of his Upakan training for more than fighting. He followed the hall, sticking close to the wall to avoid any of the creaking floorboards at the center, till he came to an opening that overlooked the ground floor. The railing had been torn away in sections, leaving openings large enough to fall through.

The room below was lit with a smattering of candles and a couple of brass lamps with polished reflectors. Amarysia stood at the center, still holding her sack. She didn't appear to be worried, but from where Ayrion stood, it was hard to tell. Very few entered a street tribe's lair without first being invited, and even then, it was typically for some kind of parley with a representative from another tribe. Amarysia kept her back straight and showed no outward sign of fear. *Good,* he thought. Fear on the streets was like blood to a school of krim. They could smell it a mile away.

With his Upakan eyes, he could see movement all the way around the room. What had she gotten herself mixed up in?

He heard voices below him. They seemed to be doing their best not to speak too loudly. He needed a better vantage point.

A small group walked out from under the balcony. At their head was a large brute of a boy. His light hair stuck out from the rest. From the way the others deferred to him, he was clearly this tribe's chieftain. Ayrion couldn't tell much more than that from where he was, but he could see the large mallet the boy was holding behind his back. Amarysia stood quietly at the center of the room, seemingly oblivious to the danger she was in.

Ayrion couldn't wait any longer. He backed to the far side of the walkway, took a deep breath, and ran for one of the openings in the railing.

Chapter 36 | Ayrion

THE FLAPS OF Ayrion's black coat opened behind him as he dropped from the second-floor balcony and hit the ground directly between the approaching convoy and Amarysia.

Amarysia shrieked and dropped her sack. Street kids everywhere dove for their cubbyholes. Their leader, clearly startled by Ayrion's sudden entrance, whipped out his large hammer as the rest of his underlings brandished whatever crude weapons they had stowed beneath their threadbare garb.

"Ayrion? What are you—"

Before Amarysia could finish her sentence, the tribal chief howled and charged. Ayrion sidestepped the heavy implement and watched as the head of the hammer swung to his left.

The boy was stronger than he looked. Using the momentum of his first swing, the kid whipped around for another try, this time aiming for Ayrion's head. Ayrion ducked and spun, letting the heavy maul hit nothing but air. The boy didn't stop. He continued to attack, howling as he went. Amarysia was yelling for them to stop.

Ayrion kept his blades sheathed. He had no intention of killing any of these kids. Instead, he continued to dance around the room, weaving in and around each swing of the hammer, while at the same time allowing his assailant to wear himself out. The boy wouldn't be able to keep it up much longer, but he wasn't about to stop of his own volition. The boy couldn't. His entire tribe was watching. His reputation as their leader was on the line. Ayrion hated embarrassing the kid like this, but he wouldn't let him hurt Amarysia.

Having chased Ayrion from one side of the open floor to the other with nothing to show for it, the tribal chief was panting. He left himself unprotected on each of his backswings. Waiting for the right moment, Ayrion sidestepped the hammer once again and then kicked the boy square in the chest, hard enough to send him flying backward with a different sort of howl.

The other boys ran to help their chief to his feet.

Ayrion headed across the room to where Amarysia was standing wide-eyed and a bit more upset than he would have expected from someone whose life he had saved. Instead of throwing her arms around his neck and thanking him for her rescue, she flew by him and threw her arms around the street thug instead.

"Are you all right?" she asked as she reached down to help the boy up.

He pushed her hand away. "Stop it!"

Ayrion watched, perplexed. Didn't she know any better than to treat the boy like a sick puppy in front of his tribe? She spun around and planted both fists firmly on her hips, fixing Ayrion with a harsh glare. "What do you think you're doing?"

"Saving your life; what does it look like? What do you think you're doing, coming down here alone in the middle of the night? Are you trying to get yourself killed?" Ayrion kept his eyes on the growing number of kids on the far side of the room as they started coming, literally, out of the woodwork. They crawled out from under the tables, from behind the support posts, through back doorways, even from small holes in the walls.

They were all staring at him in wonder. Some were pointing, others whispering.

"And what exactly did you think you were saving me from?" she asked, her fists still maintaining their spot on her hips.

"From that bruiser behind you with the sledgehammer."

"You mean Howler? The boy whose rib cage you very nearly crushed?"

The chief leaned his head back and howled. "I am no boy!" Ayrion could see where he got his name.

"Oh, shut up, Sedgewick! You are a boy. Now, do you want this food or not?" Amarysia left the young chieftain standing there with an angry pout on his face to collect her sack of pilfered goods.

Even with the large sack of food in her hand, it wasn't Amarysia everyone was staring at.

"You're him, aren't you, mister?" one of the little boys at the front asked, taking a nervous step forward. "You're . . . Death's Shadow."

Ayrion smiled. He hadn't heard that name in a very long time. Not since he wasn't much older than most of them.

"I am."

Howler gulped.

Ayrion walked across the room. Dust shot up from beneath his black boots as the loose floorboards bent under his weight. "Now, will someone kindly tell me what is going on here?"

Amarysia crossed her arms. "I would have if you hadn't decided to interfere." Some of the boys gasped at the way she addressed him.

Ayrion almost laughed but thought better of it after gauging the expression on her face. "Interfere? And what was I supposed to do, pray tell, when I catch the queen's lady-in-waiting sneaking around the palace in the middle of the night, plundering the food stores like a common burglar?"

"You were to trust she had a reason for what she was doing." Without waiting for a response from him, she turned around and started handing out the food and blankets. The boys and girls clawed at the bag to get their hands on the supplies, forcing Howler to step in and divvy out the goods himself.

Amarysia moved back alongside Ayrion as she watched the tribal chief pass out the blankets and food. "Sedgewick, I mean Howler, is my brother."

"Your brother?" Ayrion glanced at Howler, then back at Amarysia. There was a resemblance. Sedgewick's hair was lighter. Not quite as golden as Amarysia's, but clearly a family trait. He also shared her blue eyes. His features, though, weren't soft like hers. He had a strong chin and higher cheekbones.

Why did a lady-in-waiting to the queen have a brother living on the streets like a common guttersnipe? Ladies-in-waiting were chosen from noble families. Not that it would have mattered to him. He wouldn't have cared had she been born to a pig farmer.

"When Sedge and I were younger, we used to go with Mother to hand out food and blankets to the needy. She had a very large heart, you know."

"Had?"

"There was an outbreak on board one of the ships coming back from Delga. My father was on board. He hadn't realized he had caught the disease until after he had passed it to my mother. Sedge and I were lucky enough not to have caught it." She didn't need to say more. The haunted look in her eyes did the rest for her.

"I'm sorry. I know what it's like to grow up without family." Ayrion watched as Howler continued to hand out the goods. "So, how did your brother end up here? Where are your family's holdings?"

Amarysia chuckled. "Even as a young kid, Sedge always had the romantic notion of running away from home and joining a troupe. Making friends with some of the street kids we were helping was about as close as he ever got. When our parents died, our properties were repossessed by the Crown."

Ayrion grimaced but didn't say anything.

"Apparently, our father was great at organizing parties of fashion but not at keeping up with the family estate. Our taxes and debts were so far in arrears that Sedge and I were lucky to keep the clothes on our backs. Thankfully, I had already been chosen as a lady-in-waiting to the queen. It was more out of a favor to my mother than anything, I believe. Even after hearing of the scandal behind our family's sudden lack of position, the queen still kept me on as her personal attendant." Amarysia sighed. "What's done is done. I'm happy, and strangely enough, so is Sedge."

Ayrion smiled. "I would say your mother's heart lives on in you."

She turned and looked him in the eyes. "That was a beautiful thing to say." She stared a long moment before speaking. "Those grey eyes of yours really are unsettling, you know."

He chuckled. "My Upakan heritage at work."

"You never told me how you ended up in Aramoor. Did your family pass as well?" An embarrassed look crossed her face. "Oh, sorry. That didn't exactly come out the way I intended. You don't have to talk about it if you don't want to."

When a woman said that, what she really meant was, *I'm trying to politely tell you that you better talk to me.*

He was surprised how little they knew about each other. They had only shared a few meals together and a couple of walks in the gardens, during which time they mostly discussed their work—probably his fault. He had never been one for opening up to people.

"No, they haven't passed," he said with a heavy sigh. "But I'm dead to them all the same."

"If you don't want to talk about it, I understand."

Ayrion was about to continue when Howler walked over and interrupted. He had his heavy mallet up over his shoulder. "Thanks for the grub, sis. We needed it. Food's as scarce as a warm smile these days. Seems people are hoarding what they have. There've been rumors of a war with Cylmar." He glanced at Ayrion, looking for confirmation.

"Let's pray it doesn't come to that," Ayrion said, "but I would be lying to say the signs aren't there." He didn't want to give the boy any immediate information. Ayrion knew how fast news traveled in the tribes. However, a looming war with their neighbors was the very topic the High King had him and Commander Tolin discussing all night.

Her brother smiled. He had a handsome face, even if he preferred to wear a scowl around his underlings. "Best you were gone, sis, before you're missed." Sedgewick started toward the door, clearly wanting them to follow. "We wouldn't want that queen of yours waking up without you there to fluff her pillow." He smiled and opened the door. "Thanks again for the supplies. I just wish you'd quit taking so many risks. One of these days, you're gonna get caught or, worse, lead the patrollers here. You don't need to worry about us. We'll be fine."

Amarysia huffed. "You'd starve, you mean. Now come here." She engulfed him in big hug. There were a few stifled chuckles from the kids behind them, causing an embarrassed Sedgewick to pull away with a grunt.

Amarysia just smiled.

Her brother held out his hand to Ayrion with a roguish grin on his face. "Sorry about the warm welcome, Protector."

Ayrion shook the boy's hand. He had a firm grip. "Anytime. If there's anything you need, don't hesitate to ask. I know a little something about the streets myself."

"A little?" Sedge snickered. "There's not a street rat in Aramoor who doesn't know the name Death's Shadow. Thanks for sparing my life." He bowed low, showing Ayrion proper street deference.

Ayrion acknowledged the bow with a smile and a nod before walking out the front door, giving Amarysia a moment alone with her brother. Behind him, he could hear Sedge whispering to his sister.

"You didn't tell me that Death's Shadow was your suitor."

"I wouldn't exactly call him my suitor—"

"What would you call a guy who follows you all the way into Cheapside just to make sure you're safe? Does he do that for all the girls up there at the palace?"

Ayrion wanted to see the look on her face, but he forced himself to keep walking.

"Stop it, Sedge; he can hear you." Ayrion smiled at the playful tone in her voice. "I'll try to come by next week."

Once outside, Ayrion collected Amarysia's horse and waited for her to catch up before they walked up the street to where he had left his mount tied to the back of a brick depot.

"So, what would you call me?"

She glanced at him and lowered her brows. "What?"

"You said you wouldn't exactly call me your suitor. So . . . I was wondering: what would you call me?"

She nudged him in the ribs with her elbow. "I'd call you annoying." She tried hiding her smile. "Hey, you never finished your story about how you ended up in Aramoor."

"It's a long one—"

"It's a long way back to the palace."

He sighed. "I was banished."

Her smile faded. "Banished?"

"From my home."

"Your parents kicked you out?"

"No. I was banished by the Peltok. They're the heads of our clan."

"Weren't you just a kid? Why would your people banish you? That doesn't make any—"

"I killed someone."

Amarysia stopped.

"It was an accident—"

"Then why did they banish you?"

"Because of who it was that I killed."

She looked at him curiously, waiting for an answer.

"It was the clan chief's son. He challenged me in a fight for his advancement. And it didn't go well."

"So, your parents just let you go?"

"No. They pleaded with the Peltok to let me stay, but since the other members of the council were too afraid of Brim to challenge his decision, they let it stand—"

"Why didn't your parents go with you, then?"

Ayrion kicked at one of the loose cobbles. "Because I told them not to."

She looked at him like he was crazy.

"Our people are shunned wherever we go. Not that I can blame anyone, considering our profession, but there's nowhere my father or mother could have gone where they'd have found work. Without work, they'd starve."

"Family should stick together," she said, passing one final glance over her shoulder to where her brother and some of the other kids stood watching.

Ayrion pulled his horse along to catch up. He directed them to an adjoining street lined with three- and four-story homes that had remained unoccupied for the last decade or two. His horse stepped in one of the numerous potholes and whinnied, forcing Ayrion to stop.

Amarysia kept walking, not realizing he hadn't.

Ayrion leaned over and felt along the back of the horse's leg, making sure it hadn't injured itself.

There was a muffled shriek, and Ayrion looked up to see two men pulling Amarysia away from her horse, back toward a dark alley.

He ripped his blades from their sheaths and started forward. *This is about to be the worst day of these sellswords' lives.*

Chapter 37 | Ayrion

MOONLIGHT GLINTED OFF the dagger pressed against Amarysia's throat.

Ayrion slowed when he saw it.

"Toss the weapons," a voice said from the shadows of a nearby brick building.

Ayrion stopped, taking a moment to look at where it had come from, then back at the man holding Amarysia. There was no way he could reach her before the thug slit her throat.

He focused on his breathing and buried his emotions, the way his father had taught him when he was a boy. Lowering the tips of his swords, he waited.

Three more men stepped out of the shadows. This was no street tribe of orphaned children. These were Warren clan members. They directed him into the darker recesses of the alley. He didn't fight back, not with Amarysia's life on the line. One relieved Ayrion of his swords while the others attempted to thoroughly pat him down for any other weapons he might have hidden on his body.

Amarysia's hands were shaking, but her eyes remained strong.

"Don't worry," Ayrion said, trying to reassure her. "Everything will be fine, I promise." He couldn't understand why his magic hadn't alerted him. He should have sensed something was going to happen before they had been within five paces of that alley.

It didn't take long for his Upakan eyes to adjust. There were more of them than he had thought, possibly half a dozen, not including any that might be hiding farther down the alleyway.

No one said anything.

They gagged Amarysia, no doubt to keep her from alerting the city patrol, though the patrol never ventured this far south into Cheapside.

"What do you want?" Ayrion snapped. He was having trouble keeping his anger buried.

"Well, look what we have here. If it ain't the high and mighty Dark Warrior himself, come to pay us humble folks a little visit."

The voice was oddly familiar. It belonged to a tall, slender individual near the front of the group, with dark hair that fell halfway across the side of his face. He wore a brown leather coat, richly made but worn from use.

A couple of the men grabbed Ayrion's wrists. They pulled them behind his back and started to tie them off with a thick strip of leather.

"What do you fools think you're doing? Don't you know who this is? Use the manacles." The slender man walked a complete circle around Ayrion. Where had he seen him before?

The cold iron clamped shut around Ayrion's wrists. He jerked to test their strength, but they didn't budge.

"Bring them!" the slender man called, before doing an about-face and marching off in the opposite direction.

They shoved Ayrion deeper into the darkness. He twisted his head and caught a quick glimpse of Amarysia being moved in the same direction. Back on the main road, their horses were being led away. He was thankful he hadn't taken the time to saddle Shade.

Ayrion was familiar with these streets, so when his captors turned south, he knew where they were being taken—the Warrens.

The Warrens was located within the ancient ruins of what was Aramoor's original founding. It was a labyrinth of dark alleyways, abandoned warehouses, dilapidated buildings, and forgotten people. Even the city patrol, comprised mostly of former Elondrian lancers, had enough sense to steer clear of the Warrens.

Ayrion had only ever set foot in the place a few times in his life, and none of those occasions had left him with pleasant memories. He feared for Amarysia. The farther they walked, the less likely they were to make it back out.

Every city had its poor, whether by choice or circumstance. The larger the city, the larger the collection of those underprivileged. In a city the size of Aramoor, the population of unfortunates was considerable. Where there were men and women of low standing, there were always those willing to prey or profit on their situation.

If the royal palace was the heart of Aramoor, then the Warrens was its lower gut.

There was, however, a certain sort of freedom in living on the streets. Not having to worry about responsibilities, doing whatever you wanted, when you wanted. Having lived in both worlds, however, Ayrion had to admit he'd rather take on a hard day's labor if it meant not wondering where his next bed and meal would be coming from.

Ayrion's view of the streets and those living there was unlike that of the rest of those he associated with in the palace. Many, like him, had their livelihoods stripped away and ended up there by no choice of their own. However, there were plenty whose lives as vagabonds had been by choice—those who had no desire for an honest day's work; those who sought their possessions through more unsavory means.

On the streets, there was a different set of rules. Life was far more dangerous. Property belonged only to those strong enough to hold on to it. It was a harsh life but one with which Ayrion was still very familiar.

They came to a halt outside a metal door to what appeared to be a simple stone outhouse, at least from the exterior. Ayrion knew all too well where this led. He curled his hands and quietly worked his wrists back and forth in the metal cuffs. He had hoped to dig deep enough to draw blood and slip them, but the manacles were just too tight.

The lanky man in front waited for one of his men to throw back the latch and open the door. After grabbing a torch off one of the inner walls, the man turned and winked at Ayrion, then stepped inside. *What was that about?* he wondered, still unable to place the man.

One by one, the men in front entered the doorway and disappeared, leaving only himself and Amarysia along with their escorts.

Ayrion stepped inside. Instead of finding a rancid set of privies, there was a hidden circular stairwell leading down. A firm push from behind and he started forward. Behind him, Amarysia was also bundled through the entrance. The knife was no longer at her throat, but the man holding it kept her close as she followed them down.

The light from the torches reflected off the moisture seeping from the walls. The air was strong with the scent of burnt tar but free from the sharp odor of unwashed bodies and emptied chamber pots that clung to the streets above. For that, at least, Ayrion was thankful.

They descended, their muffled steps echoing off the stone encasement. No one spoke. Apart from the occasional grunt, their steps were the only sound to be heard. The stairwell finally opened into a small antechamber with a circular iron door at the far end. The front of the door was embossed with intersecting lines, similar to a cartographer's charting of city streets. Ayrion knew it to be a map of the underground tunnels within the Warrens.

Two men stood guard on either side of the entrance. They took a moment to look Ayrion over, no doubt measuring how much of a threat he posed. Their evaluation didn't last long. Ayrion tried not to look disappointed as Amarysia stepped off the landing behind him, drawing the guards' eyes.

The tall, lanky man started for the door, and both guards drew their swords. Ayrion gawked at the size of their falchions, each twice the width of a normal blade. They looked more like what he imagined troll cleavers would— if there were such things as trolls. One of the sentries pointed his blade at the dark-haired man.

"Password."

The skinny man crossed his arms and tapped his foot repeatedly on the floor. "You're kidding."

Neither guard budged.

"We just came through here, dimwits."

Still no movement.

The lanky man turned and looked at Ayrion. "You would think as long as I've lived here, these two nincompoops would have the good manners to recognize my face and let me through." He took a moment to glare at each guard in turn. "Oh, very well," he groused before straightening his shoulders and clearing his throat.

"When hope is all but lost,
And light has turned to dark.
There will a sign be given,
The rising of the marked."

Ayrion recognized the passage as a children's rhyme. His own parents had quoted it at one time or another. How odd that it would be used here, in the middle of one of the deadliest places in Aldor.

The spokesman combed an impatient hand through his hair and huffed, clearly embarrassed at having to recite a silly children's rhyme.

The guards slid their weapons back into their sheaths. One grabbed a lever connected to the outer edge of the door and flipped it back. There was a loud metallic *click* as the locking mechanism released.

Ayrion felt a twinge of dread as the rusted-out piece of metal opened. The Warren Underground was not known for mercy. They had their own set of laws, carried out by tribunal, where the heads of the clans would meet to exact their own form of justice.

Ayrion couldn't imagine what the clans would possibly want with him. Sure, he was the High King's protector, but what did that have to do with the Warrens?

Over his shoulder, he could see that Amarysia was watching him. He was proud of the way she held herself, still not showing fear. Ayrion cast a quick glance to her left at the man holding Ayrion's swords. He wanted to keep him in sight at all times. He knew the barbarism practiced in this place, and there was no way he was going to let them do to him or Amarysia what he'd seen done to others in the past. He'd kill Amarysia before he let these men lay their hands on her.

Each of the two guards placed a shoulder against the door and shoved. Light poured from the opening and bathed the small antechamber in a warm glow. Ayrion craned his neck to peek at what lay beyond.

Their tall, slender guide took a few steps into the next room and then bowed toward a raised platform with five seats. The platform had three tiers. Two high-backed chairs rested on opposite sides of the first rise, two more chairs sat atop the second rise, and a solitary throne-like seat, much larger and more grandiose than the others, sat at the top.

The Warren Tribunal was similar to the political structure of Aldor and its five kingdoms. Each clan had a single head or representative that held one of the ruling seats on the tribunal, and just as Aldor had a High King, there was a clan chieftain whose authority stood above the rest. The only way to negate a chieftain's order was by a unanimous vote from the remaining heads.

The downside to being chief, however, was that unlike the civility of a king's ordination, the clan's chieftain was chosen by the Right of Oktar. Any one of the clan heads could challenge their chieftain to combat for the throne. Some found the exercise barbaric, but when you were vying for the right to lead the least civilized members of society, all polite considerations were thrown out.

The five seats were unoccupied at present, which meant Ayrion wasn't being brought before the council. However, the assembly chamber, which was more like a throne room than a tribunal hall, was beginning to fill.

It had been a number of years since he had stepped foot in this place, but it hadn't changed all that much. Perhaps it was a bit more decorated than the last time he was there, but then again, the last time he was there, the room had been decorated with blood and viscera.

Arched pillars lined the outer perimeter, holding back the ground above them. Ayrion had always wondered by whose hands these underground lairs had been constructed. By the wear of the stone, they looked to have been created centuries before, when magic had been readily used.

Colorful tapestries rimmed the outer walls, in sharp contrast to the mellow grey of the stone room. The heavy woven material bore formal crests. Each one had its own color, emblem, and symbol. Gathered around each of those banners were men and women, adorned in garments of similar color and design. Although not apparently hostile, each group kept a wary eye on the others as they waited for whatever proceedings they had been summoned for.

The tension could be seen in the shuffling of feet, the stiffness of movements, the way eyes darted from one person to the next. You couldn't have found a more cutthroat-looking assembly in all of Aldor than the gathering in this room.

Each of the attendees was heavily armed. On the streets, whether in the Warrens or not, the ultimate code was *survival of the fittest*, and life balanced on three things: the size of your arms, the smarts in your head, and the supply of your luck. Of the three, more often than not, the last proved to be the most valuable.

Ayrion continued to struggle with the metal cuffs. The edges dug into his wrists but still didn't budge. He was going to have to figure out a way to defend himself with his hands quite literally tied behind his back.

Amarysia was moved forward and placed to his left. They had removed her gag.

Angling away from the guard, Ayrion pressed his shoulder against hers. "Are you all right?" he asked.

"I'm fine." She glanced around the room. "What do you think they want?"

"I wish I knew."

Along with the fear that something might happen to Amarysia, he had to contend with the embarrassment that he had been taken without so much as a fight. Once more, he was brought back to the question of why his magic hadn't worked. He could only think of one other time in his life when that had happened, back when he was living on the streets with—

Ayrion's eyes widened. His head shot up as he looked around for their lanky captor. *Surely, that isn't*— Their guide's back was to him as he talked to a group of angry-looking clansmen near the front. But then he turned to point at Ayrion. When he did, recognition set in.

Po? At least he thought it was. That small, chubby boy that used to follow him around everywhere he went, emulating everything he did, was now this tall, lean man who held some kind of weight within the Warren clans. *How did that happen?*

There had always been something about Po, a hidden gift, one that few knew existed. Po had the ability to negate the magic of others. Ayrion had always found it unsettling but figured it was what made Po such a valuable asset to have around during negotiations. There was always a level playing field whenever he was there.

"Bring them," the grown-up Po said as he motioned for the men guarding Ayrion and Amarysia to follow. They entered a tunnel at the back that had been hidden by one of the tapestries. Each of the other banners held similar tunnels behind them, leading back to that clan's respective residence.

Pulling the heavy material aside, Po waited for the others to pass. "She wants to see them," was all he said before turning around and marching down the dark corridor.

Ayrion decided to put his theory to the test.

"Po?"

The man's shoulders clenched. "So, you finally figured it out, huh?"

"Well, give me some credit; the last time I saw you, you were about waist high and three times as wide."

"Amazing what a little time and a life on the streets can accomplish." There was a clear undertone of disdain stemming from his words.

"Hey, it wasn't my choice for—"

"No!" Po spat, turning completely around to look Ayrion in the eyes. "It was your choice!"

"I haven't changed, Po."

"Hah!"

They came to a stop outside a wooden door marked by a shield with a bright red crest above the latch.

"Don't pretend like you know me, Ayrion, Guardian Protector of the High King," Po hissed, his words like daggers in Ayrion's chest.

Po knocked on the shield.

"Enter," said a muffled voice from the other side.

Po slid the door open. He handed his torch to one of the guards waiting in the hallway, and Ayrion and Amarysia followed him in. The room was larger than Ayrion had expected, with an almost royal feel to it. Expensive furnishings were strewn haphazardly around the space. Large swaths of satin, silk, and velvet in reds and golds draped every inch of the room.

Thick furs lined the floor in front of the hearth, where a fire was busy snapping and popping as the smoke meandered its way up the flue. How the engineers had managed to forge out a chimney so far underground was truly amazing. Oddly enough, the room carried a strong scent of burnt pine and cinnamon, not something Ayrion would have expected to find in the Warrens, but oddly familiar.

Ayrion scanned the room. Nothing about the place gave the impression of a meeting hall. It felt more like someone's personal chambers. Mounds of soft pillows lined sections of the outer wall. A hefty four-poster bed sat near the back, covered in fur. There were no lit candles, no lamps, no torches of any kind—just simple firelight. It gave the impression of a campfire where friends would gather and talk of times long past. Only now, Ayrion wasn't sure if talking was what his former friend had in mind.

"What's going on, Po?" Ayrion asked. "Why have you brought us here?"

"He hasn't changed much, has he?" a voice said from somewhere in the back behind one of the tapestries. "Always looking for answers."

Ayrion's arms prickled as he recognized its tone. It was deeper, fuller, more seductive, but somehow still the same. "Kira?"

Chapter 38 | Ayrion

A SLENDER WOMAN PUSHED aside one of the crimson draperies and stepped into the firelight. "I would recognize those grey eyes of yours anywhere, Ayri," Kira said, unashamedly batting her long lashes at him. Her deep hazel eyes reflected the light from the hearth.

"You know her?" Amarysia asked, leaning in so as not to be heard.

Ayrion nodded. "A long time ago."

Kira had grown into quite the woman. She wore fitted brown leather pants and a white laced tunic, but it wasn't her tight trousers and top that grabbed his attention. It was her long overcoat, seemingly an exact replica of his, though hers was a deep red.

Ayrion tried to rein in the mixed emotions at seeing Kira again. He remembered the first time he had seen her. It had been the day he'd first set foot in Aramoor as a thirteen-year-old boy, the day she had beaten him unconscious and stolen the clothes off his back. He had thought her pretty then. She was beautiful now.

Kira signaled the guards to leave. One of the men handed Ayrion's swords to Po before shutting the door. Kira circled them while Po moved off to one side of the hearth and poured himself half a glass of wine, which he nursed while studying Ayrion's blades.

"I've always wondered what these looked like up close," Po said. "Amazing work. Who made them?"

"A smith in Rhowynn, I am told," Ayrion said, watching the oil from Kira's leathers glisten in the light of the fire as she worked her way around him. "It's been a long time, Kira. You going to say something or just dizzy us with your prowling?"

Kira finally stopped and turned to Po. "Why are there two people here? I told you to get Ayri. Was there a sale? Kidnap one and get a free hussy for your troubles?"

Amarysia huffed.

Po swished his wine. "He was right where you said, Red. He just wasn't alone."

"How could you have possibly known where I would be?" Ayrion asked. "I hadn't even planned on leaving the palace this evening."

"We didn't. I've had people watching at all hours over the last two days, waiting for you to come out. It just happened to be tonight." Kira studied Amarysia. "So, who's this pretty little strumpet, huh?" She flicked a lock of Amarysia's hair with her finger. "I never imagined you wanting a blonde, Ayri. Your taste always ran a little . . . darker." She swung her own long raven hair around the front of her shoulder and ran a hand through the waves, giving Ayrion a sultry look.

"Like a fine wine, a man's taste betters with age," Amarysia said.

Kira sneered. Ayrion was afraid she might try to go after Amarysia, but instead, she surprised him by walking over, wrapping her arms around his neck, and giving him a hard, lingering kiss.

Ayrion froze. Her lips reminded him of desires he had thought long buried and forgotten. Kira stepped back and traced her tongue across her upper lip, giving Amarysia a victorious smirk.

Ayrion realized his mouth was hanging open and quickly shut it. He glanced at Amarysia, not knowing what to say, but her eyes were locked on Kira, evenly meeting her gaze.

"So—" His voice sounded raspy, so he cleared his throat before trying again. "Why am I here, Kira?" he asked, hoping to ease the awkward tension.

"Red," Kira said. "Only my friends call me Kira."

"I am your friend."

Kira's eyes darkened. "Perhaps, but that was many years ago."

Ayrion remained silent. She was right. He had been the one to leave. But when the king had offered him a position in the palace, how could he refuse? "Things change," he said. "Just look at you—clan chieftain. How does something like that happen, anyway?"

"Things didn't go so well for the rest of us after you left. We had to do what we could to survive."

Po grunted in agreement.

"Ruthlessness is a commodity held in high regard around here. It seems I have a knack for it." She smiled, sending cold chills crawling up his spine.

"More than a knack, I'd say," Po added, lifting his goblet in salute before downing the rest of its contents.

Ayrion was speechless. Kira had always been tough, but it was as though he were looking at two complete strangers. His face must have betrayed his thoughts, for Kira's eyes narrowed. She took two steps forward and punched him in the jaw. His head whipped to the right and he stumbled backward, nearly going to his knees.

"Don't you dare look at me with those self-righteous eyes of yours!" she roared. "I'm not ashamed of who I am or what I've done. I'm Chieftain of the Warrens! I didn't need you after all. You think you're better than us because you rub shoulders with the king? Well, you're not!" Her entire body trembled with anger.

"You're right, Kira," he said, licking the blood from his mouth. He was tempted to spit it across her white rug but thought better of it. "I don't know what you've been through. I'm sure I can't imagine. Probably don't want to. If there was a way I could go back and do it over, I would. You, Po, Reevie, and Sapphire were as close to me as any family."

Kira stiffened, and she turned her back on him. "Curse you, Ayrion. You always did have a slick tongue in that beautiful mouth of yours."

Ayrion glanced at Amarysia out of the corner of his eye. She held herself straight, not allowing emotion to show on her face.

"How're Reevie and the others?" Ayrion asked, hoping to change the subject. "Still at the orphanage?"

Kira accepted a glass of wine from Po and turned to face him. "That's why you're here," she said, her eyes weighing him, as if she was trying to decide whether or not bringing him here had been the right decision.

"What's wrong?"

She drained her glass then set it on top of a nearby cabinet. "He's missing."

Ayrion's chest tightened. It was Reevie who had shown him how to survive on the streets as a kid. His first true friend.

"What do you mean, *he's missing*?"

Kira looked at Po. "Now, I know I'm not as proper as little miss prim here, but I thought I was pretty clear in what I said. Do I need to spell it out for you? He . . . is . . . missing," she said, punctuating each word. "No longer amongst us. Completely unreachable. Vanished from sight and—"

"All right, I get the picture. What happened? How long has he been missing? How's Sapphire?"

"She's fine," Kira said. "At least, the last time I checked."

"Then what happened? Was he taken by a rival clan?"

"No," Po said, wiping his mouth with his sleeve. "Well, we're not sure. He disappeared around the same time that the vanishings started."

"Vanishings?"

Kira paced across the room, her face cut in shadow. "The last anyone saw of him was four nights ago near the upper docks between Bayside and King's Way West. He was looking for a group of street kids that had gone missing the night before. You know how sentimental Reevie is when it comes to street rats."

Ayrion could almost picture it: Reevie with his crippled leg, limping through the streets, gathering displaced children where he could.

Kira paced in front of her sofa.

"I know that look, Kira," Ayrion said. "You have your suspicions. What aren't you telling me?"

Dropping onto the cushions, Kira lounged across the sofa, letting one of her legs dangle from the end. "There's been talk about the disappearances, but no one knows what happens to them, at least not for sure. We've heard rumors of masked men roaming the streets at night and rounding up homeless from some of the outer districts, mainly the ones closest to the water."

"So, you think whoever is taking these people took Reevie?"

Kira nodded. "Possibly."

"What do you need from me? This is the Warrens we're talking about. It's not like I can just walk around and interrogate people. I wouldn't last long enough for Po there to finish his drink."

"He's got that right, Red."

Kira flipped around to plant her feet on the rug in front of her. "I don't need you here in the Warrens. I need you talking to the king. These are his citizens, after all. They're his responsibility."

Ayrion almost laughed. "Are they? The clans have made it pretty clear that short of bringing an army down here, no one is going to enforce rule over the Warrens. You pride yourselves on living outside the law, doing whatever you want, regardless of how it affects everyone else. And yet now, when you need something, you kidnap me at knifepoint and insist that it's somehow my responsibility? I am not going to bow to your whim just because you've managed to crawl your way to the top of the food chain down here."

Kira was on her feet before Ayrion could bat an eye, a knife appearing from one of her sleeves. "I'm not ashamed of what I've had to do to survive! I did what was needed. Now look at me." She gestured to her lush living quarters, then pointed the dagger at him. "Either you'll swear right here to go to the king, or you and your hussy will never leave the Warrens again."

Ayrion pulled down on the manacles, nearly forcing his shoulder joints out. She was leaving him no option. "You'll find I'm not so easy to push, Kira. Unlike the rest of those you surround yourself with, a wag from your skinny tail is hardly going to tempt me to do anything."

She flew at him.

Amarysia shrieked.

Ayrion dropped to the ground, tucking his legs through the manacles and bringing his arms back out to the front. He rolled backward and hopped to his feet about the time she struck.

She lunged for his chest. He dodged, barely, and used the manacles to block her thrust and grab her arm at the same time. She couldn't pull away. She reared back to punch him with her free hand, but he dropped to the floor, pulling her with him. With one good kick, he sent her up over his head.

Kira screamed as her momentum carried her completely over Ayrion, where she landed with a heavy thump across one of her bearskin rugs behind him. The impact knocked the breath from her lungs, and her knife clattered to a stop near the door.

Ayrion was on top of her before she had time to turn over.

Po dropped his glass in shock, the remainder of his drink spilling across the front of his tunic as he reached for the closest available weapon—one of Ayrion's blades.

"Touch it and you lose your chief," Ayrion said, wrapping his manacles around Kira's neck.

Po froze.

"He's bluffing, you idiot!" she screeched.

"You want to test that theory?"

Po didn't move.

"Amarysia, will you be so good as to get Kira's knife for me, please?"

It took a bit of maneuvering, with her arms still tied behind her back, but Amarysia managed to retrieve the dagger and give it to him.

Ayrion stood, pulling a reluctant Kira up with him. He kept the dagger close to her throat. "Now for the keys, Po." Ayrion moved behind Kira in order to keep her between Po and himself.

"You had better kill me," Kira threatened, "because if I ever get out of here, I'm coming after you."

Ayrion laughed and whispered in her ear, "Then I guess it will feel like old times, won't it?"

Po laid the sword back against the hearth and reluctantly started forward.

"That's close enough," Ayrion said when Po got within a couple of steps. "Now toss Kira the keys." Po obeyed. Ayrion tightened his grip around Kira's neck, gently prodding her to unlock the cuffs. As soon as the metal bracelets hit the ground, he walked her back a few steps and away from Po.

"Now what?" Kira asked.

"Now I want you to uncuff Amarysia."

Ayrion took the loose manacles that had been around Amarysia's wrists and placed them on Kira's.

"Po, do me a favor and walk over to Kira's bed, will you please?"

"Well, seeing as how you asked me so nice and all," he grumbled before slowly making his way over to the left side of her large overstuffed mattress.

"Now turn down the sheets."

"What?"

"You heard me: turn down the sheets."

Kira squirmed at the sight of Po dressing down her bedding.

"All right, that's good. Now let's get you tucked in for the night, shall we?"

"What?"

"Am I stuttering? Get in her bed."

"Don't you dare get in my bed, you dirty lummox!"

Po stopped with one leg halfway under what looked like silk coverings.

Ayrion pressed the knife a little tighter against Kira's neck, putting a temporary halt to her tongue. Tapping his foot, he nodded for Po to finish climbing in.

"Wonderful," Ayrion said. "Now, I don't know what kind of uncivilized behavior you're used to down here, but somehow, I doubt you sleep fully clothed."

Po's eyes widened.

"That's right. Take them off."

"But, I'll be . . . naked."

"Nothing gets by you, does it?"

"You get naked in my sheets and I'll skin you alive," Kira hissed, "right after I cut you somewhere very unpleasant."

"Now, now, Kira. What kind of way is that to talk to poor old Po?"

Amarysia giggled but quickly stifled it when Kira glanced her way.

Everyone watched while Po stripped, careful to keep the blankets and furs high enough to stave off any embarrassment.

"Come on, Ayri, is this really necessary?" Po tossed out the last of his undergarments and tucked the sheets under his arms. "It's a bit chilly in here."

"Why did you have him do that?" Amarysia asked.

"To keep him otherwise occupied. Grab his clothes. We're going to take them with us." Ayrion had another reason for keeping Po locked up in her room: namely, he needed to keep Po's magic-negating abilities as far away from him as possible. He was going to need every edge he could find if he hoped to get them out of there alive.

"Ayri, have a heart. You wouldn't walk off and leave me here in nothing but my skin, would you?"

"They'll be returned in good order, I promise. If not, I'll get you a new set." Amarysia walked over and grabbed Po's clothing, holding them out for Ayrion to inspect. "Phew." Ayrion wrinkled his nose. "You could use a new outfit anyway."

Pulling Kira over to the fireplace, Ayrion retrieved his swords. He replaced one of them in its sheath on his back and kept the other out to ensure Kira's cooperation. He handed Kira's dagger to Amarysia.

"This is what's going to happen. We are going to walk out of here the same way we came in, except this time it will be Kira who kindly volunteers to lead us out instead of Po. After her little threat of us never leaving here again, I don't plan on taking any chances."

Ayrion could almost hear Kira's teeth grinding as he raised the blade to her throat. "Let's just hope your men in the hall care about your well-being."

He pointed Kira toward the door and the waiting guards.

"Move."

Chapter 39 | Ayrion

AYRION KEPT HIS SWORD to Kira's throat as they approached the door.

He knocked once and then glanced back at the bed. "Po, it really was good to see you again. Hopefully next time it will be under . . . better circumstances."

Po grimaced.

Kira's door opened, and when the guards in the hallway saw their chief with a blade to her throat, they quickly drew their weapons.

"Tell them to drop their swords and take off their boots."

Kira tightened her shoulders. "Do as he says."

Ayrion had them toss their boots inside her room. "Now I want you to drop your trousers."

No one moved.

"Yes, you heard me. Pull off your pants."

"Do you have some kind of aversion to clothes?" Kira asked. "I don't remember you being so exciting when we were younger." She rubbed her body up against his. "You want mine as well?"

Ayrion tightened his grip on her arm. "Just tell them."

Kira nodded for them to obey.

Once her guards had undressed down to their smallclothes, they escorted Ayrion, Kira, and Amarysia back to the main room.

There was an abrupt outburst of laughter as the parade of half-naked men sauntered into the great hall. The laughter died when Kira stepped through at the edge of a blade. Suddenly, everyone was on their feet with weapons drawn.

"What's the meaning of this?" one of the men at the front demanded. By his colorful dress and demeanor, he appeared to be one of the clan heads.

This was an all-or-nothing situation. Either they would respect Kira's position as chief and let them pass, or they wouldn't, and this would get real ugly real fast. Ayrion was a match for anyone in the room, but with this many hardened cutthroats, there was no chance in Aran'gal he could fight his way out and manage to keep Amarysia alive.

"I would think the meaning should be fairly obvious," he said.

Amarysia grabbed his shoulder and whispered in his ear, "I don't think it wise to poke a hornet's nest while we're standing in the middle of it."

Ayrion simply smiled. He needed to at least appear as though he knew what he was doing. "But for those of you who are incapable of comprehending the meaning of my sword to your chief's neck, I will try to speak slowly. I am planning to walk out of here the same way I came in—unharmed." Ayrion scanned the room. He slid his blade a little higher on her neck, forcing Kira's head up.

"Do as he says!" she spat. Even being used as a shield, Kira still maintained the illusion of control. In her position, she couldn't afford to lose it.

The next few steps were going to determine whether or not they made it out alive. Ayrion and the two women slowly started across the room, heading for the circular iron door on the other side. Amarysia pressed as close as she could while they walked through the sea of angry, well-armed men and women. So far, so good. Ayrion continued to scan the faces of those they passed, watching for the first sign of aggression. They needed to get to the other side before the clans decided Kira wasn't worth it and killed them all.

They were nearly there.

"I demand the Right of Oktar!" a voice rang out near the platform.

Ayrion stopped. They were close, but not close enough to fight the rest of the way through.

"How dare you challenge me like this, Kerson!" Kira shouted, not caring one whit about Ayrion's blade at her throat.

Kerson? Ayrion had heard that name before. He was the older brother to the former chief of Hurricane, the street tribe Ayrion had joined as a child when he'd first come to Aramoor. Kerson had turned the tribe over to his younger brother Spats before Ayrion became a member.

Kerson pushed his way through the crowd, but he didn't have to push hard. The others were quick to get out of his way. Those who didn't move fast enough got thrown. He wore no shirt under his vest. And for good reason. His chest was as big as an oak, and his arms were the size of a ship's masts. He carried a battle-axe that was nearly half the size of Ayrion.

Taking one look at the brute, Ayrion knew there was no way he could afford to let Kira fight him. As much grief as she gave him, Kira was still his friend, and he didn't want to see her killed. More importantly, if she lost, they were all as good as dead. He had to think of something fast.

"Since she is under my . . . well, my care," Ayrion said, "*I* will accept that challenge for her by proxy."

Kerson stopped about ten paces away. "Huh?" The fierce mammoth cocked his head. He pushed a wad of scruffy hair out of his eyes, revealing a number of nasty scars across the top of his forehead and face. He had clearly seen the end of a knife one too many times.

Ayrion sighed. "For pity's sake. I will be her substitute. No wonder you are living underground. With people like this"—he pointed at Kerson—"wanting to be your leader, I'd be embarrassed to show my face, too." Ayrion hoped he could goad the big man into accepting.

Kira kicked him in the shin. "What are you doing, you idiot?" she muttered under her breath. "You're going to get us all killed. Shut your mouth."

Ayrion didn't respond. His eyes were on Kerson, waiting for an agreement. In the Warrens, a show of force was the only thing they respected, and Warren laws and traditions were held in high regard. There was no getting out of this.

"Well, do we have an accord?" Ayrion smirked. "That means *deal*, by the way."

Kerson looked Ayrion over and smiled. "If you want to die so badly," he said with a gruff, booming voice, "then I'll be more than happy to oblige. That means . . . *yes*."

Ayrion shifted position so Amarysia could move in behind Kira and maintain the blade at Kira's throat.

The clan members backed out of the way, giving the two fighters an open area in the center of the chamber.

Ayrion tied his hair back with a strip of cloth from his jacket pocket, then stepped into the makeshift ring, leaving the two women standing at the side. Kerson waited at the center with an eager expression.

An elderly man with a large ceremonial staff stepped from the crowd and joined them in the middle. "Let it be observed that we have a challenge for the right of chief. Anyone who interferes will forfeit their life in turn. This challenge, once invoked, cannot be undone. Are you both in agreement?"

"Wait. Are we saying that if he wins, then he becomes the new chief?" Kerson asked.

"No," the old man said. "He is fighting by proxy. He is fighting on her behalf, so whatever the outcome, it will ultimately rest on her shoulders."

"Good. Then I'll squash him like a bloodworm."

The old man looked at Ayrion, who simply nodded.

"Very well. Under the Articles of the Clans and the agreement of both parties, I declare this challenge initiated." The old man proved quite spry for his age as he sprinted back into the awaiting crowd and away from the two fighters.

Kerson unhooked his battle-axe from his side. Ayrion still couldn't get over the size of it. The handle alone was as thick as some small trees.

"Let's get this over with so I can enjoy the spoils," Kerson said, passing a lustful gaze in the women's direction.

"You just try it, Kerson!" Kira hissed from the side. "And I'll cut off your testicles and feed them to you!"

Ayrion left both his blades in their sheaths. "Are you going to talk me to death or are we going to lock steel?" he asked.

Kerson roared and swung his huge axe for Ayrion's head, but instead of ripping flesh, snapping bones, and blood soaking the crowd, his blade hit nothing but air as Ayrion ducked and spun underneath, coming out at his side. With the way Kerson was telegraphing his moves, Ayrion had no need of magic.

Kerson swung again. He was fast. His axe headed straight for the top of Ayrion's scalp as if wanting to make good on his promise of cutting Ayrion clean in two.

Ayrion sidestepped, and the axe flew by, just missing his left shoulder.

Kerson cursed and kicked, but Ayrion directed his foot away with a simple block. Kerson struck again and again, moving from one side of the ring to the other. Every time he started to get close to the edge, the ring moved as those watching jumped back to keep from being hit themselves.

"Stand still and face me like a man!" Kerson shouted.

"Fine," Ayrion said from the far side of the ring. "I promise I won't move from this spot."

"Ayrion, what are you doing?" Amarysia shouted on his left.

Kerson spun his axe in his hands as the crowd cheered him on, hungry for the kill. Seeing the bloodlust in their eyes, Ayrion almost felt sorry for Kira. He wondered how she had gotten herself tangled up in this mess.

Ayrion closed his eyes and cleared his mind, as he'd done so many times before. With Po still locked in Kira's chambers, his magic was there for the taking. He could feel Kerson's movements, hear the big man's anxious breath. The vision engulfed him.

He opened his eyes, and Kerson charged.

Stopping him would have been like stopping a boulder plummeting down the side of a mountain. Ayrion braced himself as Kerson swung with all his might.

Ayrion ducked to the left just in time to keep the axe from burying itself inside his chest. He kicked Kerson's legs out from under him with a quick snap, sending the big man tumbling headfirst into the crowd. It happened so fast, most of the onlookers were unable to dive out of the way before Kerson's thick frame slammed into them, crushing them like dried cornstalks.

Ayrion moved back toward the middle and drew one of his swords. It was time to end this.

Kerson was good and mad now. The big clansman had been belittled in front of his peers. Foul language spewed from his mouth as he threw people out of the way.

Ayrion could hear the enormous axe blade scraping the stone tiles as Kerson retrieved it from where it had fallen.

Clearly impatient to regain his lost pride, Kerson attacked. He leveled his axe and aimed for Ayrion's midriff as he ran back into the ring.

Ayrion jumped backward, letting it fly clear. He planted his feet as Kerson came again, both hands wrapped around the axe's handle, all his strength behind the swing. There was enough power there to have cut one of the stone pillars in two. Ayrion didn't bother moving. Instead, he lashed out with his blade. One swift cut and the black steel sliced straight through the handle. The axe head flew over the crowd and impaled one of the beams on the far side of the room with a loud *crack*.

Kerson looked confused as he stared at the missing head of his axe. Without warning, he pulled a dagger and ran in the opposite direction.

It took Ayrion a split second to realize what Kerson was doing, but by then, he was already too far ahead. Ayrion raced after him nonetheless.

Amarysia shrieked when she saw him coming, and Kira nearly cut her own neck trying to jump out of the way.

Kerson lunged, just missing Kira by a hand's breadth and burying his dagger in the person standing behind her. He yanked the bloody knife and spun around, but not before Ayrion hit him feet first in the right knee. There was a loud *snap*, followed by an immediate cry as Kerson dropped face-first to the ground.

Ayrion rolled to his feet and lifted his blade to put a quick end to him.

"Stop!" Kira shouted, picking herself up from where she had landed a few feet away while getting clear of Kerson's knife. "I demand the Right of Life."

The room quieted.

Kira, with her hands still bound behind her, moved alongside Ayrion. She looked down at the writhing form of Kerson.

"Do you accept my offer of life?"

This is unexpected, Ayrion thought. Or was it? Kira was using him the same way he was using her. She had always had a knack for taking a bad situation and turning it around in her favor. Apparently, nothing had changed.

Ayrion had only ever seen a Right of Life rejected once before. If an enemy's life was spared in fair combat, they were given the choice of either pledging the remainder of it to the victor or taking a swift death. Anyone who broke such a vow was assured a very long and painful death by the rest of the clans as an example to discourage others from following in the same steps.

Kerson slowly scanned the surrounding faces of the clansmen and clanswomen as they all waited to see what he would do. His teeth were bared as he gritted them against the pain. He took a moment to glare up at Ayrion and the blade hovering just above his neck. Then he turned to Kira and nodded once.

"I accept."

"Good," Kira said with a triumphant smile as she marched back to where Amarysia was waiting behind them. "I believe it's time we were going, hussy."

Ayrion sighed. Only Kira could stand there with her arms bound behind her back and still throw out orders like nothing was wrong.

It seemed almost silly to continue the charade of using their chief as a hostage, but as long as they were being let through, Ayrion figured it best to just keep going.

The crowd parted in silence as the three of them crossed the room toward the heavy iron door. Those watching were quick to give Ayrion a wide berth. No one wanted to get too close to his blade. Whispers filled the chamber behind them as they passed through the door and into the small anteroom outside.

"Aren't they going to follow us?" Amarysia asked, glancing behind her every few feet.

"Not hardly," Kira said with a grunt. "They're a pretty self-serving bunch. And it wouldn't serve them to go running up against Ayri's blades after that performance." She looked at Ayrion and smiled. "It seems luck favors me tonight. Not only did I get to spend some quality time with my favorite man in black, but he provided me with an exciting bit of entertainment, not to mention turning my biggest rival into my personal slave. You have certainly outdone yourself this time, Ayri."

Ayrion grunted.

The three made their way up the stairwell and back out onto the streets above. Under Kira's direction, they moved through the old city like ghosts floating on an evening wind. It didn't take as long getting out of the Warrens as it had to enter. Ayrion figured Kira must have taken them down a more direct path.

"Now what?" Kira asked as they crossed Mora, the street separating the Warrens from the rest of Aramoor.

"Now, I untie you and let you go."

Her eyes softened. "Just like that?"

"Just like that."

"You aren't going to arrest me or something?"

Ayrion sighed. "Kira, believe it or not, it was actually nice to see you—"

"What about Reevie? I need your help to find him—"

"See, now, was that really so difficult? Next time, Kira, try asking. It'll save us all a headache."

"But where's the fun in that?" she said with a wink.

Ayrion sighed. "I promise I'll do whatever I can to help find him and those responsible for these disappearances."

She took a moment to stare into his eyes. "I believe you," she said. She removed a gold signet ring from her finger and held it out to him.

"What's this?" he asked, turning it over. The ring bore a unique crest. It reminded Ayrion of a lion with wings.

"That ring will grant you safe passage through the Warrens. No one would dare harm anyone wearing it." She started to say something more but opted for a not-so-subtle kiss instead.

Ayrion could feel himself blushing for the second time that evening. His heart was beating so fast, he could almost hear it. He did hear Amarysia cough.

Kira released her grip and took a step back. "Keep him out of trouble, will ya?" she said to Amarysia, grinning.

Before Amarysia could respond, the clan chieftain was dashing off down the street. They watched as the lithe woman in her dark-red leather coat bounded toward the nearest alleyway and vanished into the night.

Amarysia's fingers slid into his, pulling his attention away from the vacant street.

"How do plan on looking for your friend?" she asked.

"I'll start by talking to the king."

"I can talk to the queen if you want."

He nodded. "That would be a good idea. I'm sorry you were caught in the middle of this."

"I wouldn't have been if you hadn't caught me sneaking food and blankets out of the palace. You coming to protect me was what landed us both in this." She smiled. "It seems to have worked out for the best, though. Don't you think?"

She caught him looking back toward the empty street and tugged on his hand. He could see the worry in her eyes, and he doubted it had anything to do with the mysterious kidnappings.

Chapter 40 | Valtor

ALTOR STRUMMED HIS fingers on the arm of the green-striped sofa as he and Dakaran waited for Ambassador Belkor to arrive. Valtor had chosen one of the unfrequented reading rooms on the second floor of the library as a safe place to hold their meeting. It was public enough that the ambassador wouldn't feel trapped, yet private enough that they wouldn't be disturbed.

This particular reading cubby was called the Green Room, earning its name for the remarkable overuse of green paint. All shades of green, ranging from the very dark—almost black—of the trim around the doors and shelving to the light touches found in the curtain tassels and decorative designs sewn into the upholstery. It was quite overwhelming. It was also a good explanation for why the room was so rarely used.

Like all the other rooms, there was a heavy accent of gold. From the portrait frames over the mantel to the tapestries on the walls and candelabras on the table, everything had been trimmed in gold. Even the hearth had gold-leaf etching, an extravagance that Valtor cared nothing for. The room was also equipped with a long table for studying and a sitting area in front of the fire for casual reading.

"Are you sure we won't be overheard?" Dakaran asked, not for the first time.

"I told you," Valtor said, trying not to sound too impatient with the prince, "I've warded the room. No one outside these walls will hear a thing."

Dakaran studied the door as if trying to see the magic for himself as he continued pacing in front of the hearth. The steady blaze was just what Valtor needed to break the evening chill.

The prince's presence was a gamble, one that Valtor unfortunately needed to make. There wasn't much about the prince that Valtor trusted other than that Dakaran would always do what was best for Dakaran. It appeared that the prince's momentary moderation of drink after the battle had been just that—momentary. Once again, he clutched a half-filled goblet. Thankfully, he hadn't indulged to the point of incoherence.

Dakaran stopped his pacing and turned to speak but was interrupted when the door to the reading room opened.

"What's with all the secrecy?" Ambassador Belkor asked as he stepped inside and cautiously looked around. He left the door open, probably to make a quick exit in the event his summons had been a trap. Outside the Green Room, walls of books connected by gold circular staircases and overhead walkways that crisscrossed from one aisle to the next filled the enormous chamber. The rich rosewood shelving provided quite the contrast to the deep blue-and-gold coloring of the room.

"Tell your men to remain outside," Valtor said, coming to his feet.

"How did you . . ." Belkor studied Valtor a moment, then finally turned and walked back to the door. "Remain here unless I call you." Two men wearing Cylmaran colors stepped out from behind the doorway but remained where they were. Valtor wasn't about to tell him that once the door was shut, the ambassador's guards wouldn't hear him even if he were to shout at the top of his lungs.

Valtor could see the prince was about to and quickly shook his head to deter him.

Belkor shut the door and joined the others by the fire. "Your manservant had me traipsing through every back door and side stairwell in this place."

"We apologize for the theatrics, Ambassador," Dakaran said as he gestured to an empty seat on the settee across from his, "but we wanted to make sure you were not spotted by one of our illustrious High Guard. Little escapes their notice."

The ambassador took his seat, and Valtor did the same. Belkor looked from Dakaran to Valtor and back again. "I take it I'm not here to discuss the latest fashion in women's undergarments. So, let's get on with it."

"Fine," Dakaran said, "I'll get right to the point. Overlord Saryn needs an ally on the throne of Elondria. He won't find such an ally in my father."

"Oh?" Belkor sounded both amused and curious as he leaned back in his seat. "But I take it he will in you, Prince Dakaran?"

Dakaran took a deep breath and glanced at Valtor. This was one of those defining moments when a single word would change their destiny. Valtor pushed a little magic into the prince to strengthen his resolve. Dakaran turned back to the ambassador and nodded.

"Yes."

The ambassador's eyes swung from one face to the other. "Really? And what's to keep me from going straight to the king with this news?"

Valtor let his hand brush against the side of his staff where it rested against the arm of the settee. *That would be me sucking the air from your lungs,* he thought as he leaned back against the cushions, displaying a complete lack of concern. "Compensation, for starters."

Belkor raised a brow. "Go on."

"Cylmar is a poor kingdom," Dakaran said, "with little in the way of natural resources, and its people are starving. I could change that."

"Can you fill our land with timber, game, and crops?"

"No." Dakaran leaned forward. "But if Overlord Saryn will help me seize my father's throne, I can provide him with the mining rights to the Black Hills."

Belkor grunted. "As you stated, Cylmar is a poor kingdom. How do you propose we accomplish such a feat?" He chuckled. "Lead an all-out assault on Elondria?"

"Precisely."

Belkor's smile vanished. "Are you mad? Cylmar would have no hope of winning an open conflict with Elondria. We would be completely annihilated; then what would happen to your little plan?"

"No, you wouldn't. Unlike your overlord, my father feels it his duty to attend any major battle fought by Elondrian forces. It won't have to be a full-scale assault, just enough to draw my father in."

Belkor looked confused. "Then what?"

"Then we will take it from there."

Belkor glanced at Valtor, a wary look in his eye. "It is my duty to look out for my overlord's interests, and I can tell you now, the mining rights won't be enough for him to commit the lives of his men. He will require the Black Hills themselves."

Dakaran bolted upright, sloshing his drink across the sofa. "You can't be serious! I will not give away a piece of Elondria as a bargaining chip!"

"Wake up, boy. How did you think this was going to work? That we were going to send our armies over here to get slaughtered just so you could claim your daddy's crown? Then what, trust you'd be generous enough to let us cut some rocks out of your mountains in exchange?"

Valtor laid a hand on the prince's arm and let his magic seep in. It took more than usual to calm him. If he didn't get Dakaran under control, the prince was liable to ruin their best chance at getting Rhydan off the throne.

"Give us time to consider your proposal, Ambassador," Valtor said as Dakaran relaxed in his seat. "His Highness will give you his answer before you break for home."

"Then I suggest His Highness not dawdle," Belkor said as he stood. "I leave at first light."

Valtor rose. "Thank you for your time, Ambassador." He offered the man a bow. "We wish you a pleasant night's rest."

"One can only hope," Belkor grumbled as he headed for the door. He opened it and turned. "Until tomorrow, Your Highness." The ambassador gave the prince a weighted look then left the room.

Dakaran raised his glass toward the door in salute. "I thought that went rather well, apart from him demanding a piece of Elondria."

"The ambassador was only doing his job. Besides, he has a point. It will be Cylmar who has the most invested in this endeavor. It is their right to demand what they will. And, of course, yours to accept or deny it."

Dakaran frowned. "What do you advise, then?"

Valtor yawned. "I advise that you get some sleep."

Dakaran took another sip of his wine.

"Ultimately, it doesn't matter what you offer, Your Highness. Once we see this through, there will no longer be a Cylmar to worry about. We offer Overlord Saryn one hand in peace, so he doesn't notice the other stabbing him in the back."

Early the next morning, Valtor stood in the shadows of one of the second-floor balconies and watched as Belkor's small escort of armsmen readied themselves for the rough trip west. The ambassador had just settled onto his horse when a palace courier dashed across the courtyard toward him. The young boy held up a tri-folded parchment sealed with the prince's crest.

Belkor promptly tore open the wax and unfolded the letter. The ambassador's eyes scanned the short document. Valtor could see the corners of his mouth twitch upward as he read.

Chapter 41 | Lyessa

LYESSA STRUGGLED TO catch her breath as she turned to face her attacker.

Sweat trickled down the side of her face, droplets flying into the air with every swift move of her head. Thankfully, she'd thought to tie her hair back, otherwise it would have plastered to her face and blocked her view. Several cuts across her tunic were stained with blood. The wounds weren't deep, but they were adding up.

Senses alert, she circled the man. Even though she was tall for her age, he towered over her like a giant bent on devouring her whole. Instead of a giant's thick club, he wielded a wicked rapier. He was older, at least as old as her father. But he was strong.

He lunged.

Lyessa managed to dive out of the way just as the sharp steel flew past, missing her arm by inches. She rolled and let the forward motion help bring her back to her feet as she spun around to meet the next strike. Her arms felt too heavy to lift and her chest was on fire, but she pushed through it. She didn't know how much longer she could hold off his attack.

She made the mistake of looking into his eyes. They were hard and cold. He was committed, and that frightened her more than anything. She continued to circle. Her short sword hung loosely from her hand. She wasn't sure if she had the strength to heft it one last time, but she dug deep, drawing one last cold drop from her well of determination.

She watched and waited, struggling to read the movement of the muscles in his thick arms and bare chest. His head lowered slightly, warning of another strike. *Which direction?* she wondered.

His right shoulder tensed.

There. She braced herself, carrying her sword low, trying to give him a false sense of security, a belief that she was too exhausted to raise her blade to an appropriate height. If only he knew how close to the truth that really was.

He came at her again, his right arm swinging at an angle for her head.

She anticipated the move and deflected it. He swung again, and she countered. His moves were precise. Hers were floundering. She would never beat him with the sword. He was too fast, too experienced.

She waited for the next attack. She blocked twice, his sword coming a little closer to her body each time. She took a half step to the left, making him believe she was going for his right flank. Instead, she dove to the right, wrapped both legs around his, and swept his feet out from under him.

He hit the ground with a thud, and before he had time to roll over, she was on top of him with her blade against the back of his neck.

"I yield, I yield!" he said.

She removed her blade and struggled to her feet.

The big man beside her cautiously rose. He planted his sword tip down in the dirt and without warning, reached out and grabbed her.

"I'm proud of you," he said, engulfing her in his strong arms.

Lyessa closed her eyes, melting into the embrace. It was a wonderful feeling.

All around the courtyard, many of the servants and staff were clapping and cheering. No one clapped as hard as her father, though.

Darryk released her from his grip. "By the powers, girl, your old man couldn't have done better." She beamed at her instructor's words. He had trained her since she was old enough to hold a blade.

Her father strode across the open courtyard and wrapped his arm around her shoulders, pulling her tight. Lyessa laid her cheek against his chest, a favorite spot of hers since she was a little girl sitting in his lap.

"You make your father proud," he said. "Darryk is correct; I couldn't have done better myself." He lifted her chin and looked her in the eyes. "One day, you'll thank me for putting you through this. Sidara needs a strong leader."

"It already has one," she said, wrapping her arms around his back and squeezing.

"You know what I mean."

She raised her head. "Doesn't mean I want to hear it."

"Perhaps not, but it's true."

"It might be, but not for a very, *very* long time."

"Let's hope so." He kissed the top of her head, then wrinkled his nose. "Now, go take a bath."

Darryk laughed.

"What are you laughing at, you old grizzly?" her father said. "You smell worse than she does."

"Hey, now, I don't smell *that* bad." Darryk raised his arm and took a whiff. "There, you see? Sweet as honeycakes."

Her father grimaced before turning back to her. "I forgot to mention: We have guests to entertain this afternoon. You might want to take some time to freshen up."

"Oh?"

"I've asked our gamekeeper and his sons over to discuss the troubling reports of dead animals in the woods."

Lyessa's head shot up. "They're coming here?" She released her grip around her father's waist and took a step back. That meant Ty was coming. She couldn't let him see her like this. She felt a sudden flush in her cheeks at the thought.

"Yes, why do you think I mentioned the bath?"

"And you're just telling me this now?" *What is he thinking?* "Men," she groaned. "They don't think."

"And see that Gina bandages you good and proper, you hear?" her father said, looking at the rips and gashes dotting the front and sides of her leathers. "We don't want you bleeding all over our company."

"Yes, Daddy."

Making a swift retreat toward the back patio doors, Lyessa glanced down at her state of dress. It was times like these when she wished her mother were still alive—not that she didn't wish it all the time, but there were occasions like *right now* when she could have used her advice.

Before she had managed to reach the double doors leading into her father's study, she could hear her father calling out behind her. "And have one of the servants tell Aiden—if he's even awake yet—that it would be nice if he were there for this meeting as well." She waved her hand, letting him know that she had heard him, before slipping inside. *Waking Master Lethargic up*, she mused. *Now that's a chore I'd never want.*

Aiden had been her father's latest choice of suitor. He was like all the rest— wealthy, good title, proper upbringing, and about as exciting as a rainy afternoon. She was tired of her father trying to marry her off. She was her own woman. If she ever decided she wanted to marry, it would be for love and not for political maneuvering.

After closing the doors to her chambers, Lyessa left a trail of clothing all the way to her washroom. She could hear Gina rifling around in her closet, no doubt reorganizing her dresses once again. "Gina, I need your help."

"I already have your bath prepared, Miss Lyessa," the elderly nanny said from the other room.

"Good." Lyessa pulled off the rest of her underclothes and dropped them on the floor.

"Child, what have they done to you?" Gina stood in the doorway, staring at all the new bruises and cuts lining Lyessa's chest, arms, and back. "I'm gonna have to have another talk with that father of yours," she said with a disapproving click of her tongue as she planted both fists on her hips.

"I'm fine, Gina. It's not as bad as it looks." Lyessa smiled at the old woman. Gina had been her nursemaid and nanny since birth. Apart from the years Gina had spent in Easthaven, Lyessa didn't know much about the elderly woman's past. Gina didn't speak of it, and Lyessa had never wanted to pry. She did know that Gina came from one of the Blue Islands. Every now and then, Lyessa would catch a hint of Gina's natural accent bleeding through.

"Get that pale little backside of yours into that bath before I turn it on your head," Gina said, holding one hand over her nose. To Gina, all Sidarans were pale compared to the naturally tanned skin of the islanders.

Lyessa climbed into the tub, letting the warm water ease the pain and tension she felt in her throbbing shoulders, legs, and arms. Especially her arms. She exhaled a soft moan and let her head rest against the back of the tub. "Gina, what does it feel like to fall in love?"

"Child, you are too young to be talking about love."

Lyessa opened her eyes. "I'm eighteen, a grown woman. What better time is there?"

Gina stopped her fiddling. "I guess you are, at that. Sometimes it's hard to think of you as all grown up. Seems like just yesterday you were running around here, causing all kinds of ruckus. Wait," she said with a snicker, "that *was* yesterday." Lyessa splashed her water at the old woman. "Yep, time just keeps rolling right on by, it does, leaving poor old Gina here to watch it go."

"What does it feel like, Gina?"

Gina pulled up a stool and started washing Lyessa's thick head of red curls. "It can leave you breathless, make you feel all giddy inside when you're around him. A sure sign to tell when a girl's in love, though, is the giggles. When a girl starts giggling for no good reason, you can just bet she's got herself a fella."

Lyessa smiled at the thought. "It must be wonderful."

"What's that, child?"

"To be able to marry for love. To spend the rest of your life with someone who actually likes you. To wake every morning in each other's arms." She leaned forward and wrapped her arms around her legs.

"Yes, it is," the old woman agreed. "I remember my Tomas. We had a love to fill two lifetimes."

Lyessa tilted her head back in time to see her nanny wipe at a tear before it had time to run.

"I'm sorry, Gina. I didn't mean to upset you."

"Upset me, sweet child? No, not upset. Tomas and I had forty-three wonderful years together; couldn't ask the good Creator for more than that."

"I don't love Aiden, you know." She felt her nanny stop tugging at her tangled strands.

"Well, sometimes marriage isn't about what you want or what makes you happy," Gina said, her words sounding almost forlorn. "It's about what's good for everyone else. In your case, honey, it's about what's good for Sidara."

"I don't see how marrying someone I don't love is good for anyone. Especially me," she said, mumbling the last part.

"The responsibilities of a ruler can certainly be a burden. It affords a comfortable life, but it requires much in return." Gina patted her sympathetically on the shoulder, then walked into the other room to lay out Lyessa's gown.

Chapter 42 | Ty

E VER SINCE HIS run-in with the old woman and her shop, everyone seemed to be on edge.

The last few days had seemed like torture to Ty, as his parents had demanded he stay within eyesight of the house. Especially his mother. She had always been one to worry, but this seemed different somehow. Even his sister seemed uneasy of late, no doubt due to his nearly burning her alive. She hadn't quite shunned him, but she hadn't volunteered any more walks in the woods, either. So when they had received the overlord's summons, Ty had been the first out the door.

Before he knew it, he was trotting down River Street, flanked by his brother and father. Ty managed a quick glance down Wood Lane as they passed. His eyes slid to the dark alley beside the spice merchant where he had encountered the old woman's deadly trinket shop. He shivered. Was he expecting to see the old lady standing there, waiting for him?

The council was supposed to send someone to check out his story. He wondered if she was even still there or if, having been discovered, she had moved on.

A few miles north of town, they crossed back into the Sidaran Forest. Ty took a deep breath, letting the familiar smell relax him. There was something different about it, though. Something didn't feel quite the same. A hint of danger had been growing over the last couple of weeks. It was like an itch in the middle of his back, one he could never quite reach. Was the change merely an indication of his own fears, having learned the White Tower was looking for him?

Turning east, his father led them down a dirt lane that cut farther back into the surrounding woods toward the East River. The road eventually opened into a large clearing that held the overlord's estate. Ty could only have described it as a palace, or at least as close to one as his imagination would allow.

It wasn't the first time he'd seen the property, at least from a distance. When Ty was younger, he had thought to play a prank on Lyessa by sneaking in to scare her. He hadn't realized how large the place was. He had barely made it out of the woods when a couple of Sidaran lancers on patrol nabbed him. It had been an embarrassing experience for him and his family. He hoped the overlord had forgotten about that.

The main building was at least four stories tall. Its white stone glistened as the sun peeked out from behind a cloud. Fronting the main house was a well-kept garden with fountains, pebbled paths, and strange birds with large feathery tails. Each bird stood on a pair of legs that barely looked to be more than two painted sticks.

A number of smaller outbuildings dotted the grounds, each at least three times the size of Ty's family's cottage.

The path they followed around the garden looped back toward the front of the main building and the open courtyard. A couple of attendants dressed in formal Sidaran green and gold were there to meet them. After they had dismounted, a pair of groomsmen walked their horses to the stables.

At the top of the stairs, a set of doors opened, and an angular gentleman dressed in the same colors as the staff trotted down to greet them. "Welcome, Master Kellen," the lanky man said with a swooping bow. He held his feathered hat to keep it from falling off. "Overlord Barl has been expecting you."

"Thank you, Piel."

"If you would be so good as to follow me." The tall man gestured toward the front doors and started up the steps. Ty fell in behind the others as they made their way inside.

The open foyer held two staircases—one on either side of the room—which led to a second-floor walkway that encircled most of the front entrance. The walls were lined with windows, their curtains open to let in the sun. It wasn't a very practical room, since most of the furnishings looked more for show than for use. As pristine as everything appeared, he doubted anyone had ever sat on the furniture before.

Ty smiled, and his reflection in the polished marble under his feet smiled back. He had known Lyessa was rich, but he had had no idea it was anything like this.

The chamberlain led them between the two staircases to an adjoining hallway and down a corridor to a set of golden oak doors. He knocked twice and opened.

"Master Kellen and his sons to see you, my lord."

"Thank you, Piel."

Piel pushed the door the rest of the way open, and Ty followed his father and brother in.

The afternoon sun poured in from the open drapes at the side. A set of glass doors at the back gave Ty a perfect view of the courtyard beyond.

The overlord's study didn't resemble the rest of the estate. There were no shiny marble floors, no colorful tapestries, no exotic furnishings. Instead, the room had a strong rustic flavor, with full-scribe log walls decorated in natural colors and an array of stuffed trophies from the lord's hunts.

Overlord Barl stood to greet them. Another man sitting across from the overlord rose as well. He was older than the overlord and wore a sling on his left arm.

"Master Kellen, thank you for coming," Overlord Barl said as he walked over and shook Ty's father's hand. The overlord was at least a head shorter than Ty's father and well built, with a hint of grey in his beard and hair. Ty assumed this was Lyessa's doing. He smiled, then noticed the grey in his own father's hair.

"I'd like to introduce you to our Sidaran representative, Ambassador Lanmiere." Overlord Barl turned to the ambassador. "Master Kellen is my personal gamekeeper."

The ambassador stepped forward with a friendly smile and held out his hand. Ty's father took it.

"It is a real pleasure to meet you, Master Kellen," the ambassador said.

"The pleasure is mine, Ambassador."

"And these must be your boys?"

"Yes. This is my eldest, Breen. And my youngest, Ty."

Ty followed his brother's example and bowed.

Overlord Barl brightened. "I had the opportunity of hearing our young Master Ty perform for us a couple of weeks back. Quite the talent you possess with those pipes of yours, son. Don't believe I've heard better."

Ty's cheeks flushed, and he bowed again, not knowing what else to do. "Thank you, my lord." He had forgotten all about Performance Night.

"No need to get embarrassed. If I told you what Lyessa did the first time I made her perform in public, she would probably lash me six ways to Eighthday."

"She would indeed," came a curt reply from behind them.

Ty turned to find a perfectly poised Lyessa standing in the doorway, wearing what looked to be layers of soft green chiffon with white lace trim at the collar and cuffs. The material clung to her figure in a way that nearly made him blush for looking. To Ty's dismay, standing to her left was an even more impressively arrayed Aiden. *Why is he here?*

"But some things are better left secret," she said. "Wouldn't you agree, Ty?"

Ty refused to capitulate to her teasing.

She turned her head to whisper something to Aiden, and Ty noticed a powdered-over bruise on her right cheek just below her eye. He suddenly found himself enraged, fists clenched at his side. *Had Aiden hit her?* He took a breath. *No,* he decided, dismissing the thought as soon as it came up. No one in their right mind would ever hit the overlord's daughter. Although, he had to admit there were times when he had wanted to. Knowing Lyessa, she had probably just fallen out of bed that morning.

Overlord Barl proceeded to introduce Aiden to everyone before they took their seats in front of the fire. "Aiden is staying with us for a few weeks while he inspects his family's lumber holdings here in Easthaven." The overlord was obviously proud of finding what he thought was a suitable match for his daughter. Ty wasn't so impressed.

By the time they had all found a seat around the hearth, a couple of the hired help stepped inside with trays of light snacks and some pitchers of drink. All the men, save Ty, helped themselves to a glass of the strongly spiced wine, while Ty and Lyessa opted for the apple-melon punch with a touch of honey and cinnamon.

He took a small sip and immediately relaxed. The sweetness of the honey added a wonderful blend to the apple, but not enough to overpower the flavor.

"By now, I'm sure you've noticed that our good ambassador has been recently injured," Barl said. "One of the reasons I requested your presence today is the circumstances behind those injuries." Barl turned and looked at the ambassador. "If you'd care to elaborate, Lanmiere."

Ambassador Lanmiere nodded and went on to describe his recent battle during a hunting expedition with the High King. The creatures he described were like something out of a nightmare. Ty was completely entranced. Ambassadors being torn limb from limb, horrifying creatures, mutilated bodies, feats of heroism—what wasn't to love? Even Lyessa looked excited, though she tried not to show it.

"Pardon the interruption, Ambassador," Ty's father said after the ambassador had finished describing the attack, "but did these creatures fight individually or as a pack?"

"An observant question," the ambassador said, raising his glass in acknowledgement. "It was neither. It wasn't instinctual; it seemed almost tactical."

Ty's father looked disturbed. "Are you saying they were intelligent?"

Lanmiere finished what was left in his glass and laid it to the side. "I'm saying, when I looked into their eyes, what I saw was terrifying. I saw . . . understanding." He slumped back in his chair. "Those creatures were anything but natural. I couldn't possibly guess where something like that could have come from. Maybe the Westlands, or the Caldera."

Overlord Barl looked at Ty's father. "Have you or your boys seen any signs of creatures such as these?"

"Nothing, my lord. If we had, you would have been the first to know."

The overlord seemed pensive. "There have also been reports within the last week of strange animal deaths."

"I have recently been made aware," Ty's father said. "Apparently, a few of the outlying farms have found some of their herds missing as well."

"What do you think could be causing this?" Lyessa asked unexpectedly, causing Ty to turn in his seat. She had remained quiet for the better part of the meeting. Why was she asserting herself now? Probably to impress Aiden.

"It could be a pack of timber wolves migrating down from the north," his father said.

"I don't think it is wolves," Ty said, wanting to show his worth. Besides, if there had been, he would have sensed their presence.

Lyessa turned. "Oh, and why's that?"

Not willing to back down, Ty held her gaze, then realized he'd just stuck his foot in his mouth. He couldn't tell them how he knew without revealing *how* he knew. "I just don't think it is."

Lyessa raised her brow. "Well, that was profound."

Aiden snickered.

Ty wanted to punch him in the face.

"Furgus told some of us that he found a string of ravaged conies in the woods just north of town," Breen said, nervously scratching at the side of his face. He had taken to letting his beard grow a bit thicker ever since Fraya commented on liking a man with a little scruff. "There have been dogs missing as well, and one of the local merchants found a dead horse just off the west road about three miles out of town. Something had devoured it down to its bones."

"What's so strange about that?" Aiden asked, no doubt feeling left out.

"What was strange was that the horse hadn't been there when he had ridden through earlier that morning. I've never seen a carcass completely cleaned to the bone in just a few hours. Have you?"

Aiden looked queasy, perhaps from imagining the horse's rotten carcass.

"I say we send some men out to investigate, don't you think, Father?" Lyessa asked, more of a statement than a question.

"What do you think, Kellen?" Overlord Barl asked.

Ty's father leaned forward, placing his elbows on his knees. "There is a story that my father told me when I was a boy. Like now, they had found a growing number of dead animals around the forest. It started with small rodents, and then a few cows here and there. Pretty soon, they started finding family pets missing, and eventually a few of the residents living on the outer edge of the city vanished as well."

The hair on Ty's arms stiffened.

"And then, one day, it just . . . stopped. They searched high and low for those missing families, but they were never found."

"What caused it?" Lyessa asked, her fingers nervously clutching the cup in her lap.

Ty's father shook his head. "No one knows. My granddad, and his father before him, were excellent gamesmen, but they never found a single track."

The room was silent.

Aiden looked like he was about ready to crawl under the sofa cushion.

"I'll go," Ty said, not really thinking about what he was saying beyond what would impress Lyessa.

The others turned to look at him. Lyessa seemed almost surprised, then he thought he caught the glimmer of a smile cross her lips.

"We'll make sure to do a thorough search of the surrounding woods," his father said, stealing Ty's momentary glory. "Rest easy, Your Lordship. One way or another, we will deal with the problem."

Chapter 43 | Rae

RAE HESITATED, her quivering hand held at the ready, fist clenched and knuckles white. She tried hiding her hatred, her fear, and her self-loathing. She took a deep breath to steady herself. What other choice did she have?

Rap-rap-rap. The sound of her knuckles hitting the chipped wood faded as she stood there, waiting for an answer. She tried wiping the palm of one hand across her short-cropped hair. No matter how much she tried to coax it into lying down, it seemed to have a mind of its own. She dropped her arm back to her side and nervously grabbed at her torn dress, squeezing the dirty material between her fingers.

She struggled to hold her temper in as she waited for the door to open. If she held her tongue, maybe Sylas would let her spend some time with Suri. She hadn't seen her daughter in days; the circles under her eyes and the stiffness in her limbs spoke of the sleepless nights spent pacing the cold stone of her chamber floor. Was her daughter being fed? Did she have a warm place to sleep? Worries rolled in her mind like a millstone at the grind, constantly moving but going nowhere.

Suri was kept with all the other children born at the Tower. A byproduct of men's *needs*. Something Rae knew all too well.

She tensed at the sound of the door latch being lifted.

Light spilled into the dark hallway, and her hands began to shake. The smells emanating from the room beyond were sickly familiar. She was intimately acquainted with these dismal chambers—the fireplace on the left, table and chairs on the right, cabinets of neatly stacked books, his precious tools meticulously displayed on the wall, even the damp feel of the cold stone beneath her bare feet. It turned her stomach. Worst of all was the sweat-stained mattress in the corner. She couldn't bring herself to look at it.

"Ah, come in, my dear. I've been expecting you."

She kept her head lowered as she passed, not daring to look him in the eyes. She stopped in the center of the room and waited for further instruction. It had been at least three weeks since her last visit to his chambers. With the growing number of young female wielders being brought in from the outside, she had hoped her days of use were finally numbered. It appeared her hopes had been naïve.

She clenched her fists. Her hatred for his kind was all that had kept her alive, until Suri. The thought of what her daughter would one day face made her skin crawl. Unlike her own mother, she was determined to keep that from happening, no matter the cost.

She heard the door shut behind her and on reflex started unbuttoning the back of her dress. He got upset when she wasn't submissive, and she couldn't afford to make him upset. Not today. She had managed to unfasten the last button and was pulling down the top when she felt a meaty hand slide across her neck.

"Not tonight."

She froze. He moved around to the front and sat in his rocker by the fire, watching her for a moment. Was this some sort of test? Was he waiting for something? Not knowing what else to do, she continued to pull her arms from her sleeves, one at time.

"Did you not hear me? I said not tonight."

Her heart sank. He was already in a foul mood. Quickly, she lifted her top and redid the buttons, relief flooding through her.

"I need your help," he said.

She gaped at him. *Help?* When had he ever needed her help? Her body, maybe. Her magic, quite often. But never her help. A surge of hope flooded through her, and she knew right then and there—for the chance to be with Suri, she would do anything he asked.

Chapter 44 | Orlyn

"**W**HAT IN BLAZES could have possessed Ty to go in there?" Orlyn asked as he stood outside the small trinket shop, staring up at the faded sign swinging above the door. The gloomy lane was bookended by three- and four-story buildings that blocked all light from the sun. Very few shops were in use down the narrow passageway.

"I don't see any lights on inside," Feoldor said, sounding relieved. "Maybe she's gone."

Orlyn grunted as he shifted his weight to his other foot. "If only we could be so lucky."

"This place gives me the shivers," Feoldor said, tightening his cloak around his shoulders. He eyed the windows overhead. "And I don't just mean the cold."

"Aye," Orlyn said, glancing at his longtime friend. Feoldor's chestnut hair was even more tousled than usual, strands sticking out in all directions. "Are you ready?"

Feoldor raised his hand, palm facing outward toward the lonely stretch of dark alley behind them, and the wind immediately ceased, leaving behind an eerie sort of calm.

"Now I'm ready."

Orlyn scanned both sides of the quiet lane. After assuring himself that there was no one coming, he pulled the top part of his staff out from under his robe, where he had kept it concealed as they walked down Wood Lane. The transferal crystal at the top pulsed a soft green. "Let's go."

The two men slowly made their way toward the front of the shop, carefully inspecting the door, windows, and archway for any sign of hidden traps or magical weaves. Once they were satisfied, Orlyn twisted the rusty handle and gave a small push.

The door whined on its hinges as the bell hanging from atop the jamb announced their arrival. They waited a moment to let their eyes adjust to the darkness before stepping inside.

"You see anything?" Feoldor asked, arching his neck around the side of the door to get a better look.

"No." Orlyn stepped inside. He raised his staff, and the crystal brightened. Feoldor followed him in.

"Keep your eyes open. If this woman has managed to stay hidden all this time, I doubt she is without talent."

"We could really have used Veldon," Feoldor said as he pawed nervously through some dusty odds and ends on a nearby shelf. He came away with a lamp. "If for no better reason than to give us some light." He quickly lit the wick and raised it in the air.

The inside of the shop was as run-down as its front. Dust covered the tops of the shelves, while the underneath parts were draped in webbing. It had been a while since the shop had seen a good cleaning. Orlyn swept his shop daily. If left unattended for any length of time, it would no doubt end up like this as well.

"I'll take this side," Orlyn said as he started down the left aisle. He stopped every couple of steps to listen for any sounds coming from the back room or the second floor. It felt to Orlyn like walking through an undisturbed tomb. The boards under his feet groaned with his passing.

Ty hadn't been exaggerating about the unique assortment of artifacts. Orlyn held up his staff to get a better look at the small shriveled faces hanging in the corner. "Interesting . . ."

"What is?" Feoldor asked, half whispering as he finished his survey of the right side of the room and walked over. "I found some odd weapons and a couple of shelves of old books . . . Wow! Are those real?" He joined Orlyn in staring at the heads. Feoldor was clearly having just as hard a time pulling himself away from the desiccated faces as he was. They *were* intriguing.

"We should check the back room and the upstairs residence."

Feoldor groaned. "I was afraid you were going to say that." He kept to Orlyn's heels as they headed through the open doorway leading to the back. The room was empty save for a single stool and a four-legged table with a piece of black quartz lying on top. Orlyn started for the quartz when Feoldor grabbed his arm.

"Did you hear that?"

Mangora froze. She had turned to find a more comfortable position for her back when one of the boards under her foot had groaned. The two men had stopped right above them. One was standing directly on top of the trapdoor. The dust from their footsteps filtered down through the floorboards, and she nearly sneezed. Quickly, she pinched her nose and covered her mouth.

The enormous Tallosian sharing her hiding spot was squishing her against the side wall with his shoulder. He fingered the dagger at his waist. She could feel his body tense. He seemed ready to rip through the floor and snatch the two men if they so much as looked down. She laid her hand gently on his arm and shook her head.

The floorboard above them creaked, and she shifted slightly to peek up through the cracks. Something in the taller man's hands was glowing.

"Let's check upstairs," the shorter man with the lantern said. He waited for the other man to go first.

As soon as they had left the room, Mangora breathed a short sigh of relief. She could hear their footsteps slowly scaling the stairs toward the second floor. There wasn't much up there but her bedchamber.

Pain shot up her right leg, and she elbowed Baeldor in the side. "Move over, you giant oaf," she whispered, "before I boil you from the inside out!" Mangora pushed the huge man back from where he had stepped on her foot.

"You kill me," he whispered in his rough, Tallosian dialect, "and we not fight."

Mangora was half tempted to take him up on his threat, but she held her tongue. She needed him. More importantly, she needed his people's lust for violence. The Tallosians were a savage race, and there was very little they feared. They had broken off from the rest of Aldor centuries earlier, during the height of the Wizard Wars. The superstitious fools actually believed that magic was going to eat their souls.

Luckily for her, times had grown hard for those living in the northern mountains of Tallos. Food was scarce, and some were willing to overlook their irrational fears and return to the mainland for the sake of survival, Baeldor being one of them. Although, in truth, for Baeldor and his tribe, it was more for the sake of pillaging than anything else.

Footsteps on the stairs forced them to table their conversation. The two men were coming back down.

"I told you there's no one here, Orlyn. Let's go. This place gives me the creeps."

"I want to look around the shop a little more, see what we can find."

Mangora's fists tightened, and she gritted her teeth. They had better not touch her stuff. If she found so much as a bauble missing, she would hunt them down and gut them in their sleep.

"We can look later," the shorter man said as they walked past. "Besides, it's getting late. I want to get back before dark."

"Very well," the taller man said.

Mangora heard the bell ring once, then again as the front door shut behind them.

She waited until her back couldn't take the hunched position any longer.

Baeldor huffed. "They go. Why we still in hole?"

"Because I want to make sure they're not coming back," Mangora hissed. Not wishing to spend another moment cramped in the hidey-hole alongside the smelly Northman, she finally released the trapdoor latch and pushed it open with her cane.

Baeldor leaped out in a single bound, then bent to help her up.

Having two wielders pay her a visit so soon after the faeling child had stumbled into her shop only deepened Mangora's suspicions that the ven'ae in Easthaven had been hiding him all along. Did they know who or what he was?

"How close are your men?"

Baeldor closed the trapdoor and followed her out to the front of the shop. "Close. North of town. Near fork in river." He peeked out the window a moment, then turned back around. "My men no fight magic."

"I can assure you that you will not have to." She started through her shop, checking the books on her shelf first to see if anything was missing. She chuckled when she found her lamp sitting in the same spot she had left it. Still lit. The men had probably been too scared to take it with them. "I have some associates on their way to deal with the wielder infestation in this city. Your job is to get me the boy."

"You said he magic."

"Yes, but as young as he is, I doubt he even knows how to use it. From the fear that I saw in his eyes the other day, I would be surprised if he even knew he had magic in the first place." She looked down at her hand and the mark left from where she had touched the boy. "Much more likely he has no idea who he is. Nyalis probably wanted it kept secret, even from him."

"Who this Nyalis?"

She ignored him. "We need to act quickly. If the council believes the faeling has been discovered, they will close ranks. We can't risk him going into hiding again."

She stared for a moment at the large spider ring on her right hand. She couldn't afford to lose the child now. How could she face Aerodyne if she lost her chance to grab the boy because she was overcautious?

"How many men did you bring with you?"

Baeldor straightened as he rested his huge hand on the top of his battle-axe. "All."

Mangora smiled. That was exactly what she wanted to hear.

Chapter 45 | Ferrin

FERRIN WOKE TO the sound of scraping metal.

The lock to their cell door clicked, and he rolled onto his side to get a better look. His bruised ribs brushed the stone floor, and he winced, the breath catching in his throat. He lay still, waiting. He could hear Azriel stirring in the far corner.

Here we go again.

There was a dull snap as the final pin released. The sound of rusted metal hinges grated on his already-raw nerves as his cell door swung open and three members of the Black Watch stepped inside.

The first guard held out his torch, providing just enough light for the other two to make their way across the room.

"So, what's on the schedule for today?" Ferrin asked as they each grabbed an arm. "A stroll around the gardens, perhaps, or maybe some tea by the fountain?"

The guards chuckled as they hefted him to his feet and clapped the iron bracelets around his wrists.

"Guess you'll find out soon enough," one of the guards said.

Ferrin glanced over his shoulder as they marched him toward the open door, hoping to catch a quick glimpse of his cellmate. "Don't wait up. I might be a while."

The old man shook his head, his face twisting into what Ferrin believed was a grin before the light from the torch flickered from view and they stepped into the narrow hallway beyond.

He shuffled his feet, trying to keep up as the guards half dragged, half carried him down the passageway. The sound of their boots echoed off the hollow interior of the Tower's corridors as they made their way through dark passages and circular stairwells, winding ever downward. Would this be the day he gave in? Would this be the one time he faltered? Would he fail his sister?

Ferrin took the time to study his surroundings. The inner hallways all looked the same: long, empty passageways of stone with doors interspersed every fifteen paces or so. Would it have been that difficult to stick up a nice painting or a pot of flowers? Nothing to look at but dull grey, at least in this section of the complex. The lower towers closest to the keep had marble floors with at least some semblance of design to the architecture. It might have been rather dark and disturbing, but it was better than the tedious grey of their dungeon.

There seemed to be an endless supply of cells to fill. He could tell which of the rooms were occupied by the sounds of prolonged suffering wafting eerily from underneath the doors as they passed. Men and women cried out in despair, holding on to what little hope still remained—that one of these days, the guards would show some mercy and drive a sword through their chest or drop them from the walls of the Tower and let them hit the rocks below. Either would be a kindness.

Ferrin knew this because it was how he felt most of the time.

As long as he drew breath, he was going to resist. He wouldn't succumb.

All he had left was his sense of humor, and he would wield it to the bitter end. He would cut and whack and jab with it until those around him were doubled over from its use. He laughed. He wasn't quite sure why. Maybe he was finally willing to accept his fate. Maybe Azriel's prophetic rantings were somehow taking hold. Or maybe he was just losing his mind.

"So . . ." He raised his head, his eyes hopping from one guard to the next. "What does a fellow have to do to become a member of the Black Watch, anyway? I hear the pay is pretty good. And just look at these accommodations. You can't get *this* in the city."

The guard in front turned his head as they continued their steady march. "I'm going to miss you, smith. It almost seems a shame to have to break a wit as dry as yours."

Ferrin realized he recognized the man. How could he not? Just look at that nose. *Good ol' Nostrils!* Ferrin mused. *Someone you can always count on being there when you need him the least.*

Nostrils stopped in front of a large iron door and pulled a ring of keys from his waist. Like the mouth of a great beast, it promised all those who entered a sure and painful end. Nostrils unlocked the door, and one of the guards shoved Ferrin inside. He nearly tumbled down the stairs, but he caught himself on the third or fourth step.

Screaming enfolded the small group as they stepped from the enclosed well onto the final landing and walked down a short hall. They reached the end of the corridor and strode out into a central chamber, which was cavernous in size. Stone pillars lined the outer walls, supporting whatever part of the Tower was above them. The room was lit by torches bracketed to each of the pillars. There were no windows to let in any natural light. The floor at the center of the room was made of a tile mosaic. It was dusty, but the image was still clear. It matched the one on the guards' cloaks—a sword piercing a rising sun.

Surrounding the room were thirteen doors, each with its own guard posted outside. Some doors stood open, others were shut. It didn't take great imagination to guess what was happening behind those.

Three long desks had been placed in the shape of a triangle just over the mosaic, where the black-robed members of the Legate were busy documenting whatever information the inquisitors had been able to pry from their victims. The guards marched him forward.

"Prisoner Ferrin is here for questioning as you requested, Legate," Nostrils said, awaiting a response.

An elderly man at the center table paused his scribbling long enough to take a quick look at Ferrin. "Very well." Ferrin knew him as Sticks. The man's bony arms reminded Ferrin of a pair of birchwood branches he had played swords with as a boy. Sticks scanned the papers on his desk, then gestured to his right. "Room eleven."

The guard standing outside the door opened it for them, leaving plenty of room for Ferrin and his armed escort to slip inside.

Inside, Cheeks was resting on his favorite stool in front of an already-filled rack.

The man on the rack appeared to be at least ten years Ferrin's senior. It was difficult to tell. The tortured expression on his face made him appear much older, something Ferrin understood all too well. At the end of each of his sessions, Ferrin had felt as though he'd left a few years of his life behind.

"I see you already have company," Ferrin said. "I'll come back at a more convenient time."

Cheeks turned. "Ah, my dear smith, you're just in time." The inquisitor motioned him forward. "Come, come. Take a seat. You might enjoy watching my work from a different perspective. It might give you a greater appreciation for my gifts, yes?"

"I think I have enough appreciation of your gifts already. I'll just catch up on some sleep back in my cell."

Cheeks shook with laughter, almost pitching himself from his rickety stool. "You will be the death of me, smith."

"If only," Ferrin scoffed under his breath. No one else in the room heard him, save Nostrils, and Ferrin could have sworn the man had smiled. One of the guards walked him forward and forced him into an empty seat opposite the rack. Ferrin took a moment to glance around the room, noticing the little healer was nowhere to be seen.

Cheeks pushed up from his stool and waddled over to his table of tools. Lifting the hammer, he looked it over and pursed his lips before glancing in Ferrin's direction. "Pain comes in all shapes and sizes, and our tolerance for certain kinds of pain has different levels. For example," he said, shuffling over to the rack, "our friend here has managed to withstand the knife fairly well, at least on the outside, but as you know, it's the hidden, protected areas of the body that bring the most pain."

Cheeks shook his head. "Unfortunately, those are also the worst places to apply torture, because the subject tends to lapse into a state of unconsciousness soon after the pain is applied. No, I learned long ago that the most sensitive areas are not always the best to prod.

"I should like to explain this to you later, but for now I am going to use a different form of torture." He waddled over to the rack and the weeping man strapped atop it. "The knife is an elegant tool, slicing the meat, puncturing and probing the inward parts, but with it, you get a searing pain—sharp, and relatively confined. But this," he continued, stepping in front of the prisoner and raising the hammer, "this is not so confined. It tends to spread throughout the entire limb, like so." Cheeks swung the hammer with speed, force, and precision, connecting the ball point with the man's kneecap.

Ferrin grimaced at the sound of the dull *crack*, like a rotten floorboard giving way under the weight of a heavy step. The man's knee had been shattered.

Cheeks raised his fingers in succession. "One, two, th—"

"Ahhh!" The prisoner's head bounced off the metal rungs as he screamed in pain.

"You see!" Cheeks said with a victorious grin. "There is a delay before the pain registers."

The inquisitor's brow rose as he dropped back onto his flimsy stool. "Perhaps I should pen a book." His face lifted, eyes sparkling. "Yes, that's a wonderful idea. I could pass on this wealth of information as a learning guide for new inquisitors."

"Please!" the man begged. "I've told you everything I know! Please stop!" Tears poured down the prisoner's cheeks, dripping onto his bare and bleeding chest. Ferrin watched the complete and utter collapse of the man's dignity as he cried out to the inquisitor, to the Creator, to his mother.

"Yes, yes, I believe you," he said with a flippant wave of his wrist. "You've told me everything you know."

"Then, I can go?"

"Yes, of course."

"Oh, thank you, sir, thank you. I have a wife and children, and they will surely starve without me."

Cheeks was already lost in thought again. Ferrin could see the wheels in his head turning, no doubt working out the opening lines of his new book.

"Guard!"

The latch to the door turned and the sentry stepped inside. "Yes, sir?"

"I'm through with this man. I've acquired everything I can. I believe his wielding days are over."

The prisoner's shoulders relaxed. "Yes, sir, I know now that using magic is evil. I will never do it again." A spark of hope ignited within the man's eyes.

Ferrin shook his head.

"Yes, that is most certainly true." Cheeks rose from his seat and walked back to his table and replaced the hammer within its slot. "Take him for purging."

"What?" The prisoner's legs collapsed as his spark of hope was brutally snuffed out. "But you said I was done. You said you didn't believe I would use magic anymore."

"You are correct. You are done, and I know you won't use magic anymore, since we will be ridding you of it."

Cheeks rolled his tools into a neat bundle, tucked them under his arm, and turned to Nostrils. "Send Rae in. We need our prisoner strong enough for the purging."

Nostrils opened the door, and the guard standing outside pushed Rae through.

She stumbled in, catching her fall by grabbing hold of Nostrils's arm. She recoiled quickly, as though she'd grabbed a boiling-hot kettle with her bare hands. She clearly had no love for the Tower's guards. Who could blame her? She appeared to be wearing the same torn dress Ferrin had seen her in the first time she had been there to heal his wounds. He wondered how long she had been working at the Tower.

Nostrils didn't seem to know if he should stay or leave, so he took up a position to the left of the entrance.

Rae started for the rack, then noticed Ferrin sitting in the chair next to it and stopped. Their eyes met, and Ferrin could have sworn he'd seen a quick flash of interest. But like all the other times, her head quickly lowered.

She stepped up on the base of the rack. The poor wretch on top had given up. He didn't even bother struggling against his shackles.

Ferrin felt more than a little uncomfortable sitting there watching the man's agony, so he stood and walked over to the far wall. Rae never once looked in his direction. She laid her hands on the deepest of the man's lacerations and closed her eyes.

Her hands began to glow a pale lavender. It was soft at first, then brightened as she pushed her magic deeper into him. Veins of purple expanded through his chest, lancing out from where her fingers touched his skin and spreading around the open wounds.

Ferrin recognized the shuddering effects of her magic as it forced its way through the prisoner's body—eyes widening, neck stiffening, a sharp inhalation, and then complete relaxation as the broken bones and torn flesh worked to knit themselves back together.

Ferrin wished there was something he could do for the man, but he knew better than to get involved.

Rae finished her work on the man's knee and slumped onto the nearby stool.

"Please help me!" the man begged, but Rae kept her eyes on her feet as she tried to catch her breath. How many others had she been forced to heal today?

Nostrils knocked on the door. The door opened, and the second guard stuck his head in.

"He's ready," Nostrils said, his voice holding a tinge of sympathy as he helped the other guard unshackle the man and drag him toward the doorway.

"Please, have mercy! My wife! My child! They'll starve! Please!"

The second guard punched the man in the side, and he went limp. A trail of tears and light whimpering marked their passage as they slid him through the doorway, snapping the lock back into place behind them.

Ferrin couldn't move. The look of desperation on the man's face turned his stomach. Having to stand there and let them take the man without even trying to help was one of the hardest things he'd ever had to do.

Cheeks collected his tools and left without saying a word. Strange for him.

Ferrin took a deep breath to calm his nerves as he glanced around the room, suddenly realizing they had left him alone with Rae. And the transferal!

His heart pounded in his chest. He could escape. Hadn't they realized they had left him there with Rae's crystal? He pushed off the wall. She was still slumped over on the stool, her back to him. Should he ask her for it, or should he just take it? He couldn't take a chance she'd say no. He started forward, his hands shaking. He could do this. He could take her with him. He made it about three steps, then stopped. A thought hit like the weight of the Tower crashing down on top of him. *None of it matters.*

Even if Rae gave him her transferal and he released the locks and opened the door, what then?

They were deep underground, and just outside those doors were dozens of well-trained guards, not to mention the legates and inquisitors. And even if he could somehow manipulate the metal in their blades, the guards alone were still more than capable of overpowering two underfed prisoners with their bare hands.

Ferrin almost started to cry. This must have been what that other prisoner had felt, realizing there was no hope.

He staggered back to the wall and fell against it, using its weight to keep his legs from giving out. He wanted to collapse, curl into a ball, and weep. He probably would have if not for Rae. He watched her back lift and fall under the weight of her struggling breath. She held herself up by the edges of the stool, knuckles white under the strain.

"Are you all right?"

She didn't say anything.

"Do you remember me? My name is Ferrin."

Silence.

"Where are you from?"

More silence.

"I'm from Rhowynn," he offered. "I own—" He frowned. "Or, I guess, used to own, a small smithy. It wasn't exactly Central Square. In fact, it wasn't much at all, but I had plenty of business and the work was fun. Have you ever been to Rhowynn?"

She shook her head. *Well, that's a start,* he thought.

"It's a beautiful place, nestled between the Northern Heights and Lake Baeron." He closed his eyes. "The mountains are capped with snow all year round, and the changing of the leaves during the fall adds such a contrast to the blue waters that it can take your breath away.

"During the summer, I used to take a skiff out on the lake and just float around for hours. There's no place quite as peaceful. Paddle out far enough and the only sounds you'll hear are the waves lapping against the sides of the boat." Myriah had always loved the lake. His sister would have spent every day out on it if she could.

"It's a wonderful place to live," he said.

Opening his eyes, he was surprised to find her staring at him. Her pale-green irises were filled with curiosity and something else, something he couldn't quite put a finger on.

He smiled.

She looked away.

Chapter 46 | Rae

HIS SMILE IS REVOLTING, Rae thought. *Fake. Like all the others.* There was something in the way he had described his home, though, that gave her pause. It had sounded . . . genuine.

She shook her head, tightening her resolve. She knew better than to believe him. He was a *man*, after all. And they were no better than animals. Big hairy animals, walking around on two legs instead of four. She could see through them. And they all wanted the same thing.

He probably thought that all his talk of his pretty home and his pretty mountains on his pretty lake was going to make her swoon. That he would look at her fondly with his deep brown eyes and she would simply give in. He thought wrong.

Now it was her turn to use one of *them*.

She was going take his desires and turn them against him. She saw the way he looked at her. She was going to use it to get what she wanted: time with her daughter.

She had to see her Suri.

Taking a deep breath to compose herself, she rose from the rickety old stool and turned to face him. There was curiosity in his eyes, no doubt to what lay beneath her loose garments.

She ambled over to where he stood against the wall.

He didn't move. His brows lowered slightly as he looked down at her, almost puzzled. Maybe that was just the way his face naturally looked. It was hard to tell with all that red hair covering his mouth and chin.

She stopped in front of him. He was big. He towered over her. She had to crane her neck just to look into his eyes. Not that she wanted to. It was time to get what she had come for. Sylas had promised to let her spend time with Suri if she could get the prisoner to talk. She was going to get him to talk.

She pushed aside the tattered remains of his bloodstained shirt and rested her palm against his chest. Despite his starved condition, he was muscular. "Tell me more about your home," she said, tracing her thumb across stretched skin, feeling one of the many lacerations she had healed.

He twitched, but not like she had expected. More of a recoil.

His big hand reached out and found hers. *That didn't take long,* she thought. The sooner she could get this over with the sooner she—

He pulled her hand away from his chest and released it.

What is he playing at? She was starting to lose patience. She needed to spend time with her daughter.

"My home is small but comfortable," he said. "Two stories. Nothing lavish."

She found herself nodding.

"It's in the lower town," he continued. "Not as close to the merchant district as I'd like, but close to the water, which suits me fine." She noticed a concerned look on his face, perhaps embarrassed by his low station. Most men liked to brag about possessions and abilities that far exceeded their reality.

"It doesn't matter," she said, stepping forward once again to playfully outline the wave of his muscles with her finger. "I don't care how much coin you have." Men loved it when you told them that your feelings stemmed from the way they looked and not from the size of their purse.

She stared into his eyes. Something about them was unsettling. They didn't look the same as the others. That spark of desire was missing. What was she doing wrong? He laid his warm hands on her waist. *Finally,* she thought, *here we go.*

But instead of the rough embrace she expected, she found herself being lifted off the ground and moved backward.

She had never had a man respond to her like this before. Did he not think she was attractive? She glanced at her clothing. Was it the dress? Most of the guards didn't care what she looked like—although once in the throes of passion, they usually told her how beautiful she was.

"Look, I'm not sure what you're expecting," he said, "but I think you've gotten the wrong impression."

"I'm not expecting anything," she lied. "I just wanted to hear more about your home. Did you have any family back there? A wife or maybe children?" Maybe he was already bonded and that was why he shunned her advances. Though there were plenty of men who didn't let that stop them.

He lowered his head. "No. I am not married."

"Are your parents alive? Do you have any brothers or sisters?" She needed to find something. She couldn't go back to Sylas empty-handed. He'd never let her see her Suri again.

The prisoner's eyes narrowed, but she continued to push. She needed the information. "How does your magic work?"

"Why do you ask?" There was a slight edge to his voice. The question had obviously been too direct. She clenched her fists. *Stupid.* She needed to be more careful, but time was running out.

"You've seen what I can do. I was just curious as to what your talent is. Does it hurt to use? What does it feel like? How often did you use it?"

He didn't respond except to fold his arms and cock his head awkwardly to the side. This wasn't going as she had hoped. She couldn't understand it. He simply wasn't opening up to her.

"What's going on here?" he asked.

She panicked. What could she do? She had to go all-in. It was the only way.

Her hands quivered as she slowly reached for the buttons on her dingy top.

Keeping her head lowered, she undid the first. She couldn't bring herself to look into his eyes. Instead, she focused on Suri and imagined holding her in her arms.

She undid the second, picturing the times she'd been allowed to tuck her daughter into bed. How it felt to kiss her good night, to tell her she loved her. Everything she did was for her.

She slid the third button free, and her top loosened. *This is it.* She gritted her teeth and grabbed the front. Before she could pull it down, he stepped forward and stopped her.

"You don't need to do this," he said, then turned her around, rebuttoning her top.

She was trembling, tears burning the sides of her eyes, desperate to fall, but she struggled to hold them in. She couldn't show weakness. Not to him. She stood there, unmoving, as he secured the last button. After turning her back to face him, he straightened her collar and took a step back.

She kept her gaze on the bare toes peeking out from underneath her tattered skirt.

"I'm sorry you've been placed in the middle of this," he said.

"I don't know what you're talking about," she mumbled, grabbing her dress to keep her hands from shaking. Sylas was going to be furious. She hoped he didn't use the knife again. It had taken her days to heal after the last time he'd lost his temper.

"I doubt it was your idea to come to me for information. This is the fat one's work. Only *he* would get some sick pleasure out of hurting you to get to me."

Her mind was racing. There must be a way to make this work. But he was so different from the others. She had thrown herself at him and he refused. She'd never had a man do that before. She bit her lip. Her chance to see her daughter was slipping through her fingers, and all because this *man* wasn't acting like a *man*.

"Look, I'm not saying you aren't attractive. You're a very pretty girl, but I was raised to respect women, not take advantage of them. I would never want someone using my sister like that, so I certainly wouldn't do the same. I'm sorry you were put through this."

Her head shot up. There it was, one of the answers she'd been waiting for. He did have family—*a sister*. She wondered if he realized what he had just said. It didn't appear so. Would this be enough for Sylas to let her see Suri? Then it hit her. What would Sylas do with this information? Would he go so far as to send the Watch after the man's sister? She shook her head. It didn't matter. She had to think about herself. She finally gave in and looked up. She saw concern in his eyes, remorse; she saw empathy to the point that it turned her stomach.

She looked away. She couldn't bear his kind gaze any longer.

"Look," he said. "I might have a way to get us—"

The latch on the door behind her released, and she scurried to the other side of the room before he could finish what he was saying.

It opened partway, and a guard peeked inside. It was the one with the big nose.

"Time to go, smith."

"What, no interrogation today?"

The guard marched by her and placed the iron cuffs back on the man's wrists. "Apparently not."

"I guess there is a Creator after all."

The guard shook his head. "If there is, he doesn't visit this place."

Not waiting around to see what would happen next, Rae spared a quick glance at the scruffy prisoner and found him staring at her. The look of pity on his face hurt worse than she would have thought. A twinge of regret knotted in her stomach, and she pushed it aside as she slipped out the door.

The thought of wrapping her arms around her little girl had her scurrying for the inquisitor's quarters.

Chapter 47 | Ayrion

AYRION

"WAR, YOUR MAJESTY?" Ayrion asked. He leaned back against the table holding documents that he, alongside Commander Tolin and the king, had been poring over for the better part of two days. "Have we really exhausted all other options?"

Ayrion wasn't overly surprised with the decision—in fact, he'd been expecting it—but with everything that had been happening with the Warrens, and the kidnappings, and Dakaran, the last thing he needed right now was a war to deal with. There hadn't been a declaration of war between kingdoms since long before Ayrion's lifetime, back during the rule of Rhydan's grandfather.

"I don't see how we have any other choice," Rhydan said as he paced in front of the hearth. "I've met with Overlord Saryn on several occasions. We've sent lancers to push their armsmen back. We've cut off supplies. We've even threatened retaliation. But nothing has worked." Rhydan turned to Tolin. "Commander?"

Tolin stared up at the large map on the wall. "Overlord Saryn has left us little option. His raids are increasing." The commander pointed to a spot just south of the Black Hills along the border. "Our scouts tell us that he is amassing troops just west of Belbridge. Actions speak louder than anything, Your Majesty. And Overlord Saryn's actions tell me that war has already been declared."

"The question is why?" Ayrion said, joining Tolin and the king in front of the map. "What does he hope to gain? Elondria is far superior. We have more soldiers, more supplies, better equipment. Even if they conscripted every able body in Cylmar, they wouldn't be able to marshal a force half the size of ours. It doesn't make sense."

"Desperation rarely does," Rhydan said.

"Desperation for what, though? More land? He has to know this is a losing endeavor."

"Insanity, then." Rhydan looked up at the map. "But I agree. This move is far too bold for Saryn. There's something else at work here. I only wish I knew what it was."

"I don't like it either," Tolin interjected, "but we can't leave our border cities to be ransacked by an opposing army."

The king looked at the commander. "How soon can you have your men ready to march?"

"By the end of the week, Your Majesty," Tolin said without the slightest hesitation. He had clearly anticipated the question—another fine quality of an effective leader.

It was Ayrion who was feeling ineffective. He felt like a showman at a carnival, juggling a dozen blades, never knowing when he was going to miss and grab the wrong end. He still needed to figure out what to do about Reevie.

Rhydan took a deep breath. Ayrion could hear frustration in the exhale. "Do it, Commander."

"Very well, Your Majesty." Tolin turned to leave.

"Just a moment, Commander," Ayrion said, stopping Tolin before he made it to the door. This might be his last chance to do something about the kidnappings.

"I almost hate to bring this up, Your Majesty," Ayrion said, "especially with everything else that is going on, but I've recently been informed of a string of abductions around the Warrens. I was wondering if it would be possible to assign the city patrol to investigate."

"I've already been made aware," Rhydan said.

Ayrion's head lifted. "You have? Why wasn't I informed? Have the patrollers already been sent—"

"No, they haven't."

"Why not?"

"Because I was only just informed a couple of days ago," Rhydan said sharply.

"What are you planning to do? . . . Your Majesty," Ayrion added belatedly.

Rhydan grunted irritably. "I've assigned an inspector to look into it."

"Only one?" Ayrion's heart sank. Reevie's life depended on the king's help. It had been far too long since he had taken the time to visit his old friend. He blamed himself. Reevie had taken Ayrion's parting hard, and it had hurt their friendship. Even though Ayrion tried to get by and see him when he could, their relationship had never been the same. He had hoped to fix that.

"Not to be cynical," Tolin said, "but this is the Warrens we're talking about. People disappear there all the time, usually by a knife in the back and a quick drop in the bay."

Ayrion clenched his fists. "Just because a person lives on the streets doesn't make them a criminal."

"No. But their reputation does. The Warrens has made no qualms about the fact that they will allow no rule over their own. They're outlaws, common thieves."

"They are citizens of Aramoor."

Tolin opened his mouth but held back.

Ayrion should have known he wouldn't receive any sympathy from Tolin, whose father had been murdered by a street thug when he was just a boy. The commander was a man of principle, as straight as the law itself. Ayrion, on the other hand, knew what it was like to steal an apple from the fruit cart just to survive. Life wasn't as clean as Tolin thought it was.

"You've never shown this kind of interest in the Warrens before," Rhydan asked. "Why now?"

Rhydan's statement hit harder than Ayrion had expected. Ayrion had been one of the lucky few to make it off the streets. He should have spent more time trying to help others to as well. He had been so focused on his duties, especially once he'd accepted the role of Guardian Protector, that he hadn't taken the time to look back.

"Because a very close friend of mine might have been one of those who was taken."

Rhydan leaned against the hearth. "I'm sorry to hear that. Do we know for sure that these *are* kidnappings? Could it simply be people leaving the city?"

"No, Your Majesty. There've been sightings of hooded men rounding people up in the night."

"Do we know why they are being taken?" Tolin asked.

Ayrion shook his head. "No one seems to know. My contacts within the Warrens simply said people were being taken and no one has seen them since."

Ayrion couldn't fault their skepticism. It wasn't like he hadn't shared it himself at first. But Kira wouldn't have gone to the trouble of kidnapping him if she hadn't been worried. And she certainly wouldn't have used Reevie as a bargaining chip unless it were true.

"I'll assign one of the patrol offices to look into the matter," Rhydan said, then glanced at the commander. "Can you spare some men to give support?"

Tolin looked at Ayrion, then back at the king, and nodded.

"Excellent," Rhydan said as he walked back to this desk. "The last thing we need is a citywide panic, or citizens worried they'll be snatched out of their beds." He took a seat and started shuffling through some papers. "If there's nothing more, gentlemen, I'll bid you good morning. I have other affairs that need attending to before our journey to the border."

Ayrion joined Tolin in bowing. "By your leave, Your Majesty."

The king raised his hand without looking up, and Ayrion and Tolin left.

Ayrion shut the door behind them, and the two walked back to their offices on the first floor.

"I'm sorry if I came off as harsh," Tolin said, "but the Warrens have been a plague on Aramoor for decades. I'm not saying that everyone on the streets is a criminal. We still have homeless. I understand that. That's not going to change. But the Warrens act as though it is above the law."

"I don't disagree. Even the street tribes are afraid of the Warrens."

"Then I'm confused. Why are we trying to help them?"

"Because the new head of the clans is a former acquaintance." Ayrion didn't want to go into the details of how close that acquaintance was. "And I believe that if given support, she could turn the underground around." Maybe that was stretching it a bit.

"I'll make sure the patrollers receive a squad of lancers," Tolin said. "I promised the king I would. But don't expect more. In my opinion, Aramoor would be better off if that place were leveled."

Ayrion could see there was no dissuading his former commander, so he dropped the issue.

They walked on in silence for some time before Tolin finally turned to speak. "You'll need to come by the house for dinner sometime. Tirana was asking about you the other day, complaining how seldom we do any entertaining. You'll have to invite Captain Barthol and his wife as well. Kensey was very kind to Tirana."

"I'd be happy to," Ayrion said as they stopped outside Tolin's office, only a couple of doors down from Ayrion's. "Just tell me when."

Tolin opened the door. "I'll discuss it with Tirana and get back with you. Oh, and be sure to invite Amarysia."

Ayrion smiled as the commander shut the door.

Tolin had been hinting for some time that Ayrion needed to move his relationship with Amarysia forward before someone else snatched her up. Deep down, he was afraid that with his line of work, he would make her a soon-to-be widow.

Ayrion glanced at the clan ring on his smallest finger. He needed to let Kira know that the king was looking into the matter, but after their last meeting, he was feeling a little anxious about organizing another. And then there was the question of whether he should tell Amarysia he was planning on seeing the elusive clan chief again. If he did, she might insist on coming.

Chapter 48 | Dakaran

$\mathcal{T}$HE QUEEN'S GILDED chamber door opened without a sound.

Dakaran stood in the hallway just outside and watched Amarysia step out and close the door behind her. She was carefully balancing a tray of empty cups, plates, and a crystal pitcher of what looked like his mother's favorite apricot tea. She hadn't seen him.

He downed the rest of his glass and quietly walked up behind her.

She turned and hit him with the tray. "Oh, Your Highness. I'm so sorry. I didn't see you there."

Dakaran smiled as he steadied the tray as best he could, keeping its contents from pouring across the front of his white lace tunic and vest. His hands were shaking as much as hers.

"Let me help you with that," he said softly. He couldn't believe his luck. He'd been trying to find a way to get her alone, and here she was, not only without an escort but in need of his help. "Where are you going? You shouldn't be carrying this. We have servants for that."

"I don't mind."

"Nonsense. That's what they're here for." He took the tray and shoved it at a guard outside his mother's door. "Dispose of these."

The guard nearly dropped his halberd as he tried to keep from spilling anything.

Amarysia looked as perplexed as the guard. "Uh . . . thank you, Your Highness." She bowed and then turned to leave.

"Actually, I find myself free at the moment," he said, trying his best to look at her eyes instead of her figure. The meeting with his mother would have to wait. "I'll walk with you."

"There's no need, Your Highness. I'm sure you have more important things to do than escort me to the kitchens."

Dakaran smiled at her selflessness. Amarysia had always impressed him, ever since his mother had taken her on as a lady-in-waiting. Unlike the other women at court, she had never tried to garner his attention, and she genuinely seemed to care about the queen.

"No, I insist," he said, putting a hand to her waist and directing her down the hall. "Our meeting like this must be fate." He tried to take deep breaths to help ease his mind. How many glasses had he filled this morning? Four? Five?

Amarysia cleared her throat and offered another timid smile. "Um, yes. I'm . . . I'm sure it was."

"You're the most beautiful woman in the palace, you know," he blurted out, unable to think of what else to say. He couldn't go wrong, complimenting a woman's beauty. He'd learned that early on.

She looked away, almost embarrassed. "The prince is too kind."

"Not at all." He tightened his grip. She was trembling. He couldn't help but admire the way her dress hinted at what the fabric kept hidden. Her pouty lips seemed to be calling his name, daring—no, begging—him to partake.

His eagerness to find an opportunity to be close to her kept him from paying attention to where they were heading. It wasn't until they had passed through the open atrium on the main floor and down the officers' hallway that he realized where they were. But by then, it was too late.

Amarysia stopped a few doors down from Ayrion's office. The blasted man was standing in the doorway, chatting with one of the palace guards.

Ayrion turned when he saw them, dismissing the guard. Dakaran met his gaze, pulling Amarysia closer. He was pleased to see the tension on Ayrion's face.

"Your Highness," Ayrion said with a very slight nod of his head. He glanced at Amarysia. "I was just coming to look for you, my lady. Are we still on for dinner?"

"I've just asked the young lady to join me for a meal in the banquet hall," Dakaran lied.

"I . . . uh . . ." She glanced at both men. "I . . ."

"I understand," Ayrion said, offering her a sympathetic look, as if sharing a meal with Dakaran was something to be pitied.

Dakaran's blood boiled. "And what is it exactly that you understand? That an offer from the High Prince is more desired than one from a common soldier?" He pulled Amarysia even closer.

Ayrion's grey eyes darkened. "Let go, Dakaran. You're hurting her."

"How dare you order me around, and in my own house, no less! Who do you think you are, street rat?" Dakaran whirled on Amarysia. "I bet you didn't know that our Guardian here was nothing more than a worthless street scamp when my father found him. A thieving little pickpocket. No doubt he told you that he was highborn."

Dakaran turned his attention back to Ayrion. "Ever since we were kids, you always had your nose stuck in the air."

"Leave her out of this, Dakaran. It's me you're angry with." Ayrion stepped into the center of the hall, hands loose at his sides.

Dakaran ground his teeth. "You'd love that, wouldn't you?" he spat. "To have me face you in open combat so you can cut me down? That might work on the battlefield, but here in the palace, we do things a bit differently. For example, all I need to do is call the guards and have them put you under arrest for open defiance, or for threatening the royal family, or for . . . well, anything I want, actually. It would be the word of a guttersnipe against the prince of Elondria. Who do you think they'll believe?"

"They'll believe the guttersnipe," an all-too-familiar voice said behind them. He turned to see his father, arms crossed, face as hard as an anvil. The look in the king's eyes momentarily cleared his head. His father looked ashamed. "You might be the crown prince, but as long as I am king, a man's word will be measured by his actions. Sadly, it's a conviction that I've been unable to pass along to you."

Rhydan turned to Ayrion. "Guardian, would you be so kind as to take our young Amarysia here to the kitchens for a bite to eat? She looks nearly faint."

Dakaran reluctantly released his grip. The look on Amarysia's face as Ayrion wrapped his arm protectively around her made his stomach tighten. He felt like he'd just been kicked by a mule. Once again, Ayrion had been chosen over him. Even his father preferred the street rat over his own son.

"What are you doing, Dakaran? You have an entire court of women throwing themselves at you, yet you pursue a woman who is already taken?" His father stared at him, his eyes measuring, calculating. "This has nothing to do with the lady, does it? This is about hurting Ayrion."

Dakaran didn't know what he hated more: what his father was saying or the fact that he might have been right.

His father shook his head. "Somehow, I feel like this is my fault. Maybe if I'd been stronger with you . . ." He sighed. "This childish petulance does not befit a High Prince. If you don't get yourself under control, Dakaran, I'll have no choice but to pull you from the line of succession."

"What? You can't do that! I'm your son!" Dakaran shook with rage. His mind had never been so clear, the wine dissipating under the heat of his anger.

"You're a drunkard. Now, get on with you. Your mother was expecting you some time ago."

Dakaran almost reached for his sword, then realized he wasn't carrying one. Under the circumstances, that might have been a good thing. He stormed back the way he'd come, his thoughts a blur, and for once not from wine. How dare his father threaten to remove him from the succession! He was the High Prince. He had never even considered this a possibility. He had been hesitant at first with Valtor's plans of seizing the throne from his father. But no more.

"Snap out of it!"

Dakaran jumped. Where was he? He'd been so focused on his father, he hadn't noticed his own chief advisor standing in the middle of the hall he'd just turned down. He'd nearly run the man over.

Valtor looked even thinner than normal, if that was possible. His eyes had dark rings. Did the man ever sleep? His wolf-head staff rested comfortably in his hands. Dakaran never had liked the way the vicious animal seemed to watch him.

"Did you hear him, Valtor? He actually threatened to cut me from the line of succession. My own father!"

Valtor grinned, which Dakaran found even more unsettling for reasons he couldn't explain. "Then I bring good tidings indeed, Your Highness." Valtor scanned the empty passageway before leaning in a little closer. "Cylmar has answered our call. Your father is readying his forces. Things are falling into place."

Chapter 49 | Ayrion

A YRION SAT ALONE in the dark.

The park bench was cold and stiff, much like his present mood. All during his meal with Amarysia, he had debated whether or not to mention his upcoming meeting with Kira. She had been especially perceptive this evening, asking him twice before their food had even arrived if there was something wrong. He'd assured her there wasn't, but he could tell she didn't believe him.

To her credit, she'd let the matter drop. He had almost told her before they'd kissed good night, but he'd been afraid that bringing it up *then* would have made him look guilty. He groaned and twisted his fingers through his hair.

He hated feeling like this.

He enjoyed order, routine, discipline. And if this roiling pit of emotions was a normal part of being involved with someone, then maybe he was being too hasty. All these *feelings* were clouding his judgment. A foggy mind in his line of work could get him killed, or worse, cause those under his protection to be killed.

"Why does it have to be so complicated?" he asked the star-filled sky above, watching his breath mist in front of his face.

"Because life is complicated."

Ayrion turned in his seat. Across the street, a shape detached itself from the corner building. He hated the way Kira was able to keep him on edge. Her red leather coat glistened in the light of the streetlamps as she crossed the lane and stepped into the park. He couldn't help but notice the extra undulation from her hips as she sashayed up to his bench and took a seat.

"Talk to yourself much?" she asked with a grin.

"After having been kidnapped and dragged underground, I find myself doing a number of strange things of late."

"Oh?" she asked, batting her long eyelashes.

"Like checking every alleyway for ruffians before crossing," he said with a smirk.

"I'm glad to see I'm having an effect."

"Like a bad rash," he mumbled.

Her eyes narrowed. "Here." She handed back the clan ring he had sent as an invitation for their meeting. "As much as I enjoy admiring your beautiful face, Ayri, it's getting chilly. Cold weather and leather don't mix well, you know." She looked down at her leather pants and smiled. "So, what do you want?"

Blunt as always. "I spoke with the king."

Surprise flickered across her face. "I didn't think I'd hear from you again after what happened last time, let alone that you'd actually meet with the king on our behalf."

"I told you I would. I keep my promises."

She stared at him, her brown eyes boring a hole straight through his face. The growing silence was awkward.

"Why would you think otherwise?" he asked.

She pulled a pearl-handled dagger from her jacket and casually spun it between her fingers. "I guess I'm not used to it. Honesty, that is. Not exactly a commodity in great supply in the Warrens."

Ayrion felt sorry for her. And Po. He was glad Reevie and Sapphire had managed not to get sucked into their world. He wished there was some way to help get them out of the clans and into an honest profession. He could probably find work at the palace for them, but he doubted they would accept. He smiled at the thought of Kira waiting tables and turning down bedsheets.

"You think what I said was funny?"

"No, I was just . . . thinking."

"Well, quit it! The last time you resorted to thinking, I ended up bound by my own shackles in front of my men, with Po naked in my bed." She scrunched her nose. "Not exactly the outcome I had envisioned. Even if you did manage to put a stop to that traitorous son of a faerie, Kerson, it still doesn't negate the fact that you and thinking just don't belong in the same room together."

He smiled. He had missed her fiery temper and loose tongue.

"There you go again with your smiling."

"Sorry."

"So, out with it. What did the king have to say? Is he going to help us or not?"

"He is. But not without hesitation."

Her knife stopped spinning. "What do you mean?"

"He agreed to assign one of the patrol offices to investigate the matter, along with a squad of lancers."

"Doesn't sound hesitant to me," she said.

"That's because you didn't let me finish."

She motioned for him to continue.

"He had originally assigned a single investigator. The only reason he granted additional resources was because I practically begged him for them.

Tolin certainly was no help. If he had his way, he'd send the entire army in to flush the Warrens out."

"Commander Tolin?"

Ayrion nodded. "Don't get me wrong. He's a good man. He just . . ." Ayrion sighed. "Until you live on the streets, you can't very well judge them, you know."

She nodded.

He found it easy to talk with Kira about this. Probably because she understood in a way others didn't.

"Is the commander going to be a problem?" she asked.

"No. He gave his word, and there's no one more honorable. If you can get the clan heads to agree to work with the patrollers, you might be able to make something happen. At the very least, the extra armsmen on patrol should chase away whoever is doing this, if only for a while."

Kira stared at her small belt dagger as she continued to spin it around her knuckles. "I think I can do that. I'll hold a meeting of the heads to discuss it." She cast a sideways glance. "How will I be able to get back in touch with you?"

How *could* she get in touch with him? It wasn't like she could walk in and request an audience. He glanced at the ring she had given him and realized he could do the same. From his finger he pulled his High Guard ring, given to him upon his induction into the king's service. The silver piece had a smooth black stone bearing the High Guard symbol of a silver falcon. "After you meet with the clans, get this ring to Loren. He's one of the royal hostlers, and a friend. He'll be able to get it to me."

She took the ring and turned it over with her fingers, then glanced at his other hand. "Not that ring?"

Ayrion lifted his right hand. It held a plain black onyx ring with the crest of his Upakan tribe etched in white at the center. Memories flooded through him as he pictured the look in his father's eyes when he had given it to him. It was the day Ayrion had been banished from his home. The last time Ayrion had seen his family. His father had told him it would always be there to remind him of who he was.

"No."

"So touchy." She smirked. "Afraid I might steal it." She twirled her fingers through her black hair.

The first day he'd stepped foot in Aramoor all those years ago, it was Kira and her tribe who had greeted him. And by greeted, that meant she had robbed him and left him lying in a puddle of rainwater, half naked and waiting to die.

Kira unbuttoned the top of her leather jacket and tucked his ring into her brassiere with a shameless smirk. After twitching back and forth to make sure it wasn't going to fall back out, she scooted across the seat and leaned in.

Without thinking, Ayrion reached out and grabbed her shoulders. They were strong. Not the shoulders of a genteel woman, but instead a woman who had struggled every day of her life for the chance to have one more. But instead of pulling her to him, he pushed her away.

"I'm with someone, Kira."

She grinned. "Not right now."

He grunted.

"She wouldn't have to know."

"I would know." He stood from his seat and took a step away, trying to prove he had the fortitude not to give in to temptation. She remained where she was. "Maybe if circumstances had been different . . ." He didn't finish the sentence. He knew she understood. "I'll be waiting for that ring."

Kira stood. "She's a lucky woman. Faithfulness is a rare virtue." She turned and started to walk away.

"If you want our help," Ayrion called after her, "be sure to meet with the clans soon. The king is preparing a declaration of war against Cylmar. We will be heading to the border as early as the end of next week. Arrangements are already underway."

"War?" She stopped and turned back around. She had a worried look on her face. "I take it you'll be going?"

"Of course. Where the king goes, I go."

She didn't say anything for a moment. "Do me a favor and don't get yourself killed."

"Why, Kira, that almost sounded like you cared."

"I don't," she said with a smirk. "But I just gave you my best ring."

Ayrion shook his head as he watched her disappear back into the night.

Chapter 50 | Ferrin

ERRIN WOKE TO THE sound of Azriel groaning in his sleep. Reluctantly, he crawled across the floor to see if the old man had twisted himself up in his chains during the night, as was his common practice. Ferrin went to shake his shoulder when Azriel suddenly lurched forward, causing Ferrin to stumble backward.

The old man's eyes snapped open, and Ferrin shuddered. They were completely white. Azriel was babbling incoherently. Was this another vision? He had never seen his cellmate like this before. He didn't know if he should try to intervene.

Ferrin decided to keep his distance. After a few minutes, the mumbling stopped. Azriel blinked, coughed, and then glanced around the room as if not quite sure where he was. When he saw Ferrin, he sighed. His irises had returned to their normal emerald green.

"What are you looking at, my boy?"

"I don't know. You tell me. Are you all right?"

Azriel raised his hand. "Just give me some time to catch my breath. I had another vision."

"I gathered that. Never seen anyone's eyes do that before except on a corpse."

Azriel chuckled. "I might look like a corpse, but I assure you, I'm very much alive."

Ferrin reclined on his haunches and waited. Long moments passed, and when Azriel didn't say anything more, Ferrin grew impatient. "Well?"

Azriel lifted his head. "*Well,* what?"

"Well, are you going to tell me about the vision, or are you going to keep it to yourself?"

The old man studied Ferrin for a moment. "It wasn't clear. Actually, the images couldn't have been more confusing had they come from a drunken Tonga troll." Ferrin tried picturing one of the greenish beasts with a barrel of stout ale in its hand and then gave up. "I will say this, though. Your time here is coming to an end, one way or another."

Ferrin could almost feel his heart pounding. "Are you saying we are going to escape?"

"I'm saying you'd better try, and soon."

Now his heart really was pounding. What had the old man seen? Were they going to send him for purging? He needed to get out of there, but to do that, he needed to get his hands on one of those crystals. Rae was his only hope. Unfortunately, after the misplaced passion and subsequent awkwardness of their last meeting, he wasn't sure how he was going to manage it.

"Oh, and whatever you do," Azriel said, "don't antagonize him."

"Antagonize who?"

The lock on the door suddenly snapped open, and the latch pulled back.

"It's time to go, smith."

Today, the Black Watch ushered him down a route he didn't recognize. They didn't go outside along the west bulwark; instead, they continued downward into the lower parts of the Tower complex. He scanned every new chamber, hall, and passageway, trying to memorize the way, repeating to himself the succession of doorways they maneuvered through, as well as any noticeable architecture that might aid him in his eventual escape, if the chance ever presented itself. At the very least, it gave him something to focus on besides whatever form of torture they had awaiting him next.

If he'd seen one hallway in the White Tower, he'd seen them all—slate-grey stone, rusty torch rings, thin arrow-slit windows, and the occasional rat that scurried from one cell to the next. He realized there was no hope of memorizing the route.

The air grew stale as they continued to circle their way farther into the bowels. He had never been this far down before.

Gradually, the air started to warm. His teeth quit their chattering, and the chill bumps along his arms began to recede. The torches on the walls, which had at first grown farther apart, now stopped altogether. The darkness left him with the eerie feeling that wherever they were going, it would leave him wishing he was back on the rack.

The flickering light from the handheld torch at the front of the procession revealed walls and a ceiling made not of stone but of compacted earth and rock. Small roots poked their way out of the packed crevices. The smell of the soil, even though stale, left him feeling homesick. He closed his eyes for a moment and tried to imagine a warm summer day spent wandering the forests that bordered the western edge of Rhowynn: the birds in song, the cool breeze sweeping off the Northern Heights, the soft pine needles rustling underfoot.

He was jolted back to reality when a guard shoved him forward.

A soft light appeared ahead, revealing the end of the tunnel they were currently trudging through. When Ferrin stepped out of the confined passageway, his jaw dropped in wonder. A vast chasm stood before him with a wide fissure that plummeted hundreds of feet into darkness below. An enormous stone bridge spanned from their tunnel across the chasm to the other side.

Putting his hands on the protective wall at the side of the bridge, Ferrin leaned over and gaped at a river of magma below. From this height, the blazing liquid appeared to be nothing more than a thin string of light rambling through the cavernous opening. They had to be somewhere deep within the core of the Razor Spine Mountains.

"Impressive, isn't it?" Nostrils said, cautiously joining Ferrin at the edge.

"It is," Ferrin admitted, taking a step back.

Rays of jade-colored light filled the cavern, bright enough to illuminate the bridge and give its passengers a clear guide across. It didn't take Ferrin long to find its source: large crystal formations that seemed to be growing straight out of the rock above him. Each produced an unusual iridescence. *Incredible,* Ferrin thought.

The bridge was massive. An entire company of lancers could have crossed in formation. He couldn't even perceive the work and planning required to create something on this scale.

At the far end of the bridge stood a bulwark carved straight out of the mountain. The pillars and arches of its gate towered a long way overhead. Nostrils came to a halt in front of two enormous doors, whose gold plating sparkled fiercely in the light of his torch. Six men in white robes stood watch, three on either side.

The doors were engraved with scenes from someone's worst nightmares. Twelve robed figures were depicted around a circle of stone pillars marked with symbols Ferrin had never seen before. Behind the pillars, a dark pool, and inside the pool, shadowy beings trying to claw their way out. At the center of the circle stood a broad, leafless tree, its limbs reaching in all directions, and in front of the tree, an altar. There was a person on the altar bound by what looked like the tree's branches, his head back and mouth wide as if screaming. A second person stood at the head of the altar with an open book, watching as something rose from the prostrate man's open mouth. It was vaguely similar in shape to the shadowy people in the pool. Were those supposed to be . . . souls?

Ferrin shivered. *What in the name of all that's holy is going on down here?*

"What is this place?" he asked.

"This is the Chamber of Purging," Nostrils said, and ordered his men forward.

Even the guards seemed hesitant to open the double doors. Instead of handles and latches, each door had a large gold-plated ring. Four members of Nostrils's guard stepped forward and joined those already at the doors. Together, they grabbed hold of one of the rings, planted their feet, and pulled. The doors parted, releasing a flood of amber light.

Nostrils took the lead, and Ferrin followed him in, his legs quivering, more from seeing the doors than from their trek down.

The chamber on the inside was similar to that on the out: cavernous. Ferrin looked up, but the ceiling, if there was one, was lost in darkness. Formations of lime grew down from the dark recesses above and up from the solid rock below. They reminded Ferrin of the teeth of some great beast, with the doorway for its maw.

Near the center of the room lay the ring of stones depicted on the doors. Behind the stones and surrounding the rear of the enclave was a large reservoir of dark liquid. Its placid surface swallowed the light of the torches. Unlike the depiction on the doors, though, the waters weren't moving.

Ferrin looked away but shuddered when he saw the enormous tree at the center of the stone pillars. It was even more disturbing here than on the door. Its gnarled branches spread out as if beckoning all to come and take shade under them.

Two men walked along the outer rim of the stones, heading in their direction. Ferrin recognized the bloody robes of his pale, tattooed tormentor instantly, but the other man he had not seen before. He was a good head taller than Cheeks, but even through his thick scarlet clothing, Ferrin could tell the man was quite thin. His dark, sunken eyes suited his long, angular face. He turned and looked at Ferrin. And something about his gaze made Ferrin want to look away, but he didn't. Whoever this man was, he was dangerous.

Cheeks promptly bowed with such deference that, had he bent any farther, it would have required two men to lift him back up. The inquisitor waddled over to Ferrin, and one of the guards tightened his hold on Ferrin's shackles.

"If I were you, my dear smith, I would listen very carefully to what the Archchancellor has to say. They could well be the last words you'll ever hear." Cheeks squared his shoulders and marched past.

To Ferrin's surprise, the guards followed, pushing the door closed behind them.

He was alone.

He turned to face the Archchancellor. The very man responsible for his imprisonment and torture. Would killing him save the life of his sister? Would cutting off the head bring down the beast, or would the Tower simply replace him with another? Either way, it would certainly make him feel better. He shifted one leg back to get a better position to charge. The man might have been taller than Ferrin, but judging by his gaunt frame, Ferrin could snap him in half.

Ferrin clenched his fists. *Wait for it.* Suddenly, he heard Azriel's warning in the back of his mind, and something about it stopped him. The old seer had told him not to do anything. Why? Had he seen something? Would something bad happen to him if he tried? Reluctantly, he took a deep breath and slowly exhaled, letting go of the tension and giving up his one chance at killing the head of the Tower.

"Ferrin, isn't it?" the robed figure asked as he casually flicked his hand at Ferrin. "You won't be needing those."

Ferrin's shackles opened and fell from his wrists, clanging loudly on the rock below. He gaped. Now he knew why Azriel had warned him not to antagonize the man. He was a wielder.

"Forgive me," the Archchancellor said, taking a couple of steps forward.

"Where are my manners?" He raised a hand to his chest. "My name is Valtor. I'm the Archchancellor of the White Tower. And I need your help."

Ferrin did a poor job of hiding his confusion as he sneered at the man. "And why for the love of Aldor would I *ever* want to help you or your Tower with anything?"

The Archchancellor grinned. "I was told you were one to speak your mind." He tapped the tips of his fingers together. "Good. I don't care to mince words either."

Ferrin remained silent, poised to run or attack if needed—not that he figured he would get very far with either approach. The Archchancellor was obviously a man who knew his capabilities and had no fear of what Ferrin might attempt.

"I would like to tell you a story, Ferrin, if I may."

Ferrin shrugged. It wasn't like he had a choice.

"It's about a little boy who was born . . . different from everyone around him. He could do things no one else could. Because of this difference, he was shunned by not only the other children, but by his own family. Those who had promised to love him and protect him wanted nothing more than to be rid of him."

Ferrin's brow tightened. This story sounded familiar.

"Do you know why they did this?" Valtor asked.

Fear, Ferrin thought.

The Archchancellor nodded as though he could hear Ferrin's thoughts. "Fear. They were afraid of what he could do, and yet, at the same time, they were jealous of his gifts." Valtor's smile vanished, his mouth twisting into something resembling scorn. "They wanted the power he had. The little boy didn't understand why they were treating him the way they were. Helpless as he was, he tried to fit in, forcing himself to contain his abilities. He locked them away in a deep, dark place, never to let them out again.

"However, the boy soon discovered it was impossible to contain who he was. He might as well have decided to stop breathing."

Ferrin's shoulders slumped. He remembered what that hurt and confusion had felt like the moment his uncle had sold him to Pinon the peddler. Ferrin ground his teeth. Reliving his worst memories was tougher than an hour under Cheeks's knife—quite possibly under the wiggler, even.

"And so, one night, he found himself awakened to the sound of familiar whispers and a large sack shoved over his head."

Ferrin cocked his head. That hadn't happened to him.

"They stuffed him in the sack and carried him away," the Archchancellor continued. "He could hear the voice of his father trying to console his crying mother. He could also hear his older brothers laughing as they followed nearby. He didn't understand what was going on. He thought it was all just a game, until the arms that were carrying him disappeared, and he plummeted into icy waters below."

Ferrin grimaced. He knew all too well the pain of having those dearest to him discard him like a worn-out piece of cloth. He also knew what it felt like to be manipulated, and as touching as the Archchancellor's story was, he wasn't about to let himself be used.

Valtor lifted his head. "I was that little boy."

A heavy blanket of silence enclosed the cavern as the Archchancellor studied Ferrin's face, obviously hoping to have connected in some way.

"You had me going there for a moment," Ferrin said, "what with that whole little-boy-hated-by-his-family routine. Playing on my childhood experiences to gain sympathy." Ferrin started clapping. "Masterful performance."

The muscles in Valtor's face tightened.

"If you have any hope of me believing any of that rubbish, though, then I have a question for you."

Valtor sneered but eventually nodded.

"Why in the Defiler's name are you hunting down and murdering the very people you *should* be protecting?"

The smile slid back across the Archchancellor's face like a snake through tall grass, attempting to catch its prey unaware. "Because, my oh-so-unobservant friend, there is a war coming: a confrontation that has been building for centuries between those with magic and those without. A battle the likes of which we have not seen since the time of the Great Purge. And I will do everything in my power to see our side victorious."

The Archchancellor began to pace as he continued. "The White Tower was built by the great wizard Aerodyne and his followers after they had thrown the faeries out of our realm. But after the Wizard Wars, it was repurposed by the jun'ri," he said the name as though spitting out a sour grape, "for the purpose of separating wielders from their magic.

"During those earlier years, thousands of our kind were butchered for nothing more than being different. Wielders became the sport of the jun'ri kings. They had special arenas made where they would pit one against another. They would organize great hunts, where instead of chasing stag or boar or bear, they would chase wielders and mount their heads as trophies."

Ferrin's stomach turned the more he listened.

"The faeries were the ones responsible for creating the durma collars," the Archchancellor continued. "Despicable creations. They were used to—"

Ferrin raised his hand. "I've heard enough. I get it. Magic good . . . collars bad. And before you take me down another history lesson from two millennia ago, how about explaining to me what you think *you* are doing here!" Ferrin counted off his fingers. "You hunt wielders, you imprison them, you torture them, and the Defiler only knows what you do to them down here. How are you any different?"

"What I do, I do for the greater good! Not because I want to. But because I have to."

"The blazes you do! Leaders have been using that excuse to justify their actions since the dawn of man!"

"The difference is," Valtor said, "I will use what I gain here to fight against our oppressors and protect future generations from suffering another Great Purge. And if a few of us have to be sacrificed for that to happen . . . then so be it."

Ferrin sneered. "I take it you won't be volunteering to be one of those?"

Valtor collected himself. "Like all the rest, I am offering you a choice. Having someone of your talent here to help us create weapons would be of great importance to our fight, so here is my proposition. Help me forge our weapons, and I'll see to it that you and your family remain safe."

"And if I refuse?"

"You'll undergo the purging process, where we will take your abilities and use them anyway."

Ferrin studied Valtor's face. "If you have a way of taking my magic from me, then why are we even having this conversation? I assume there's more to it than merely killing me and taking what I possess?"

Valtor chuckled. "They said you had a head on your shoulders. You are correct. It is one thing to gain another's powers, but it's something altogether different to try to use them. And since you already possess a working knowledge of weaponry, it is in my best interest to keep you whole."

Ferrin didn't respond. At least now he knew for sure what they wanted from him.

"I will give you time to decide," Valtor said as he turned and headed for the entrance. "Make no mistake: Whether you cooperate or not, I will have your magic. I can't risk wielders giving their services to the other side."

"How long do I have to decide?"

The Archchancellor raised his arm, and the enormous doors swung open like they were made of hollow wood. "I will return in a couple of days for your answer," he said on the way out.

Ferrin was left standing in the silence of the empty chasm, listening to the sound of his own thoughts as though they echoed off the stone around him. A couple of days? That wasn't much time.

Chapter 51 | Ty

TY STIFLED A YAWN. He wasn't used to rising before the sun, but after a cold wash and a quick meal of yesterday's leftovers, he helped his brother load up the horses so they could make an early start of it.

They each carried a strung bow, a quiver of arrows, a long dagger on their belts, and a boot knife. They also took two travel bags with some pork and cheese and a couple of bladders of water in case they didn't return until after dark.

"Here, I'll take those," Breen said, walking around to collect the brace of throwing knives from Ty. "You couldn't hit the broad side of the barn from five paces."

"I'm not *that* bad."

"The last time I tried teaching you how to throw, even the horses had enough sense to get out of the way."

Ty huffed and rubbed Waddle's neck. "You weren't scared, were you?"

Waddle whinnied and stuck his tongue out.

Ty waited until Breen wasn't looking, then returned the gesture.

The sun was just peeking through the trees by the time they mounted. Breen led the way as he directed Ty toward the north trail behind their cottage. Ty's fingers tightened on the reins, as he was feeling a bit anxious about hunting down an unknown predator. After listening to Ambassador Lanmiere talk about the monstrous creatures he had faced with the king, Ty was beginning to rethink his decision. Who cared what Lyessa thought, anyway?

"Wish Father was here," Ty said, scanning the woods as if he expected some gruesome beast to come leaping out and swallow him whole.

"We could wait till he finishes his meetings with the council," Breen said.

"But that could take days."

"This was your idea, remember? You're the one who went and volunteered us to go looking for this . . . whatever it is."

Ty groaned. He hated when his brother was right. "I know. I just . . . it would be easier with Father here."

"Well, he's busy cleaning up your other mess."

Ty grimaced.

"Leave it to you to go walking right into a witch's den just to hide from a girl." Breen shook his head, almost chuckling. "The sooner you two admit your feelings and get it over with, the safer the rest of us will be."

Ty's head shot up. "I don't have any feelings for her."

"The Defiler you don't. There's enough tension between you two to snap an oak."

Ty ground his teeth but held off arguing. Instead, he reached out with his magic and let it drift into the forest ahead. He could feel the life within—the trees, ancient as they were; the animals scurrying this way and that, searching out their next meal. He wasn't sure what to look for, but he had the distinct impression that if it showed up, he'd know it.

So far, he felt nothing out of the ordinary.

Normally, he wouldn't have given his magic a second thought. He'd been using it—at least, this part of it—since he was a child. But ever since discovering his new abilities, Ty's life had been turned upside down. Things had gotten completely out of control: the White Tower, the Black Watch, scary witches, strange beasts attacking the High King, and now a possible creature lurking in the forest. Not to mention the fact that he could light things on fire whether he wanted to or not.

Ty missed the simple life he used to have, where all he had to worry about was getting his chores done for the day, or getting back at Breen for his latest prank, or picking on Adarra while she read. He started to smile at the fond memories, but a nagging sensation in the pit of his stomach drove the pleasant thoughts away.

They weren't alone.

He stopped.

"What's wrong?" Breen asked, pulling back on the reins as well to look at the surrounding trees.

"I don't know." Ty twisted in his saddle, but other than the strange sensation in his gut, he couldn't see or hear anything. Even the birds continued their song, clearly not threatened. "Probably nothing."

Breen stared at him a moment, measuring his reaction, but eventually started back down the trail. An hour later, they reached a narrow section of the East River. The water was deep enough to be over their heads, but the current wasn't too strong. Ty was thankful they weren't attempting to cross during the rainy season. The river had been known to pull horses under.

Ty hopped off Waddle and walked down to the bank. He watched as the water slowly meandered along, cutting a clean trail through the forest.

Traveling the river with Breen had always been one of Ty's fondest pastimes. They would spend days fishing, swimming, and exploring the vast expanse of its ever-flowing body. His father had always said it was one of the great natural beauties of Aldor. The water was cold but clear, right down to the rocky bottom. The overhanging forest on either side maintained a constant shade during the day for bargemen as they carried freight up and down its length.

Ty sat on a large rock and started pulling off his boots. He stuffed them, along with his pants, shirt, and two pairs of socks, in one of the sacks and remounted. His brother had already done the same and was guiding his horse toward the river's edge.

"Keep the supplies out of the water," Breen called back over his shoulder as he headed into the river, holding his food sack and weapons in one hand and the reins in the other.

Ty nodded and grabbed his supplies. He shivered when the water hit his bare feet and rose above his knees. His teeth started chattering once it reached his waist. "Hurry up, Waddle," he said, urging his horse to swim faster. "It's freezing in here."

Once on the opposite bank, they re-dressed.

They spent the entire morning traveling in a northeasterly direction, carefully searching the densely wooded area between Easthaven and Reed Marsh. They maintained a safe distance from the marsh, though. The things that made their home in there were best left alone.

The sun was high enough now to peek through the trees, and Ty was anxious for the warmth. So far, they'd spotted nothing suspicious, and Ty was beginning to wonder if the unease he was feeling was due to nerves rather than some unknown animal.

Breen raised his hand. Ty pulled back on the reins, watching as his brother hopped down from Acorn and gingerly speared something just off the trail with a stick. He offered it to Ty, who found himself pinching his nose as he came face-to-face with the clean-picked bones of what had once been a large tree-rat. By the smell, its death had been fairly recent, maybe a day or two.

"What do you see?" Breen asked as he held the skeleton up for Ty to get a better look.

"What do you mean, what do I see? I see a dead animal."

Breen huffed. "But what else? Take a good look."

Ty studied the bones. Something about them did look strange. "Those marks on the skull." It was like something had peeled the flesh off, then taken a dull knife and started carving lines across the top. Some were deeper than others.

Breen nodded. "They're teeth marks," he said, swinging the end of the branch back his way. He studied the skull. "I can't even begin to guess what did this. Never seen marks like this before. And where's the skin? If it had been eaten by a hawk, or fox, or coyote, they would have left the fur—or at least the tail. But all I see are bones." With a grunt, his brother tossed the branch, along with the remains, back into the brush. "Let's keep moving."

The farther they traveled, the stronger the smell of death became. By the time the sun was directly overhead, they were surrounded by it. Skeletal remains littered the path along the trail ahead. The feeling of dread was so pervasive that Ty had stopped using his magic altogether. It was making him sick to his stomach.

"We need to check in on old Dorbin," Breen said as he bit off a chunk of dried meat and passed the rest to Ty. Ty tried taking a small bite but eventually spit it out and passed it back. He didn't think he could get it down, not the way his stomach was feeling. "I'd feel a whole lot better knowing he was all right."

Ty took a quick pull from his water pouch, then signaled he was ready. He tried once more to reach out with his senses, but like the other times, came back empty. There was something out there, but he couldn't tell what or even where it was. He really wished his father were there.

They traveled another mile or so before Breen came to a stop.

Ty moved Waddle closer to Acorn and his brother. "What do you hear?"

"Nothing," Breen said, glancing around cautiously. "Silent as a ryu before it pounces."

Ty was feeling more than a little antsy. A branch snapped in the distance, and Ty jumped. Breen simply smiled.

They pushed ahead. Twice, they came across what appeared to be a feeding ground, the forest floor glistening with mounds of small animal bones.

"I don't like this," Ty whispered. "Maybe we should turn around."

"You're the one who got us out here." Breen's voice was barely above a whisper as he lifted his bow and nocked an arrow.

"I'd say we got the proof we needed. I think it's time we headed back."

Breen swung down from Acorn and wrapped the reins around a small tree.

"What are you doing?"

"We should be able to see Dorbin's place from the top of this ridge."

Ty slid off Waddle and tied him to the same tree. He grabbed his bow and followed his brother up the hill.

Ty crested the rise and froze. The entire floor of the glen below was covered in bones, like a carpet of winter snow covering the ground. Dorbin's cabin sat at the center, seemingly untouched. Breen grabbed his shoulder and jerked him down behind some loose brush.

There was a strange clicking sound off in the distance, like a knife puncturing the brittle bark of an old hemlock.

"What could have possibly done this?" Ty whispered, not really wanting to know.

"We need to find out."

Ty gritted his teeth. "Are you crazy?"

Breen pointed toward the front of the cabin. Ty followed his aim and regretted it. There on the front porch, lying in a fetal position, were the remains of a human carcass. Unlike the rest of the smaller animals, Dorbin had not yet been completely devoured. Everything from the waist down was missing. Part of his backbone hung below his opened stomach. The rest was obviously being saved for later.

Ty turned and heaved. He lost his entire breakfast and last night's dinner in one outpour. He wiped his mouth with his jacket sleeve and swallowed hard against the growing surge threatening to overwhelm him. The hairs on his arms and neck were up and dancing. Something was coming. Careful not to look at the cabin again, he reached out with his magic, afraid of what he might find. This time he was met with a response, one solitary thought: *Hunger!*

"I can feel it, Breen," Ty whispered.

His brother turned to look at him. "What do you mean? You can talk to it? What is it?"

Sweat broke out across Ty's forehead. "I don't know. Whatever it is, it's dangerous. It's like nothing I've ever felt before."

Breen glanced once more out across the silent glen. "There's nothing more we can do here. Let's go."

"Go where?" Ty rushed back down the side of the hill after his brother, careful to avoid any loose twigs or branches that might give away their presence.

"Let's go find out what we're dealing with."

Ty felt the air being sucked from his lungs. "I just told you it was dangerous."

"All the more reason to find out what it is."

"How about we come back with a hunting party? Or a full regiment of Sidaran lancers?"

Breen clearly wasn't listening. Ty mounted and quietly followed his foolhardy brother as he directed them off the beaten path and deeper into the woods. Breen had them going farther west, back toward the clicking they had heard earlier.

Ty's eyes darted in all directions for any sign of movement. The closer they got, the slower they went. Pretty soon, Breen was off his horse and signaling Ty to do the same. Reluctantly, he climbed down.

Every hair on his body was standing on end. He could feel the creature. It was close. Its hunger for blood was insatiable. Was it the same creature that had attacked the king? This was insane. It had taken an entire company of the king's finest, plus the Guardian Protector, to keep the king safe. There were only the two of them.

After traveling awhile on foot, Breen motioned for them to get down on all fours.

Once down, Ty propelled himself forward with his hands and knees through a thick patch of undergrowth. The clicking was coming from somewhere on the other side. Sliding alongside his brother, he peered through the brush. As soon as he did, the clicking stopped.

Ty froze, his eyes darted left and right, trying to find the origin of the noise. There was a hidden alcove of rock about twenty feet away, burrowed deep into the ground. The open mouth was large enough for a grown man to stand up in. The smell of rotting flesh and moist fur had Ty nearly ready to choke.

Where is it?

Something nudged Ty's foot, and he almost screamed. It was Breen. He could have strangled his brother if he hadn't been so worried about being eaten alive like poor Dorbin. Slowly, he twisted his head around. His brother raised a single finger off the ground and pointed to the left of the giant burrow. Ty didn't see anything. Why couldn't he see it? Then his brother's finger rose a little higher and Ty looked up.

He froze all over again. Halfway up the tree, a branch moved. A branch unlike any he'd seen before. It was covered in coarse brown hair instead of bark. Then another branched moved a little farther down. Then another. His breath caught in his throat. They weren't branches. They were . . . *legs*.

His eyes bulged as he watched the enormous spider lower itself from the top of the tree. The sharp points at the ends of each leg made a dull clicking sound as they punctured the bark.

Ty tried to swallow but couldn't. His mouth was as dry as a shriveled cucumber. They should have waited for their father. Why had he been in such a rush to impress Lyessa? *Stupid!* He only hoped his death would haunt her the rest of her life.

Even seeing the spider, Ty could hardly believe its size. It stopped every so often to shift position, as if looking for something. *Can it sense me?* Ty panicked. Why hadn't he thought about that before? Maybe this creature was magical. Maybe it could tell when there was other magic around it.

Breen tapped the side of his arm, and he flinched. He hadn't realized he'd been holding his breath. He released it slowly. The spider reached the bottom of the tree and crawled into its burrow. It disappeared into the shadows, forcing Ty to strain to hear how far in it had crawled, or if it was just sitting at the edge waiting to jump out.

They remained where they were a few more minutes, which to Ty felt like days, before finally getting up the courage to move. Ty followed Breen's example and slowly scooted back out of the undergrowth.

Quietly, they made their way back to where they had left the horses. For the first time, Ty breathed a small sigh of relief at the sight of Waddle. Without saying a word, he mounted, and the two headed back the way they had come. Once they reached the trail, Breen urged them to go faster. Ty didn't argue.

They didn't bother undressing this time. They took the river, clothes and all.

"We need to warn the townsfolk to stay out of the forest," Breen said as he snapped Acorn's reins.

Ty grimaced as the image of the old hermit lying there on his front porch replayed in his mind. With a sharp kick to Waddle's flank, Ty followed his brother south toward home.

Chapter 52 | Valtor

VALTOR STOOD AT the center of the platform and concentrated on the smooth stone resting in the palm of his outstretched hand. Calling out in the ancient Fae tongue, Valtor watched as the single rune that was etched into the top of the stone glimmered.

Surrounding the platform were thirteen stone pyres, each with its own rune carved into the front. Piles of coal rested on top of each pyre, waiting to be ignited. One by one, the runes awoke, until all thirteen had spread their pale-green light across the platform.

Valtor lowered his hand, careful to keep the stone pressed against his skin. Scrying stones only worked if the user maintained contact. Resting against his staff, he waited.

Soon, the coals burst to life. Flames of the same pale green shot into the air, sending shadows fleeing in all directions. It didn't take long for the flames to take the shapes of thirteen robed individuals, one for each pyre. Unlike the incantus crystal Valtor sometimes used when talking with Mangora, the scrying chamber allowed him to meet with a group of people no matter how far away.

The scrying chamber was a remarkable feat of magical ingenuity. Each person represented was able to see not only Valtor but each other as well. It had been designed with a certain equality to it. Thirteen pyres forming a complete circle around the platform so that no *one* individual stood above the rest. The flames, even though translucent at times, spared no detail when manifesting their images. Valtor could even see the rings on some of their fingers.

"Remove your hoods," he said. "We have no secrets here."

The twelve bulradoer, along with Mangora, complied by pulling back the cowls of their black robes.

"For those of you who don't know, the faeling has been located."

Excited murmurs spread around the platform.

"It's about time," Topin said. The tall bulradoer to Valtor's left shifted impatiently.

"Where is he?" someone behind him asked. Valtor turned and locked eyes with the woman on the fifth pyre. The scar on her right cheek was mostly covered by her full head of frizzy red hair.

"Ah, Lenara, I understand why you of all people would have an interest in the child's whereabouts. However, given your colossal failure to retrieve him the first time, I have another task in mind for you."

Her raspberry eyes grew cold. "It wasn't our fault. Nyalis beat us there."

"Yes," Mangora spouted from her pyre on the left, "and there were three of you and only one of him."

"He's also a full wizard with nearly a thousand years of experience!" Lenara snapped.

"Enough," Valtor said, putting an end to the debate before it got any more heated. The last thing he needed was to lose another one of his bulradoer because they picked a fight with the wrong witch. "I will have need of your services here at the Tower," he said to Lenara. "There is a particularly interesting wielder who I require your help with."

"Who is this wielder?" Selma asked on Valtor's left. She was taller than the other women present, with straight brown hair and a long face to match. Her left eye twitched, a nervous tic Valtor had grown accustomed to since elevating her to the position of bulradoer. "I would be glad to offer my assistance."

"I am more than capable of handling a single wielder," Lenara said, giving Selma a hard glare. "Keep to your own tasks."

Selma was always eager to offer her assistance. A little *too* eager, Valtor thought. Being the newest to the ranks, she felt like she had the most to prove. As annoying as her persistence was, it was nice to know he always had someone there willing to please.

Valtor turned his attention back to Lenara. "The wielder I speak of is a metallurgist who also happens to be a gifted weaponsmith."

"What do you need from me?" Lenara asked.

Valtor turned back around. "If we can't get the metallurgist to cooperate, I will need your help in purging him."

She nodded.

"Where did we find this metallurgist?" Mangora asked.

"The Black Watch found him in Rhowynn. Some minor lord turned him in for reasons no one seems to know." He turned around. "Speaking of new recruits," he said, looking at Horvah. The weasel of a man on his right never seemed to cease rubbing his hands together. "How goes it with the enrollment?"

"Ah, Your Eminence, it goes well. Yes, it goes very well indeed."

He even sounded like a weasel, Valtor thought, with his enthusiastic chirping.

"The numbers are up, up, up. We are seeing a steady flow of enlistment from three of the five kingdoms, although we are definitely seeing the largest influx coming out of Cylmar. I don't think the people there much care for the way their overlord treats them, like second-class citizens, you know. Sidara, however, is proving to be the most difficult of the five. Overlord Barl has no love for magic, but he has less love for the Tower."

"Sidara will be dealt with," Valtor said.

The short bulradoer bowed. "That is good to hear, Your Eminence. Good news, indeed."

"Not soon enough," Mangora griped.

Valtor ignored her.

"I'm also going to send five of you to Easthaven to help Mangora root out a wielder council that is protecting the faeling child."

"What do you want done with them once they are found?" Rukar asked. He stood on the pyre to the left of Mangora. The Cylmaran wasn't a tall man, but he was well built, with dark skin, a strong face, and a head of greasy hair that had been slicked back. He was rarely seen without at least a handful of weapons on his person. At the moment, he seemed to be carrying only a short mace.

"Extract as much information as you can. We need to know what they do. Once you're finished . . . kill them."

This brought a smile to many of the bulradoer's faces.

"I want a permanent Black Watch contingent in Easthaven. As Horvah has so graciously pointed out, Sidara is the only kingdom so far in which we haven't been able to build ties. Overlord Barl hasn't been the most receptive of hosts. See that we change that."

"How do you suggest we do that?" Topin asked, still fidgeting impatiently.

"I hear he has a rather beautiful daughter," Valtor said. "I'm sure you can find a way to use that to your advantage."

A couple of the men murmured with excitement, eager to be amongst those chosen to aid Mangora. Their appetites had grown dangerous of late, but after spending the last year weeding out a number of their ranks, Valtor couldn't be too choosy.

"And what is it that our illustrious leader will be engaged with during this time?" Mangora groused, always there to push his patience.

"I will be accompanying our young prince to the battlefield."

"So, your war has finally come to fruition," Lenara said, her words sounding more a question than statement. "What is to be gained from this maneuvering?"

Valtor smiled. "A new king."

Chapter 53 | Ayrion

AYRION RUBBED HIS hands together as he stepped out of his tent near the center of camp. There was a strong chill in the air, his breath visible in the early morning fog. This was a bad time to have to start a campaign, with winter just around the corner. Then again, he didn't expect it would last that long.

The journey from Aramoor to the Elondrian border had taken less than two weeks, a feat that impressed Ayrion, considering the size of the caravan that had followed the bulk of the army. Apart from the ranks of fighting men and the cooks to keep them fed, there were wranglers to tend horses, healers to patch up the wounded, and wagoners to transport provisions, as well as an entire supply train of craftsmen and tradesmen, all necessary to meet the needs of an ongoing campaign.

He stood there a moment, watching the soldiers scurry from one assignment to the next, all in full battle gear. The skirmishes with Cylmar were now almost a daily occurrence, and the soldiers needed to be in a constant state of readiness. But for all the pressure and planning and sleepless nights involved in running a campaign, it wasn't Cylmar holding Ayrion's thoughts at the moment. It was Reevie.

Ayrion had spent every night leading up to their departure scouring the city for some evidence of what had happened to his friend. He had even joined a couple of search teams Kira had put together, but to no avail. Each night, he went out. Each morning, he came back even more depressed than before. Amarysia had begged him to sleep, but how could he do that knowing his friend was out there, somewhere, in need of rescuing?

Then he ran out of time to do either.

Ayrion yawned and wandered over to one of the water barrels and splashed some on his face. The chill cleared his mind, if momentarily. Drying his face with a nearby cloth, he put his gloves back on.

"Good morning, Guardian," one of the runners said on his way by.

"Good morning." Ayrion glanced at Tolin's tent, then stopped the runner. "Do you know if the commander is in?"

Commander Tolin's tent was just to the left of Ayrion's. It was larger than his own, but it doubled as the central command post for the entire army. At any given time, a steady stream of officers and runners could be seen entering with reports and exiting with orders. However, the command post seemed to be deserted at present.

The young runner, who wasn't much older than thirteen or fourteen, stopped and stood to attention. "He's not, sir. I saw him heading toward the rise about a half hour ago, sir."

Ayrion was impressed by the boy's assertiveness. It reminded him of his earlier years and the excitement in being brought to be a part of something important.

"Thank you."

The boy tried to hold a serious look as he bowed. "Can I do anything for the Guardian?"

Ayrion smiled. "You've done enough already. You're dismissed, *soldier*."

The lad saluted and then took off running before Ayrion thought to ask him whether he had seen the king accompanying Tolin. Ayrion shook his head; the lack of sleep was getting to him. And since his men hadn't woken him, they must have agreed. He was sure he had Barthol to thank for that kindness.

Ayrion yawned once more and spared a quick glance at the king's quarters just across the way. The king's tent was no larger than Ayrion's. In fact, Rhydan traveled with accommodation little better than the officers serving under him. He had even been known to take his meals in the general mess with the common soldiers. It was no wonder his men loved and respected him.

Dakaran, on the other hand, traveled with a full retinue to service his whims. Ayrion had watched in wonder as a caravan of servants had set up his rather gaudy tent, which happened to be right next to the king's. Why would anyone need a chifforobe in the middle of a war camp? If the enemy were to break through, Dakaran's tent would be the first they attacked, believing it was the king's. Ayrion wondered if that wouldn't be such a bad thing.

Ayrion made his way through the bustling city of canvas, weaving in and around the bivouacs and small cooking fires already lit for the lancers' morning rations.

Atop a small rise in back of the Elondrian forces sat the staging area for the king. The crimson-and-gold canopy was set high enough on the hill for the king to have a perfect view of the Cylmaran army on the other side of the valley.

At the base of the rise was the encampment of the High Guard. Ayrion's men, in their notable black and silver, were preparing their breakfasts as he passed through. Those closest stood and saluted.

Ayrion nodded and moved up the slope through the ranks. Once at the peak, he took a moment to let the early morning sun warm the back of his neck. A couple of his men were standing guard outside the open flap at the front of the king's pavilion, letting Ayrion know that Rhydan was indeed inside.

Wanting to clear his head before meeting with the king and Commander Tolin, he walked over to the edge of the rise and looked out across the two opposing armies. The open expanse of borderland between them lay in peaceful silence at the moment. What could have been used as farmland was now tilled underfoot by men rushing to kill one another. Instead of seed being scattered across the upturned soil, bodies were strewn, and instead of manure, the land was fertilized with their blood.

Ayrion finally turned and headed for the pavilion.

The king and the commander looked up as he stepped inside.

"Guardian, I'm glad you're here." Rhydan motioned him to the table. "We were just looking over the plans from last night."

Ayrion passed Dakaran, who was slouched in a chair in the corner, nursing a glass of wine. Like his father, he had donned his armor, not that he ever intended to join in the fighting. Unlike his father's, Dakaran's armor was spotless. Ayrion could have seen his own reflection in the shine. Rhydan's, however, although buffed and polished, was worn from use with scratches, chinks, and dents the royal smithy had been unable to completely remove.

Why had the prince chosen to come at all? Ayrion could see the glint of pride it gave Rhydan to have his son at least passively involved in Elondrian affairs, but Ayrion couldn't help but wonder if that involvement would prove to be a good thing. Elondria would never survive a king like Dakaran.

Ayrion tipped his head to Dakaran in acknowledgement, then stepped alongside Rhydan and looked down at the planning stretched across the table. Tolin had blocked out the formations, with pikemen at the front to stop the initial charge, archers at the sides to force the enemy to leave their fronts unguarded, and cavalry ready to flank, driving wedges through the opposing force.

"What are your thoughts?"

Ayrion scanned the vellum scrolls. "I believe the commander has done a remarkable job. The offensive is direct. It plays to our strength of numbers but at the same time leaves us with options."

Tolin cocked his head. "I'm sensing a *but* here."

"To be honest," Ayrion admitted with a little reluctance, "I still find myself asking what Overlord Saryn has up his sleeve." Ayrion pointed out at the battlefield beyond the entrance. "Saryn has never made an appearance in battle before. He prefers to let his generals run his wars while he keeps to the safety of his castle in Ecrin. Yet here he is, on the front lines, fighting a battle hardly in his favor."

Tolin crossed his arms. "Our scouts have reported no hidden armsmen. No extra recruitment. No reinforcements. What you see before you is the extent of their offensive. I don't know what else he could be planning."

"Saryn is no fool," Ayrion said. "He wouldn't be here if he didn't believe he could win."

"I still say he's after the Black Hills," Dakaran said from his corner. "His people are starving, and he knows the resources in those mountains could support them for years to come. He's desperate."

"Dakaran makes a valid point," Rhydan acknowledged. "Most animals would rather run and hide than fight, but you back one into a corner and . . ." He shrugged.

Still, they were missing something. Ayrion turned back to the table. "All the same, I would feel better, Your Majesty, if you remained here behind the lines."

Rhydan straightened. "I will not sit and watch as my men fight and die while I do nothing."

"We do not consider your presence here as nothing, Your Majesty," Tolin said. "Having you with us is a show of strength. The men fight for their king."

Dakaran stood. "I agree with the commander, Father," he said, setting his glass aside. "You need to be kept safe. If something were to happen to you, it would be just as great a tragedy for the kingdom as losing the battle."

"And I will be here to see to that protection, my king," Ayrion said, for once finding himself in agreement with Dakaran.

Rhydan's shoulders lowered slightly.

"Do you think that wise, Guardian?" Dakaran asked.

All three men turned to look at the prince.

"What I meant to say is, I would have thought your talents would be better used to see a swift end to this conflict, on the battlefield."

"The duty of the Guardian Protector and High Guard has always been to the king's safety," Ayrion said. "Commander Tolin and his lancers are more than capable of handling the offensive."

Dakaran opened his mouth to argue.

"Enough of this," the king said. "It's settled. I will direct from here. Ayrion and his men will guard the rise, and the commander has the field. Now, Commander, how about showing me once more what you have planned for this third division."

All eyes returned to the plans. All eyes save Dakaran's.

Chapter 54 | Tolin

BREAKFAST CONSISTED OF a piece of fruit and a wedge of cheese, barely chewed and hastily swallowed. It was all Tolin had time for as he assembled his division heads to go over the battle plans. The meeting hadn't taken long. They were quick to listen and even quicker to obey. He had trained them well.

Tolin was a man of strict order and discipline. He believed a successful army was a prepared army. The way to win was to plan for every possible outcome, thereby mitigating the likelihood of surprise. He loved to watch a well-planned strategy come to life, all the pieces fitting perfectly together to form the whole.

Tolin stepped from his tent and returned the salutes of the two sentries posted outside. He wanted to get a closer look at the enemy ranks. Waving off his escort, he marched through the camp toward the front lines. Men hopped to attention with fist to chest when they saw him. He held his head high. He couldn't afford to show any signs of weakness to his men. They needed their leader to be strong, someone they believed could take them to victory.

Leaders who couldn't earn their men's respect had to resort to fear. Tolin had never found that a viable tactic. He smiled and nodded at a group of lancers casting dice around one of the fires. They started to rise, but he waved them off, motioning for them to continue.

He left the main encampment and headed southwest to where one of the cavalry units had been stationed next to the archer mounds. It seemed he wasn't the only one interested in the enemy's position. He found Ayrion and Captain Barthol already there.

"They seem to be waiting for something," Ayrion said, acknowledging Tolin's arrival. The Guardian had a leather-bound ocular up to his eye for a closer look.

Tolin stared out across the open expanse. "Any idea as to what?"

"None. That's what worries me." Ayrion handed Tolin the spyglass.

Tolin held it up to his eye. The men on the Cylmaran side didn't appear to be in any great hurry. They meandered from one campfire to the next, some half dressed, all seemingly unaware of the army on this side making ready for war. Tolin could have sworn some of the men looked drunk. A fight broke out at one of the fires, and soldiers—if you could call them that—stood round to watch and cheer on the contenders.

"A disgrace, if you ask me," Tolin said as he handed the ocular back to Ayrion, who in turn passed it to Barthol.

The captain took a quick look and shook his head. "My mother always warned us boys before we went a-courtin': 'Just because she looks sweet and smells sweet don't mean that she is.'" He crossed his massive arms and nodded toward the enemy ranks. "It's the *easy* victories that tend to be the most difficult, and costly."

Tolin nodded. "If it seems too good to be true . . ."

"Commander?"

"Over here, son," Barthol said to one of the runners.

The boy rushed over when he spotted Tolin, stopping only long enough to salute before shoving one of the communication pouches in Tolin's direction.

Tolin took the pouch, unhooked the top, and removed the rolled missive inside. He read it twice, then handed the carrier back to the boy. "Tell them I'll be there shortly."

"Yes, sir," the boy said with a deep bow, and then off he went.

Tolin turned to Ayrion. "I've just been informed that the scouts we sent out last night have returned. I'd like you to sit in on their debriefing. They were supposed to have been back hours ago. This late arrival has me concerned."

Ayrion turned to look at Barthol.

"Don't worry," Barthol said. "I'll see to the guard." He saluted Tolin. "Commander."

Tolin reciprocated and watched as the big man disappeared back into the sea of rankers behind them. He liked Barthol. He was fiercely loyal to Ayrion.

"A good man," Tolin said as he and Ayrion headed back to the command post to meet with the pathfinders.

"To a fault."

"Reminds me of Asa. I wouldn't be half the commander you see today without the overcaptain's support."

As they made their way toward the center of the encampment, Tolin could almost feel the weight of unease resting on his men. The laughter and boasting and song had all but died. Most of the men stuck to their tents and fires, weapons within arm's reach. What they weren't saying spoke volumes—conversations consisting of everything except what lay ahead. He would have almost preferred the fighting to waiting for it.

Two soldiers guarding the command post pulled back the flap for them to enter. Stepping into the dimly lit tent, Tolin wrinkled his nose at the smell of horse lather and hard sweat. Overcaptain Asa stood to the left of the entrance, and four men waited in front of Tolin's desk. Tolin was glad to see Asa there. He could certainly use an extra set of eyes, or in Asa's case, *eye*. Judging by the scouts' appearance, they had seen some rough road over their evening's excursion.

Ayrion stood off to the side and watched the men.

The pathfinders weren't wearing the same livery as the lancer corps. Instead, they wore an assortment of thick furs. From a distance, they must have looked more like a pack of ratty badgers than a team of Elondrian scouts.

Tolin directed his attention to the man on the right. "Terris, let's start with you and Ellson."

Terris, a middle-aged man with disheveled hair draping his shoulders and a full beard covering his face, stepped forward and pulled off his fur cap before offering a quick salute. "Sir, Ellson and I, we rode south along the Pyruvian River before cutting west around the Cylmaran forces. We spent the remainder of the night in Cylmaran territory, looking for signs of troop movement, but I'm happy to report we found none. Only local traffic." He saluted again and stepped back.

"So why the late return?" Tolin asked.

"We rode farther than originally expected. Wanted to make sure we didn't miss anything."

Tolin glanced at Ellson. "Anything to add, son?" Ellson was the youngest of the pathfinders. He'd been with them only a couple of months. His hair was shoulder-length and tucked behind his ears.

Ellson ripped his hat off and stepped forward. "No, sir," he said with an awkward bow, followed closely with a salute as if he wasn't sure which he was supposed to do.

Tolin almost chuckled but bit his lip to hold it in. "Very well."

Ellson stepped back into line.

"Did you follow the main road into Cylmar?" Overcaptain Asa asked from behind them.

"Yes, sir," Terris replied, casting a quick glance over his shoulder. "As well as fields and forests that could be used to conceal their movements, but still nothing."

"Very well," Tolin said, turning to the next set. "Merrick, what about you and Bayle?"

Merrick, a short man with a barrel chest and a squared-off goatee that didn't quite fit his chubby face, stepped forward and saluted. "Sir, we would have been back sooner as well, but Bayle's horse picked up a rock in its shoe, and we had to stop for a smithy. Our route took us north toward the base of the Black Hills and then west around the Cylmaran ranks, but we found no signs of additional forces."

Merrick saluted and stepped back beside Bayle, a former merchant sailor who'd traded his life on the sea for the possibility of exploring new territories as an Elondrian scout.

"Didn't we send out three sets?" Tolin asked.

"You did, sir," Merrick said. "Roan and Arnst haven't returned."

"I don't like it, Commander," Asa said behind them, adjusting his eye patch. "Those two had the least distance to travel."

"Where were they sent?" Ayrion asked.

Merrick looked at Ayrion. "The passes leading into the Black Hills—"

"Aye," Asa butted in. "We don't want those flamin' Cylmarans sneakin' up our backsides in the middle of the night."

"Anything back there besides the mines?" Ayrion asked.

"No, sir," Merrick said. "The main pass leads straight through to Cylmar. There's only one branch, and it'll take you back to the mines."

Tolin looked at the four men standing in front of his desk. "If something has happened to those scouts, we need to know."

Merrick saluted. "I can ride, sir. Roan and Arnst are friends, and if something did happen, I'd want to know as well." His words got quick nods of agreement from the other three.

That was the kind of dedication Tolin appreciated. The other pathfinders looked up to Merrick. He was the kind of man who led by example. "How soon can you leave?"

"We'll need fresh mounts and supplies," Merrick said. He pursed his lips. "I would say within the next half hour."

"Very well. Grab some breakfast on the way out." Tolin stood from his seat. "Keep up the good work, gentlemen. You're dismissed." He waited for the three men to leave before turning to Asa. "What do you think?"

"I try not to. That's your job."

Tolin grunted. He should have seen that coming.

"But," Asa continued, "if you're asking what my guts is telling me, I'd have to say . . . nothing good."

Chapter 55 | Dakaran

AFTER THE MEETING between his father, Commander Tolin, and Ayrion, Dakaran decided to head back to his tent. All their talk of strategies and troop placement had given him a headache—one that could be assuaged only with a thick mattress and a soft pillow.

Their discussion of why Overlord Saryn had instigated this war had him worried. What would happen if his father found out? Dakaran would be executed for treason. Then again, after his father's threats of pulling him from succession, what option did he have?

He raised his glass but noticed it was empty. Probably for the best. He needed a clear head, anyway. He had to think this through.

Could he really go through with killing his father? The more he thought about it, the more it plagued him. His stomach twisted with nervous apprehension. He stopped a moment to lean against a rack of pikes to catch his breath. How had this gone so far?

His hands were shaking by the time he reached his tent. A couple of

Valtor's guards stood just outside, their white uniforms a stark contrast to the brightly colored canvas. One lifted the front flap, and Dakaran entered. He walked around a large drapery that acted as a makeshift privacy wall and headed into the main chamber. His tall crimson-robed advisor stood over one of the tables in the center of the room. The miter atop his head reminded him of one of the palace spires, its design much like the crenellation of a battlement.

"Where've you been?" Dakaran asked with a slur even he noticed. He walked over to a second, smaller table he used for his meals and started to pour some more wine but caught himself and opted for the pitcher of water instead. "I was looking for you earlier, but no one saw you leave."

"I can come and go without being seen, Your Highness," Valtor said with a very small bow. "A most helpful trait if you find yourself enabling two opposing forces."

Dakaran took a seat on the sofa to stop his head from spinning. "Are we doing the right thing?"

Valtor lowered the book he'd been reading. His eyes were blank. "A little late for second thoughts, Your Highness."

"I just . . ." Dakaran wrung his hands. "Murdering the *king*." He couldn't bring himself to say *my father*. "Maybe we—"

"Your Highness." Valtor snapped the book shut and placed it on the table. "The pieces have already been put in motion. Even if you wanted to, you couldn't reset the board. And I don't know why you would." Valtor grabbed his staff on his way around the table. "Your father has already threatened to pull you from the succession. He clearly plans to choose someone else."

Ayrion, Dakaran guessed. The pounding in his head suddenly lifted, and his thoughts grew clearer. Valtor was right. What would he do? Warn his father? That would certainly see him in chains, if not on the chopping block. No. The only way he would sit on the throne was if his father was no longer on it.

"Everything will be fine," Valtor said, turning back to the table. He placed his staff against the edge, freeing his hands to collect some papers. "I have a few minor wrinkles that need smoothing."

Dakaran raised his head. "Oh?"

"Nothing for you to worry about, Your Highness."

Dakaran watched from his seat with a careful yet somewhat blurry eye as Valtor packed a couple of books into his riding satchel, grabbed his staff, and made his way to the front of the tent.

Valtor bowed. "By your leave?"

Dakaran dismissed him with a half-hearted wave, then rolled over on his back and stared at the designs stitched into the material overhead. He could hear the tent flap dropping back into place.

He closed his eyes, feeling his headache returning once more. His advisor was right about one thing: they *had* gone too far to turn back.

Chapter 56 | Merrick

MERRICK WAS THE OLDEST of the pathfinders. He'd been a scout in the Elondrian forces for nearly thirty years. The others looked up to him. It was his duty to keep them safe. In a way, he was their commander; at least, that's what he liked to tell them. So, when a couple of his men turned up missing, he was going to be the first to volunteer to go after them.

"Nothing here, Merrick," Terris said as he scoured one side of the crossroad to the other, stopping every so often to study the tracks. Merrick held the reins to Terris's horse as the man continued searching for signs of recent travel. "Just the same as it was when Ellson and I came through here last night."

Along with Merrick, Terris was another who'd spent his life in the king's service. Of their group, Terris was considered the quiet one, which only meant he didn't voice every thought that came traipsing through his mind. He had a good head on his shoulders. He thought things through before acting. Although, with a couple of stout drinks in him—preferably Bristonian White—he'd sing you a tune that would make a Tallosian blush.

Merrick had only gotten his friend drunk in that way once or twice, and only when the mood was so dour that his men required something extreme to pull them out.

"And you and Ellson headed east, while Roan and Arnst went north?" Merrick asked.

"Yes, sir," Ellson butted in eagerly on his left. They called him the *kid*. He was the youngest of the lot. Barely nineteen. His father had been a pathfinder as well, so when Ellson received his papers, he couldn't wait to join up. Merrick gave it six months before the enthusiasm wore off. In the meantime, he'd taken the kid under his wing. Merrick and his wife, Taleen, had never been able to have children, so he tended to look out for the younger ones.

Merrick turned his horse northward. "We best be pressing on." He handed Terris back his horse's reins, and once mounted, they rode through the rest of the morning and into the afternoon before reaching the first pass.

The fissure leading into the Black Hills was wide enough to fit at least four haulers. It was used specifically for mining, but because of the increase in raiders coming out of Cylmar, it had been closed for the season.

Merrick swung down from his horse and studied the packed clay and rock around the mouth of the ravine.

"What do you think?" Terris asked as he guided his horse up alongside Merrick.

"There's been recent movement. Can't tell how many. But if I were to guess, I'd say not more than half a dozen tracks have come and gone through here in the last couple of days."

"The rain holding off is a good thing," Terris said.

There were deep grooves in the rock where heavy wagons, laden with the newly mined ore, had traveled on their way to Aramoor for processing.

"I'll be a-scoutin' ahead, boss," Bayle said in his deep seafaring accent. Without waiting for acknowledgement, Bayle guided his horse into the pass at a slow trot and disappeared around the first turn.

Merrick sighed and shook his head. If there was one thing he could say about Bayle, it was that the man was as stubborn as a two-headed donkey, and just as loud. Bayle was a gruff, in-your-face sort of fellow, but he could read just about any track and smell rain at least a day off. Merrick never could figure out how he did it. It had something to do with all his years at sea.

Merrick stood from where he'd been kneeling and glanced up the road they'd been traveling. "One of us needs to ride north and make sure nothing is moving south from the second pass. I'd hate to get stuck in here with no way to retreat."

"I'll go!" Ellson said, almost shouting. He brushed aside the long dirty-blonde hair covering the left side of his face. His eyes were wide with excitement.

"I don't know," Merrick said, trying to let the boy down easily. The lad was too green to be let off the leash. "Terris would stand a better chance of reading the signs and—"

"No, Commander, I can do it! Give me a chance. I promise I won't let you down."

"I'm not worried about you letting me down. I'm just . . ."

"It doesn't look like there's been any movement, Merrick," Terris said, looking down from his horse. He shrugged. "You're going to have to loosen the reins at some point."

Merrick grunted. He hated when Terris was right, which was generally most of the time. Another reason why he liked having him around. Merrick tended to let his emotions cloud his better judgment, and Terris was a good counterbalance.

"Fine. But you turn back at the first sign of trouble. You hear me? There are no heroes here."

Ellson was beaming from ear to ear. "You won't be disappointed, sir." He actually saluted.

"I better not," Merrick said, shouting after him as the boy swung his horse

around and galloped north. "I don't want to have to explain to your father how
you went and got yourself killed by not listening!"

Ellson didn't slow as he headed up the main road. He did manage a quick
wave behind him, though.

Merrick shook his head. "Foolish upstart. Too eager to prove himself."

"Reminds me of another young man I knew a long time ago," Terris said
with a cheeky grin in Merrick's direction.

"Oh, shut up."

The two men mounted and made their way into the pass. The echoes from
their horses' hooves reverberated off the solid walls rising hundreds of feet into
the air. The passage held an eerie sense of finality. Merrick couldn't seem to
shake the uneasy feeling snaking its way up his back.

Rounding the first corner, they found Bayle kneeling beside his horse,
searching the ground for recent activity. Merrick reined in alongside. He
watched as the stout sailor moved across the rock, looking for fresh tracks.

"I be seein' two recent sets leadin' in," he said, glancing at the overlaying
dust, "but I don't be seein' any leadin' out."

"If I remember correctly," Terris said beside Merrick, "the pass splits a
couple of miles ahead. The left will take you out toward the Cylmaran side of
the mountains, and the right takes you back toward the mines."

Bayle climbed back into his saddle. "After you, boss."

"We'll take it slow." Merrick twisted in his saddle to glance at the passage
behind them. "If Ellson hasn't caught up to us by the time we reach the fork,
we'll leave a marker for him to follow." Markers were a common trait amongst
scouts. Anything from a notch in the bark of a tree to scoring the side of a rock.

The other two flanked him as they continued toward the next curve.
Merrick kept a close eye on the trail for any indication as to what had happened
to their missing comrades. So far, he hadn't seen anything out of the ordinary.
It was hard to tell, though, on such a solid surface. Roan and Arnst had been
with his team for the last three years. They were good men. Both had wives.

Arnst had a young daughter. He hoped the men were all right.

The clopping of their horses' hooves was the only sound present within the vast corridor of stone. The unease he was feeling before had grown. It slithered down his back like fingertips stroking his skin. He rubbed the back of his neck.

"Something doesn't feel right," Terris said, twisting around in his saddle to look behind them.

Merrick agreed.

"What be that?" Bayle asked, bringing them to a stop.

Merrick strained to hear what Bayle had, but the only sound was the howling of the wind as it occasionally whipped through the tunnels from the peaks above.

"That *be* your imagination," Terris mumbled.

By midafternoon, they had managed to reach the forked split in the pass. Merrick climbed down along with the others and walked the open ground around both trailheads, trying to piece together which direction Roan and Arnst might have taken the previous night.

"It appears they took the pass toward the mines," Terris said, moving some pebbles with the toe of his boot to get a good look at the hoofprints underneath.

Merrick checked the left fork. "I'm not seeing any recent tracks heading back toward the other end of the pass."

"That not be makin' a lick a sense," Bayle said. "Why would ye be a-headin' toward the mines if ye be lookin' for armsmen comin' from Cylmar? That trail be only one way."

"Well, something obviously gave them cause to search the ironworks," Terris said, glancing down the left fork.

Merrick didn't like what he was seeing. "Let's eat a quick bite and give Ellson a chance to catch up before moving farther in."

The three ate in silence, keeping a close eye on the trails ahead and the one behind. A quarter of an hour passed, and still no Ellson. Merrick rewrapped the rest of his food and stuffed it back in the satchel. "We can't wait any longer."

Bayle walked over to the right fork, the one leading back to the mines, and scored a simple mark on the wall with another rock, signaling the direction they were taking.

"Make sure it's clear to see," Terris said. "The last time we tried following some of your marks, we nearly ended up in Keldor."

Bayle huffed and dug a little deeper. "There," he said. "Satisfactory?"

Terris smiled. The two picked at each other like an old married couple.

Merrick waited for Bayle to remount before they headed in.

They continued the rest of the way in silence. An hour later, the pass opened into a large canyon that held the mines, the ironworks, and the distribution center. Wooden buildings serving as a small functioning community for the workers dotted the cavern floor. Everything lay in silence. An entire town without a single person in sight.

"Right spooky, it is," Bayle remarked as he scanned the gorge.

"Aye," Terris said. "Reminds me of some of those abandoned cities in Keldor after Mount Ash blew her top. Entire towns left for the land to reclaim. Father and I ran across one when trapping along the Ryne River back when I was just a lad. We took shelter in one of the homes to get out of the rain." Terris shivered slightly. "I think I would have preferred the rain. The ghosts of those who died haunted the place. I spent the entire night listening to footsteps moving from room to room."

Bayle made the sign of an *X* on his chest and spat off to the side. The former sailor was as superstitious as they came.

"Quit messing with the man," Merrick said to Terris as he swung down from his horse. "You're even starting to give me the shakes."

Terris only smiled.

"Let's split up and see if we can't cover more ground," Merrick said. "With Ellson still gone, Terris, you take Bayle with you around the right side, and I'll take the left. We'll meet by those loading docks over there." He pointed to a couple of dilapidated buildings corralled together near the back of the gorge.

Terris slid off his horse and drew his sword.

Merrick untied his bow. "I'll see you fellas on the other side." He nocked an arrow and started toward the first building, his horse following naturally. The building wasn't much to look at: wooden slats nailed together to form four walls, small glass-pane windows boarded over. The single stone chimney at the back certainly wouldn't have kept out the winter cold. He glanced over his shoulder and caught a glint of Bayle's battle-axe as he and Terris approached one of the buildings on the other side of the canyon.

Merrick stepped up on the front porch, keeping a close eye on where he planted his feet. The boards groaned underneath him as he headed for the front door. He reached out, still maintaining a solid hold on his bow, and pushed down on the latch. He nudged the door with his boot, and it slid open with a slow, annoying creak.

Quietly, he stepped inside. He swung his bow left to right, scanning the room. The place was dark save for the rays of light piercing the cracks in the shutters, revealing a heavy amount of dust floating in the air. The building appeared to be a barracks. Small empty cots lined the two outer walls, leaving a narrow walkway down the middle. Not finding any signs of life, he left, closing the door behind him.

One by one, he checked every building around the left perimeter of the ironworks, but to no avail. The place was truly devoid of life. Terris and Bayle were waiting for him by the loading docks as he approached.

"The place is empty, Merrick," Terris said. "No sign of Roan and Arnst anywhere."

"Best we be headin' back, then," Bayle said, sounding relieved.

Merrick wasn't feeling so relieved. There were two scouts, comrades, who were unaccounted for. He wasn't leaving until they were found. "There's still one place we haven't checked."

Bayle shook his head. "I ain't going in there."

"If it was you missing, I'm sure you'd want us to leave no stone unturned."

Bayle grumbled something under his breath but didn't argue.

Terris didn't give his opinion. Instead, he walked over to where they had tied off the horses on one of the corral railings and grabbed a lantern. He lit the wick and started for the mouth of the largest mine.

Merrick had been hoping not to have to enter the mines, but there was nowhere else his men could have gone. He lifted his bow. "Keep your eyes open."

"Did you think I'd be closing 'em?"

Merrick rolled his eyes. Bayle was somewhat of an acquired taste. He always looked at the glass as half empty and was never shy about letting you know.

"Here, I'll carry that," Bayle said as he grabbed the lantern from Terris.

"Hold it steady," Terris scolded, tripping on one of the cart rails that led down into the bowels of the mountain.

"Sorry 'bout that," Bayle said, holding the lantern up. "I've got me a fear of dark spaces. Why'd you think I first chose the sea as me trade?"

"Because no one on land wanted you," Terris mocked.

Bayle chuckled, the light shaking as he did.

The farther into the mine they went, the damper it became. Merrick could no longer see the tunnel entrance behind them. They were completely surrounded by darkness. Apart from their own nervous breaths, the only noise to be heard was the shuffle of gravel under their feet.

Bayle continued to swing the lantern slowly from one side to the other, its light barely enough to see where to place their feet.

"Wait," Merrick whispered. "I think I hear something ahead."

The other two stopped to listen.

The air had turned sour, the smell of mildew and soil replaced by something much stronger. Something Merrick was all too familiar with.

"What is it?" Terris asked.

"It be a warning for us to leave," Bayle said.

He turned and started to oblige, but Terris snatched the lantern back out of his hand before he could. "Fine. If you want to go back, be my guest. But the lantern's mine, so we'll be taking it with us."

Bayle huffed and turned back around. "I don't like it," he said, keeping his voice lowered. "We shouldn't be here. Why would Roan and Arnst have come in this place? It don't be makin' no sense."

The sound ahead was beginning to grow. It was strange, almost like an underground river with its waters echoing off the inside of the rock walls.

"Come on," Merrick said, starting forward once again. "We've come this far."

Terris moved alongside him, holding out the lantern for them to see. They hadn't made it twenty feet when there was a loud crash behind them.

Merrick spun and drew his bowstring, only to find Bayle lying flat on his face.

"What happened?" Merrick walked over and helped Terris haul the plucky man back to his feet.

"What's it look like? I fell," Bayle barked. He brushed off his knees and turned around to see what he'd tripped on. "Sweet mother's milk."

Terris held up the lantern, his eyes bulged. "Merciful Creator."

"What is it?" Merrick asked as he moved to the side to get a better look, the suffocating stench already telling him what he'd find.

"It's a piece of a leg, I think," Terris said, then raised his hand and pointed to the far wall. "There's more."

Pieces of bodies were gathered in a pile on the right side of the tunnel, the flesh mostly chewed off, and recently.

Terris leaned over. "Is it . . ."

Merrick nodded. He couldn't bring himself to say it out loud. He recognized Roan's knife. Roan had won it off him a few years back. He always wore it at the front of his belt just to tease him. Merrick snarled. "They deserved better than this." He could feel his temperature rising. He wanted to find who'd done this to his men and return the favor.

"Who could have done this?" Terris asked, kneeling to examine some of the remains.

"More like *what*," Merrick corrected.

"I don't care," Bayle said. "I say we be goin' before it does the same to us."

"We're not leaving until we find out what happened," Merrick hissed. "We owe them that much."

Raising his bow once more, he crept his way toward the next corner of the tunnel.

Thankfully, the others followed, since they had the lantern.

There was a sliver of light ahead, coming from just around the next bend. They laid the lantern down far enough back to keep from displaying their shadows on the wall. Merrick pressed against the stone and stepped right to the edge.

"What's that noise?" Bayle whispered, barely loud enough to hear. "It be soundin' like . . . like . . ."

Without saying another word, they peered around the corner. Merrick froze. On the other side was an enormous cavern, its walls lined with multiple tunnels, each heading in a separate direction. At the center was a large fire pit, where flames cast eerie shadows across the entire hollowed-out fissure. And surrounding the flames was the source of their fear.

Hor'hounds. Hundreds of them.

Chapter 57 | Merrick

MERRICK COULD BARELY believe his eyes.

The stories told of these ancient creatures didn't come close to doing them justice, and they were every bit as frightening. Thick, matted fur coated their wide, muscular frames. Dagger-size fangs hung from long, angular snouts, and their yellow eyes glowed near the fire. Each hound was large enough to ride.

Hor'hounds were said to be one part canine, one part wolf, and one part dark magic. They had been created during the Wizard Wars but driven back into the frozen Northlands and sealed beyond the great wall of Bel'Taag during the time of the Great Purge. Merrick wondered how they had managed to end up in an abandoned mine here in the middle of the Black Hills.

The entire place reeked of moist rock, burnt coal, and wet dog. As frightening as it was to see these creatures, something else caused his bowels to squeeze. In the middle of the horde stood a solitary figure draped in a dark shroud.

"Patience, my friends, your time is coming," the robed figure soothed. It was a man. He sounded aged. The hor'hounds turned to look at the figure standing in their midst. "Tomorrow, you will feast on the flesh of kings."

The creatures howled in response, nearly paralyzing Merrick in fear. It took everything he had to force himself to edge away from the corner, pushing Terris and Bayle along with him.

Bayle grabbed the lantern behind them, and the three made a run for it.

They had to make it out of there alive. It wasn't just their lives at stake; it was the entire Elondrian army, including the High King himself. What had they gotten themselves mixed up in?

Twice, Merrick stumbled and almost went down. Both times, he caught himself, forcing his legs to keep running. He glanced over his shoulder to see if they'd been spotted or if the creatures were giving chase. Nothing so far.

Not only was Merrick the oldest, but he was the shortest as well, making it more difficult to keep up with the other two. Bringing up the rear meant he had the least light available to see with. Every time he turned to look, all he saw was blackness.

Up ahead, the mouth of the tunnel finally came into view. They were almost there.

Terris, with his longer legs and leaner frame, was the first to burst from the mine; Bayle was right behind, huffing and puffing the entire way.

Merrick stumbled through, hardly able to catch his own breath. By the time he reached his horse, it was coming in short, raspy draws. He was too winded to even give orders. As it happened, he didn't need to. Both Bayle and Terris were already mounted and snapping reins by the time Merrick had swung his leg over. He slid his arrow back in its quiver and hooked his bow around his shoulder. Digging in his boots, he took off after the other two as they raced through the abandoned buildings for the pass ahead.

Terris was the first to reach the mouth of the pass, Bayle nipping at his heels. Merrick twisted in his saddle to get one last look at the mine. Nothing seemed to be following. He breathed a small sigh of relief as he turned back around and concentrated on keeping his horse away from the larger rock.

The thought of slowing down through the treacherous curves never even crossed his mind as he pushed his horse as hard as he dared. They made great time through the pass leading back to the main fork. Rounding the last bend, they spotted the split in the channel ahead.

"Don't slow down!" Merrick shouted ahead.

They hit the intersection, and Terris's horse reared, nearly throwing him out of the saddle.

"Watch out!" Bayle shouted, jerking his horse to a stop as he reached for his axe.

Merrick pulled back on his reins just in time to keep from hitting Bayle, but not before seeing an enormous hor'hound step out from behind the right fork. It must have been guarding the tunnel leading back to Cylmar. Why hadn't they seen it before?

Merrick barely had time to unhook his bow and nock an arrow before the creature attacked, its fangs wide for the kill. Bayle threw himself off his horse as the creature tore into them.

Terris's horse was thrown against the mountain wall. The lanky man screamed in pain as his leg was crushed between the horse and the rock. His quick thinking kept him alive as he unsheathed his sword in time to land a solid blow to the side of the hound's head, deflecting it far enough to keep from reaching him.

Merrick drew his bowstring and released, but the hound bounded off the wall and he missed. "Blood and ash!" He grabbed another arrow, holding on to this horse with his legs.

"Hold on, Terris, I'm a-comin'!" Bayle shouted as he climbed back into his saddle and swung his horse around. He rode in behind the hound, swinging his axe to keep the creature's attention away from Terris, who was desperately trying to free his leg.

With Bayle coming up behind it, the hound turned and came straight for Merrick.

"I got you this time, you ugly excuse for a mangy mutt!" Merrick drew again. The creature leaped into the air, and Merrick released. He heard the hor'hound howl as he threw himself out of the saddle. The creature soared right over his horse, landing on the other side. It would have ripped him in half had he still been there.

Merrick rolled back to his hands and knees, the beast not twenty paces away. His arrow was protruding from its left shoulder. The hound tried ripping it out with its jaws, only managing to snap the shaft in half. Merrick climbed to his feet and reached for another arrow, but his quiver was gone. Frantically, he looked around, spotting it up against the far wall. He'd never reach it in time.

The creature turned and looked at him, its jaws parting, allowing long runs of saliva to hang from the corners as it barked out its challenge and charged.

Merrick drew his sword with one hand and his dagger with the other. He knew he didn't stand a chance, but he held his ground. He wasn't about to leave this world whimpering like a coward.

The hor'hound reached him with two powerful leaps. Merrick swung with everything he had as he leaped to the side. He felt the impact of the creature's paw as it hurled him through the air. He landed in a heap, all air knocked from his lungs. His fingers still gripped his sword, but his dagger was gone. He saw it planted in the hound's side, just behind the left shoulder.

The creature howled in fury. Merrick would have liked to do the same, but he was too busy trying to suck the wind back in. Everything around him started to blur. He shook his head, trying to clear his vision. He couldn't lose focus. He had to keep moving.

As fast as he could, he crawled toward the side of the pass. He couldn't understand why the creature hadn't finished him off. A shout from behind brought him around in time to see Bayle barreling down on the hound. The creature drove straight for the wall and then leaped off it, angling back around for Bayle.

Bayle managed one swing of his axe before the creature knocked his horse out from under him and sent him tumbling. He cut a deep wound in the front of the hound's chest before the impact ripped his axe from his fingers. Bayle shouted like a man possessed, then hit the ground and didn't move.

Come on. Get up, you ornery cuss! Merrick wasn't sure if he was talking to Bayle or himself. He fought his way back to his feet. He had to draw the hound away from his men. He shouted as he pushed himself up with his sword. "Here I am! Come and get me! I'm right here!"

Terris was lying against the far wall, unable to do anything but watch, his leg no doubt shattered.

Merrick stumbled forward into the middle of the pass.

The hor'hound spared a passing glance his way, but with easier prey lying in front of it, Merrick was ignored.

Merrick watched helplessly as the hound closed in on Bayle. There wasn't anything he could do. He was too far away. Merrick grabbed his bow and hobbled across the ravine as fast as he could, desperate to reach his quiver of arrows.

Bayle started moving, but not soon enough. He tried crawling toward his axe, but the creature kicked it back across the stone. It was playing with him. Taunting him.

"Hang me from the yardarm and watch me dance!" Bayle spat as he tried crawling away from the creature. In true sailor fashion, he spouted language that could have been uttered only by a true seafaring man. He let fly every name in the book, and a few he'd evidently created specially for just such an occasion.

Merrick grabbed his quiver, but by then, the creature had lunged for Bayle.

Bayle raised his arm in a desperate attempt to protect his head, and the hor'hound sank its huge fangs straight through to the bone. Bayle screamed as the creature shook him like a doll. He pounded on the top of its head with his free hand.

Merrick yanked an arrow from the quiver and turned to draw. As soon as he did, something came flying out of the tunnel behind them. It was Ellson. He had his sword in hand as he rode straight for the beast. There was no fear at all. The boy leaped from his horse, his sword in the air, ready to plunge.

The hound release Bayle's arm and turned, snatching Ellson right out of the air like a dog with a stick. The boy didn't stand a chance. He screamed as the hound bit down on his shoulder and neck.

"No!" Merrick fired his bow and the arrow flew true, catching the hound in the side. It dropped Ellson, but even from where Merrick was standing, he could see it wasn't going to matter. Half the boy's neck was missing.

Merrick could barely see for the tears. He drew another arrow and nocked, his hands shaking with rage. He screamed and fired again, this time catching the hor'hound straight in the chest. It faltered.

He didn't have time to draw again as the creature rushed him, its massive paws scattering gravel and rock in all directions. He threw the bow down and raised his sword. If he was going down, he was taking this thing with him. He aimed for the mouth. He was going to drive it straight through its head when it opened for him.

"Come and get it!" he shouted.

Merrick waited till the last possible moment, then drove his sword home.

He missed, catching only the outer lip as the hound turned its head at the last moment. The creature's shoulder hit Merrick, and he could feel his ribs pop. He slid across the gravel, barely able to move. He knew he wasn't getting back up. It was over. His men were going to die because he didn't have the strength to keep fighting. He'd led them straight into a trap. He went to raise his sword but realized it wasn't there. He'd lost it in the fall.

He grabbed the only weapon he had left: the knife in his boot.

The hor'hound stood over him, its teeth dripping Ellson's blood across his face. The creature actually had the audacity to smile. It raised its head and howled. Merrick raised his dagger, but before he had time to swing, the hound shrieked and dropped on top of him.

Merrick wheezed as the impact knocked the air from his lungs all over again. There was only one thought that flooded his mind: *Kill it!*

He plunged his dagger into the unmoving creature's back. Then he pulled it out and did it again. And again. He kept stabbing until his arm gave out. Once his mind cleared enough to realize the animal was dead, he struggled to push the lifeless carcass off his legs.

Struggling to his feet, he noticed Bayle's battle-axe sticking out of the creature's neck and yanked the blade free. He limped over to where Bayle was sitting beside Ellson's body. There was no need to ask if he was dead. The boy's eyes were wide and lifeless.

"Foolish child!" Merrick said, practically falling down beside him. "Why did he do it? Why couldn't it have been me?" Merrick leaned over and closed Ellson's eyes respectfully. "We will take the body with us. He deserves a proper burial."

"Aye," Bayle said, wincing as he cradled his ruined arm.

Merrick ripped off his sleeve and started tying off Bayle's wounds to keep him from bleeding to death. It didn't look good. He wasn't sure the man would make it back to camp.

He left Bayle and limped over to where Terris was trying his best to make it up with one leg. "How bad is it?"

"Bad enough." He yelped as Merrick pulled him the rest of the way up.

"We need to get out of here before we run into more."

"How's Bayle's arm?" Terris asked.

Merrick shook his head. "Not looking good. If we don't hurry, he'll bleed out before we make it back."

Merrick collected the skittish horses, which surprisingly had not run off during the fighting—a true testament to their battle training. Bayle's horse was too badly injured to take with them, so he rode double with Merrick. They used Ellson's horse to transport the boy's body back to his parents.

After everyone had mounted, they headed out. The pace was slower but steady. The late evening sky had begun to darken as they rounded the last curve leading out of the pass. Thankfully, they hadn't encountered any more of the creatures.

"Let's move," Merrick said as he spurred his animal faster. "We need to warn the king."

Chapter 58 | Orlyn

ORLYN FOUND HIMSELF whistling as he wrapped the final purchase of the day. He'd already hung the CLOSED sign on the door to keep other customers from entering.

The sun had crossed behind the shops on the other side of the street a couple of hours earlier, signaling to his stomach that supper was just around the corner. He could hardly wait. He had ordered a side of ham from the butcher and was going to pick it up on his way home.

He handed Sorna her bag of dorak root, and she handed him three coppers.

"Will I be seeing you at Performance Night next week, Orlyn?" his final customer asked with a lingering smile. Sorna had been pursuing Orlyn for nearly twenty years, ever since her husband had died in a milling accident. With all the coin she'd spent at his shop, she could have opened her own apothecary.

"I don't know," he said, his stomach wanting to hurry her along. "But there's a good possibility."

Sorna wasn't exactly unattractive: stately silver hair cut to the shoulders, a kind smile with bright eyes that made Orlyn want to fall into them. Most importantly, she was tall enough for him to kiss and could make a dry goose taste like stuffed pheasant. His stomach grumbled at the thought. Unfortunately, she also had seven children, and even though fully raised, Orlyn had always feared they would reject another man taking their father's place.

"I will save you a seat," she said with a wink as she closed the door behind her.

After a while, it occurred to him that he was standing in the middle of the shop with a stupid grin on his face. He shook his head and chuckled. "You old fool." Pushing his feelings aside, he locked the door and closed the curtains. "Good night and sweet dreams, my beauties," he said as he turned back to his plants. They were his family. He loved each and every one them.

With a whistle, he started refilling his jars. It had been a fairly busy day, and he had quite a few to top up. He began at the back, as was his custom since those were typically less used, and began working his way forward, one shelf at a time.

The bell on the front door rang.

Orlyn looked up from where he'd been refilling another bottle of coneflower. "I thought I locked that." *Too bad they don't make a tonic for being old and senile.* He grabbed the side of the shelf and hauled himself back to his feet.

"We're closed. Try back tomorrow." When no answer came and the bell didn't ring to signal that whoever it was had left, he made his way through the aisles to the front. Couldn't they see the sign on the door? He stepped out from the center aisle and looked around. There was no one there. *That's strange.* He checked the door. It was locked.

He turned around and jumped. There was a man leaning against one of the shelves he'd just walked past. "Oh, my!" He grabbed his chest. "You startled me. How did you . . ." He glanced at the locked door, then back at the man.

The stranger was tall. Not as tall as Orlyn but broader in the shoulders, and younger by a good twenty years. He wasn't wearing the white robes of the Watch, but that didn't mean he didn't work for them. Besides, his darker skin gave him away as someone not from the area.

"Are you the apothecary?"

A rather strange question, Orlyn thought, while standing in the middle of an apothecary's shop. "My name is Orlyn. Can I help you with something?"

"Yes, I believe you can." The man's smile matched his hair—greasy with a slick edge. He held Orlyn's gaze, never blinking.

Orlyn slowly made his way toward the first row of shelves. "As I said earlier, I'm closed for the day. Can your business wait until the morrow?"

"Afraid not," the man said, taking a step forward.

Orlyn took a matching step back. His staff was in the storage room. Something told him he would need it. "I'm sorry," he said, "unless this is an emergency, I'm going to have to ask you to leave." He retreated another two steps.

The way the man kept smiling filled Orlyn with concern.

"Where are you going?"

"I . . . I just need to get something from the storage room."

"Something like this?"

Orlyn stopped, his eyes bulging. The man was holding his staff. He could see the runes from where he was standing, and his transferal nestled into the top. Who was this man?

No longer hiding his intentions, Orlyn started moving backward. The front door was locked. If he could reach the storage room—

The intruder rushed him.

Orlyn grabbed the nearest set of shelves and heaved with all his might.

The man was light on his feet and dove out of the way before the shelves hit him.

Glass shattered and flew across the floor as jars of herbs hit the ground and spread their contents in all directions. Orlyn hated doing it, but it gave him the time he needed to make it down the aisle. He practically hopped the counter and grabbed the door to the back. He could hear the crunching of glass behind him as his assailant rushed across the shop. Orlyn flung the door open, jumped inside, and swung it shut before the man had made it over the counter.

He locked the handle and quickly pushed a table in front for weight.

The man on the other side was doing his best to kick it down.

Behind him were two doors: one leading to the alley behind his shop, the other to the second-floor residence. If he could make it outside before the man broke through, he might be able to lose him in the backstreets.

Orlyn turned and charged across the room. Thankfully, he hadn't locked the back door yet. He flung it open and found himself face-to-face with a second robed individual. Before he could shut the door, the man blew some kind of powder in Orlyn's face.

Orlyn staggered backward. He recognized the pungent scent of ether. "Ah, chicken stink," he mumbled just before his knees buckled and everything went black.

A wave of cold water snapped Orlyn back to consciousness. He let out a strangled hoot. Where was he? What happened? He tried to swallow, then realized he'd been gagged. He felt like he'd been kicked in the gut. There was a funny taste in his mouth, like vinegar and pine sap.

His mind started to clear, and he remembered the attack. His staff? Where was his staff? He tried to turn to see if he could find it, but he couldn't move. His hands and feet were bound to his chair. What was going on?

"He's awake, missus," a voice said in the darkness.

Orlyn squinted, trying to see who was out there. The room was dim. He could just make out the white cloak of a Black Watch guard nearby, empty pail in hand.

Orlyn shook his head, trying to rid himself of the water dripping from his beard, bangs, and brows. His eyes were adjusting. A single torch on the wall revealed the silhouettes of several people near the door, but he couldn't see who they were.

Simple panel boards lined the floor and walls. There were cots down both sides of the room and wall racks between each bed for storing weapons. Unfortunately, the racks were empty—not that he could have done anything even had they been fully stocked. It looked like he was being held in one of the Sidaran barracks.

A figure shuffled forward, completely cloaked in black. "Is this him?" The woman's voice sounded at least a hundred years old. Orlyn strained to catch a glimpse of the face beneath the cowl, but it was useless. He could barely see three paces in front of his chair. Regardless, he was afraid he knew exactly who this was.

"That's him," another woman replied from somewhere to his right. Her voice shook as she spoke. "He . . . he used his magic plants to try to seduce me." A couple of the guards chuckled. "You just ask Felina if he didn't. She'll tell you I speak the truth."

Helene? Orlyn couldn't believe it. He'd been handed over to the White Tower by Helene Tunsfield, the stupid woman who had accused him of using magic when she had seen a plant move.

"If I had stayed in his shop a moment longer," she said, "I shudder to think what might have happened to my womanly virtue."

"From the look of you," one of the guards said, "not much."

The three men laughed.

"I'm just doing my duty as an upstanding citizen of Easthaven."

Orlyn could almost hear the stiffness in Helene's voice. He could picture her chin held high as she justified her actions.

"Of course you are, my dear." The black-robed woman waved her hand.

"I'm through with her."

Just when Orlyn thought Helene could stoop no lower, she opened her mouth. "Do I . . . do I collect some sort of compensation for this?"

"Compensation?"

"You know . . . reward."

"Of course, my dear." Again, the old woman waved for the guards to take her.

"What do we do with her?" the guard with the bucket asked.

"We can't have her or her friend running their mouths in town. Put them with the others."

"What?" Helene squealed.

"They'll make fine washerwomen for the Tower. Blood is so difficult to get out of white, you know."

Helene let out an ear-piercing shrill. "No! You can't do this! Do you know who I am? Who my husband is? I'm the one who told you about the apothecary!"

"Yes, you have proven to have surprisingly loose lips, *Your Ladyship*. I'm sure there are many more wielders here you'll be willing to expose before the inquisitors are done with you."

Orlyn heard a loud *thump*. From the sound of it, Helene had passed out, and no one had bothered to catch her. *Poor Helene.* Had he not been gagged, he might have joined the others in their laughter. If he was to be taken to the White Tower, it was a comfort to know he'd be keeping such fine company.

He could hear Helene's shoes scraping the floor as the guards dragged her out the door. A surprisingly silent Felina was ushered out right behind her, whimpering so hard that she was shaking from head to toe.

The cloaked woman turned. "You are on the council, are you not?"

Orlyn could just make out the tip of her nose from beneath her hood. He tried to tell her he didn't know what she was talking about, but the gag muffled every word. The woman, who Orlyn was sure was the witch Ty had run into, stepped forward and removed his gag. She had the most withered hands he'd ever seen.

"Ah, much better," he mumbled, working his tongue around in his mouth, trying to draw saliva.

"Tell me about the boy," she said, taking a small step back. She braced herself with her cane.

"Boy? What boy? As it happens, I have no children. My poor Nora, Creator rest her soul, was barren." He let his shoulders sag.

The old woman lifted her withered hand and slid a single curved nail down the side of his face. "No children? What a shame, and from such a fine specimen as yourself."

"Isn't that so. I'm sure I would have sired quite a resplendent brood."

The witch lowered her hood. Orlyn tried to mask a shudder. *I hope she's not volunteering,* he thought.

She didn't just sound like she was a hundred years old—she looked it as well. Her skin was wrinkled like an old peach and hung from her neck like the jowls of a bloodhound. Her white hair, or what was left of it, draped the sides of her face. Her eyes were brown and sunken, and her nose was even more bulbous than his own. Quite a terrifying face to come across in the dark.

"Don't make me ask again," she said. "I would hate to ruin such handsome features." She smiled and playfully tugged on his beard. He yelped when her ring snagged on a few of his long whiskers. The ring was a spider, eight legs wrapped around her finger with a crystal for its belly. The stone pulsed a deep red, erasing any doubt about whether she was a wielder.

"Madam, if I knew what boy you were referring to, I might be better able to answer your rather vague question."

Her hand shot out of her robe and grabbed his throat, nails digging into his flesh. She yanked his head forward until their noses touched. "The faeling. Tell me where he is."

Orlyn gulped. How did she know what Ty was? What else did she know?

"Fae-what? Tell you where who is? I don't know what you're talking about." He could feel something running down his neck—probably blood from where the woman's nails dug into his flesh. "Madam, if you have mistakenly taken me for some wielder of magic on the word of a chinwagger like Helene Tunsfield, then you have been sadly duped. Helene Tunsfield would sell out her own family if she thought it would better her standing in the community. There has been a grave misunderstanding here." Orlyn continued to struggle against his bindings. They seemed to be loosening. Or maybe that was just wishful thinking. "Now, if you were to release me, I would be more than willing to keep this whole miscarriage of justice to myself."

The old woman's laugh sent a tinge of dread up his legs. "You're a very convincing liar, my dear apothecary, but . . ." She turned toward the door. "Bring it!"

The man with the slick hair who had attacked Orlyn in his shop stepped out from the shadows. He was holding Orlyn's staff. The intricate detailing of the vines and runes glistened in the light of the torch.

Orlyn fought against his ropes. He pulled with everything he could muster. If he could just get his hands on it . . .

The old woman snatched the staff from the man. "What do you call this?" She held it in front of Orlyn to taunt him.

He took a moment to look it over. It appeared undamaged. Good. The crystal was still resting at the top. "It looks like a rather decorative walking stick."

She released his neck and backhanded him across the face. His head whipped hard to the right. He hadn't expected such strength from someone so frail-looking. The side of his face burned. He checked his teeth with his tongue to make sure they were still there.

"I've never seen a staff like this before," she said, studying the runes. "Where did you get it?"

"My father."

"Your father? And where is he?"

Orlyn sighed. "Nowhere you can reach him. Although I'd be happy to help you try."

The witch cackled. "I applaud your efforts, apothecary. Your loyalty is touching." She began to pace. "Now tell me of the boy. Has he reached his full potential? Does he even know who he is?"

Orlyn decided to drop the pretense and try a more forward tactic. "Of course he knows who he is, and he's more powerful than you can possibly imagine."

She paused a moment but held her smile. "Not quite the impression I got after he ran screaming from my shop like a frightened child in the woods on Dark Winter's Eve."

Orlyn's stony gaze crumbled, leaving behind a sad smirk. *Yep, that sounds like Ty.*

"So, let's start again, shall we?" the sorceress said as she rounded the back of his chair, her cane tapping the floorboards. Orlyn could feel her hot breath against the side of his face. "Tell you what. You answer just one question for me and I'll make sure you live long enough to see the White Tower. If not, this room is going to be the last thing you'll ever see."

Orlyn gritted his teeth.

"Tell me. Where is the boy?"

Orlyn stopped wrestling against the ropes and leaned forward as far as he could. "I'll die first."

The witch studied his face. "I believe you. I can see it in your eyes. You *would* be willing to sacrifice your life for him." She raised her hand, signaling to those behind her. "But would you be willing to sacrifice someone else's?"

The door opened, and three people walked in—two guards and someone in the middle. Orlyn squinted, but he couldn't tell who it was because of the bag over their head.

"Who are you people? What do you want?"

The woman's voice had Orlyn gasping for breath. *Sorna?*

The guards put a chair directly in front of Orlyn and forced her into it. They ripped the bag off her head, and Orlyn's hopes withered. It was Sorna. There were tears in her eyes. She had bruises on her face and a split lip. Why had they taken her? Had they seen them talking before he'd closed up the shop?

It took her a moment to adjust to the dim light. "Orlyn?" Her eyes widened. "Orlyn!" She tried to stand, but one of the guards shoved her back down.

"Orlyn, what's going on? Why are you just—" Then she noticed his bindings, and she leaned forward to reach him, but the guard yanked her back once again. "What did they do to you?" She looked around the room frantically. "Who are these people?"

"Let her go! She has nothing to do with this."

The old woman moved around to the side. "Oh, I'd say she has everything to do with this."

"To do with what?" Sorna asked. "What's going on?"

The two guards grabbed Sorna's arms, and she shrieked. Orlyn jerked on his bindings, nearly tipping his chair over.

"Get your hands off her!"

She tried to fight them off, but one clap to the side of her head put a quick stop to it.

"Stop!" Orlyn couldn't move. He couldn't do anything but watch.

She sat there trembling like a frightened animal and let them tie her arms behind the chair.

It was one thing for Orlyn to be willing to suffer to keep Ty safe, but how could he be expected to allow Sorna to? She was an innocent.

"Rukar tells me you have a fondness for this woman."

The man with the greasy hair on Orlyn's right smiled.

"Says she has a fondness for you, too." The witch looked at Sorna. "Is that right, dear? Do you care for this man?"

Sorna looked at Orlyn, then back at her. "Why does it matter? What do you want?"

"Answer the question." The old woman nodded to the men standing behind Sorna, and one of them yanked Sorna's arms backward. Orlyn heard a *pop*.

Sorna screamed.

"Stop it, curse you!" Orlyn yanked and wrenched, nearly pulling his own arms out of their sockets as he fought to break free.

"Answer the question. Do you care for this man?"

"Yes, yes," Sorna said, tears streaking down both cheeks.

The old woman gestured for them to release her arms. Sorna slumped in her chair, not daring to look up.

"Good. Let's hope he reciprocates that affection."

"It'll be all right," Orlyn said, attempting to comfort her. "Look at me. It will be all right."

"It will be if you answer my question," the witch said as she watched the two of them with a certain amount of glee in her eyes. She looked at Sorna. "It occurs to me that perhaps you aren't as familiar with this man as you should be."

Orlyn sneered. It was all he could do.

The old woman smiled. "My name is Mangora. I'm a representative of the White Tower."

"You're a witch, you mean," Orlyn said.

Sorna's eyes widened.

"And you're a wielder," Mangora shot back.

Sorna's eyes widened even farther. She stared at Orlyn, confusion on her face.

"Now that that's out of the way," Mangora said. "I'm here because the Tower has been informed of a growing number of dissidents living in Easthaven. Wielders hiding amongst you."

"You being one of them!" Orlyn was nearly panting from anger.

"These ven'ae have been harboring someone. Someone the Tower has been hunting for a very long time." Mangora hobbled over to Sorna, placed her fingers around her neck, then smiled at Orlyn. "So, I'll ask you one last time, apothecary. Where is the boy?"

"Let her go, witch," Orlyn demanded. "I'm the one you want."

"No. You're not." She tightened her grip, and Sorna started to gasp for air, blood oozing around Mangora's nails.

"Please," Sorna stuttered under the witch's grip, "I've got children."

"Then maybe I should have them brought in for questioning as well."

Sorna's mouth opened and shut as she gasped for breath. Desperation flooded her eyes as she stared at Orlyn, begging him to help her.

Every muscle in Orlyn's body strained to the point of snapping. He couldn't let them kill Sorna. But he couldn't betray Ty.

Sorna's face began turning a pale blue. She was suffocating right in front of him. Orlyn's mind cried out, searching for some way to justify this.

Ty, at least, could defend himself. He had the council to protect him. Sorna had no one. She didn't even know why this was happening.

"I won't ask again," Mangora said, squeezing all the harder. "Where is the boy?"

Chapter 59 | Ferrin

ERRIN GASPED.

The inhalation was sharp. A familiar wave of ice coursed through his body. Peering out through swollen eyes, he watched as Rae worked her hands across another deep laceration, sliding her fingers halfway to his navel. The skin rewove and the pain in his chest dulled, leaving only the intense throbbing of his fingers.

One by one, she pulled the thick wedges from under what remained of Ferrin's fingernails. Cheeks had spent a remarkable amount of time tapping them in. Ferrin had passed out more than once, only to be revived for another round. He couldn't understand why the inquisitor was continuing his sessions. He'd thought that since they had given him a final ultimatum, they would leave him to think about it. Clearly, he was wrong.

Ferrin knew his time was running out. His meeting with the Archchancellor in the chamber below had told him as much. He could either use his gifts for the Tower or have them stripped away by other means. Azriel had said Ferrin would be leaving the Tower one way or the other. Ferrin hoped it was with his soul still intact.

With the last of the small shards removed from his fingers, Rae pushed her healing into the damaged tips. He took a slow breath in through his nose and exhaled the same way. The intense throbbing was nothing more than a distant memory, a memory he would relive over and over again unless he found a way to escape. His only hope was Rae and her transferal.

He looked into her eyes. All he saw was hopelessness. He saw a woman with nothing left to live for. He could almost understand. If not for Myriah, he would have given in long before. Rae held his gaze a moment longer before removing her bloodstained hands from his chest.

Ferrin twisted in his restraints. "Thank you."

She quickly withdrew and glanced back down at the floor. Her dark-brown hair hung in strands to block her face.

"No need to thank me," Cheeks called out from across the room. His back was to Ferrin as he fumbled through his bag of utensils. "What should we try next? Ah, here we go." The inquisitor turned and held out a hammer in one hand and a long nail in the other.

Ferrin tensed. He knew what was coming. Cheeks enjoyed finding new and creative places to insert his nails. The last time had been between Ferrin's toes. More than once, he had required healing just to revive him from unconsciousness. He almost longed for those moments. It was the only time he truly felt nothing.

"Now, where were we? Oh, right, your wielder friends in Rhowynn. I want the names of those on the council."

"What council?" Cheeks was no longer asking him to join the Tower. In fact, the inquisitor had quit mentioning making weapons altogether. It seemed that all he cared about now was finding more wielders to persecute.

"Don't play coy with me, smith. A city the size of Rhowynn would have a rather large wielder council. I want their names."

The inquisitor stepped up on the base of the rack and pressed the tip of the nail against the back of Ferrin's hand just behind the center knuckle. Beads of sweat dotted Ferrin's forehead. How long had it been since the last time Cheeks had used the nail? *Was it last week, or the week before, or yesterday?* Time seemed meaningless in the Tower. As often as he was tortured, one session tended to blur into the next. He wasn't even sure how long it had been since his capture. Had it been days? Weeks? Months? It felt like years.

"So, where shall we start, hmm? With your friends?" Cheeks studied Ferrin's eyes. "No, perhaps not." He lifted the nail and tapped the head against his chin in thought. "How about your family?" The inquisitor's eyes suddenly brightened. "How about . . . a sister?"

Ferrin didn't move. *How could he possibly know about . . .* He almost raised his head, giving away his panic, but then thought better of it as he realized the inquisitor was more than likely just probing for something to use. Then he thought some more. No. It was more than probing. Cheeks had specifically mentioned a *sister*. Why would he . . . Then it hit him.

Ferrin turned his head and caught Rae's eye. She quickly looked away but not before he had seen the guilt. She had betrayed him. Worse, she had betrayed his sister. As badly as Rae was treated, how could she offer up another for them to use?

Ferrin was furious; his fists clenched tight enough to feel his newly healed nails digging into his palms. Worse, he was furious with himself for having given away the information. His mind raced. Even if they knew he had a sister, how would they ever find her? For a brief moment, he felt an overwhelming sense of relief, until he remembered that the Black Watch had already been to his home. They knew where he lived. Relief was quickly replaced with panic.

The inquisitor glanced at Rae. "Yes, my dear Rae is quite the treasure, isn't she?" Cheeks looked at Ferrin, pursed his lips, then stepped down off the rack. "It's getting late. I think I'll let you mull this over tonight. As you're sitting in your cell, I want you to imagine all the wonderful new experiences I will introduce your sister to once we bring her in."

Ferrin yanked against his shackles, letting the metal dig into his wrists as he fought to get his hands on Cheeks. His hatred burned like a forge's fire. He leaned forward and met the tattooed inquisitor's blue eyes. "You go near my sister, and I promise you, transferal or not, I will chase you all the way to the Pits of Aran'gal, into the arms of the Defiler himself if I have to. There is nowhere you will be able to hide from me."

Cheeks stepped back up onto the base of the rack and looked Ferrin in the eyes. With one hand, he reached out and pinched Ferrin's cheek. "You're so cute when you're angry." He chuckled all the way back to the table, where he collected his bag of tools.

"Finish up with our smith, my dear. He seems to be bleeding again." Cheeks waddled over to the door. "Then I want to see you in my chambers. I have a gift for you." Rae's fingers tightened hard on her skirt.

As angry as he was, Ferrin couldn't help but feel pity for the healer. There was no telling what the inquisitor had done to get her to betray him. Maybe he could use that in some way to help him escape. Help them both escape.

Rae was evidently through for the night, which meant the inquisitors would have no further need for her transferal. At least, he hoped not. This was his one chance. But how could he persuade her to let him use it?

One of the guards in the hallway shut the creaking door behind Cheeks and snapped the lock back into place. It took a while for Rae to move, most likely too embarrassed by what she'd done.

Ferrin watched as she finally started across the room, her head lowered, not daring to look him in the eyes. She placed her hands on his arm where he'd cut it struggling against the manacles.

"Why did you do it?" he asked, trying his best not to sound too sharp. He kept reminding himself that she was a victim too. "I would have thought you of all people would be the last to want to help them."

She sent a wave of healing through him. His arm glowed a pale lavender as the magic did its work. He felt the chill crawl up his arm.

She didn't respond.

"I guess I was wrong. You really are one of them," he said, hoping to force her to say something—anything—as long as it opened a dialogue.

She passed him a fleeting look as she moved to the other side of the rack and began to heal his other arm. As quick as the glance had been, he had seen the anger in her eyes, or maybe it was hurt. He wasn't sure. He relaxed his head back against the rack, trying to think of what he could say to persuade her to help him. It wasn't looking good so far. If only he could—

"I have a daughter."

Ferrin lifted his head. *A daughter?* That was unexpected.

"She's six. She was born here, like me. Like my mother before me."

Born here? The time Ferrin had spent in the White Tower was bad enough, let alone the time Azriel had spent, but he couldn't imagine having been born and raised into a life such as this. Could he use this somehow to convince her?

"When my nana's gift of healing was discovered, they decided to try making more of us. When my abilities became apparent, they thought they had found a way to keep an ongoing supply of healers around." He could hear the contempt in her voice. "So, eventually, I was forced to give birth to Suri."

Ferrin wasn't sure how to respond. His previous anger at her betrayal had all but withered, paling in comparison to what she had suffered already. They were using her daughter the same way they planned on using Myriah. He had to try appealing to her on that level. He had to make her see how Myriah was—

"Why didn't you take me?"

Ferrin was taken aback. "What?" He wasn't sure he had heard her correctly. His mind conjured images of their previous encounter, when she had tried to seduce him. It was an image he would like to forget. It had obviously been a ruse to extract information from him. But then why would it matter to her now? Was she going to try again?

"Why didn't you take me?" she asked.

Ferrin was sure his face was red as a beet. "I told you why. It wasn't right."
She looked confused. But was it genuine? He had to take the chance. "Look, I
have no idea what it's been like for you to live in a place like this. The horrors
you've seen, the atrocities that have been done to you. I can't imagine, and
quite honestly, I don't want to. But please understand, not everyone is like
what you see here."

She listened in silence, studying his face.

"Come with me and find out."

Her eyes widened, and she immediately grabbed for the folds of her dress.
"I'm sorry about your sister," she said, "but I have to watch out for my Suri.
She's all I've got, and they won't let me see her unless I help them get what
they want. She's just a little girl." Tears flowed down her dimpled cheeks.

"Then help me," Ferrin pleaded. "We can leave together."

She shook her head, shuffling backward slowly. He was losing her.

"I understand that you love your daughter. The same way I love my sister.
Do you really want her to have to live through what you have been made to
suffer?"

Rae stopped. Her eyes lifted.

"Save her from that. Please, Rae, come with me. This is our one chance."

She nervously glanced around the room. "When?"

"Tonight."

"How?"

Ferrin's eyes lowered to the chain around her neck. "I'm going to need to
borrow that."

Chapter 60 | Tolin

TOLIN STEPPED OUT of his tent and rubbed his eyes. Where had the night gone? The sun was barely peeking above the rise behind them, leaving a pale, dismal sort of feeling in the air. The battlefield had remained quiet over the last day and a half. The Cylmaran army on the other side still seemed to be waiting for something.

The smell of breakfast being cooked over what remained of last night's campfires had his stomach rumbling. He had managed an odd hour here or there for rest, but not enough to make a difference. In fact, he felt worse now for having tried.

He grabbed a biscuit and stuffed a couple slabs of bacon in between on his way through the camp toward the rise.

The High Guard were up, fed, and ready for battle. Ayrion had done a remarkable job in training his men. Tolin passed through their ranks, nodding here and there as some of the guards stood to acknowledge him. Each guard wore one sword at their waist and one on their back. They weren't your average broadswords, either—they were shorter, more versatile. He didn't know how he felt about fighting with more than one sword at a time. He preferred wielding a sword with reach. He liked to keep his enemy at a distance.

Tolin reached the top of the rise and found the king and Ayrion already inside the pavilion, glancing over maps and battle-drawn sketches of troop movements and blocking. Surprisingly, the prince was there as well. It was strange to see him out of his tent before noon. He was reclining in his usual spot in the corner, a bored look on his face. Tolin shook his head. If Dakaran had been his son, he'd have knocked some sense into him. Dakaran almost made Tolin glad that he and his wife had never had kids.

"I wonder if there's such a thing as being too prepared," the king joked as he thumbed through the mountain of sketches Tolin had drafted for the king's approval. He looked up at Tolin and raised his eyebrows. "Commander, you look about how I feel."

Tolin grunted. "Like I haven't slept in three weeks?"

"That, and you haven't had a decent meal in about as long."

Tolin glanced at Ayrion, and they both smiled.

"Has there been any word from the scouts you sent?" Ayrion asked. "Has the missing team made it back?"

"No," Tolin said, frustrated by the situation. "The only word we've—"

"Your Majesty!" One of the black-and-silver-clad guards stuck his head in the doorway. "You need to see this!"

What now? Tolin wondered. Had the Cylmarans attacked? Would he be a bad commander if he hoped they had?

"What is it?" Rhydan asked.

Tolin followed the king out into the early morning haze.

The guard pointed north. "There, Your Majesty!"

Tolin turned and looked north toward the Black Hills. His mouth opened in awe. He couldn't believe what he was seeing. Up out of the mountains rose a pillar of red fire. It erupted from the center of the small range, reaching all the way to the heavens above. The brilliance of the flame was particularly prominent against the dull grey of the pre-dawn sky.

"What do you make of that, Commander?" the king asked, transfixed on the aberration.

Tolin had to remind himself to close his mouth. "I'm not a betting man, Your Majesty, but that looks like a clear opening signal to me."

"At least now we know why Saryn has risked this campaign," Ayrion said.

"Aye," Tolin agreed. "He's clearly aligned himself with wielders."

"And powerful ones, by the look of it," Ayrion added, staring at the spectacle.

How was this going to affect their strategy? "Where's that Archchancellor gotten himself off to?" Tolin glanced around the rise. "This is supposed to be his area of expertise, isn't it?"

All three men turned and looked at Dakaran.

Dakaran shrugged, looking as perplexed as the rest of them. Then again, the prince always seemed to look a bit bewildered.

Rhydan grabbed his helm and waited for his attendants to begin strapping on the rest of his armor.

Tolin stepped back inside the pavilion and retrieved his own helmet. He needed to get to the command post and meet with his division captains. He walked back outside and raised his fist to his chest. "By your leave, Your Majesty."

Rhydan's arms were out to the side as his groomsmen helped him with his plate, but he managed a nod. "May the Creator guide your sword, Commander."

Tolin bowed for a final time and left.

He marched through the encampment. Men scurried like mice in a field when a hawk showed up. They were well trained, but they were still men. And although they were managing to put up a good front, he could see the fear in their eyes. They knew what they were about to face. They knew that they, or someone they knew, would probably never see another sunrise. That was the life of a lancer.

Loren, one of the hostlers on duty, waited outside Tolin's tent with his horse ready and saddled. The young man rubbed the animal with long, nervous strokes. Tolin smiled. "There's nothing wrong with being afraid."

"I'm sorry, sir," the embarrassed lad said as he attempted to straighten his shoulders. "I don't know what came over me."

"Fear is a valuable tool."

The hostler looked at him like he'd lost his mind.

"No, it's true. Fear keeps us sharp, keeps our minds active. It keeps us alive. Show me a man without fear, and I'll show you a fool. Just remember, without fear, there can be no courage."

The wiry lad wiped a strand of hair from his face. "I never thought of it like that. Thank you, sir."

"Take heart, lad. When the time comes for courage, I'm sure you'll do us proud."

The young man nodded with a half smile and went back to his grooming.

The ominous signal fire was still burning in the early morning sky behind them as Tolin neared the command post. On either side of the tent were stations of runners whose job it was to transport information from the command post to the officers in the field. The boys looked worried. Many a runner had been brought down by a stray arrow or an unexpected opening in the lines where the enemy had broken through.

Tolin marched inside, took a seat behind his desk, and began looking over their plans, trying to factor in this new development. Would Cylmar's use of wielders change things? How many wielders did they have? What could they do besides throw fire all the way into the flaming sky? Tolin hit the top of his table with his fist. *Too many unanswered questions.* He shouted for the head runner.

"Elior!"

A short man with greying hair, wearing Elondrian crimson and gold, shuffled through the front flaps, dragging a gimp leg behind him. He had the appearance of having seen one too many battles in his time. "You called, sir?"

Tolin admired the man. He was considered a good luck charm by most in the camp. Even at his age, Elior felt like there was always more he could do. The man would never be able to participate in battle, but his ability to keep the runners moving more than made up for his physical limitations.

"Have we heard back from those scouts we sent out yesterday?"

"No, sir. No one has returned since this morning. If I might ask, sir, where were they headed?"

Tolin lifted his head from his papers and sighed. "The Black Hills."

"Oh." Elior rubbed his forehead. "That's not good." He glanced over his shoulder at the pillar of fire.

"No, it's not. If you do hear anything, let me know immediately."

"Yes, sir!" the old runner said crisply. "Will that be all, sir?"

"Yes, you're dismissed."

"Very good, sir."

Elior was turning to leave when the tent flap rustled, and another lancer slammed into him and knocked him off his feet. The soldier grabbed the old runner before he hit the ground.

"Don't mind me," Elior said, getting back to his feet.

"Sorry, I didn't see you sta—"

"Exactly my point."

"Are you okay?" Tolin asked, halfway out of his seat.

Elior waved him off. "I'm fine, Commander. These young bucks nowadays." He shook his head and hustled his way outside.

The soldier turned back to Tolin. "I'm sorry, sir, but you might want to see this."

Tolin left the table and stepped outside to get a better look.

The pillar of red flame was gone.

"Send runners to have the men ready their positions. It appears our time has just run out."

Chapter 61 | Tolin

THE EASTERN SKY darkened as a fresh storm rolled in. The morning sunlight was completely overshadowed by clouds and mist, promising a rain-soaked battle. Lightning flashed across the sky, followed closely by a loud clap of thunder.

Tolin watched from atop his painted warhorse as the Cylmaran army closed ranks on the other side of the valley.

"Looks to be a bad one!" Overcaptain Asa said as he tightened his grip on his horse's reins. His long grey-streaked hair had been pulled tight behind his head and tied off with a leather strap. The sullen patch over his eye and long scar down the side of his face lent him the appearance of a warrior stepping out of some mythical tale.

"It does indeed." It was dangerous for horsemen to ride into battle across sodden ground, but it seemed they weren't going to have a choice.

"Any word from those flaming scouts?" Asa asked.

"Nothing. I don't like it."

"I don't like soggy bread, stale cheese, or watered-down ale. Three sets of missing scouts has me downright nauseous."

Asa had always been one to turn a phrase.

Tolin watched the enemy form ranks. The Cylmaran army was at best a disorganized grouping of ragtag armsmen, whose premier battle strategy was to aim in one direction and charge when someone gave the signal. Their armor was piecemeal at best, and their uniforms consisted mostly of whatever they happened to be wearing at the time, which made it fairly easy for both sides to spot the other. However, with rain moving in, nobody would be seeing much of anything.

"I believe it's time for us to part ways, Commander," Asa said as he tugged anxiously on his ducktail beard. He flipped up his eye patch and rubbed his finger around the inner edge of his empty socket. He seemed to take perverse pleasure in watching Tolin squirm.

Tolin smiled at his crazy, battle-hardened friend. He held out his arm. "To victory!"

Asa took it. "To the swift death of our enemies and to the women who await our return!"

Asa spun his horse and dug in his heels, speeding off toward his cavalry unit. Tolin wondered if this would be the last time he would ever speak to his old friend. He had lost a lot of men along the way. That was the harsh reality of living by the sword.

The rain thickened, the drops washing down his face, forcing him to shake them off. His shoulder-length hair had been tied back with a crimson strap to keep from getting in his eyes.

The Cylmaran troops were just now reaching the halfway point as they slow-marched across the open field. It seemed their horsemen, few as they were, had been added to their frontal assault. *That was a mistake.*

On his side, he watched as Captain Janus and Captain Bashan ordered their men to brace their pikes to meet a mounted charge.

Behind the pikes, Captain Nadeer stood with flags raised while his bowmen spread out in a staggered line formation. They drew their strings and waited. Nadeer was a good man, a veteran of several campaigns. He was also one of the best marksmen Tolin had ever seen, able to hit the red from three hundred paces.

A horn sounded from somewhere behind the Cylmaran lines, and they charged, their battle cries drowned out momentarily by another roll of thunder.

The enemy ranks tore across the valley floor like a tidal wave ready to make land.

Nadeer's flag came down, and the Elondrian bowmen fired their first volley.

Tolin held his breath and counted—a tradition of his—as the deadly cloud raced toward the oncoming soldiers. *One. Two. Three. Four.* He exhaled as the wall of shafts fell across the front of the Cylmaran ranks.

Men were chopped down in large swathes, arrows piercing arms, legs, chests, and heads. Those in front looked more like pincushions than men. The screams of the wounded and dying were masked only in part by the blood-frenzied roar issuing from those coming up behind as they continued to close the distance on the Elondrian lancers.

The Cylmarans' mounted regiment had suffered tremendous damage from the initial rain of the bowmen. By the time the horses reached the front of the Elondrian lines, there was hardly a quarter of them left. Many of their riders were clearly inexperienced in warfare; having seen the dark wave of arrows, they had tried turning their horses to flee. But the stampede of men behind them trampled them to death, horse and all.

"Fools, the lot of them."

The Cylmaran armsmens' strategy of attack was direct. Their soldiers drew on what they knew—blunt force and animalistic aggression. They were familiar with ravaging villages, fighting farmhands, and raping women, not standing toe to toe with well-armed and well-trained troops.

Their weapons consisted of battle-axes, war hammers, and maces. Apparently, in Cylmaran eyes, the larger the weapon, the fiercer they appeared.

Their army crossed to within fifty paces. Tolin gripped his reins in anticipation of the clash. He could hear Nadeer ordering his longbowmen into a defensible retreat, while at the same time, Undercaptain Bellos and his ranks of crossbowmen stepped into position.

"Fire at will!" Bellos shouted, and his men released their bolts into the front line of the Cylmarans. Chaos ensued as men stumbled over the bodies of their fallen, trying to reach the Elondrian line.

The crossbowmen retreated just as the front ranks of the Cylmaran army broke across the Elondrian pikes. Tolin held his breath once again. The sound of the impact could be heard even above the storm. It was like a wave crashing against the side of a cliff.

Tolin couldn't pull his eyes away from the carnage below. The bodies piled in front of the pole-bearers. The great pikes skewered two, sometimes three men at a time. All of the ballads ever sung and masterpieces painted fell unequivocally short of capturing the sheer horror of a single battle. They sang of the glories of victory, the spoils of conquest, the nobility of war; but had they ever sought an honest answer from a veteran of the horrors of hand-to-hand combat, they would know that there is nothing glorious or noble to be found in the slaughter of men.

The rain washed across the battlefield in heavy sheets.

Tolin shifted position in his saddle as he scanned the carnage. His fingers tightened anxiously on the reins. He didn't like sitting still while his men fought and died in front of him.

The forward momentum of the Cylmaran army had stalled as it struggled to push through the Elondrian front line. It was time for the cavalry. Tolin knew it was best to wait until the other side was standing still to bring in the mounted troops. It was easier to hit an object that wasn't moving.

Tolin moved his horse out in front. On the far side of the field, Asa's unit was moving into position as well.

Taking one last survey of the landscape, Tolin waved his horsemen into position at the edge of the gently rising slope. His painted stallion pranced to the front. Another crash of lightning lit the battlefield ahead.

Anticipating his maneuvers, Captain Janus and Captain Bashan signaled their footmen forward while Nadeer and Bellos moved their bowmen behind the large earthen mounds flanking the sides of the field. From there, they had the advantage of herding the enemy's ranks back to the center.

Turning in his saddle, Tolin drew his sword, the leather grip familiar between his gloved fingers. He raised the blade over his head and shouted loudly. "For Elondria!"

The loud ring of steel behind him sent a shiver of excitement rushing through his bones as his men echoed his call. "For Elondria!"

The ground rumbled with the surge of riders tearing down the slope and across the field.

As much as he hated war, there were times like these when he found a certain thrill galloping at the head of a stampede of horsemen—sword drawn, teeth bared, hair rippling in the wind. He could feel his heart racing and his mind coming into focus as they neared the wall of Cylmaran armsmen. It was terrifying. It was exhilarating. It was the rush.

The faces of the enemy came into view. They had no idea what was about to hit them. Or maybe they did. He could see the horror in the eyes of the closest. Taking a deep breath, he raised his sword in the air and roared as they tore into the Cylmaran army's right flank.

His horse trampled those unable to get out of the way. He swung his arm with the fury of a madman, cutting, slicing, stabbing. Tolin's heart raced. It was the rush.

A large cleaver swung in his direction. He sent it flying, along with half the owner's arm still holding it. From one side of his horse to the other, he struck, severing limb from torso. Like an artist, he painted his canvas with blood-filled strokes. Men cried out in rage, cried out in terror, cried out for mercy. But there was none to be had. It was the rush.

He took a deep cut to his left leg, but he hardly felt it, the rush keeping him focused on nothing but the next kill. Tolin kicked a soldier in the face as the man raised his axe, then stabbed him through the chest. Tolin didn't let up. He forced his cavalry onward. They couldn't slow down. If his charge faltered before exiting, they would be cut to pieces.

With everything he had, Tolin pushed his men forward. Like an arrowhead, they tore through the Cylmaran ranks without slowing.

He felt another cold slice of pain as one of their blades deflected off his sword and opened the top of his forearm. He struck the man with the hilt of his sword while catching another in the chest with his boot. The pain was beginning to push past the rush. He could feel blood flowing from the open wound on his arm. He couldn't succumb now.

Angling his horse back the way they had come, Tolin urged his riders on. He kept his mind focused on the poor farmers whose lands these savages had burned, whose daughters and wives they had raped, whose sons they had killed. It fueled his rage.

The perimeter of the Cylmaran forces was just ahead. He blocked another strike on his left and opened a soldier's neck on his right with a swift backswing.

A sigh of relief escaped his lips as they cut their way back out to open ground. He led his men up a small slope on the side before turning. The V-shaped hole they had dug into the enemy's flank had momentarily halted their advance, allowing the Elondrian lancers to push their way through. He needed to return to the command center to prepare for their next engagement, and to see if there had been any further orders from the king.

On the other side of the battlefield, Tolin caught a glimpse of Asa and his men fighting their way out of the Cylmaran lines. The overcaptain swung his battle-axe as he directed his regiment away from the main force.

"Commander!"

Tolin turned to find one of Elior's war-runners heading in his direction. Tolin rode to meet him. The young man looked like a half-drowned tabby just pulled from the river.

"What is it?" Tolin asked, shouting to be heard above the sudden roll of thunder.

"Three of the scouts have returned, sir." The runner looked close to panic. "Sir, you need to hear their report immediately."

Chapter 62 | Tolin

AWAVE OF TREPIDATION washed over Tolin as he entered his
tent and saw the battered state of the three pathfinders. They looked like
they'd fought their way through the entire Cylmaran army to get there.

"What happened? Did you find the other scouts?"

The three men struggled just to remain standing. Terris had a splint on his
shattered leg, Bayle sported a bloody sling around his arm, and Merrick tried
to support them both.

"We did, Commander," Merrick said with a weary look in his eyes. "Or at
least what was left of them. But there is another force massing in the hills, and
I'm sure they're already on their way by now. It's like no force we've ever seen
before."

"What are you talking about?" Tolin's mind was racing. "How many
wielders did you see?"

"Wielders? What wielders, sir?"

"You said you just came from the Black Hills, didn't you?"

"Yes, sir."

"Didn't you see the enormous blaze of fire?"

The scouts looked at each other in bewilderment. "No, sir. What fire?"

"Then what kind of force are you talking about? How many men?" *Has Overlord Agnar sent Keldoran troops to help the Cylmarans undermine the king's position?*

"They not be *men*, sir," Bayle said, eyes wide.

"Not men?" Tolin was about to lose it. "What the blazes are you three talking about?"

"They be . . ."

Merrick cleared his throat. "Commander, they were hor'hounds."

Tolin felt the air wheeze from his lungs.

"Our search led us to the caves within the ironworks," Merrick said, still keeping his shoulder under Terris. The unstable tracker teetered on one leg. "We saw a dark figure calling them forth. We didn't stay to see more. On the way out, we ran into one of the beasts and had to fight our way out of the pass."

Tolin looked at the men. "One hor'hound did all that?"

"Yes, sir."

"We lost Ellson as well," Terris added, gritting his teeth in pain as he tried to keep to one leg.

"Aye, that we did," Bayle said. "We rode as fast as our poor injured horses would allow, hoping to stay ahead of them—"

Tolin didn't let him finish. "How many?"

Merrick looked at the others, then back at Tolin. "Hundreds."

Tolin dropped into his seat. "How is that possible? We haven't seen or even heard of a hor'hound for centuries." Of everything Tolin had planned for, he could not have foreseen something like this. He needed to warn the king. "Get to the healers and see to your injuries," he snapped.

The three men bowed and departed.

"Elior, send word to the king that a force of hor'hounds has been spotted.

Tell him I recommend an immediate retreat. We don't want to be caught in a fight on two fronts." Tolin quickly wrote a missive for the runner to dispatch, stamping it with his official seal. "And send runners to Asa and the other captains. Tell them to be ready to start pulling our lancers back."

"Yes, sir!" Elior said, not bothering to even salute as he began barking orders, shoving his stunned runners into motion.

"Hor'hounds?" This time it was Asa who nearly knocked poor Elior off his feet as he came charging through the front. He shook his head, flinging water like a wooly sheepdog. "Did the scouts' rutty breath smell of ale when they reported this? Did you get yourself a good whiff?"

"How did you already hear about it? I just found out myself," said Tolin.

"Good news travels fast. Bad news, even faster."

Tolin huffed. "To answer your question, no, they weren't drunk. Although I'm sure they would rather have been."

"Huh?"

"One of them looked like he'd gone three rounds with Barthol, the second couldn't walk from a shattered leg, the third was holding an arm that looked to have been half torn off, and the fourth . . . well, he didn't come back at all. So, yes, I'm sure they'd have preferred to be sitting around getting sloshed."

Asa wiped his face. "So it's true?"

Tolin nodded. "Which means we need to secure our position immediately. I can only guess the direction they'll be hitting us from." He glanced down at the maps on the table and circled a section with his finger. "We need to move our lancers south, right here. It will give our pikemen a chance to change direction. If we face north, that will put the Cylmarans between us and the hounds."

Asa walked over to have a look. "Aye, that will help."

"Have Nadeer and Bellos pull the bowmen in behind the lancers to protect their flanks. Give them plenty of space to fire on whatever's coming. The more lethal we are from a distance, the fewer of the creatures we'll have to face up close. I don't know about you, but I don't relish the thought of going toe to toe with a hor'hound."

"Neither do I," Asa said, giving his beard a tug. "Do you think the stories about them are true?"

"I reckon we're about to find out."

"The mounted regiments are going to be the defining factor in this outcome. They'll be the only ones capable of matching the creatures' speed and size."

"I'll be flamin' hanged if I allow a pack of mangy fleabags to overrun us!" Asa spat.

"The cavalry is yours," Tolin said. "I will direct from here. Can you handle that?"

Asa stared down the point of his nose at Tolin with his one and only eye. "Who do you think you're talkin' to? I was gonna insist on it. We need our commander . . . commanding, not stickin' his neck out there for the enemy to get an easy strike at. Besides," he said, clearing his throat, "with you out of the way, I can take all the glory for myself."

Tolin would have laughed if the situation hadn't been so dire. At least one of them still had a sense of humor.

The evening light waned. The rain looked to have settled in for the long haul.

Both sides were feeling the strain of battle when the first of the hor'hounds made its appearance. Ethereal baying announced their arrival shortly before they hit the back of the Cylmaran ranks.

Chaos ensued as the creatures bounded out of the shadows, little more than specters in the storm. They tore through the back of the Cylmarans' already-muddled formations, apparently not distinguishing one side from the other.

Maybe he'd been wrong, Tolin thought. Maybe the hounds weren't in league with the Cylmarans after all. Was this a third army coming to join the fight?

Tolin knew the next few moments would determine not only the course of this battle, but whether any of the humans fighting in it would survive. If they were to stand any chance at all, he needed to turn an enemy into an ally.

As fast as Elior could send his runners, Tolin ordered the Elondrian forces to cease their attacks on the Cylmarans and focus on fighting this new, deadly foe.

Chapter 63 | Asa

"WELL, AIN'T THIS a sight!" Asa shouted to his men as he unstrapped his large battle-axe. "One moment, we're killin' them, and the next, we're savin' their sorry backsides!"

The battle in front of him looked more like a circus than a war. The cold rain had transformed a countryside valley into a mire of mud, clay, and human remains. The Cylmarans had been caught entirely unprepared as the enormous beasts tore their way through the rear flank. The armsmen stampeded toward the Elondrian lancers as they fought to escape.

Asa leaned over the side of his horse and spat. "Like herding cattle!" He pointed at the enemy lines as they scattered and fled. "Just look at 'em! Cowards, every last flaming one of 'em!"

He squeezed his hands. They were getting cold. He couldn't afford for them to go numb, especially not in the middle of a charge.

Behind him, his men were ready—as ready as they could be, knowing what they were up against. He had to admit the thought of directing a battle charge against a horde of creatures from another age brought a certain amount of vitality back to his weary bones. It was the chance of a lifetime. This was what he had been born for. This was what, most likely, he'd die for.

Instead of dividing his riders as they had against the Cylmaran flanks, Asa had brought the entire contingent together. One unit, one strike force that could be used to match the creatures' speed and size. They needed to strike the hor'hounds where they could do the most damage. A straight-on assault wouldn't work. It would be easier to knock them off balance from the side, driving his lancers in and out of their flanks—pierce and run, pierce and run. Never striking the same place twice, yet cutting down their numbers and giving the Elondrian footmen a chance to counter.

They couldn't wait any longer.

Asa raised his axe for his men to see and drove his heels into his horse. He felt like Faylorn of old, galloping toward a horde of Khuls. But instead of wild half-human cannibals with file-sharpened teeth, he faced giant wolflike monsters with dagger-sized claws and fangs.

Glancing over his shoulder, Asa saw that his men—*Creator love 'em*—were still there and looking as determined as ever. They would sing songs about this day. Tales would be told of this battle for years to come. Asa was proud to be leading these men into what could be their final charge.

He held his axe high again as they drew down on the creatures' left flank. "For Elondria!"

The men behind him repeated his cry. His breath caught in his throat. *Twenty paces. Ten paces. Five . . .*

He shouted again, even louder, his voice becoming hoarse. "For the KING!"

They slammed into the hor'hounds' unprotected side. The creatures in front dropped on impact as the unit punched its way like a great spear deep into the side of the pack. The hounds were every bit as tall as the horses. Asa swung for their necks and open flanks, cutting at anything within reach, while urging his horse to keep going. The rain did little to wash away the beasts' pungent stench.

The hounds were everywhere. Asa attacked from both sides of his horse as he fought to keep them moving. He began to turn the momentum, angling his men back out. He couldn't afford to get caught inside the creatures' ranks.

Behind him, he could hear steel against hides and the shouts of his men as they fought to escape. To his right, one of the hounds grabbed the lancer next to him, sinking its teeth in. With a twist of the beast's head, the man's arm was ripped off completely. The pale look of shock on the young soldier's face as he turned to Asa for help had Asa wanting to retch. Asa turned and swung his double-sided axe, burying it in the top of the creature's head. Its mouth went slack, dropping the man's arm. The soldier slumped forward in his saddle.

Their drive was beginning to falter. If they didn't break free soon, they were going to be overrun. Swinging to the left, Asa opened the neck of another hound as it attempted to reach for his horse. He couldn't tell how close they were to the outer lines because of the rain. Panic set in. Had they driven too far into the belly of the pack to get back out?

He jerked his arm back, narrowly escaping one hound's jaws. He twisted in the saddle and clipped the side of the beast's head as he rode by.

By now, their momentum had slowed to the point that the creatures were able to shift direction, forcing Asa and his men to face them head-on. Asa could see the edge of the hounds' ranks just ahead. He kicked his horse all the harder, desperately fighting to reach their line.

He swiped at a hound on his left but missed when the creature reared on its back legs and swung for him. Asa turned his shoulder to protect his front, and the creature's claws tore into the side of his arm. With nothing left but his legs to steer his horse, he turned his steed directly into the hound, not giving it the advantage of reach again. He buried his axe in the creature's neck, taking nearly half its head off in the process. The warm blood running down his arm was a relief from the freezing rain. His fingers were already going numb.

Another ranker on his right went down, his horse knocked out from under him. Asa grabbed the man's arms and tried hauling him onto his own horse, but one of the creatures bit down on the soldier's leg. There was a brief tug-of-war between Asa and the hor'hound.

"Help me!" the man cried out.

Asa swung his axe, but the hound was out of reach. Asa's grip was slipping. He'd hang before he let another one of his own be taken if there was a chance to save him. Using his legs, he turned his horse into the creature and swung again.

Suddenly, the man tore free of the hound's grasp with a sharp cry, and Asa managed to pull him over the side of his own horse. The lancer was delirious, mumbling incoherently. Glancing over his shoulder, Asa saw the man's foot hanging from the creature's teeth.

Asa kicked his horse forward. They were almost there. He fought like a madman, his axe swinging from one side to the other. His face and hands and uniform were covered in blood. He held on to his mount with his knees as he hacked his way back into the open.

Asa nearly cried as his men reached open ground once again. Behind him, the hor'hounds' advance had been thwarted. He hoped it was enough to help the lancers get into place. Asa quickly directed his men back toward the staging area to drop off their wounded.

His arm throbbed from where the creature had gouged it. He needed to get it wrapped before going back out, or he would have a hard time wielding a weapon. Looking again at the men behind him, he doubted whether they could handle another charge.

But what choice did they have?

Chapter 64 | Ayrion

A S THE BATTLE raged across the valley below, Ayrion and Rhydan watched from their perch on top of the rise.

The hor'hounds were every bit as ferocious as any of the stories Ayrion had ever heard. They looked like giant wolves. Giant, horse-sized wolves, if that was possible.

"Where could they have come from?" Rhydan asked, wiping the rain from his face as he stared out at the battlefield through his eyepiece. "It's not like they could simply travel across Elondria without being seen. Look at them. They're enormous. How can we possibly fight something like this? And where in the name of Aldor did Saryn ever manage to find these things?"

"I don't believe this has anything to do with Cylmar, Your Majesty," Ayrion said. "They're killing more of them than they are of us."

"Maybe Overlord Saryn thought he could control them?"

"I don't think anyone can control this."

Rhydan nodded in agreement.

The only thing keeping the creatures from completely overrunning their forces was the company of mounted lancers. Asa's regiments had managed to thwart the hounds momentarily, giving the pikemen enough time to get into place amongst the Cylmaran troops. It looked like the cavalry had taken serious losses, though. Far fewer had come out than had gone in. Ayrion doubted if they could manage another ride.

"That's one way to stop a war of men." Rhydan balked, lowering his ocular. "Send in a horde of creatures from another age, and all thoughts of killing each other vanish."

The hor'hounds fought as a single unit. They didn't have the size and agility of the three monsters they had encountered during the king's hunt, but their numbers more than made up for the difference. Many of the hor'hounds were skewered on the lancers' long poles, but those behind used the fallen as bridges to jump over the poles and reach the men on the other side. There was no honor amongst these beasts, apparently, only an insatiable hunger.

"How much longer can our men stand such punishment?" the king asked, almost to himself.

Ayrion wasn't sure Rhydan was expecting an answer, so he didn't give one. Instead, he continued to study the battle below. From behind their protective mounds, the archers unleashed waves of arrows into the hor'hounds' open flanks. The creatures were falling, but only after each had been pierced by numerous arrows. And there were always more to take their places.

Ayrion couldn't believe the strength of these creatures. Even with the Cylmarans turning to fight alongside the Elondrian soldiers—recognizing it as their only hope of survival—they hardly seemed to be slowing them down.

"We need to get you out of here, sire," Ayrion said. "If the commander can't hold them back, we can't guarantee your safety."

This time, Rhydan didn't protest. He just nodded. "I've never left—"

A horn sounded from the base of the rise. Even over the downpour, he could hear the shout of orders and clash of steel.

Another streak of lightning lit the sky, and Ayrion spotted them. A pack of hor'hounds had appeared out of nowhere and were clawing their way through Ayrion's men below. They must have broken away from the main force before the initial attack and made their way around the side of the rise. This was a planned attack. They knew exactly where to go. *How is that possible?*

"Protect the king!" Ayrion shouted at the cluster of High Guard standing in front of the pavilion. They were an elite group that Ayrion had specifically chosen as the king's shadow, never to leave his side. They had to stop the creatures before they reached the top of the rise. The best bet was to keep them pinned on the slope. If they reached the top, there would be no way to stop them.

In one swift move, Ayrion leaped onto Shade and galloped down the side of the mountain—rock face on his left, sheer drop on his right. The flaps of his black overcoat billowed out behind him, opening like the wings of a nighthawk. His twin blades were out of their sheaths and held at the ready. The jeweled eyes of each dragon crossguard sparkled in the harsh light of the storm. Ayrion took a deep breath and focused. Underneath him, Shade moved with the grace of something otherworldly, his muscular frame tearing up the ground as he raced to carry his rider to the skirmish below.

Ahead, the creatures were tearing through the High Guard front lines. It was one thing to see these things from a distance, but they were even more terrifying up close. Whatever their fangs latched on to was torn apart. His men were thrown back and forth across the front of the rise. But it didn't stop them. They carried a sword in each hand. No shields; shields were for defense. The High Guard had been trained to attack.

"On your right!" Barthol bellowed as a group of hounds tried to skirt the edge of the rise. The men in black moved as one, cutting off the beasts' attempt. These hounds hadn't yet encountered soldiers this well trained.

Reaching the first of the creatures, Ayrion jumped from his saddle and slammed into the closest hound, burying both swords in its rancid pelt. Ayrion yanked the blades free and noticed Shade had pulled away from the fighting and moved farther up the slope, waiting for his call. He'd never met a horse quite like Shade.

Ayrion spun on the next creature. He could feel his magic rising. "Don't fail me now," he said, his words misting into the cold air as he saw the hound's mouth opening for him. Before it could clamp shut, Ayrion was gone, three steps over with his sword raised. One swift chop, and he opened the hor'hound's neck. It was dead before it knew what hit it.

Another vision, and he hopped backward as a set of claws dug into the ground where he'd been standing. He plunged black steel through the creature's heart. It was like slicing through a day-warm cantermelon—no resistance. He loved his blades. Two creatures down without so much as a whimper, and Ayrion hopped over them to battle the next.

He fought his way to Barthol. The huge captain held two of the hounds at bay at once, giving his men time to finish them off.

"Pull back!" Ayrion shouted to the first wave of guards. They quickly grabbed their wounded and retreated as fresh reinforcements from the third and fourth blocks moved in to take over. Ayrion admired the discipline his men showed. It was inspiring. The quick rotation gave the first and second regiments time to catch their breath as they prepared to take the next wave.

"I count at least fifty, could be more!" Barthol shouted as he hacked the head off another hound. Instead of falling back with the others from the first and second blocks, the captain remained where he was for another round of fighting. Barthol was an enormous man, but even he was looking winded.

Momentarily distracted by his friend, Ayrion dove to the side to escape one set of claws but was hit by another. The creature tore through his newly mended coat. Thankfully, the heavy leather kept the lacerations on his arm from being too serious. He dropped to one knee and cut the legs out from under the creature before it could try again, then drove his sword through the mouth of another.

They just kept coming. The hor'hounds made another push for the edge. Whatever was driving them, they were clearly after what was at the top. Ayrion couldn't help but notice the similarities between the attack on the king's hunt and this one. Something bigger was going on, and Rhydan was at the heart of it.

"On my right!" Ayrion yelled as soon as he saw the shift. Guards rushed to Ayrion, blocking the hounds' attempt to break through. A few of his men went over the side with the hounds. Each death ripped a hole in Ayrion's chest, threatening to overwhelm him. These weren't just his men. They were his friends. His family. He'd trained each and every one of them.

Barthol was the next to go down. He was there one minute, shouting and hacking, and the next, he'd disappeared between two hounds near the mountain's face.

"Barthol!" Ayrion lunged at the closest hound, chopping its muzzle clean off and leaving it to drool blood down the front of its hide.

Ayrion cut his way through the next hor'hound and found Barthol on the flat of his back. The only thing keeping the hound's fangs from reaching his neck was the blade of his sword between its jaws, like a dog holding on to a stick in its mouth.

Ayrion ducked as another vision spared his back from being ripped open. He dropped to the ground and rolled under the creature. With a single thrust, he pushed his blade up and through the side of the hound's chest.

"Get this flaming mutt off me!" Barthol shouted.

Ayrion sprang to his feet, but three more hounds had managed to get between him and Barthol while he was down. He fought with everything he had, but he could see he wasn't going to make it. He cut the front legs off the first hor'hound. *One down. Two more to go.* He turned to the second, but before he could raise his swords, fresh guards appeared out of nowhere to help. From the corner of his eye, Ayrion caught the mark of the crown and sword on their black uniforms.

"What do you think you're doing?" he roared. "You should be protecting the king!"

"They are!" Rhydan bellowed as he charged in beside Ayrion, thrusting his longsword into the closest creature with the fury of a man who had just spent the better part of the day watching his soldiers being slaughtered.

"Get back, Your Majesty! I can't protect you from down here."

"About as much as you can from *up there* if these creatures get past!"

Ayrion didn't have time to argue. He jumped over the king's fresh kill and bounded on top of the hound still fighting to sink its teeth into Barthol. The hound's head jerked upward, rattled by the sudden weight on its back. Completely forgetting about Barthol, the creature bucked once, twice, three times, trying to unseat its unwelcome rider.

Ayrion grabbed its mane and barked a laugh. *Look at me! I'm riding a hor'hound!* He was sure those watching thought he had lost his mind. The monstrous animal leaped dangerously close to the ledge before Ayrion rammed his sword through its distended backbone. Blood soaked the front of his coat as the creature went down, and Ayrion spat the salty tang from his mouth.

The creatures never slowed. With the king's help, Ayrion lifted Barthol to his feet and moved him toward the back lines as fresh recruits rushed in to fill their spots. His men were down to only two blocks.

"You see!" Barthol said, spitting out a wad of wet fur. "This is why I won't allow the wife to get a pet! Flaming things shed everywhere!"

Ayrion and Rhydan laughed as they helped the large captain over to a boulder at the side.

"Where's Dakaran?" Ayrion asked.

"Where do you think?" Rhydan said with an embarrassed look as he glanced back up the rise toward the top.

At least he wouldn't have to watch out for both of them, Ayrion thought as he fought to catch his breath.

"We're losing too many men. At this rate, we're not going to have enough to rotate out. When that happens . . ."

Chapter 65 | Asa

$\mathcal{T}$HE CYLMARAN SOLDIERS proved little help.

They flailed with their gaudy cleavers and axes, with no cohesive strategy. It was every man for himself, and their ranks were swallowed by the Elondrian forces as they either were pushed to the back or struggled to hold the flanks in between the lancer formations.

The hor'hounds were going down, but so were the lancers. The temporary halt that Asa's cavalry had managed to secure was now gone, and the creatures were pushing forward once again, but not as swiftly.

Asa shifted in his saddle to get a look at his men. He'd lost nearly a third in their last charge. Many of those still riding were injured, but not badly enough to be left out. He turned and looked out across the field. If they could manage one more charge, it might be enough to turn the tide. It looked as though the hor'hound lines had thinned enough to drive straight through. It was a risk he had to take. He couldn't wait on orders. Tolin trusted him to make decisions in the field. Asa wasn't about to let him down.

"Ready yourselves!" he shouted, and the ring of steel filled the air behind him as swords were drawn down the line. He didn't know what to say to them. Tolin had always been the one to inspire the troops. When Asa opened his mouth, whatever came out usually had the commander blushing. "We are men of Elondria . . ." That was about as far as he got. "Flame it! Let's send these bung-licking fleabags back to the pits they came from! *On me!*"

Asa kicked his horse into motion, battle-axe in the air. The ground shook as his men tore down the slope toward the creatures. Rain pelted his face. It was cold, biting all the way to the bone. He shook his head to keep the drops out of his eyes.

Twenty paces. Fifteen paces.

His breathing slowed. His mind focused.

Ten paces. Five paces.

The hounds turned at the last moment to face the charge.

The cavalry hit the horde like a sledgehammer, punching through the lines, their momentum alone carrying them deep inside. Asa swung and chopped, hacked and cut, his axe growing heavy in his hands, his arms wanting to drop. But he couldn't afford to let them. They had to push through. They had to keep moving.

He turned his shoulder and was nearly knocked from his horse by a stray paw that had been meant for the soldier behind him.

"What I'd give for two eyes!" he shouted, not really caring who heard. Being unable to see anything on one side made it difficult to judge where to swing. He righted himself and continued kicking his horse. They couldn't afford to stop.

Another hor'hound lunged, its mouth wide. Asa widened it farther with one hard swing, his axe tearing off the lower half of its face. The creature dropped, writhing in the mud. The horses trampled over it.

The thrill that had threatened to overwhelm him earlier—the thought of great songs being written about the lancers' charge—had soured in his gut.

"Forward!" he shouted as his battle-worn arm continued to swing his axe at the hungry creatures around him. *Cut.* He severed one's head. *Cut.* He hacked two more. *Cut.* He watched a piece of a massive paw sail through the air, then cleaved the neck of the hound it came from. All he knew to do was to keep cutting, to keep pushing forward. The farther they charged, the slower their movement became, until finally they didn't move at all.

"Captain!" one soldier yelled beside him, then went down, horse and rider together. The hounds had changed tactics. They were now going for the horses, realizing that bringing down the horse would bring down the rider. His men were dropping all around him. Asa's right leg was bleeding through the openings in his armor, where the daggerlike claws had torn through.

All around him came the clash of steel, the cries of battle, and the howls of their enemy. The cacophony would have driven fear into the most valiant of hearts.

Asa clenched his teeth and brought his axe up and around, ramming the blade deep inside the chest of the nearest hound. The creature slumped to the side with an ugly whine. Behind him, his men, now stationary, were giving everything they had just to keep the animals at bay. He could see the other side of the horde, but barely. It was too far to make it.

He was down to about half his riders. Those who had managed to remain mounted were unable to move.

Asa raised his axe once more to give encouragement to those behind when his horse stumbled over a fallen hor'hound, sending him tumbling across the ravaged bodies of his men. Struggling back to his feet, he shook the rain from his face in time to see a hound lunge for him.

Asa jumped to the side, barely avoiding its teeth as he raked his axe across the creature's shoulder. The hound reared, and Asa buried his blade in its chest. He had barely managed to yank the axe free when he was struck from the side.

The impact threw him into the mud. He rolled, still managing to hold his weapon. Twisting around, he severed one of the hound's front legs. It dropped beside him, and he finished the beast with a single overhead swing.

He pulled his axe from the corpse and turned for the next attack, but there was none. His men, those that were still mounted, had moved their horses in to protect him. They fought to keep the creatures back. One small group amidst so many. He knew how this would end. It had been a gamble from the start. He only hoped their sacrifice would make a difference.

The hor'hounds pressed in, blood on their teeth and death in their eyes. Asa could hear the sound of Elondrian footmen somewhere off to his right, but they were too far away to manage a rescue. One by one, the horses were taken down as his men fought to hold the creatures off.

Now on foot, they pressed together in a single cluster. Back to back, they swung wildly at the encroaching creatures. It was a hopeless endeavor. The only choice left was to go out with honor.

Flaming hounds! If this was to be his end, Asa was going to take as many with him as he could. He stumbled through the mud and attacked, piercing the closest creature's thick hide with a *thud*. It howled and snapped at him, but he managed to jump out of the way just in time.

From the right, another hound broke through the lines and plowed into the men, knocking him from his feet. Asa landed on his face in the mud. He barely had time to wipe it from his eye when searing pain shot through his right leg. He howled as ferociously as any hound, twisting to find the creature that had clamped its jaw just below his knee. Its teeth had punctured his armor; it felt as though they had pierced to the bone. He'd suffered wounds before, but this was unlike anything he'd felt.

Everything went black for a second, and he frantically slapped himself in the face to keep from passing out. He couldn't afford to lose consciousness.

The hound began to drag him from his men.

The few remaining lancers fought to reach him, but each attempt was thrown back by another hor'hound. Asa went to swing his axe, but it wasn't in his hands. Desperately, he clawed at the ground, fighting to keep the creature from gaining any more leverage. The pain was unbearable. His body spasmed and he heaved. But there wasn't enough in him to come out. He was losing feeling in the leg altogether. At that moment, he wasn't sure if that wasn't a good thing.

The hor'hound took another step back, and the fire in his leg returned as the creature pulled him with it. He couldn't believe his leg was still attached. It must have been the armor. Frantically, he pried a broadsword from one of the dead and swung it at the creature. Though the swing was weak, he managed to connect with the top of its skull, peeling away a large chunk of fur. The hor'hound didn't even flinch.

Asa tried using his other leg to dig into the mud, but he was losing strength. He had to do something. Doubling down on the pain, he gathered whatever energy he had left and heaved himself into a sitting position and plunged the blade into the hound's closest eye. The creature howled, and Asa howled right along with it as the hor'hound's fangs withdrew from his leg.

He rolled to the side and drove the sword into its exposed chest. The hound collapsed beside him, splattering water and mud across his face. Using the sword for leverage, he tried making it to his feet but collapsed. Two of his men managed to grab his arms and pull him back into the circle. He crawled to one knee and picked up his fallen axe. He didn't have enough strength to lift it. He propped it up to use as a crutch.

This was it. The end to the Elondrian cavalry. He couldn't have chosen a better way to die than surrounded by men such as these.

He drew up every last ounce of willpower and made it to his feet. He might not have been able to swing his axe, but he still had the ability to wield one last weapon. He opened his mouth.

"You flaming sons of—"

He was cut short by the blare of a lancer's signal horn to his right.

He turned his head. Where had that—

He heard it again. Louder.

Behind him, a group of riders charged through the hounds, Commander Tolin himself at the head. It looked like the commander had rounded up every last one of his staff, including the runners and the cooks—even his young hostler.

Asa nearly choked when he saw old Elior riding in behind them, swinging his sword around and having more fun than a seventy-year-old should have been able to. He didn't know whether to laugh or cry.

"Looks like you could use a hand!" Tolin shouted.

"And a leg!"

A couple of Asa's men helped him up onto one of the fallen lancers' mounts. Another man jumped on behind him. There weren't enough horses to go around, so they were riding two, even three, to a horse. Asa bit down against the pain in his leg but managed to turn the horse about and follow Tolin and his riders out. He was surprised at how close they had been to escaping.

The Elondrian bowmen focused their fire on the hor'hounds' right flank, keeping them from completely enclosing the mounted riders before they had the opportunity to make it through.

"What took you so long? I almost flaming died back there!"

Tolin laughed. "I'm a busy man."

Asa grunted. "Impeccable timing, I must say."

"Can't let you have all the glory, now can I?"

Asa wiped his face with a bloodstained glove, wincing at every jolt of the horse's hooves. "Right about now, I don't mind sharing!"

It looked as though the creatures' numbers had decreased significantly since their last charge. His horsemen had managed to keep the hounds off balance long enough for the lancers to overpower the creatures' momentum.

For the first time since the conflict began, Asa thought he could see an end in sight.

Chapter 66 | Ayrion

THE HIGH GUARD was down to a single unit.

Ayrion's men were being picked off one by one as he fought to keep them alive. But he was only one man. His arms felt as heavy as tree trunks and his chest burned with every breath. His men believed he was something more than human, something near divine. He could do things no person should have been able to do. He had lived through encounters that would have killed a dozen men. Yet, for all his abilities, he was powerless to stop this slaughter. He was barely able to keep his own life from being snuffed out.

Ayrion flung his hair from his face, moving to block two more hor'hounds from breaking through the outer lines. His swords never slowed. The first creature went for his legs, but his magic interceded. He moved just in time to kick the hound away and use its momentum to carry him up and over the second. He slid both blades through the creature's neck before his feet hit the ground, then whipped around and cut through the back legs of the first.

The creature howled and fell, snapping at him as it did. The king brought his sword down across its neck to finish it off.

Ayrion moved back between Barthol and Rhydan. He was panting, hardly able to catch his breath. He wouldn't be able to do that again—at least not the jumping.

The High Guard continued to give ground. Little by little, they had worked their way back up the incline until they were almost at the top of the rise. Ayrion had hoped to keep the hounds held farther down, but their surge was relentless, and his men's numbers were quickly diminishing.

The last few surviving members blocked, slashed, and stabbed with what little resolve they had left. Ayrion fought to stay in front of the king, his swords feeling like lead weights in his hands. He'd been fighting nearly the entire time. Only once had he stopped to rest, and that was after saving Barthol. He should have made himself rest, too. What good was having magic if he was too weak to use it?

He looked at his men. So few left. Was there even a purpose for this senseless slaughter? There had to be.

Four creatures remained, but their determination was only heightened by their diminished numbers. They drove all the harder, not caring whether they lived or died. They seemed to have no fear at all.

"On your right, sir!" Barthol shouted as he pulled his sword from a downed creature and tried to cut at the one bounding by him. He missed.

Ayrion turned but not before the hound had thrown Barthol from his feet and latched on to Rhydan's sword arm. The king yelled and started punching the creature with his free hand.

Ayrion ran to help but was stopped when a second creature lunged between them. He nearly didn't get out of the way in time. He swung and caught the hound in the side of its shoulder. It opened a deep wound but didn't deter the creature. They were clearly after the king, and now that they had him, they weren't about to let him go.

He swung high, ducking just in time to miss having his head snapped between the hound's fangs. He lunged, and the creature reared, keeping clear of Ayrion's blades. After being hit by them already, it didn't appear to want to attempt it again.

"Get to the king!" he yelled at whichever of his guards were still left. *Where is Dakaran?* They could have used those flaming Black Watch right about now. Ayrion saw one young guard run forward.

The hor'hound continued to dance in front of Ayrion, lunging in, backing off, making sure to keep him occupied, never getting close enough for Ayrion to use his blades. Ayrion's magic let him see when the creature would attack, but nothing more. It was a defensive tool, not an offensive one.

Ayrion caught a brief glimpse of the king being dragged by the arm toward the back of the rise. If Rhydan went over, there would be no help for him. Ayrion couldn't wait. He had to try something different. The hound came at him from the side. It clearly wanted to rip him in two. But this time, he didn't dodge or duck or sidestep. This time, he let the creature have him. The hound spread its jaws. Ayrion waited until the creature's momentum couldn't be stopped, then turned and rammed his right sword straight through its mouth.

He yelled as the creature's fangs caught his forearm, his hand reaching clear to the back of the beast's throat as he pushed his sword straight through the back of its head. The creature was dead before it hit the ground.

He yanked his sword free, not bothering to look at his injured arm, and half ran, half stumbled for the king. Barthol and two other guards were busy with a hor'hound of their own, while a third guard was trying desperately to free Rhydan. They were near the edge of the slope. The backside of the rise wasn't as sheer a drop as the front, but it was enough to lose footing.

The young guard fought to free the king's arm. He swung at the creature's head, cutting a deep gash down the side of its ear. Before he could land another hit, the hor'hound slashed him across the front with its claws. The guard looked stunned, his sword falling behind him as he dropped to his knees. There was nothing Ayrion could do for him. He had to get to the king.

The hound had one foot off the rise. Rhydan shouted as he dug his boots into the ground. One strong pull and it would be over. The hound would crush him as they rolled down the side.

Ayrion was nearly there, but he wasn't going to make it in time to reach the creature. He only had once choice, and he could see it in the king's eyes as Ayrion raised his sword and leaped.

His sword came down with a swift stroke and cut the king's arm off just below the elbow. The hound went over the side, still clutching the king's forearm between its teeth.

Rhydan never made a sound. He pushed himself back up to a sitting position and looked down at his stump of an arm. "Thank you," he said through gritted teeth. "Now tie this thing off." He shook his head. "Ellise is going to kill me."

Ayrion ripped the sleeve off the dead guard's shirt and tied it around Rhydan's arm, then he cut some more and pressed it against the wound. "Here. Hold this over it."

The king jerked at the pressure.

Behind them, Barthol and the last two remaining guards finished off the final hound.

"Victory, Your Majesty," Ayrion said, looking for any reason to give the king hope.

Rhydan tried to smile, but it came out more of a grimace. They needed to get him to a healer immediately.

Ayrion could feel the blood running down his own arm from where he had cut it in the creature's mouth. He didn't have time to worry about it, though, not with his king bleeding to death in front of him.

Barthol rushed over, took one look at the king's arm, then turned to Ayrion. "I thought we were supposed to save him, not help the creatures kill him."

"He did what was needed," Rhydan mumbled as Ayrion and Barthol lifted him to his feet. Rhydan's legs were shaking. Ayrion's were as well. The two remaining guards joined them at the ledge as they took a moment to look over the side. The hor'hound was gone.

"Where'd it go?" Barthol asked, trading places with one of the guards so he could get a closer look. The guard put his shoulder up under the king's arm.

"Back to wherever it came from, most likely," Ayrion said. He stepped back from the edge and started to turn when he was struck with another vision.

"No!" he screamed, but it was too late.

Already facing Barthol, he did the only thing he could. He raised his foot and kicked his friend over the edge of the rise.

A hail of bolts descended upon them.

Ayrion's back and chest were on fire. He tried to breathe but coughed up blood instead. Beside him, the last of his men fell facedown in the mud. The king released his grip and dropped to one knee, two crossbow bolts sticking through the back of his plated armor. *No! This can't be happening!* They'd just won. They'd defeated the hor'hounds. His head spun.

He looked down, noticing the black tip of a bolt sticking from his chest. Where had that come from? He dropped to his knees, coughing more blood. He couldn't seem to think straight. Who was doing this? Had the Cylmarans sent assassins?

He raised his hand, but it was empty. Where were his swords? He looked down. They were lying beside him. Why were they beside him and not in his hands?

Another sharp sensation pierced his body, and he cried out, dropping to all fours. Everything felt wrong. His thoughts slowed to a crawl. Was he having another vision? Why wasn't he being pulled back? No. This was different. It was lasting too long.

Ayrion turned. The king looked as bewildered as he.

He saw movement and turned to see white-robed guards coming his way. *Finally,* he thought. Why hadn't they helped sooner? Then he noticed they were carrying crossbows.

Rhydan turned as well.

Valtor and Dakaran stepped out from behind the Black Watch and walked over to stand in front of where the king knelt, gasping for breath.

"Dakaran . . . son?" The king held out a hand for help.

Dakaran turned his head away, not able to look at his father.

"Do it, Dakaran!" Valtor hissed as he thrust his sword into the prince's hands. "This is what you came for, so finish it."

"Son, please."

Dakaran looked at his father, then at Valtor, and finally shook his head. "No." His hands were trembling. "No. I can't do this." He threw the blade down and ran back to the pavilion.

Rhydan stared after his son, disbelief on his face.

Ayrion couldn't believe Dakaran had hated his father so much as to let this happen.

"It's too late to turn back now," Valtor shouted after him. "Oh, well, I guess I should have expected it." He leaned over and picked up the sword from where it had fallen in the mud. "You've raised quite the coward, my king," Valtor said as he stood over Rhydan. "It will make him that much easier to manipulate once he takes your place on the throne."

Rhydan tried to grab the Archchancellor's robe but missed and fell forward.

Valtor smiled.

"No!" Ayrion fought to move, but his arms and legs wouldn't budge. All he could do was watch.

"Why are you doing this?" Rhydan asked, his words garbled as he looked up at Valtor.

"Because it needs to be done." The Archchancellor stepped forward and thrust the blade through the gap in Rhydan's armor under his arm. Rhydan eyes widened as he spat blood and collapsed. His helm fell from his head and sank into the mud beside him. He looked at Ayrion and exhaled for the last time.

Ayrion screamed.

Valtor turned and nodded at one of the Tower's guards, who stepped forward and raised his crossbow. Ayrion barely felt the bolt as it drove through his back.

The last thing he saw was his king lying motionless in the mud while the rain rolled down his face, mixing with the blood seeping from his broken body. Then everything went numb and darkness took over.

Chapter 67 | Dakaran

YESTERDAY'S STORM HAD finally passed, and a new day was creeping over the horizon.

An unwelcome chill in the air clung to Dakaran like a wet shirt, dampening his already-sour mood as he followed the Tower's guards down the rise while they carried his father's body ceremoniously toward camp. They placed his father in the back of a wagon with all the honor befitting a king fallen in battle. Valtor ordered the cart be draped with the Elondrian flag. Dakaran noticed his father had been re-dressed, no doubt to hide the obvious reason for his death. Valtor had thought of everything.

Dakaran's hands shook as he placed the crown back on his father's head. He then turned to address the lancers that had gathered to pay their respects.

"They were the bravest of us," he said, his voice cracking. He didn't have to fake the tears streaking his cheeks as he looked once more at his father's lifeless body. The king's arms had been folded, his fingers gripping the pommel of his sword.

"The High King and the Guardian Protector fought with the courage of true Elondrian warriors. They gave their lives for their country. They shall be remembered as heroes, not only of Elondria but of all Aldor."

Many of the lancers bowed their heads in respect, many tearful.

"We ride for Aramoor in the morning."

"Your Highness." Commander Tolin stepped forward. "What shall we do about the Cylmarans? We're holding Overlord Saryn and Ambassador Belkor for questioning. They are both demanding to speak with you."

There was a strange look on the commander's face.

Does he know? Dakaran wondered. Had Saryn betrayed him? This whole situation had gone from bad to worse. There weren't supposed to be prisoners, let alone Saryn himself. What if the overlord talked?

"They're spouting something about a bargain."

"Bargain?" Dakaran flushed. He glanced at Valtor, but the man's face was as empty as an unwritten letter. What was he going to do? He had to get rid of them. What would his father have done? No. He couldn't think about that. He turned back to the commander.

"Here's my *bargain*, Commander. Tell them Cylmar is no more. Tell them their families will live as outcasts and their children and grandchildren shall curse their names. Then remove their heads." He turned to walk away.

"Your Highness, what about our dead? They should be laid to rest with dignity, not left for the birds."

Dakaran took in the concerned faces of the lancers surrounding him. "You are correct, Commander." He smiled, but there was an edge to his voice. "That is why I have arranged for the local citizenry of Belbridge to give them a proper burial." He needed to remember to do that. "They can benefit from the extra coin we will provide for their services, and we can make for Aramoor with all haste in order to bury my father."

"But, Your Highness, should we not look for survivors in hope of—"

"Commander! Are you saying the burial of the High King is not of immediate importance?" This man was going to be a problem. One of his first actions as king would be to get rid of him. The king had been killed on *his* watch, after all.

Tolin glanced around hesitantly. "No, Your Highness, I didn't mean to imply—"

"Good. Then as the new king of Elondria, I am giving you an order. Leave them to the people of Belbridge. I want to make for Aramoor as soon as possible." He held Tolin's gaze and waited.

Tolin finally bowed his head. "Very well, Your Highness, if that is your wish."

"It is," Dakaran said as he headed for his tent. He balled his fists to keep them from trembling. He held his shoulders straight as he walked back toward the center of camp. He was starting to feel like a king.

"Masterfully done, Your Highness," Valtor said as they entered his tent. The Archchancellor's praise slid around Dakaran like a python ready to squeeze. "Showing authority right from the start will make them realize you are not a weak king." Valtor moved behind the desk and began packing some books inside an open case. "On that note, I strongly advise the prince to execute Overlord Saryn's entire family as well. The last thing you want is for his progeny to become an eventual thorn in your side. It would set a strong precedent in case others would dare rise up against you."

Dakaran cringed. "That sounds a bit much. Killing his entire family could spark another uprising."

"They have nothing to rise against us with. Their army has been defeated. Besides, the way Saryn treated his people, I wouldn't be surprised if they sang your praises in the streets."

Valtor had a point. Saryn had been quite the tyrant. But apart from what to do about him and his family, they had a much larger problem to face.

"Your scheming might have gained us the throne, but in doing so, you've left us vulnerable to our enemies. We've lost more than half our army, not to mention the entire High Guard. How are we going to defend ourselves against the other kingdoms if they decide to take advantage of the situation?"

"Do you think me a fool, Your Highness?"

Dakaran wondered if the question was supposed to be rhetorical.

"I have no intention of leaving Elondria without defense. There was more than one reason why we needed this war. It's not enough to simply remove the king. We needed to remove his support. The Elondrian lancers were loyal not just to the Crown, but to your father—especially those of the old guard like Commander Tolin. You saw the way he challenged you in front of his men. You will need to remove him and others loyal to him as soon as possible."

"But how are we going to replace the men we've lost? It's not like soldiers grow on trees."

"Grow on trees? What an interesting concept." Valtor shuffled through some papers on his desk. "We can start by replacing the fallen with men from the White Tower. The Black Watch will be loyal—not to the kingdom or to Aramoor, but to you."

Dakaran cocked his head. "The Black Watch serves the White Tower—"

"Yes. And as head of the Tower, I dictate what those services are for. I propose a merging. Your father has always kept the Tower at arm's length. I recommend using it."

Dakaran crossed the room and poured himself a glass of wine. Events were moving too quickly for him to keep up. He didn't like the idea of being reliant on Valtor. "What do we do about Ayrion and his men? We can't very well let Tolin see them lying out there with arrows sticking out of their backs."

"It has already been taken care of." Valtor continued gathering his books and paraphernalia. "My men stand guard on the rise as we speak, and the bodies are being hidden in the surrounding foliage to its rear. No one will be the wiser. But if they ask, we will tell them that we buried what little remains the hor'hounds left." Valtor looked up from his packing. "Now, about Saryn and the ambassador?"

"I suppose you have a point," Dakaran said, still not liking the idea of execution but not seeing any other way around it.

"Very good. I'll have the executioner notified at once."

Dakaran lowered himself into his chair with a heavy sigh before taking another gulp of wine. He couldn't believe they had managed to pull it off. *King Dakaran.* He smiled, then the image of his father keeling over in the mud, looking up at him, ripped it away.

Chapter 68 | Ferrin

ERRIN'S TIME HAD finally arrived. Either he would make it out tonight, or he wouldn't make it out at all. He wiped his sweaty palms down the back side of his torn trousers. He knew he'd never get another chance like this.

No one had ever escaped the White Tower. He was determined to be the first. He had to. His sister's life depended on it. Drat! *His* life depended on it. It had been Ferrin's experience that life rarely gave you what you wanted. So, when Rae handed over her crystal, at great risk to herself, he knew he had to make it count.

His plan, what little there was of it, was straightforward. He would use the crystal to open the doors leading to the Hall of Inquisition. From there he'd collect Rae and, if possible, her daughter, then make his way out of the stronghold. Along the way, he'd somehow manage to grab a uniform to disguise himself, and from there get a horse and hope they'd open the gates for them to leave. And all of this would hinge on whether the information he had gleaned from the guards was even slightly accurate.

Ferrin groaned. Who was he kidding? This was the most ridiculous plan he'd ever heard of. He stood a better chance of sprouting wings and flying out than he did of this plan working. But what choice did he have? Either he tried or he waited for the Archchancellor to rip his soul from his body. And that didn't sound pleasant at all.

He slipped his hand into the side pocket of his trousers, his fingers tightening around the small piece of rock. Pulling it out by its tarnished chain, he slid the transferal over his head and around his neck, dropping it beneath what little remained of his soiled tunic.

As soon as the crystal touched his skin, it activated. And as long as he kept it within a certain distance of his body, he could use its powers to enhance his natural abilities. However, the opposite was also true. The farther away it was, the weaker its use. Ferrin could already feel the change within himself. He could do more than sense the metal in the room; he could touch it, smell it, taste it. He breathed it in. It had been a long time since this part of him had been awoken.

"Last chance," Ferrin said, walking over to where his roommate sat, bound in the far corner of their cell. "You can still come with us."

Azriel leaned his head back against the wall, skin blotched, hair falling out, clothes all but gone. "Alas, no," he said. "My path is here. There is another who will need my help, and like you, his destiny is yet to be shaped. We each have our role to play in this pattern of life, and this is mine. But I pray for the Creator's blessings for your journey."

"I'm going to miss you, old man," Ferrin said, kneeling beside him. He grabbed the cuffs digging into the old man's feet and concentrated.

"What are you doing?" Azriel asked.

Ferrin smiled. His magic flooded through him like the bellows of a great forge, building the flames within, stoking the fire with each new breath. He had forgotten how much he'd missed that sensation. How good it had made him feel. The piece that was missing had finally returned. He rubbed his thumbs gently around the inner edge of the rusty manacles. The hard iron was like clay in his hands. It stretched and formed around his fingers, bending to his will.

Once finished, he started on the other foot, then the wrists and neck. By the time he was through, each of the manacles had been widened by at least a finger, allowing for a more comfortable fit. As a finishing touch, he smoothed the sharp edges that were clawing into the seer's skin.

"That's better," Ferrin said. "They shouldn't cut anymore. How does it feel?"

Azriel moved his hands and feet around. "Better." He laid a shaky hand on the side of Ferrin's face. "Thank you, Ferrin. May the Creator guide you down the right path. Oh, and don't be afraid to accept help from others, even if it comes from the most . . . unlikely of places."

Ferrin stared at the man. *Was that a prayer or a vision?*

He finally shrugged and headed for the door. In his hand he held a small clump of metal he had managed to extract from the seer's anklets. He lifted it up to the keyhole and let his magic take over. The metal took on a life of its own, growing directly into the lock. He could feel it forming into place, settling against the tumblers before hardening back into solid form.

Ferrin flipped his wrist, and the lock snapped. He pulled back the inner latch and cracked the door ajar, peering out into the dark passageway beyond. He waited, listening for any sound of movement in the corridor. Satisfied that no guards were patrolling within earshot, he opened the door far enough to slip through. Before he did, he turned back around.

"Is there anyone I can contact for you? Let them know you're alive?"

Azriel's head lifted slightly. "I have a son, or at least, I did. He was only a boy when I was taken, and that was—" He raised his hand and began counting his fingers. "Well, more years than I care to remember. He would be a grown man by now, with kids of his own."

"What's his name?" Ferrin asked. "Where does he live?"

"We had a small place in the Sidaran Forest. Not sure if it's still there. Quiet little place, you know? The kind where a man can do some serious thinking and never have to worry about neighbors wanting to get into your business."

Azriel was rambling. Again.

"He won't be there, though," he said. "He never enjoyed the solitude it provided—always wanted to be going into town to see his friends. Of course, he wouldn't have admitted it, but I knew it was more than just his friends he was going to see. Yep, when a boy his age starts pickin' flowers on the side of the road, and it ain't for his mother, well, there's only one other explanation."

Ferrin shook his head. "Yes, but what's his name?"

Azriel's head pivoted in his direction. "What's that? Whose name?"

"Your son . . . in Sidara. What's his name?"

"Kellen," Azriel said proudly. "His name is Kellen. We had a cottage just outside of Easthaven."

Kellen. Easthaven. Ferrin locked the information away for later as he tried to burn Azriel's image deep into the recesses of his mind, never wanting to forget the time he had spent in this place or the friend he had made in doing so.

"Till we meet again, my friend," Ferrin said with a forced smile.

Azriel lifted his hand. "Till we meet again."

Ferrin moved back into the corridor and forced the door shut behind him, locking it into place. He paused for a moment to wipe his eyes. Leaving the old man there proved more difficult than he expected.

There were no torches on the walls in this section of the Tower. There were, however, arrow slits on the opposite wall, allowing for a little guidance to see by. He proceeded down the corridor to his right, keeping to the balls of his feet to soften his passage across the cold stone.

He stopped at the corner and peeked around the edge slowly. No guards had been posted outside the door leading down to the lower corridors. *Good. At least one part of what they told me was true. Now to find the storage rooms.*

Behind the door was a winding stairwell, one he had taken numerous times. No torches or arrow slits to light the path, so he used his hands to feel his way down. He counted the doors as he passed them, continuing until he reached door number twelve.

One more flight down and he would leave the prison ward behind. He could see light ahead. He stopped at the open archway and listened. He couldn't hear anything, so he stepped off the landing and into the long hallway beyond. The stairwell on the other side of the hall led down to the lower levels. The guards had taken him this way plenty of times, so it was familiar.

The stone in this section of the Tower was smoother. There were two torches. One on Ferrin's side of the corridor and one on the other, leaving the center of the hall cloaked in shadow. A number of doors were interspersed on the right side, with chairs in between. There were even a few tapestries adding a touch of color to the walls. The guards had told him that some members of the Legate used these rooms as offices, which meant he was going to have to be extra cautious in case they were working at this time of night.

Quietly, he crept down the long hallway, keeping a close eye on each door he passed, checking to see if there was any light seeping underneath.

He made it past the third door when he heard something ahead. Without thinking, he dropped to his stomach just as one of the Tower's guards stepped into the hall from the open stairwell ahead. He didn't think the man had seen him.

Quickly, he crawled into a nearby doorway, stood, and pressed himself against the stone, hoping the guard would pass by without noticing. Trying the handle, he realized it was unlocked. There was no light coming from the other side, so he eased it open. To his surprise, it swung with minimal resistance and noise. Once inside, Ferrin closed it behind him and waited. *With my luck, this is probably his bedchamber, and he's just getting off a two-day shift.*

Holding his breath, Ferrin whispered a silent prayer into the darkness as he anxiously listened to the guard's approach. From just outside the door, the noise of the sentry's passing went abruptly still.

Ferrin grabbed the small piece of metal that he had used as a makeshift key from his pocket, effortlessly shaping it into a point. It wasn't long enough to make a dagger, but he could use it to puncture the man's neck.

He flattened himself against the wall again and waited. What was the guard doing out there? Why hadn't he heard anything? Then, for no apparent reason, the guard's boots started up once again and he continued down the hall.

Ferrin released the breath he'd been holding as the footsteps faded altogether. Not wanting to waste time, he made his way around the room quickly, hands held out in front as he tried to determine where he was and if there was anything worth pilfering.

He knocked over a chair, banged his knee on a desk, and tripped over a small trunk, allowing him to test the cleanliness of the floor with the side of his face. Picking himself back up, he found a large cabinet near the back of the room. It held an assortment of odds and ends but, more importantly, also an empty shoulder pack. He couldn't tell what each item on the shelf was simply by touch, so he had to guess which to take and which to leave behind.

He found something that felt like a tinderbox with the striker inside. There were a couple of candles, a small lantern, stacks of paper, and a quill—which he left behind—plus rows of oddly shaped bottles. Again, not important, since he had no idea what they held. He moved from there to the desk, where he found more paper and writing utensils, which made sense if these were a legate's quarters.

He was about to leave when his hands stumbled across a hidden cubby up under the desk. No one sitting there would have found it by sight alone, but since he was using his hands, he had. He reached inside and pulled out a small bag. It felt like a purse. He bounced it in his hand. It was quite heavy. He smiled and stuffed it in his sack.

Back at the door, he listened for any shuffling of feet before stepping out into the corridor.

His stride increased with each new step. Time was running short. Ferrin glanced down at the bag and smiled. *Maybe my luck is finally starting to turn.*

There was a noise behind him. *Then again, maybe not.*

He sprinted for the open stairwell ahead, practically diving onto the hard steps. He clutched his bag of stolen goods to his chest to keep them from banging on the stone. One good thing about having no boots was that his footsteps were almost silent.

He'd have preferred the boots.

Ferrin wiped a sheen of nervous sweat from his forehead and rubbed the corner of his knee where it had smashed on the second step. Carefully, he crept down the remaining stairs, pleading reverently that there be no one on their way up. To his relief, the stairwell was empty.

The landing at the bottom opened into a circular vestibule with multiple corridors leading off in different directions. It wasn't much to look at. A couple of torches revealed at least twelve-foot ceilings, decorative archways around each passage, and the same slate-grey stone as most of the buildings. The room was twenty paces across, perhaps—a simple intersection to wherever one needed to go.

Ferrin took a moment to replay the route in his mind. Where had they said the storage rooms were? He knew the second corridor on the left would take him down to the Hall of Inquisition, but he needed to make a quick stop first.

The entry arches all looked the same. His eyes scanned the passageways on the right side. *Third corridor on the right . . . Fourth door on the left. Or was it fourth on the right and third on the left?* Hugging the walls, he made his way around the room to the third opening on the right. From there, he silently counted off the doors. *One, two, three, and—here we go—four . . . pantry storage. At least, I hope it is.*

To his surprise, the door was unlocked and the room already lit by a bracketed torch. *Rather nice of them to have this waiting for me.* He pushed the door closed behind him and dropped back the latch. It didn't take long to realize that he had either forgotten how to count to four or had mixed up the information he had gleaned from his captors. There was no food in sight; however, there were blankets, linens, and pillows aplenty.

Ferrin stuffed a couple of blankets inside his pouch. While leaning over to extract a small coil of twine, he heard the latch on the door behind him flip open.

His back was to the door, and there was nowhere to go, so he didn't move. He reached in his pocket and grabbed the small metal poker.

"Who are you?" the guard demanded.

Ferrin turned.

He sighed when he saw there was only the one guard. But how long until more showed up? "I'm Ferrin," he said. "I was told to take extra blankets to the inquisitors' quarters for the cold."

The man's eyes narrowed. His hand gripped the hilt of his sword, which was still sheathed for the moment, thankfully.

"Look," Ferrin said, "they're going to be pretty upset if I don't deliver them. And trust me, coming from someone who knows what they're like when they're angry"—he lifted the bottom of his ripped tunic, revealing the half-healed lacerations across his waistline—"you don't want to get them upset."

Ferrin didn't give the guard time to think and moved to step around him, but the guard grabbed him on the way past.

"Wait."

Ferrin obeyed. His hand was still clutching the small piece of metal in his right trouser pocket. He slowly started to lift it out.

"Better take a few more just in case." The guard stepped into the room, hefting a couple more blankets from one of the bottom shelves and tucking them under Ferrin's arm.

Ferrin smiled. "You have a point. Better safe than sorry." He bowed his head respectfully. "Thank you."

He ducked through the doorway into the dimly lit hallway beyond and retraced his steps to the circular vestibule. This time, he took the second archway on the left, the one leading down to the inquisitors' chambers. He couldn't afford to keep rummaging around for the food stores, not while there was a guard watching him. He would have to try again on the way out.

Chapter 69 | Ferrin

FERRIN STUCK THE metal rod into the compact lock on the heavy iron door. The metal morphed once again, nudging the tumblers into position, and the door opened.

Was he doing the right thing? The last place he wanted to be right now was down in the Hall of Inquisition, but it was the only way to get to Rae's sleeping quarters, and she was depending on him. For a brief moment, he hesitated. It would be much easier to escape without having to worry about a woman and a child. The longer he stayed in the Tower, the greater the risk of capture. He shoved the thought aside. He'd never be able to live with himself if he left them there.

Resolving to what he needed to do, he put his weight against the door and pushed. It opened with a whine. He stepped into the torch-lit stairwell on the other side and closed the door. He didn't bother locking it, in case he needed to make a swift exit. He shifted the travel pack on his shoulder and started down the stairs. A twinge of fear washed over him. It was understandable. Every time he'd descended these steps, it was to spend another session on the rack.

The stairwell ended in a small corridor, the Hall of Inquisition just ahead. He stopped just inside the mouth of the passageway and took a moment to look around at the enormous chamber beyond. It was the first time he'd seen it empty. The three desks in the center where the legates performed their menial tasks were neatly aligned, papers stacked on all corners, and chairs carefully tucked underneath.

It looked like everyone was in bed. Ferrin breathed a short sigh of relief and stepped into the room. He kept his back pressed against the wall as he worked his way around to the single passageway on the other side, which led back to the sleeping quarters.

He tried recalling the exact instructions Rae had given him to find her room. Everything depended on him *not* choosing the wrong door. She had told him to take the second corridor on—

Someone screamed.

Ferrin dropped to the floor once again, not that it would have done him much good. He would have been spotted easily from anywhere in the chamber. He waited a moment, then lifted himself back onto his knees. He noticed light coming from the base of one of the doors opposite him. It was door eleven. He'd seen the inside of that room more than once himself.

The woman screamed again. He rose quickly to his feet. The agonizing echoes from the lingering cry reverberated off the vaulted walls.

He knew that voice. It was Rae!

This changed everything. The plan had been to meet in her room so they could leave without anyone knowing. Why was she here? Had they discovered she didn't have her crystal? Had she given him up? Sweat broke out on his forehead.

No. They wouldn't be torturing her if she had. Then again, they'd probably torture her either way.

No longer worrying about making noise, he raced across the atrium and tried his best to peer through the keyhole. The light was too dim to see.

With sweaty hands, he hefted the latch and slid the door open. For the first time, with just a little magical help, it didn't squeal.

His fists clenched when he saw Cheeks standing over his set of tools at the table. His back was to the door, so he didn't see Ferrin slip in. The rack in the center of the room was locked in an upright position, with Rae fastened to it. Her arms and legs looked barely long enough to reach the manacles. The front of her shirt had been ripped open, and blood was pouring from deep slashes running down her chest and stomach. Tears streamed down her face as she sobbed.

As soon as she saw him, her head lifted.

Ferrin raised his finger to his lips. He eased the door shut behind him, lifting the latch and gently lowering it into place. He moved back into the shadows at the edge of the door. He could feel the fire of his magic rising, his rage pulling it forth. The metal called to him. He could feel the rack—every bar, every bolt, every inch of its despicable frame.

From the corner of his eye, he caught some movement.

A little girl curled into a ball off to the side was whimpering as she rocked back and forth against the wall. She had to be Rae's daughter.

"Where is the transferal, Rae?" Cheeks demanded, walking back to the rack and striking her across the face. His tone rested somewhere between rage and fear. It was a side of Cheeks that Ferrin had not seen before. The pale-faced sadist brandished a large knife and wiped the side of it across the soft skin of her neck.

Ferrin stepped quietly, moving farther into the room. He didn't want to spook the inquisitor and have him slit her throat by accident.

"And don't tell me you lost it," Cheeks said, sliding the flat side of the blade down her chest and across her stomach. "We both know you did no such thing. Don't make me cut you again. I would hate to see something so beautiful ruined for life."

She glanced past the inquisitor for a brief moment and looked at Ferrin.

He raised his finger to his lips once again and shook his head. She must have gotten the message because she quickly looked away.

Cheeks started to turn.

Ferrin froze.

"Why won't you believe me?" Rae asked, causing the inquisitor to turn back around.

Ferrin exhaled.

Cheeks shook his knife at her. "Did you give it to the smith? I just sent a contingent of guards to check on him. One way or another, I'm going to find out."

Ferrin almost choked. He must have missed them on his way down, but only just. How was that possible? Talk about a lucky coincidence. An image of Azriel popped into his mind, and he wondered if luck had had anything to do with it—or not.

"I didn't give it to him."

"Then tell me who has the transferal!"

Ferrin couldn't take it any longer. He stepped out of the shadows. "I do."

Cheeks nearly fell off the back of the rack's platform. He reached out and grabbed hold of the hoist wheel to keep from tipping over completely.

Ferrin used the distraction and charged.

Cheeks turned and swung widely with his blade. Still trying to balance, his aim was off. Ferrin blocked with his arm and slammed his elbow into Cheeks's side, spinning the big man around and off the rack.

Ferrin hopped up on the base and grabbed the braces around Rae's ankles. As soon as his hands touched the iron, his magic came alive. He ripped the cuffs open, then did the same for her arms. Before he could pull her down, though, Cheeks came at him, this time with the stone blade Ferrin was used to seeing him with.

Ferrin ducked and kicked the inquisitor in the gut, but Cheeks had his footing now and barely moved. Ferrin reached behind him and grabbed one of the rack's bars. It twisted in his hand to form the shape of a simple dagger. It certainly wasn't anything he could sell at market, but its edge was sharp.

Ferrin stepped down off the rack to face the inquisitor. "I've been waiting to do this for a long time." His legs were shaking, sleep deprivation and malnourishment catching up with him, but his determination was stronger than ever.

Cheeks snarled, but Ferrin could see the man's hands were shaking. He'd never had to face one of his subjects before. Not when the other person was on equal footing.

Cheeks lunged, but his size made his movements slow and unwieldy.

Ferrin dodged the blow and grabbed the inquisitor's wrist. He spun it around and locked the elbow, then brought his other hand down and snapped the bone.

The stone blade skittered across the floor as Ferrin counted.

"One. Two—"

"Ahhh!" Cheeks screamed, his body stiffening as his head reared backward. His arm hung at an unnatural angle at his side.

"You're right," Ferrin said. "There is a time delay."

Cheeks stumbled backward and glanced at the door.

"Don't even think about—"

Before Ferrin could finish, Cheeks turned and bolted. If he called for help, it was over.

Ferrin ran after him. Much lighter on his feet than the obese inquisitor, he dove and hit Cheeks in the back of his knees. The collision sent Cheeks forward, bouncing off the door and landing on his face in the corner.

Cheeks curled against the wall to protect himself.

"Get up," Ferrin said, standing over him with his knife.

The man didn't move.

Ferrin stuck the tip of the blade to the side of Cheeks's face. "I said, get up!"

Cheeks obeyed. With Ferrin's help, the big man finally made it to his feet. Cheeks didn't say a word, his teeth gritted against the pain of his broken arm.

"Move." Ferrin poked him in the back with the knife, and Cheeks waddled back to the center of the room, cradling his arm. Ferrin stepped up on the rack and gently lifted Rae off the bars, placing her against the far wall beside her daughter. Keeping a close eye on Cheeks, he retrieved a clean blanket from his sack by the door and cut it into strips to wrap her chest.

Cheeks didn't move. He stood quietly on the right side of the rack, opposite his tools. Blood dripped from his mouth and nose from where his face had hit the floor.

Ferrin didn't have time to bother with him. As much as he would have liked to repay Cheeks for the hours he'd spent being tortured at his hands, the fact was that escaping was more important. Even so, Ferrin couldn't take the chance of the man raising the alarm.

"Get on the rack," Ferrin said, starting across the room toward Cheeks.

The inquisitor hesitated. "What?"

Ferrin aimed his blade at Cheeks's midsection. "I said, get on the rack."

"What are you going to do?" Cheeks asked, hobbling up onto the base and turning around.

Ferrin shoved him backward, pressing him against the rack. Seizing the iron with his magic, he snapped shut all four clamps around Cheeks's wrists and ankles.

Cheeks didn't even bother fighting against the restraints. He sneered, suddenly regaining his backbone. "What now?"

Ferrin stared at the helpless inquisitor, not ignoring the irony of the situation.

"If you kill me, the others will know."

Ferrin felt conflicted. He didn't know whether his desire for vengeance and retribution was stronger than his sense of morality. It had been well-tested during his time in the White Tower. He lifted his blade up to Cheeks's neck.

"Keep talking."

Cheeks grinned, his teeth red with blood. "Every member of the Inquisition has been linked with a layered spell. It informs the others immediately if one of us were to meet an untimely end."

"I don't believe you."

"What do you think these runes on my head were for? Decoration? Look around you!" Cheeks spat, wincing from having moved his broken arm. "You know what we do here? We work with the most dangerous people in Aldor. Of course we have a system of protection in place."

"It only works if I kill you?"

Cheeks started to nod.

"So, what happens when I do this?" Ferrin ripped open the front of the man's robe and slid his knife across the fat man's chest.

Cheeks shouted, his head ricocheting off the back of the rack.

"Hmm." Ferrin glanced around the room. "I guess nothing."

Ferrin realized he was enjoying this a little too much and wondered, for a brief moment, if this was what it felt like for Cheeks. The very thought of comparing himself to the sadistic inquisitor turned his stomach; he lowered his blade. He walked over and grabbed a soiled rag off the table and stuffed it in the inquisitor's mouth, then bent one of the metal bars over it, holding it in.

He walked over to where Rae was sitting against the wall with Suri. She struggled to her feet when she saw him coming.

"We need to go," he said. "If the inquisitor was telling the truth and has sent guards up to check my cell, then they'll have seen I'm not there by now and have started looking. Our only hope is that this is the last place they'd think to look."

Ferrin leaned over. "I'll carry Suri if you'll get the gear." It took a moment to pry Rae's daughter from her hands, but she finally relinquished her hold. Ferrin walked the little girl over to where he had left his travel bag at the entrance and laid her down beside it. He knelt to look inside.

"Rae! No!" Cheeks shouted.

Ferrin turned. Rae had left her place by the wall and was now standing in front of the inquisitor. She had removed his gag. Ferrin's eyes widened when he saw the stone blade clutched in her other hand.

"Think of Suri," the inquisitor pleaded. "I'm her father."

"Not anymore."

Ferrin stood. "Don't do it, Rae! What if he's telling the truth? You could alert the rest of the Inquisition."

She turned and looked at Ferrin. He saw it in her eyes. There was no stopping her.

Ferrin ran as fast as he could, but he wasn't fast enough.

A wet choking sound was all he heard as she slid the stone blade through Cheeks's neck. The inquisitor's blue eyes flared, and his body jerked.

"What have you done?" Ferrin hissed as he jumped up on the rack and pulled the knife out. He tried covering the wound with his hand. "Rae, you need to save him."

Rae looked at Cheeks, wiped the blood from her hands on the front of her dress, and casually strolled across the room to where her daughter sat digging around inside Ferrin's bag. Ferrin tried to stem the bleeding as best he could, but even he could see there was no hope for the man. Not without Rae.

Ferrin glanced over his shoulder. "What if he was telling the truth?"

The look in Rae's eyes said she didn't care.

Ferrin finally released Cheeks's neck. There was nothing more he could do. The man wasn't dead, but he would be soon. Ferrin wiped the blood from his hands on the front of his tattered trousers and did the same to the stone blade before tucking it into the back of his pants. He grabbed the inquisitor's tools and stuffed the case inside his travel sack.

Ferrin lifted Suri and opened the door. "We have to go."

Rae slid out the door first and disappeared into the outer chamber. Ferrin paused a moment to take one final look around the small stone room, ending on Cheeks. The blood flowing from his neck was a colorful contrast to the stark white of his robes. It was a pathetic and yet disturbingly satisfying end to his tormentor. He couldn't help but feel a little vindicated.

He turned to leave when he noticed the inquisitor's tattoos begin to shift color. They went from black to a pale chartreuse. Within seconds, they were a fiery red.

Ferrin sighed. "Just my luck."

Chapter 70 | Ferrin

FOLLOWING ON RAE'S HEELS, Ferrin raced across the open atrium and into the small hallway leading up and out of the Hall of Inquisition. They had barely made it halfway down the corridor when the sound of booted feet filled the main chamber behind them. Ferrin didn't turn to look.

"I guess Cheeks was telling the truth."

Rae grunted and headed up the stairs in front of him. Ferrin took them two at a time, Suri bouncing in his arms the entire way. The little girl giggled as if it were all good fun. They reached the top, and Ferrin put his shoulder to the door with a shove. *Good.* It was still unlocked.

He could see torchlight below as men in white robes, black robes, and some without any robes at all sprinted up the stairwell behind them. The door opened far enough for them to get through. Ferrin could see the glint of blades in the hands of some as he stepped out of the stairwell and put his weight into moving the large iron door back into place.

He didn't have time to lock it. The first of those giving chase had reached the other side and was pushing against him. The door began to give way. Drawing on his magic, he melded the door to the surrounding wall and then smelted the hinges and handle for good measure.

"Let's see you try getting out of there."

"Give her to me," Rae said as she tried to snatch Suri out of Ferrin's arms.

Ferrin held her back. "You can't carry her. You're wounded. Now which way to get out of here?"

Rae huffed but finally gave in. "This way!" She took off running for the first hallway on the right.

Ferrin chased after her. "Are you sure you know where you're going?"

She looked at him and sneered. "This is my home." She cut down the corridor, her bare feet padding on the stone.

Can't argue with that, he thought as he raced to catch up. For someone so small, she was very swift. His eyes scanned the dim area ahead, and he spotted her standing at a second entranceway on the right, motioning for him to hurry.

Rae checked Suri quickly once he reached her. The girl was playing a game of seeing how many of Ferrin's whiskers she could pull out. What he wouldn't give, he thought, for a sharp knife and some soap.

As soon as Rae was sure her daughter was fine, she started running again. Ferrin raced to keep up, struggling to match her pace. His body was weak, but he pushed through it. Every now and then, she'd stop and let him catch up.

The White Tower was alive with the shouts of the Black Watch running to and fro, searching for any sign of the escaped prisoners. Each time they were about to be discovered, Rae would usher them into an adjoining hall, or side room, or even a broom closet till the threat had passed. She hadn't been exaggerating when she'd said she knew her way around the enormous construct. If it had been left to Ferrin, they would have been lost or captured before now. But no matter how many times she would angle off in one direction to avoid a passing patrol, she would always manage to get them back to where they needed to be.

Around the next junction was another long corridor. He could hear the clanging of swords and armor coming from behind. The guards were getting close. Again, he dashed after Rae. His arms were beginning to tire under the strain of Suri's weight.

Just ahead, the latch to the next doorway pulled back and a white-robed guard stepped through. Rae tripped over her own feet trying to stop, and Ferrin nearly tripped over her.

The hall was too dark to make out the guard's face. How many others were waiting on the other side of the door? The clamor of the Watch behind them was getting louder; pretty soon, they would be cornered. There was only one option. He thrust Suri into Rae's arms and pulled the stone blade from his back pocket.

"Smith, is that you?"

Ferrin stopped. The voice was familiar. A torch appeared from the other side of the door, lighting the man's face.

"This way!" Nostrils said, motioning for them to follow. "Hurry."

Rae shook her head. She wasn't moving. At any moment, the guards were going to come rushing into the corridor behind them. Ferrin had to do something. Leaning over, he grabbed both Rae and Suri, lifted them off the ground, and ran for the door.

"I've been waiting for you," the captain said, ushering them through just as the first of the Black Watch rounded the far end of the hall behind them.

Nostrils quickly shut the door but stayed in the hall to talk with the Tower guards.

"What do you think you're doing?" Rae hissed as Ferrin put her and Suri down. His arms were shaking. He'd thought carrying Suri was bad.

"I'm saving your life. You're welcome."

She kicked him in the shin. "And how do you know he's not leading them right to us?"

"I don't," he admitted. "But what other option did we have?" He walked over and stuck his ear to the door.

"We could have—"

"Quiet," Ferrin said, raising his hand. "I'm trying to listen."

He caught snatches of what they said.

"Haven't seen them . . ."

". . . south corridors."

A moment later, Ferrin stepped back as the door squeaked open and Nostrils stepped through. "I don't know how you've made it this far without being caught," he said, shutting the door. "Absolute miracle, if you ask me."

"Why are you helping us?" Ferrin asked, unconcerned about the skepticism in his voice. "How did you know we'd be here?"

"Someone told me you would."

Ferrin raised his knife and shoved Nostrils back against the wall. "Told you? Who told you?"

The captain gulped. "Look, I've been waiting for a long time to get out of this place. I'm just as much a prisoner here as you."

Ferrin's scowl clearly didn't go unnoticed, and the captain revised his statement.

"Sorry. Maybe not *like* you, but when I first signed up, I didn't know what I was getting myself into. And once you're here, it's not like you can tell them you've changed your mind and want to leave."

Ferrin lowered his blade and moved back. Nostrils rubbed at the spot on his neck where the knife had been.

"Here, help me with this." He handed Ferrin another large travel sack and then hefted two of his own before turning and heading down the dark corridor.

"What's all this?" Ferrin asked as hurried to catch up. Rae and Suri were right beside him.

"Supplies—"

"You never answered my question. Who told you we'd be here?"

"I was getting to that," Nostrils said. "A few months ago, I was called to one of the upper cells to calm a prisoner. When I got there, he asked to speak with me alone. I figured, how bad could it be? He was chained to a wall."

Ferrin's head rose.

"So, I shut the door and listened. And what he had to say left me feeling hopeful for the first time in a long while."

Nostrils pulled them to a halt at the end of another small corridor. He listened for a brief moment, and then nodded to the far-left stairwell before they began to move once again.

"Anyway, the old man said he knew that I wanted to leave the Tower and that it was going to happen. But I had to wait. He said I needed to help you three escape. Well, he didn't exactly specify *you* three in particular. He just said a man, a woman, and a small child. And here you are. He also gave me explicit instructions about what I was to do and where I was to wait for you."

Ferrin smiled as he thought about Azriel's earlier statement of aid coming from unexpected sources. For the first time in his life, Ferrin wondered if there truly was a Creator and whether his own life had a larger purpose in His plan— or if this was all just some elaborate coincidence.

"So," Nostrils said with a shrug as they continued, "when I heard there were three people trying to escape, I knew it had to be you. I was waiting in the exact spot he told me, and sure enough, there you were."

They rounded the next corner and walked face-first into a small company of armed guards.

Everyone stopped. Ferrin's eyes danced from one person to the next. They looked just as confused as Ferrin.

"So, did he tell you what to do here?" Rae asked.

Nostrils was the first to break the deadly silence as he dropped his two bags. "Found them!" he said, throwing on a wide smile and extending his arms.

No one moved.

"Yeah, caught them wandering the halls. No need to worry; just on our way back to the Inquisition. Everything's under control."

We're all going to die, Ferrin thought.

The guards' hands slid to the hilts of their swords. Thankfully, they weren't wearing armor like some of the others.

Ferrin shoved Suri back into her mother's arms and grabbed the dead inquisitor's stone blade from his belt. With a roar that caused Nostrils to jump, Ferrin leaped at the closest guard. The man didn't even have time to draw his sword.

Ferrin hit him with the full strength of a smith, ripping through his neck and nicking the bone on the way through. The guard grabbed his throat and tried to scream, but it came out as a sickening sort of burble.

He was on the second man by the time Nostrils had drawn his sword and charged the third. The guard swung for Ferrin's head, but he ducked and plunged his knife into the man's chest once, twice, three times, and then flung his body to the side.

Nostrils finished off his opponent with a thrust to the open midsection, and the fourth and final guard took off running.

Ferrin started to go after him, but Nostrils pulled him back. "We don't have time, smith. It'll take a while to get back to the south side of the tower, and we need to get out of here, preferably without being seen."

"And how in the name of Aldor are we going to do that?"

"Ahem." Rae held the top of a dead guard's uniform in her free hand.

Ferrin grinned. "I knew there was a reason I brought you along."

Rae's demeanor hardened. "Brought *me* along? I think you got that backward, bush-face."

Ferrin rubbed his unkempt beard and smiled.

They worked as fast as humanly possible to undress the two guards, cleaning as much of the blood off as they could. After putting on the dead men's uniforms, Nostrils led them to one of the not-so-known side exits. One, he said, had been used by the Black Watch back when this part of the stronghold had been a barracks. They'd since moved the Watch's quarters closer to the main keep.

The corridors on this side of the stronghold were much colder than those farther in, leaving Ferrin thankful that the guard's boots had been large enough to fit him. A thick layer of dust on the floor made hiding their passage almost impossible.

Ferrin was practically trembling with excitement when Nostrils opened the final door and he caught his first glimpse of freedom. Stepping outside, Ferrin swelled his chest with a deep gulp of fresh air. It smelled like horse manure, but he wasn't complaining. His breath turned to mist in front of his face as he exhaled.

"Now what?" he asked.

"You wait here while I find us horses. The stables are just on the other side of that rock."

There were trees and vines blocking most of the entrance, with a small beaten path leading around a large outcropping of stone. Ferrin couldn't see a stable from where they were, but he could certainly smell it.

"Aren't they going to question why you need three horses?"

"Not if I outrank them," Nostrils said with a smile. "Besides, it's not unusual to have more than one unit on patrol at night, especially with the increase in numbers we've seen lately. Wait here and stay out of sight. I'll be back with the horses."

Ferrin directed Rae to a cluster of rocks off to the side of the entrance. "Stay here."

"Where are you going?" she asked.

"I'm going to make sure we get those horses."

"You're going to get us caught, you mean."

Ferrin ignored her and started down the path. It wasn't that he didn't trust Nostrils, especially having watched him kill one of his own men, but he wasn't taking any chances.

Ferrin crouched behind a large boulder and peeked around the edge. He could see the stable in the distance. It wasn't as big as he would have expected, considering the size of the White Tower, but it was probably only one of many. He straightened his new white robe and headed for the front. He kept a slow pace so as not to attract attention. There didn't seem to be anyone else about.

He could hear voices coming from inside. One of them was Nostrils, and he didn't sound pleased.

"What do you mean, I can't have the horses? Me and my men are on patrol tonight. What's your name, ranker?"

"The name's Tadis, sir. I'm sorry, but I've got my orders. No one's to get a horse until the prisoners are found."

Ferrin stood just outside the entrance and peered through the wooden slats. Nostrils had his back to the door, and the other man—wearing the familiar white of the Black Watch—stood about three feet to his right, holding a set of reins.

"You see these stripes, son? They mean *I* give the orders. And I'm ordering you to give—"

"They've escaped the Tower!" Ferrin shouted and charged into the barn, panting as though he'd just run up half the mountainside. "Captain, they've made it outside the walls. I've been ordered to inform you that you are to take a small contingent and guard the pass, just in case."

"No one has ever escaped the Tower!" Nostrils bellowed, catching on. "And they certainly won't on my watch."

The stable hand looked from Nostrils to Ferrin then back to Nostrils. He wasn't sure what to do.

"Well, you heard him, soldier. Saddle three horses, and be quick about it!"

Not wanting to disobey orders or get into trouble with the captain, Tadis rushed off to get the horses ready. It wasn't long before all three were saddled and waiting.

"Be sure to shut these doors as soon as we leave," Nostrils said as he mounted. "And keep your eyes open. You never know where they might be."

"Yes, sir," the stable hand said with a sharp salute to his chest.

Ferrin mounted and followed Nostrils out the door, leading the third horse besides. A quick glance back showed the man shutting the doors behind them. Ferrin chuckled.

They rode the horses back around to where they had left Rae. Before Ferrin had even managed to dismount, she and Suri were scrambling out from behind the rocks.

"It's about time," she stated. She stopped when she saw the horses. She looked ready to bolt.

"What's wrong?" Ferrin asked. She looked like she'd never seen a horse before.

"I'm not getting on one of those."

"You will if you want to get out of here."

Ferrin had to practically force her up onto the animal. Rae fought him the whole way up. Once mounted, she was stiff as a board. He was going to hand Suri up in front of her but changed his mind. "You've never ridden a horse, have you?"

She didn't move anything but her head, and only enough to shake it slowly.

Ferrin sighed. "This isn't going to work." He looked at Nostrils, who was busy tying off their supplies. "You'll have to ride with one and I'll take the other."

"Fine by me," he said, "but hurry."

Ferrin carried Suri over to where Nostrils was swinging onto his mount. He handed her up and then headed back for his horse. "Scoot back," he told Rae. "I need to get on."

Rae didn't move. She looked terrified.

After a bit of jostling, Ferrin managed to get his foot in the stirrup and lift his leg around front without knocking her off. This was going to be a rough ride.

He glanced at Nostrils and nodded.

"Now hold on." He tried grabbing her arms, but she twisted and turned to keep him from reaching them. "Stop!" he shouted, finally yanking her arms around his waist. "You've got to hold on to me or you're going to fall off."

She jerked her arms back as soon as he let go.

"Fine." He kicked his horse, and it leaped forward.

She squealed, and her arms flung around his waist.

He gasped for breath. "Not so tight."

She didn't loosen her grip.

Ferrin kept just behind Nostrils as they made their way down the mountainside. In the moonlight, they appeared to be nothing more than a small group on night patrol, making their typical sweep of the Tower's base.

To Ferrin's surprise, the bridge gate was still open. Apparently, word hadn't reached there yet of their escape. Then again, the guards probably still believed the prisoners were somewhere inside the Tower.

With Nostrils taking the lead, they pushed the horses forward, keeping to a slow canter across the massive bridge. Ferrin stayed toward the middle, not bothering to get close enough to the edge to see what was below. He didn't really care. He'd seen it before when he'd first arrived, from the back of a prison wagon.

Once across, they headed directly for the two monolithic stone sentinels that guarded the Pass of Arnon. He'd forgotten how unnerving the two robed figures were, both with cowls covering their faces, each holding an enormous sword cut from the same stone as the mountain.

Before passing between the gigantic figures, Ferrin brought his horse to a stop and turned.

"What are you doing?" Rae asked. "Why are you stopping?"

"Quiet," he said. He studied the upper towers to the left of the main keep. He knew that somewhere within the twisted labyrinth of hallways, stairwells, and inner corridors lay an old man, his white hair falling out, his wrinkled skin cut and torn. He was bound by fate and magic to serve the Creator's purpose, patiently waiting for the next poor soul to save.

How long he would have to wait, Ferrin didn't know.

"I'll miss you, old man." Not bothering to wipe the tears from his eyes, he turned his horse back toward the Pass of Arnon. He gave his reins a light snap, and the four of them disappeared into the night.

Chapter 71 | Ty

"**WE'VE GOT TO DO SOMETHING**," Ty said as he thought about poor Orlyn being questioned by the Black Watch. "We can't just leave him there."

At the head of the dinner table, his father scooped up a second helping of vegetable soup and poured it into his bowl. "The council is working on a way to get him out, but we can't risk jumping in feet first without exposing the rest of us." He nodded in Ty's direction. "That includes you."

"I don't care about me. We need to save Orlyn."

"Well, your mother and I care about you, and so does the council. I just hope the Tower guards don't leave before we have a chance to act."

"What can I do?" Ever since his induction into the wielder council, they had kept Ty at arm's length, never really letting him get more involved. He was tired of being treated like a piece of his mother's special cookware—too fragile for everyday use, only brought out when company was expected.

"Best you stay as far away from the Black Watch as possible," his mother said from the other end of the table. "We can't afford you getting dragged into this."

"Why not? I'm not afraid."

"You know very well why not," his father said, jabbing his spoon in Ty's direction. "We were charged with your protection. And protect you we will."

"I have just as much right to fight as the rest of you."

"It has nothing to do with rights. It has to do with our duty to keep you safe."

"But I have magic too. I can—"

"You don't know what you have," his father said. "You accidentally transported the entire East Inn into the Sidaran Forest while playing a flute." He shook his head. "It's best you leave this to us."

"I didn't actually move the inn," he grumbled.

"Regardless, you're too young and too inexperienced."

"I'm sixteen. And I'd hardly—"

A loud knock on the front door nearly made him jump in his seat. Adarra and his mother did. Before his father had even scooted his chair back, Ty was up and heading across the room.

"Ty, get back here." His father's tone was anything but jovial.

Ty ignored him and kept going. Did they think he was too young even to answer the door? He was nearly there when a second knock resounded.

"Hold your horses! I'm coming!" He jerked the latch open, and the blood drained from his face.

He half choked. "Overlord Barl? What are you doing here?" *That was a stupid question to ask.* "I mean, how can we help you?" He tried a formal bow but gave up halfway through, too rattled at having just told the overlord of Sidara to hold his horses.

Behind him, Ty could hear the rest of his family hopping to their feet, spoons dropping and dishes clanging as his father made a swift approach.

"Your Lordship, how can we be of service?" His father gestured toward the front room. "Please, will you come inside?"

"You know, I don't believe I've been in this cottage since I was a boy," Barl said. "It was my great-grandfather who built it, you know." His hand reached out and gently rubbed across the doorpost, where there were periodic markings, starting at knee height and working their way up. "I rather enjoyed spending my summers here as a child." He took a step back to glance around the homestead, and in doing so, revealed that he wasn't alone.

Ty flushed when he spotted Lyessa standing directly behind her father. She looked different from the last time they'd met. Instead of one of the frilly dresses he was used to seeing her in, she wore a pair of light-brown breeches, a white shirt, and a dark coat with grey fur trim. The euphoria of the moment was cut short, however, when he noticed Aiden strolling up the walkway behind her.

"Is everything all right, young Ty?" Overlord Barl asked.

Ty snapped to. "No, my lord, I mean, yes, my lord. I mean—" *For pity's sake, what do I mean?* "I'll see to your horses." He shied past their guests and made a quick retreat for the corral, where the overlord's guards were already stabling the animals. Ty counted twelve lancers in Overlord Barl's patrol, all wearing armor, each bearing the symbolic tree of the Sidaran crest.

He kept an eye on Lyessa as he rubbed down one of the mares. He watched, as subtly as possible, as she spoke a few words to her father and then started in his direction. Ty turned his head, not wanting to appear too obvious as she closed in on the gated pen.

"So, how is our young Master Ty doing today?" she asked, leaning across the top rail.

Ty looked up from his grooming to see a friendly smile. Aiden, on the other hand, looked positively green with envy as he approached to join them. Ty smiled back. Maybe all was *not* lost when it came to Lyessa.

"He's doing as well as can be expected," Ty said, trying to be pleasant. "And how is Your Ladyship today?" He held out a small bucket of oats for the horse, and it happily thrust its muzzle in and chomped down.

"Have there been any new sightings of the creature roaming through the woods?" she asked eagerly. "That's why we're here, you know. Father and his patrol met me and Aiden at the Sidaran border yesterday. They were escorting us back from Aiden's family's estate in Highcrest."

Ty grunted. *Who cares about Aiden's family's estate?* Ty glanced at their cottage and sighed. Who was he kidding? His family didn't even own their home. It belonged to the overlord.

"So, is it true?" she asked.

"What?"

"Have you seen the beast?"

Ty nodded. "Yes. I've seen it." He set the now-empty oat bucket down and stepped over to the railing. "Breen and I went out a few days ago to scout the woods east of town." He took a deep breath and shook his head. "It was horrifying."

"What was horrifying?" Aiden asked, stepping a little closer.

Lyessa's eyes brightened in anticipation.

Ty was enjoying this. He had them eating out of his hands. "We found its feeding ground. An entire valley filled with nothing but bones and rotten corpses."

Aiden's mouth twisted with skepticism, but his eyes were wide all the same.

"Where?" Lyessa asked.

"Just north of the East River," he said, pointing back behind the house.

Lyessa looked uneasy as she turned her head in that direction. "Did you get a look at it?" she asked. "Was it like the creature Ambassador Lanmiere described?"

"No. It was much, much worse. We tracked it to its lair. A giant tunnel leading deep into the ground. It smelled like . . . like death."

"What did it look like?" she asked, practically leaning over the railing.

"Like nothing I've ever seen. It was a spider."

Aiden laughed. "All this fuss for a spider?"

"A spider the size of a mountain bear," Ty snapped.

Just when Ty thought Aiden couldn't laugh any harder, he did. It took all of Ty's restraint to keep from punching his powdered face. Even Lyessa was trying her best not to snicker. She held her hand to her mouth and looked down the wooden fence rail as if to measure its straightness.

Ty ground his teeth. Who cared if they didn't believe him? He knew it was true.

"What a crock of targ dung," Aiden said as he pulled Lyessa back from the railing. "Let's go see what they're discussing inside, shall we?" Aiden continued shaking his head as he directed Lyessa toward the front of the house. "Bear-sized spiders, indeed."

Ty kicked the feed bucket, and it bounced off the rail, nearly hitting one of the horses. What did Lyessa see in that stupid fluffed-up boor? Was his family's big estate all she cared about?

After taking a moment to cool down, he joined the rest of his family inside the front room. Ty sat in the corner and listened patiently as his brother relayed their expedition into the Sidaran Forest.

Barl leaned forward, resting his elbows on his knees. "So, you're saying you've seen this creature? It actually exists?"

"Yes, my lord. We tracked it to its nest."

"This is rich," Aiden butted in. "Go on, Ty, tell them what you said you saw. When you hear this, my lord, you're going to have a good laugh."

Everyone turned to look at Ty, but he was too furious to say anything. If he had, it was sure to be the wrong thing. He suddenly felt the heat of his magic rising. Quickly, he took a deep breath and a gulp to fight it back down.

"Well, go on, Ty, tell him."

The overlord looked at Ty, then back at Aiden. "What's this about?" Barl demanded.

Ty's father spoke up. "The creature is an arachnobe."

"Ha! You see," Aiden said victoriously. "Wait . . . a what? Ty said it was a giant bear-spider."

"An arachnobe *is* a spider," Ty's father said. "Well, sort of. They're monstrous creatures whose nests are said to populate the deeper hollows of the Razor Spine Mountains. They are rarely seen, and only when they come out to feed."

"There hasn't been a record of an arachnobe in Sidara for the last four or five decades," Barl said, sounding more uncertain with each passing word. "Surely you're mistaken."

"I only wish I were. There can be no mistake. Both my sons saw it. They tracked it to its burrow but thought it unwise to linger. Arachnobes have an extremely keen sense of smell."

After a few worried looks and hushed whispers, Barl finally spoke. "I don't like it, Kellen. Just the threat of such a creature could spread a panic that would prove truly devastating to Easthaven."

"How so, Father?" Lyessa asked. "If people will just stay clear of the woods, maybe it will move on."

"These woods provide food and shelter to our entire community. How long do you think it will take before the merchants stop shipping their freight downriver through the forest? It would devastate our trade routes." Barl stared at his lap for a moment. "No. We cannot allow this to continue. I'll take a regiment of our lancers in to find this creature and destroy it if I have to."

"My sons and I can track it for you, my lord."

What about Orlyn? Ty wanted to ask but caught himself.

"Excellent. The sooner we rid ourselves of this creature, the better. Word is already traveling through Easthaven. I've received at least a dozen missives from—"

The front door flew open, and one of the overlord's guards rushed in. "My lord, there are riders approaching!"

The expression on the lancer's face had everyone hopping out of their seats.

Chapter 72 | Ty

TY

T HE OVERLORD'S PATROL stood with swords drawn, taking up a
protective stance in front of the cottage as they waited for Overlord Barl
and the others to join them outside.

Ty followed on the heels of his father, hoping to get a better look at the
horsemen who were just now turning off the main road and riding toward the
house. A thick cloud of dirt and dust followed in their wake, masking their true
number. Ty couldn't help but notice that there were far more of them than
there were in the overlord's guard.

The savage-looking group finally came to a stop across the yard, a stone's
throw from the house. Ty wondered what they wanted. Were they there to see
Overlord Barl? The tingling feeling running down the back of his neck said
otherwise.

Once the dust had settled, Ty was able to get a better count. There looked
to be around thirty riders. They certainly weren't from Easthaven, or Sidara,
for that matter. Their garb consisted mostly of haphazard pieces of strange furs

and leathers. Black and white markings were painted across their arms and faces. Some wore masks made from pieces of human skull. Their long, matted hair was braided halfway down their backs, making them seem more rabid animal than human. Where had they come from?

At the front of the pack rode one of the biggest men Ty had ever seen— bigger than Breen or Ty's father, even. The battle-axe strapped to his horse looked like it weighed at least twenty pounds. Similar to many of the others, his face had been painted black with white stripes running diagonally across his cheeks, nose, and eyes.

Ty's father turned to Breen. "Get the weapons."

Breen disappeared back inside the house as the big horseman spoke to the men riding behind him. Ty didn't recognize a single word. Whatever the man said, it brought a round of laughter. They appeared to be staring at Lyessa, his mother, and Adarra.

"Do you recognize their dress?" his mother asked, her voice hardly above a whisper.

"Their wraps are similar to those of tribal Northmen," Ty's father said.

"Tallosians?"

"Aye," Barl agreed. "They look ready for war."

"You can tell all that just by looking at the furry cloaks?" Aiden asked.

"That's not fur," Barl said.

Aiden took a step forward. "Looks like fur to me."

Barl kept his eyes on the horsemen. "They're human scalps."

Aiden gulped and stepped back.

Ty's father glanced at Barl. "The question is, what do they want with us?"

"Only one way to find out." Barl cleared his throat and took a step forward. "What is your business here?" He waited but didn't receive a reply. "Do you know who I am?"

The big man at the front hocked a couple of times and spat a large wad out in front of his horse, then wiped his mouth. "An overfed, underbred sow, by the look of ya!" He spoke in a rather broken form of Aldoran.

Barl clenched his fists. "I am Overlord Barl! And I demand to know what you want."

With at least thirty armed men looking like they'd rather eat them than talk, Ty didn't think that *demanding* was the best way to start.

The lead Tallosian held Barl's gaze. "Baeldor is name. And what I want, to you is no concern."

Barl looked at Ty's father. "What did he say?"

Ty's father shook his head.

Ty caught movement out of the corner of his eye as his brother slid out the front door. He had three strung bows leaning to the left of the entry, along with their quarrels. There were also a few swords and a belt of throwing knives. The other brace of knives was probably hidden somewhere underneath his brother's cloak.

A haggard voice behind the Northmen brought Ty's attention back around to the front. "We want the boy!"

An unpleasant feeling rose in the pit of Ty's stomach, much like when he first realized he'd just eaten a bad pick of mushrooms—nauseous, woozy, and dreading what came next. He knew that voice. It was burned into his memory. He couldn't have forgotten it had he wanted to. And he certainly did want to.

"What boy?" Barl demanded. "What are you talking about?"

The cluster of horsemen parted, and a lone rider trotted forward, the hood of her black robe pulled tight so as not to show her features. The rider was small by comparison as she passed between the enormous savages, but each Tallosian turned their head away so as not to cast their eyes in her direction.

Ty gulped. He didn't need to see her face to know who was behind the dark cowl. They were there for him.

The hooded figure came to a halt beside the large spokesman and pointed her bony finger at Ty. "We want him!"

Aiden was standing next to Ty. His face paled as he lifted a quivering finger and pointed at himself. "Me? You want me?"

"Not you, you overdressed peacock!" The witch pointed again. "Him!"

Aiden moved quickly to the side as the rest of their group turned to look at Ty.

Ty didn't move. He couldn't. He was doing everything he could just to keep his bladder from leaking down the front of his trousers.

"We've been searching for you for sixteen years, boy. Then, for no reason at all, you up and walk right into my shop. You recognize your work?" She pulled back the arm of her robe and held out her hand for everyone to see the disfigurement.

"What is she talking about, Ty?" Lyessa asked, moving a little closer.

He didn't know what to say without revealing his magic to the overlord and his men. And Lyessa. Especially Lyessa. He had the sinking feeling it wasn't going to matter.

Ty's father spoke in his place. "You said, 'We have been searching.' Who are you referring to?"

The woman smiled. "I think you already know the answer to that."

Ty wheezed as he felt his last ounce of hope vanish into the cold air. She wasn't *hiding* from the White Tower. She *was* the White Tower.

Ty's father placed an arm around Ty's shoulders. "There's no way in the Pits of Aran'gal that you or any member of the White Tower are going to get your hands on my son."

"What's going on here, Kellen?" Barl asked. He looked back at the woman. "I demand to know who you are."

The robed figure removed her hood. Her shriveled features were quite unmistakable. "My name is Mangora," she said and pointed at Ty once more, "and that boy does not belong to you."

"He most certainly does!" Ty's mother stated, hands on her hips. "We raised him, fed him, clothed him, and loved him. That makes him ours in my book."

"Foolish woman, do you even know what he is?"

What I am? What kind of a question is that? Ty wondered. From the peculiar looks of those standing around, Ty felt like one of the oddities he might pay to see at the traveling circus. For a couple of coppers, he could look at the strange hairy woman, or the man with two heads, or the little boy with six fingers and toes, or his favorite, the owl-man who could turn his head almost all the way around.

Ty had always worried that if people found out what he could do, he would end up like one of those sad performers, traveling from town to town while people handed over their hard-earned coinage to gawk and laugh and stare.

At that moment, he could think of no place he would rather be than there.

"From the look on your face, I see that you do." Mangora leaned back in her saddle. "I take it Nyalis told you all about our young faeling."

Ty's head shot up. "Faeling? What's a faeling?"

His father's grip tightened on his shoulder.

"Ah, so, he didn't tell you everything." Mangora cackled. "Wizards aren't exactly in the habit of sharing information. They tend to be too tight-lipped for their own good. And on the rare occasion one does open up, it generally comes out more in half-truths and riddles than anything else."

What was she talking about? What was a faeling?

"He told us enough," Ty's father said.

"Did he, now? Then you know how dangerous the boy could be to us all?"

A memory of Adarra on fire suddenly flashed in Ty's head. His hands started shaking, and he grabbed the legs of his trousers. Was she right? Was he growing too dangerous to be around?

Barl was now staring at Ty as well.

"He needs to be kept under constant supervision, for his sake and ours," Mangora said. "The White Tower has the means to make that happen. It's the only safe place for him."

"The Defiler it is!" His father was irate. "The White Tower is nothing more than a lie! All it seeks is power. I know why you want my son. The same reason you've been rounding up every other wielder you can get your hands on. If I didn't know any better, I'd say your Archchancellor was looking to start a war. We won't let that happen, even if we have to go to the High King himself."

"Oh, my, I see you haven't heard." Mangora raised a shriveled hand to her mouth. "But of course you haven't, living way out here so far from civilization. Rhydan is dead!"

"What?" Barl took a step forward. "You lie!"

"Even now, His Highness, Prince Dakaran, is being crowned." Mangora smiled. "Changes are coming."

"There are still those of us out here willing to fight," Ty's father said.

"Oh, I take it you are referring to your coalition of wielders? Your council here in Easthaven is being dealt with as we speak."

"What have you done?" Ty's father asked, looking even more worried than Barl.

Mangora didn't answer. Her laugh was brittle and sharp.

"What council in Easthaven?" Barl asked. "What's going on here, Kellen?" Lyessa's father, even though a decent sort of man, was still against open wielding. He had never taken harsh action against wielders in Sidara, but he had made it clear it would not be tolerated within city limits.

Ty's father looked flustered. He clearly hadn't expected to be divulging a secret of this magnitude right in front of the Sidaran overlord. "It's nothing, my lord. Something we can discuss at a later time."

"No. We can discuss it now. I want to know what's going on."

"My lord, you know me. Have I ever lied to you?"

Barl cleared his throat. "After what I've just heard, I'm not sure."

"Have I ever done anything to hurt you or Easthaven?"

"Not as far as I know, but—"

"Then trust me now. Protecting Ty is more important than anything. I wager the most important thing you'll ever do."

Barl turned and looked at Ty.

"I believe him, Father," Lyessa said, taking a couple of steps closer to Ty. "We need to help him."

Barl shifted from one foot to the other, his fingers caressing the jeweled hilt of his longsword.

Across the yard, the Northmen also eagerly fingered their cleavers, axes, hammers, and flails.

"We only want the boy," Mangora said. "Turn him over, and I'll let the rest of you live."

"Like anyone actually believes *that's* going to happen," Adarra said under her breath, drawing a few uneasy glances. "What?" she said, holding a book under her arm. "It's true. They're not going to leave here *without* Ty, and we're not going to let them leave here *with* him." She shrugged. "Seems pretty obvious to me."

Ty shook his head. His sister, ever the scholar.

Across the way, Baeldor released the strap on his battle-axe.

A deathly silence swept across the open yard as each side waited to see what the other would do.

To everyone's amazement, it was Aiden who made the first move. He grabbed Ty and tried to drag him forward. "Quit being so selfish, Ty! Can't you see it's the only way to save the rest of us?"

Ty was too shocked even to fight back.

"My lord!" Aiden called to Lyessa's father. "They only want Ty! Do it to save your daughter! Do it to save—" Before he could finish the sentence, a gloved fist caught him square in the face and knocked him clean off his feet.

Holding a bloody nose and whimpering through the oncoming tears, Aiden looked up to see Lyessa staring down at him. "You coward. What kind of a man are you?" She shook her hand from where she had punched him. "Wow, that hurt."

The Tallosians on the other side of the yard burst into laughter at the sight of a slender young woman knocking a grown man on his backside.

"What will it be, then?" Mangora asked. "These men grow impatient. I can't hold them back forever. You can either turn the boy over and I let you live—or not, and I let them do what they do best." She extended her disfigured hand toward them. "The choice is yours."

Barl looked at Ty, then at his daughter, then at Ty's father. Ty could see the conflict in his eyes. On the one hand, he didn't seem to have any love for the White Tower, but on the other, his daughter's life was in jeopardy.

Ty couldn't let this happen. As much as he detested Aiden, he was right. He couldn't just let his entire family be murdered because of him. His parents might have felt he was too young to make his own decisions, but this *was* his decision. His and his alone. Besides, if he was growing too dangerous, maybe it would be safer if he left.

Before the overlord could say anything, Ty stepped forward. "If you give your word they won't be harmed, I'll go with you."

"Over my dead body you will!" Ty's father butted in as he grabbed Ty by the shoulder and yanked him back, nearly tearing the buttons off his shirt. "Now get behind me! That wizard said if the White Tower were to get their hands on you, it would be the end of us all."

Ty's father turned to Barl. "My lord, I apologize for getting you and your daughter into the middle of this, but you can't believe for one moment that she'll live up to her word and let you go. The White Tower lives by anonymity. They won't allow any witnesses to survive."

Barl's eyes narrowed. He turned to his men. "Draw your swords." Barl drew his as well. "I don't know what you've gotten me into, Kellen, but it had better be worth it."

"More than you know."

"Pity," Mangora said as she turned to the large Northman sitting across from her. "Don't damage the boy. The Archchancellor wants him alive."

There was hunger in Baeldor's eyes as he stared at those gathered in front of the house. "What we do with rest?"

Mangora smiled. "Kill them!"

Chapter 73 | Ty

TY HEARD THE TWANG of a bowstring behind him and felt the wind of an arrow fly past his ear. He knew its intended target, and like their father, Breen never missed.

Mangora didn't flinch.

She swiped her hand across her face, and the shaft veered into one of the horsemen just behind. The masked man glanced down at the fletching end of the shaft protruding from his chest. A gurgling cough escaped his mouth before he dropped from his horse.

Rage burned in the witch's eyes. She raised her hand and effortlessly conjured a ball of red flame.

"You had your chance!" she hissed, releasing it straight at the front line.

Ty dove out of the way, along with everyone else, as the fiery ball impacted the ground behind him, sending dirt in all directions. It hadn't been close enough to hit him, but he wasn't taking any chances.

Aiden shrilled and ran for the house. Ty hopped to his feet and turned to see if anyone had been hurt. Surprisingly, the flames had missed them all.

Ty started to raise his hand and summon his own fire, then recoiled. No. The last time he'd summoned it, his sister had nearly lost her life. He couldn't take that kind of a chance.

Another ball erupted from Mangora's palm, its light reflecting off a menacing grin.

He had to do something.

Mangora raised her hand to throw.

In a state of panic, Ty lashed out with the one bit of magic he knew he could trust. He reached out to every animal within a hundred paces and pushed a single thought. *Jump!*

Mangora's horse, along with all the Northmen's, leaped in unison. Tallosians flew through the air like leaves in an autumn breeze. The few who managed to retain their reins fought to keep their mounts from trampling those on the ground.

Mangora had been thrown backward as well. Two of the Tallosians helped her to her feet.

Run! Ty commanded. The horses stampeded back toward the road, dragging a few of their riders along with them.

Breen rushed by with an armful of weapons, tossing Ty his bow and his sword on the way forward.

Taking advantage of the diversion, Ty's father slung a belt of knives across his chest and nocked his bow. Ty stuck his sword tip down into the ground and readied his bow. His hands were quivering. He wondered if he'd be able to hit anything.

Ty's father pulled back on his large recurve. There were very few men who could manage the bow's draw. "I count a full company," he said to Barl. "They outnumber us two, maybe three to one."

Ty's father released and killed two Tallosians at once. It was a remarkable shot—one that only his father or brother could have made. The arrow drove straight through the back of one and into the chest of the other. The man in front died instantly. The second fumbled around with the weight of the other attached to him before finally tipping over.

"Two-to-one odds?" Barl said, rocking anxiously. "Then that should make it just about even, wouldn't you say?" He tightened his two-handed grip on his sword as the savages bellowed their war cry.

The Northmen rushed across the yard like a black wave of death. Ty's brother and father managed to launch two more volleys before they tossed their bows back in exchange for their braces of knives, which they began to throw.

Ty's entire body shook as he stood just behind the others, firing a couple more shots before the Northmen hit the front line. He hit one man in the shoulder. The Tallosian barely stumbled, raised his cleaver, and continued running.

Ty tossed his bow behind him and grabbed his sword in case they broke through. His father and brother fought like he'd never seen before. Hacking and slashing, stabbing and chopping at any Tallosian that came within reach.

A ball of fire struck one of the Sidaran guards to the right. The flesh on the front of the guard's body cooked off his bones in mere moments. The smell of roasted flesh had Ty doubling over, heaving what little supper he had managed to get down before the overlord's arrival.

Ty felt helpless as he watched his protectors fight to hold back the tide. He had never witnessed a true battle before—only heard of them in stories and song. They were nothing like this. This was horrifying.

A spray of warm liquid struck him across his chest and face. He turned to see one of the Sidaran lancers with Baeldor's axe buried in his chest. The huge Northman had to struggle to pull his blade free from the man's torso as another lancer charged in to take his place.

The sharp iron flavor in Ty's mouth brought him back from his momentary stupor as the realization of what he was tasting dawned on him. He doubled over once more, wiping his tongue with the clean side of his sleeve.

"Ty! Look out!" his brother shouted off to his right.

Ty raised his sword. One of the Tallosians had broken through. Ty swung his blade to keep the man from taking off his leg. He wondered if the message about *not killing* him had registered with the rest of the face-painted savages. Their swords collided. The jolt of the impact ran all the way up Ty's arm. The Northman swung high, forcing Ty to counter with an overhead block, but as soon as his sword arm went up, the man kicked him in the chest.

Ty flew backward, the air expelled from his lungs. He landed on top of his mother's winter daisies and rolled. His chest was on fire; no doubt some ribs were broken. He couldn't breathe. Panic set in and he started gasping. Where was the Northman? He turned and found the savage momentarily distracted by one of Barl's lancers. The lancer managed to wound him and knock him off his feet before another Tallosian hopped in to take his place.

The injured savage made it to his knees and looked at Ty. Ty reached for his sword and realized it wasn't there. *Where is it?* Spinning around, he found it lying against the stone foundation of the house.

Behind him, the Tallosian was back on his feet, cleaver in hand. Ty crawled as fast as he could. The Northman charged. Half the man's face was covered in bleached bone, the other half in white paint. Ty froze. There was no way to reach his weapon before the Northman had him. He raised his arms defensively as the Northman raised his blade. The savage made it within three paces when Ty's brother barreled past and slammed into the man.

Ty could hear bones snapping as the Northman flew through the air. His mask was torn from his face, revealing a look of utter shock and pain. This time, he didn't get back up.

"Get your sword!" Breen shouted as he ran back to the front.

Ty scrambled for his blade. He grabbed it and started back toward the fighting. He could see Mangora back behind the Tallosians, clearly not wanting to get too close. She released another ball of fire straight for Barl and Ty's father. Ty's father threw himself into the overlord and knocked him out of the way. The flames lit up another one of the Sidaran lancers on the left, along with two Northmen. Either her aim was terrible or she didn't care who she killed, as long as she succeeded.

They were sitting targets. But what could he do? His fire was out of the question. He'd just as likely kill his own people as theirs. Could he create one of those air shields he'd seen Mangora use on Breen's arrow?

Quickly, Ty moved back toward the front of the house, keeping as far from the actual fighting as possible. It wouldn't do him any good to create an air shield if some Northman chopped his head off while he wasn't looking.

He had no idea if this would work, or if he even had the kind of magic that would allow him to try. Pushing doubt aside, Ty reached out and focused on the air around him. He swiped his hand to the side like he had seen her do. Nothing. He aimed his palm toward the ground and imagined a puff of wind striking the loose dirt. Nothing.

Pulling back, he searched for the warming sensation within him that always seemed to precede his abilities, but he couldn't seem to find it. He took a deep breath to calm himself and closed his eyes momentarily. This time, instead of trying to release air from his hands, he decided to reach out and grab the wind as though it were a tangible object.

Suddenly, he felt the heat of his magic rise inside him as his fingers brushed through the air, leaving a tingling sensation across his skin. He opened his eyes and swiped his hand upward as if swatting at a fly. A small gust of wind hit him in the face and rustled his hair. It was working.

Movement out of the corner of his eye broke his concentration. Ty barely had time to turn when he caught a fist to the side of his head. There was a flash of white light followed by immense pain as he hit the ground. It felt like the man had punched his jaw right off his face. Opening his eyes, Ty felt to make sure it was still there. Everything was spinning. He had managed to hold on to his sword this time, but without seeing where to strike, it didn't do him a whole lot of good. He swung widely in all directions.

By the time he made it to all fours and turned, he was knocked to the side as someone rushed in to face the Tallosian for him. His jaw dropped, causing him to howl in pain. It was Lyessa, her bright red hair flinging back and forth as she went toe to toe with the huge savage.

He couldn't believe it. Not only was she managing to block the man's assault, but she was leading him around like a first-year cadet.

Ty had never seen anything like it before. It was like watching a dance. She dodged and spun, deflected and sidestepped, her long hair whipping with each new parry and whirl. The Northman bared his teeth, not able to land a single hit. He growled at her.

Hopping to the side, she deflected the man's lunge and decapitated him with one swift cut. His head hit the dirt and rolled in Ty's direction. Ty didn't move, still in shock at seeing Lyessa suddenly transformed into a crazed sword-master.

"What are you gawking at, you idiot?!" she screamed as she grabbed the front of his tunic and yanked him to his feet. One of her sleeves had been cut and was hanging open at the elbow. Ty noticed the extensive scarring on her forearm.

"What just . . . where did you learn . . . who are you?"

"I'm the person who just saved your scrawny backside. Now pick up that sword and get ready to fight!"

There was no hesitation. Ty grabbed his blade and stood beside her.

"By the way," she said over her shoulder. "You fight like a girl."

Ty grimaced. Twice now he'd been saved by someone else, and this time, it was Lyessa. It was as though she were a whole different person. He kind of liked it.

Three more men broke through the lines, each with a mask covering the whole of their face. Lyessa took the first two. Ty waited for the third to come to him. Lifting his sword, he successfully blocked the first swing. The weight of the impact nearly tore the weapon from his hands, and he stumbled backward.

This was nothing like the wooden swordplay he and his brother used to engage in when they were younger. His hands throbbed with each successful block. Instead of a sword, his attacker wielded a large club with pieces of sharp metal attached to the end.

"Ty, hang on!" Lyessa shouted over her shoulder, but she was busy holding back the other two.

Ty ducked as the huge club drove for his head, then deflected a second attempt with his sword. The savage never slowed. He swung his club around, and Ty hopped to the left, barely dodging the blow. He waited for the Tallosian to raise his weapon again, then plunged his sword through his unguarded thigh. It went in more easily than he'd expected.

The Tallosian shouted. Ty tried to yank his blade free, but the Northman knocked it from his hands with the club, leaving a deep, bloody gash across Ty's forearm. Ty cried out and stumbled backward. The masked man took the advantage and swept Ty's legs out from under him.

With Ty's sword still sticking out of his leg, the angry Northman placed his foot on Ty's chest. "Mangora says we keep you alive." He pointed the tip of his club at the top of Ty's head. "But you no need that." The Northman's speech might have been broken with an unusual dialect, but Ty had no problem understanding his meaning.

The big savage drew an ugly-looking knife from his boot and held it up for Ty to see. The handle was constructed from what looked like part of a leg bone. With a smile, he glanced at the top of Ty's head. "Pretty hair."

Ty didn't have time to think. Throwing away all restraint, he dove within himself and gathered the heat of his magic. He could feel it rising, starting from his gut and spreading outward. He didn't try forcing it. This time, he let it come on its own. It poured through him like an open dam.

The Northman grabbed a handful of Ty's blonde strands and lowered the knife to make the first cut. Somewhere in the distance, Ty could hear people screaming his name, but he put it aside as he drew the wind to him, almost as though he were inhaling it.

He let his magic take control. He turned himself over to it, releasing all inhibitions, all doubt. With an upward thrust of his hands, he hit the savage with everything he had. The man let go of Ty's hair and flew into the air, over the top of the other fighters, and disappeared into the forest beyond. His screams trailed after him. There was no telling how far he went.

Ty crawled back to his feet in time to see Lyessa stab her final attacker in the foot, forcing him to lose balance before she finished him with a swift thrust to his chest. She had some bruising around her left eye and a small cut over her brow from where the Northman must have gotten in a solid punch.

"What was that?" she asked, looking in the general direction of where Ty had just sent the Tallosian.

An unnerving scream brought them both around as another lancer caught fire. He was standing directly in front of Barl. The red-hot flames ate through the bottom half of the man's uniform, skin, flesh, and bone as he collapsed to the ground.

Ty looked at Lyessa. "We've got to stop her."

Chapter 74 | Orlyn

ORLYN SAT, waiting patiently for his next session with the sorceress Mangora.

It had been two days since his abduction. Two days since they had used Sorna to try to get him to talk. Two days since he had given in. The shame of what he'd done burned inside him. And to make matters worse, they had taken Sorna anyway. No doubt she was sharing a ride with Helene and Felina, on their way to the White Tower.

He wanted to die. Why hadn't they killed him yet?

The drugs they had been giving him were finally beginning to dissipate. Since the day Orlyn had accepted an apprenticeship with his father, it had been clear that he had a natural affinity with flora. His father had always believed it was due to his own quality as a teacher, but his mother had known different. She had encouraged Orlyn to explore his capabilities, but in a way that was kept secret from others.

Orlyn had never been willing to sell an herb to a customer without first trying it himself. Because of this policy, his body had developed a natural immunity to a great number of drugs and potions. But whatever the crone had been giving him was unlike anything he had ever experienced.

He had both seen and heard things that weren't there: voices out of the dark, people from his past who had long since died. It was disturbing on levels even he was unaccustomed to. He was having a hard time keeping his mind focused on what was real and what wasn't.

There were times he wondered if his betrayal had been a mere side effect of the drugs. Maybe he hadn't betrayed his friends. Maybe the witch had never captured Sorna. Maybe it was all a dream. A nightmare. The more he tried to convince himself, the more he realized the truth: he had sacrificed his oath to save a woman he cared about.

From his lonely seat inside the darkened barracks, Orlyn thought he heard a commotion in the next room. *Another hallucination?* He didn't even bother lifting his head. He wondered how this one would end. The last one had ended with his head being chopped off—a very unpleasant feeling.

The noise in the next room was getting louder. It sounded like a tavern brawl, with voices raised and the sounds of steel and wind. *Wind?* That couldn't be right. Then again, when were any of his hallucinations right? Whatever it was, it was getting closer.

He could hear heavy thumps, like bodies being thrown against the walls. He forced his head up from where it had been propped against his chest and tried peeking out through his swollen eyes.

The door to his makeshift prison burst open, just before being ripped completely off its hinges and sucked back into the other room and out of sight. Orlyn squinted until his eyes managed to adjust to the additional light. He could hear footsteps running in his direction. They must have become tired of questioning him and were finally going to finish him off.

"Get up, you old fool! We're here to rescue you."

Orlyn's eyes opened the rest of the way. He didn't need to see the man to recognize his gruff voice.

"Feoldor?"

"Who else would be willing to stick their precious neck out for you? Can't leave you alone for a minute. Next thing we know, you're up and getting yourself captured by the Black Watch."

"Are they still here?"

"Who?" Feoldor asked as he worked to free Orlyn's hands.

"The Watch," Orlyn said frantically. Maybe they still had time to stop them before they took Sorna.

"I didn't see any on the way in. Why? You want me to call them for you?" Feoldor ripped off the last of the rope tying Orlyn to his chair.

Orlyn rubbed his wrists, then quickly began searching through the numerous pockets inside his robes. The guards had confiscated most everything of substance, leaving behind a few pockets containing some loose herbs, seeds, and powders. Either they hadn't noticed them when they'd patted him down or they hadn't thought them important enough to remove.

"Are you just going to sit around all day or are you going to give us a hand?" Feoldor griped.

Orlyn struggled to his feet. "Did anyone ever tell you you're about as ugly as a sniffer's backside?"

Feoldor's smile said it all. "Yep, he's still Orlyn."

"Who else would I be, you sotted nincompoop? Now get me out of here." He went to take a step, but his legs gave out. He would have landed on his face but for a small pair of sturdy shoulders underneath him. Looking down, he saw a bright, childlike smile beaming his way. "Gilly, is that you?"

"It's Gilly," the dwarf replied as he positioned himself under Orlyn's arm.

Feoldor had a stout hold of his other shoulder, balancing him. "We thought you could use a hand."

Orlyn grunted. "I could have used that hand days ago. Now hurry. We need to stop the Watch before they leave town."

"Why?"

"They have Sorna."

"Your Sorna?"

"She's not my . . . oh, never mind. Just move."

Orlyn attempted to put one foot in front of the other as the blood slowly worked its way back into his limbs. They started into the next room, but Feoldor stopped before they had gotten much farther than the door.

"Why are we stopping?"

"Because I thought you might want this." Feoldor leaned over and grabbed something from behind where the door had been moments earlier. "Found it on the two men left guarding the place."

Orlyn's eyes bulged at the sight of his staff. He nearly tipped his helpers over as he reached for it. He hugged it to him. He had thought it gone for good. Mangora must have been holding on to it for leverage.

Quickly, they crossed the room and cut down a side corridor, leading to an exit between the buildings. The barracks were always quiet this time of year. Most of the lancers were volunteers from all across Sidara and were needed at home during the colder months to support their families, leaving the garrison to those lancers who lived in and around Easthaven.

Feoldor pushed up on the latch and slid the door open. They stepped out into the afternoon sun and stopped. They examined the narrow alleyway before stepping out.

"How did you fight your way through the guard?" Orlyn asked.

"It wasn't hard; there weren't but two, and they were a mite puny if you ask me."

"Seems a little odd, doesn't it?"

Feoldor didn't respond right away. "Didn't think about it at the time."

After limping down the narrow space between the barracks and the mess hall, they stopped just within the shadows and studied the empty yard ahead. The south gate was off to the right and the north gate lay in front of them. To their left were a couple of smaller buildings, along with one of the stables.

There was no movement anywhere. Even though the barracks weren't housing their full complement, there should have at least been a modicum of Sidaran lancers about. But right then, the place looked completely abandoned. The hairs on the back of Orlyn's neck began to prickle.

"Finally, something is going our way," Feoldor said as he started forward.

"Wait." Having finally gotten some feeling back in his extremities, Orlyn grabbed the back of Feoldor's cloak and pulled him backward.

"Wait? You were just telling me we should have come for you sooner. Now you're telling us to wait? Make up your mind, would you?"

"Doesn't this seem a little too easy? Where are the lancers? Where are the rest of the Black Watch? Where's that sorceress?" She had to be around there somewhere, he thought.

"Sorceress? What sorceress? No one said anything about a sorceress." Feoldor cast his eyes about the yard. "She's here too?"

A wave of heat rose from the passageway behind them.

Orlyn turned. "Look out!" Flames shot down the alley, heading directly for them. He dove into the dirt next to Gilly. The fire was intense, but instead of roasting them alive, the ball flew up into the air and dissipated.

"That was a close one," Feoldor said, lowering his hands. The crystal in his bracelet was glowing a pale blue.

Orlyn used his staff to get to his feet. He felt strong when holding it. "What happened?"

"I just saved your life. Again."

"Look!" Orlyn shouted, pointing back down the alley behind them. A black-robed figure was heading their way. Whoever it was, it was clear they had sent the fire.

"I'd say we've worn out our welcome," Feoldor said, "but that seems a bit obvious."

Orlyn turned back around. "Run!"

The three raced across the open yard, heading for the north gate. They made it about twenty paces when two more black-robed figures stepped out from the side of one of the buildings in front of them, blocking their way.

Orlyn turned with the others but stopped when the wielder who had tried to scorch them stepped out of the alleyway behind them. To their left, a fourth and fifth were walking across the yard.

"It's the bulradoer," Feoldor whispered nervously.

What are the bulradoer doing in Easthaven? Orlyn, of course, knew the answer. They had come for Ty. And he'd been the one to give him up. He tried to push his guilt aside. It wouldn't serve him now. He had to focus.

How were they going to fight five bulradoer? "You two certainly know how to pull off a rescue."

"Shut it, you old windbag," Feoldor spouted. "I didn't see you doing anything back there to get yourself out of this mess. We were just trying to help."

"Yeah? Well, the next time, try to do a better job of it!"

Gilly remained completely silent as usual, his head shifting from one dark wielder to another. In his right hand, the large crystal he normally kept hidden in his pocket was pulsing a deep blue.

By the time the men had finished arguing, the five bulradoer had them completely surrounded. The three council members put their backs to each other and braced for the inevitable.

They didn't have a prayer—not that Orlyn wasn't saying one. Even with Feoldor's gift as a vanti and Gilly's voda abilities, they weren't going to be a match for five of the White Tower's wielders. Orlyn's eye caught something to his left, and he glanced over his shoulder. He was hoping to find the rest of the wielder council coming to save them, but instead found Captain Hatch leading his guards out from behind one of the far buildings near the south gate. This was quite the ambush.

Wait! If Hatch and his men were still there, that meant Sorna was as well.

There was still a chance.

"When Mangora told us we could net the entire wielder council at once if we had the patience to wait, I had no idea it would be so *formidable* a foe." The speaker was the only one of the dark wielders to have his cowl drawn back. It was the same slick-haired man Orlyn had encountered in his shop. The bulradoer smiled. Orlyn had to admit the three of them did look quite the sight—one decrepit old man, one arrogant fool, and a dwarf thrown in for good measure.

"Or maybe we've got you right where we want you," Feoldor said, sounding as brash as ever.

The bulradoer took a step forward. "Actually, what I think is that if you had a lick of real ability between the three of you, we would have already—"

A torrent of fire flew out of a building on their right and engulfed one of the bulradoer. The woman inside the dark robes shrilled. She ran in circles, her robes melting to her body as she burned alive in front of them.

"Like I said," Feoldor exclaimed with a smile, "right where we want you."

A door to one of the side buildings opened, and Veldon came charging out, sending balls of fire in all directions and yelling like a man possessed. The ring on his right hand pulsed a bright red.

The bulradoer moved back, conjuring shields to stave off the unexpected attack as they scrambled to join ranks. Feoldor joined Veldon and unleashed a hammer of wind, throwing two of the wielders at least ten feet before they hit the ground.

"Clear!" Veldon shouted behind him.

Fraya was the next out, with Reloria bringing up the rear, holding a pink bonnet to the top of her head as she ran for the three men.

"What were you thinking, bringing them here?" Orlyn asked.

"I'd like to see you try stopping them," Veldon shouted, sending another wave of fire barreling toward the dark-robed wielders.

Not letting a clear opportunity pass, one of the bulradoer sent a fist of flame directly at the two helpless women as they ran across the yard. Feoldor turned and threw a gust of air into the fire's path and sent it off course. It was just enough to miss them but not enough to miss setting the front of the building they had just exited aflame.

"What are you fools doing?" Orlyn shouted at Fraya and Reloria as they ran up behind them.

"I'm a healer," Fraya said emphatically. "You'll need me."

"And I'm not about to sit at home alone while the rest of you take on the Tower," Reloria said, offering a wink in Feoldor's direction.

Orlyn huffed. He turned to say something more when he noticed the runes on his staff were glowing. *What's this?* They'd never done that before. His transferal always flared when he used his floratide gifts, but never the runes.

A surge of power rushed through the wood and into him as the runes awoke. He gulped at the unexpected sensation. Like chill bumps on a cold morning, his skin began to tingle. He could feel his strength returning. It was intoxicating, more euphoric than eating an entire bag of tellareen mushrooms. And he would know.

No one said a word as the two groups of wielders faced off, ten long paces between them. Even the Black Watch had enough sense to stay back.

Orlyn scanned the now-unhooded assembly before him: three men and a woman. He knew better than to take any of these wielders lightly. They had no need for transferals. Their powers came through the spoken word, incantation, and runes, something they had certainly been studying and perfecting for years. Each of them was no doubt trained in warfare, unlike the Easthaven Council.

Each side waited to see what the other would do. And, of course, Feoldor was the first to speak.

"So, who's laughing now?"

Orlyn tightened his grip as the bulradoer raised their arms. "I guess we're about to find out."

Chapter 75 | Adarra

ADARRA, NEVER HAVING witnessed combat other than what she had read in her books, nervously cracked her knuckles as she watched the battle taking place outside the window.

"They're too far apart," she said to herself. "The line will never hold." Little by little, they were losing ground. "There's too many of them."

As much reading as she had done, she had found little in the way of military tactics. She had scoured most of the local book merchants. Her favorite was Book Bees. The owner, Townsend, had named the shop after his two favorite pastimes: collecting books and keeping bees. He had always found her ability to retain what she read fascinating, and had allowed her to come and read whenever she wanted, free of charge.

While studying his collection of new and used books, she had managed to get her hands on a secondhand copy of the *Sidaran Lancer Guide*. It was given to first-year cadets as part of a foundational course in understanding basic principles, like weaponry and armor and their proper use; divisions of formation like infantry, cavalry, archers, and pikemen. It also spoke of basic guard, stance, and footwork, but nothing of their application when defending against a horde of savage Northmen, whose only form of strategy was to muscle their way through any defense.

Her mother stood by the doorway, sword in hand. With no other weapons available, Adarra had found one of her father's sickles in the kitchen. He had carried it in before supper to remind him it needed a whetstone taken to it before he went to bed.

Behind her, Aiden sat in the corner, his sword across his lap as he stared blankly at its design.

Adarra had been a bit smitten with Aiden since first having seen him at Performance Night. He was tall with dark hair, a strong chin, and green eyes like her father and older brother. But after witnessing such cowardice earlier, Aiden's outward beauty had dissolved while his inward character shone through.

"They need your help," she said desperately.

Aiden didn't even look up.

"Even Ty's out there, and he's the one we're trying to protect." Adarra wished she better understood the implications of who her brother was. In all her reading, she had never come across a single mention of the word *faeling*. But she wasn't too surprised, considering all books related to the practice of magic had been banned centuries before.

Aiden finally lifted his head. "Don't look at me. I'm not going out there and getting myself killed. Like you said, it's Ty they want."

And Adarra hadn't thought she could have loathed him more. "Are you really that stupid? You heard the witch. They're going to kill us all! You have a sword; go use it!"

"I can't."

"Yes, you can."

"No, I can't!"

"Why not?" Her face was flushed.

Aiden turned his head away. "Because I don't know how. I wear it for decoration. All right?"

His cheeks were red. Adarra wasn't sure whether it was due to rage or embarrassment.

Aiden fiddled with the sword. "I thought it made me look . . . courageous."

Adarra shook her head. For once, she was without words.

"Besides," he said, "it's not exactly a real sword." He held it out for inspection. "It's completely dull. It wouldn't cut a loaf of bread."

That was probably the most honest statement she'd heard come out of Aiden's mouth. She almost felt sorry for him. Had he not been so ridiculously good-looking, she'd have found it a lot easier to hate him.

The back door to the kitchen flew open with a loud crash that brought everyone around with a start. Pieces of splintered wood slid across the floor as two men in rough leather and patched furs stepped inside. Adarra grabbed her sickle and turned. Aiden hopped to his feet, eyes as wide as two persimmons.

The shorter of the two Northmen walked across the kitchen and stopped at the edge of the main room, about twenty feet from where they were standing. He held a cutlass in one hand, a weapon generally favored by seafarers. The second Northman stopped alongside him.

It wouldn't have mattered what the second Northman carried. The man was enormous. Every bit the size of her brother and father. He wore a half-mask with black markings. It looked as though he had dipped his fingers in some kind of ink and smeared them across the white bone. And if his size wasn't enough to frighten her to death, he carried an axe over his shoulder that was as tall as she was.

"See, they are here, Jonas," the shorter man on the right said, pointing his cutlass in their direction. His speech seemed to come a bit easier than the others'. At least she was able to understand it.

The big Tallosian on the left wiped his hand down the side of his hardened face. He didn't say anything, but he couldn't seem to pull his eyes off of her. He spared a passing glance at Aiden and her mother, but his attention went right back to her. He noticed the sickle in her hand but didn't appear to give it much thought. Holding her with his gaze, he turned and said something to the shorter man, ending the conversation with the word *Damar*. Adarra figured it must be the smaller man's name.

Adarra's mother moved in front of her and raised her sword.

The smaller man, Damar, smiled. "I love mine warm and full of fight."

"How dare you!" Aiden bellowed uncharacteristically, raising his own sword. "You will not touch a single hair of their heads or . . ." He puffed out his chest as far as it would go. "Or I'll be forced to run you through."

Damar laughed. "Look, Jonas. It is a man. Look at his purty hair."

"You'll pay for that, you dirty savage!" Aiden shouted back, his face as red as his crimson vest. He started forward but didn't make it as far as the rocking chair before Adarra's mother grabbed hold of his jacket.

"Get back here, you fool, before you get yourself killed!"

The two Northmen slowly made their way farther into the main room. The big one, Jonas, followed Damar, careful to stay a step or two behind. They were now within ten feet, almost enough to touch blades if extended completely.

Adarra's mother held her old sword out in front of her. "You stay back, you hear me?"

Ignoring her warning, Damar took another step forward, his eyes glistening with excitement.

Adarra's knuckles were white around her sickle's wooden handle. Images of effective stances from the lancer guidebook flashed into her mind. Her legs were shaking as she tried to mimic what she'd seen—left leg front, right leg back. She turned and spared a quick glance out the window behind her. There was no one there to help. She thought about screaming to get her father's attention, but that might provoke the two Northmen to attack.

"Don't you come any closer," her mother said. "I'm warning you!"

"Why? You cut me?" the smaller man jeered, taking another step forward. They were now within swinging distance.

"Take another step and find out," her mother countered.

Damar's eyes danced with eager anticipation, then with sudden concern as her mother's blade flew at his face. He blinked, but his reflexes took over.

The two swords clanged as Damar blocked the attack. He grabbed the front of her top and jerked her forward, trying to kiss her forcibly.

The savage shouted something in his own language and backhanded her across the face with a closed fist. Her mother's head spun around, and she landed in a heap on the floor. She didn't move.

Damar grabbed his mouth. "She bites!" He wiped at the blood now flowing from the jagged teeth marks in his lower lip.

Jonas bellowed out a hard laugh. He said something to Damar that was no doubt meant to humiliate him further.

Damar's face darkened.

Jonas kept back, seemingly none too eager to join in his comrade's fun.

"You want blood?" Damar spat, looking down at her mother. "I give you blood!" He raised his cutlass.

Adarra was out of time. She raised her sickle but was thrown aside as Aiden shouted and rushed past, his sword poised to swing. Adarra was speechless. So was Damar, but it didn't stop him from meeting Aiden's swing with one of his own.

The two swords connected.

Adarra couldn't tell who was more surprised, Aiden or Damar, when Aiden's sword burst into a dozen pieces and flew across the room, leaving him completely open to Damar's quick backswing. The sword sliced him shoulder to navel. Aiden staggered backward with a look of horror. He glanced down at the blood leaking through his beautiful silk shirt. He screamed and dropped to the floor, crawling as fast as he could for the back wall.

Damar smiled at his wounded prey, giving no thought to Adarra. Maybe he believed she was too frightened or too shocked to do anything but stand there. He was right. She was terrified. *Think, Adarra!* This wasn't some children's tale where the good guys always won. This was real! *The sickle.* Her mind raced as it tore through countless books for the information she needed. The sickle. It was a cutting instrument, not for thrusting. It had a sharp point but only good if used from the side, overhead, or . . . *Oh, hang it! Just swing!*

Damar stepped over Aiden and raised his blade, giving her the perfect target.

The weapon seemed such a light thing in her hand as her adrenaline kicked in. She didn't bother shouting; she simply held the handle with both hands and swung with all her might. She aimed for the softest part of the body, giving her the greatest chance of cutting straight through without catching a bone.

Damar turned but not quickly enough. He howled as the curved blade sliced straight through the soft underside of his stomach like a hot knife through butter, carving out a thick portion to spread.

His guts had been split wide open, revealing a mass of entrails. His cutlass dropped from his hands as he tried to hold his insides in. He fell to the floor with a thump, his body convulsing.

"Damar!" Jonas swung his axe.

Adarra threw herself backward, the only thing she could think to do to keep from being cut in half by the huge blade. She landed hard, seeing white dots when she did. She lost focus for a brief moment.

Jonas leaned over to check his companion, then mumbled something under his breath and stood. Adarra raised her sickle but already knew it was a useless effort. He would split it like kindling and nail her to the floor in the process.

She gritted her teeth and stared up into his eyes. She wouldn't leave this world a coward.

He took a step forward and stood over her. *His mistake.* She swung her sickle for his right ankle. She was going to cut his leg off if it was the last thing she did. It probably would be.

Without the least bit of effort, he raised his foot and kicked the tool out of her hands. It flew across the room and nearly hit Aiden as it bounced off the right wall. He turned and looked down at her.

What was he waiting for? "Just do it!"

Gong! Suddenly Jonas's eyes rolled up in his head, and he pitched forward. She squealed as the huge Northman landed right on top of her, his bone mask splitting into pieces when it struck the floor.

"Here, give me your hands," her mother said as she rushed over to help her out from under the man. Her mother had to lay her skillet down to pull.

Adarra worked her way out from under the Tallosian. She thought about gutting him as well but just couldn't bring herself to do it. There was something about the way he had looked at her.

A raspy groan from the corner diverted her attention, and she quickly rushed to Aiden's side. Her mother was already there, pressing her hand against the gaping wound.

The left side of her mother's face was already swelling from Damar's fist. "We need to stop the bleeding," her mother said as they pressed against the gushing wound.

Aiden lay there, trying his best not to whimper.

"Hang on, Aiden," Adarra said, her hands still trembling. "I'll . . . I'll get some cloths."

Chapter 76 | Ty

"I'VE GOT TO STOP HER," Ty said, more to himself than anything. His words were meant to be a call to action, a way to muster what courage he had left and to force him to act. However, the cries of death as men were chopped down around him seemed to cloud his thoughts and unhinge his nerve. Even worse was the witch and her magic. They didn't stand a chance against such odds, and he knew it.

What was left of the lord's guard continued to fall to the Tallosians' numbers. They were still heavily outmatched, even if the savages' ranks had been halved by the highly trained Sidaran soldiers.

It was chaos. Blood everywhere. Ever since Ty had begun to use magic to defend himself, the Northmen had given up their attempts at capturing him unharmed and were now trying to do whatever they could to incapacitate him.

On his left, Ty watched in awe as his older brother fought like a wild animal against the ferocious scalp-wearing Northmen trying to flank him. He cut and slashed with his dagger while blocking and thrusting with his sword.

Overlord Barl and a few of his lancers were holding off another siege on Ty's right, the Northmen being led by Baeldor.

Near the center, Ty's father matched the Tallosians strike for strike; he used his strength to his advantage as he threw back his opponents' advances, cutting down one after the other. But there were just too many of them.

"Behind you!" Lyessa shouted.

Ty turned and frantically raised his hands and conjured a small shield of air. The Tallosian's mace slammed against the barrier, throwing Ty backward. He hit the ground, rolled, and was back on his feet with another shield as the mace came down again. This time, Ty used it to deflect instead of taking the full force of the blow.

The heavyset Tallosian looked as though someone had used his head to begin demonstrating the most proficient form of scalping, then changed their mind halfway through. He was missing half the hair on one side.

The Northman swung again and again, but each time, Ty managed to repel the blows.

Lyessa killed one man on their right, and while Ty kept his half-scalped attacker preoccupied, she turned and stuck her sword through his back. He fell forward, and Ty hopped out of the way to keep from getting hit.

"Pay attention!" she shouted. "I can't do everything." Lyessa had become his guardian. Ty had found it embarrassing at first, but it was growing on him.

Mangora was working her way around the back of the Tallosians, clearly looking for an opening to reach either Ty's father or Overlord Barl. Both men were too preoccupied fending off the Northmen to see the danger they were in.

Ty started forward.

Lyessa grabbed him by the arm. "Where do you think you're going?"

"I'm going after Mangora."

"Then I'm coming too."

They headed right, working their way around the back of the fighting as they matched pace with the witch. The numbers on both sides had been cut severely—more so on the Tallosians' side than theirs. His mind raced as he tried to figure out how he was going to stop her. Sure, he had a little control over the wind, but so did she . . . and a lot more.

Barl shouted, momentarily pulling their attention away from Mangora. The overlord's men were holding back a group of Northmen on their right, leaving Barl to face Baeldor on his own.

As proficient as he was with a blade, Barl was clearly outmatched in both age and strength. The huge Northman muscled his way through Barl's defenses with little effort. Barl continued to swing, desperately trying to keep away from the enormous man's axe.

"Father!" Lyessa ran for him but was forced to give way as another Northman broke through the line. The man didn't need a mask. His face was covered with the whitened flesh of numerous scarred-over injuries. Over his head, he spun a long flail.

Lyessa dove out of the way, and Ty barely had time to raise another shield before the spiked ball hit. It spun Ty completely around, causing the edge of the ball to graze his arm before impacting the ground beside him, flinging dirt and debris around his legs.

Ty bit down and grabbed his arm, the blood making his hand slip. He didn't have time to scream; the sudden surge of adrenaline fueled his anger. The man swung again, barely missing Lyessa's head as she dove to the left and rolled.

They didn't have time for this.

The big Tallosian yanked the flail back for another swing.

Ty didn't give him the chance. He gathered the wind. Breathed it in as if swelling his chest with an enormous gulp. It came easier this time. Instead of using it as a shield, he lashed out at the ugly savage. The force of the blow struck the man in the chest like a battering ram hoisted by a team of rock trolls.

The Tallosian plowed into the dirt, his chest completely caved in. The man's lifeless eyes stared up at him, blood seeping from both, along with his nose, mouth, and ears.

Barl cried out, drawing Ty's attention away from the gruesome sight. The overlord had been injured. He was bleeding from his shoulder. With a hard kick, Baeldor swept his legs out from under him.

Barl fell, his sword hitting the ground beside him. He tried grabbing for it as he crawled back to his knees, but Baeldor kicked it out of reach. The Tallosian didn't waste any time as he moved around front, seemingly to taunt the overlord before killing him.

Ty was too far away to do anything. He raised his hands to try drawing the wind, but before he could do anything with it, Lyessa grabbed Ty's discarded bow, nocked, aimed, and released in one swift, beautiful move. The arrow flew true.

Baeldor screamed and dropped to his knees.

Ty released his hold on the wind when he saw her arrow sticking from the huge Northman's left eye. Ty couldn't believe the man was still alive, but he was.

The Tallosian's axe fell from his fingers as he struggled to pull the shaft free. Overlord Barl, with what looked to be every last bit of strength he possessed, hefted himself onto his good leg, wrapped his bloody fingers around the momentarily forgotten weapon, and hefted it into the air.

With a roar, Barl swung the axe and separated the Northman's head from his body. It rolled across the ground and stopped with his face looking up at the sky, wearing a dumb look of disbelief.

The Tallosian warriors, having seen their leader beheaded, began backing away.

"What do you think you're doing?" Mangora shrilled, filling the ground behind them with fire. "Kill them! Kill them all!"

The Northmen were clearly more afraid of her than of the lancers, as they regathered their courage and attacked. Barl's men were down to a mere handful, and those who still stood were bleeding or worse. Their numbers had thinned to the point of being completely overrun. It was only a matter of time now.

Ty spun at the sound of his father's cry. One of the savages had managed to impale him in the shoulder with a dagger. Ty's father punched the man in the face, then pulled the blade out and gave it back to him, straight through his neck. The Northman gasped and dropped. But his death left a clear opening for Mangora.

She grinned as she raised her arms, summoning her fire.

Ty's instinct kicked in, and he struck his father with a wave of air that sent him flying to the left, out of the path of the flames.

The old woman screeched as her attack shot through their ranks, doing nothing more than scorching the ground in front of the house.

Both the Tallosians and the lancers moved to keep from getting hit. The shift in position left a large gap down the middle of the fighting, a clean opening for her to walk through.

Ty quickly moved into the gap.

His father was back on his feet and heading for him. "Ty! Move!"

Ty raised his hand. "No. Stay back!" There was nothing his father could do—or anyone else, for that matter. He was the only one who stood a chance.

"Ty!" Lyessa tried to reach him as well, but he used the wind to force her back, careful not to throw her like he had his father.

He turned and looked at Mangora. "You want me. Here I am." Ty raised his hands but hesitated. He was afraid of the fire. Afraid of what he might do with it. What if he couldn't control it? The image of his sister engulfed in blue flames reemerged.

Mangora smiled. "You clearly have no idea how to use your abilities. Come with me, and I'll pull my men back. Save your family before it's too late."

For a brief moment, Ty let the possibility take root. *No.* There was only one way to save his family. He had to release the fire. He had to give himself over to the magic. He could feel it. The burning swelled, begging to be released.

He raised his hands, and they immediately burst into flame.

Mangora flinched. She looked as though she hadn't expected him to be able to wield fire. "Last chance, boy. Come with me or watch your family die."

Ty gritted his teeth. "Never."

"So be it." Her hands ignited, and she released a pillar of red-hot flame straight at him.

His eyes widened. Capturing him was clearly no longer an option. He stretched out his hands, and liquid flames blue as a midday sky poured from both. The fire was unlike anything he'd ever felt before. It erupted from him in a torrent, nearly stealing his breath. He squinted against its brilliance.

The two streams connected, releasing red and blue ribbons of fire that burned everything they touched to ash. The flames fought back and forth, working their way from one side of the breach to the other as the two battled to overpower each other.

Mangora's face twisted with rage. Her lips curled upward, revealing a crooked set of yellowing teeth. "Give it up, boy! I've spent more years mastering my craft than you've been alive."

Ty kept his eyes on the flame. He didn't dare drop his focus. One slip and there'd be nothing stopping her from making pyres of them all.

"What happened to taking me alive?" His words were muffled under the strain.

Mangora sneered. "If the Tower can't have you, I'll make sure no one does."

Ty fought to hold on to his magic. It was like wrestling a wild animal, one fighting to break free. What he did, he did on pure instinct.

"I can feel you weakening," she said. "Stop while you can. I promise to be lenient." Mangora's breathing was growing heavier.

Ty wanted to lash out at her, to tell her what he really thought of her, but she was right. He didn't have the strength. So he kept his mouth shut. Beads of sweat dripped from his eyebrows and nose and chin as he concentrated on the flames. The heat was suffocating. He might not have been able to feel his own fire, but hers was enough to roast on.

Ty heard the familiar hum of a bowstring, and an arrow flew past. Mangora raised one of her hands and swiped it away, never losing a moment's concentration.

She was strong. Ty couldn't have managed something like that. His knees were already buckling, and his breathing shallow and raspy. The red flames were inching closer and closer. It took everything he had just to slow them down.

Mangora's chin was quivering, her eyes blinking uncontrollably. Maybe she wasn't holding it together as much as she wanted him to believe. Another arrow flew by. Breen moved to Ty's left to get a better shot.

This time, Mangora sent a surge of air and Breen went tumbling out of view. Ty couldn't worry about him. He kept his focus on Mangora, digging deep, trying to scoop out whatever reserves he had left. With Breen's help, he had managed to push his stream back toward the center once again.

Mangora was now shaking nearly as much as Ty. He had to hold out just a little longer.

One of Ty's legs wavered, and he went to one knee.

Seeing him go down, Mangora released a loud, high-pitched roar and sent one final pulse through the two streams. Ty emptied every last bit of magic he had in order to keep her attack from consuming him.

The two interconnecting lines of flame erupted with a loud crack of thunder, and he flew backward head over heels.

Everything went black before Ty hit the ground.

Muffled voices broke the silence, and he could feel his body being lifted. "He's not breathing!" someone said. Strangely enough, Ty hadn't noticed until right then.

"Move! Let me through!" The voice sounded like his sister's. Suddenly, he felt a sharp pain in his chest like someone had decided to make sure he was dead by beating on him with one of the Northmen's war hammers. Without warning, the air rushed back into his lungs, and he inhaled a deep gulp. He started coughing uncontrollably.

"Wha . . . what happened?" He was still dazed. "Who was punching me?"

"I wasn't punching you, doofus," Adarra said. "I was trying to get you to breathe."

"What?"

"It'll take too long to explain."

Lyessa hovered nearby. "What happened to his . . . his hair?"

Ty lifted his hand to rub the top of his head. Had the Northmen scalped him?

"It's white," she said, "like an old man's."

"Quiet, Lyessa," her father said, trying to offer a rebuke. He was rather preoccupied with studying the change himself.

Why is everyone standing around? Did we win? "Where are the Northmen?"

Lyessa grunted. "One look at the two of you lighting up the yard and they took off running for the trees. Don't think we'll be seeing them again anytime soon."

Breen steadied Ty as he struggled to stand. Ty held his brother's arm until he regained his balance. He glanced across the yard and spotted a lump on the other side, which had to be Mangora. She was beginning to stir.

Ty's father drew his bowstring and released. The arrow veered into the woods after deflecting off another one of her shields. "Get back to the house!"

Breen helped Ty across the yard, and Lyessa her father. Ty's father was the last one through the door. He shut it behind them and moved to join Ty at the window to see what Mangora would do next.

She released another high-pitched squeal as she made it to her feet. She looked around, realizing her warriors had abandoned her.

"We should go out there and finish her off," Breen said.

His father grabbed Breen's arm. "No. Not while your brother is down. It's one thing to fight against sword and axe; it's another to stand against that kind of magic."

"Hide, you cowards!" the old woman shouted, hatred filling her words. "Hide behind your walls of wood and stone! They will not save you from what is coming!" She raised her arm in the direction of the northwest woods and released some kind of red pulse into the trees. "Come to me!"

"Who is she talking to?" Ty's mother asked, trying to peek around the others.

Ty glanced at Breen. He had a sinking feeling he knew the answer.

Chapter 77 | Orlyn

"**A** LOT OF GOOD that flaming wizard's horn did us!" Feoldor shouted. "What's the point in having a way to signal a wizard if he doesn't even show up?"

From beneath their robes, the four remaining bulradoer in front of them drew the most unusual weapons Orlyn had ever seen, each one a handle without a blade.

Feoldor looked ready to offer one of his typical biting comments when the slick-haired man mumbled something under his breath, and the spiked head of a mace formed in blue flame at the top of the rod he was holding.

Orlyn gasped, as did the rest of the council members, when the other three bulradoer did the same: a gold-flame whip, an orange-flame sword, and a red-flame battle-axe. The woman on the right holding the golden whip demonstrated its potency by flinging it at one of the barracks porches. The lash cut straight through the main beam and half the porch collapsed.

"Is it too late to run?" Feoldor asked, eyes wide.

Orlyn opened his mouth but was cut short when the bulradoer attacked.

Veldon and Feoldor held the front line as they blasted the Tower's wielders with fire and wind. Reloria, Gilly, and Fraya hung back, ready to offer assistance if needed.

The building on their right was still burning. Orlyn could feel the heat as it spread toward the front wall.

In front of him, one of the bulradoer had managed to break off from the others. Using a conjured shield to stave off Veldon's assaults, he worked his way around the left flank to where Orlyn had taken up position. Orlyn didn't have much in the way of offensive magic. His staff was the only weapon he possessed.

The runes on his staff continued to glow as they supplied him with added strength. He wouldn't have been capable of standing otherwise. Whatever it was doing to him, he felt tougher. Quickly, he moved into position.

The bulradoer was quite a bit shorter, but the orange-flame longsword in his hands made up the difference. The bulradoer swung for Orlyn's head. Orlyn did the only thing he could: he raised his staff and prayed, knowing he'd likely be cut in half.

The transferal at the top pulsed a bright green as the bulradoer's sword came down. Sparks of orange and green shot into the air as flame and wood connected with a searing hiss. The arcane runes interwoven around the staff's outer edge were as radiant as the bulradoer's sword.

The bulradoer looked shocked, mirroring Orlyn's own face. How was he still alive? Not only had the sword not cut through the wood, but it hadn't even left a mark.

Back and forth they fought, striking, blocking, lunging, and circling around to start the cycle over again. Orlyn thanked his father for all the years of training he'd been forced to endure as a child. It seemed his instincts hadn't dulled too much over the years.

His arms were growing heavy, though. He hadn't had a full night's rest or a decent meal in days.

A few steps away, Veldon and Feoldor fought as a single unit. The portmaster's fire roared in waves as Feoldor cast volley after volley of hardened air, blocking the returning fire from the bulradoer and deflecting their magical weapons.

Orlyn spun the base of his quarterstaff downward to keep his opponent's blade from taking off his left leg. He winced at the searing heat. Flipping the staff back up, he thrust the end directly into the man's face, forcing the wielder back. It was a fairly obvious move, but Orlyn needed to put some distance between them in order to think. His opponent was much younger and more agile than he had been even twenty years ago. He wasn't going to win by trading blows.

Orlyn fumbled through his pockets as the bulradoer shook off the near miss and started for him again. Orlyn smiled when his hand reached the third pocket down on the right. *Good.* It was still there.

Lowering his staff, he ducked underneath another lunging assault. He could feel the heat passing overhead. Quickly, Orlyn shook the sweat from his face and turned as the bulradoer recovered from the swing to prepare for another. Orlyn waited till the bulradoer's arms were raised to strike, then threw a handful of ground valerian into the man's face and sprang out of the way.

As soon as the powder hit the man's eyes, the bulradoer yelled, and his weapon lowered, giving Orlyn the opening he needed. Pivoting on his back leg, Orlyn swung his staff with all his might. There was a loud *crack* as it connected with the side of the bulradoer's head. The dark wielder spat blood, and his sword dropped from his hands. Whatever magic had created the impressive blade vanished as soon as it left his fingers.

The hilt hit the ground, its wielder soon after.

Orlyn leaned over and picked the weapon up, hoping it would work for him as well. No such luck.

"Orlyn, behind you!"

Orlyn spun at Fraya's warning and found the spiked ends of a blue mace swinging in his direction. He raised his staff as fast as he could, but his counter wasn't quick enough. He managed to keep the spikes from embedding in his skull, but the deflection sent a couple of the tips tearing into his left shoulder instead.

The impact on his staff and shoulder sent him spinning backward. He lost his footing and went down, crying out as excruciating pain ripped through the left side of his body. He landed on his face. Somehow, the staff's power kept him lucid. He gripped it to his chest as he rolled over and glanced at the wound. There should have been a lot more blood. Then he noticed his flesh had been seared shut, no doubt from the heat of the weapon itself.

Behind him, Fraya jumped to her feet and ran for him.

"No!" he hollered, trying to wave her off. It didn't do any good. Above everything else, Fraya was a healer, and like most healers, she put others before herself.

The bulradoer was only steps away.

"I see you found your staff after all, old man." It was the same slick-haired man who'd taken him from his shop.

Orlyn struggled to lift his staff, but it was no use. He couldn't move his arm.

"Pity it won't—"

The bulradoer suddenly flew to the side, doing a complete flip in the air before landing a good ten paces away.

On his right, Feoldor threw Orlyn a quick nod as Fraya slid to a stop beside him and grabbed his ruined shoulder, causing him to yelp.

He tried to push her away, but his arms were too weak. "I'm already done for, child. Get back to the others."

She ran her hands across the wound on his shoulder. Orlyn's eyes bulged as he felt a wash of icy cold flood through his body, nearly taking his breath away all over again.

The bulradoer made it back to his feet and started for them, keeping a better eye on the other two council members this time. His hair wasn't quite so slick anymore.

"Hate killing something so pretty," the man said as he approached, giving Fraya a wide grin. "But we can't have you healing him, now, can we?" The wielder pivoted on his heels and raised the mace over his head.

"Fraya! Move!"

Fraya never even flinched.

Orlyn closed his eyes and waited for the impact. But instead of hearing the sound of a sickening thud and feeling the spray of Fraya's blood across the side of his face, Orlyn heard an unexpected howl. He opened his eyes as the dark wielder dropped his weapon. The conjured end disappeared.

The slick-haired man twisted around, trying to reach at something behind him. A thick black bolt was sticking out of his right shoulder.

Orlyn turned to find a senile-looking elderly man stepping out of a nearby doorway with an enormous double-bolt crossbow pressed to his chest.

"That'll teach you to come to Eaththaven looking for trouble!" Eliab shouted. The old Harbor House gatekeeper limped his way to the end of the open porch and fired off another round. The bulradoer was ready this time and deflected the quarrel up and off to the right.

Saleena joined Eliab on the porch, yanking another bolt from his quiver and handing it to him. Orlyn was glad to see the healer had decided to stick around, especially considering she wasn't even a wielder.

Orlyn half expected to see Sheeva next. They could really use her gifts right about now. But the white-haired assassin was literally nowhere to be seen. Why hadn't she shown up to help?

With the bulradoer's attention momentarily split between trying to remove the bolt from his shoulder and blocking the ones being fired at him, Orlyn managed to recover enough strength to crawl back toward the stables, where Gilly was guarding Reloria.

Finally giving up on pulling the bolt free, the bulradoer snapped the shaft in half and pulled the remaining piece the rest of the way through. He knelt and grabbed his weapon. As soon as his fingers wrapped around the handle, its blue flames burst to life, and the mace's spiked ball rose into place. Instead of coming straight for them, he was forced to continue blocking Eliab's bolts.

Whatever Fraya was doing to Orlyn with her magic was clearly working. He had never before allowed a healer to use magic on him when natural herbs would have sufficed. But now he was starting to wonder why he'd never tried it. The pain had lessened to a dull ache, and the muscle and skin were knitting back into place. Soon he found he was able to move his shoulder.

Fraya dropped to her knees beside him and hung an arm over the long trough where Gilly was stirring the water with his magic.

Orlyn knelt beside her. "Are you all right, Fraya? Is there anything I can do?"

"No," she said softly. "I need to rest and gather my strength."

"Here," Reloria said as she pushed her way through. "Eat this." She pulled an apple from her bag and handed it to Fraya. She looked at Orlyn. "I'll see to her. You go deal with those black-robed vermin."

Orlyn stood and tested his range of motion, encouraged by the fact that he didn't fall flat on his face as soon as he reached his feet. He grabbed his staff, and the runes brightened. Once again, he could feel their power flowing through him, adding their strength to his own. He barely had time to see if everything was working when the slick-haired bulradoer found an opening and charged.

Orlyn threw himself in front of the others and blocked the blazing weapon with his staff. The runes pulsed as blue and green sparks rained down on them. With each strike of the bulradoer's mace, the ancient symbols brightened. He hoped their power wouldn't run out.

Though strong in his own right, the dark wielder had obviously never been taught the fine art of defense. With a weapon like his, it was no wonder. Its magic seemed unstoppable. Why would its wielder need to worry about such things as the proper placement of his hands to gain the most momentum or the suitable width and angle of his swing to avoid leaving his front exposed?

"It's not the weapon that makes the warrior," Orlyn's father used to say. "It's knowing how to wield it."

Orlyn waited for the man to come back around with another wild swing. He dodged to the side and hit his exposed sternum with a swift jab. The bulradoer doubled over, gasping for breath. Orlyn spun his staff and landed a precise strike to the top of the man's wrist, forcing his hand to open.

The mace fell from his fingers and tumbled just as Orlyn swept his legs out from under him, sending the bulradoer onto his back.

Orlyn raised his staff to finish him but was hindered when the female bulradoer on his right sent her golden whip in his direction. He raised his staff to protect his head. It sounded like a crack of lightning as the tail end of her whip connected with the magical length of wood. The unexpected attack forced Orlyn back toward the others, giving the slick-haired man on the ground the chance to retrieve his weapon. Again.

Orlyn was getting sick and tired of the man's apparent good fortune.

"Looks like we got here just in time," Saleena said as she and Eliab moved in behind Gilly near the stable doors.

"I appreciate the help," Orlyn said, keeping his eye on the bulradoer in front of him. He seemed to be holding back to nurse the hole in his shoulder.

On his right, Veldon and Feoldor might have been holding the line, but they were being herded slowly in his direction as they fought against the other two bulradoer at the edge of the barracks. They were only about fifteen feet from the stable. The taller man with the red-flame axe struck from the front, while the woman—moving along the porch of the last building—came at them from the right, looking for an opening in Feoldor's shields.

"Reloria! Look out!" Orlyn shouted. The female bulradoer suddenly changed her attack away from Feoldor and sent her whip toward the rest of the council huddled near the stable.

This time, it was Gilly's quick reaction that saved their lives. He raised his blue crystal to create a sheet of ice from the water in the trough, blocking the lash.

Reloria screamed as the bulradoer's whip deflected off the ice and cut through the top of her pink bonnet, just missing her head by a finger. She dove behind the trough.

The bulradoer recoiled for another try. But before she could, Feoldor turned and sent a hammer of air careening into her side, and she was sent tumbling into the building. Halfway through the front window, she unleashed a single swing of her whip that caught Feoldor in the back.

He yelled and went down face-first into the dirt.

Reloria shrieked, jumping up from her spot behind the trough to run for Feoldor.

Orlyn rushed to help them pull Feoldor out of the way but was cut short when the slick-haired bulradoer came at him from the side. Orlyn dodged the first swing and blocked the second. He spun left, hoping to draw the bulradoer away from the others.

Even with the added strength from his staff, he could feel the strain of what seemed an unending fight catching up. His white knuckles clutched the wood as he angled his staff and deflected the mace away from his head. He then countered with a hard swing of his own that forced the bulradoer to give ground.

In the quick glimpses afforded Orlyn while he struggled to keep his staff moving, he could see the others dragging Feoldor back toward the stables and away from the immediate battle. On his right, Veldon was struggling to hold the axe-wielding bulradoer at bay by sending wave after wave of fire careening into the man's shield. The look in the portmaster's eyes said he wasn't going to be able to hold out much longer.

Chapter 78 | Ty

BODIES LITTERED the front lawn.

It was a colorful mosaic—the aftermath of human confrontation, the dying and the already dead.

Outside their cottage, all was silent. On the inside, ears strained and eyes shifted as the surviving members of the recent battle waited with bated breath for whatever dark thing was about to be unleashed.

Ty's sister and mother moved about, washing wounds, smearing salves, and applying bandages.

Only two of the Sidaran lancers had survived the Tallosian assault, but both had sustained wounds that left them incapacitated. If it hadn't been for Adarra's knowledge of medicine, neither would have survived long. Ty's father had a knife wound to his shoulder, Ty's brother had multiple lacerations on both arms and a cut to his midsection, Lyessa had a few deep bruises and some minor cuts on the arm and forehead, and Overlord Barl had a wounded shoulder as well as a nasty gash down his leg that left him hobbling. The worst, though, was poor Aiden. His face was pale as he lay on the sofa, coughing up mouthfuls of blood. Adarra was doing everything she could to keep him from dying.

Then there was the Northman.

"We should kill him and be done with it," Barl said, looking down in disgust at the Tallosian captured by Adarra and her mother, "before he wakes and tries killing us all."

"He's not going anywhere," Ty's father said. "He's bound hand and foot."

Breen had helped Adarra move the savage over to the side and out of the way.

"Besides," his father said, "if we manage to survive this, it might be wise to have someone around to interrogate."

Barl looked at the savage and nodded, but he didn't look happy about it.

From his spot in the corner, Ty stretched out his senses, hoping to catch a glimpse of what they were going to face. He was weak, too weak to even stand, and the amount of magic he was able to expend was almost nonexistent. But in the distance, a shape started to form in the back of his mind. It wasn't the first time he had encountered this dark sentience. The last time had been while overlooking a valley of dry bones. A dark consciousness that held but a single thought: to feed!

"It's coming," he said, almost as an afterthought.

"What's coming?" his father asked. "Is it the creature?" Ty's mother held a mug of tea halfway to Ty's father's swollen lips, urging him to drink.

Ty nodded and closed his eyes once more. "It's almost here." He could feel it. But this time, it was much larger by comparison—much, much larger. He opened his eyes. "And it's not alone."

Ty was the first to notice the clicks. His father's head was the second to lift, and then his brother's, as the cracking and snapping reached their trained ears. One by one, the others noticed it too.

"What could be making such a noise?" Barl asked as he hobbled over to the front window to get a better look. He glanced around the yard. "There's nothing there."

Holding a clean dressing to his shoulder, Ty's father made his way over to stand beside the overlord.

Ty took a moment to gain his own footing, testing his strength. He closed his eyes in concentration as he attempted to reach his magic. It was no use. And ever since Fraya's admission that using too much magic could kill the wielder, Ty wasn't in favor of pushing it.

By the time everyone had reached the bay window at the front, the faint clicking had grown to a low rumble. Ty, along with everyone else, searched for some indication of its origin.

Ty shuddered. "They're here."

"Where?" Lyessa asked.

"There." Ty's father pointed toward the western edge of the woods.

Everyone bunched as tight as they could to peer out the window at the copse of trees on the far side of the house.

"I don't see anything," Barl grunted in exasperation.

"Me either," Lyessa said, trying to poke her head around her father's.

"Not there." Ty's father raised his finger. "There."

All heads tilted back, shifting focus from the ground to the tops of the trees as the first of the huge spiders made their way out of the uppermost branches.

"By the unholy powers!" Barl didn't even try to hide the tremor in his voice.

Spiders poured out by the dozens. The trees were alive with movement as they skittered down the sides and across the yard, stopping to feast on the dead.

Ty watched as one enormous spider, much larger than the others, crawled out of the woods and made its way across the lawn to Mangora's side. The witch rubbed her hand across the thick hide of the horse-sized monster.

"There it is," his father said. "The mother arachnobe."

Lyessa's father placed a hand on Ty's shoulder. "Son, we're going to need your help, now more than ever."

"I'm sorry, my lord, but I've got nothing left."

"Well, I . . ." The overlord cleared his throat. "I'm sure you'll think of something." He patted Ty gently, trying to look reassuring. Instead, he looked like a man who'd just received word that his house had burned, his wife had left him, and his daughter had run off with the town drunk.

"Ty, there's nothing to be ashamed of," his father said. "You fought well."

Ty nodded as his father went to inspect Breen's wounds. "How are you holding up?"

Breen winced. "I've been better."

"Here. You might need these." He handed Breen one of their swords and leaned his large recurve up against the side of the table, along with a few of their remaining arrows.

Breen took the bow, pulling back on the string to test his strength. "I'm good." Gently, he prodded his wrapped midsection. "There's nothing like killing a few dozen Northmen to loosen the joints for a horde of spiders." His smile was less than convincing.

His father gave Breen a proud slap on the back, causing him to wince.

"Here," Adarra said, holding out a small leather pouch for her mother to take.

"What's this?"

"It's the last of my hemper vine."

Ty's mother looked confused.

"It helps reduce swelling from"—she glanced around sheepishly—"bug bites."

There was a brief silence before the entire company burst into laughter.

The amusement was short-lived, as the sound of the approaching horde grew louder.

Ty's father turned to the others. "We need to barricade ourselves in."

Chapter 79 | Orlyn

ELDON WAS STRUGGLING on Orlyn's right. They had been pushed nearly all the way back to where the others were huddled in front of the stables. There was nowhere else for them to go. Behind them, Gilly was busy keeping his trough of water moving, waiting to raise another protective sheet of ice if needed.

Orlyn swung low, the sweat that poured down his face threatening to cloud his vision. This time, the slick-haired bulradoer was barely able to block as he managed to catch the tip of Orlyn's staff with his mace. The man was favoring his injured wrist. Orlyn had no qualms about taking advantage of that as he forced him to defend his weaker side.

A loud *crack* on the right made them all jump. It was the sound of wooden planks breaking under too much pressure. Orlyn glanced to his right in time to see the front of the half-torn-down building suddenly explode outward.

The fighters broke off their engagement to shield themselves from the glass and debris as the female bulradoer emerged. Her face was bruised and bleeding.

She scanned the group, and when she saw Feoldor lying on his back near the front of the stables, she reignited her golden-flamed whip. She wiped the blood from her mouth and headed straight for him.

"Get him out of there!" Orlyn shouted. There was nothing he could do. He swung his staff back around in time to keep the blue-flamed mace from caving in the top of his head. He struck the weapon away and was about to catch the bulradoer on his injured side when a loud shrill stopped him.

Behind him, Reloria, who had been nursing a near-dead Feoldor, leaped to her feet and charged the oncoming bulradoer. The look of shock on the bulradoer's face was nearly a match for his own as Reloria ran at the woman—arms flailing, pink hat flying from her head, locks of hair waving out behind her. She looked like a mother hen rushing in to protect her chicks from a fox, knowing she had no hope of surviving but willing all the same.

Orlyn didn't want to watch, but he couldn't seem to pull himself away. The slick-haired bulradoer seemed to have the same inclination, as he turned as well.

The female bulradoer smiled as she uncurled her whip, ready to split Reloria in two. She swung, and the golden lash cut through the porch's one remaining post on its way to do the same to Reloria. The flame sizzled and hissed, and then vanished as a huge spear of ice flew past Reloria and impaled the bulradoer through the chest, sending her flying to her back.

The woman's body slid backward down the end of the frozen spike until she reached the dirt and went still.

Orlyn heard Gilly clap in victory, but the slick-haired bulradoer's roar quickly drowned it out. Orlyn barely got his staff up in time to keep the blue mace from taking off the front of his face. The scalding flames stopped a few inches from his head.

"Gilly, behind you!" Reloria screamed.

Orlyn heard Eliab's crossbow twang. What was happening? He blocked and countered with a swift swing at the slick-haired man's head. The bulradoer ducked and spun away, giving Orlyn a brief chance to glance over his shoulder.

Behind them, Captain Hatch and the Black Watch were moving in through the north gate to flank them. Orlyn panicked. There was nothing they could do. Eliab and Gilly had no way of defending themselves against Hatch and his men.

Another twang and a second white-robed guard went down with one of Eliab's bolts in his chest.

The rest charged.

Frantically, Orlyn turned and deflected his attacker's next swing and then raised his staff as though aiming for the bulradoer's head. The man was too busy watching Orlyn's hands to worry about anything else, so he swung high, leaving himself completely open.

Orlyn took it. He reversed direction mid-swing and smashed the top of the man's foot with all the force he could muster. The bulradoer howled and was momentarily thrown off balance. Orlyn pivoted and swung as hard as he could for the bulradoer's bad arm. A *crack*, another howl, and the fiery mace once again winked out as it hit the ground.

The bulradoer dove for his weapon, but Orlyn wasn't about to let him have it again. He brought the full force of his quarterstaff down across the top of the slick-haired man's head, leaving him unconscious in the dirt. Orlyn grabbed the silver rod and stuffed it into one of his pockets, then ran to help the others.

Three more of the Tower's guards went down, shards of ice sticking from their torsos. Gilly stood over the near-empty trough, looking perplexed. Other than Eliab's sword and Gilly's small dagger, not one of the other council members had a weapon to fight with.

From behind them, a lance of fire flew over their heads and struck the ground in front of the oncoming Watch, breaking their advance. Orlyn turned to see Veldon twisting back around as he conjured another ball of flame and sent it careening against the shield of the bulradoer he was facing.

They couldn't count on Veldon being able to do that again.

Orlyn quickly searched his pockets. He knew he had felt them earlier. But where? He started pulling out handfuls of powders, seeds, and herbs from various tucked-away spaces, the contents raining down across his feet as he tried finding what he was looking for. He needed to organize his robes better. They were all about to die because he couldn't be bothered enough to clean out his pockets.

Finally, he pulled his hand from the fourth pocket on the right and shouted at Gilly, "How much water is left?"

Gilly looked into the trough and shook his head.

"Give me something. Anything!"

Gilly reached in and scooped up a small handful of water, barely enough to fill the bottom of a glass, and threw it at Orlyn.

Orlyn didn't need much. He raised his hand high enough for the water to hit the seeds, then turned and threw them at the Tower's guards. With a hard thrust, he planted his staff in the dirt. As soon as the seeds landed in front of Hatch and his men, Orlyn released his floratide magic into them, and they burst to life.

Roots burrowed into the soil while vines sprouted from the tops. Within moments, half the men had been entangled in creepers. The plants continued to grow as they wrapped themselves around the guards, pulling them down, squeezing the life from them.

Those who weren't hacking at the plants to save the others continued after Hatch.

Orlyn poured life into his seeds as Eliab and Gilly bravely held the line. They didn't hold for long. Gilly was the first to go down. Orlyn couldn't see what had happened from where he was standing, but the poor dwarf hadn't stood a chance. All he had to defend himself was a short dagger—certainly no match for the Watch's swords.

Eliab, on the other hand, wielded his blade like a master. The former captain of the Sidaran Guard had slit the throat of one guard and skewered another when a blade caught his side. He cut the legs out from the man before finally going down.

Orlyn held his focus as he continued to kill as many guards as he could with the thick vines. With no one left but himself to protect the women, he shuffled over to where they were busy standing over Feoldor.

Reloria rose to his right. She clutched her jeweled pendant in one hand and raised the other in the direction of the oncoming rush. The armed men stumbled to a halt. Some of them tripped and went down as they spat, hacked, and vomited. Orlyn could only imagine what someone as angry as Reloria had caused them to choke on.

Unfortunately, Captain Hatch was too enraged to care. He hacked and spat a wad out to the side, then turned to his men behind him. "Get back in line, you sons of goats!" he roared. He kicked Gilly's body out of the way as he started forward. He stopped about ten feet from where they were and gasped when he saw Saleena.

"How? I saw you die. What kind of evil is this?"

Orlyn released his hold on the plants. There wasn't much more he could do with them, anyway. He needed to focus on the fight in front of him. Reloria and Saleena stood protectively over Fraya as she worked to keep Feoldor alive. Behind them, Orlyn could hear Veldon's fire still beating away against the bulradoer's shield. He had to be near exhaustion.

Orlyn raised his staff, and the runes glowed. He let its energy flow through him. He was near exhaustion himself. He stepped forward, and Hatch hesitated, not sure what to expect. The Watch clearly had a respectful fear of wielders.

Orlyn's staff might have had magic, but it was a weapon best used to defend against other magic, not half a dozen sword-wielding members of the Black Watch. Unfortunately, it was the only weapon they had.

He swung his staff at the first three guards who came at him. He hit one, missed the second, and took a deep cut to his arm from the third. Rocks flew past Orlyn's head and bounced helplessly off the guards' armor as Reloria and Saleena offered their last desperate attempt to save themselves.

The guards came at him again, and Orlyn continued swinging, trying to hold the men at bay. He was even managing it for a time until someone threw a dagger and hit him in the shoulder. The sudden jolt caused him to drop his staff, while one of the other guards opened his leg with a single cut, and he went to his knees.

Reloria and Saleena yelled at him to get up, but he knew he couldn't.

Orlyn couldn't believe it was going to end like this. He was proud of their council, though. They had fought against unbelievable odds.

"Kill him," Hatch said.

The guard stepped forward. He couldn't have been much more than twenty. About the age his son might have been if his wife hadn't lost him in childbirth. There was a certain amount of trepidation in the guard's steps, but he raised his sword anyway.

Orlyn kept his eyes open as he faced what he hoped would be a quick end. The guard swung for his neck, but the blade stopped with a clang just a few inches from his face.

The guard looked down at his sword curiously, then gasped when blood erupted from a hole in the side of his neck. The young man's garbled screams ended with his eyes rolling into the back of his head before he collapsed in the dirt beside him.

Both Reloria and Saleena shrieked as a second guard went down, his throat opened from ear to ear.

There was only one person Orlyn knew to be capable of doing this. Why had she waited so long to come?

Panic ensued as men began to swing their blades in all directions, doing more damage to themselves than anything else. Others took off running, swearing curses on all who practiced magic.

"Get back here, you cowards!" Hatch screamed as he, too, flung his blade from side to side, fighting against an invisible force. He turned, and his eyes caught Fraya. Her hands were glowing as she knelt beside Feoldor. "For my brother!" he shouted and charged.

Orlyn tried to get to his feet, but the deep wound across his leg had him collapsing on his side.

"No!" Saleena leaped in front of Fraya, and the captain's steel slid in one side and out the other.

Hatch pulled the blade from Saleena's chest, and her limp body fell backward on top of Fraya, knocking her to the ground.

"That's one less bit of evil in this world," the captain said as he turned to Fraya and raised his blade once more.

He stiffened as the tip of a sword ripped through the front of his white uniform. He dropped to his knees in front of Fraya, confusion on his face. His sword fell from his hand as he sat there looking at her.

A small woman with short white hair appeared beside him.

The captain looked up, then coughed blood as he released his final breath. His head lowered to his chest, and if not for the sword sticking through it, he would have looked like a man in prayer. Orlyn could have sworn he saw relief in the captain's eyes.

With the death of three of their own, and the Black Watch either dead or fleeing, the remaining bulradoer withdrew his attacks on Veldon long enough to make a retreat. The slick-haired bulradoer Orlyn had been fighting had apparently snuck off, no doubt when he realized he no longer had a weapon.

After checking to see if there was anything that could be done for Saleena, Fraya moved to help Orlyn, but he pushed her off. "Go see to Gilly and Eliab. They might yet be alive. I'll be here when you get back." She nodded and headed for the old gatekeeper and the dwarf. Her legs looked unstable.

Veldon dropped down beside where Orlyn was sitting and weakly pointed at Reloria lying unconscious on the ground beside Feoldor. "Reloria?"

"She's fine," Orlyn said, biting back the pain in his shoulder and legs, "just had a bit of a fainting spell."

Veldon reached for the dagger sticking from Orlyn's shoulder.

"No, no, no. Let's wait for the healer."

"Right. Probably a good idea." Veldon studied the dagger a moment. "Fine-looking handle, though."

Orlyn looked at Veldon, and they both chuckled.

Orlyn's chest seized, and he started to cough. "Don't make me laugh. Here, help me up." With Veldon's help, he managed to make it to his feet. They slowly limped over to where Fraya was tending to their fallen comrades.

To everyone's amazement, Eliab was still alive, if only barely.

Fraya infused the old gatekeeper with as much of her magic as she could, and with what strength she still had, she turned to Gilly. She reached her hand out, and he hopped to his feet.

"Are they gone?"

No one said anything, too shocked at the little man's sudden recovery.

"I thought you were dead," Orlyn said, just as stunned as the rest.

"That's what I wanted them to think." He held up his right arm, where he had sustained a slight cut.

Orlyn sighed. If he'd had an ounce of strength, he'd have smacked the dwarf over the head with his staff.

Fraya was too weak to provide any sort of full healing, but after removing Orlyn's dagger, she did manage to close the wounds enough to keep infection from setting in, promising to continue once her strength had returned.

Orlyn turned to thank the white-haired assassin for saving their lives and to give her a stout scolding for not having come sooner, but Sheeva had already vanished.

"Where did she run off to?"

"Who?" Veldon asked.

"Sheeva. We could have used her a lot sooner." Orlyn stared down at Saleena's lifeless body.

"If she had been here to help, we—"

"She was busy releasing the prisoners they had captured to take to the White Tower. Did you know they had Sorna?"

Orlyn sighed. He took back all the bad things he'd thought about their resident assassin. She had clearly proven more honorable than him.

"We need to ride for Kellen's immediately," Orlyn said.

"Why?" Fraya asked as she rested against the stable wall, looking about as pale as Feoldor and Eliab.

"Ty's in danger."

Veldon rubbed the top of his balding head. "From who? What's going on?"

Orlyn lowered his eyes. "I'm afraid I've done something rather terrible."

Chapter 80 | Ty

"**W**HAT IF WE made a run for it?" Barl asked, using his sheathed sword like a cane as he helped stack loose chairs in front of the bay windows. "If we could make it to the horses . . ." The overlord didn't finish his thought. He shook his head and sighed.

Even Ty could see that wouldn't work.

"We wouldn't make it ten feet before they ripped us apart," his father said as he helped Breen lift the heavy oak table into place. "They have the house completely surrounded. The only reason the witch hasn't sent them in is because she's still hoping to get her hands on Ty."

Barl snorted and moved over to the fireplace, resting one arm on the mantel. He watched Ty's father and Breen as they upturned the kitchen table to barricade the front window.

Ty helped move some of the furniture. He was feeling a little better, having downed some of the leftovers from their earlier meal. He still wasn't up to using magic, but he felt like he could make good use of the sword Lyessa had given him. It had belonged to one of the dead lancers outside. He held the weapon, wanting to get used to its weight in his hands. The leather binding felt oddly comforting. He loosened his grip when he noticed his knuckles turning white.

Behind him, Adarra and Lyessa dragged an unresponsive Aiden from the center of the room over to the far wall, alongside the other two injured lancers. Meanwhile, Breen and Ty's mother went from room to room locking down windows, latching shutters, and barring doors.

Ty watched from the corner as his father counted the arrows in his quiver. Looking around the room, Ty studied the drawn faces. He was feeling it too—the thought of what was coming. He would rather have faced an entire army of Tallosian savages than what was scurrying around outside. He hated spiders. Even though he could communicate with them, he still detested them. And now he was facing ones as big as Waddle.

He had tried to push a command at the arachnobes, but they didn't appear to listen.

The sound of hundreds of legs skittering across the yard, up the trees, and over the roof of their dwelling was enough to not only put him on edge but also throw him clear over it. Short of a miracle, there was no way out of this one, and Ty had certainly used his last miracle during the previous battle.

Ty's mother gently interlocked her fingers with her husband's as they stood off to the side. "We are together," she said. "I couldn't ask for more than that."

"Aye. We've been blessed with a wonderful family. No man could count himself more fortunate." He leaned over and kissed the top of her head.

Overlord Barl had an arm wrapped around Lyessa. The overlord's eyes were heavy under the emotion of whatever they were quietly discussing—no doubt their final goodbyes.

"What are they waiting for?" Barl finally asked, turning back to the others. "Why don't they just get it over with?"

As if in answer to his question, Mangora's voice rang out above the clatter of the creatures as they feasted on the flesh outside. "This is your last chance!"

Ty peeked through a crack between the table and the rocker, where Adarra often read.

Mangora stood on the other side of the yard. "Well? What will it be? Do you come out, or do we come in?"

Ty's father took a step toward the pile of furniture. "You step foot in this house, and I give you my word, you'll never step out again!"

Mangora shrilled, and the legion of spiders rained down on them.

With the glass already missing from the window, Ty's father released the last of his arrows in between the table and piled chairs. The spiders screeched and hissed as the long shafts hit their marks. Green blood sprayed across the front of the barricade as they continued their advance.

Breen stood in front of Ty and unloaded the last of his as well. Each shot landed true, bringing down three more. "Six down . . . hundreds to go," he said over his shoulder with a wink.

Ty caught Breen's bow as he tossed it behind him. His brother raised an axe he'd confiscated from one of the Northmen and joined the others in chopping off spider legs as fast as they poked their way through. Large angular limbs wrapped in slick leathery sinew flopped at Ty's feet, saturating the floor with their blood. The stench was unbearable. He tried not to vomit.

Ty spotted an opening near Lyessa where one of the spiders was pushing back Adarra's rocker. He leaped at the hole and drove his blade through the opening. The spider on the other side shrilled, and a squirt of warm green blood shot back and hit him in the face. In all the excitement, he had forgotten to close his mouth.

He shouted at the top of his lungs and spat all over the floor. "Flaming toadstools! That stuff is wretched!" He did his best to purge his tongue with the back of his sleeve.

On his right, Lyessa was laughing. "That'll teach you to keep your mouth shut!" She chopped off another set of furry legs at the joint as they struggled to break through the wooden barrier.

A loud crash from one of the back rooms brought them all around with a start. "They're in the house!" his father shouted and ran for the hallway just as the first of the spiders burst through Adarra's bedroom door.

Ty pulled back from his place at the wall to see if his father needed his help.

"Kellen!"

Ty's father turned, and Ty's mother tossed him one of her large kitchen knives. Grabbing it out of the air, he launched it down the hall, driving it deep between the spider's three eyes. Flailing and hissing, it lurched forward but only managed a few confused steps before collapsing. The next one was already working its way over when his father met it with a resounding battle cry. He held it at bay, slicing and stabbing as best he could in such a confined space. As it reared, he thrust his sword into its lower abdomen. It slumped and died atop the other.

His father's clothes were soaked in spider blood, and his skin had begun to turn a faint green. "This stuff reeks!" he said, flinging the excess goo from his arms like a dog shaking water from its coat.

"We need help out here!" Barl bellowed from the front, the chairs being pushed back by the overwhelming onslaught.

Ty jumped back into place as another of the spiders started squeezing through the far-left side. He struck the first leg, but his swing hadn't been enough to cut all the way through. He tried yanking the blade free, but it was lodged tight. He angled himself to get a better pull, but a second leg punched through and hit him in the gut, and he tumbled backward, unable to breathe. His hands slid across the blood-soaked boards as he struggled to get back onto his feet.

Breen jerked Ty up to help him stand. "Go protect Adarra!" He grabbed Ty's sword from where it had been stuck and tossed it to him before chopping the creature's leg off with his axe.

Ty scooted back to where Adarra was busy working to heal Aiden and the two lancers. He was clearly in the way. He had never taken to combat like his older brother. His father had been a good teacher, but Ty had always found it a bit rigorous. Now he wished he had paid better attention. He was determined that if the Creator saw fit to allow them to survive, he was going to learn.

An arm wrapped around his shoulder, and he jumped.

"Your brother just wants to make sure you're protected," his mother said. She glanced down at Adarra. "Now you make sure *they* are."

Ty nodded and raised his sword. Nothing was going to get to them as long as he was there.

His father roared as he cut the legs out from another spider in mid-lunge. He'd been forced to give ground as the spiders pressed their way down the hall. He was now fighting from the entranceway, which allowed him a greater range of motion with his swing.

Lyessa was knocked down momentarily, and Ty started for her, but before he had made it two steps, she was back on her feet and stabbing a smaller spider trying to squeeze its way underneath the table. It quickly retreated.

On the right side, where the barricade was weakest, the first of the larger arachnobes finally gained a foothold. Lyessa's back was turned, and she didn't see the deadly creature behind her. Barl dove in front of his daughter and thrust his sword into its lower abdomen. The eight-legged monster reeled and hissed in rage before leaking the last of its life across an end table Ty's father had made from an old poplar that had fallen on the barn some years back.

Unfortunately, the creature's dead weight knocked the overlord off his feet, leaving him unable to stop the next spider from crawling inside. Barl shouted his loathing for the creature as the spider stabbed the end of its spear-like leg into his calf.

Lyessa wove her way around its legs with amazing speed, working to get to her father while Breen held the others at bay. There were just too many. She wasn't going to make it. With a frustrated scream, she leaped on top of the creature's back and drove her dagger to the hilt through the top of its head. It flinched once and went still.

Ty rushed forward and hacked off the leg that was holding the overlord. He helped her drag her father out from under the dead creature and back toward the others that his sister and mother were busy nursing.

Without waiting to see how her father was doing, Lyessa grabbed her sword and rushed back to the front to help Breen. With Barl down, Ty didn't hesitate. He lifted his sword and retook his spot on the left side. He hacked and stabbed until his arms felt ready to give out, and then he hacked and stabbed some more. They were barely slowing the creatures down.

There was a clatter near the rear of the kitchen, followed by pots and pans clanging, and dishes breaking. Ty glanced behind him. The top half of the kitchen door had been ripped open, and a single spider was trying to push its way inside, but it was met with his mother's iron skillet. The impact sounded like the tolling of the Sidaran Senate's bell. With the creature still dazed, his mother buried a meat cleaver in its thick sinew. And then she did it again and again until even the leftover spasms had ceased.

"Nilla?" his father called from the front hall.

"Fine," she shouted as she maneuvered a nearby cabinet into place in front of the door.

Ty turned and plunged his sword deep into the mouth of the next spider. Its fangs were as big as his hands. The thought of being struck by one kept his arms moving. But for each one he killed, there were five more to take its place. Those they killed were hauled off by the others to make room for the next wave.

On his right, Lyessa's father hobbled back to the front between Lyessa and Breen. The overlord had one sword to hold himself up and another to kill anything that poked through the barricade.

Behind him, Ty's father shouted. Ty watched him cut half a leg off the next spider coming over the pile and, with a lunging thrust, drive his blade through its open maw.

Barl stumbled back to avoid being hit by another spider and tripped over the severed legs at his feet. He reached out on instinct and grabbed the nearest object available—Lyessa—to keep from pitching over altogether. But instead of stopping his fall, he merely pulled her down on top of him, giving the spiders a clear opening.

One of the smaller spiders forced its way through the barricade.

"Hey! Over here!" Ty shouted, trying to steer the spider's attention away from Lyessa and her father. Ty shrilled as one of the spiders coming through his side of the barricade cut a gash down his arm. He turned and killed the beast with a single thrust to its head. He pulled his sword free and turned to help Lyessa, but Adarra was already racing across the room with one of their father's sickles.

She screamed and brought the farming instrument around in a wide arc. The blade passed through the creature's outer hide as easily as a stalk of sun-kissed wheat. She pulled the blade out and hit it again. The beast hissed and collapsed, leaving Adarra drenched in spider yuck as Lyessa once again pulled her father to safety.

Ty thought he heard something behind him and turned to see how his mother and father were doing. His heart stopped.

"Father!" Ty screamed, his breath catching in his throat.

Ty's father spun around.

Two spiders had somehow managed to push their way through the back door and were now standing over his mother. She wasn't moving.

His father shouted for Breen, leaving the spiders in the hall as he ran for the kitchen.

"Ty! Hold the front!" Breen said as he rushed to take their father's place and keep the creatures from overrunning them.

Ty couldn't focus. He barely heard his brother. All he could think about was the two spiders on top of his mother. Throwing everything else aside, he left the barricade and ran for the kitchen.

Ahead, Ty's father chopped the front legs off the first spider. It hissed, and he kicked it to the side as he lunged at the second. The second spider reared and hit him in the arm. Ty could see the blood, but it didn't stop his father.

Ty leaped at the first creature. He called it every name in the book. It lunged, but he dodged to the right and landed a solid cut to its side. The creature hissed and swept Ty's legs out from under him, and he landed on his face. The floor was slick with spider goo, making it hard to gain his footing. He barely had time to turn over before the spider was on top of him. It was even uglier underneath. Its mandibles clicked open and shut as they sought to latch on to his neck. Using his legs, he kicked up and flipped the creature over.

On the other side of the kitchen, his father blocked the second spider's legs, and then, with a powerful swing, he cut the arachnobe in half, his blade hitting the narrow section dividing its lower and upper abdomen.

Ty spun around and rolled back onto his feet. He had to get to his mother. He was halfway there when he felt a sharp pain in his left shoulder. At first, he thought it was the markings on his arm growing once again, but then he remembered that was his right shoulder. He turned his head and screamed.

It was the arachnobe. The spider had sunk its fangs into the top of his arm.

He screamed again. By the time he'd thought to use his blade, his father's sword had flown past and buried itself inside the creature's head. Its mouth opened, releasing him, and Ty fell to the floor. The pain was excruciating. It ran the entire length of his body, but he pushed it aside. He crawled as fast as he could to where his father was cradling his mother's head in his lap.

"Mama? Mama, can you hear me?" He glanced down at her ravaged body and cried. Along with the numerous punctures and lacerations, there were places where the spiders had already started eating.

She opened her eyes, and Ty held her gaze. He couldn't imagine how she had managed to survive this long. Why had she not cried out? Why had he not turned around sooner?

She opened her mouth, blood leaking from the corners. "My brave little boy."

Ty's father laid his hand on her cheek and smiled, tears marking the front of his face. "Hang on, Nilla. Just breathe. I'm here." His voice was cracking.

She looked up at him and smiled, then her eyes went blank and her head dropped to the side.

At that moment, Ty didn't care if the spiders ate them all. He leaned back and screamed.

Chapter 81 | Ty

TY FELT DEAD INSIDE.

He stood from his mother's broken body and lifted his sword, its edges slick with green blood. If it was the last thing he did, he was going to cut that witch's head off. And Creator help anything that stood in his way.

His anger woke something deep inside. He could feel it stirring, something dark and powerful. He felt strangely numb. The pain from his earlier wounds vanished. His fingers tightened around the grip of his sword as he started for the front door.

He took two steps into the main room . . . and collapsed. He watched as the floor leaped into the air and hit him in the face. Or was it his face hitting the floor? Something didn't feel right. He couldn't move his legs.

"Ty! What happened?" He felt his father's arms lift him to his knees.

The room was beginning to spin. "I . . . I don't know." He looked down at his lower half. "I can't feel my legs."

His father winced as he pulled back the top of Ty's overcoat where the spider had latched on to his arm. "This doesn't look good. We need to see if Adarra can do anything for it."

Ty retched, and strangely enough, the room finally stopped spinning. His father carried him over to the left side of the family room and laid him beside Aiden.

Ty watched his brother fighting to hold back the spiders in the hall. On his left, more spiders were pushing their way through the front barricade. Lyessa and her father were being forced farther back into the room. Adarra swung her sickle, cutting off legs as fast as she could, but there were just too many of them.

Ty knew it was over. They had lost, and there was nothing he could do about it. Some great wielder he'd turned out to be. If the White Tower had known how pathetic he was, they wouldn't have wasted so much time and energy looking for him. He had been too weak to make a difference, and now they were all going to suffer his mother's fate.

He started crying. He couldn't hold it in. His emotions overwhelmed him, and he let them sweep him away in their tide.

From somewhere outside, an explosion rocked the cottage. The spiders halted their attack, then one by one retreated out the toppled blockade or through the bedroom windows. Something was diverting their attention—something more pressing than their tiny band of half-dead fighters.

There was another crash of thunder. The entire house shook as if lightning had struck it. With the creatures evacuating, the group hobbled to the barricade to see if they could catch a glimpse of what was happening.

"Help me up," Ty said as he anxiously raised one arm.

His father leaned over and picked him up. Carefully, they maneuvered in and around the carcasses littering the floor, making their way toward a small section of collapsed debris near the front door. The oak table had all but toppled, leaving an open window to the front yard.

Outside, the horde of massive bloodthirsty arachnobes was being corralled by a wall of golden fire, or at least Ty thought it was fire. There was something strange about it. It didn't quite move like fire, more like some kind of golden liquid.

"*Suethian Duwanite!*"

Standing on their side of the barricade was an old man. Long white hair swirled around his head as he wielded what appeared to be a sword of golden flame. With each swing, the white-haired man cut down any spider not shut off by the fiery blockade.

Ty could see Mangora through the gold-colored wall. She was riding atop the mother arachnobe. "This isn't over, wizard!" she shouted over the cacophony of her eight-legged army. She sent a spear of flame at the old man, but it didn't make it past the fire.

Mangora shrilled and quickly disappeared into the woods, taking her spider army with her.

"*Tares'ayden!*" The old man lowered his hands, and the golden barricade vanished into the ground. He waited for the last of the spiders to retreat before turning around. "You can come out now." His fiery blade faded and then dissipated altogether, leaving nothing more than the hilt, which he tucked into one of the folds of his robe.

Breen was the first one out the door, his axe raised. He stood on the front steps and looked around the yard. "Looks clear," he said.

"Here, take your brother," Ty's father said as walked through the door and handed Ty off before strolling out to talk with the old man.

"What happened to you?" Breen asked.

"Spider bit me," Ty said.

Breen winced.

"You said you would return," Ty's father said as he approached who Ty could only guess was the wizard everyone had been talking about.

The old man smiled. "I told you I would."

His father glanced back at the house, tears still in his eyes. "I wish it had been sooner." He waved for Breen and the others to join him.

Ty bounced in his brother's arms as they started forward. As they neared the wizard, Ty could see the weathered look of age in the man's face. He had clearly lived a hard life.

The rest of those in the house followed Breen and Ty across the yard, stepping over and around the fallen, Overlord Barl helped along by Lyessa and Adarra.

As soon as everyone had gathered, Ty's father made introductions. "This is Nyalis. He was the wizard who brought Ty to us sixteen years ago." He then introduced the rest to Nyalis.

The old man nodded a greeting to each but brightened when he came to Ty. "Ah, my young faeling, we meet again." He rubbed a hand through Ty's hair. "The white suits you, I think." His smile was warm, almost fatherly, the sound of his voice calming.

"He needs help," Breen said as he held Ty out to the wizard.

Nyalis pulled back the torn material and sniffed Ty's arm. Ty yelped as his shirt was peeled from the open wound.

The wizard's nose wrinkled. "Oh, dear. That does smell bad, doesn't it?"

"Can you heal him?" Adarra asked. "You are a wizard, aren't you?"

"The last wizard," Nyalis said with a wave of his arm. "At least for now." He gave Adarra a cheeky grin. "To answer your question—yes, I can heal him, but not here."

"Why not?" Adarra asked before Ty got the chance. She stepped closer to inspect the wound herself.

"Because, my dear, the . . ."

Nyalis was cut off at the sound of approaching horses.

Everyone turned and quickly raised their weapons.

A band of ragged, half-dead riders rounded the trees on the far side of the lane leading back to the homestead. It was the wielder council. They looked to be in little better shape than Ty, barely holding on to their horses.

Veldon was in the lead. Behind him was Reloria, who rode double with Feoldor. Feoldor looked about as cheerful as ever.

Orlyn was next, his long staff lying across his lap. Ty craned his neck to get a better look. *Is his staff . . .* It was. It was glowing. "Breen, do you see that?" Ty looked up to see if his brother had noticed, but Breen was too busy staring at the next horse in line. Or, more importantly, the one holding its reins.

Fraya held on to Gilly as the dwarf bounced around in front of her with a childlike grin. Ty found himself bouncing too, while Breen started for her horse.

Eliab rode at the end of their small caravan. The toothless gatekeeper had his large double-strung crossbow resting in a holster on the side of his saddle. The man looked like he was about to fall off his horse, wincing at every jolt.

"What in the flaming Pits of Aran'gal happened here?" Feoldor bellowed as Ty and Breen walked past on their way to Fraya's horse.

"We fought an army of Tallosian savages and a horde of giant spiders," Ty said.

"You don't say." Feoldor slowly swung off his horse with Reloria's help.

Ty lost sight of them as Breen carried him farther down. "Are you all right?" Breen called up to Fraya as they approached. The way his brother was fidgeting back and forth, Ty could tell he wanted to help her down but couldn't—not with Ty in his arms.

"I'm fine." She managed a firm squeeze on Breen's arm once she was back on solid ground. She quickly turned her attention to Ty. "What happened?"

"I was bitten by one of those huge spiders." Ty tried to move his hand to point behind them, but it barely made it past his chest before giving out.

"Is that what happened to your hair?" she asked as she ran her fingers across the top of his head. Even Gilly stopped long enough to touch it.

Why was everyone so fascinated with his hair? It wasn't like they hadn't seen white hair before. He wished he had a mirror so he could see for himself.

"No," Breen said. "The bite happened afterward."

She looked at the wound and started to place her hand over it, but Breen held her off. "Don't bother. The wizard said it couldn't be healed here."

"Why not?"

Breen shrugged. "Don't know. You'll have to ask him."

Ty started bouncing again as Breen escorted Fraya back to where the others were gathering around Nyalis.

"And where's that white-haired assassin of ours gotten off to?" Feoldor asked. "I thought I saw her horse on the way in. Every time we turn around, she's done vanished."

Feoldor had barely gotten the words out of his mouth when Sheeva suddenly appeared beside him. He stumbled backward with a yelp, griping under his breath as he scratched at his side whiskers. "Comes and goes whenever she wants . . . never can keep track of her, the shifty little witch."

"Overlord Barl? What are you doing here?" Veldon asked with a quick bow once he recognized who it was he was standing in front of. "And Lady Lyessa?" He bowed once again.

The others followed his example as Veldon rubbed his soiled hankie across the top of his head.

Barl nodded. "I take it this is the council you were speaking of, Kellen?" He looked them over. "It appears the witch underestimated them as well."

"Well, you certainly picked a fine time to show up," Feoldor said, eyeing Nyalis. "Could have used your help back in town fighting off those wretched bulradoer, not to mention their Black Watch dogs."

"As much as I'd like to, I can't be in all places at all times," the old man said with a harsh grunt. "I'm a wizard, not the Creator. There are other people and places in need of my assistance—"

"And who could have possibly been in as much need as us?"

Reloria jabbed Feoldor in the side.

"What?" Feoldor said. "It's an honest question."

Nyalis looked irritated. "A band of Ashanti healers on a pilgrimage to the

City of the Forgotten, if you must know," he said. "Unlike you, they had no means of protecting themselves. But as soon as I heard the horn, I came straight here."

"How did you travel all the way from . . ." Feoldor glanced at the others, and seeing the stern looks on their faces, he folded his arms with a huff. "Oh, never mind." Unwilling to capitulate, he mumbled the last bit under his breath. "We wouldn't have lost poor Saleena if you had been a little quicker about it."

"Saleena's dead?" Ty's father asked.

Veldon nodded, then went on to describe the battle they had fought against the bulradoer and the Black Watch. He told of Captain Hatch's death and of Saleena's sacrifice. He also told them of the bulradoer's magical weapons.

"They are called ter'aks," Nyalis said. "A favored weapon of wizards." He glanced at Orlyn. "That's quite the staff you have there. Might I see it?"

Orlyn handed it over for him to study. The runes didn't seem to be glowing at the moment. Maybe they never had been. Maybe it had been a trick of the light. Or maybe the spider bite was making him see things.

"How did you come by it?" Nyalis asked.

Orlyn glanced at the decorative length of timber and smiled. "It's been in my family for generations."

"Hmm." The old wizard nodded but didn't say anything more as he handed it back to its owner. There was something in Nyalis's eyes, though, that said he knew more.

Ty's father then told the council of their battle against the Northmen, of Ty's standoff with the witch—which led to the discoloration of his hair—and the horrific battle against the arachnobes. He also told them of Ty's mother. Ty wanted to cry, but for some reason his tears wouldn't come.

"So, what's wrong with him?" Reloria asked as she, along with some of the others, gathered to take a closer look.

"I was . . ." Ty started to say, but the words seemed to shrivel and die in his mouth. Ty's left arm hung from his side. He couldn't move it enough to raise it back into place. Whatever was happening to him was spreading.

"He was bitten by one of the arachnobes," his father finally said.

"Does it hurt?" Gilly asked as he tried standing on tiptoes to look at the ugly wound.

Ty shook his head. At least he was still able to do that much.

Sheeva pointed at Ty's white hair then back at hers and smiled. Ty couldn't help but wonder if he was somehow related to the strange yellow-eyed assassin. *Wouldn't that be something?*

Orlyn started rummaging through the pockets of his robe. "I might have something here. If not, I'm sure Fraya can manage a little help until she gains her strength back."

"I'm afraid not," Nyalis said, digging around in his own robes.

Orlyn stopped his searching and joined the others in staring at the old wizard.

"Like I was telling them earlier, the poison inside of Ty isn't natural. It's been altered by magic, and dark magic at that." He pulled out a small pellet, stuffed it in Ty's mouth, and pinched his nose. "Swallow."

Ty didn't have much of a choice. His eyes watered as he tried sucking the sticky substance down. Whatever it was, it tasted terrible, at least at first, then it tasted like raspberry preserve. He turned his head, and Miss Reloria winked at him.

"What I just gave you will not heal you. It's only a temporary relief meant to slow the poison's spread."

"So, he *can* be healed?" his father asked as he picked up Ty's limp arm and laid it back on his chest. Ty tried to smile but found his mouth no longer worked.

"Yes. We've caught it in time. A day or two longer, and even I could do nothing for him."

Ty wanted to shout at them. If it was so deadly, then why were they still standing there talking? He tried again to open his mouth, but it wouldn't cooperate. His entire body was numb. The pain was gone, but so was everything else. He couldn't even feel Breen's arms under him anymore. He wasn't sure if it was due to the poison or whatever Nyalis had just given him.

Ty's eyes were beginning to weigh heavy. He let them slip shut as he listened.

"Times are changing," the wizard said.

"You can say that again," he heard Feoldor counter.

"And we need to be prepared. We can no longer hide in the shadows and hope to remain unnoticed. The Dark Wizard stirs within Aran'gal, and this age is coming to an end. If we're not ready to meet it, I'm afraid the world we know will not survive."

Everyone was quiet. Ty tried to open his eyes to see what was happening, but his lids wouldn't move. He felt the brush of a hand on his forehead, and a soft voice lulled him even deeper into the blackness of sleep.

"Rest now, my little faeling. Your journey has only just begun."

Chapter 82 | Zynora

IT HAD BEEN two days since the Elondrian army had left for their march back to Aramoor. The cold Èshan winds, hinting of winter's coming, had managed to suppress the stench of decay from the bodies spotting the desolate landscape.

Zynora took a moment to look out across the battlefield. She shook her head, the gold charms around her silk scarf dangling in the breeze. The valley looked like a patch of diseased skin waiting for its pustules to burst and seep. How long would it take to be usable again?

"How soon till the townsfolk begin the burial process, you reckon?" she asked her husband, Tameel, as she pulled her aged hand from the pocket of yet another fallen lancer. The rings on her knobby fingers kept getting stuck on the lining. She huffed and scanned the contents. "Hmm, five coppers." She clicked her tongue and moved on to the next.

Tameel swept the long ends of his purple headband back over his shoulder as he looked up from his own pickpocketing. "I would say we have today, maybe tomorrow, before they start." He took a moment to scratch the top of his head. His feathery white hair poked out and over the silk wrap like water erupting from a small fountain.

Zynora maneuvered around one of the fallen horses to get at a rather nice-looking dagger hanging from a soldier's belt.

They had heard about the forthcoming battle while passing through Belbridge on their way to Keldor and decided to stay for a couple of days to see if they could wait it out.

It had been a lucrative decision.

Zynora studied the small parchment that held their quickly sketched map. They had scouted the encampment a day or two before it had begun, passing themselves off as Belbridge merchants and offering whatever services the soldiers said they needed.

"Once we finish here, we should make for that rise." She pointed behind them on the east side of the valley. "The king spent most of his time near the top. If there's anything of value, that will be the place to look."

Tameel grumbled. "That's a long way up, and I'm not as young as I used to be."

"If I can do it, so can you."

It took a while, but after scouring the bodies of the High Guard and keeping well clear of the cadavers of monstrous creatures that spotted the ground, they finally reached the top of the rise. To their disappointment, they didn't find so much as a single tent wedge.

"Surely they had to have left something?" Tameel said as he carefully scanned the ground. "Why was this place so thoroughly cleaned, while everything else lies in ruin?"

"Maybe someone beat us here." Zynora took a moment to look out over the battlefield below. She could see why the king had chosen this spot. It was quite the view. Beautiful, in fact. If she didn't count the corpses littering the landscape.

"Impossible," Tameel said. "We were here before they finished breaking camp. Make sure to grab *him*."

Zynora turned to see what her husband was referring to. Just inside a thicket on the back side of the rise, a rather enormous stallion shook its head. She hadn't noticed it before. Its black coat had kept it hidden.

"I guarantee he'll be worth a hefty bag of gold," Tameel said. "He looks bred for royalty."

A white mark ran from the forehead to its nostrils. It was certainly a beautiful animal.

"I wonder why they left him."

He husband shrugged as he continued scouring the open ground. "Aha! At last. We have our first artifact!" He held up a broken piece of quarrel. "Looks to have come from a crossbow."

Zynora snorted and kept going. "What are you doing back here?" she said to the horse, letting him sniff her hand before approaching. She tried to coax him out, but he didn't seem to want to move. He whinnied and ruffled his mane but kept his gaze on something farther in. "What is it, boy?" she asked, rubbing her hand down his strong neck. His hair was matted with a mix of blood and dirt.

The undergrowth was too thick for him to get through, but she managed to shimmy past some of the smaller bushes, taking the time to unhook her colorful skirt from the briars. There was something back there after all. She took a couple of steps closer, then stopped when she realized it was a pile of bodies. More of the black-uniformed soldiers. What were they doing back there? Then she noticed the bolts sticking from their backs.

"I think I know where your bolt came from," she called back to Tameel. She walked over to search their pockets. "Come now, quit being so difficult," she said to the first, trying to shove the man off the pile after deciding he had nothing of value to salvage. She reached for the next. Her hand was halfway in when the pile suddenly moved.

She shrieked and yanked her hand out, tripping over her skirt and landing halfway in the bushes behind her.

A moment later, Tameel broke through the scrub, his belt knife in hand. "What's going on? Are you all right?"

"It moved."

Tameel looked around. "What moved?"

"The pile," she said, pointing at the bodies. "I think someone's alive in there."

Her husband helped her back to her feet, then turned and looked at the dead soldiers. "They have bolts in their backs."

"Very observant, my love."

Tameel took a step back. "I think it's best we were going. Whatever intrigues are being played here, we shouldn't get involved."

Before Zynora could say anything, a groan rose from somewhere near the bottom of the pile.

"The Rhivanni don't turn their backs on those in need."

Tameel huffed. "They do if they know what's good for them."

"Get down here and help me, old man, or you'll get no supper tonight."

Tameel huffed but finally knelt and started rolling the bodies back.

They were nearing the end of the pile when they finally spotted movement from the man on the very bottom.

They worked to remove the man's thick leather coat. It had three holes in the back. She noticed the bolts had been snapped off. Probably from the weight of the other men being thrown on top of him.

"Careful," Tameel said as Zynora jerked on the sleeve. "That could be worth something if he doesn't make it."

She shook her head. "Hand me your knife."

Tameel gave her his belt knife, and with a steady hand she cut open the back of the man's black tunic.

"Careful, now. We could still sell that, you know."

Zynora rolled her eyes. "And who do you reckon is going to buy a shirt with three holes?" They stared at the three similar holes in the man's back, pieces of the bolts still rising from the skin. The blood seeping out of the wounds was clotted and dark. "Cut me some cloth from one of the other tunics," she said, passing the knife back to her husband. "We need to slow the bleeding enough to get him to the wagon."

"How is he not dead already?"

Zynora pursed her lips. "If I was to guess, I'd say the pressure of the other men on top of him held back the bleeding long enough for him to survive."

"The Great Father must be looking out for him."

She instinctively touched a few of the gold charms dangling from her headdress at the naming of the Great Father.

Tameel handed her the material he'd cut from the other soldiers.

"We need to get him back to the wagon so I can work on him."

"Will he make it that far?"

Zynora looked around. "Use the mud. It should be enough to stop the blood till then."

"Wife, you have a stout mind in that beautiful head of yours," Tameel remarked with an affectionate smile. He thrust his hand deep into the waterlogged soil and pulled out a fist of dark mire. It oozed between his fingers as he squeezed. He gently packed the three wounds before firmly applying the cloth bandages on top.

They struggled to load the half-dead man onto the stallion, which surprisingly hadn't moved from its position.

Zynora grabbed the horse's reins, expecting a fight, but before she even got the chance to tug, the horse walked out of the thicket and headed directly for the descending path. With the horse in the lead, they carried the man back down the rise, along with a couple more purses and an assortment of weapons.

They directed the horse to a small copse of trees just south of the rise, where they had hidden the covered wagon that was their home while traveling.

The wagon's faded and chipped green and gold paint was in desperate need of another coat. Her husband kept promising he'd get around to it but never seemed to find the time. Tinkers tended to be on the road more often than not. Selling their wares was the only way they knew to provide for themselves, a trait passed down for generations.

It was quite the task getting the wounded man inside. Tameel opened the back door of the wagon and tried pulling from his end, while Zynora pushed from hers. Eventually, they managed it. Once in, they muscled him onto a small built-in cot they had been using for additional storage space. Zynora rummaged through the glass jars and vials she had stockpiled on shelves above the cot.

"Will he live, wife?"

Zynora clicked her tongue. "He probably won't last till evening, but at least we can sleep tonight with a clear conscience." She sat on a stool by the man's bed as she cleaned the mud from his back and applied one salve after another in an attempt to battle the infection.

"I am a daughter of the Dar'Rhivanni," she huffed. "A student of the healing arts of Kojzu. This will not beat me." She held her hands over the wounds and closed her eyes. It had been a long time since she had resorted to magic.

"*Zintari Freyestra.*" She drew on the magical healing elements all Rhivanni women were instructed in since birth. "*Zintari Folduru.*" She wasn't as powerful as a full healer, but she knew enough to get by.

Her palms radiated a soft violet as she sent the simple spell down through the open wounds and into the pus-yellow infection beneath. The area around his back glowed violet as well, just under the skin.

There was a lot of death surrounding the man's wounds. She didn't know if she could heal it. She'd never tried to heal someone this far gone before. It was dangerous. If she expended too much, it could kill her as well.

She could feel her own energy leaving her body. She was barely able to concentrate. She was numb all over. She couldn't risk going any further. Quickly, she released the spell, and the light soon faded, and the color vanished. The inside of the wagon started to spin, and she slumped beside the man's cot, resting her head on the edge of the straw mattress. "I'm getting too old for this," she sighed, before exhaustion took her and she passed out.

Zynora woke to the sway of the wagon. How long had she been asleep? She raised herself from where Tameel had obviously placed her on some blankets on the floor. She smiled. *Good man.*

The sun was shining through the front hatch leading to the driver's seat. Was it still the afternoon, or had she slept straight through to the next day?

She tried to stand, but her legs gave out halfway up. "I'm not that old," she barked, then glanced at her knobby knees poking out from beneath her skirt and huffed. Twisting around, she grabbed the stool and pulled it over for leverage. With its help, she made it up far enough to plop down on top.

The young man appeared to be sleeping. His chest rose and fell in a slow, rhythmic fashion. She reached over to pull up his blanket from where it had slipped, and his eyes opened.

She gasped. "Tameel!"

Her husband turned around from his seat on the driver's bench and peeked inside. "Ah, you're finally up. I was beginning to worry you were going to sleep today away as well."

"Our guest is awake," she said.

Tameel pulled back on the reins, and the wagon lurched to a stop, forcing Zynora to grab some crates to keep from getting pitched off her stool.

"How is he?" Tameel asked as he climbed through the hatch and into the back. "He hasn't moved much since yesterday. Neither have you, for that matter. They say sleep grows more frequent with age, but that was ridiculous."

"Oh, stop your whining. At least I don't keep the horses up with my snoring."

She fought back a yawn. She had never felt so weak. Resuscitating the man's life had nearly cost her her own. She made a point not to tell Tameel how close to death she had come.

Her husband hobbled across the wagon and stood behind her stool. "Well, son, you gave us quite the start. Didn't think you was going to make it. Your fever didn't break until sometime in the night."

The young man struggled to push himself into a sitting position as he glanced around the wagon. He looked down at his state of undress, a patchwork quilt covering his lower half. His chest was completely wrapped in a white binding.

"Wa . . ." he rasped, tried again, then shook his head and pointed to his mouth.

Zynora pointed to one of the smaller barrels on the side. "He wants something to drink."

Tameel dipped a cup into the water barrel and handed it to her.

She held the tin mug to the man's lips, and he tried gulping it down. "Slowly," she scolded gently. "You don't want to drink it too fast. There you go."

He finished off what was in the cup and fell back against the feather pillows. "Thank you," he said. His bright-grey eyes scanned the cramped quarters of their wagon.

"Where am I?"

"You are safe." She wiped his moist forehead with a cloth.

Tameel laid a hand on her shoulder. "I'm Tameel, and this beautiful young thing is my wife, Zynora."

Zynora blushed and playfully slapped at his hand.

"I take it you are Upakan," he said. "What's your name, young man?"

There was a long, uncomfortable silence, and a look of panic crossed the young man's face. "I . . . I don't know."

The End of
Book One of
The Aldoran Chronicles

Dear Reader,

I HOPE YOU enjoyed this first book in the Aldoran Chronicles series. If you found the story entertaining and would like to see more, then please consider helping me reach that goal by leaving a quick review on Amazon.

Reviews are very important. They help encourage other readers to try the book while at the same time showing Amazon that the book is worth promoting. Reviews don't need to be long or involved, just a sentence or two that tells people what you liked about the book in order to help readers know why they might like it too.

Thank you in advance!

Love fantasy merchandise? Stop by the ***Aramoor Market*** and take a look at the new Aldoran store. New arrivals every month.

<www.store.michaelwisehart.com>>

Free Offer

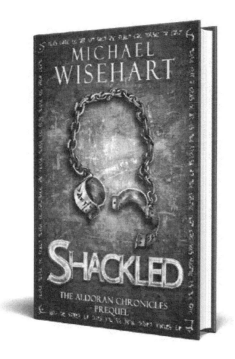

I F YOU WOULD LIKE to know more about Ferrin's captured and imprisonment within the White Tower, I have written the first of the Aldoran Chronicles prequels just for you. More importantly, it's FREE. Type in the address below to get your book: *Shackled*

« www.michaelwisehart.com/shackled-wt »

Born in a world where magic is not only feared, but outlawed, Ferrin's choice to use his abilities brings the Black Watch to his doorstep. While caged alongside a helpless band of half-starved wielders, he formulates a strategy to escape. Armed with nothing more than his sarcastic wit and the determination to never give in, Ferrin attempts the impossible.

Author's Note

YOU CAN LEARN more about the World of Aldor on my website. If you haven't taken the time to peruse, I believe you'll find it both educational and entertaining. Don't forget to read the *History of Aldor* while you're there. It will give you a better understanding behind the internal struggles and conflicts taking place between those with magic and those without.

Stop by and say hello!

« michaelwisehart.com »

« facebook.com/MichaelWisehart.author »

Acknowledgements

I THANK GOD for the doors and windows He's allowed to open in order for me to reach this point.

I want to thank my parents, *Mickey and Julie Wisehart,* for their unending loyalty, encouragement, and support over the years. None of this would be possible without you. Love you both.

I want to thank my Author Team, whose endless talent, time, and dedication have made this project possible:

AUTHOR TEAM

I want to thank my illustrator, who has a talent for taking verbose descriptions and turning them into stunning works of art—*Jack Adams*

I want to thank my cartographer, who patiently worked with me and my continual need to tweak things, and still managed to produce one incredible map for the capital city of Easthaven—*Elwira Pawlikowska*

I want to thank my cartographer, who managed to take a maze of jumbled ideas and turn them into the capital city of Aramoor—*RenflowerGrapx*

I want to thank my content editor, who has spent countless hours advising me on the proper structure of my thoughts—*Nathan Hall*

I want to thank my line editor, who managed to take a floundering script and turn it into something readable—*Danae Smith*

I want to thank my copy editors, whose careful eyes have made my book shine—*Richard Shealy, Mia Darien, Tammy Salyer, Crystal Watanabe*

I want to thank my Beta Team, who took precious time out of their busy schedule to suffer through the first, second, and third drafts in order to leave such valuable feedback as to help me make this book worth reading— (alphabetical order) *Tom Barone, Kylie Betzner, Toni Betzner, Jeff Boles, Roger Bopp, Mary Bradshaw, Linden Brinks, Melody Brocke, Meredith Burnette, Rachel*

Rene, Micah Clark, Raymond Clarke, Emily Coda, Bridgett Cox, Lindsay Cyr, Jeff Davis, Karen Furk, Melissa Holmes, Chester Hendrix, Leigh Herring, Sahar Itani, Pamela Johnson, Clement Joly, Katie Kowalski, Breanna Lawrence, Peter Lynch, Amanda Matula, Michael O'Steen, Salvitor Patricola, Maegan Penley, Julie Petkovsky, Daniel Pinkoski, Dave Place, Sharon Rhoads, Bill Rueth, Lynnette Short, Danae Smith, Jason Smith, Ethan Starnes, Phil Brown, Alida Van Pelt, Charlotte Walters, Renee Webb, Ali Weber, Peter Wiebe, Jeff Wilson, and Ruth Zellers.

About the Author

MICHAEL WISEHART graduated with a bachelor's degree in business before going back to school for film and starting his own production company. As much as he enjoyed film work, the call of writing a novel got the better of him, and on April 14, 2014, he started typing the first words of what would become two epic fantasy series: The Aldoran Chronicles and the Street Rats of Aramoor.

He currently lives and writes in South Georgia.

Sneak Peek | Chapter 1

Banished (The Street Rats of Aramoor: Book 1)

"ᶆOVE IT, AYRION! You stop, you die." My words echoed off the mountainside as I fought to make it up the steep granite wall in front of me. The shelf I needed to reach was close. I was nearly there. The excitement of finishing before the others had me climbing even faster. My right hand slipped, and for a moment, the only things that stood between me and the deadly rocks below were my left hand and a few hundred feet of nothing.

This is what I get for yelling at myself.

A freezing gust of wind lashed against me, whipping me around. Even in the middle of the night, I could see the ruins of the Lost City in the distance.

My home had never looked so small. Dragon Fang was the tallest of the peaks in the Northern Heights, and it was the final stage of the Tri'Nephrin. We weren't expected to climb all the way to the summit, only to the top of Howling Gorge.

I kicked my legs and twisted around to find another hold. The wind shrilled as it pushed through the gaps in the deep ravine, coming in heavy gusts.

The rock face was sharp in some places, smooth in others. From one swing to the next, you never knew what you were going to get. Deep crevices and cracks made for strong grips if you could find them, as long as you stayed away from the ones with webbing. One bite from the wrong spider and it would be a quick trip down.

I found another handhold a few feet to my right. I had to hurry; my fingers weren't going to hold much longer. I waited for the next gust to pass and then kicked out and swung for it. My fingers latched on to the textured part of the rock, and I let go with my left hand to reach for the next one up. Just as I did, the rock gave way, and time seemed to stop. I felt what it was like to fly, suspended in the air, as free as a bird.

The moment didn't last.

Before my mind had even registered what had happened, I was falling. I tried to scream, but the wind ripped the air from my lungs. I looked down and watched as the ground grew closer. This was it. My short life was over, all thirteen years of it. I'd spent my entire life training to become an Upakan warrior, the youngest to ever claim the title, and here I was, about to die before completing my first real advancement. Worse yet was the thought that after working so hard to get a full day's lead ahead of Flon and the other trainees, they were going to find my bloody remains, laugh, and go on without me.

It's amazing what runs through your mind before you die. I closed my eyes and waited for the impact.

My head cleared, and I realized I was still hanging by my left hand, my body swaying against the side of the mountain. My stomach heaved from the sensation of having fallen to my death. I swallowed, forcing myself to take a breath as I tried to slow the beating in my chest. Even knowing how my magic worked, I still had a hard time getting used to it.

The visions were so real.

My knuckles were white as I held on to the small crack in the rock with everything I had. I couldn't feel my fingers. Any moment, they were going to give way. Frantically, I searched for another hold. Thanks to my vision, I knew where *not* to grab, so I swung for a small outcropping just above it.

It held.

I pulled myself up and reached for another just under the shelf I was trying to reach. The ledge over my head extended too far out for me to climb. I considered my options. It seemed my only choice was a bad one. Almost as bad as having decided to undergo the Tri'Nephrin in the first place. No one had ever attempted to complete the advancement course at my age. It was unheard of. The course was made for trainees at least three or four years my senior.

On my left, about six or seven feet below me, was a small section of rock jutting out from a wall adjacent to the one I was clinging to. It was just enough to stand on, but not much more. The only way I could see to reach it was by jumping.

Now would have been a good time to have anchored a rope to the wall, but since I had left my pack below in order to increase the speed of my climb, not to mention the bragging rights, I had to make do without it. Instead, I opted to use one of my picks. Letting go with my right hand, I grabbed it from its holder at my waist.

Not wanting to give myself time to reconsider, I planted both feet and aimed myself at the shelf. "Here goes nothing." I released my grip and kicked off the wall.

The wind pounded in my ears as I flew across the gorge. My eyes never left the small outcropping on the other side. My feet landed first, and then the rest of me hit the side of the mountain. A sharp pain tore through my legs and chest where they struck the hard granite, letting me know I was still alive.

I slammed my pick into a small crevice and yanked myself back against the wall. I released a heartfelt sigh of relief as my face pressed against the cold stone. This was as good a time as any to take a breather. My hands were shaking as they clung to the pick's handle. My legs weren't doing much better.

I glanced over my right shoulder at the shelf above me. It was so close and yet just out of reach. As desperate as I was to finish, I needed to slow down and think. The other trainees hadn't made it this far. They were probably still in the caverns below the city, trying to get through the previous three obstacles. Not a single trainee had volunteered to team with me, so I had gone on alone. I wasn't too worried. I worked better alone.

My fingers prickled as the blood and feeling returned. I gave them a few more minutes to rest before moving on. Carefully, I tapped the end of the pick to release it from the rock, then slipped it back into its hoop at my waist and started climbing.

The problem now was that to reach the final shelf, I was going to need to jump back across the gorge. Unfortunately, the two walls separated farther up, making a jump all but impossible.

"Why is it never easy?" I moaned. Talking to myself helped. I was an excellent conversationalist. I very rarely argued, but if I did, it was for a good cause.

My anticipation grew as I climbed high enough to see over the top of the shelf and spot the five flags bracketed to the walls on the other side, one for each of the trainees. Mine was second from the left—a black background with a white rune at the center. The rune was from the Old Tongue and supposedly stood for my name, *Ayrion*. There were few who could still read the ancient language, so I had to take their word for it.

At the back of the rise was a door with torches on either side. Behind the door was a set of tunnels leading down to the bottom of the gorge. In the old days, they had used rises like this as lookouts for oncoming armies. No guards were in sight, which wasn't too surprising, considering they wouldn't have expected the trainees to make it this far for at least another day.

A little farther up, I found a small outcropping for my feet, which took some of the weight off my arms. I rested as I studied the gulf between me and the ledge where I needed to be. It was too far to jump. I didn't need a vision to tell me how stupid I'd be to try it. Yet that was exactly what I needed to do.

I studied the wall above me and then looked back at the shelf. What was I going to do? The only way to make it that far would be to jump from higher up to add distance. Even then, I wasn't sure it would be enough. And if it was, it would be a very hard landing.

I took an extra few seconds to let the blood flow back into my arms while I looked for the next set of holds I'd need to reach to get high enough to attempt something this ridiculous. Two deep breaths, and I reached for the first of what looked like eight pulls.

The first wasn't a problem; it was close enough to reach without having to stretch. But the next two were a different matter. There were no toeholds for my boots, which meant I had to heft my entire weight with my arms. The fourth and fifth had small ledges beneath, large enough to place the tip of one boot. I used them to ease some of the weight on my arms as I readied myself for the final three pulls up to where I estimated I needed to be to make the jump across.

By the time I'd reached the top of the narrow ledge on my side of the gorge and stood looking across to where I needed to jump, I had all but talked myself out of it. If it weren't for the fact that I had nowhere else to go, I would have been tempted to give up and climb back down. But I'd rather fall to my death than let Flon and the others see me quit. So, I pushed all doubt and fear aside and focused on the task. Even from this height, I could see I wasn't going to be able to jump far enough to land on the shelf, which meant I needed to try something else.

I could have kicked myself for not taking the full pack of supplies offered before the climb. I figured the lighter load would cut my climbing time down and allow me to gain even more distance from my fellow trainees. That had been a mistake. That grapple would have come in rather handy right about now. In fact, if I had carried it along, I probably wouldn't have been forced to resort to such a foolish stunt.

Without the grapple and rope, my only options were my picks. I removed both from their holders and held them in front of me, testing their balance. Each had a small leather loop at the end of the handle for me to stick my wrist through in case my hand slipped.

I took a moment to glance over the side one last time. It was a long way down. At least it would be a quick death if I missed.

Tightening my grip, I concentrated on what I was about to do, picturing it in my mind—the jump, the swing of the picks, the jerk as they struck the ledge. Each time, the image ended with me falling to my death. So far, I hadn't received another vision, so maybe I would make it. Then again, my visions only gave me a few seconds' warning. With my luck, the vision would come halfway across the gorge and make me miss the strike.

I walked back from the ledge until I reached the face of the mountain behind me. I needed as much room to run as I could manage.

My breath coursed through my lungs—in and out. In and out. I started counting down.

Three. I locked my fingers around my picks.

Two. My legs tightened, and I bent to run.

One. I screamed, hit three steps, and pushed off the ledge as hard as I could.

There was no question. I wasn't going to make it.

I raised my picks and swung at the top of the ledge.

They missed.

My picks sparked as they scraped down the side of the shelf, one of them snagging on a boulder protruding from the bottom. The force of the catch nearly pulled my arm from its socket. I screamed in pain. My fingers came loose, and for a moment, I was hanging from the side of the mountain with nothing but a leather strap holding me up.

I looked down and wished I hadn't. The fear of heights had been trained out of me years before, but something about hanging there by my pick's strap had me on the verge of losing my stomach. I closed my eyes and fought through the pain, praying to anyone who'd listen that my strap wouldn't break.

Opening my eyes, I raised my other pick and swung. It stuck.

"Come on, Ayrion! Pull!" I bit down and hauled myself up with one arm, far enough to pry loose the first pick and reach for something higher. I swung, but the rock I hit gave way, raining pieces down on my face. I shook my head and tried again. The pick held. I tested its weight before releasing the other.

Arm over arm, I swung and pulled, swung and pulled, until I reached the top of the shelf and crawled over the edge. I rolled onto my back, panting harder than I ever had before.

I couldn't move.

My entire body was shaking. I couldn't believe I'd made it. That was by far the stupidest thing I'd ever done, and yet the most thrilling. I wished the other trainees had been there to see it. I shook my head. No. If they had been, that would mean they had made it up the mountain in front of me, and I wasn't about to wish for that.

The wind howled above me as I lay there gasping for breath, and the moon flooded the top of the rise with pale light. With what strength I had left, I rolled onto my side and tried to stand, but sitting with my back against one of the smaller boulders on the side of the rise was as far as I got. I looked out over the edge of the cliff into the depths of the gorge below, and I wondered if all of this was really worth it. Did I really want to become a warrior after all?

I got my answer when my legs pushed the rest of me up to a standing position. From there, I hobbled over to where the flags waved in their brackets and lifted the black one with the white rune. I tucked it under my arm, hobbled over to the door, and knocked. While waiting for someone to open, I raised my hands to the torches to warm them.

It was a while before someone lifted the latch on the other side of the door and the hinges groaned. I stepped back to keep from getting hit.

A short man with a round face stuck his head out, took one look at me, and then went back inside. "Hey, Jesup. You were right. It was a knock."

"Here, let me see." A taller man with a rather bulbous nose stuck his head out, then finally opened the door the rest of the way. "I don't believe it. How'd you get up here?"

"I climbed."

The man stepped around me and scanned the top of the shelf. He turned back around. "Where's your pack?"

"I didn't carry one."

"What do you mean, you didn't carry one? How'd you climb up here without a pack?"

"I used my hands and my picks." I patted the picks where they hung at my sides.

The two men stared at me like they'd seen a specter.

"Well, I never," the second guard said as he scratched the top of his head and glanced at the first. "Mark this down, Argust. Could be for the records."

I smiled. I couldn't wait to see the others' faces when I walked in carrying my flag a full day in front of the others. They couldn't deny me my right to be there anymore.

Character Glossary

Abbet Lydale [*ă -bit/lĭ-del*] Easthaven fuller. Town drunk.

Acorn [*ā -corn*] Breen's horse.

Adarra [*uh-dar-uh*] Sister of Ty and Breen. Daughter of Kellen and Nilla.

Aerodyne [*air-o-dine*] The founder of the first Wizard Order. Known as the Dark One.

Agnar [*ag-nar*] Overlord of Keldor.

Aiden Raycrest [*aye-den/ray-crest*] Son of wealthy millworks owner in Highcrest. Lyessa's fiancé.

Amarysia [*am-uh-ree-see-uh*] Lady-in-waiting to High Queen Ellise.

Arina Respuel [*uh-ree-nuh/res-pee-ule*] Overcaptain Barthol's daughter.

Arnoni [*ar-non-ee*] Night Walker whom Kellen's great-great-grandfather saved and received a moonstone for his generosity.

Arnst [*arn-st*] Elondrian scout.

Asa [*ace-uh*] Overcaptain under Tolin.

Ayrion [*air-ee-un*] Known as Death's Shadow. Guardian Protector of the High King. Upakan heritage.

Azriel [*az-ree-el*] Seer inside of the White Tower. Ferrin's roommate.

Baeldor [*bay-el-dor*] Leader of Tallosian war party.

Barl [*barl*] Overlord of Sidara. Father of Lyessa.

Barthol Respuel [*bar-thol/res-pee-ule*] Captain of High Guard under Ayrion.

Bartimus [*bar-tĭ-mus*] Fool who went in search of a wife and had a song written about his experience.

Bashan [*bay-shun*] Undercaptain in charge of the Elondrian foot soldiers under Captain Janus.

Basil Kilburn [*bace-le/kill-bern*] Cooper's son. Local bully who went to school with Ty. Dared him to jump into East River.

Bayle [*bay-ul*] Elondrian scout, partner to Merrick. Seafaring accent. Wields a battle-axe.

Belkor [*bel-kor*] Ambassador to Cylmar.

Bellar [*bel-ar*] Bulradoer from Elondria.

Bellos [*bel-lō-ce*] Captain in charge of Elondrian crossbowmen.

Bezaleel [*bez-uh-leel*] Former Archchancellor.

Black Watch [*black/watch*] Group of mercenaries sent to round up magic wielders.

Breen [*breen*] Brother of Ty.

Bue Aboloff [byoo/*ab-o-loff*] Husband of Noreen. Innkeeper. Chef.

Calina Tirfing [*cuh-lee-nuh*] Class beauty. Justice Tirfing's only daughter.

Cheeks/Sylas [*sī-lus*] Sadistic inquisitor in the White Tower.

Clye Durran [*klī/dir-an*] Former Easthaven cooper and storyteller.

Dak [*dak*] Bully in Easthaven. Tried dunking Ty in a pickle barrel.

Dakaran [*duh-kar-un*] High Prince of Elondria. Son of Rhydan and Ellise.

Damar [*duh-mar*] Mercenary hired by Baeldor and Mangora to fight Ty's family.

Darryk [*dare-ick*] Lyessa's martial trainer in weapons and combat.

Derryk Lahorn [*dare-ick/luh-horn*] Tal Lahorn's oldest son. Died from a brain fever.

Dorbin [*dor-bin*] Old hermit living outside of Easthaven.

Eliab [*ee-lie-ub*] Gatekeeper for the Easthaven Harbor House.

Elior [*el-ee-or*] Head of Elondrian war-runners.

Ellise [*el-leece*] High Queen of Elondria.

Ellson [*el-son*] Elondrian scout, partner to Terris.

Ethen [*ee-thin*] Local carpenter.

Felina [*fel-ee-nuh*] Citizen of Easthaven. Friend of Helene.

Feoldor [*fay-ol-dor*] Member of Easthaven Wielder Council. Glassblower. Vanti.

Ferrin [*fare-in*] Rhowynn weaponsmith. Imprisoned in the White Tower.

Forel [*for-el*] Member of Tallosian war party.

Fraya Lahorn [*fray-uh/luh-horn*] Daughter of Tal Lahorn. Member of Easthaven Wielder Council. Healer.

Furgus McKesh [*fer-gus/mc-kesh*] Easthaven blacksmith.

Gilly [*gil-ee*] Member of Easthaven Wielder Council. Dwarf. Voda.

Gina [*gee-nuh*] Nanny to Lady Lyessa.

Gunther Mezard [*gun-ther/mez-ard*] Chandler in Easthaven.

Gyin [*guy-in*] Ambassador to Briston.

Hatch [*hach*] Captain of Black Watch riders.

Heglith [*heg-lith*] Black Watch rider under Captain Hatch.

Helene Tunsfield [*hel-een/tuns-field*] Citizen of Easthaven. Friend of Felina.

Heleyna [*hel-ee-nuh*] Mother of Lyessa. Deceased.

Horvah [*hor-vuh*] Weaselly bulradoer in charge of the Tower's recruitment.

Janus [*jan-us*] Captain of Elondrian foot soldiers.

Jaylen [*jay-len*] Black Watch rider under Captain Hatch.

Jonas [*joe-nus*] Member of the Tallosian war party.

Josten [*joss-ten*] Mill owner in Easthaven.

Kassyna Lahorn [*kuh-see-nuh/luh-horn*] Wife of Tal Lahorn. Deceased.

Kellen [*kel-en*] Adoptive father of Ty, gamekeeper.

Kensey Respuel [*kin-zee/res-pee-ule*] Overcaptain Barthol Respuel's wife

Kerson [*kir-son*] Warren clansman who challenges the Right of Oktar.

Kira [*keir-ruh*] Street tribe chief Ayrion grew up with. Head of the Warren clans.

Lanmiere [*lan-meer*] Ambassador to Sidara.

Lenara [*len-ar-uh*] Bulradoer from Cylmar.

Lerra [*lare-uh*] The name of Tameel's wagon.

Loren [*lor-en*] High Guard ostler.

Luc Kilburn [*luke*] Town cooper.

Lugar [*loo-gar*] Head of the Harbor House in Duport. Trusted friend of Veldon.

Lyessa [*lee-es-uh*] Daughter of Overlord Barl and Lady Heleyna.

Mangora [*man-gor-uh*] Dark witch in Easthaven.

Marta [*mar-tuh*] Legate Superior at the White Tower.

Medarin [*meh-dar-in*] Bulradoer. Outspoken against Valtor's rise to Archchancellor.

Merrick [*mare-ick*] Elondrian scout. Husband of Taleen.

Meyrose [*may-rose*] Overlord of Briston.

Myriah [*mer-eye-uh*] Sister to Ferrin. Lives in Rhowynn.

Nadeer [*nuh-deer*] In charge of the Elondrian longbowmen.

Narri Lahorn [*nar-ee/luh-horn*] Youngest son of Tal.

Nierdon [*nee-air-dun*] Ambassador to Keldor.

Nilla [*nee-luh*] Adoptive mother of Ty. Wife of Kellen.

Nora [*nor-uh*] Orlyn's dead wife.

Noreen Aboloff [*nor-een/ab-o-loff*] Wife of Bue. Runs the East Inn.

Nostrils [*noss-trolls*] Captain in the service of the Black Watch.

Nyalis [*nee-al-is*] Last of the Aerodyne Wizards.

Old Man Wyker [*wick-er*] Owns a distillery in Easthaven.

Orlyn [*or-lin*] Member of the Easthaven Wielder Council. Apothecary. Floratide.

Peyla [*pee-luh*] Easthaven baker's wife.

Piel [*pee-el*] Head butler to Overlord Barl.

Pinon [*pĭ-non*] Peddler that Ferrin is sold to as a child by his uncle. Former captain in the Keldoran army.

Po [*poe*] Street kid Ayrion grew up with. Second in command under Kira.

Rae [*ray-uh*] Healer in the White Tower. Mother of Suri.

Raguel [*rah-gool*] Master painter who after the death of his wife turned to morbid depictions of humanity.

Reevie [*ree-vee*] Childhood best friend of Ayrion.

Reloria [*reh-lor-ee-uh*] Member of the Easthaven Wielder Council. Telasaro. Owns the Easthaven Sweet Shop.

Rhydan [*rī-dun*] High King of Elondria.

Roan [*rone*] Elondrian scout.

Rowen [*roe-win*] Apprentice to Valtor. Has an ugly deformity on the side of his face.

Rukar [*roo-kar*] Bulradoer. Well built. Dark skin with strong face. Always seen with a handful of weapons.

Saleena [*suh-lee-nuh*] Physicker captured near Reed Marsh by the Black Watch.

Saryn [*sar-in*] Overlord of Cylmar. Wages war against Elondria.

Sedgewick [*sej-wik*] Younger brother of Amarysia. Nickname is Sedge or Howler. Aramoor street tribe chief.

Selma [*sell-muh*] Bulradoer. Tall with straight brown hair and a long face. She has a nervous twitch in her left eye.

Shade [*shade*] Ayrion's black warhorse.

Sheeva [*shee-vuh*] New member of Easthaven Wielder Council. From Duport. Short-cut blonde hair. Night Walker. Invisibility. Assassin.

Sil'foren [*sil-for-in*] Factory owner in Aramoor who uses street urchins as forced labor.

Soren [*sor-en*] Black Watch rider under Captain Hatch.

Sorna Blaudell [*sor-nuh/blah-dell*] Widow who has had her sights set on Orlyn for the last twenty years.

Suri [*sir-ee*] Daughter of Rae.

Syglara [*sig-lar-uh*] Queen of the Spiders.

Tadis [*tay-diss*] Stablehand at the White Tower.

Tal Lahorn [*tal/luh-horn*] Father of Fraya. Easthaven farmer.

Taleen [*tuh-leen*] Wife of Merrick who longed to live in the city.

Tameel [*tuh-meel*] Tinker. Husband of Zynora. Part of the Dar'Rhivanni.

Tate [*tayt*] Young street kid who Valtor's henchmen kidnap.

Terris [*tare-iss*] Elondrian scout with scraggy hairy and beard. Broadsword. Slight country accent.

Tess Lahorn [*tess/luh-horn*] Youngest daughter of Tal.

Thistle [*thiss-le*] Adarra's mare.

Tirana [*tir-ah-nuh*] Wife of Commander Tolin.

Tolin [*tol-in*] Commander of the Elondrian Forces under King Rhydan.

Tolvin [*tol-vin*] Bulradoer from Elondria.

Topin [*toe-pin*] Bulradoer.

Trepin Odel [*trep-in/o-del*] Town cobbler.

Tulvik [*tul-vik*] Wealthy lord who owns an estate north of the Tansian River.

Ty [*tī*] Bearer of the Mark, adopted son of Kellen and Nilla. Brother to Breen and Adarra. Faeling.

Valtor [*val-tor*] Birth name is Milo. [*my-lo*] Archchancellor of the White Tower.

Veldon [*vel-dun*] Portmaster for Easthaven. Leader of Easthaven Wielder Council. Incidi.

Waddle [*wŏd-el*] Ty's horse.

Widow Windel [*win-dul*] Crazy woman who dressed her pony in her husband's suit and tried to marry him.

Your Highness [*yor/hi-ness*] Kellen's horse, a bit high spirited, chestnut in color.

Zynora [*zin-or-uh*] Wife of Tameel. Tinker. Part of the Dar'Rhivanni.

Stop by and visit:

www.michaelwisehart.com

Made in the USA
Coppell, TX
03 September 2021

61750544R00374